SWORDS' MASTERS

SWORDS'
MASTERS

SWORDS AGAINST WIZARDRY
THE SWORDS OF LANKHMAR
SWORDS AND ICE MAGIC

Fritz Leiber

GUILDAMERICA
B O O K S™

Published by arrangement with
The Berkley Publishing Group
200 Madison Avenue
New York, New York 10016

Printed in the United States of America

Quality Printing and Binding by:
Berryville Graphics
P.O. Box 272
Berryville, VA 22611 U.S.A.

AUTHOR'S FOREWORD

The list below is the proper order of the six books in the saga of the Gray Mouser and Fafhrd, beginning with the one containing two tales of Fafhrd's and the Mouser's lives before their meeting and also the yarn of that definitive encounter:

SWORDS AND DEVILTRY
SWORDS AGAINST DEATH
SWORDS IN THE MIST
SWORDS AGAINST WIZARDRY
THE SWORDS OF LANKHMAR
SWORDS AND ICE MAGIC

That plural "swords" sounds a bit monotonous, yet it seemed wise to make a clear link between the six books, especially since Fafhrd and the Gray Mouser are undoubtedly the greatest swordsmen who ever lived, or will ever live, in any of the many universes—having their many adventures, encountering many other proficient swordsmen and most evil and clever villains, fierce beasts and supernatural monsters, wizards of the vastest sorcerous skill, and delectable girls a-plenty, some of the last having great wisdom and character.

—FRITZ LEIBER

CONTENTS

SWORDS AGAINST WIZARDRY

THE SWORDS OF LANKHMAR

SWORDS AND ICE MAGIC

SWORDS AGAINST WIZARDRY

This book is dedicated to
HARRY OTTO FISCHER,
who first explored Quarmall
and who wrote ten thousand of these words,
here unchanged,
about that subterranean kingdom.

Additionally, Part Two of his novel—
Stardock—is dedicated to
those two hardy cragsmen,
Poul Anderson and Paul Turner.

AUTHOR'S INTRODUCTION

Swords Against Wizardry is the fourth book of the Saga of Fafhrd and the Grey Mouser, immediately following *Swords in the Mist* and followed by *The Swords of Lankhmar.* The two heroes have been comrades in adventure for about a decade.

In 1936 my comrade Harry Otto Fischer conceived, began, and abandoned the story "The Lords of Quarmall." Twenty five years later I decided I was up to the pleasant task of solving the mysteries of the tale and completing it without changing his words at all, except to add details of plot. Harry, in some ways a very patient person, laconically commented that he was glad to discover at last how his story ended.

The sections Harry wrote are the history of Quarmall and the introduction of its lord and Flindach, beginning with the last paragraph on page 93 and ending at the top of 101; the chess game between Gwaay and Hasjarl, 112 to 120; the cremation of Quarmal, 128 to 134; parts of the Mouser's spell, 134; and the idea of the Mouser's tunnel journey, 146.

Now Harry's home is in the hilly city of Clarksburg in the Appalachian heartland, while I bivouac in another hilly city on the West Coast, but the comradeship is as always.

Fritz Leiber
San Francisco,
Oct. 19, 1973

Grand Pennon

Petty Pennon

5

6

White
Waterfall

OBELISK
POLARIS

●●●●● Route Kranarch & Gnarfi
●●●● Route of Fafhrd & Mouser
1. The Needle's Eye
2. The Tresses
3. The Ladder
4. Snow ridge corniced to east
5. White Fang
6. Gran Hanack
7. The Great Chimney

THE WEST WALLS OF STARDOCK AND OBELISK POLARIS

I
IN THE WITCH'S TENT

THE HAG BENT over the brazier. It's upward-seeking gray fumes inter-
wove with strands of her downward dangling, tangled black hair. Its
glow showed her face to be as dark, jagged-featured, and dirty as the
new-dug root-clump of a blackapple tree. A half century of brazier
heat and smoke had cured it as black, crinkly, and hard as Mingol
bacon.

Through her splayed nostrils and slack mouth, which showed a few
brown teeth like old tree stumps irregularly fencing the gray field of
her tongue, she garglingly inhaled and bubblingly expelled the
fumes.

Such of them as escaped her greedy lungs tortuously found their
way to the tent's saggy roof, resting on seven ribs down-curving from
the central pole, and deposited on the ancient rawhide their tiny dole
of resin and soot. It is said that such a tent, boiled out after decades or
preferably centuries of use, yields a nauseous liquid which gives a
man strange and dangerous visions.

Outside the tent's drooping walls radiated the dark, twisty alleys of
Illik-Ving, an overgrown and rudely boisterous town, which is the
eighth and smallest metropolis of the Land of the Eight Cities.

While overhead there shivered in the chill wind the strange stars of
the world of Nehwon, which is so like and unlike our own world.

Inside the tent, two barbarian-clad men watched the crouching witch across the brazier. The big man, who had red-blond hair, stared somber-eyed and intently. The little man, who was dressed all in gray, drooped his eyelids, stifled a yawn, and wrinkled his nose.

"I don't know which stinks worse, she or the brazier," he murmured. "Or maybe it's the whole tent, or this alley muck we must sit in. Or perchance her familiar is a skunk. Look, Fafhrd, if we must consult a sorcerous personage, we should have sought out Sheelba or Ningauble before ever we sailed north from Lankhmar across the Inner Sea."

"They weren't available," the big man answered in a clipped whisper. "Shh, Gray Mouser, I think she's gone into trance."

"Asleep, you mean," the little man retorted irreverently.

The hag's gargling breath began to sound more like a death rattle. Her eyelids fluttered, showing two white lines. Wind stirred the tent's dark walls—or it might be unseen presences fumbling and fingering.

The little man was unimpressed. He said, "I don't see why we have to consult anyone. It isn't as if we were going outside Nehwon altogether, as we did in our last adventure. We've got the papers—the scrap of ramskin parchment, I mean—and we know where we're going. Or at least you say you do."

"Shh!" the big man commanded, then added hoarsely, "Before embarking on any great enterprise, it's customary to consult a warlock or witch."

The little man, now whispering likewise, countered with, "Then why couldn't we have consulted a civilized one?—any member in good standing of the Lankhmar Sorcerers Guild. He'd at least have had a comely naked girl or two around, to rest your eyes on when they began to water from scanning his crabbed hieroglyphs and horoscopes."

"A good earthy witch is more honest than some city rogue tricked out in black cone-hat and robe of stars," the big man argued. "Besides, this one is nearer our icy goal and its influences. You and your townsman's lust for luxuries! You'd turn a wizard's workroom into a brothel."

"Why not?" the little man wanted to know. "Both species of glamour at once!" Then, jerking his thumb at the hag, "Earthy, you said? Dungy describes her better."

"Shh, Mouser, you'll break her trance."

"Trance?" The little man reinspected the hag. Her mouth had shut and she was breathing wheezingly through her beaky nose alone, the fume-sooty tip of which sought to meet her jutting chin. There was a faint high wailing, as of distant wolves, or nearby ghosts, or perhaps just an odd overtone of the hag's wheezes.

The little man sneered his upper lip and shook his head. His hands shook a little too, but he hid that. "No, she's only stoned out of her skull, I'd say," he commented judiciously. "You shouldn't have given her so much poppy gum."

"But that's the entire intent of trance," the big man protested. "To lash, stone, and otherwise drive the spirit out of the skull and whip it up mystic mountains, so that from their peaks it can spy out the lands of past and future, and mayhaps other-world."

"I wish the mountains ahead of *us* were merely mystic," the little man muttered. "Look, Fafhrd, I'm willing to squat here all night—or at any rate for fifty more stinking breaths or two hundred bored heartbeats—to pleasure your whim. But has it occurred to you that we're in danger in this tent? And I don't mean solely from spirits. There are other rogues than ourselves in Illik-Ving, some perhaps on the same quest as ours, who'd dearly love to scupper us. And here in this blind leather hut we're deer on a skyline—or sitting ducks."

Just then the wind came back with its fumblings and fingerings, and in addition a scrabbling that might be that of wind-swayed branch tips or of dead men's long fingernails a-scratch. There were faint growlings and wailings too, and with them stealthy footfalls. Both men thought of the Mouser's last warning. Fafhrd and he looked toward the tent's night-slitted skin door and loosened their swords in their scabbards.

At that instant the hag's noisy breathing stopped and with it all other sound. Her eyes opened, showing only whites—milky ovals infinitely eerie in the dark root-tangle of her sharp features and stringy hair. The gray tip of her tongue traveled like a large maggot around her lips.

The Mouser made to comment, but the out-thrust palm-side of Fafhrd's spread-fingered hand was more compelling than any *shh*.

In a voice low but remarkably clear, almost a girl's voice, the hag intoned:

> "For reasons sorcerous and dim
> You travel toward the world's frost rim. . . ."

"Dim" is the key word there, the Mouser thought. *Typical witchy say-nothing. She clearly knows naught about us except that we're headed north, which she could get from any gossipy mouth.*

"You north, north, north, and north must go
  Through dagger-ice and powder-snow . . ."

More of the same, was the Mouser's inward comment. *But must she rub it in, even the snow? Brr!*

"And many a rival, envy-eyed,
  Will dog your steps until you've died. . . ."

Aha, the inevitable fright-thrust, without which no fortune-tale is complete!

"But after peril's cleansing fire
  You'll meet at last your hearts' desire . . ."

And how pat the happy ending! Gods, but the stupidest palm-reading prostitute of Ilthmar could—

"And then you'll find—"

Something silvery gray flashed across the Mouser's eyes, so close its form was blurred. Without a thought he ducked back and drew Scalpel.

The razor-sharp spear-blade, driven through the tent's side as if it were paper, stopped inches from Fafhrd's head and was dragged back.

A javelin hurtled out of the hide wall. This the Mouser struck aside with his sword.

Now a storm of cries rose outside. The burden of some was, "Death to the strangers!" Of others, "Come out, dogs, and be killed!"

The Mouser faced the skin door, his gaze darting.

Fafhrd, almost as quick to react as the Mouser, hit on a somewhat irregular solution to their knotty tactical problem: that of men besieged in a fortress whose walls neither protect them nor permit outward viewing. At first step, he leaped to the tent's central pole and with a great heave drew it from the earth.

The witch, likewise reacting with good solid sense, threw herself flat on the dirt.

"We decamp!" Fafhrd cried. "Mouser, guard our front and guide me!"

And with that he charged toward the door, carrying the whole tent with him. There was a rapid series of little explosions as the somewhat brittle old thongs that tied its rawhide sides to its pegs snapped.

The brazier tumbled over, scattering coals. The hag was overpassed. The Mouser, running ahead of Fafhrd, threw wide the door-slit. He had to use Scalpel at once, to parry a sword thrust out of the dark, but with his other hand he kept the door spread.

The opposing swordsman was bowled over, perhaps a bit startled at being attacked by the tent. The Mouser trod on him. He thought he heard ribs snap as Fafhrd did the same, which seemed a nice if brutal touch. Then he was crying out, "Veer left now, Fafhrd! Now to the right a little! There's an alley coming up on our left. Be ready to turn sharp into it when I give the word. Now!" And grasping the door's hide edges, the Mouser helped swing the tent as Fafhrd pivoted.

From behind came cries of rage and wonder, also a screeching that sounded like the hag, enraged at the theft of her home.

The alley was so narrow that the tent's sides dragged against buildings and fences. At the first sign of a soft spot in the dirt underfoot, Fafhrd drove the tent-pole into it, and they both dashed out of the tent, leaving it blocking the alley.

The cries behind them grew suddenly louder as their pursuers turned into the alley, but Fafhrd and the Mouser did not run off overswiftly. It seemed certain their attackers would spend considerable time scouting and assaulting the empty tent.

They loped together through the outskirts of the sleeping city toward their own well-hidden camp outside it. Their nostrils sucked in the chill, bracing air funneling down from the best pass through the Trollstep Mountains, a craggy chain which walled off the Land of Eight Cities from the vast plateau of the Cold Waste to the north.

Fafhrd remarked, "It's unfortunate the old lady was interrupted just when she was about to tell us something important."

The Mouser snorted. "She'd already sung her song, the sum of which was zero."

"I wonder who those rude fellows were and what were their motives?" Fafhrd asked. "I thought I recognized the voice of that aleswiller Gnarfi, who has an aversion to bearmeat."

"Scoundrels behaving as stupidly as we were," the Mouser answered. "Motives?—as soon impute 'em to sheep! Ten dolts following an idiot leader."

"Still, it appears that someone doesn't like us," Fafhrd opined.

"Was that ever news?" the Gray Mouser retorted.

II
STARDOCK

EARLY ONE EVENING, weeks later, the sky's gray cloud-armor blew away south, smashed and dissolving as if by blows of an acid-dipped mace. The same mighty northeast wind contemptuously puffed down the hitherto impregnable cloud wall to the east, revealing a grimly majestic mountain range running north to south and springing abruptly from the plateau, two leagues high, of the Cold Waste—like a dragon fifty leagues long heaving up its spike-crested spine from icy entombment.

Fafhrd, no stranger to the Cold Waste, born at the foot of these same mountains and childhood climber of their lower slopes, named them off to the Gray Mouser as the two men stood together on the crunchy hoarfrosted eastern rim of the hollow that held their camp. The sun, set for the camp, still shone from behind their backs onto the western faces of the major peaks as he named them—but it shone not with any romanticizing rosy glow, but rather with a clear, cold, detail-pinning light fitting the peaks' dire aloofness.

"Travel your eye to the first great northerly upthrust," he told the Mouser, "that phalanx of heaven-menacing ice-spears shafted with dark rock and gleaming green—that's the Ripsaw. Then, dwarfing them, a single ivory-icy tooth, unscalable by any sane appraisal—the Tusk, he's called. Another unscalable then, still higher and with south wall a sheer precipice shooting up a league and curving outward toward the needletop: he is White Fang, where my father died—the canine of the Mountains of the Giants.

"Now begin again with the first snow dome at the south of the chain," continued the tall fur-cloaked man, copper-bearded and copper-maned, his head otherwise bare to the frigid air, which was as quiet at ground level as sea-deep beneath storm. "The Hint, she's named, or the Come On. Little enough she looks, yet men have frozen nighting on her slopes and been whirled to death by her whimsical queenly avalanches. Then a far vaster snow dome, true queen to the Hint's princess, a hemisphere of purest white, grand enough to roof the council hall of all the gods that ever were or will be—she is Gran Hanack, whom my father was first of men to mount and master. Our town of tents was pitched *there* near her base. No mark of it now, I'll guess, not even a midden.

"After Gran Hanack and nearest to us of them all, a huge flat-topped pillar, a pedestal for the sky almost, looking to be of green-shot snow but in truth all snow-pale granite scoured by the storms: Obelisk Polaris.

"Lastly," Fafhrd continued, sinking his voice and gripping his smaller comrade's shoulder, "let your gaze travel up the snow-tressed, dark-rocked, snowcapped peak between the Obelisk and White Fang, her glittering skirt somewhat masked by the former, but taller than they as they are taller than the Waste. Even now she hides behind her the mounting moon. She is Stardock, our quest's goal."

"A pretty enough, tall, slender wart on this frostbit patch of Nehwon's face," the Gray Mouser conceded, writhing his shoulder from Fafhrd's grip. "And now at last tell me, friend, why you never climbed this Stardock in your youth and seized the treasure there, but must wait until we get a clue to it in a dusty, hot, scorpion-patrolled desert tower a quarter world away—and waste half a year getting here."

Fafhrd's voice grew a shade unsure as he answered, "My father never climbed her; how should I? Also, there were no legends of a treasure on Stardock's top in my father's clan . . . though there was a storm of other legends about Stardock, each forbidding her ascent. They called my father the Legend Breaker and shrugged wisely when he died on White Fang. . . . Truly, my memory's not so good for those days, Mouser—I got many a mind-shattering knock on my head before I learned to deal all knocks first . . . and then I was hardly a boy when the clan left the Cold Waste—though the rough hard walls of Obelisk Polaris had been my upended playground. . . ."

The Mouser nodded doubtfully. In the stillness they heard their tethered ponies munching the ice-crisped grass of the hollow, then a faint unangry growl from Hrissa the ice-cat, curled between the tiny fire and the piled baggage—likely one of the ponies had come cropping too close. On the great icy plain around them, nothing moved— or almost nothing.

The Mouser dipped gray lambskin-gloved fingers into the bottom of his pouch and from the pocket there withdrew a tiny oblong of parchment and read from it, more by memory than sight:

> "Who mounts white Stardock, the Moon Tree,
> "Past worm and gnome and unseen bars,
> "Will win the key to luxury:
> "The Heart of Light, a pouch of stars."

Fafhrd said dreamily, "They say the gods once dwelt and had their smithies on Stardock and from thence, amid jetting fire and showering sparks, launched all the stars; hence her name. They say diamonds, rubies, smaragds—all great gems—are the tiny pilot models the gods made of the stars . . . and then threw carelessly away across the world when their great work was done."

"You never told me that before," the Mouser said, looking at him sharply.

Fafhrd blinked his eyes and frowned puzzledly. "I am beginning to remember childhood things."

The Mouser smiled thinly before returning the parchment to its deep pocket. "The guess that a pouch of stars might be a bag of gems," he listed, "the story that Nehwon's biggest diamond is called the Heart of Light, a few words on a ramskin scrap in the topmost room of a desert tower locked and sealed for centuries—small hints, those, to draw two men across this murdering, monotonous Cold Waste. Tell me, Old Horse, were you just homesick for the miserable white meadows of your birth to pretend to believe 'em?"

"Those small hints," Fafhrd said, gazing now toward White Fang, "drew other men north across Nehwon. There must have been other ramskin scraps, though why they should be discovered at the same time, I cannot guess."

"We left all such fellows behind at Illik-Ving, or Lankhmar even, before we ever mounted the Trollsteps," the Mouser asserted with complete confidence. "Weak sisters, they were, smelling loot but quailing at hardship."

Fafhrd gave a small headshake and pointed. Between them and White Fang rose the tiniest thread of black smoke.

"Did Gnarfi and Kranarch seem weak sisters?—to name but two of the other seekers," he asked when the Mouser finally saw and nodded.

"It could be," the Mouser agreed gloomily. "Though aren't there any ordinary travelers of this Waste? Not that we've seen a man-shaped soul since the Mingol."

Fafhrd said thoughtfully, "It might be an encampment of the Icy Gnomes . . . though they seldom leave their caves except at High Summer, now a month gone. . . ." He broke of, frowning puzzledly. "Now how did I know that?"

"Another childhood memory bobbing to the top of the black pot?" the Mouser hazarded. Fafhrd shrugged doubtfully.

"So, for choice, Kranarch and Gnarfi," the Mouser concluded. "Two strong brothers, I'll concede. Perhaps we should have picked a fight with 'em at Illik-Ving," he suggested. "Or perhaps even now . . . a swift march by night . . . a sudden swoop—"

Fafhrd shook his head. "Now we're climbers, not killers," he said. "A man must be all climber to dare Stardock." He directed the Mouser's gaze back toward the tallest mountain. "Let's rather study her west wall while the light holds.

"Begin first at her feet," he said. "That glimmering skirt falling from her snowy hips, which are almost as high as the Obelisk—that's the White Waterfall, where no man may live.

"Now to her head again. From her flat tilted snowcap hang two great swelling braids of snow, streaming almost perpetually with avalanches, as if she combed 'em day and night—the Tresses, those are called. Between them's a wide ladder of dark rock, marked at three points by ledges. The topmost of the three ledge-banks is the Face—d'you note the darker ledges marking eyes and lips? The mid-most of the three is called the Roosts; the lowermost—level with Obelisk's wide summit—the Lairs."

"What lairs and roosts there?" the Mouser wanted to know.

"None may say, for none have climbed the Ladder," Fafhrd replied. "Now as to our route up her—it's most simple. We scale Obelisk Polaris—a trustworthy mountain if there ever was one—then cross by a dippling snow-saddle (there's the danger-stretch of our ascent!) to Stardock and climb the Ladder to her top."

"How do we climb the Ladder in the long blank stretches between the ledges?" the Mouser asked with childlike innocence, almost. "That is, if the Lairers and Roosters will honor our passports and permit us to try."

Fafhrd shrugged. "There'll be a way, rock being rock."

"Why's there no snow on the Ladder?"

"Too steep."

"And supposing we climb it to the top," the Mouser finally asked, "how do we lift our black-and-blue skeletonized bodies over the brim of Stardock's snowy hat, which seems to outcurve and downcurve most stylishly?"

"There's a triangular hole in it somewhere called the Needle's Eye," Fafhrd answered negligently. "Or so I've heard. But never you fret, Mouser, we'll find it."

"Of course we will," the Mouser agreed with an airy certainty that almost sounded sincere, "we who hop-skip across shaking snow bridges and dance the fantastic up vertical walls without ever touching hand to granite. Remind me to bring a longish knife to carve our initials on the sky when we celebrate the end of our little upward sortie."

His gaze wandered slightly northward. In another voice he continued, "The dark north wall of Stardock now—that looks steep enough, to be sure, but free of snow to the very top. Why isn't that our route —rock, as you say with such unanswerable profundity, being rock."

Fafhrd laughed unmockingly. "Mouser," he said, "do you mark against the darkening sky that long white streamer waving south from Stardock's top? Yes, and below it a lesser streamer—can you distinguish that? That second one comes through the Needle's Eye! Well, those streamers from Stardock's hat are called the Grand and Petty Pennons. They're powdered snow blasted off Stardock by the northeast gale, which blows at least seven days out of eight, never predictably. That gale would pluck the stoutest climber off the north wall as easily as you or I might puff dandelion down from its darkening stem. Stardock's self shields the Ladder from the gale."

"Does the gale never shift around to strike the Ladder?" the Mouser inquired lightly.

"Only occasionally," Fafhrd reassured him.

"Oh, that's great," the Mouser responded with quite overpowering sincerity and would have returned to the fire, except just then the darkness began swiftly to climb the Mountains of the Giants, as the sun took his final dive far to the west, and the gray-clad man stayed to watch the grand spectacle.

It was like a black blanket being pulled up. First the glittering skirt of the White Waterfall was hidden, then the Lairs on the Ladder and then the Roosts. Now all the other peaks were gone, even the Tusk's and White Fang's gleaming cruel tips, even the greenish-white roof of

Obelisk Polaris. Now only Stardock's snow hat was left and below it the Face between the silvery Tresses. For a moment the ledges called the Eyes gleamed, or seemed to. Then all was night.

Yet there was a pale afterglow about. It was profoundly silent and the air utterly unmoving. Around them, the Cold Waste seemed to stretch north, west, and south to infinity.

And in that space of silence something went whisper-gliding through the still air, with the faint rushy sound of a great sail in a moderate breeze. Fafhrd and the Mouser both stared all around wildly. Nothing. Beyond the little fire, Hrissa the ice-cat sprang up hissing. Still nothing. Then the sound, whatever had made it, died away.

Very softly, Fafhrd began, "There is a legend. . . ." A long pause. Then with a sudden headshake, in a more natural voice: "The memory slips away, Mouser. All my mind-fingers couldn't clutch it. Let's patrol once around the camp and so to bed."

From first sleep the Mouser woke so softly that even Hrissa, back pressed against him from his knees to his chest on the side toward the fire, did not rouse.

Emerging from behind Stardock, her light glittering on the southern Tress, hung the swelling moon, truly a proper fruit of the Moon Tree. Strange, the Mouser thought, how small the moon was and how big Stardock, silhouetted against the moon-pale sky.

Then, just below the flat top of Stardock's hat, he saw a bright, pale blue twinkling. He recalled that Ashsha, pale blue and brightest of Nehwon's stars, was near the moon tonight and he wondered if he were seeing her by rare chance through the Needle's Eye, proving the latter's existence. He wondered too what great sapphire or blue diamond—perhaps the Heart of Light?—had been the gods' pilot model for Ashsha, smiling drowsily the while at himself for entertaining such a silly, lovely myth. And then, embracing the myth entirely, he asked himself whether the gods had left any of their full-scale stars, unlaunched, on Stardock. Then Ashsha, if it were she, winked out.

The Mouser felt cozy in his cloak lined with sheep's-wool and now thong-laced into a bag by the horn hooks around its hem. He stared long and dreamily at Stardock until the moon broke loose from her and a blue jewel twinkled on top of her hat and broke loose too—now Ashsha surely. He wondered unfearfully about the windy rushing he and Fafhrd had heard in the still air—perhaps only a long tongue of a storm licking down briefly. If the storm lasted, they would climb up into it.

Hrissa stretched in her sleep. Fafhrd grumbled low in a dream, wrapped in his own great thong-laced cloak stuffed with eiderdown.

The Mouser dropped his gaze to the ghostly flames of the dying fire, seeking sleep himself. The flames made girl-bodies, then girl-faces. Next a ghostly pale green girl-face—perhaps an afterimage, he thought at first—appeared beyond the fire, staring at him through close-slitted eyes across the flame tops. It grew more distinct as he gazed at it, but there was no trace of hair or body about it—it hung against the dark like a mask.

Yet it was weirdly beautiful: narrow chin, high-arched cheeks, wine-dark short lips slightly pouted, straight nose that went up without a dip into the broad, somewhat low forehead—and then the mystery of those fully lidded eyes seeming to peer at him through wine-dark lashes. And all, save lashes and lips, of palest green, like jade.

The Mouser did not speak or stir a muscle, simply because the face was very beautiful to him—just as any man might hope for the moment never to end when his naked mistress unconsciously or by secret design assumes a particularly charming attitude.

Also, in the dismal Cold Waste, any man treasures illusions, though knowing them almost certainly to be such.

Suddenly the eyes parted wide, showing only the darkness behind, as if the face were a mask indeed. The Mouser did start then, but still not enough to wake Hrissa.

Then the eyes closed, the lips puckered with taunting invitation; then the face began swiftly to dissolve as if were being literally wiped away. First the right side went, then the left, then the center, last of all the dark lips and the eyes. For a moment the Mouser fancied he caught a winy odor; then all was gone.

He contemplated waking Fafhrd and almost laughed at the thought of his comrade's surly reactions. He wondered if the face had been a sign from the gods, or a sending from some black magician castled on Stardock, or Stardock's very soul perhaps—though then where had she left her glittering tresses and hat and her Ashsha eye?—or only a random creation of his own most clever brain, stimulated by sexual privation and tonight by beauteous if devilishly dangerous mountains. Rather quickly he decided on the last explanation and he slumbered.

Two evenings later, at the same hour, Fafhrd and the Gray Mouser stood scarcely a knife cast from the west wall of Obelisk Polaris, building a cairn from pale greenish rock-shards fallen over the mil-

lennia. Among this scanty scree were some bones, many broken, of
sheep or goats.

As before, the air was still though very cold, the Waste empty, the
set sun bright on the mountain faces.

From this closest vantage point the Obelisk was foreshortened into
a pyramid that seemed to taper up forever, vertically. Encouragingly,
his rock felt diamond-hard while the lowest reaches of the wall at any
rate were thick with bumpy handholds and footholds, like pebbled
leather.

To the south, Gran Hanack and the Hint were hidden. To the
north White Flag towered monstrously, yellowish white in the sunlight, as if ready to rip a hole in the graying sky. Bane of Fafhrd's
father, the Mouser recalled.

Of Stardock, there could be seen the dark beginning of the wind-
blasted north wall and the north end of the deadly White Waterfall.
All else of Stardock the Obelisk hid.

Save for one touch: almost straight overhead, seeming now to come
from Obelisk Polaris, the ghostly Grand Pennon streamed southwest.

From behind Fafhrd and the Mouser as they worked came the tantalizing odor of two snow hares roasting by the fire, while before it
Hrissa tore flesh slowly and savoringly from the carcass of a third
she'd coursed down. The ice-cat was about the size and shape of a
cheetah, though with long tufty white hair. The Mouser had bought
her from a far-ranging Mingol trapper just north of the Trollsteps.

Beyond the fire the ponies eagerly chomped the last of the grain,
strengthening stuff they'd not tasted for a week.

Fafhrd wrapped his sheathed longsword Graywand in oiled silk
and laid it in the cairn, then held out a big hand to the Mouser.

"Scalpel?"

"I'm taking my sword with me," the Mouser stated, then added
justifyingly, "it's but a feather to yours."

"Tomorrow you'll find what a feather weighs," Fafhrd foretold.
The big man shrugged and placed by Graywand his helmet, a bear's
hide, a folded tent, shovel and pickax, gold bracelets from his wrists
and arms, quills, ink, papyrus, a large copper pot, and some books and
scrolls. The Mouser added various empty and near-empty bags, two
hunting spears, skis, an unstrung bow with a quiver of arrows, tiny
jars of oily paint and squares of parchment, and all the harness of the
ponies, many of the items wrapped against damp like Graywand.

Then, their appetites quickening from the roast-fumes, the two
comrades swiftly built two top courses, roofing the cairn.

Just as they turned toward supper, facing the raggedly gilt-edged flat western horizon, they heard in the silence the rushy sail-like noise again, fainter this time but twice: once in the air to the north and, almost simultaneously, to the south.

Again they stared around swiftly but searchingly, yet there was nothing anywhere to be seen except—again Fafhrd saw it first—a thread of black smoke very near White Fang, rising from a point on the glacier between that mountain and Stardock.

"Gnarfi and Kranarch, if it be they, have chosen the rocky north wall for their ascent," the Mouser observed.

"And it will be their bane," Fafhrd predicted, up-jerking his thumb at the Pennon.

The Mouser nodded with less certainty, then demanded, "Fafhrd, what *was* that sound? You've lived here."

Fafhrd's brow crinkled and his eyes almost shut. "Some legend of great birds . . ." he muttered questioningly, ". . . or of great fish— no, that couldn't be right."

"Memory pot still seething all black?" the Mouser asked. Fafhrd nodded.

Before he left the cairn, the Northerner laid beside it a slab of salt. "That," he said, "along with the ice-filmed pool and herbage we just passed, should hold the ponies here for a week. If we don't return, well, at least we showed 'em the way between here and Illik-Ving."

Hrissa smiled up from her bloody tidbit, as if to say, "No need to worry about me or my rations."

Again the Mouser woke as soon as sleep had gripped him tight, this time with a surge of pleasure, as one who remembers a rendezvous. And again, this time without any preliminary star-staring or flame-gazing, the living mask faced him across the sinking fire: every same expression-quirk and feature—short lips, nose and forehead one straight line—except that tonight it was ivory pale with greenish lips and lids and lashes.

The Mouser was considerably startled, for last night he had stayed awake, waiting for the phantom girl-face—and even trying to make it come again—until the swelling moon had risen three handbreaths above Stardock . . . without any success whatever. His mind had known that the face had been an hallucination on the first occasion, but his feelings had insisted otherwise—to his considerable disgust and the loss of a quarter night's sleep.

And by day he had secretly consulted the last of the four short stanzas on the parchment scrap in his pouch's deepest pocket:

Who scales the Snow King's citadel
  Shall father his two daughter's sons;
Though he must face foes fierce and fell,
  His seed shall live while time still runs.

Yesterday that had seemed rather promising—at least the fathering and daughters part—though today, after his lost sleep, the merest mockery.

But now the living mask was there again and going through all the same teasing antics, including the shuddersome yet somehow thrilling trick of opening wide its lids to show not eyes but a dark backing like the rest of the night. The Mouser was enchanted in a shivery way, but unlike the first night he was full-mindedly alert and he tested for illusions by blinking and squinting his own eyes and silently shifting his head about in his hood—with no effect whatever on the living mask. Then he quietly unlaced the thong from the top hooks of his cloak—Hrissa was sleeping against Fafhrd tonight—and slowly reached out his hand and picked up a pebble and flicked it across the pale flames at a point somewhat below the mask.

Although he knew there wasn't anything beyond the fire but scattered scree and ringingly hard earth, there wasn't the faintest sound of the pebble striking anywhere. He might have thrown it off Nehwon.

At almost the same instant, the mask smiled tauntingly.

The Mouser was very swiftly out of his cloak and on his feet.

But even more swiftly the mask dissolved away—this time in one swift stroke from forehead to chin.

He quickly stepped, almost lunged, around the fire to the spot where the mask had seemed to hang, and there he stared around searchingly. Nothing—except a fleeting breath of wine or spirits of wine. He stirred the fire and stared around again. Still nothing. Except that Hrissa woke beside Fafhrd and bristled her moustache and gazed solemnly, perhaps scornfully, at the Mouser, who was beginning to feel rather like a fool. He wondered if his mind and his desires were playing a silly game against each other.

Then he trod on something. His pebble, he thought, but when he picked it up, he saw it was a tiny jar. It could have been one of his own pigment jars, but it was too small, hardly bigger than a joint of his thumb, and made not of hollowed stone but some kind of ivory or other tooth.

He knelt by the fire and peered into it, then dipped in his little finger and gingerly rubbed the tip against the rather hard grease inside. It came out ivory-hued. The grease had an oily, not winy odor.

The Mouser pondered by the fire for some time. Then with a glance at Hrissa, who had closed her eyes and laid back her moustache again, and at Fafhrd, who was snoring softly, he returned to his cloak and to sleep.

He had not told Fafhrd a word about his earlier vision of the living mask. His surface reason was that Fafhrd would laugh at such calf-brained nonsense of smoke-faces; his deeper reason the one which keeps any man from mentioning a pretty new girl even to his dearest friend.

So perhaps it was the same reason which next morning kept Fafhrd from telling his dearest friend what happened to him late that same night. Fafhrd dreamed he was feeling out the exact shape of a girl's face in absolute darkness while her slender hands caressed his body. She had a rounded forehead, very long-lashed eyes, in-dipping nose bridge, apple cheeks, an impudent snub nose—it *felt* impudent!—and long lips whose grin his big gentle fingers could trace clearly.

He woke to the moon glaring down at him aslant from the south. It silvered the Obelisk's interminable wall, turning rock-knobs to black shadow bars. He also woke to acute disappointment that a dream had been only a dream. Then he would have sworn that he felt fingertips briefly brush his face and that he heard a faint silvery chuckle which receded swiftly. He sat up like a mummy in his laced cloak and stared around. The fire had sunk to a few red ember-eyes, but the moonlight was bright and by it he could see nothing at all.

Hrissa growled at him reproachfully for a silly-sleep-breaker. He damned himself for mistaking the afterimage of a dream for reality. He damned the whole girl-less, girl-vision-breeding Cold Waste. A bit of the night's growing chill spilled down his neck. He told himself he should be fast asleep like the wise Mouser over there, gathering strength for tomorrow's great effort. He lay back and after some time he slumbered.

Next morning the Mouser and Fafhrd woke at the first gray of dawn, the moon still bright as a snowball in the west, and quickly breakfasted and readied themselves and stood facing Obelisk Polaris in the stinging cold, all girls forgotten, their manhood directed solely at the mountain.

Fafhrd stood in high-laced boots with newly-sharpened thick hobnails. He wore a wolfskin tunic, fur turned in but open now from neck to belly. His lower arms and legs were bare. Short-wristed rawhide gloves covered his hands. A rather small pack, wrapped in his cloak, rode high on his back. Clipped to it was a large coil of black hempen rope. On his stout unstudded belt, his sheathed ax on his right side balanced on the other a knife, a small waterskin, and a bag of iron spikes headed by rings.

The Mouser wore his ramskin hood, pulled close around his face now by its drawstring, and on his body a tunic of gray silk, triple layered. His gloves were longer than Fafhrd's and fur-lined. So were his slender boots, which were footed with crinkly behemoth hide. On *his* belt, his dagger Cat's Claw and his waterskin balanced his sword Scalpel, its scabbard thonged loosely to his thigh. While to his cloak-wrapped pack was secured a curiously thick, short, black bamboo rod headed with a spike at one end and at the other a spike and large hook, somewhat like that of a shepherd's crook.

Both men were deeply tanned and leanly muscular, in best trim for climbing, hardened by the Trollsteps and the Cold Waste, their chests a shade larger than ordinary from weeks of subsisting on the latter's thin air.

No need to search out the best-looking ascent—Fafhrd had done that yesterday as they'd approached the Obelisk.

The ponies were cropping again, and one had found the salt and was licking it with his thick tongue. The Mouser looked around for Hrissa to cuff her cheek in farewell, but the ice-cat was sniffling out a spoor beyond the campsite, her ears a-prick.

"She makes a cat-parting," Fafhrd said. "Good."

A faint shade of rose touched the heavens and the glacier by White Fang. Scanning toward the latter, the Mouser drew in his breath and squinted hard, while Fafhrd gazed narrowly from under the roof of his palm.

"Brownish figures," the Mouser said at last. "Kranarch and Gnarfi always dressed in brown leather, I recall. But I make them more than two."

"I make them four," Fafhrd said. "Two strangely shaggy—clad in brown fur suits, I guess. And all four mounting from the glacier up the rock wall."

"Where the gale will—" the Mouser began, then looked up. So did Fafhrd.

The Grand Pennon was gone.

"You said that sometimes—" the Mouser started.

"Forget the gale and those two and their rough-edged reinforcements," Fafhrd said curtly. He faced around again at Obelisk Polaris. So did the Mouser.

Squinting up the greenish-white slope, head bent sharply back, the Mouser said, "This morning he seems somewhat steeper even than that north wall and rather extensive upward."

"Pah!" Fafhrd retorted. "As a child I would climb him before breakfast. Often." He raised his clenched right rawhide glove as if it held a baton, and cried, "We go!"

With that he strode forward and without a break began to walk up the knobbly face—or so it seemed, for although he used handholds he kept his body far out from the rock, as a good climber should.

The Mouser followed in Fafhrd's steps and holds, stretching his legs farther and keeping somewhat closer to the cliff.

Midmorning and they were still climbing without a break. The Mouser ached or stung in every part. His pack was like a fat man on his back, Scalpel a sizable boy clinging to his belt. And his ears had popped five times.

Just above, Fafhrd's boots clashed rock-knobs and into rock-holes with an unhesitating mechanistic rhythm the Mouser had begun to hate. Yet he kept his eyes resolutely fixed on them. Once he had looked down between his own legs and decided not to do that again.

It is not good to see the blue of distance, or even the gray-blue of middle distance, below one.

So he was taken by surprise when a small white bearded face, bloodily encumbered, came bobbing up alongside and past him.

Hrissa halted on a ledgelet by Fafhrd and took great whistling breaths, her tufted belly-skin pressing up against her spine with each exhalation. She breathed only through her pinkish nostrils because her jaws were full of two snow hares, packed side by side, with dead heads and hindquarters a-dangle.

Fafhrd took them from her and dropped them in his pouch and laced it shut.

Then he said, just a shade grandiloquently, "She has proved her endurance and skill, and she has paid her way. She is one of us."

It had not occurred to the Mouser to doubt any of that. It seemed to him simply that there were three comrades now climbing Obelisk Polaris. Besides, he was most grateful to Hrissa for the halt she had brought. Partly to prolong it, he carefully pressed a handful of water from his bag and stretch it to her to lap. Then he and Fafhrd drank a little too.

All the long summer day they climbed the west wall of the cruel but reliable Obelisk. Fafhrd seemed tireless. The Mouser got his second wind, lost it, and never quite got his third. His whole body was one great leaden ache, beginning deep in his bones and filtering outward, like refined poison, through his flesh. His vision became a bobbing welter of real and remembered rock-knobs, while the necessity of never missing one single grip or foot-placement seemed the ruling of an insane schoolmaster god. He silently cursed the whole maniacal Stardock project, cackling in his brain at the idea that the luring stanzas on the parchment could mean anything but pipe dreams. Yet he would not cry quits or seek again to prolong the brief breathers they took.

He marveled dully at Hrissa's leaping and hunching up beside them. But by mid-afternoon he noted she was limping and once he saw a light blood-print of two pads where she'd set a paw.

They made camp at last almost two hours before sunset, because they'd found a rather wide ledge—and because a very light snowfall had begun, the tiny flakes sifting silently down like meal.

They made a fire of resin-pellets in the tiny claw-footed brazier Fafhrd packed, and they heated over it water for herb tea in their single narrow high pot. The water was a long time getting even luke-warm. With Cat's Claw the Mouser stirred two dollops of honey into it.

The ledge was as long as three men stretched out and as deep as one. On the sheer face of Obelisk Polaris that much space seemed an acre, at least.

Hrissa stretched slackly behind the tiny fire. Fafhrd and the Mouser huddled to either side of it, their cloaks drawn around them, too tired to look around, talk, or even think.

The snowfall grew a little thicker, enough to hide the Cold Waste far below.

After his second swallow of sweetened tea, Fafhrd asserted they'd come at least two-thirds of the way up the Obelisk.

The Mouser couldn't understand how Fafhrd could pretend to know that, any more than a man could tell by looking at the shoreless waters of the Outer Sea how far he'd sailed across it. To the Mouser they were simply in the exact center of a dizzily tip-tilted plain of pale granite, green-tinged and now snow-sprinkled. He was still too weary to outline this concept to Fafhrd, but he managed to make himself say, "As a child you would climb up and down the Obelisk before breakfast?"

"We had rather late breakfasts then," Fafhrd explained gruffly.

"Doubtless on the afternoon of the fifth day," the Mouser concluded.

After the tea was drunk, they heated more water and left the hacked and disjointed bits of one of the snow hares in the fluid until they turned gray, then slowly chewed them and drank the dull soup. At about the same time Hrissa became a little interested in the flayed carcass of the other hare set before her nose—by the brazier to keep it from freezing. Enough interested to begin to haggle it with her fangs and slowly chew and swallow.

The Mouser very gently examined the pads of the ice-cat's paws. They were worn silk-thin, there were two or three cuts in them, and the white fur between them was stained deep pink. Using a feather touch, the Mouser rubbed salve into them, shaking his head the while. Then he nodded once and took from his pouch a large needle, a spool of thin thong, and a small rolled hide of thin, tough leather. From the last he cut with Cat's Claw a shape rather like a very fat pear and stitched from it a boot for Hrissa.

When he tried it on the ice-cat's hind paw, she let it be for a little, then began to bite at it rather gently, looking up queerly at the Mouser. He thought, then very carefully bored holes in it for the ice-cat's non-retracting claws, then drew the boot up the leg snugly until the claws protruded fully and tied it there with the drawstring he'd run through slits at the top.

Hrissa no longer bothered the boot. The Mouser made others, and Fafhrd joined in and cut and stitched one too.

When Hrissa was fully shod in her four clawed paw-mittens, she smelled each, then stood up and paced back and forth the length of the ledge a few times, and finally settled herself by the still-warm brazier and the Mouser, chin on his ankle.

The tiny grains of snow were still falling ruler-straight, frosting the ledge and Fafhrd's coppery hair. He and the Mouser began to pull up their hoods and lace their cloaks about them for the night. The sun still shone through the snowfall, but its light was filtered white and brought not an atom of warmth.

Obelisk Polaris was not a noisy mountain, as many are—a-drip with glacial water, rattling with rock slides, and even with rock strata a-creak from uneven loss or gain of heat. The silence was profound.

The Mouser felt an impulse to tell Fafhrd about the living girl-mask or illusion he'd seen by night, while simultaneously Fafhrd considered recounting to the Mouser his own erotic dream.

At that moment there came again, without prelude, the rushing in the silent air and they saw, clearly outlined by the falling snow, a great flat undulating shape.

It came swooping past them, rather slowly, about two spear-lengths out from the ledge.

There was nothing at all to be seen except the flat, flakeless space the thing made in the airborne snow and the eddies it raised; it in no way obscured the snow beyond. Yet they felt the gust of its passage.

The shape of this invisible thing was most like that of a giant skate or stingray four yards long and three wide; there was even the suggestion of a vertical fin and a long, lashing tail.

"Great invisible fish!" the Mouser hissed, thrusting his hand down in his half-laced cloak and managing to draw Scalpel in a single sweep. "Your mind was most right, Fafhrd, when you thought it wrong!"

As the snow-sketched apparition glided out of sight around the buttress ending the ledge to the south, there came from it a mocking rippling laughter in two voices, one alto, one soprano.

"A sightless fish that laughs like girls—most monstrous!" Fafhrd commented shakenly, hefting his ax, which he'd got out swiftly too, though it was still attached to his belt by a long thong.

They crouched there then for a while, scrambled out of their cloaks, and with weapons ready, awaited the invisible monster's return, Hrissa standing between them with fur bristling. But after a while they began to shake from the cold and so they perforce got back into their cloaks and laced them, though still gripping their weapons and prepared to throw off the upper lacings in a flash. Then they briefly discussed the weirdness just witnessed, insofar as they could, each now confessing his earlier visions or dreams of girls.

Finally the Mouser said, "The girls might have been riding the invisible thing, lying along its back—and invisible too! Yet, what *was* the thing?"

This touched a small spot in Fafhrd's memory. Rather unwillingly he said, "I remember waking once as a child in the night and hearing my father say to my mother, '. . . like great thick quivering sails, but the ones you can't see are the worst.' They stopped speaking then, I think because they heard me stir."

The Mouser asked, "Did your father ever speak of seeing girls in the high mountains—flesh, apparition, or witch, which is a mixture of the two; visible or invisible?"

"He wouldn't have mentioned 'em if he had," Fafhrd replied. "My mother was a very jealous woman and a devil with a chopper."

The whiteness they'd been scanning turned swiftly to darkest gray. The sun had set. They could no longer see the falling snow. They pulled up their hoods and laced their cloaks tight and huddled together at the back of the ledge with Hrissa close between them.

Trouble came early the next day. They roused with first light, feeling battered and nightmare-ridden, and uncramped themselves with difficulty while the morning ration of strong herb tea and powdered meat and snow were stewed in the same pot to a barely uncold aromatic gruel. Hrissa gnawed her rewarmed hare's bones and accepted a little bear's fat and water from the Mouser.

The snow had stopped during the night, but the Obelisk was powdered with it on every step and hold, while under the snow was ice—the first-fallen snow melted by yesterday afternoon's meager warmth on the rock and quickly refrozen.

So Fafhrd and the Mouser roped together, and the Mouser swiftly fashioned a harness for Hrissa by cutting two holes in the long side of an oblong of leather. Hrissa protested somewhat when her forelegs were thrust through the holes and the ends of the oblong double-stitched together snugly over her shoulders. But when an end of Fafhrd's black hempen rope was tied around her harness where the stitching was, she simply lay down flat on the ledge, on the warm spot where the brazier had stood, as if to say, "This debasing tether I will not accept, though humans may."

But when Fafhrd slowly started up the wall and the Mouser followed and the rope tightened on Hrissa, and when she had looked up and seen them still roped like herself, she followed sulkily after. A little later she slipped off a bulge—her boots, snug as they were, must have been clumsy to her after naked pads—and swung scrabbling back and forth several long moments before she was supporting her own weight again. Fortunately the Mouser had a firm stance at the time.

After that, Hrissa came on more cheerily, sometimes even climbing to the side ahead of the Mouser and smiling back at him—rather sardonically, the Mouser fancied.

The climbing was a shade steeper than yesterday with an even greater insistence that each hand- and foothold be perfect. Gloved fingers must grip stone, not ice; spikes must clash through the brittle stuff to rock. Fafhrd roped his ax to his right wrist and used its hammer to tap away treacherous thin platelets and curves of the glassy frozen water.

And the climbing was more wearing because it was harder to avoid tenseness. Even looking sideways at the steepness of the wall tightened the Mouser's groin with fear. He wondered *what if the wind should blow?*—and fought the impulse to cling flat to the cliff. Yet at the same time sweat began to trickle down his face and chest, so that he had to throw back his hood and loosen his tunic to his belly to keep his clothes from sogging.

But there was worse to come. It had looked as though the slope above were gentling, but now, drawing nearer, they perceived a bulge jutting out a full two yards some seven yards above them. The under-slope was pocked here and there—fine handholds, except that they opened down. The bulge extended as far as they could see to either side, at most points looking worse.

They found themselves the best and highest holds they could, close together, and stared up at their problem. Even Hrissa, a-cling by the Mouser, seemed subdued.

Fafhrd said softly, "I mind me now they used to say there was an out-jutting around the Obelisk's top. His Crown, I think my father called it. I wonder . . ."

"Don't you know?" the Mouser demanded, a shade harshly. Standing rigid on his holds, his arms and legs were aching worse than ever.

"O Mouser," Fafhrd confessed, "in my youth I never climbed Obelisk Polaris farther than halfway to last night's camp. I only boasted to raise our spirits."

There being nothing to say to that, the Mouser shut his lips, though somewhat thinly. Fafhrd began to whistle a tuneless tune and carefully fished a small grapnel with five dagger-sharp flukes from his pouch and tied it securely to the long end of their black rope still coiled on his back. Then stretching his right arm as far out as he might from the cliff, he whirled the grapnel in a smallish circle, faster and faster, and finally hurled it upward. They heard it clash against rock somewhere above the bulge, but it did not catch on any crack or hump and instantly came sliding and then dropping down, missing the Mouser by hardly a handbreadth, it seemed to him.

Fafhrd drew up the grapnel—with some delays, since it tended to catch on every crack or hump below them—and whirled and hurled it again. And again and again and again, each time without success. Once it stayed up, but Fafhrd's first careful tug on the rope brought it down.

Fafhrd's sixth cast was his first really bad one. The grapnel never went out of sight at all. As it reached the top of the throw, it glinted for an instant.

"Sunlight!" Fafhrd hissed happily. "We're almost to the summit!"

"That 'almost' is a whopper, though," the Mouser commented, but even he couldn't keep a cheerful note out of his voice.

By the time Fafhrd had failed on seven more casts, all cheerfulness was gone from the Mouser again. His aches were horrible, his hands and feet were numbing in the cold, and his brain was numbing too, so that the next time Fafhrd cast and missed, he was so unwise as to follow the grapnel with his gaze as it fell.

For the first time today he really looked out and down. The Cold Waste was a pale blue expanse almost like the sky—and seeming even more distant—all its copses and mounds and tiny tarns having long since become pinpoints and vanished. Many leagues to the west, almost at the horizon, a jagged pale gold band showed where the shadows of the mountains ended. Midway in the band was a blue gap— Stardock's shadow continuing over the edge of the world.

Giddily the Mouser snatched his gaze back to Obelisk Polaris . . . and although he could still see the granite, it didn't seem to count any more—only four insecure holds on a kind of pale green nothingness, with Fafhrd and Hrissa somehow suspended beside him. His mind could no longer accept the Obelisk's steepness.

As the urge to hurl himself down swelled in him, he somehow transformed it into a sardonic snort, and he heard himself say with daggerish contempt, "Leave off your foolish fishing, Fafhrd! I'll show you now how Lankhmarian mountain science deals with a trifling problem such as this which has baffled all your barbarian whirling and casting!"

And with that he unclipped from his pack with reckless speed the thick black bamboo pike or crook and began cursingly with numb fingers to draw out and let snap into place its telescoping sections until it was four times its original length.

This tool of technical climbing, which indeed the Mouser had brought all the way from Lankhmar, had been a matter of dispute between them the whole trip, Fafhrd asserting it was a tricksy toy not worth the packing.

Now, however, Fafhrd made no comment, but merely coiled up his grapnel and thrust his hands into his wolfskin jerkin against his sides to warm them and, mild-eyed, watched the Mouser's furious activity. Hrissa shifted to a perch closer to Fafhrd and crouched stoically.

But when the Mouser shakily thrust the narrower end of his black tool toward the bulge above, Fafhrd reached out a hand to help him steady it, yet could not refrain from saying, "If you think to get a good enough hold with the crook on the rim to shinny up that stick—"

"Quiet, you loutish kibitzer!" the Mouser snarled and with Fafhrd's help thrust pike-end into a pock in the rock hardly a finger's length from the rim. Then he seated the spiked foot of the pole in a small, deep hollow just above his head. Next he snapped out two short recessed lever-arms from the base of the pole and began to rotate them. It soon became clear that they controlled a great screw hidden in the pole, for the latter lengthened until it stood firmly between the two pocks in the rock, while the stiff black shaft itself bent a little.

At that instant a sliver of rock, being pressed by the pole, broke off from the rim. The pole thrummed as it straightened and the Mouser, screaming a curse, slipped off his holds and fell.

It was good then that the rope between the two comrades was short and that the spikes of Fafhrd's boots were seated firmly, like so many demon-forged dagger-points, in the rock of his footholds—for as the strain came suddenly on Fafhrd's belt and on his rope-gripping left hand, he took it without plummeting after the Mouser, only bending his knees a little and grunting softly, while his right hand snatched hold of the vibrating pole and saved it.

The Mouser had not even fallen far enough to drag Hrissa from her perch, though the rope almost straightened between them. The ice-cat, her tufted neck bent sharply between foreleg and chest, peered down with great curiosity at the dangling man.

His face was ashen. Fafhrd made no mark of that, but simply handed him the black pole, saying, "It's a good tool. I've screwed it back short. Seat it in another pock and try again."

Soon the pole stood firm between the hollow by the Mouser's head and a pock a hand's width from the rim. The bowlike bend in the pole faced downward. Then they put the Mouser first on the rope, and he went climbing up and out along the pole, hanging from it back downward, his boot-edges finding tiny holds on the pole's section-shoulders —out into and over the vast, pale blue-gray space which had so lately dizzied him.

The pole began to bend a little more with the Mouser's weight, the pike-end slipping a finger's span in the upper pock with a horrible tiny grating sound, but Fafhrd gave the screw another turn and the pole held firm.

Fafhrd and Hrissa watched the Mouser reach its end, where he paused briefly. Then they saw him reach up his left arm until it was out of sight to the elbow above the rim, meanwhile gripping with his right hand the crook and twining his legs around the shaft. He appeared to feel about with his left hand and find something. Then he moved out and up still further and very slowly his head and after it, in a sudden swift sweep, his right arm went out of sight above the rim.

For several long moments they saw only the bottom half of the bent Mouser, his dark crinkly-soled boots twined securely to the end of the pole. Then, rather slowly, like a gray snail, and with a final push of one boot against the top of the crook, he went entirely out of sight.

Fafhrd slowly paid out rope after him.

After some time the Mouser's voice, quite ghostly yet clear, came down to them: "Hola! I've got the rope anchored around a boss big as a tree stump. Send up Hrissa."

So Fafhrd put Hrissa on the rope ahead of him, knotting it to her harness with a sheepshank.

Hrissa fought desperately for a moment against being swung into space, but as soon as it was done hung deathly still. Then as she was drawn slowly up, Fafhrd's knot began to slip. The ice-cat swiftly snatched at the rope with her teeth and gripped it far back between her jaws. The moment she came near the rim, her clawed mittens were ready and she scrabbled and was dragged out of sight.

Soon word came down from the Mouser that Hrissa was safe and Fafhrd might follow. He frowningly tightened the screw another half turn, though the pole creaked ominously, and then very gently climbed out along it. The Mouser now kept the rope taut from above, but for the first stretch it could hardly take more than a few pounds of Fafhrd's weight off the pole.

The upper spike once again grated horribly a bit in its pock, but it still held firm. Helped more by the rope now, Fafhrd got his hands and head over the rim.

What he saw was a smooth, gentle rock slope, which could be climbed by friction, and at the top of it the Mouser and Hrissa standing backgrounded by blue sky and gilded by sunlight.

Soon he stood beside them.

The Mouser said, "Fafhrd, when we get back to Lankhmar remind me to give Glinthi the Artificer thirteen diamonds from the pouch of them we'll find on Stardock's hat: one for each section and joint of my climbing pole, one each for the spikes at the ends and two for each screw."

"Are there two screws?" Fafhrd asked respectfully.

"Yes, one at each end," the Mouser told him and then made Fafhrd brace the rope for him so that he could climb down the slope and, bending all his upper body down over the rim, shorten the pole by rotating its upper screw until he was able to drag it triumphantly back over the top with him.

As the Mouser telescoped its sections together again, Fafhrd said to him seriously, "You must thong it to your belt as I do my ax. We must not chance losing Glinthi's help on the rest of this journey."

Throwing back their hoods and opening their tunics wide to the hot sun, Fafhrd and the Mouser looked around, while Hrissa luxuriously stretched and worked her slim limbs and neck and body, the white fur of which hid her bruises.

Both men were somewhat exalted by the thin air and filled brain-high with the ease of mind and spirit that comes with a great danger skillfully conquered.

Rather to their amazement, the southward swinging sun had climbed barely halfway to noon. Perils which had seemed demihours long had lasted minutes only.

The summit of Obelisk Polaris was a great rolling field of pale rock too big to measure by Lankhmar acres. They had arrived near the southwest corner, and the gray-tinted stone meadow seemed to stretch east and north almost indefinitely. Here and there were hummocks and hollows, but they swelled and dipped most gently. There were a few scattered large boulders, not many, while off to the east were darker indistinct shapes which might be bushes and small trees footed in cracks filled with blown dirt.

"What lies east of the mountain chain?" the Mouser asked. "More Cold Waste?"

"Our clan never journeyed there," Fafhrd answered. He frowned. "Some taboo on the whole area, I think. Mist always masked the east on my father's great climbs—or so he told us."

"We could have a look now," the Mouser suggested.

Fafhrd shook his head. "Our course lies there," he said, pointing northeast, where Stardock rose like a giantess standing tall but asleep, or feigning sleep, looking seven times as big and high at least as she had before the Obelisk hid her top two days ago.

The Mouser said, a shade dolefully, "All our brave work scaling the Obelisk has only made Stardock higher. Are you sure there's not another peak, perhaps invisible, on top of her?"

Fafhrd nodded without taking his eyes off her, who was empress without consort of the Mountains of the Giants. Her Tresses had grown to great swelling rivers of snow and now the two adventurers could see faint stirrings in them—avalanches slipping and tumbling.

The Southern Tress came down in a great dipping double curve toward the northwest corner of the mighty rock summit on which they stood.

At the top, Stardock's corniced snow hat, its upper rim glittering with sunlight as if it were edged around with diamonds, seemed to nod toward them a trifle more than it ever had before, and the demurely-eyed Face with it, like a great lady hinting at possible favors.

But the gauzy, long pale veils of the Grand and Petty Pennons no longer streamed from her Hat. The air atop Stardock must be as still at the moment as it was where they stood upon the Obelisk.

"What devil's luck that Kranarch and Gnarfi should tackle the north wall the one day in eight the gale fails!" Fafhrd cursed. "But 'twill be their destruction yet—yes, and of their two shaggy-clad henchmen too. This calm can't hold."

"I recall now," the Mouser remarked, "that when we caroused with 'em in Illik-Ving, Gnarfi drunken-claimed he could whistle up winds —had learned the trick from his grandmother—and could whistle 'em down too, which is more to the point."

"The more reason for us to hasten!" Fafhrd cried, upping his pack and slipping his big arms through the wide shoulder straps. "On, Mouser! Up, Hrissa! We'll have a bite and sup before the snow ridge."

"You mean we must tackle that freezing, treacherous problem today?" demurred the Mouser, who would dearly have loved to strip and bake in the sun.

"Before noon!" Fafhrd decreed. And with that he set them a stiff walking pace straight north, keeping close to the summit's west edge, as if to countermand from the start any curiosity the Mouser might have about a peek to the east. The latter followed with only minor further protests; Hrissa came on limpingly, lagging at first far behind, but catching up as her limp went and her cat-zest for newness grew.

And so they marched across the great, strange rolling granite plain of Obelisk's top, patched here and there with limestone stretches white as marble. Its sun-drenched silence and uniformity became eerie after a bit. The shallowness of its hollows was deceptive: Fafhrd noted several in which battalions of armed men might have hidden acrouch, unseen until one came within a spear's cast.

The longer they strode along, the more closely Fafhrd studied the rock his hobnails clashed. Finally he paused to point out a strangely rippled stretch.

"I'd swear that once was seabottom," he said softly.

The Mouser's eyes narrowed. Thinking of the great invisible fishlike flier they had seen last evening, its raylike form undulating through the snowfall, he felt gooseflesh crawling on him.

Hrissa slunk past them, head a-weave.

Soon they passed the last boulder, a huge one, and saw, scarcely a bowshot ahead, the glitter of snow.

The Mouser said, "The worst thing about mountain climbing is that the easy parts go so quickly."

"Hist!" warned Fafhrd, sprawling down suddenly like a great four-legged water beetle and putting his cheek to the rock. "Do you hear it, Mouser!"

Hrissa snarled, staring about, and her white fur bristled.

The Mouser started to stoop, but realized he wouldn't have to, so fast the sound was coming on: a general high-pitched drumming, as of five hundred fiends rippling their giant thick fingernails on a great stone drumhead.

Then, without pause, there came surging straight toward them over the nearest rock swelling to the southeast, a great wide-fronted stampede of goats, so packed together and their fur so glossy white that they seemed for a flash like an onrushing of living snow. Even the great curving horns of their leaders were ivory-hued. The Mouser noted that a stretch of the sunny air just above their center shimmered and wavered as it will above a fire. Then he and Fafhrd were racing back toward the last boulder with Hrissa bounding ahead.

Behind them the devil's tattoo of the stampede grew louder and louder.

They reached the boulder and vaulted atop it, where Hrissa already crouched, hardly a pounding heartbeat before the white horde. And well it was that Fafhrd had his ax out the instant they won there, for the midmost of the great billies sprang high, forelegs tucked up and head bowed to present his creamy horns—so close Fafhrd could see their splintered tips. But in that same instant Fafhrd got him in his snowy shoulder with a great swashing deep-cleaving blow so heavy that the beast was carried past them to the side and crashed on the short slope leading down to the rim of the west wall.

Then the white stampede was splitting around the great boulder, the animals so near and packed that there was no longer room for leaping, and the din of their hooves and the gasping and now the frightened bleating was horrendous, and the caprid stench was stifling, while the boulder rocked with their passage.

In the worst of the bruit there was a momentary downrushing of air, briefly dispelling the stench, as something passed close above their heads, rippling the sky like a long flapping blanket of fluid glass, while through the clangor could be heard for a moment a harsh, hateful laughter.

The lesser tongue of the stampede passed between the boulder and the rim, and of these goats many went tumbling over the edge with bleats like screams of the damned, carrying with them the body of the great billy Fafhrd had maimed.

Then as sudden in its departure as a snow squall that dismasts a ship in the Frozen Sea, the stampede was past them and pounding south, swinging east somewhat from the deadly rim, with the last few of the goats, chiefly nannies and kids, bounding madly after.

Pointing his arm toward the sun as if for a sword-thrust, the Mouser cried furiously, "See there, where the beams twist all askew above the herd! It's the same flier as just now overpassed us and last night we saw in the snowfall—the flier who raised the stampede and whose riders guided it against us! Oh, damn the two deceitful ghostly bitches, luring us on to a goaty destruction stinking worse than a temple orgy in the City of Ghouls!"

"I thought this laughter was far deeper," Fafhrd objected. "It was not the girls."

"So they have a deep-throated pimp—does that improve them in your eyes? Or your great flapping love-struck ears?" the Mouser demanded angrily.

The drumming of the stampede had died away even swifter than it had come and in the new-fallen silence they heard now a happy half-obstructed growling. Hrissa, springing off the boulder at stampede-end, had struck down a fat kid and was tearing at its bloodied white neck.

"Ah, I can smell it broiling now!" the Mouser cried with a great smile, his preoccupations altering in less than an instant. "Good Hrissa! Fafhrd, if those be treelets and bushes and grass to the east—and they must be that, for what else feeds these goats?—there's sure to be dead wood—why, there may even be mint!—and we can . . ."

"You'll eat the flesh raw for lunch or not at all!" Fafhrd decreed fiercely. "Are we to risk the stampede again? Or give the sniggering flier a chance to marshal against us some snow lions?—which are sure to be here too, to prey on the goats. And are we to present Kranarch and Gnarfi the summit of Stardock on a diamond-studded silver platter?—if this devil's lull holds tomorrow too and they be industrious strong climbers, not nice-bellied sluggards like one I could name!"

So, with only a gripe or two more from the Mouser, the kid was swiftly bled, gutted and skinned, and some of its spine-meat and haunches wrapped and packed for supper. Hrissa drank some more blood and ate half the liver and then followed the Mouser and Fafhrd as they set off north toward the snow ridge. The two men were chewing thin-sliced peppered collops of raw kid, but striding swiftly and keeping a wary eye behind for another stampede.

The Mouser expected now at last to get a view of the eastern depths, by peering east along the north wall of Obelisk Polaris, but here again he was foiled by the first great swell of the snow-saddle.

However, the northern view was fearsomely majestic. A full half league below them now and seen almost vertically on, the White Waterfall went showering down mysteriously, twinkling even in the shadow.

The ridge by which they must travel first curved up a score of yards, then dipped smoothly down to a long snow-saddle another score of yards below them, then slowly curved up into the South Tress, down which they could now plainly see avalanches trickling and tumbling.

It was easy to see how the northeast gale, blowing almost continually but missing the Ladder, would greatly pile up snow between the taller mountain and the Obelisk—but whether the rocky connection between the two mountains underlay the snow by only a few yards or by as much as a quarter league was impossible to know.

"We must rope again," Fafhrd decreed. "I'll go first and cut steps for us across the west slope."

"What need we steps in this calm?" the Mouser demanded. "Or to go by the west slope? You just don't want me to see the east, do you? The top of the ridge is broad enough to drive two carts across abreast."

"The ridge-top in the wind's path almost certainly overhangs emptiness to the east and would break away," Fafhrd explained. "Look you, Mouser; do I know more about snow and ice or do you?"

"I once crossed the Bones of the Old Ones with you," the Mouser retorted, shrugging. "There was snow there, I recall."

"Pooh, the mere spillings of a lady's powderbox compared to this. No, Mouser, on this stretch my word is law."

"Very well," the Mouser agreed.

So they roped up rather close—in order, Fafhrd, Mouser, and Hrissa—and without more ado Fafhrd donned his gloves and thonged his ax to his wrist and began cutting steps for them around the shoulder of the snow swell.

It was rather slow work, for under a dusting of powder snow the stuff was hard and for each step Fafhrd must make at least two cuts—first an in-chopping backhand one to make the step, then a down-chop to clear it. And as the slope grew steeper, he must make the

steps somewhat closer together. The steps he made were rather small,
at least for his great boots, but they were sure.

Soon the ridge and the Obelisk cut off the sun. It grew very chill.
The Mouser closed his tunic and drew his hood around his face, while
Hrissa, between her short leaps from step to step, performed a kind of
tiny cat-jig on them, to keep her gloved paws from freezing. The
Mouser reminded himself to stuff them a bit with lamb's wool when
he renewed the salve. He had his pike out now, telescoped short and
thonged to his wrist.

They passed the shoulder of the swell and came opposite the beginning of the snow-saddle, but Fafhrd did not cut steps up toward it.
Rather, the steps he now was cutting descended at a sharper angle
than the saddle dipped, though the slope they were crossing was becoming quite steep.

"Fafhrd," the Mouser protested quietly, "we're heading for
Stardock's top, not the White Waterfall."

"You said, 'Very well,'" Fafhrd retorted between chops. "Besides,
who does the work?" His ax rang as it bit into ice.

"Look, Fafhrd," the Mouser said, "there are two goats crossing to
Stardock along the saddletop. No, three."

"We should trust goats? Ask yourself why they've been sent."
Again Fafhrd's ax rang.

The sun swung into view as it coursed southward, sending their
three shadows ranging far ahead of them. The pale gray of the snow
turned glittery white. The Mouser unhooded to the yellow rays. For a
while the enjoyment of their warmth on the back of his head helped
him keep his mouth shut, but then the slope grew steeper yet, as
Fafhrd continued remorselessly to cut steps downward.

"I seem to recall that our purpose was to *climb* Stardock, but my
memory must be disordered," the Mouser observed. "Fafhrd, I'll take
your word we must keep away from the top of the ridge, but do we
have to keep away so *far*? And the three goats have all skipped
across."

Still, "'Very well,' you said," was all Fafhrd would answer, and
this time there was a snarl in his voice.

The Mouser shrugged. Now he was bracing himself with his pike
continuously, while Hrissa would pause studyingly before each leap.

Their shadows went less than a spear's cast ahead of them now,
while the hot sun had begun to melt the surface snow, sending down
trickles of ice water to wet their gloves and make their footing unsure.

Yet still Fafhrd kept cutting steps downward. And now of a sudden he began to cut them downward more steeply still, adding with taps of his ax a tiny handhold above each step—and these handholds were needed!

"Fafhrd," the Mouser said dreamily, "perhaps an ice-sprite has whispered to you the secret of levitation, so that from this fine takeoff you can dive, level out, and then go spiring to Stardock's top. In that case I wish you'd teach myself and Hrissa how to grow wings in an instant."

"Hist!" Fafhrd spoke softly yet sharply at that instant. "I have a feeling. Something comes. Brace yourself and watch behind us."

The Mouser drove his pike in deep and rotated his head. As he did, Hrissa leaped from the last step behind to the one on which the Mouser stood, landing half on his boot and clinging to his knee—yet this done so dexterously the Mouser was not dislodged.

"I see nothing," the Mouser reported, staring almost sunward. Then, words suddenly clipped: "Again the beams twist like a spinning lantern! The glints on the ice ripple and wave. 'Tis the flier come again! Cling!"

There came the rushing sound, louder than ever before and swiftly mounting, then a great sea-wave of air, as of a great body passing swiftly only spans away; it whipped their clothes and Hrissa's fur and forced them to cling fiercely to their holds, though Fafhrd made a full-armed swipe with his ax. Hrissa snarled. Fafhrd almost louted forward off his holds with the momentum of his blow.

"I'll swear I scored on him, Mouser," he snarled, recovering. "My ax touched something besides air."

"You harebrained fool!" the Mouser cried. "Your scratches will anger him and bring him back." He let go of the chopped ice-hold with his hand and, steadying himself by his pike, he searched the sun-bright air ahead and around for ripples.

"More like I've scared him off," Fafhrd asserted, doing the same. The rush sound faded and did not return; the air became quiet, and the steep slope grew very still; even the water-drip faded.

Turning back to the wall with a grunt of relief, the Mouser touched emptiness. He grew still as death himself. Turning his eyes only he saw that upward from a point level with his knees the whole snow ridge had vanished—the whole saddle and a section of the swell to either side of it—as if some great god had reached down while the Mouser's back was turned and removed that block of reality.

Giddily he clung to his pike. He was standing atop a newly created snow-saddle now. Beyond and below its raw, fresh-fractured white eastern slope, the silently departed great snow-cornice was falling faster and faster, still in one hill-size chunk.

Behind them the steps Fafhrd had cut mounted to the new snow rim, then vanished.

"See, I chopped us down far enough only in the nick," Fafhrd grumbled. "My judgment was faulty."

The falling cornice was snatched downward out of sight, so that the Mouser and Fafhrd at last could see what lay east of the Mountains of the Giants: a rolling expanse of dark green that might be treetops except that from here even giant trees would be tinier than grass blades—an expanse even farther below them than the Cold Waste at their backs. Beyond the green-carpeted depression, another mountain range loomed like the ghost of one.

"I have heard legends of the Great Rift Valley," Fafhrd murmured. "A mountainsided cup for sunlight, its warm floor a league below the Waste."

Their eyes searched.

"Look," the Mouser said, "how trees climb the eastern face of Obelisk almost to his top. Now the goats don't seem so strange."

They could see nothing, however, of the east face of Stardock.

"Come on!" Fafhrd commanded. "If we linger, the invisible growl-laughtered flier may gather courage to return despite my ax-nick."

And without further word he began resolutely to cut steps onward . . . and still a little down.

Hrissa continued to peer over the rim, her bearded chin almost resting on it, her nostrils a-twitch as if she faintly scented gossamer threads of meat-odor mounting from the leagues' distant dark green, but when the rope tightened on her harness, she followed.

Perils came thick now. They reached the dark rock of the Ladder only by chopping their way along a nearly vertical ice wall in the twinkly gloom under a close-arching waterfall of snow that shot out from an icy boss above them—perhaps a miniature version of the White Waterfall that was Stardock's skirt.

When they stepped at last, numb with cold and hardly daring to believe they'd made it, onto a wide dark ledge, they saw a jumble of bloody goat tracks in the snow around.

Without more warning than that, a long snowbank between that step and the next above reared up its nearest white end a dozen feet and hissed fearsomely, showing it to be a huge serpent with head as big as an elk's, all covered with shaggy snow-white fur. Its great violet eyes glared like those of a mad horse and its jaws gaped to show slashing-teeth like a shark's and two great fangs jetting a mist of pale ichor.

The furred serpent hesitated for two sways between the nearer, taller man with flashing ax and the farther, smaller one with thick black stick. In that pause Hrissa, with snarling hisses of her own, sprang forward past the Mouser on the downslope side and the furred serpent struck at this newest and most active foe.

Fafhrd got a blast of its hot acrid breath, and the vapor trail from its nearer fang bathed his left elbow.

The Mouser's attention was fixed on a fur-wisped violet eye as big as a girl's fist.

Hrissa looked down the monster's gaping dark red gullet rimmed by slaver-swimming ivory knives and the two ichor-jetting fangs.

Then the jaws clashed shut, but in the intervening instant Hrissa had leaped back more swiftly even than she'd advanced.

The Mouser plunged the pike-end of his climbing pole into the glaring violet eye.

Swinging his ax two-handed, Fafhrd slashed at the furry neck just back of the horse-like skull, and there gushed out red blood which steamed as it struck the snow.

Then the three climbers were scrambling upward, while the monster writhed in convulsions which shook the rock and spattered with red alike the snow and its snow-white fur.

At what they hoped was a safe distance above it, the climbers watched it dying, though not without frequent glances about for creatures like it or other perilous beasts.

Fafhrd said, "A hot-blooded serpent, a snake with fur—it goes against experience. My father never spoke of such; I doubt he ever met 'em."

The Mouser answered, "I'll wager they find their prey on the east slope of Stardock and come here only to lair or breed. Perhaps the invisible flier drove the three goats over the snow-saddle to lure this one." His voice grew dreamy. "Or perhaps there's a secret world inside Stardock."

Fafhrd shook his head, as if to clear it of such imagination-snaring visions. "Our way lies upward," he said. "We'd best be well above the Lairs before nightfall. Give me a dollop of honey when I drink," he added, loosening his water bag as he turned and scanned up the Ladder.

From its base the Ladder was a dark narrow triangle climbing to the blue sky between the snowy, ever-tumbling Tresses. First there were the ledges on which they stood, easy at first, but swiftly growing steeper and narrower. Next an almost blank stretch, etched here and there with shadows and ripplings hinting at part-way climbing routes, but none of them connected. Then another band of ledges, the Roosts. Then a stretch still blanker than the first. Finally another ledge-band, narrower and shorter—the Face—and atop all what seemed a tiny pen-stroke of white ink: the brim of Stardock's pennonless snowy hat.

All the Mouser's aches and weariness came back as he squinted up the Ladder while feeling in his pouch for the honey jar. Never, he was sure, had he seen so much distance compressed into so little space by vertical foreshortening. It was as if the gods had built a ladder to reach the sky, and after using it had kicked most of the steps away. But he clenched his teeth and prepared to follow Fafhrd.

All their previous climbing began to seem book-simple compared to what they now struggled through, step by straining step, all the long summer afternoon. Where Obelisk Polaris had been a stern schoolmaster, Stardock was a mad queen, tireless in preparing her shocks and surprises, unpredictable in her wild caprices.

The ledges of the Lairs were built of rock that sometimes broke away at a touch, and they were piled with loose gravel. Also, the climbers made acquaintance with Stardock's rocky avalanches, which brought stones whizzing and spattering down around them without warning, so that they had to press close to the walls and Fafhrd regretted leaving his helmet in the cairn. Hrissa first snarled at each pelting pebble which hit near her, but when at last struck in the side by a small one, showed fear and slunk close to the Mouser, trying until rebuked to push between the wall and his legs.

And once they saw a cousin of the white worm they had slain rear up man-high and glare at them from a distant ledge, but it did not attack.

They had to work their way to the northernmost point of the topmost ledge before they found, at the very edge of the Northern Tress, almost underlying its streaming snow, a scree-choked gulley which narrowed upward to a wide vertical groove—or chimney, as Fafhrd called it.

And when the treacherous scree was at last surmounted, the Mouser discovered that the next stretch of the ascent was indeed very like climbing up the inside of a rectangular chimney of varying width and with one of the four walls missing—that facing outward to the air. Its rock was sounder than that of the Lairs, but that was all that could be said for it.

Here all tricks of climbing were required and the utmost of main strength into the bargain. Sometimes they hoisted themselves by cracks wide enough for finger- and toeholds; if a crack they needed was too narrow, Fafhrd would tap into it one of his spikes to make a hold, and this spike must, if possible, be unwedged after use and recovered. Sometimes the chimney narrowed so that they could walk up it laboriously with shoulders to one wall and boot soles to the other. Twice it widened and became so smooth-walled that the Mouser's extensible climbing-pike had to be braced between wall and wall to give them a necessary step.

And five times the chimney was blocked by a huge rock of chockstone which in falling had wedged itself fast, and these fearsome obstructions had to be climbed around on the outside, generally with the aid of one or more of Fafhrd's spikes driven between chockstone and wall, or his grapnel tossed over it.

"Stardock has wept millstones in her day," the Mouser said of these gigantic barriers, jerking his body aside from a whizzing rock for a period to his sentence.

This climbing was generally beyond Hrissa and she often had to be carried on the Mouser's back, or left on a chockstone or one of the rare paw-wide ledges and hoisted up when opportunity offered. They were strongly tempted, especially after they drew death-weary, to abandon her, but could not forget how her brave feint had saved them from the white worm's first stroke.

All this, particularly the passing of the chockstones, must be done under the pelting of Stardock's rock avalanches—so that each new chockstone above them was welcomed as a roof, until it had to be surmounted. Also, snow sometimes gushed into the chimney, overspilling from one of the snowy avalanches forever whispering down the North Tress—one more danger to guard against. Ice water runneled too from time to time down the chimney, drenching boots and gloves and making all holds unsure.

In addition, there was less nourishment in the air, so that they had more often to halt and gasp deeply until their lungs were satisfied. And Fafhrd's left arm began to swell where the venomous mist from the worm's fang had blown around it, until he could hardly bend its swollen fingers to grip crack or rope. Besides, it itched and stung. He plunged it again and again into snow to no avail.

Their only allies on this most punishing ascent were the hot sun, heartening them by its glow and offsetting the growing frigidity of the thin still air, and the very difficulty and variety of the climb itself, which at least kept their minds off the emptiness around and beneath them—the latter a farther drop than they'd ever stood over on the Obelisk. The Cold Waste seemed like another world, poised separate from Stardock in space.

Once they forced themselves to eat a bite and several times sipped water. And once the Mouser was seized with mountain sickness, ending only when he had retched himself weary.

The only incident of the climb unrelated to Stardock's mad self occurred when they were climbing out around the fifth chockstone, slowly, like two large slugs, the Mouser first this time and bearing Hrissa, with Fafhrd close behind. At this point the North Tress narrowed so that a hump of the North Wall was visible across the snow stream.

There was a whirring unlike that of any rock. Another whirring then, closer and ending in a *thunk*. When Fafhrd scrambled atop the chockstone and into the shelter of the walls, he had a cruelly barbed arrow through his pack.

At cost of a third arrow whirring close by his head, the Mouser peeped out north with Fafhrd clinging to his heels and swiftly dragging him back.

" 'Twas Kranarch all right; I saw him twang his bow," the Mouser reported. "No sight of Gnarfi, but one of their new comrades clad in brown fur crouched behind Kranarch, braced on the same boss. I couldn't see his face, but 'tis a most burly fellow, short of leg."

"They keep apace of us," Fafhrd grunted.

"Also, they scruple not to mix climbing with killing," the Mouser observed as he broke off the tail of the arrow piercing Fafhrd's pack and yanked out the shaft. "Oh, comrade, I fear your sleeping cloak is sixteen times holed. And that little bladder of pine liniment—it got holed too. Ah, what fragrance!"

"I'm beginning to think those two men of Illik-Ving aren't sportsmen," Fafhrd asserted. "So . . . up and on!"

They were all dog-weary, even cat-Hrissa, and the sun was barely ten fingerbreadths (at the end of an outstretched arm) above the flat horizon of the Waste; and something in the air had turned Sol white as silver—he no longer sent warmth to combat the cold. But the ledges of the Roosts were close above now, and it was possible to hope they would offer a better camp site than the chimney.

So although every man and cat muscle protested against it, they obeyed Fafhrd's command.

Halfway to the Roosts it began to snow, powdery grains falling arrow-straight like last night, but thicker.

This silent snowfall gave a sense of serenity and security which was

most false, since it masked the rockfalls which still came firing down
the chimney like the artillery of the God of Chance.

Five yards from the top a fist-size chunk struck Fafhrd glancingly
on the right shoulder, so that his good arm went numb and hung
useless, but the little climbing that remained was so easy he could
make it with boots and puffed-up, barely-usable left hand.

He peeped cautiously out of the chimney's top, but the Tress here
had thickened up again, so that there was no sight of the North Wall.
Also the first ledge was blessedly wide and so overhung with rock
that not even snow had fallen on its inner half, let alone stones. He
scrambled up eagerly, followed by the Mouser and Hrissa.

But even as they cast themselves down to rest at the back of the
ledge, the Mouser wriggling out of his heavy pack and unthonging
his climbing-pike from his wrist—for even *that* had become a torturesome burden—they heard a now-familiar rushing in the air and
there came a great flat shape swooping slowly through the sun-
silvered snow which outlined it. Straight at the ledge it came and this
time it did not go past, but halted and hung there, like a giant devil
fish nuzzling the sea's rim, while ten narrow marks, each of suckers in
line, appeared in the snow on the ledge's edge, as of ten short tentacles gripping there.

From the center of this monstrous invisibility rose a smaller snow-
outlined invisibility of the height and thickness of a man. Midway up
this shape was one visible thing: a slim sword of dark gray blade and
silvery hilt, pointed straight at the Mouser's breast.

Suddenly the sword shot forward, almost as fast as if hurled, but
not quite, and after it, as swiftly, the man-size pillar, which now
laughed harshly from its top.

The Mouser snatched up one-handed his unthonged climbing pike
and thrust at the snow-sketched figure behind the sword.

The gray sword snaked around the pike and with a sudden sharp
twist swept it from the Mouser's fatigue-slack fingers.

The black tool, on which Glinthi the Artificer had expended all the
evenings of the Mouth of the Weasel three years past, vanished into
the silvery snowfall and space.

Hrissa backed against the wall frothing and snarling, a-tremble in
every limb.

Fafhrd fumbled frantically for his ax, but his swollen fingers could
not even unsnap the sheath binding its head to his belt.

The Mouser, enraged at the loss of his precious pike to the point
where he cared not a whit whether his foe was invisible or not, drew

Scalpel from its sheath and fiercely parried the gray sword as it came streaking in again.

A dozen parries he had to make and was pinked twice in the arm and pressed back against the wall almost like Hrissa, before he could take the measure of his foe, now out of the snowfall and wholly invisible, and go himself on the attack.

Then, glaring at a point a foot above the gray sword—a point where he judged his foe's eyes to be (if his foe carried his eyes in his head)—he went stamping forward, beating at the gray blade, slipping Scalpel around it with the tiniest disengages, seeking to bind it with his own sword, and ever thrusting impetuously at invisible arm and trunk.

Three times he felt his blade strike flesh and once it bent briefly against invisible bone.

His foe leaped back onto the invisible flier, making narrow footprints in the slush gathered there. The flier rocked.

In his fighting rage the Mouser almost followed his foe onto that invisible, living, pulsating platform, yet prudently stopped at the brink.

And well it was he did so, for the flier dropped away like a skate in flight from a shark, shaking its slush into the snowfall. There came a last burst of laughter more like a wail, fading off and down in the silvery murk.

The Mouser began to laugh himself, a shade hysterically, and retreated to the wall. There he wiped off his blade and felt the stickiness of invisible blood, and laughed a wild high laugh again.

Hrissa's fur was still on end—and was a long time flattening.

Fafhrd quit trying to fumble out his ax and said seriously, "The girls couldn't have been with him—we'd have seen their forms or footprints on the slush-backed flier. I think he's jealous of us and works against 'em."

The Mouser laughed—only foolishly now—for a third time.

The murk turned dark gray. They set about firing the brazier and making ready for night. Despite their hurts and supreme weariness, the shock and fright of the last encounter had excited new energy from them and raised their spirits and given them appetites. They feasted well on thin collops of kid frizzled in the resin-flames or cooked pale gray in water that, strangely, could be sipped without hurt almost while it boiled.

"Must be nearing the realm of the Gods," Fafhrd muttered. "It's said they joyously drink boiling wine—and walk hurtlessly through flames."

"Fire is just as hot here, though," the Mouser said dully. "Yet the air seems to have less nourishment. On what do you suppose the Gods subsist?"

"They are ethereal and require neither air nor food," Fafhrd suggested after a long frown of thinking.

"Yet you just now said they drink wine."

"Everybody drinks wine," Fafhrd asserted with a yawn, killing the discussion and also the Mouser's dim, unspoken speculation as to whether the feebler air, pressing less strongly on heating liquid, let its bubbles escape more easily.

Power of movement began to return to Fafhrd's right arm and his left was swelling no more. The Mouser salved and bandaged his own small wounds, then remembered to salve Hrissa's pads and tuck into her boots a little pine-scented eiderdown tweaked from the arrow-holes in Fafhrd's cloak.

When they were half laced up in their cloaks, Hrissa snuggled between them—and a few more precious resin-pellets dropped in the brazier as a bedtime luxury—Fafhrd got out a tiny jar of strong wine of Ilthmar, and they each took a sup of it, imagining those sunny vineyards and that hot, rich soil so far south.

A momentary flare from the brazier showed them the snow falling yet. A few rocks crashed nearby and a snowy avalanche hissed, then Stardock grew still in the frigid grip of night. The climbers' aerie seemed most strange to them, set above every other peak in the Mountains of the Giants—and likely all Nehwon—yet walled with darkness like a tiny room.

The Mouser said softly, "Now we know what roosts in the Roosts. Do you suppose there are dozens of these invisible mantas carpeting around us on ledges like this, or a-hang from them? Why don't they freeze? Or does someone stable them? And the invisible folk, what of them? No more can you call 'em mirage—you saw the sword, and I fought the man-thing at the other end of it. Yet invisible! How's that possible?"

Fafhrd shrugged and then winced because it hurt both shoulders cruelly. "Made of some stuff like water or glass," he hazarded. "Yet pliant and twisting the light less—and with no surface shimmer. You've seen sand and ashes made transparent by firing. Perhaps there's some heatless way of firing monsters and men until they are invisible."

"But how light enough to fly?" the Mouser asked.

"Thin beasts to match thin air," Fafhrd guessed sleepily.

The Mouser said, "And then those deadly worms—and the Fiend

knows what perils above." He paused. "And yet we must still climb Stardock to the top, mustn't we? Why?"

Fafhrd nodded. "To beat out Kranarch and Gnarfi . . ." he muttered. "To beat out my father . . . the mystery of it . . . the girls . . . O Mouser, could you stop here any more than you could stop after touching half of a woman?"

"You don't mention diamonds any more," the Mouser noted. "Don't you think we'll find them?"

Fafhrd started another shrug and mumbled a curse that turned into a yawn.

The Mouser dug in his pouch to the bottom pocket and brought out the parchment and blowing on the brazier read it all by the resin's last flaming:

> Who mounts white Stardock, the Moon Tree,
>   Past worm and gnome and unseen bars,
> Will win the key to luxury:
>   The Heart of Light, a pouch of stars.
> The gods who once ruled all the world
>   Have made that peak their citadel,
> From whence the stars were one time hurled
>   And paths lead on to Heav'n and Hell.
> Come, heroes, past the Trollstep rocks.
>   Come, best of men, across the Waste.
> For you, glory each door unlocks.
>   Delay not, up, and come in haste.
> Who scales the Snow King's citadel
>   Shall father his two daughters' sons;
> Though he must face foes fierce and fell,
>   His seed shall live while time still runs.

The resin burnt out. The Mouser said, "Well, we've met a worm and one unseen fellow who sought to bar our way—and two sightless witches who might be Snow King's daughters for all I know. Gnomes now—they would be a change, wouldn't they? You said something about Ice Gnomes, Fafhrd. What was it?"

He waited with an unnatural anxiety for Fafhrd's answer. After a bit he began to hear it: soft regular snores.

The Mouser snarled soundlessly, his demon of restlessness now become a fury despite all his aches. He shouldn't have thought of girls —or rather of one girl who was nothing but a taunting mask with pouting lips and eyes of black mystery seen across a fire.

Suddenly he felt stifled. He quickly unhooked his cloak and despite

Hrissa's questioning mew felt his way south along the ledge. Soon snow, sifting like ice needles on his flushed face, told him he was beyond the overhang. Then the snow stopped. Another overhang, he thought—but he had not moved. He strained his eyes upward, and there was the black expanse of Stardock's topmost quarter silhouetted against a band of sky pale with the hidden moon and specked by a few faint stars. Behind him to the west, the snowstorm still obscured the sky.

He blinked his eyes and then he swore softly, for now the black cliff they must climb tomorrow was a-glow with soft scattered lights of violet and rose and palest green and amber. The nearest, which were still far above, looked tinily rectangular, like gleam-spilling windows seen from below.

It was as if Stardock were a great hostelry.

Then freezing flakes pinked his face again, and the band of sky narrowed to nothing. The snowfall had moved back against Stardock once more, hiding all stars and other lights.

The Mouser's fury drained from him. Suddenly he felt very small and foolhardy and very, very cold. The mysterious vision of the lights remained in his mind, but muted, as if part of a dream. Most cautiously he crept back the way he had come, feeling the radiant warmth of Fafhrd and Hrissa and the burnt-out brazier just before he touched his cloak. He laced it around him and lay for a long time doubled up like a baby, his mind empty of everything except frigid blackness. At last he slumbered.

Next day started gloomy. The two men chafed and wrestled each other as they lay, to get the stiffness a little out of them and enough warmth in them to rise. Hrissa withdrew from between them limping and sullen.

At any rate, Fafhrd's arms were recovered from their swelling and numbing, while the Mouser was hardly aware of his own arm's little wounds.

They breakfasted on herb tea and honey and began climbing the Roosts in a light snowfall. This last pest stayed with them all morning except when gusty breezes blew it back from Stardock. On these occasions they could see the great smooth cliff separating the Roosts from the ultimate ledges of the Face. By the glimpses they got, the cliff looked to be without any climbing routes whatever, or any marks at all—so that Fafhrd laughed at the Mouser for a dreamer with his tale of windows spilling colored light—but finally as they neared the cliff's base they began to distinguish what seemed to be a narrow crack—a hairline to vision—mounting its center.

They met none of the invisible flat fliers, either a-wing or a-perch, though whenever gusts blew strange gaps into the snowfall, the two adventurers would firm themselves on their perches and grip for their weapons, and Hrissa would snarl.

The wind slowed them little though chilling them much, for the rock of the Roosts was true.

And they still had to watch out for stony peltings, though these were fewer than yesterday, perhaps because so much of Stardock now lay below them.

They reached the base of the great cliff at the point where the crack began, which was a good thing, since the snowfall had grown so heavy that a hunt for it would have been difficult.

To their joy, the crack proved to be another chimney, scarcely a yard across and not much more deep, and as knobbly inside with footholds as the cliff outside was smooth. Unlike yesterday's chimney, it appeared to extend upward indefinitely without change of width and as far as they could see there were no chockstones. In many ways it was like a rock ladder half sheltered from the snow. Even Hrissa could climb here, as on Obelisk Polaris.

They lunched on food warmed against their skins. They were afire with eagerness, yet forced themselves to take time to chew and sip. As they entered the chimney, Fafhrd going first, there came three faint growling booms—thunder perhaps and certainly ominous, yet the Mouser laughed.

With never-failing footholds and opposite wall for backbrace, the climbing was easy, except for the drain on main strength, which required rather frequent halts to gulp down fresh stores of the thin air. Only twice did the chimney narrow so that Fafhrd had to climb for a short stretch with his body outside it; the Mouser, slighter framed, could stay inside.

It was an intoxicating experience, almost. Even as the day grew darker from the thickening snowfall and as the crackling booms returned sharper and stronger—thunder now for sure, since they were heralded by brief palings up and down the chimney—snow-muted lightning flashes—the Mouser and Fafhrd felt as merry as children mounting a mysterious twisty stairway in a haunted castle. They even wasted a little breath in joking calls which went echoing faintly up and down the rugged shaft as it paled and gloomed with the lightning.

But then the shaft grew by degrees almost as smooth as the outer cliff and at the same time it began gradually to widen, first a hand-breadth, then another, then a finger more, so that they had to mount more perilously, bracing shoulders against one wall and boots against the other and so "walking" up with pushes and heaves. The Mouser drew up Hrissa and the ice-cat crouched on his pitching, rocking chest—no inconsiderable burden. Yet both men still felt quite jolly—so that the Mouser began to wonder if there might not be some actual intoxicant in air near Heaven.

Being a head or two taller than the Mouser, Fafhrd was better equipped for this sort of climbing and was still able to go on at that moment when the Mouser realized that his body was stretched almost straight between shoulders and boot soles—with Hrissa a-crouch on him like a traveler on a little bridge. He could mount no farther—and was hazy about how he had managed to come this far.

Fafhrd came down like a great spider at the Mouser's call and seemed not much impressed by the latter's plight—in fact, a lightning flash showed his great bearded face all a-grin.

"Abide you here a bit," he said. " 'Tis not so far to the top. I think I glimpsed it the last flash but one. I'll mount and draw you up, putting all the rope between you and me. There's a crack by your head—I'll knock in a spike for safety's sake. Meanwhile, rest."

Whereupon Fafhrd did all of these things so swiftly and was on his upward way again so soon that the Mouser forebore to utter any of the sardonic remarks churning inside his rigid belly.

Successive lightning flashes showed the Northerner's long-limbed form growing smaller at a gratifyingly rapid rate until he looked hardly bigger than a trap spider at the end of his tube. Another flash and he was gone, but whether because he had reached the top or passed a bend in the chimney the Mouser couldn't be sure.

The rope kept paying upward, however, until there was only a small loop below the Mouser. He was aching abominably now and was also very cold, but gritted his teeth against the pain. Hrissa chose this moment to prowl up and down her small human bridge, rest-lessly. There was a blinding lightning flash and a crash of thunder that shook Stardock. Hrissa cringed.

The rope grew taut, tugging at the belt of the Mouser, who started to put his weight on it, holding Hrissa to his chest, but then decided to wait for Fafhrd's call. This was a good decision on his part, for just then the rope went slack and began to fall on the Mouser's belly like a stream of black water. Hrissa crouched away from it on his face. It came pelting endlessly, but finally its upper end hit the Mouser under the breastbone with a snap. The only good thing was that Fafhrd didn't come hurtling down with it. Another blinding mountain-shaking crash showed the upper chimney utterly empty.

"Fafhrd!" the Mouser called. "*Fafhrd!*" There came back only the echo.

The Mouser thought for a bit, then reached up and felt by his ear for the spike Fafhrd had struck in with a single offhand slap of his ax-hammer. Whatever had happened to Fafhrd, nothing seemed to remain to do but tie rope to spike and descend by it to where the chimney was easier.

The spike came out at the first touch and went clattering shrilly down the chimney until a new thunderblast drowned the small sound.

The Mouser decided to "walk" down the chimney. After all, he'd come up that way the last few score of yards.

The first attempt to move a leg told him his muscles were knotted by cramp. He'd never be able to bend his leg and straighten it again without losing his purchase and falling.

The Mouser thought of Glinthi's pike, lost in white space, and he slew that thought.

Hrissa crouched on his chest and gazed down into his face with an expression the next levin-glare showed to be sad yet critical, as if to ask, "Where is this vaunted human ingenuity?"

Fafhrd had barely eased himself out of the chimney onto the wide, deep rock-roofed ledge at its top, when a door two yards high, a yard wide, and two spans thick had silently opened in the rock at the back of the ledge.

The contrast was most remarkable between the roughness of that rock and the ruler-flat smoothness of the dark stone forming the thick sides of the door and the lintel, jambs, and threshold of the doorway.

Soft pink light spilled out and with it a perfume whose heavy fumes were cargoed with dreams of pleasure barges afloat in a rippling sunset sea.

Those musky narcotic fumes, along with the alcoholic headiness of the thin air, almost made Fafhrd forget his purpose, but touching the black rope was like touching Hrissa and the Mouser at its other end. He unknotted it from his belt and prepared to secure it around a stout rock pillar beside the open door. To get enough rope to make a good knot he had to draw it up quite tight.

But the dream-freighted fumes grew thicker, and he no longer felt the Mouser and Hrissa in the rope. Indeed, he began to forget his two comrades altogether.

And then a silvery voice—a voice he knew well from having heard it laugh once and once chuckle—called, "Come in, barbarian. Come in to me."

The end of the black rope slipped from his fingers unnoticed and hissed softly across the rock and down the chimney.

Stooping a little, he went through the doorway which silently closed behind him just in time to shut out the Mouser's desperate call.

He was in a room lit by pink globes hanging at the level of his head. Their soft warm radiance colored the hangings and rugs of the room, but especially the pale spread of the great bed that was its only furniture.

Beside the bed stood a slim woman whose black silk robe concealed all of her except her face, yet did not disguise her body's sleek curves. A black lace mask hid the rest of her.

She looked at Fafhrd for seven thudding heartbeats, then sat down on the bed. A slender arm and hand clothed all in black lace came from under her robe and patted the spread beside her and rested there. Her mask never wavered from Fafhrd's face.

He shouldered out of his pack and unbuckled his ax belt.

The Mouser finished pounding all the thin blade of his dagger into the crack by his ear, using the firestone from his pouch for hammer, so that sparks showered from every cramped stroke of stone against pommel—small lightning flashes to match the greater flares still chasing up and down the chimney, while their thunder crashed an obbligato to the Mouser's taps. Hrissa crouched on his ankles, and from time to time the Mouser glared at her, as if to say, "Well, cat?"

A gust of snow-freighted wind roaring up the chimney momentarily lifted the lean shaggy beast a span above him and almost blew the Mouser loose, but he tightened his pushing muscles still more and the bridge, arching upward a trifle, held firm.

He had just finished knotting an end of the black rope around the dagger's crossguard and grip—and his fingers and forearms were almost useless with fatigue—when a window two feet high and five wide silently opened in the back of the chimney, its thick rock shutter sliding aside, not a span away from the Mouser's inward shoulder.

A red glow sprang from the window and somewhat illumined four faces with piggy black eyes and with low hairless domes above.

The Mouser considered them. They were all four of extreme ugliness, he decided dispassionately. Only their wide white teeth, showing between their grinning lips which almost joined ear to swinish ear, had any claim to beauty.

Hrissa sprang at once through the red window and disappeared. The two faces between which she jumped did not flicker a black button-eye.

Then eight short brawny arms came out and easily pried the Mouser out and lifted him inside. He screamed faintly from a sudden increase in the agony of his cramps. He was aware of thick dwarfish bodies clad in hairy black jerkins and breeks—and one in a black hairy shirt—but all with thick-nailed splay-feet bare. Then he fainted.

When he came to, it was because he was being punishingly massaged on a hard table, his body naked and slick with warm oil. He was in a low, ill-lit chamber and still closely surrounded by the four dwarves, as he could tell from the eight horny hands squeezing and thumping his muscles before he ever opened his eyes.

The dwarf kneading his right shoulder and banging the top of his spine crinkled his warty eyelids and bared his beautiful white teeth bigger than a giant's in what might be intended for a friendly grin. Then he said in an atrocious Mingol patois, "I am Bonecracker. This is my wife Gibberfat. Cosseting your body on the larboard side are my brothers Legcruncher and Breakskull. Now drink this wine and follow me."

The wine stung, yet dispelled the Mouser's dizziness, and it was certainly a blessing to be free of the murderous massage—and also apparently of the cramp-lumps in his muscles.

Bonecracker and Gibberfat helped him off the slab while Legcruncher and Breakskull rubbed him quickly down with rough towels. The warm low-ceilinged room rocked dizzily for a moment; then he felt wondrous fine.

Bonecracker waddled off into the dimness beyond the smoky torches. With never a question the Mouser followed the dwarf. Or were these Fafhrd's Ice Gnomes? he wondered.

Bonecracker pulled aside heavy drapes in the dark. Amber light fanned out. The Mouser stepped from rock-roughness onto down-softness. The drapes swished to behind him.

He was alone in a chamber mellowly lit by hanging globes like great topazes—yet he guessed they would bounce aside like puffballs if touched. There was a large wide couch and beyond it a low table against the arras-hung wall with an ivory stool set before it. Above the table was a great silver mirror, while on it were fantastic small bottles and many tiny ivory jars.

No, the room was not altogether empty. Hrissa, sleekly groomed, lay curled in a far corner. She was not watching the Mouser, however, but a point above the stool.

The Mouser felt a shiver creeping on him, yet not altogether one of fear.

A dab of palest green leaped from one of the jars to the point Hrissa was watching and vanished there. But then he saw a streak of reflected green appear in the mirror. The riddlesome maneuver was repeated, and soon in the mirror's silver there hung a green mask, somewhat clouded by the silver's dullness.

Then the mask vanished from the mirror and simultaneously reappeared unblurred hanging in the air above the ivory stool. It was the mask the mouser knew achingly well—narrow chin, high-arched cheeks, straight nose and forehead.

The pouty wine-dark lips opened a little and a soft throaty voice asked, "Does my visage displease you, man of Lankhmar?"

"You jest cruelly, O Princess," the Mouser replied, drawing on all his aplomb and sketching a courtier's bow, "for you are Beauty's self."

Slim fingers, half outlined now in pale green, dipped into the unguent jar and took up a more generous dab.

The soft throaty voice that so well matched half the laughter he had once heard in a snowfall, now said, "You shall judge all of me."

Fafhrd woke in the dark and touched the girl beside him. As soon as he knew she was awake too, he grasped her by the hips. When he felt her body stiffen, he lifted her into the air and held her above him as he lay flat on his back.

She was wondrous light, as if made of pastry or eiderdown, yet when he laid her beside him again, her flesh felt as firm as any, though smoother than most.

"Let us have a light, Hirriwi, I beg you," he said.

"That were unwise, Faffy," she answered in a voice like a curtain of tiny silver bells lightly brushed. "Have you forgotten that now I am wholly invisible?—which might tickle some men, yet you, I think . . ."

"You're right, you're right, I like you real," he answered, gripping her fiercely by the shoulders to emphasize his feelings, then guiltily jerking away his hands as he thought of how delicate she must be.

The silver bells clashed in full laughter, as if the curtain of them had been struck a great swipe. "Have no fears," she told him. "My airy bones are grown of matter stronger than steel. It is a riddle beyond your philosophers and relates to the invisibility of my race and of the animals from which it sprang. Think how strong tempered glass can be, yet light goes through it. My cursed brother Faroomfar has the strength of a bear for all his slimness while my father Oom-forafor is a very lion despite his centuries. Your friend's encounter with Faroomfar was no final test—but oh how it made him howl—Father raged at him—and then there are the cousins. Soon as this night be ended—which is not soon, my dear; the moon still climbs—you must return down Stardock. Promise me that. My heart grows cold at the thought of the dangers you've already faced—and was like ice I know not how many times this last three-day."

"Yet you never warned us," he mused. "You lured me on."

"Can you doubt why?" she asked. He was feeling her snub nose then and her apple cheeks, and so he felt her smile too. "Or perhaps you resent it that I let you risk your life a little to win here to this bed?"

He implanted a fervent kiss on her wide lips to show her how little true that was, but she thrust him back after a moment.

"Wait, Faffy dear," she said. "No, wait, I say! I know you're greedy and impetuous, but you can at least wait while the moon creeps the width of a star. I asked you to promise me you would descend Stardock at dawn."

There was a rather long silence in the dark.

"Well?" she prompted. "What shuts your mouth?" she queried impatiently. "You've shown no such indecision in certain other matters. Time wastes, the moon sails."

"Hirriwi," Fafhrd said softly, "I must climb Stardock."

"Why?" she demanded ringingly. "The poem has been fulfilled. You have your reward. Go on, and only frigid fruitless perils await you. Return, and I'll guard you from the air—yes, and your companion too—to the very Waste." Her sweet voice faltered a little. "O Faffy, am I not enough to make you forego the conquest of a cruel mountain? In addition to all else, I love you—if I understand rightly how mortals use that word."

"No," he answered her solemnly in the dark. "You are wondrous, more wondrous than any wench I've known—and I love you, which is not a word I bandy—yet you only make me hotter to conquer Stardock. Can you understand that?"

Now there was silence for a while in the other direction.

"Well," she said at length, "you are masterful and will do what you will do. And I have warned you. I could tell you more, show you reasons counter, argue further, but in the end I know I would not break your stubbornness—and time gallops. We must mount our own steeds and catch up with the moon. Kiss me again. Slowly. So."

The Mouser lay across the foot of the bed under the amber globes and contemplated Keyaira, who lay lengthwise with her slender apple green shoulders and tranquil sleeping face propped by many pillows.

He took up the corner of a sheet and moistened it with wine from a cup set against his knee and with it rubbed Keyaira's slim right ankle —so gently that there was no change in her narrow bosom's slow-paced rise and fall. Presently he had cleared away all the greenish unguent from a patch as big as half his palm. He peered down at his handiwork. This time he expected surely to see flesh, or at least the green cosmetic on the underside of her ankle, but no, he saw through the irregular little rectangle he'd wiped only the bed's tufted coverlet reflecting the amber light from above. It was a most fascinating and somewhat unnerving mystery.

He glanced questioningly over at Hrissa, who now lay on an end of the low table, the thin-glassed, fantastic perfume bottles standing around her, while she contemplated the occupants of the bed, her white tufted chin set on her folded paws. It seemed to the Mouser that she was looking at him with disapproval, so he hastily smoothed back unguent from other parts of Keyaira's leg until the peephole was once more greenly covered.

There was a low laugh. Keyaira, propped on her elbows now, was gazing at him through slitted heavy-lashed eyelids.

"We invisibles," she said in a humorous voice truly or feignedly heavy with sleep, "show only the outward side of any cosmetic or raiment on us. It is a mystery beyond our seers."

"You are Mystery's queenly self a-walk through the stars," the Mouser pronounced, lightly caressing her green toes. "And I the most fortunate of men. I fear it's a dream and I'll wake on Stardock's frigid ledges. How is it I am here?"

"Our race is dying out," she said. "Our men have become sterile. Hirriwi and I are the only princesses left. Our brother Faroomfar hotly wished to be our consort—he still boasts his virility—'twas he you dueled with—but our father Oomforafor said, 'It must be new blood—the blood of heroes.' So the cousins and Faroomfar, he much against his will, must fly hither and yon and leave those little rhymed lures written on ramskin in perilous, lonely spots apt to tempt heroes."

"But how can visibles and invisibles mate?" he asked.

She laughed with delight. "Is your memory *that* short, Mouse?"

"I mean, have progeny," he corrected himself, a little irked, but not much, that she had hit on his boyhood nickname. "Besides, wouldn't such offspring be cloudy, a mix of seen and unseen?"

Keyaira's green mask swung a little from side to side. "My father thinks such mating will be fertile and that the children will breed true to invisibility—that being dominant over visibility—yet profit greatly in other ways from the admixture of hot, heroic blood."

"Then your father commanded you to mate with me?" the Mouser asked, a little disappointed.

"By no means, Mouse," she assured him. "He would be furious if he dreamt you were here, and Faroomfar would go mad. No, I took a fancy to you, as Hirriwi did to your comrade, when first I spied on you on the Waste—very fortunate that was for you, since my father would have got your seed, if you had won to Stardock's top, in quite a different fashion. Which reminds me, Mouse, you must promise me to descend Stardock at dawn."

"That is not so easy a promise to give," the Mouser said. "Fafhrd will be stubborn, I know. And then there's that other matter of a bag of diamonds, if that's what a pouch of stars means—oh, it's but a trifle, I know, compared to the embraces of a glorious girl . . . still . . ."

"But if I say I love you?—which is only truth. . . ."

"Oh Princess," the Mouser sighed, gliding his hand to her knee. "How can I leave you at dawn? Only one night . . ."

"Why, Mouse," Keyaira broke in, smiling roguishly and twisting her green form a little, "do you not know that every night is an eternity? Has not any girl taught you that yet, Mouse? I am astonished. Think, we have half an eternity left us yet—which is also an eternity, as your geometer, whether white-bearded or dainty-breasted, should have taught you."

"But if I am to sire many children—" the Mouser began.

"Hirriwi and I are somewhat like queen bees," Keyaira explained, "but think not of that. We have eternity tonight, 'tis true, but only if we make it so. Come closer."

A little later, plagiarizing himself somewhat, the Mouser said softly, "The sole fault of mountain climbing is that the best parts go so swiftly."

"They can last an eternity," Keyaira breathed in his air. "Make them last, Mouse."

Fafhrd woke shaking with cold. The pink globes were gray and tossing in icy gusts from the open door. Snow had blown in on his clothes and gear scattered across the floor and was piled inches deep on the threshold, across which came also the only illumination—leaden daylight.

A great joy in him fought all these grim gray sights and conquered them.

Nevertheless he was naked and shivering. He sprang up and beat his clothes against the bed and thrust his limbs into their icy stiffness.

As he was buckling his ax belt, he remembered the Mouser down in the chimney, helpless. Somehow all night, even when he'd spoken to Hirriwi of the Mouser, he'd never thought of that.

He snatched up his pack and sprang out on the ledge. From the corner of his eye he caught something moving behind him. It was the massive door closing.

A titan gust of snow-fisted wind struck him. He grabbed the rough rock pillar to which he'd last night planned to tie the rope and hugged it tight. The gods help the Mouser below! Someone came sliding and blowing along the ledge in the wind and snow and hugged the pillar lower down.

The gust passed. Fafhrd looked for the door. There was no sign of it. All the piled snow was redrifted. Keeping close hold of pillar and pack with one hand, he felt over the rough wall with the other. Fingernails no more than eyes could discover the slightest crack.

"So you got tossed out too?" a familiar voice said gayly. "*I* was tossed out by Ice Gnomes, I'll have you know."

"Mouser!" Fafhrd cried. "Then you weren't—? I thought—"

"You never thought of me once all night, if I know you," the Mouser said. "Keyaira assured me you were safe and somewhat more than that. Hirriwi would have told you the same of me if you'd asked her. But of course you didn't."

"Then you too—?" Fafhrd demanded, grinning with delight.

"Yes, Prince Brother-in-Law," the Mouser answered him, grinning back.

They pommeled each other around the pillar a bit—to battle chill, but in sheer high spirits too.

"Hrissa?" Fafhrd asked.

"Warm inside, the wise one. They don't put out the cat here, only the man. I wonder, though. . . . Do you suppose Hrissa was Keyaira's to begin with and that she foresaw and planned . . ." His voice trailed off.

No more gusts had come. The snowfall was so light they could see almost a league—up to the Hat above the snow-streaked ledges of the Face and down to where the Ladder faded out.

Once again their minds were filled, almost overpowered by the vastness of Stardock and by their own predicament: two half-frozen mites precariously poised on a frozen vertical world only distantly linked with Nehwon.

To the south there was a pale silver disk in the sky—the sun. They'd been abed till noon.

"Easier to fashion an eternity out of an eighteen-hour night," the Mouser observed.

"We galloped the moon deep under the sea," Fafhrd mused.

"Your girl promise to make you go down?" the Mouser asked suddenly.

Fafhrd nodded his head. "She tried."

"Mine too. And not a bad idea. The summit smells, by her account. But the chimney looks stuffed with snow. Hold my ankles while I peer over. Yes, packed solid all the way down. So—?"

"Mouser," Fafhrd said, almost gloomily, "whether there's a way down or no, I must climb Stardock."

"You know," the Mouser answered, "I am beginning to find something in that madness myself. Besides, the east wall of Stardock may hold an easy route to that lush-looking Rift Valley. So let's do what we can with the bare seven hours of light left us. Daytime's no stuff to fashion eternities."

Mounting the ledges of the Face was both the easiest and hardest climbing they'd had yet to do. The ledges were wide, but some of them sloped outward and were footed with rotten shale that went skidding away into space at a touch, and now and again there were brief traverses which had to be done by narrow cracks and main strength, sometimes swinging by their hands alone.

And weariness and chill and even dizzying faintness came far quicker at this height. They had to halt often to drink air and chafe themselves. While in the back of one deep ledge—Stardock's right eye, they judged—they were forced to spend time firing the brazier with all the remaining resin-pellets, partly to warm food and drink, but chiefly to warm themselves.

Last night's exertions had weakened them too, they sometimes thought, but then the memories of those exertions would return to strengthen them.

And then there were the sudden treacherous wind gusts and the constant yet variable snowfall, which sometimes hid the summit and sometimes let them see it clear against the silvery sky, with the great white out-curving brim of the Hat now poised threateningly above them—a cornice like that of the snow-saddle, only now they were on the wrong side.

The illusion grew stronger that Stardock was a separate world from Nehwon in snow-filled space.

Finally the sky turned blue and they felt the sun on their backs—they had climbed above the snowfall at last—and Fafhrd pointed at a tiny nick of blue deep in the brim of the Hat—a nick just visible above the next snow-streaked rock bulge—and he cried, "The apex of the Needle's Eye!"

At that, something dropped into a snowbank beside them, and there was a muffled clash of metal on rock, while from snow a notched and feathered arrow-end stuck straight up.

They dodged under the protective roof of a bigger bulge as a second arrow and a third clashed against the naked rock on which they'd stood.

"Gnarfi and Kranarch have beaten us, curse 'em," Fafhrd hissed, "and set an ambush for us at the Eye, the obvious spot. We must go roundabout and get above 'em."

"Won't they expect that?"

"They were fools to spring their ambush too soon. Besides, we have no other tactic."

So they began to climb south, though still upward, always keeping rock or snow between them and where they judged the Needle's Eye to be. At last, when the sun was dropping swiftly toward the western horizon, they came swinging back north again and still upward, stamping out steps now in the steepening bank of snow that reversed its curve above them to make the brim of the Hat that now roofed them ominously, covering two-thirds of the sky. They sweated and shook by turns and fought off almost continuous bouts of giddy faintness, yet still strove to move as silently and warily as they might.

At last they rounded one more snow bulge and found themselves looking down a slope at the great bare stretch of rock normally swept by the gale that came through the Needle's Eye to make the Petty Pennon.

On the outward lip of the exposed rock were two men, both clad in suits of brown leather, much scuffed and here and there ripped, showing the inward-turned fur. Lank, black-bearded, elk-faced Kranarch stood whipping his arms against his chest for warmth. Beside him lay his strung bow and some arrows. Stock boar-faced Gnarfi knelt peeping over the rim. Fafhrd wondered where their two brown-clad bulky servitors were.

The Mouser dug into his pouch. At the same moment Kranarch

saw them and snatched up his weapon, though rather more slowly than he would have in thicker air. With a similar slowness the Mouser drew out the fist-size rock he had picked up several ledges below for just such a moment as this.

Kranarch's arrow whistled between his and Fafhrd's heads. A moment later the Mouser's rock struck Kranarch full on his bow-shoulder. The weapon fell from his hand and that arm dangled. Then Fafhrd and the Mouser charged recklessly down the snow slope, the former brandishing his unthonged ax, the latter drawing Scalpel.

Kranarch and Gnarfi received them with their own swords, and Gnarfi with a dagger in his left hand as well. The battle that followed had the same dreamlike slowness as the exchange of missiles. First Fafhrd's and the Mouser's rush gave them the advantage. Then Kranarch's and Gnarfi's great strength—or restedness, rather—told, and they almost drove their enemy off the rim. Fafhrd took a slash in the ribs which bit through his tough wolfskin tunic, slicing flesh and jarring bone.

But then skill told, as it generally will, and the two brown-clad men received wounds and suddenly turned and ran through the great white pointy-topped triangular archway of the Needle's Eye. As he ran Gnarfi screeched, "Graah! Kruk!"

"Doubtless calling for their shaggy-clad servants or bearers," the Mouser gasped in surmise, resting sword arm on knee, almost spent. "Farmerish fat country fellows those looked, hardly trained to weapons. We need not fear 'em greatly, I think, even if they come to Gnarfi's call." Fafhrd nodded, gasping himself. "Yet they climbed Stardock," he added dubiously.

Just then there came galloping through the snowy archway on their hind legs with their nails clashing the windswept rock and their fang-edged slavering red mouths open wide and their great-clawed arms widespread—two huge brown bears.

With a speed which their human opponents had been unable to sting from them, the Mouser snatched up Kranarch's bow and sent two arrows speeding, while Fafhrd swung his ax in a gleaming circle and cast it. Then the two comrades sprang swiftly to either side, the Mouser wielding Scalpel and Fafhrd drawing his knife.

But there was no need for further fighting. The Mouser's first arrow took the leading bear in the neck, his second straight in its red mouth-roof and brain, while Fafhrd's ax sank to its helve between two ribs on the trailing bear's left side. The great animals pitched forward in their blood and death throes and rolled twice over and went tumbling ponderously off the rim.

"Doubtless both shes," the Mouser remarked as he watched them fall. "Oh those bestial men of Illik-Ving! Still, to charm or train such beasts to carry packs and climb and even give up their poor lives . . ."

"Kranarch and Gnarfi are no sportsmen, that's for certain now," Fafhrd pronounced. "Don't praise their tricks." As he stuffed a rag into his tunic over his wound, he grimaced and swore so angrily that the Mouser didn't speak his quip: *Well, bears are only shortened bearers. I'm always right.*

Then the two comrades trudged slowly under the high tentlike arch of snow to survey the domain, highest on all Nehwon, of which they had made themselves masters—refusing from light-headed weariness to think, in that moment of triumph, of the invisible beings who were Stardock's lords. They went warily, yet not too much so, because Gnarfi and Kranarch had run scared and were wounded not trivially—and the latter had lost his bow.

Stardock's top behind the great toppling snow wave of the Hat was almost as extensive north to south as that of Obelisk Polaris, yet the east rim looked little more than a long bowshot away. Snow with a thick crust beneath a softer layer covered it all except for the north end and stretches of the east rim, where bare dark rock showed.

The surface, both snow and rock, was flatter even than that of the Obelisk and sloped somewhat from north to south. There were no structures or beings visible, nor signs of hollows where either might hide. Truth to tell, neither the Mouser nor Fafhrd could recall ever having seen a lonelier or barer place.

The only oddity they noticed at first were three holes in the snow a little to the south, each about as big as a hogshead but having the form of an equilateral triangle and apparently going down through the snow to the rock. The three were arranged as the apex of another equilateral triangle.

The Mouser squinted around closely, then shrugged. "But a pouch of stars could be a rather small thing, I suppose," he said. "While a heart of light—no guessing its size."

The whole summit was in bluish shadow except for the northernmost end and for a great pathway of golden light from the setting sun leading from the Needle's Eye all the way across the wind-leveled snow to the east rim.

Down the center of this sunroad went Kranarch's and Gnarfi's running footsteps, the snow flecked here and there with blood. Otherwise the snow ahead was printless. Fafhrd and the Mouser followed those tracks, walking east up their long shadows.

"No sign of 'em ahead," the Mouser said. "Looks like there *is* some route down the east wall, and they've taken it—at least far enough to set another ambush."

As they neared the east rim, Fafhrd said, "I see other prints making north—a spear's cast that way. Perhaps they turned."

"But where to?" the Mouser asked.

A few steps more and the mystery was solved horribly. They reached the end of the snow and there on the dark bloodied rock, hidden until now by the wind-piled margin of the snow, sprawled the carcasses of Gnarfi and Kranarch, their middle clothes ripped away, their bodies obscenely mutilated.

Even as the Mouser's gorge rose, he remembered Keyaira's lightly-spoken words: "If you had won to Stardock's top, my father would have got your seed in quite a different fashion."

Shaking his head and glaring fiercely, Fafhrd walked around the bodies to the east rim and peered down.

He recoiled a step, then knelt and once more peered.

The Mouser's hopeful theory was prodigiously disproved. Never in his life had Fafhrd looked straight down half such a distance.

A few yards below, the east wall vanished inward. No telling how far the east rim jutted out from Stardock's heart-rock.

From this point the fall was straight to the greenish gloom of the Great Rift Valley—five Lankhmar leagues, at least. Perhaps more.

He heard the Mouser say over his shoulder, "A path for birds or suicides. Naught else."

Suddenly the green below grew bright, though without showing the slightest feature except for a silvery hair, which might be a great river, running down its center. Looking up again, they saw that the sky had gone all golden with a mighty afterglow. They faced around and gasped in wonder.

The last sunrays coming through the Needle's Eye, swinging southward and a little up, glancingly illumined a transparent, solid symmetric shape big as the biggest oak tree and resting exactly over the three triangular holes in the snow. It might only be described as a sharp-edged solid star of about eighteen points, resting by three of those on Stardock and built of purest diamond or some like substance.

Both had the same thought: that this must be a star the gods had failed to launch. The sunlight had touched the fire in its heart and made it shine, but for a moment only and feebly, not incandescently and forever, as it would have in the sky.

A piercingly shrill, silvery trumpet call broke the silence of the summit.

They swung their gaze north. Outlined by the same deep golden sunlight, ghostlier than the star, yet still clearly to be seen in some of its parts against the yellow sky, a tall slender castle lifted transparent walls and towers from the stony end of the summit. Its topmost spires seemed to go out of sight upward rather than end.

Another sound then—a wailing snarl. A pale animal bounded toward them across the snow from the northwest. Leaping aside with another snarl from the sprawled bodies, Hrissa rushed past them south with a third snarl tossed at them.

Almost too late they saw the peril against which she had tried to warn them.

Advancing toward them from west and north across the unmarked snow were a score of sets of footprints. There were no feet in those prints, nor bodies above them, yet they came on—right print, left print, appearing in succession—and ever more rapidly. And now they saw what they had missed at first because viewed end-on: above each paired set of prints a narrow-shafted, narrow-bladed spear, pointed straight toward them, coming on as swiftly as the prints.

They ran south with Hrissa, Fafhrd in the lead. After a half dozen sprinting steps the Northerner heard a cry behind him. He stopped and then swiftly spun around.

The Mouser had slipped in the blood of their late foes and fallen. When he got to his feet, the gray spear points were around him on all sides save the rim. He made two wild defensive slashes with Scalpel, but the gray spear points came in relentlessly. Now they were in a close semicircle around him and hardly a span apart, and he was standing on the rim. They advanced another thrust and the Mouser perforce sprang back from them—and down he fell.

There was a rushing sound and chill air sluiced Fafhrd from behind and something sleekly hairy brushed his calves. As he braced himself to rush forward with his knife and slay an invisible or two for his friend, slender unseen arms clasped him from behind and he heard Hirriwi's silvery voice say in his ear, "Trust us," and a coppery-golden sister voice say, "We'll after him," and then he found himself pulled down onto a great invisible pulsing shaggy bed three spans above the snow, and they told him "Cling!" and he clung to the long thick unseen hair, and then suddenly the living bed shot forward across the snow and off the rim and there tilted vertically so his feet pointed at the sky and his face at the Great Rift Valley—and then the bed plunged straight down.

The thin air roared past and his beard and mane were whipped back by the speed of that plunge, but he tightened his grip on the handfuls of invisible hair and a slender arm pressed him down from either side, so that he felt through the fur the throbbing heartbeat of the great invisible carpet-like creature they rode. And he became aware that somehow Hrissa had got under his arm, for there was the small feline face beside his, with slitted eyes and with beard-tuft and ears blown back. And he felt the two invisible girls' bodies alongside his.

He realized that mortal eyes, could such have watched, would have seen only a large man clasping a large white cat and falling headfirst through empty space—but he would be falling much faster than any man should fall, even from such a vast height.

Beside him Hirriwi laughed, as if she had caught his thought, but then that laughter broke off suddenly and the roaring of the wind died almost to utter silence. He guessed it was because the swiftly thickening air had deafened him.

The great dark cliffs flashing upward a dozen yards away were a blur. Yet below him the Great Rift Valley was still featureless green— no, the larger details were beginning to show now: forests and glades and curling hair-thin streams and little lakes like dewdrops.

Between him and the green below he saw a dark speck. It grew in size. It was the Mouser!—rather characteristically falling headfirst, straight as an arrow, with hands locked ahead of him and legs pressed together behind, probably in the faint hope that he might hit deep water.

The creature they rode matched the Mouser's speed and then gradually swung its plunge toward him, flattening out more and more from the vertical, so that the Mouser was pressed against them. Arms visible and invisible clasped him then, pulling him closer, so that all five of the plungers were crowded together on that one great sentient bed.

The creature's dive flattened still more then, halting its fall—there was a long moment while they were all pressed stomach-surgingly tight against the hairy back, while the trees still rushed up at them— and then they were coasting above those same treetops and spiraling down into a large glade.

What happened next to Fafhrd and the Mouser went all in a great tumbling rush, much too swiftly: the feel of springy turf under their feet and balmy air sluicing their bodies, quick kisses exchanged, laughing, shouted congratulations that still sounded all muffled like ghost voices, something hard and irregular yet soft-covered pressed into the Mouser's hands, a last kiss—and then Hirriwi and Keyaira had broken away and a great burst of air flattened the grass and the great invisible flier was gone and the girls with it.

They could watch its upward spiraling flight for a little, however, because Hrissa had gone away on it too. The ice-cat seemed to be peering down at them in farewell. Then she too vanished as the golden afterglow swiftly died in the darkening sky overhead.

They stood leaning together for support in the twilight. Then they straightened themselves, yawning prodigiously, and their hearing came back. They heard the gurgling of a brook and the twittering of birds and a small, faint rustle of dry leaves going away from them and the tiny buzz of a spiraling gnat.

The Mouser opened the invisible pouch in his hands.

"The gems seem to be invisible too," he said, "though I can feel 'em well enough. We'll have a hard time selling them—unless we can find a blind jeweler."

The darkness deepened. Tiny cold fires began to glow in his palms: ruby, emerald, sapphire, amethyst, and pure white.

"No, by Issek!" the Gray Mouser said. "We'll only need to sell them by night—which is unquestionably the best time for trade in gems."

The new-risen moon, herself invisible beyond the lesser mountains walling the Rift Valley to the east, painted palely now the upper half of the great slender column of Stardock's east wall.

Gazing up at that queenly sight, Fafhrd said, "Gallant ladies, all four."

III
THE TWO BEST THIEVES IN LANKHMAR

THROUGH THE MAZY avenues and alleys of the great city of Lankhmar, Night was a-slink, though not yet grown tall enough to whirl her black star-studded cloak across the sky, which still showed pale, towering wraiths of sunset.

The hawkers of drugs and strong drinks forbidden by day had not yet taken up their bell-tinklings and thin, enticing cries. The pleasure girls had not lit their red lanterns and sauntered insolently forth. Bravos, desperadoes, procurers, spies, pimps, conmen, and other malfeasors yawned and rubbed drowsy sleep from eyes yet thick-lidded. In fact, most of the Night People were at supper. Which made for an emptiness and hush in the streets, suitable to Night's slippered tread. And which created a large bare stretch of dark thick, unpierced wall at the intersection of Silver Street with the Street of the Gods, a crossing-point where there habitually foregathered the junior executives and star operatives of the Thieves Guild; also meeting there were the few free-lance thieves bold and resourceful enough to defy the Guild and the few thieves of aristocratic birth, sometimes most brilliant amateurs, whom the Guild tolerated and even toadied to, on account of their noble ancestry, which dignified a very old but most disreputable profession.

Midway along the bare stretch of wall, where none might conceivably overhear, a very tall and a somewhat short thief drifted together. After a while they began to converse in prison-yard whispers.

A distance had grown between Fafhrd and the Gray Mouser during their long and uneventful trek south from the Great Rift Valley. It was due simply to too much of each other and to an ever more bickering disagreement as to how the invisible jewels, gift of Hirriwi and Keyaira, might most advantageously be disposed of—a dispute which had finally grown so acrimonious that they had divided the jewels, each carrying his share. When they finally reached Lankhmar, they had lodged apart and each made his own contact with jeweler, fence or private buyer. This separation had made their relationship quite scratchy, but in no way diminished their absolute trust in each other.

"Greetings, Little Man," Fafhrd prison-growled. "So you've come to sell your share to Ogo the Blind, or at least give him a viewing?—if such expression may be used of a sightless man."

"How did you know that?" the Mouser whispered sharply.

"It was the obvious thing to do," Fafhrd answered somewhat condescendingly. "Sell the jewels to a dealer who could note neither their night-glow nor daytime invisibility. A dealer who must judge them by weight, feel, and what they can scratch or be scratched by. Besides, we stand just across from the door to Ogo's den. It's very well guarded, by the by—at fewest, ten Mingol swordsmen."

"At least give me credit for such trifles of common knowledge," the Mouser answered sardonically. "Well, you guessed right; it appears that by long association with me you've gained some knowledge of how my wit works, though I doubt that it's sharpened your own a whit. Yes, I've already had one conference with Ogo, and tonight we conclude the deal."

Fafhrd asked equably, "Is it true that Ogo conducts all his interviews in pitchy dark?"

"Ho! So there are some few things you admit not knowing! Yes, it's quite true, which makes any interview with Ogo risky work. By insisting on absolute darkness, Ogo the Blind cancels at a stroke the interviewer's advantage—indeed, the advantage passes to Ogo, since he is used by a lifetime of it to utter darkness—a long lifetime, since he's an ancient one, to judge by his speech. Nay, Ogo knows not what darkness is, since it's all he's ever known. However, I've a device to trick him there if need be. In my thick, tightly drawstringed pouch I carry fragments of brightest glow-wood, and can spill them out in a trice."

Fafhrd nodded admiringly and then asked, "And what's in that flat case you carry so tightly under your elbow? An elaborate false history of each of the jewels embossed in ancient parchment for Ogo's fingers to read?"

"There your guess fails! No, it's the jewels themselves, guarded in clever wise so that they cannot be filched. Here, take a peek." And after glancing quickly to either side and overhead, the Mouser opened the case a handbreadth on its hinges.

Fafhrd saw the rainbow-twinkling jewels firmly affixed in artistic pattern to a bed of black velvet, but all closely covered by an inner top consisting of a mesh of stout iron wire.

The Mouser clapped the case shut. "On our first meeting, I took two of the smallest of the jewels from their spots in the box and let Ogo feel and otherwise test them. He may dream of filching them all, but my box and the mesh thwart that."

"Unless he steals from you the box itself," Fafhrd agreed. "As for myself, I keep my share of the jewels chained to me." And after such precautionary glances as the Mouser had made, he thrust back his loose left sleeve, showing a stout browned-iron bracelet snapped around his wrist. From the bracelet hung a short chain which both supported and kept tightly shut a small, bulging pouch. The leather of the pouch was everywhere sewed across with fine brown wire. He unclicked the bracelet, which opened on a hinge, then clicked it fast again.

"The browned-iron wire's to foil any cutpurse," Fafhrd explained offhandedly, pulling down his sleeve.

The Mouser's eyebrows rose. Then his gaze followed them as it went from Fafhrd's wrist to his face, while the small man's expression changed from mild approval to bland inquiry. He asked, "And you trust such devices to guard your half of the gems from Nemia of the Dusk?"

"How did you know my dealings were with Nemia?" Fafhrd asked in tones just the slightest surprised.

"Because she's Lankhmar's only woman fence, of course. All know you favor women when possible, in business as well as erotic matters. Which is one of your greatest failings, if I may say so. Also, Nemia's door lies next to Ogo's, though that's a trivial clue. You know, I presume, that seven Kleshite stranglers protect her somewhat overripe person? Well, at least then you know the sort of trap you're rushing into. Deal with a woman!—surest route to disaster. By the by, you mentioned 'dealings.' Does that plural mean this is not your first interview with her?"

Fafhrd nodded. "As you with Ogo. . . . Incidentally, am I to understand that you trust men simply because they're men? That were a greater failing than the one you impute to me. Anyhow, as you with Ogo, I go to Nemia of the Dusk a second time, to complete our deal. The first time I showed her the gems in a twilit chamber, where they appeared to greatest advantage, twinkling just enough to seem utterly real. Did you know, in passing, that she always works in twilight or soft gloom?—which accounts for the second half of her name. At all events, as soon as she glimpsed them, Nemia greatly desired the gems —her breath actually caught in her throat—and she agreed at once to my price, which is not low, as basis for further bargaining. However, it happens that she invariably follows the rule—which I myself consider a sound one—of never completing a transaction of any sort with a member of the opposite sex without first testing them in amorous commerce. Hence this second meeting. If the member be old or otherwise ugly, Nemia deputes the task to one of her maids, but in my case, of course . . ." Fafhrd coughed modestly. "One more point I'd like to make: 'overripe' is the wrong expression. 'Full-bloomed' or 'the acme of maturity' is what you're looking for."

"Believe me, I'm sure Nemia is in fullest bloom—a late August flower. Such women always prefer twilight for the display of their 'perfectly matured' charms," the Mouser answered somewhat stifledly. He had for some time been hard put to restrain laughter, and now it appeared in quiet little bursts as he said, "Oh, you great fool! And you've actually agreed to go to bed with her? And expect not to be parted from your jewels (including family jewels?), let alone not be strangled, while at that disadvantage? Oh, this is worse than I thought."

"I'm not always at such a disadvantage in bed as some people may think," Fafhrd answered with quiet modesty. "With me, amorous play sharpens instead of dulls the senses. I trust you have as much luck with a man in ebon darkness as I with a woman in soft gloom. Incidentally, why must you have two conferences with Ogo? Not Nemia's reason, surely?"

The Mouser's grin faded and he lightly bit his lip. With elaborate casualness he said, "Oh, the jewels must be inspected by the Eyes of Ogo—*his* invariable rule. But whatever test is tried, I'm prepared to out-trick it."

Fafhrd pondered, then asked, "And what, or who are, or is, the Eyes of Ogo? Does he keep a pair of them in his pouch?"

"Is," the Mouser said. Then with even more elaborate casualness, "Oh, some chit of a girl, I believe. Supposed to have an intuitive faculty where gems are concerned. Interesting, isn't it, that a man as

clever as Ogo should believe such superstitious nonsense? Or depend
on the soft sex in any fashion. Truly, a mere formality."

" 'Chit of a girl,' " Fafhrd mused, nodding his head again and yet
again and yet again. "That describes to a red dot on each of her
immature nipples the sort of female you've come to favor in recent
years. But of course the amorous is not at all involved in this deal of
yours, I'm sure," he added, rather too solemnly.

"In no way whatever," the Mouser replied, rather too sharply.
Looking around, he remarked, "We're getting a bit of company, despite the early hour. There's Dickon of the Thieves Guild, that old
pen-pusher and drawer of the floor plans of houses to be robbed—I
don't believe he's actually worked on a job since the Year of the
Snake. And there's fat Grom, their sub-treasurer, another armchair
thief. Who comes so dramatically a-slither?—by the Black Bones, it's
Snarve, our overlord Glipkerio's nephew! Who's that he speaks to?—
oh, only Tork the Cutpurse."

"And there now appears," Fafhrd took up, "Vlek, said to be the
Guild's star operative these days. Note his smirk and hear how his
shoes creak faintly. And there's that gray-eyed, black-haired amateur,
Alyx the Picklock—well, at least her boots don't squeak and I rather
admire her courage in adventuring here, where the Guild's animosity
toward freelance females is as ill a byword as that of the Pimps Guild.
And, just now turning from the Street of the Gods, who have we but
Countess Kronia of the Seventy-seven Secret Pockets, who steals by
madness, not method. There's one bone-bag I'd never trust, despite
her emaciated charms and the weakness you lay to me."

Nodding, the Mouser pronounced, "And such as these are called
the aristocracy of thiefdom! In all honesty I must say that notwith-
standing your weaknesses—which I'm glad you admit—one of the
two best thieves in Lankhmar now stands beside me. While the other,
needless to say, occupies my ratskin boots."

Fafhrd nodded back, though carefully crossing two fingers.

Stifling a yawn, the Mouser said, "By the by, have you yet any
thought about what you'll be doing after those gems are stolen from
your wrist, or—though unlikely—sold and paid for? I've been approached about—or at any rate been considering a wander toward—
in the general direction of the Eastern Lands."

"Where it's hotter even than in this sultry Lankhmar? Such a stroll
hardly appeals to me," Fafhrd replied, then casually added, "In any
case, I've been thinking of taking ship—er—northward."

"Toward that abominable Cold Waste once more? No, thank you!"
the Mouser answered. Then, glancing south along Silver Street,

where a pale star shone close to the horizon, he went on still more briskly, "Well, it's time for my interview with Ogo—and his silly girl Eyes. Take your sword to bed with you, I advise, and look to it that neither Graywand nor your more vital blade are filched from you in Nemia's dusk."

"Oh, so first twinkle of the Whale Star is the time set for your appointment too?" Fafhrd remarked, himself stirring from the wall. "Tell me, is the true appearance of Ogo known to anyone? Somehow the name makes me think of a fat, old, and overlarge spider."

"Curb your imagination, if you please," the Mouser answered sharply. "Or keep it for your own business, where I'll remind you that the only dangerous spider is the female. No, Ogo's true appearance is unknown. But perhaps tonight I'll discover it!"

"I'd like you to ponder that your besetting fault is over-curiosity," said Fafhrd, "and that you can't trust even the stupidest girl to be always silly."

The Mouser turned impulsively and said, "However tonight's interviews fall out, let's rendezvous after. The Silver Eel?"

Fafhrd nodded and they gripped hands together. Then each rogue sauntered toward his fateful door.

The Mouser crouched a little, every sense a-quiver, in space utterly dark. On a surface before him—a table, he had felt it out to be—lay his jewel box, closed. His left hand touched the box. His right gripped Cat's Claw and with that weapon nervously threatened the inky darkness all around.

A voice which was at once dry and thick croaked from behind him, "Open the box!"

The Mouser's skin crawled at the horror of that voice. Nevertheless, he complied with the direction. The rainbow light of the meshed jewels spilled upward, dimly showing the room to be low-ceilinged and rather large. It appeared to be empty except for the table and, indistinct in the far left corner behind him, a dark low shape which the Mouser did not like. It might be a hassock or a fat, round, black pillow. Or it might be . . . The Mouser wished Fafhrd hadn't made his last suggestion.

From ahead of him a rippling, silvery voice quite unlike the first called, "Your jewels, like no others I have ever seen, gleam in the absence of all light."

Scanning piercingly across the table and box, the Mouser could see no sign of the second caller. Evening out his own voice, so it was not breathy with apprehension, but bland with confidence, he said, to the emptiness, "My gems are like no others in the world. In fact, they come not from the world, being of the same substance as the stars. Yet you know by your test that one of them is harder than diamond."

"They are truly unearthly and most beautiful jewels," the sourceless silvery voice answered. "My mind pierces them through and through, and they are what you say they are. I shall advise Ogo to pay your asking price."

At that instant the Mouser heard behind him a little cough and a dry, rapid scuttling. He whorled around, dirk poised to strike. There was nothing to be seen or sensed, except for the hassock or whatever, which had not moved. The scuttling was no longer to be heard.

He swiftly turned back, and there across the table from him, her front illumined by the twinkling jewels, stood a slim naked girl with pale straight hair, somewhat darker skin, and overlarge eyes staring entrancedly from a child's tiny-chinned, pouty-lipped face.

Satisfying himself by a rapid glance that the jewels were in their proper pattern under their mesh and none missing, he swiftly advanced Cat's Claw so that its needle point touched the taut skin between the small yet jutting breasts.

"Do not seek to startle me so again!" he hissed. "Men—aye, and girls—have died for less."

The girl did not stir by so much as the breadth of a fine hair; neither did her expression nor her dreamy yet concentrated gaze change, except that her short lips smiled, then parted to say honey-voiced, "So you are the Gray Mouser. I had expected a crouchy, sear-faced rogue, and I find . . . a prince." The very jewels seemed to twinkle more wildly because of her sweet voice and sweeter presence, striking opalescent glimmers from her pale irises.

"Neither seek to flatter me!" the Mouser commanded, catching up his box and holding it open against his side. "I am inured, I'll have you know, to the ensorcelments of all the world's minxes and nymphs."

"I speak truth only, as I did of your jewels," she answered guilelessly. Her lips had stayed parted a little and she spoke without moving them.

"Are you the Eyes of Ogo?" the Mouser demanded harshly, yet drawing Cat's Claw back from her bosom. It bothered him a little, yet only a little, that the tiniest stream of blood, like a black thread, led down for a few inches from the prick his dirk had made.

Utterly unmindful of the tiny wound, the girl nodded. "And I can see through you, as through your jewels, and I discover naught in you but what is noble and fine, save for certain small subtle impulses of violence and cruelty, which a girl like myself might find delightful."

"There your all-piercing eyes err wholly, for I am a great villain," the Mouser answered scornfully, though he felt a pulse of fond satisfaction within him.

The girl's eyes widened as she looked over his shoulder somewhat apprehensively, and from behind the Mouser the dry and thick voice croaked once more, "Keep to business! Yes, I will pay you in gold your offering price, a sum it will take me some hours to assemble. Return at the same time tomorrow night and we will close the deal. Now shut the box."

The Mouser had turned around, still clutching his box, when Ogo began to speak. Again he could not distinguish the source of the voice, though he scanned minutely. It seemed to come from the whole wall.

Now he turned back. Somewhat to his disappointment, the naked girl had vanished. He peered under the table, but there was nothing there. Doubtless some trapdoor or hypnotic device . . .

Still suspicious as a snake, he returned the way he had come. On close approach, the black hassock appeared to be only that. Then as the door to the outside slid open noiselessly, he swiftly obeyed Ogo's last injunction, snapping shut the box, and departed.

Fafhrd gazed tenderly at Nemia lying beside him in perfumed twilight, while keeping the edge of his vision on his brawny wrist and the pouch pendant from it, both of which his companion was now idly fondling.

To do Nemia justice, even at the risk of imputing a certain cattiness to the Mouser, her charms were neither overblown, nor even ample, but only . . . sufficient.

From just behind Fafhrd's shoulder came a spitting hiss. He quickly turned his head and found himself looking into the crossed blue eyes of a white cat standing on the small bedside table beside a bowl of bronze chrysanthemums.

"Ixy!" Nemia called remonstratingly yet languorously.

Despite her voice, Fafhrd heard behind him, in rapid succession, the click of a bracelet opening and the slightly louder click of one closing.

He turned back instantly, to discover only that Nemia had meanwhile clasped on his wrist, beside the browned-iron bracelet, a golden one around which sapphires and rubies marched alternately in single file.

Gazing at him from betwixt the strands of her long dark hair, she said huskily, "It is only a small token which I give to those who please me . . . greatly."

Fafhrd drew his wrist closer to his eyes to admire his prize, but mostly to palpate his pouch with the fingers of his other hand, to assure himself that it bulged as tightly as ever.

It did, and in a burst of generous feeling he said, "Let me give you one of my gems in precisely the same spirit," and made to undo his pouch.

Nemia's long-fingered hand glided out to prevent. "No," she breathed. "Let never the gems of business be mixed with the jewels of pleasure. Now if you should choose to bring me some small gift tomorrow night, when at the same hour we exchange your jewels for my gold and my letters of credit on Glipkerio, underwritten by Hisvin the Grain Merchant . . ."

"Right," Fafhrd said briefly, concealing the relief he felt. He'd been an idiot to think of giving Nemia one of the gems—and with it a day's opportunity to discover its abnormalities.

"Until tomorrow," Nemia said, opening her arms to him.

"Until tomorrow, then," Fafhrd agreed, embracing her fervently, yet keeping his pouch clutched in the hand to which it was chained— and already eager to be gone.

The Silver Eel was far less than half filled, its candles few, its cup-bearers torpid, as Fafhrd and the Gray Mouser entered simultaneously by different doors and made for one of the many empty booths.

The only eye to watch them at all closely was a gray one above a narrow section of pale cheek bordered by dark hair, peering past the curtain of the backmost booth.

When their thick table-candles had been lit and cups set before them and a jug of fortified wine, and fresh charcoal tumbled into the red-seeded brazier at table's end, the Mouser placed his flat box on the table and, grinning, said, "All's set. The jewels passed the test of the Eyes—a toothsome wenchlet; more of her later. I get the cash tomorrow night—all my offering price! But you, friend, I hardly thought to see you back alive. Drink we up! I take it you escaped from Nemia's divan whole and sound in organs and limbs—as far as you yet know. But the jewels?"

"They came through too," Fafhrd answered, swinging the pouch lightly out of his sleeve and then back in again. "And I get my money tomorrow night . . . the full amount of my asking price, just like you."

As he named those coincidences, his eyes went thoughtful.

They stayed that way while he took two large swallows of wine. The Mouser watched him curiously.

"At one point," Fafhrd finally mused, "I thought she was trying the old trick of substituting for mine an identical but worthlessly filled pouch. Since she'd seen the pouch at our first meeting, she could have had a similar one made up, complete with chain and bracelet."

"But was she—?" the Mouser asked.

"Oh no, it turned out to be something entirely different," Fafhrd said lightly, though some thought kept two slight vertical furrows in his forehead.

"That's odd," the Mouser remarked. "At one point—just one, mind you—the Eyes of Ogo, if she'd been extremely swift, deft, and silent, might have been able to switch boxes on me."

Fafhrd lifted his eyebrows.

The Mouser went on rapidly, "That is, if my box had been closed. But it was open, in darkness, and there'd have been no way to reproduce the varicolored twinkling of the gems. Phosphorous or glow-wood? Too dim. Hot coals? No, I'd have felt the heat. Besides, how get that way a diamond's pure white glow? Quite impossible."

Fafhrd nodded agreement, but continued to gaze over the Mouser's shoulder.

The Mouser started to reach toward his box, but instead with a small self-contemptuous chuckle picked up the jug and began to pour himself another drink in a careful small stream.

Fafhrd shrugged at last, used the back of his fingers to push over his own pewter cup for a refill, and yawned mightily, leaning back a little and at the same time pushing his spread-fingered hands to either side across the table, as if pushing away from him all small doubts and wonderings.

The fingers of his left hand touched the Mouser's box.

His face went blank. He looked down his arm at the box.

Then to the great puzzlement of the Mouser, who had just begun to fill Fafhrd's cup, the Northerner leaned forward and placed his head ear-down on the box.

"Mouser," he said in a small voice, "your box is buzzing."

Fafhrd's fragrant wine puddled and began to run toward the glowing brazier.

"When I touched the box, I felt vibration," Fafhrd went on bemusedly. "It's buzzing. It's still buzzing."

With a low snarl, the Mouser slammed down the jug and snatched the box from under Fafhrd's ear. The wine reached the brazier's hot bottom and hissed.

He tore the box open, opened also its mesh top, and he and Fafhrd peered in.

The candlelight dimmed, but by no means extinguished the yellow, violet, reddish, and white twinkling glows rising from various points on the black velvet bottom.

But the candlelight was quite bright enough also to show, at each such point, matching the colors listed, a firebeetle, glowwasp, nightbee, or diamondfly, each insect alive but delicately affixed to the floor of the box with fine silver wire. From time to time the wings or wingcases of some buzzed.

Without hesitation, Fafhrd unclasped the browned-iron bracelet from his wrist, unchained the pouch, and dumped it on the table.

Jewels of various sizes, all beautifully cut, made a fair heap.

But they were all dead black.

Fafhrd picked up a big one, tried it with his fingernail, then whipped out his hunting knife and with its edge easily scored the gem.

He carefully dropped it in the brazier's glowing center. After a bit it flamed up yellow and blue.

"Coal," Fafhrd said.

The Mouser clawed his hands over his faintly twinkling box, as if about to pick it up and hurl it through the wall and across the Inner Sea.

Instead he unclawed his hands and hung them decorously at his sides.

"I am going away," he announced quietly, but very clearly, and did so.

Fafhrd did not look up. He was dropping a second black gem in the brazier.

He did take off the bracelet Nemia had given him; he brought it close to his eyes, said, "Brass . . . glass," and spread his fingers to let it drop in the spilled wine. After the Mouser was gone, Fafhrd drained his brimming cup, drained the Mouser's and filled it again, then went on supping from it as he continued to drop the black jewels one by one in the brazier.

Nemia and the Eyes of Ogo sat cozily side by side on a luxurious divan. They had put on negligees. A few candles made a yellowish dusk.

On a low, gleaming table were set delicate flagons of wines and liqueurs, slim-stemmed crystal goblets, golden plates of sweetmeats and savories, and in the center two equal heaps of rainbow-glowing gems.

"What a quaint bore barbarians are," Nemia remarked, delicately stifling a yawn, "though good for one's sensuous self, once in a great while. This one had a little more brains than most. I think he might have caught on, except that I made the two clicks come so exactly together when I snapped back on his wrist the bracelet with the false pouch and at the same time my brass keepsake. It's amazing how barbarians are hypnotized by brass along with any odd bits of glass colored like rubies and sapphires—I think the three primary colors paralyze their primitive brains."

"Clever, *clever* Nemia," the Eyes of Ogo cooed with a tender caress. "My little fellow almost caught on too when I made the switch, but then he got interested in threatening me with his knife. Actually jabbed me between the breasts. I think he has a dirty mind."

"Let me kiss the blood away, darling Eyes," Nemia suggested. "Oh, dreadful . . . dreadful."

While shivering under her treatment—Nemia had a slightly bristly tongue—Eyes said, "For some reason he was quite nervous about Ogo." She made her face blank, her pouty mouth hanging slightly open.

The richly draped wall opposite her made a scuttling sound and then croaked in a dry, thick voice, "Open your box, Gray Mouser. Now close it. Girls, girls! Cease your lascivious play!"

Nemia and Eyes clung to each other laughing. Eyes said in her natural voice, if she had one, "And he went away still thinking there was a real Ogo. I'm quite certain of that. My, they both must be in a froth by now."

Sitting back, Nemia said, "I suppose we'll have to take some special precautions against their raiding us to get their jewels back."

Eyes shrugged. "I have my five Mingol swordsmen."

Nemia said, "And I have my three and a half Kleshite stranglers."

"Half?" Eyes asked.

"I was counting Ixy. No, but seriously."

Eyes frowned for half a heartbeat, then shook her head decisively. "I don't think we need worry about Fafhrd and the Gray Mouser raiding us back. Because we're girls, their pride will be hurt, and they'll sulk a while and then run away to the ends of the earth on one of those adventures of theirs."

"Adventures!" said Nemia, as one who says, "Cesspools and privies!"

"You see, they're really weaklings," Eyes went on, warming to her topic. "They have no drive whatever, no ambition, no true passion for money. For instance, if they did—and if they didn't spend so much time in dismal spots away from Lankhmar—they'd have known that the King of Ilthmar has developed a mania for gems that are invisible by day, but glow by night, and has offered half his kingdom for a sack of star-jewels. And then they'd never have had even to consider such an idiotic thing as coming to us."

"What do you suppose he'll do with them? The King, I mean."

Eyes shrugged. "I don't know. Build a planetarium. Or eat them." She thought a moment. "All things considered, it might be as well if we got away from here for a few weeks. We deserve a vacation."

Nemia nodded, closing her eyes. "It should be absolutely the opposite sort of place to the one in which the Mouser and Fafhrd will have their next—ugh!—adventure."

Eyes nodded too and said dreamily, "Blue skies and rippling water, spotless beach, a tepid wind, flowers and slim slavegirls everywhere . . ."

Nemia said, "I've always wished for a place that has no weather, only perfection. Do you know which half of Ilthmar's kingdom has the least weather?"

"Precious Nemia," Eyes murmured, "you're so civilized. And so very, very clever. Next to one other, you're certainly the best thief in Lankhmar."

"Who's the other?" Nemia was eager to know.

"Myself, of course," Eyes answered modestly.

Nemia reached up and tweaked her companion's ear—not too painfully, but enough.

"If there were the least money depending on that," she said quietly but firmly, "I'd teach you differently. But since it's only conversation . . ."

"Dearest Nemia."

"Sweetest Eyes."

The two girls embraced and kissed each other fondly.

The Mouser glared thin-lipped across a table in a curtained booth in the Golden Lamprey, a tavern not unlike the Silver Eel.

He rapped the teak before him with his fingertip, and the perfumed stale air with his voice, saying, "Double those twenty gold pieces and I'll make the trip and hear Prince Gwaay's proposal."

The very pale man opposite him, who squinted as if even the candlelight were a glare, answered softly, "Twenty-five—and you serve him for one day after arrival."

"What sort of ass do you take me for?" the Mouser demanded dangerously. "I might be able to settle all his troubles in one day—I usually can—and what then? No, no preagreed service; I hear his proposal only. And . . . thirty-five gold pieces in advance."

"Very well, thirty gold pieces—twenty to be refunded if you refuse to serve my master, which would be a risky step, I warn you."

"Risk is my bed-mate," the Mouser snapped. "Ten only to be refunded."

The other nodded and began slowly to count rilks onto the teak. "Ten *now*," he said. "Ten when you join our caravan tomorrow morning at the Grain Gate. And ten when we reach Quarmall."

"When we first glimpse the spires of Quarmall," the Mouser insisted.

The other nodded.

The Mouser moodily snatched the golden coins and stood up. They felt very few in his fist. For a moment he thought of returning to Fafhrd and with him devising plans against Ogo and Nemia.

No, never! He realized he couldn't in his misery and self-rage bear the thought of even looking at Fafhrd.

Besides, the Northerner would certainly be drunk.

And two, or at most three, rilks would buy him certain tolerable and even interesting pleasures to fill the hours before dawn brought him release from this hateful city.

Fafhrd was indeed drunk, being on his third jug. He had burnt up all the black jewels and was now with the greatest delicacy and most careful use of the needle point of his knife, releasing unharmed each of the silver-wired firebeetles, glowwasps, nightbees, and diamondflies. They buzzed about erratically.

Two cupbearers and the chucker-out had come to protest, and now Slevyas himself joined them, rubbing the back of his thick neck. He had been stung and a customer too. Fafhrd had himself been stung twice, but hadn't seemed to notice. Nor did he now pay the slightest attention to the four haranguing him.

The last nightbee was released. It careened off noisily past Slevyas' neck, who dodged his head with a curse. Fafhrd sat back, suddenly looking very wretched. With varying shrugs the master of the Silver Eel and his three servitors made off, one cupbearer making swipes at the air.

Fafhrd tossed up his knife. It came down almost point first, but didn't quite stick in the teak. He laboriously scabbarded it, then forced himself to take a small sip of wine.

As if someone were about to emerge from the backmost booth, there was a stirring of its heavy curtains, which like all the others had stitched to them heavy chain and squares of metal, so that one guest couldn't stab another through them, except with luck and the slimmest stilettos.

But at that moment a very pale man, who held up his cloak to shield his eyes from the candlelight, entered by the side door and made to Fafhrd's table.

"I've come for my answer, Northerner," he said in a voice soft yet sinister. He glanced at the toppled jugs and spilled wine. "That is, if you remember my proposition."

"Sit down," Fafhrd said. "Have a drink. Watch out for the glow-wasps—they're vicious." Then, scornfully, "Remember! Prince Hasjarl of Marquall—Quarmall. Passage by ship. A mountain of gold rilks. Remember!"

Keeping on his feet, the other amended, "Twenty-five rilks. Provided you take ship with me at once and promise to render a day's service to my prince. Thereafter by what further agreement you and he arrive at."

He placed on the table a small golden tower of pre-counted coins.

"Munificent!" Fafhrd said, grabbing it up and reeling to his feet. He placed five of the coins on the table and shoved the rest in his pouch, except for three more, which scattered dulcetly across the floor. He corked and pouched the third wine jug. Coming out from behind the table, he said, "Lead the way, comrade," gave the squinty-eyed man a mighty shove toward the side door, and went weaving after him.

In the backmost booth, Alyx the Picklock pursed her lips and shook her head disapprovingly.

IV
THE LORDS OF QUARMALL

THE ROOM WAS dim, almost maddeningly dim to one who loved sharp detail and the burning sun. The few wall-set torches that provided the sole illumination flamed palely and thinly, more like will-o'-the-wisps than true fire, although they released a pleasant incense. One got the feeling that the dwellers of this region resented light and only tolerated a thin mist of it for the benefit of strangers.

Despite its vast size, the room was carved all in somber solid rock—smooth floor, polished curving walls, and domed ceiling—either a natural cave finished by man or else chipped out and burnished entirely by human effort, although the thought of that latter amount of work was nearly intolerable. From numerous deep niches between the torches, metal statuettes and masks and jeweled objects gleamed darkly.

Through the room, bending the feeble bluish flames, came a perpetual cool draft bringing acid odors of damp ground and moist rock which the sweet spicy scent of the torches never quite masked.

The only sounds were the occasional rutch of rock on wood from the other end of the long table, where a game was being played with black and white stone counters—that and, from beyond the room, the ponderous sighing of the great fans that sucked down the fresh air on its last stage of passage from the distant world above and drove it

through this region . . . and the perpetual soft thudding of the naked feet of the slaves on the heavy leather tread-belts that drove those
great wooden fans . . . and the very faint mechanic gasping of those
slaves.

After one had been in this region for a few days, or only a few
hours, the sighing of the fans and the soft thudding of the feet and the
faint gaspings of the tortured lungs seemed to drone out only the
name of this region, over and over.

"Quarmall . . ." they seemed to chant. "Quarmall . . . Quarmall
is all . . ."

The Gray Mouser, upon whose senses and through whose mind
these sensations and fancies had been flooding and flitting, was a
small man strongly muscled. Clad in gray silks irregularly woven,
with tiny thread-tufts here and there, he looked restless as a lynx and
as dangerous.

From a great tray of strangely hued and shaped mushrooms set
before him like sweetmeats, the Mouser disdainfully selected and nibbled cautiously at the more normal looking, a gray one. Its perfumy
savor masking bitterness offended him and he spat it surreptitiously
into his palm and dropped that hand under the table and flicked the
wet chewed fragments to the floor. Then, while he sucked his cheeks
sourly, the fingers of both his hands began to play as slowly and
nervously with the hilts of his sword Scalpel and his dagger Cat's
Claw as his mind played with his boredoms and murky wonderings.

Along each side of the long narrow table, in great high-backed
chairs widely spaced, sat six scrawny old men, bald or shaven of dome
and chin, and chicken fluted of jowl, and each clad only in a neat
white loincloth. Eleven of these stared intently at nothing and perpetually tensed their meager muscles until even their ears seemed to
stiffen, as though concentrating mightily in realms unseen. The
twelfth had his chair half turned and was playing across a far corner
of the table the board-game that made the occasional tiny rutching
noises. He was playing it with the Mouser's employer Gwaay, ruler
of the Lower Levels of Quarmall and younger son to Quarmal, Lord
of Quarmall.

Although the Mouser had been three days in Quarmall's depths he
had come no closer to Gwaay than he was now, so that he knew him
only as a pallid, handsome, soft-spoken youth, no realer to the
Mouser, because of the eternal dimness and the invariable distance
between them, than a ghost.

The game was one the Mouser had never seen before and quite
tricky in several respects.

The board looked green, though it was impossible to be certain of colors in the unending twilight of the torches, and it had no perceptible squares or tracks on it, except for a phosphorescent line midway between the opponents, dividing the board into two equal fields.

Each contestant started the game with twelve flat circular counters set along his edge of the board. Gwaay's counters were obsidian-black, his ancient opponent's marble-white, so the Mouser was able to distinguish them despite the dimness.

The object of the game seemed to be to move the pieces randomly forward over uneven distances and get at least seven of them into your opponent's field first.

Here the trickiness was that one moved the pieces not with the fingers but only by looking at them intently. Apparently, if one gazed only at a single piece, one could move it quite swiftly. If one gazed at several, one could move them all together in a line or cluster, but more sluggishly.

The Mouser was not yet wholly convinced that he was witnessing a display of thought-power. He still suspected threads, soundless air-puffings, surreptitious joggings of the board from below, powerful beetles under the counters, and hidden magnets!—for Gwaay's pieces at least could by their color be some sort of lodestone.

At the present moment Gwaay's black counters and the ancient's white ones were massed at the central line, shifting only a little now and then as the push-of-war went first a nail's breadth one way, then the other. Suddenly Gwaay's rearmost counter circled swiftly back and darted toward an open space at the board's edge. Two of the ancient's counters formed a wedge and thrust across the midline through the weak point thus created. As the ancient's two detached counters returned to oppose them, Gwaay's end-running counter sped across. The game was over—Gwaay gave no sign of this, but the ancient began fumblingly to return the pieces to their starting positions with his fingers.

"Ho, Gwaay, that was easily won!" the Mouser called out cockily. "Why not take on two of them together? The oldster must be a sorcerer of the Second Rank to play so weakly—or even a doddering apprentice of the Third."

The ancient shot the Mouser a venomous gaze. "We are, all twelve of us, sorcerers of the First Rank and have been from our youth," he proclaimed portentously. "As you should swiftly learn were one of us to point but a little finger against you."

"You have heard what he says," Gwaay called softly to the Mouser without looking at him.

The Mouser, daunted no whit, at least outwardly, called back. "I still think you could beat two of them together, or seven—or the whole decrepit dozen! If they are of First Rank, you must be of Zero or Negative Magnitude."

The ancient's lips worked speechlessly and bubbled with froth at that affront, but Gwaay only called pleasantly, "Were but three of my faithful magi to cease their sorcerous concentrations, my brother Hasjarl's sendings would burst through from the Upper Levels and I would be stricken with all the diseases in the evil compendium, and a few others that exist in Hasjarl's putrescent imagination alone—or perchance I should be erased entirely from this life."

"If nine out of twelve must be forever a-guarding you, they can't get much sleep," the Mouser observed, calling back.

"Times are not always so troublous," Gwaay replied tranquilly. "Sometimes custom or my father enjoins a truce. Sometimes the dark inward sea quiets. But today I know by certain signs that a major assault is being made on the liver and lights and blood and bones and rest of me. Dear Hasjarl has a double coven of sorcerers hardly inferior to my own—Second Rank, but High Second—and he whips them on. And I am as distasteful to Hasjarl, oh Gray Mouser, as the simple fruits of our manure beds are to your lips. Tonight, furthermore, my father Quarmal casts his horoscope in the tower of the Keep, high above Hasjarl's Upper Levels, so it befits I keep all ratholes closely watched."

"If it's magical helpings you lack," the Mouser retorted boldly, "I have a spell or two that would frizzle your elder brother's witches and warlocks!" And truth to tell the Mouser had parchment-crackling in his pouch one spell—though one spell only—which he dearly wanted to test. It had been given him by his own wizardly mentor and master Sheelba of the Eyeless Face.

Gwaay replied, more softly than ever, so that the Mouser felt if there had been a yard more between them he would not have heard, "It is your work to ward from my physical body Hasjarl's sword-sendings, in particular those of his great champion he is reputed to have hired. My sorcerers of the First Rank will shield off Hasjarl's sorcerous *billets-doux*. Each to his proper occupation." He lightly clapped his hands together. A slim slavegirl appeared noiselessly in the dark archway beyond him. Without looking once at her, Gwaay softly commanded, "Strong wine for our warrior." She vanished.

The ancient had at last laboriously shuffled the black and white counters into their starting positions and Gwaay regarded his thoughtfully. But before making a move, he called to the Mouser, "If time still hangs heavy on your hands, devote some of it to selecting the reward you will take when your work is done. And in your search overlook not the maiden who brings you the wine. Her name is Ivivis."

At that the Mouser shut up. He had already chosen more than a dozen expensive be-charming objects from Gwaay's drawers and niches and locked them in a disused closet he had discovered two levels down. If this should be discovered, he would explain that he was merely making an innocent preselection pending final choice, but Gwaay might not view it that way and Gwaay was sharp, judging from the way he'd noted the rejected mushroom and other things.

It had not occurred to the Mouser to preempt a girl or two by locking her in the closet also, though it was admittedly an attractive idea.

The ancient cleared his throat and said chucklingly across the board, "Lord Gwaay, let this ambitious sworder try his sorcerous tricks. Let him try them on me!"

The Mouser's spirits rose, but Gwaay only raised palm and shook his head slightly and pointed a finger at the board; the ancient began obediently to think a piece forward.

The Mouser's spirits fell. He was beginning to feel very much alone in this dim underworld where all spoke and moved in whispers. True, when Gwaay's emissary had approached him in Lankhmar, the Mouser had been happy to take on this solo job. It would teach his loud-voiced sword-mate Fafhrd a lesson if his small gray comrade (and brain!) should disappear one night without a word . . . and then return perchance a year later with a brimful treasure chest and a mocking smile.

The Mouser had even been happy all the long caravan trip from Lankhmar south to Quarmall, along the Hlal River and past the Lakes of Pleea and through the Mountains of Hunger. It had been a positive pleasure to loll on a swaying camel beyond reach of Fafhrd's hugeness and disputatious talk and boisterous ways, while the nights grew ever bluer and warmer and strange jewel-fiery stars came peering over the southern horizon.

But now he had been three nights in Quarmall since his secret coming to the Lower Levels—three nights and days, or rather one hundred and forty-four interminable demi-hours of buried twilight—and he was already beginning in his secretest mind to wish that Fafhrd were here, instead of half a continent away in Lankhmar—or even farther than that if he'd carried out his misty plans to revisit his northern homeland. Someone to drink with, at any rate—and even a roaring quarrel would be positively refreshing after seventy-two hours of nothing but silent servitors, tranced sorcerers, stewed mushrooms, and Gwaay's unbreakable soft-tongued equanimity.

Besides, it appeared that all Gwaay wanted was a mighty sworder to nullify the threat of this champion Hasjarl was supposed to have hired as secretly as Gwaay had smuggled in the Mouser. If Fafhrd were here, he could be Gwaay's sworder, while the Mouser would have better opportunity to peddle Gwaay his magical talents. The one spell he had in his pouch—he had got it from Sheelba in return for the tale of the Perversions of Clutho—would forever establish his reputation as an archimage of deadly might, he was sure.

The Mouser came out of his musings to realize that the slavegirl Ivivis was kneeling before him—for how long she had been there he could not say—and proffering an ebony tray on which stood a squat stone jug and a copper cup.

She knelt with one leg doubled, the other thrust behind her as in a fencing lunge, stretching the short skirt of her green tunic, while her arms reached the tray forward.

Her slim body was most supple—she had the difficult pose effortlessly. Her fine straight hair was pale as her skin—both a sort of ghost color. It occurred to the Mouser that she would look very well in his closet, perhaps cherishing against her bosom the necklace of large black pearls he had discovered piled behind a pewter statuette in one of Gwaay's niches.

However, she was kneeling as far away from him as she could and still stretch him the tray, and her eyes were most modestly downcast, nor would she even flicker up their lids to his gracious murmurings—which were all the approach he thought suitable at this moment.

He seized the jug and cup. Ivivis drooped her head still lower in acknowledgment, then flitted silently away.

The Mouser poured a finger of blood-red, blood-thick wine and sipped. Its flavor was darkly sweet, but with a bitter undertaste. He wondered if it were fermented from scarlet toadstools.

The black and white counters skittered rutchingly in obedience to Gwaay's and the ancient's peerings. The pale torch flames bent to the unceasing cool breeze, while the fanslaves and their splayed bare feet on the leather belts and the great unseen fans themselves on their ponderous axles muttered unendingly, "Quarmall . . . Quarmall is downward tall . . . Quarmall . . . Quarmall is all. . . ."

In an equally vast room many levels higher yet still underground— a windowless room where torches flared redder and brighter, but their brightness nullified by an acrid haze of incense smoke, so that here too the final effect was exasperating dimness—Fafhrd sat at the table's foot.

Fafhrd was ordinarily a monstrously calm man, but now he was restlessly drumming fist on thumb-root, on the verge of admitting to himself that he wished the Gray Mouser were here, instead of back in Lankhmar or perchance off on some ramble in the desert-patched Eastern Lands.

The Mouser, Fafhrd thought, might have more patience to unriddle the mystifications and crooked behavior-ways of these burrowing Quarmallians. The Mouser might find it easier to endure Hasjarl's loathsome taste for torture, and at least the little gray fool would be someone human to drink with!

Fafhrd had been very glad to be parted from the Mouser and from his vanities and tricksiness and chatter when Hasjarl's agent had contacted him in Lankhmar, promising large pay in return for Fafhrd's instant, secret, and solitary coming. Fafhrd had even dropped a hint to the small fellow that he might take ship with some of his Northerner countrymen who had sailed down across the Inner Sea.

What he had not explained to the Mouser was that, as soon as Fafhrd was aboard her, the longship had sailed not north but south, coasting through the vast Outer Sea along Lankhmar's western seaboard.

It had been an idyllic journey, that—pirating a little now and then, despite the sour objections of Hasjarl's agent, battling great storms and also the giant cuttlefish, rays, and serpents which swarmed ever thicker in the Outer Sea as one sailed south. At the recollection Fafhrd's fist slowed its drumming and his lips almost formed a long smile.

But now this Quarmall! This endless stinking sorcery! This torture-besotted Hasjarl! Fafhrd's fist drummed fiercely again.

Rules!—he mustn't explore downward, for that led to the Lower Levels and the enemy. Nor must he explore upward—that way was to Father Quarmal's apartments, sacrosanct. None must know of Fafhrd's presence. He must satisfy himself with such drink and inferior wenches as were available in Hasjarl's limited Upper Levels. (They called these dim labyrinths and crypts *upper!*)

Delays!—they mustn't muster their forces and march down and smash brother-enemy Gwaay; that was unthinkable rashness. They mustn't even shut off the huge treadmill-driven fans whose perpetual creaking troubled Fafhrd's ears and which sent the life-giving air on the first stages of its journey to Gwaay's underworld, and through

other rock-driven wells sucked out the stale—no, those fans must
never be stopped, for Father Quarmal would frown on any battle-
tactic which suffocated valuable slaves; and from anything Father
Quarmal frowned on, his sons shrank shuddering.

Instead, Hasjarl's war-council must plot years-long campaigns
weaponed chiefly with sorcery and envisioning the conquest of
Gwaay's Lower Levels a quarter tunnel—or a quarter mushroom
field—at a time.

Mystifications!—mushrooms must be served at all meals but never
eaten or so much as tasted. Roast rat, on the other hand, was a delicacy to be crowed over. Tonight Father Quarmal would cast his own
horoscope and for some reason that superstitious starsighting and
scribbling would be of incalculable cryptic consequence. All maids
must scream loudly twice when familiarities were suggested to them,
no matter what their subsequent behavior. Fafhrd must never get
closer to Hasjarl than a long dagger's cast—a rule which gave Fafhrd
no chance to discover how Hasjarl managed never to miss a detail of
what went on around him while keeping his eyes fully closed almost
all the time.

Perhaps Hasjarl had a sort of short-range second sight, or perhaps
the slave nearest him ceaselessly whispered an account of all that
transpired, or perhaps—well, Fafhrd had no way of knowing.

But somehow Hasjarl could see things with his eyes shut.

This paltry trick of Hasjarl's evidently saved his eyes from the
irritation of the incense smoke, which kept those of Hasjarl's sorcerers and of Fafhrd himself red and watering. However, since Hasjarl
was otherwise a most energetic and restless prince—his bandy-legged
misshapen body and mismated arms forever a-twitch, his ugly face
always grimacing—the detail of eyes tranquilly shut was peculiarly
jarring and shiversome.

All in all, Fafhrd was heartily sick of the Upper Levels of Quarmall
though scarcely a week in them. He had even toyed with the notion
of double-crossing Hasjarl and hiring out to his brother or turning
informer for his father—although they might, as employers, be no
improvement whatever.

But mostly he simply wanted to meet in combat this champion of
Gwaay's he kept hearing so much of—meet him and slay him and
then shoulder his reward (preferably a shapely maiden with a bag of
gold in her either hand) and turn his back forever on the accursed
dim-tunneled whisper-haunted hill of Quarmall!

In an excess of exasperation he clapped his hand to the hilt of his
longsword Graywand.

Hasjarl saw that, although Hasjarl's eyes were closed, for he quickly pointed his gnarly face down the long table at Fafhrd, between the ranks of the twenty-four heavily-robed, thickly-bearded sorcerers crowded shoulder to shoulder. Then, his eyelids still shut, Hasjarl commenced to twitch his mouth as a preamble to speech and with a twitter-tremble as overture called, "Ha, hot for battle, eh, Fafhrd boy? Keep him in the sheath! Yet tell me, what manner of man do you think this warrior—the one you protect me against—Gwaay's grim man-slayer? He is said to be mightier than an elephant in strength, and more guileful than the very Zobolds." With a final spasm Hasjarl managed, still without opening his eyes, to look expectantly at Fafhrd.

Fafhrd had heard all this sort of worrying time and time again during the past week, so he merely answered with a snort:

"Zutt! They all say that about anybody. I know. But unless you get me some action and keep these old flea-bitten beards out of my sight—"

Catching himself up short, Fafhrd tossed off his wine and beat with his pewter mug on the table for more. For although Hasjarl might have the demeanor of an idiot and the disposition of a ocelot, he served excellent ferment of grape ripened on the hot brown southern slopes of Quarmall hill . . . and there was no profit in goading him.

Nor did Hasjarl appear to take offense—or if he did, he took it out on his bearded sorcerers, for he instantly began to instruct one to enunciate his runes more clearly, questioned another as to whether his herbs were sufficiently pounded, reminded a third that it was time to tinkle a certain silver bell thrice, and in general treated the whole two dozen as if they were a roomful of schoolboys and he their eagle-eyed pedagogue—though Fafhrd had been given to understand that they were all magi of the First Rank.

The double coven of sorcerers in turn began to bustle more nervously, each with his particular spell—touching off more stinks, jiggling black drops out of more dirty vials, waving more wands, pin-stabbing more figurines, finger-tracing eldritch symbols more swiftly in the air, mounding up each in front of him from his bag more noisesome fetishes, and so on.

From his hours of sitting at the foot of the table, Fafhrd had learned that most of the spells were designed to inflict a noisome disease upon Gwaay: the Black Plague, the Red Plague, the Boneless Death, the Hairless Decline, the Slow Rot, the Fast Rot, the Green Rot, the Bloody Cough, the Belly Melts, the Ague, the Runs, and even the footling Nose Drip. Gwaay's own sorcerers, he gathered, kept warding off these malefic spells with counter-charms, but the idea was to keep on sending them in hopes that the opposition would some day drop their guard, if only for a few moments.

Fafhrd rather wished Gwaay's gang were able to reflect back the disease-spells on their dark-robed senders. He had become weary even of the abstruse astrologic signs stitched in gold and silver on those robes, and of the ribbons and precious wires knotted cabalistically in their heavy beards.

Hasjarl, his magicians disciplined into a state of furious busyness, opened wide his eyes for a change and with only a preliminary lip-writhe called to Fafhrd, "So you want action, eh, Fafhrd boy?"

Fafhrd, mightily irked at the last epithet, planted an elbow on the table and wagged that hand at Hasjarl and called back, "I do. My muscles cry to bulge. You've strong-looking arms, Lord Hasjarl. What say you we play the wrist game?"

Hasjarl tittered evilly and cried, "I go but now to play another sort of wrist game with a maid suspected of commerce with one of Gwaay's pages. She never screamed even once . . . then. Wouldst accompany me and watch the action, Fafhrd?" And he suddenly shut his eyes again with the effect of putting on two tiny masks of skin— yet shut them so firmly there could be no question of his peering through the lashes.

Fafhrd shrank back in his chair, flushing a little. Hasjarl had divined Fafhrd's distaste for torture on the Northerner's first night in Quarmall's Upper Levels and since then had never missed an opportunity to play on what Hasjarl must view as Fafhrd's weakness.

To cover his embarrassment, Fafhrd drew from under his tunic a tiny book of stitched parchment pages. The Northerner would have sworn that Hasjarl's eyelids had not flickered once since closing, yet now the villain cried, "The sigil on the cover of that packet tells me it is something of Ningauble of the Seven Eyes. What is it, Fafhrd?"

"Private matters," the latter retorted firmly. Truth to tell, he was somewhat alarmed. The contents of the packet were such as he dared not permit Hasjarl see. And just as the villain somehow knew, there was indeed on the top parchment the bold black figure of a seven-fingered hand, each finger bearing an eye for a nail—one of the many signs of Fafhrd's wizardly patron.

Hasjarl coughed hackingly. "No servant of Hasjarl has private matters," he pronounced. "However, we will speak of that at another time. Duty calls me." He bounded up from his chair and fiercely eyeing his sorcerers cried at them barkingly, "If I find one of you dozing over his spells when I return, it were better for him—aye, and for his mother too—had he been born with slave's chains on his ankles!"

He paused, turning to go, and pointing his face at Fafhrd again, called rapidly yet cajolingly, "The girl is named Friska. She's but seventeen. I doubt not she will play the wrist game most adroitly and with many a charming exclamation. I will converse with her, at length. I will question her, as I twist the crank, very slowly. And she will answer, she will comment, she will describe her feelings, in sounds if not in words. Sure you won't come?" And trailing an evil titter behind him, Hasjarl strode rapidly from the room, red torches in the archway outlining his monstrous bandy-legged form in blood.

Fafhrd ground his teeth. There was nothing he could do at the moment. Hasjarl's torture chamber was also his guard barrack. Yet the Northerner chalked up in his mind an intention, or perhaps an obligation.

To keep his mind from nasty unmanning imaginings, he began carefully to reread the tiny parchment book which Ningauble had given him as a sort of reward for past services, or an assurance for future ones, on the night of the Northerner's departure from Lankhmar.

Fafhrd did not worry about Hasjarl's sorcerers overlooking what he read. After their master's last threat, they were all as furiously and elbow-jostlingly busy with their spells as so many bearded black ants.

Quarmall was first brought to my attention *(Fafhrd read in Ningauble's little handwritten, or tentacle-writ book)* by the report that certain passageways beneath it ran deep under the Sea and extended to certain caverns wherein might dwell some remnant of the Elder Ones. Naturally I dispatched agents to probe the truth of the report: two well-trained and valuable spies were sent (also two others to watch them) to find the facts and accumulate gossip. Neither pair returned, nor did they send messages or tokens in explanation, or indeed word of any sort. I was interested; but being unable at that time, to spare valuable material on so uncertain and dangerous a quest, I bided my time until information should be placed at my disposal (as it usually is).

After twenty years my discretion was rewarded. *(So went the crabbed script as Fafhrd continued to read.)* An old man, horribly scarred and peculiarly pallid, was fetched to me. His name was Tamorg, and his tale interesting in spite of the teller's incoherence. He claimed to have been captured from a passing caravan when yet a small lad and carried into captivity within Quarmall. There he served as a slave on the Lower Levels, far below the ground. Here there was no natural light, and the only air was sucked down into the mazy caverns by means of large fans, treadmill-driven; hence his pallor and otherwise unusual appearance.

Tamorg was quite bitter about these fans, for he had been chained at one of those endless belts for a longer time than he cared to think about. (He really did not know exactly how long, since there was, by his own statement, no measure of time in the Lower Levels.) Finally he was released from his onerous walking, as nearly as I could glean from his garbled tale, by the invention or breeding of a specialized type of slave who better served the purpose.

From this I postulate that the Masters of Quarmall are sufficiently interested in the economics of their holdings to improve them: a rarity among overlords. Moreover, if these specialized slaves were bred, the life-span of these overlords must perforce be longer than ordinary; or else the cooperation between father and son is more perfect than any filial relationship I have yet noted.

Tamorg further related that he was put to work digging, along with eight other slaves likewise taken from the treadmills. They were forced to enlarge and extend certain passages and chambers; so for another space of time he mined and buttressed. This time must have been long, for by close cross-questioning I found that Tamorg digged and walled, single-handed, a passage a thousand and twenty paces long. These slaves were not chained, unless maniacal, nor was it necessary to bind them so; for these Lower Levels seem to be a maze within a maze, and an unlucky slave once strayed from familiar paths stood small chance of retracing his steps. However, rumor has it, Tamorg said, that the Lords of Quarmall keep certain slaves who have memorized each a portion of the ever-extending labyrinth. By this means they are able to traverse with safety and communicate one level to the other.

Tamorg finally escaped by the simple expedient of accidentally breaking through the wall whereat he dug. He enlarged the opening with his mattock and stooped to peer. At that moment a fellow workman pushed against him and Tamorg was thrust head-foremost into the opening he had made. Fortunately it led into a chasm at the bottom of which ran a swift but deep underground stream, into which Tamorg fell. As swimming is an art not easily forgotten, he managed to keep afloat until he reached the outer world. For several days he was blinded by the sun's rays and felt comfortable only by dim torchlight.

I questioned him in detail about the many interesting phenomena which must have been before him constantly but he was very unsatisfactory, being ignorant of all observational methods. However I placed him as gatekeeper in the palace of D—whose coming and going I desired to check upon. So much for that source of information.

My interest in Quarmall was aroused *(Ningauble's book went on)* and my appetite whetted by this scanty meal of facts, so I applied myself toward getting more information. Through my connection with Sheelba I made contact with Eeack, the Overlord of Rats; by holding out the lure of secret passages to the granaries of Lankhmar, he was persuaded to visit me. His visit proved both barren and embarrassing. Barren because it turned out that rats are eaten as a delicacy in Quarmall and hunted for culinary purposes by well-trained weasels. Naturally, under such circumstances, any rat within the walls of Quarmall stood little chance of doing liaison work except from the uncertain vantage of a pot. Eeack's personal cohort of countless rats, evil-smelling and famished, consumed all edibles within reach of their sharp teeth; and out of pity for the plight in which I was left Eeack favored me by cajoling Scraa to wake and speak with me.

Scraa *(Ningauble's notes continued)* is one of those eon-old roaches who existed contemporaneously with those monstrous reptiles which once ruled the world, and whose racial memories go back into the mistiness of time before the Elder Ones retreated from the surface. Scraa presented me the following short history Quarmall neatly inscribed on a peculiar parchment composed of cleverly welded wing-cases flattened and smoothed most subtly. I append his document and apologize for his somewhat dry and prosy style.

"The city-state of Quarmall houses a civilization almost unheard of in the sphere of anthropoid organization. Perhaps the closest analogy which might be made is to that of the slave-making ants. The domain of Quarmall is at the present day limited to the small mountain, or large hill, on which it stands; but like a radish the main portion of it lies buried beneath the surface. This was not always so.

"Once the Lords of Quarmall ruled over broad meadows and vast seas; their ships swam between all known ports and their caravans marched the routes from sea to sea. Slowly from the fertile valleys and barren cliffs, from the desert spots and the open sea the grip of Quarmall loosened; not willingly but ever forced did the Lords of Quarmall retreat. Inexorably they were driven, year by year, generation by generation, from all their possessions and rights; until finally they were confined to that last and staunchest stronghold, the impregnable castle of Quarmall. The cause of this driving is lost in the dimness of fable; but it was probably due to those most gruesome

practices which even to this day persuade the surrounding country-
side that Quarmall is unclean and cursed.

"As the Lords of Quarmall were pushed back, driven in spite of
their sorceries and valor, they burrowed under that last, vast stronghold ever deeper and ever broader. Each succeeding Lord dug more
deeply into the bowels of the small mount on which sat the Keep of
Quarmall. Eventually the memory of past glories faded and was forgotten and the Lords of Quarmall concentrated on their mazy tunneling to the exclusion of the outer world. They would have forgotten
the outer world entirely but for their constant and ever increasing
need of slaves and of sustenance for those slaves.

"The Lords of Quarmall are magicians of great repute and adepts
in the practice of the Art. It is said that by their skill they can charm
men into bondage both of body and of soul."

So much did Scraa write. All in all it is a very unsatisfactory bit of
gossip: hardly a word about those intriguing passageways which first
aroused my interest; nothing, about the conformation of the Land or
its inhabitants; not even a map! But then poor ancient Scraa lives
almost entirely in the past—the present will not become important to
him for another eon or so.

However I believe I know two fellows who might be persuaded to
undertake a mission there. . . . *(Here Ningauble's notes ended, much to
Fafhrd's irritation and suspicious puzzlement—and carking shamed discom-
fort too, for now he must think again of the unknown girl Hasjarl was
torturing.*

Outside the mount of Quarmall the sun was past meridian and
shadows had begun to grow. The great white oxen threw their
weight against the yoke. It was not the first time nor would it be the
last, they knew. Each month as they approached this mucky stretch of
road the master whipped and slashed them frantically, attempting to
goad them into a speed which they, by nature, were unable to attain.
Straining until the harness creaked, they obliged as best they could:
for they knew that when this spot was pulled the master would reward them with a bit of salt, a rough caress, and a brief respite from
work. It was unfortunate that this particular piece of road stayed
mucky long after the rains had ceased; almost from one season to the
next. Unfortunate that it took a longer time to pass.

Their master had reason to lash them so. This spot was accounted
accursed among his people. From this curved eminence the towers of
Quarmall could be spied on; and more important these towers looked
down upon the road, even as one looking up could see them. It was

not healthy to look on the towers of Quarmall, or to be looked upon by them. There was sufficient reason for this feeling. The master of the oxen spat surreptitiously, made an obvious gesture with his fingers, and glanced fearfully over his shoulder at the sky-thrusting lacy-topped towers as the last mudhole was traversed. Even in this fleeting glance he caught the glimpse of a flash, a brilliant scintillation, from the tallest keep. Shuddering, he leaped into the welcome covert of the trees and thanked the gods he worshiped for his escape.

Tonight he would have much to speak of in the tavern. Men would buy him bowls of wine to swill, and bitter beer of herbs. He could lord it for an evening. Ah! but for his quickness he might even now be plodding soulless to the mighty gates of Quarmall; there to serve until his body was no more and even after. For tales were told of such charmings, and of other things, among the elders of the village: tales that bore no moral but which all men did heed. Was it not only last Serpent Eve that young Twelm went from the ken of men? Had he not jeered at these very tales and, drunken, braved the terraces of Quarmall? Sure, and this was so! And it was also true that his less brave companion had seen him swagger with bravado to the last, the highest terrace, almost to the moat; then when Twelm, alarmed at some unknown cause, turned to run, his twisted-arched body was pulled willy-nilly back into the darkness. Not even a scream was heard to mark the passing of Twelm from this earth and the ken of his fellowmen. Juln, that less brave or less foolhardy companion of Twelm, had spent his time thenceforth in a continual drunken stupor. Nor would he stir from under roofs at night.

All the way to the village the master of the oxen pondered. He tried to formulate in his dim peasant intellect a method by which he might present himself as a hero. But even as he painfully constructed a simple, self-aggrandizing tale, he bethought himself of the fate of that one who had dared to brag of robbing Quarmall's vineyards; the one whose name was spoken only in a hushed whisper, secretly. So the driver decided to confine himself to facts, simple as they were, and trust to the atmosphere of horror that he knew any manifestation of activity in Quarmall would arouse.

While the driver was still whipping oxen, and the Mouser watching two shadow-men play a thought-game, and Fafhrd swilling wine to drown the thought of an unknown girl in pain—at that same time Quarmal, Lord of Quarmall, was casting his own horoscope for the coming year. In the highest tower of the Keep he labored, putting in order the huge astrolabe and the other massive instruments necessary for his accurate observations.

Through curtains of broidery the afternoon sun beat hotly into the small chamber; beams glanced from the polished surfaces and scintillated into rainbow hues as they reflected askew. It was warm, even for an old man lightly gowned, and Quarmal stepped to the windows opposite the sun and drew the broidery aside, letting the cool moorbreeze blow through his observatory.

He glanced idly out the deep-cut embrasures. In the distance down past the terraced slopes he could see the little, curved brown thread of road which led eventually to the village.

Like ants the small figures on it appeared: ants struggling through some sticky trap; and like ants, even as Quarmal watched, they persisted and finally disappeared. Quarmal sighed as he turned away from the windows. Sighed in a slight disappointment because he regretted not having looked a moment sooner. Slaves were always needed. Besides, it would have been an opportunity for trying out a recently invented instrument or two.

Yet it was never Quarmal's way to regret the past, so with a shrug he turned away.

For an old man Quarmal was not particularly hideous until his eyes were noticed. They were peculiar in their shape and the ball was a rich ruby-red. The dead-white iris had that nauseous sheen of pearly iridescence found only in the sea dwellers among living creatures; this character he inherited from his mother, a mer-woman. The pupils, like specks of black crystal, sparkled with incredible malevolent intelligence. His baldness was accentuated by the long tufts of coarse black hair which grew symmetrically over each ear. Pale, pitted skin hung loosely on his jowls, but was tightly drawn over the high cheekbones. Thin as a sharpened blade, his long jutting nose gave him the appearance of an old hawk or kestrel.

If Quarmal's eyes were the most arresting feature in his countenance, his mouth was the most beautiful. The lips were full and ruddy, remarkable in so aged a man, and they had that peculiar mobility found in some elocutionists and orators and actors. Had it been possible for Quarmal to have known vanity, he might have been vain about the beauty of his mouth; as it was this perfectly molded mouth served only to accentuate the horror of his eyes.

He looked up veiledly now through the iron rondures of the astrolabe at the twin of his own face pushing forth from a windowless square of the opposite wall: it was his own waxen life-mask, taken within the year and most realistically tinted and blackly hair-tufted by his finest artist, save that the white-irised eyes were of necessity closed—though the mask still gave a feeling of peering. The mask was the last in several rows of such, each a little more age-darkened than the succeeding one. Though some were ugly and many were elderly-handsome, there was a strong family resemblance between the shut-eyed faces, for there had been few if any intrusions into the male lineage of Quarmall.

There were perhaps fewer masks than might have been expected, for most Lords of Quarmall lived very long and had sons late. Yet there were also a considerable many, since Quarmall was such an ancient rulership. The oldest masks were of a brown almost black and not wax at all but the cured and mummified face skins of those prime-val autocrats. The arts of flaying and tanning had early been brought to an exquisite degree of perfection in Quarmall and were still prac-ticed with jealously prideful skill.

Quarmal dropped his gaze from the mask to his lightly-robed body. He was a lean man, and his hips and shoulders still gave evidence that once he had hawked, hunted, and fenced with the best. His feet were high-arched and his step was still light. Long and spatulate were his knob-knuckled fingers, while fleshy muscular palms gave witness to their dexterity and nimbleness, a necessary advantage to one of his calling. For Quarmal was a sorcerer, as were all the Lords of Quarmall from the eon-mighty past. From childhood up through manhood each male was trained into his calling, like some vines are coaxed to twist and thread a difficult terrace.

As Quarmal returned from the window to attend his duties he pondered on his training. It was unfortunate for the House of Quarmall that he possessed two instead of the usual single heir. Each of his sons was a creditable necromancer and well skilled in other sciences pertaining to the Art; both were exceedingly ambitious and filled with hatred. Hatred not only for one another but for Quarmal their father.

Quarmal pictured in his mind Hasjarl in his Upper Levels below the Keep and Gwaay below Hasjarl in his Lower Levels . . . Hasjarl cultivating his passions as if in some fiery circle of Hell, making en-ergy and movement and logic carried to the ultimate the greatest goods, constantly threatening with whips and tortures and carrying through those threats, and now hiring a great brawling beast of a man to be his sworder . . . Gwaay nourishing restraint as if in Hell's frigidest circle, trying to reduce all life to art and intuitive thought, seeking by meditation to compel lifeless rock to do his bidding and constrain Death by the power of his will, and now hiring a small gray man like Death's younger brother to be his knifer. . . . Quarmal thought of Hasjarl and Gwaay and for a moment a strange smile of fatherly pride bent his lips and then he shook his head and his smile became stranger still and he shuddered very faintly.

It was well, thought Quarmal, that he was an old man, far past his prime, even as magicians counted years, for it would be unpleasant to cease living in the prime of life, or even in the twilight of life's day. And he knew that sooner or later, in spite of all protecting charms and precautions, Death would creep silently on him or spring suddenly from some unguarded moment. This very night his horoscope might signal Death's instant escapeless approach; and though men lived by lies, treating truth's very self as lie to be exploited, the stars remained the stars.

Each day Quarmal's sons, he knew, grew more clever and more subtle in their usage of the Art which he had taught them. Nor could Quarmal protect himself by slaying them. Brother might murder brother, or the son his sire, but it was forbidden from ancient times for the father to slay his son. There were no very good reasons for this custom, nor were any needed. Custom in the House of Quarmall stood unchallenged, and it was not lightly defied.

Quarmal bethought him of the babe sprouting in the womb of Kewissa, the childlike favorite concubine of his age. So far as his precautions and watchfulness might have enforced that babe was surely his own—and Quarmal was the most watchful and cynically realistic of men. If that babe lived and proved a boy—as omens foretold it would be—and if Quarmal were given but twelve more years to train him, and if Hasjarl and Gwaay should be taken by the fates or each other . . .

Quarmal clipped off in his mind this line of speculation. To expect to live a dozen more years with Hasjarl and Gwaay growing daily more clever-subtle in their sorceries—or to hope for the dual extinguishment of two such cautious sprigs of his own flesh—were vanity and irrealism indeed!

He looked around him. The preliminaries for the casting were completed, the instruments prepared and aligned; now only the final observations and their interpretation were required. Lifting a small leaden hammer Quarmal lightly struck a brazen gong. Hardly had the resonance faded when the tall, richly appareled figure of a man appeared in the arched doorway.

Flindach was Master of the Magicians. His duties were many but not easily apparent. His power carefully concealed was second only to that of Quarmal. A wearied cruelty sat upon his dark visage, giving him an air of boredom which ill matched the consuming interest he took in the affairs of others. Flindach was not a comely man: a purple wine mark covered his left cheek, three large warts made an isosceles triangle on his right, while his nose and chin jutted like those of an old witch. Startlingly, with an effect of mocking irreverence, his eyes were ruby-whited and pearly-irised like those of his lord; he was a younger offspring of the same mer-woman who had birthed Quarmal —after Quarmal's father had done with her and following one of Quarmall's bizarre customs, had given her to *his* Master of the Magicians.

Now those eyes of Flindach, large and hypnotically staring, shifted, uneasily as Quarmal spoke: "Gwaay and Hasjarl, my sons, work today on their respective Levels. It would be well if they were called into the council room this night. For it is the night on which my doom is to be foretold. And I sense premonitorily that this casting will bear no good. Bid them dine together and permit them to amuse one another by plotting at my death—or by attempting each other's."

He shut his lips precisely as he finished, and looked more evil than a man expecting Death should look. Flindach, used to terrors in the line of business, could scarcely repress a shudder at the glance bestowed on him; but remembering his position he made the sign of obeisance, and without a word or backward look departed.

The Gray Mouser did not once remove his gaze from Flindach as the latter strode across the domed dim sorcery chamber of the Lower Levels until he reached Gwaay's side. The Mouser was mightily intrigued by the warts and wine mark on the cheeks of the richly-robed witch-faced man, and by his eerie red-whited eyes, and he instantly gave this charming visage a place of honor in the large catalog of freak-faces he stored in his memory vaults.

Although he strained his ears, he could not hear what Flindach said to Gwaay or what Gwaay answered.

Gwaay finished the telekinetic game he was playing by sending all his black counters across the midline in a great rutching surge that knocked half his opponent's white counters tumbling into his loin-clothed lap. Then he rose smoothly from his stool.

"I sup tonight with my beloved brother in my all-revered father's apartments," he pronounced mellowly to all. "While I am there and in the escort of great Flindach here, no sorcerous spells may harm me. So you may rest for a space from your protective concentrations, oh my gracious magi of the First Rank." He turned to go.

The Mouser, inwardly leaping at the chance to glimpse the sky again, if only by chilly night, rose springily too from his chair and called out, "Ho, Prince Gwaay! Though safe from spells, will you not want the warding of my blades at this dinner party? There's many a great prince never made king 'cause he was served cold iron 'twixt the ribs between the soup and the fish. I also juggle most prettily and do conjuring tricks."

Gwaay half turned back. "Nor may steel harm me while my sire's hand is stretched above," he called so softly that the Mouser felt the words were being lobbed like feather balls barely as far as his ear. "Stay here, Gray Mouser."

His tone was unmistakably rebuffing, nevertheless the Mouser, dreading a dull evening, persisted, "There is also the matter of that serious spell of mine of which I told you, Prince—a spell most effective against magi of the *Second* Rank and lower, such as a certain noxious brother employs. Now were a good time—"

"Let there be no sorcery tonight!" Gwaay cut him off sternly, though speaking hardly louder than before. " 'Twere an insult to my sire and to his great servant Flindach here, a Master of Magicians, even to think of such! Bide quietly, swordsman, keep peace, and speak no more." His voice took on a pious note. "There will be time enough for sorcery and swords, if slaying there must be."

Flindach nodded solemnly at that and they silently departed. The Mouser sat down. Rather to his surprise, he noted that the twelve aged sorcerers were already curled up like pillbugs on their sides on their great chairs and snoring away. He could not even while away time by challenging one of them to the thought-game, hoping to learn by playing, or to a bout at conventional chess. This promised to be a most glum evening indeed.

Then a thought brightened the Mouser's swarthy visage. He lifted his hands, cupping the palms, and clapped them lightly together as he had seen Gwaay do.

The slim slavegirl Ivivis instantly appeared in the far archway. When she saw that Gwaay was gone and his sorcerers slumbering, her eyes became bright as a kitten's. She scampered to the Mouser, her slender legs flashing, seated herself with a last bound on his lap, and clapped her lissome arms around him.

Fafhrd silently faded back into a dark side passage as Hasjarl came hurrying along the torchlit corridor beside a richly robed official with hideously warted and mottled face and red eyeballs, on whose other side strode a pallid comely youth with strangely ancient eyes. Fafhrd had never before met Flindach or, of course, Gwaay.

Hasjarl was clearly in a pet, for he was grimacing insanely and twisting his hands together furiously as though pitting one in murderous battle against the other. His eyes, however, were tightly shut. As he stamped swiftly past, Fafhrd thought he glimpsed a bit of tattooing on the nearest upper eyelid.

Fafhrd heard the red-eyeballed one say, "No need to run to your sire's banquet-board, Lord Hasjarl. We're in good time." Hasjarl answered only a snarl, but the pale youth said sweetly, "My brother is ever a baroque pearl of dutifulness."

Fafhrd moved forward, watched the three out of sight, then turned the other way and followed the scent of hot iron straight to Hasjarl's torture chamber.

It was a wide, low-vaulted room and the brightest Fafhrd had yet encountered in these murky, misnamed Upper Levels.

To the right was a low table around which crouched five squat brawny men more bandy-legged than Hasjarl and masked each to the upper lip. They were noisily gnawing bones snatched from a huge platter of them, and swilling ale from leather jacks. Four of the masks were black, one red.

Beyond them was a fire of coals in a circular brick tower half as high as a man. The iron grill above it glowed redly. The coals brightened almost to white, then grew more deeply red again, as a twisted half-bald hag in tatters slowly worked a bellows.

Along the walls to either side, there thickly stood or hung various metal and leather instruments which showed their foul purpose by their ghostly hand-and-glove resemblance to various outer surfaces and inward orifices of the human body: boots, collars, masks, iron maidens, funnels, and the like.

To the left a fair-haired pleasingly plump girl in white under tunic lay bound to a rack. Her right hand in an iron half-glove stretched out tautly toward a machine with a crank. Although her face was tear-streaked, she did not seem to be in present pain.

Fafhrd strode toward her, hurriedly slipping out of his pouch and onto the middle finger of his right hand the massy ring Hasjarl's emissary had given him in Lankhmar as token from his master. It was of silver, holding a large black seal on which was Hasjarl's sign: a clenched fist.

The girl's eyes widened with new fears as she saw Fafhrd coming.

Hardly looking at her as he paused by the rack, Fafhrd turned toward the table of masked messy feathers, who were staring at him gape-mouthed by now. Stretching out toward them the back of his right hand, he called harshly yet carelessly, "By authority of this sigil, release to me the girl Friska!" From mouth-corner he muttered to the girl, "Courage!"

The black-masked creature who came hurrying toward him like a terrier appeared either not to recognize at once Hasjarl's sign or else not to reason out its import, for he said only, wagging a greasy finger, "Begone, barbarian. This dainty morsel is not for you. Think not to quench your rough lusts here. Our Master—"

Fafhrd cried out, "If you will not accept the authority of the Clenched Fist one way, then you must take it the other." Doubling up the hand with the ring on it, he smashed it against the torturer's suet-shining jaw so that he stretched himself out on the dark flags, skidded a foot, and lay quietly.

Fafhrd turned at once toward the half-risen feasters slapping Gray-wand's hilt but not drawing it, he planted his knuckles on his hips and, addressing himself to the red mask, he barked out rather like Hasjarl, "Our Master of the Fist had an afterthought and ordered me to fetch the girl Friska so that he might continue her entertainment at dinner for the amusement of those he goes to dine with. Would you have a new servant like myself report to Hasjarl your derelictions and delays? Loose her quickly and I'll say nothing." He stabbed a finger at the hag by the bellows, "You!—fetch her outer dress."

The masked ones sprang to obey quickly enough at that, their tucked-up masks falling over their mouths and chins. There were mumblings of apology, which he ignored. Even the one he had slugged got groggily to his feet and tried to help.

The girl had been released from her wrist-twisting device, Fafhrd supervising, and she was sitting up on the side of the rack when the hag came with a dress and two slippers, the toe of one stuffed with oddments of ornament and such. The girl reached for them, but Fafhrd grabbed them instead and, seizing her by the left arm, dragged her roughly to her feet.

"No time for that now," he commanded. "We will let Hasjarl decide how he wants you trigged out for the sport," and without more ado he strode from the torture chamber, dragging her beside him, though again muttering from mouth-side, "Courage."

When they were around the first bend in the corridor and had reached a dark branching, he stopped and looked at her frowningly. Her eyes grew wide with fright; she shrank from him, but then firming her features she said fearful-boldly, "If you rape me by the way, I'll tell Hasjarl."

"I don't mean to rape but rescue you, Friska," Fafhrd assured her rapidly. "That talk of Hasjarl sending to fetch you was but my trick.

Where's a secret place I can hide you for a few days?—until we flee
these musty crypts forever! I'll bring you food and drink."

At that Friska looked far more frightened. "You mean Hasjarl
didn't order this? And that you dream of escaping from Quarmall?
Oh stranger, Hasjarl would only have twisted my wrist a little longer,
perhaps not maimed me much, only heaped a few more indignities,
certainly spared my life. But if he so much as suspected that I had
sought to escape from Quarmall . . . Take me back to the torture
chamber!"

"That I will not," Fafhrd said irkedly, his gaze darting up and
down the empty corridor. "Take heart, girl. Quarmall's not the wide
world. Quarmall's not the stars and the sea. Where's a secret room?"

"Oh, it's hopeless," she faltered. "We could never escape. The stars
are a myth. Take me back."

"And make myself out a fool? No," Fafhrd retorted harshly. "We're
rescuing you from Hasjarl and from Quarmall too. Make up your
mind to it, Friska, for I won't be budged. If you try to scream I'll stop
your mouth. *Where's a secret room?*" In his exasperation he almost
twisted her wrist, but remembered in time and only brought his face
close to hers and rasped, "*Think!*" She had a scent like heather underlying the odor of sweat and tears.

Her eyes went distant then and she said in a small voice, almost
dreamlike, "Between the Upper and the Lower Levels there is a great
hall with many small rooms adjoining. Once it was a busy and teem-
ing part of Quarmall, they say, but now debated ground between
Hasjarl and Gwaay. Both claim it, neither will maintain it, not even
sweep its dust. It is called the Ghost Hall." Her voice went smaller
still. "Gwaay's page once begged me meet him a little this side of
there, but I did not dare."

"Ha, that's the very place," Fafhrd said with a grin. "Lead us to it."

"But I don't remember the way," Friska protested. "Gwaay's page
told me, but I tried to forget . . ."

Fafhrd had spotted a spiral stair in the dark branchway. Now he
strode instantly toward it, drawing Friska along beside him.

"We know we have to start by going down," he said with rough
cheer. "Your memory will improve with motion, Friska."

The Gray Mouser and Ivivis had solaced themselves with such
kisses and caresses as seemed prudent in Gwaay's Hall of Sorcery, or
rather now of Sleeping Sorcerers. Then, at first coaxed chiefly by
Ivivis, it is true, they had visited a nearby kitchen, where the Mouser
had readily wheedled from the lumpish cook three large thin slices of

medium-rare unmistakable rib-beef, which he had devoured with great satisfaction.

At least one of his appetites mollified, the Mouser had consented that they continue their little ramble and even pause to view a mushroom field. Most strange it had been to see, betwixt the rough-finished pillars of rock, the rows of white button-fungi grow dim, narrow, and converge toward infinity in the ammonia-scented darkness.

At this point they had become teasing in their talk, he taxing Ivivis with having many lovers drawn by her pert beauty, she stoutly denying it, but finally admitting that there was a certain Klevis, page to Gwaay, for whom her heart had once or twice beat faster.

"And best, Gray Guest, you keep an eye open for him," she had warned, wagging a slim finger, "for certain he is the fiercest and most skillful of Gwaay's swordsmen."

Then to change this topic and to reward the Mouser for his patience in viewing the mushroom field, she had drawn him, they going hand in hand now, to a wine cellar. There she had prettily begged the aged and cranky butler for a great tankard of amber fluid for her companion. It had proved to the Mouser's delight to be purest and most potent essence of grape with no bitter admixture whatever.

Two of his appetites now satisfied, the third returned to the Mouser more hotly. Hand-holding became suddenly merely tantalizing and Ivivis' pale green tunic no more an object for admiration and for complements to her, but only a barrier to be got rid of as swiftly as possible and with the smallest necessary modicum of decorousness.

Himself taking the lead, he drew her as directly as he could recall the route, and with little speech, toward the closet he had preempted for his loot, two levels below Gwaay's Hall of Sorcery. At last he found the corridor he sought, one hung to either side with thick purple arras and lit by infrequent copper chandeliers which hung each from the rock ceiling on three copper chains and held three thick black candles.

This far Ivivis followed him with only the fewest flirtatious balkings and a minimum of wondering, innocent-eyed questions as to what he intended and why such haste was needful. But now her hesitations became convincing, her eyes began to show a genuine uneasiness, or even fearfulness, and when he stopped by the arras-slit before the door to his closet and with the courtliest of lecherous smirks he could manage indicated to her that they had reached their destination, she drew sharply back, stifling an exclamation with the flat of her hand.

"Gray Mouser," she whispered rapidly, her eyes at once frightened and beseeching, "there is a confession I should have made earlier and now must make at once. By one of those malign and mocking coincidences which haunt all Quarmall, you have chosen for your hidey-hole the very chamber where—"

Well it was for the Gray Mouser then that he took seriously Ivivis' look and tone, that he was by nature sense-aware and distrustful, and in particular that his ankles now took note of a slight yet unaccustomed draft from under the arras. For without other warning a fist pointed with a dark dagger punched through the arras-slit at his throat.

With the edge of his left hand, which had been raised to indicate to Ivivis their bedding-place, the Mouser struck aside the black-sleeved arm.

The girl exclaimed, not loudly, "Klevis!"

With his right hand the Mouser caught hold of the wrist going by him and twisted it. With his spread left hand he simultaneously rammed his attacker in the armpit.

But the Mouser's grip, made by hurried snatch, was imperfect. Moreover, Klevis was not minded to resist and have his arm dislocated or broken in that fashion. Spinning with the Mouser's twist, he also went into a deliberate forward somersault.

The net result was that Klevis lost his cross-gripped dagger, which clattered dully on the thick-carpeted floor, but tore loose unhurt from the Mouser and after two more somersaults came lightly to his feet, at once turning and drawing rapier.

By then the Mouser had drawn Scalpel and his dirk Cat's Claw too, but held the latter behind him. He attacked cautiously, with probing feints. When Klevis counterattacked strongly, he retreated, parrying each fierce thrust at the last moment, so that again and again the enemy blade went whickering close by him.

Klevis lunged with especial fierceness. The Mouser parried, high this time and not retreating. In an instant they were pressed body to body, their rapiers strongly engaged near their hilts and above their heads.

By turning a little, the Mouser blocked Klevis' knee driven at his groin. While with the dirk Klevis had overlooked, he stabbed the other from below, Cat's Claw entering just under Klevis' breastbone to pierce his liver, gizzard, and heart.

Letting go his dirk, the Mouser nudged the body away from him and turned.

Ivivis was facing them, with Klevis' punching-dagger gripped ready for a thrust.

The body thudded to the floor.

"Which of us did you propose to skewer?" the Mouser asked.

"I don't know," the girl answered in a flat voice. "You, I suppose."

The Mouser nodded. "Just before this interruption, you were saying, 'The very chamber where—' What?"

"—where I often met Klevis, to be with him," she replied.

Again the Mouser nodded. "So you loved him and—"

"Shut up, you fool!" she interrupted. *"Is he dead?"* There were both deep concern and exasperation in her voice.

The Mouser backed along the body until he stood at the head of it. Looking down, he said, "As mutton. He was a handsome youth."

For a long moment they eyed each other like leopards across the corpse. Then, averting her face a little, Ivivis said, "Hide the body, you imbecile. It tears my heartstrings to see it."

Nodding, the Mouser stooped and rolled the corpse under the arras opposite the closet door. He tucked in Klevis' rapier beside him. Then he withdrew Cat's Claw from the body. Only a little dark blood followed. He cleaned his dirk on the arras, then let the hanging drop.

Standing up, he snatched the punching-dagger from the brooding girl and flipped it so that it too vanished under the arras.

With one hand he spread wide the slit in the arras. With the other he took hold of Ivivis' shoulder and pressed her toward the doorway which Klevis had left open to his undoing.

She instantly shook loose from his grip, but walked through the doorway. The Mouser followed. The leopard look was still in both their eyes.

A single torch lit the closet. The Mouser shut the door and barred it.

Ivivis snarled at him, summing it up: "You owe me much, Gray Stranger."

The Mouser showed his teeth in an unhumorous grin. He did not stop to see whether his stolen trinkets had been disturbed. It did not even occur to him, then, to do so.

Fafhrd felt relief when Friska told him that the darker slit at the very end of the dark, long, straight corridor they'd just entered was the door to the Ghost Hall. It had been a hurrying, nervous trip, with many peerings around corners and dartings back into dark alcoves while someone passed, and a longer trip vertically downward than Fafhrd had anticipated. If they had now only reached the top of the

Lower Levels, this Quarmall must be bottomless! Yet Friska's spirits had improved considerably. Now at times she almost skipped along in her white chemise cut low behind. Fafhrd strode purposefully, her dress and slippers in his left hand, his ax in his right.

The Northerner's relief in no wise diminished his wariness, so that when someone rushed from an inky tunnel-mouth they were passing, he stroked out almost negligently and he felt and heard his ax crunch halfway through a head.

He saw a comely blond youth, now most sadly dead and his comeliness rather spoiled by Fafhrd's ax, which still stood in the great wound it had made. A fair hand opened and the sword it had held fell from it.

"Hovis!" he heard Friska cry. "O gods! O gods that are not here. Hovis!"

Lifting a booted foot, Fafhrd stamped it sideways at the youth's chest, at once freeing his ax and sending the corpse back into the tunneled dark from which the live man had so rashly hurtled.

After a swift look and listen all about, he turned toward Friska where she stood white-faced and staring.

"Who's this Hovis?" he demanded, shaking her lightly by the shoulder when she did not reply.

Twice her mouth opened and shut again, while her face remained as expressionless as that of a silly fish. Then with a little gasp she said, "I lied to you, barbarian. I have met Gwaay's page Hovis here. More than once."

"Then why didn't you warn me, wench?" Fafhrd demanded. "Did you think I would scold you for your morals, like some city graybeard? Or have you no regard at all for your men, Friska?"

"Oh, do not chide me," Friska begged miserably. "Please do not chide me."

Fafhrd patted her shoulder. "There, there," he said. "I forget you were shortly tortured and hardly of a mind to remember everything. Come on."

They had taken a dozen steps when Friska began to shudder and sob together in a swiftly mounting crescendo. She turned and ran back, crying, "Hovis! Hovis, forgive me!"

Fafhrd caught her before three steps. He shook her again and when that did not stop her sobbing, he used his other hand to slap her twice, rocking her head a little.

She stared at him dumbly.

He said not fiercely but somberly, "Friska, I must tell you that Hovis is where your words and tears can never again reach him. He's dead. Beyond recall. Also, I killed him. That's beyond recall too. But you are still alive. You can hide from Hasjarl. Ultimately, whether you believe it or not, you can escape with me from Quarmall. Now come on with me, and no looking back."

She blindly obeyed, with only the faintest of moanings.

The Gray Mouser stretched luxuriously on the silver-tipped bear-skin he'd thrown on the floor of his closet. Then he lifted on an elbow and, finding the black pearls he'd pilfered, tried them against Ivivis' bosom in the pale cool light of the single torch above. Just as he'd imagined, the pearls looked very well there. He started to fasten them around her neck.

"No, Mouser," she objected lazily. "It awakens an unpleasant memory."

He did not persist, but lying back again, said unguardedly, "Ah, but I'm a lucky man, Ivivis. I have you and I have an employer who, though somewhat boresome with his sorceries and his endless mild speaking, seems a harmless enough chap and certainly more endurable than his brother Hasjarl, if but half of what I hear of that one is true."

The voice of Ivivis briskened. "You think Gwaay harmless?—and kinder than Hasjarl? La, that's a quaint conceit. Why, but a week ago he summoned my late dearest friend, Divis, then his favorite concubine, and telling her it was a necklace of the same stones, hung around her neck an emerald adder, the sting of which is infallibly deadly."

The Mouser turned his head and stared at Ivivis. "Why did Gwaay do that?" he asked.

She stared back at him blankly. "Why, for nothing at all, to be sure," she said wonderingly. "As everyone knows, that is Gwaay's way."

The Mouser said, "You mean that, rather than say, 'I am wearied of you,' he killed her?"

Ivivis nodded. "I believe Gwaay can no more bear to hurt people's feelings by rejecting them than he can bear to shout."

"It is better to be slain than rejected?" the Mouser questioned ingenuously.

"No, but for Gwaay it is easier on his feelings to slay than to reject. Death is everywhere here in Quarmall."

The Mouser had a fleeting vision of Klevis' corpse stiffening behind the arras.

Ivivis continued, "Here in the Lower Levels we are buried before we are born. We live, love, and die buried. Even when we strip, we yet wear a garment of invisible mold."

The Mouser said, "I begin to understand why it is necessary to cultivate a certain callousness in Quarmall, to be able to enjoy at all any moments of pleasure snatched from life, or perhaps I mean from death."

"That is most true, Gray Mouser," Ivivis said very soberly, pressing herself against him.

Fafhrd started to brush aside the cobwebs joining the two dust-filmed sides of the half open, high, nail-studded door, then checked himself and bending very low ducked under them.

"Do you stoop too," he told Friska. "It were best we leave no signs of our entry. Later I'll attend to our footprints in the dust, if that be needful."

They advanced a few paces, then stood hand in hand, waiting for their eyes to grow accustomed to the darkness. Fafhrd still clutched in his other hand Friska's dress and slippers.

"This is the Ghost Hall?" Fafhrd asked.

"Aye," Friska whispered close to his ear, sounding fearful. "Some say that Gwaay and Hasjarl send their dead to battle here. Some say that demons owing allegiance to neither—"

"No more of that, girl," Fafhrd ordered gruffly. "If I must battle devils or liches, leave me my hearing and my courage."

They were silent a space then while the flame of the last torch twenty paces beyond the half shut door slowly revealed to them a vast chamber low-domed with huge, rough black blocks pale-mortared for a ceiling. It was set out with a few tatter-shrouded furnishings and showed many small closed doorways. To either side were wide rostra set a few feet above floor level, and toward the center there was, surprisingly, what looked like a dried-up fountain pool.

Friska whispered, "Some say the Ghost Hall was once the harem of the father lords of Quarmall during some centuries when they dwelt underground between Levels, ere this Quarmal's father coaxed by his sea-wife returned to the Keep. See, they left so suddenly that the new ceiling was neither finish-polished, nor final cemented, nor embellished with drawings, if such were purposed."

Fafhrd nodded. He distrusted that unpillared ceiling and thought the whole place looked rather more primitive than Hasjarl's polished and leather-hung chambers. That gave him a thought.

"Tell me, Friska," he said. "How is it that Hasjarl can see with his eyes closed? Is it that—"

"Why, do you not know that?" she interrupted in surprise. "Do you not know even the secret of his horrible peeping? He simply—"

A dim velvet shape that chittered almost inaudibly shrill swooped past their faces and with a little shriek Friska hid her face in Fafhrd's chest and clung to him tightly.

In combing his fingers through her heather-scented hair to show her no flying mouse had found lodgment there and in smoothing his palms over her bare shoulders and back to demonstrate that no bat had landed there either, Fafhrd began to forget all about Hasjarl and the puzzle of his second sight—and his worries about the ceiling falling in on them too.

Following custom, Friska shrieked twice, very softly.

Gwaay languidly clapped his white, perfectly groomed hands and with a slight nod motioned for the waiting slaves to remove the platters from the low table. He leaned lazily into the deep-cushioned chair and through half-closed lids looked momentarily at his companion before he spoke. His brother across the table was not in a good humor. But then it was rare for Hasjarl to be other than in a pet, a tempter, or more often merely sullen and vicious. This may have been due to the fact that Hasjarl was a very ugly man, and his nature had grown to conform to his body; or perhaps it was the other way around. Gwaay was indifferent to both theories; he merely knew that in one glance all his memory had told him of Hasjarl was verified; and he again realized the bitter magnitude of his hatred for his brother. However, Gwaay spoke gently in a low, pleasant voice:

"Well, how now, Brother, shall we play at chess, that demon game they say exists in every world? 'Twill give you a chance to lord it over me again. You always win at chess, you know, except when you resign. Shall I have the board set before us?" and then cajolingly, "I'll give you a pawn!" and he raised one hand slightly as if to clap again in order that his suggestion might be carried out.

With the lash he carried slung to his wrist Hasjarl slashed the face of the slave nearest him, and silently pointed at the massive and ornate chessboard across the room. This was quite characteristic of Hasjarl. He was a man of action and given to few words, at least away from his home territory.

Besides, Hasjarl was in a nasty humor. Flindach had torn him from his most interesting and exciting amusement: torture! And for what? thought Hasjarl: to play at chess with his prigish brother; to sit and look at his pretty brother's face; to eat food that would surely disagree with him; to wait the answer to the casting, which he already knew—

had known for years; and finally to be forced to smile into the horrible blood-white eyes of his father, unique in Quarmall save for those of Flindach, and toast the House of Quarmall for the ensuing year. All this was most distasteful to Hasjarl and he showed it plainly.

The slave, a bloody welt swift-swelling across his face, carefully slid the chessboard between the two. Gwaay smiled as another slave arranged the chessmen precisely on their squares; he had thought of a scheme to annoy his brother. He had chosen the black as usual and he planned a gambit which he knew his avaricious opponent couldn't refuse; one Hasjarl would accept to his own undoing.

Hasjarl sat grimly back in his chair, arms folded. "I should have made you take white," he complained. "I know the paltry tricks you can do with black pebbles—I've seen you as a girl-pale child darting them through the air to startle the slaves' brats. How am I to know you will not cheat by fingerless shifting your pieces while I deep ponder?"

Gwaay answered gently, "My paltry powers, as you most justly appraise them, Brother, extend only to bits of basalt, trifles of obsidian and other volcanic rocks conformable to my nether level. While these chess pieces are jet, Brother, which in your great scholarship you surely know is only a kind of coal, vegetable stuff pressed black, not even in the same realm as the very few materials subject to my small magickings. Moreover, for you to miss the slightest trick with those quaint slave-surgeried eyes of yours, Brother, were matter for mighty wonder."

Hasjarl growled. Not until all was ready did he stir; then, like an adder's strike, he plucked a black rook's pawn from the board and with a sputtering giggle, snarled: "Remember, Brother? It was a pawn you promised! Move!"

Gwaay motioned the waiting slave to advance his king's pawn. In like manner Hasjarl replied. A moment's pause and Gwaay offered his gambit: pawn to king-bishop's fourth! Eagerly Hasjarl snatched the apparent advantage and the game began in earnest. Gwaay, his face easy-smiling in repose, seeming to be less interested in the game than in the shadow play of the flickering lamps on the figured leather upholsterings of calfskin, lambskin, snakeskin, and even slaveskin and nobler human hide; seeming to move offhand, without plan, yet confidently. Hasjarl, his lips compressed in concentration, was intent on the board, each move a planned action both mental and physical. His concentration made him for the moment oblivious of his brother, oblivious of all but the problem before him; for Hasjarl loved to win beyond all computation.

It had always been this way; even as children the contrast was apparent. Hasjarl was the elder; older by only a few months which his appearance and demeanor lengthened to years. His long, misshapen torso was ill-borne on short bandy legs. His left arm was perceptibly longer than the right; and his fingers, peculiarly webbed to the first knuckle, were gnarled and stubby with brittle striated nails. It was as if Hasjarl were a poorly reconstructed puzzle put together in such fashion that all the pieces were mismated and awry.

This was particularly true of his features. He possessed his sire's nose, though thickened and coarse-pored; but this was contradicted by the thin-lipped, tightly compressed mouth continually pursed until it had assumed a perpetual sphincterlike appearance. Hair, lank and lusterless, grew low on his forehead; and low, flattened cheekbones added yet another contradiction.

As a lad, led by some perverse whim, Hasjarl had bribed, coaxed, or more probably browbeaten one of the slaves versed in surgery to perform a slight operation on his upper eyelids. It was a small enough thing in itself, yet its implications and results had affected the lives of many men unpleasantly, and never ceased to delight Hasjarl.

That merely the piercing of two small holes, centered over the pupil when the eyes were closed, could produce such qualms in other people were incredible; but it was so. Featherweight grommets of sleekest gold, jade or—as now—ivory—kept the holes from growing shut.

When Hasjarl peered through these tiny apertures it gave the effect of an ambush and made the object of his gaze feel spied upon; but this was the least annoying of his many irritating habits.

Hasjarl did nothing easily but he did all things well. Even in swordplay his constant practice and overly long left arm made him the equal of the athletic Gwaay. His administration of the Upper Levels over which he ruled was above all things economical and smooth; for woe betide the slave who failed in the slightest detail of his duties. Hasjarl saw and punished.

Hasjarl was well nigh the equal of his teacher in the practice of the Art; and he had gathered about him a band of magicians almost the caliber of Flindach himself. But he was not happy in his prowess so hardly won, for between the absolute power which he desired and the realization of that desire stood two obstacles: the Lord of Quarmall whom he feared above all things; and his brother Gwaay whom he hated with a hatred nourished on envy and fed by his own thwarted desires.

Gwaay, antithetically, was supple of limb, well-formed and good to look upon. His eyes, wide-set and pale, were deceptively gentle and kindly; for they masked a will as strong and capable of action as coiled spring-steel. His continual residence in the Lower Levels over which he ruled gave to his pallid smooth skin a peculiar waxy luster.

Gwaay possessed that enviable ability to do all things well, with little exertion and less practice. In a way he was much worse than his brother: for while Hasjarl slew with tortures and slow pain and an obvious personal satisfaction, he at least attached some importance to life because he was so meticulous in its taking; whereas Gwaay smiling gently would slay, without reason, as if jesting. Even the group of sorcerers which he had gathered about him for protection and amusement was not safe from his fatal and swift humors.

Some thought that Gwaay was a stranger to fear, but this was not so. He feared the Lord of Quarmall and he feared his brother; or rather he feared that he would be slain by his brother before he could slay him. Yet so well were his fear and hatred concealed that he could sit relaxed, not two yards from Hasjarl, and smile amusedly, enjoying every moment of the evening. Gwaay flattered himself on his perfect control over all emotion.

The chess game had developed beyond the opening stage, the moves coming slower, and now Hasjarl rapped down a rook on the seventh rank.

Gwaay observed gently, "Your turreted warrior rushes deep into my territory, Brother. Rumor has it you've hired a brawny champion out of the north. With what purpose, I wonder, in our peace-wrapped cavern world? Could he be a sort of living rook?" He poised, hand unmoving over one of his knights.

Hasjarl giggled. "And if his purpose is to slash pretty throats, what's that to you? I know naught of this rook-warrior, but 'tis said—slaves' chat, no doubt—that you yourself have had fetched a skilled sworder from Lankhmar. Should I call him a knight?"

"Aye, two can play at a game," Gwaay remarked with prosy philosophy and lifting his knight, softly but firmly planted it at his king's sixth.

"I'll not be drawn," Hasjarl snarled. "You shall not win by making my mind wander." And arching his head over the board, he cloaked himself again with his all-consuming calculations.

In the background slaves moved silently, tending the lamps and replenishing the founts with oil. Many lamps were needed to light the council room, for it was low-ceiled and massively beamed, and the arras-hung walls reflected little of the yellow rays and the mosaic floor was worn to a dull richness by countless footsteps in the past.

From the living rock this room had been carved; long forgotten hands had set the huge cypress beams and inlaid the floor so cunningly. Those gay, time-faded tapestries had been hung by the slaves of some ancient Lord of Quarmall, who had pilfered them from a passing caravan, and so with all the rich adornments. The chessmen and the chairs, the chased lamp sconces and the oil which fed the wicks, and the slaves which tended them: all was loot. Loot from generations back when the Lords of Quarmall plundered far and wide and took their toll from every passing caravan.

High above that warm, luxuriously furnished chamber where Gwaay and Hasjarl played at chess, the Lord of Quarmall finished the final calculations which would complete his horoscope. Heavy leather hangings shut out the stars that had but now twinkled down their benisons and dooms. The only light in that instrument-filled room was the tiny flare of a single taper. By such scant illumination did custom bid the final casting be read, and Quarmal strained even his keen vision to see the Signs and Houses rightly.

As he rechecked the final results his supple lips writhed in a sneer, a grimace of displeasure. *Tonight or tomorrow,* he thought with an inward chill. *At most, late on the morrow.* Truly, he had little time.

Then, as if pleased by some subtle jest, he smiled and nodded, making his skinny shadow perform monstrous gyrations on the curtains and brasured wall.

Finally Quarmal laid aside his crayon, and taking the single candle lighted by its flame seven larger tapers. With the aid of this better light he read once more the horoscope. This time he made no sign of pleasure or any other emotion. Slowly he rolled the intricately diagramed and inscribed parchment into a slender tube, which he thrust in his belt; then rubbing together his lean hands he smiled again. At a nearby table were the ingredients which he needed for his scheme's success: powders, oils, tiny knives, and other materials and instruments.

The time was short. Swiftly he worked, his spatulate fingers performing miracles of dexterity. Once he went on an errand to the wall. The Lord of Quarmall made no mistakes, nor could he afford them.

It was not long before the task was completed to his satisfaction. After extinguishing the last-lit candles, Quarmal, Lord of Quarmall, relaxed into his chair and by the dim light of a single taper summoned Flindach, in order that his horoscope might be announced to those below.

As was his wont, Flindach appeared almost at once. He presented himself confronting his master with arms folded across his chest, and head bowed submissively. Flindach never presumed. His figure was illuminated only to the waist, above that shadow concealed whatever expression of interest or boredom his warted and wine-marked face might show. In like manner the pitted yet sleeker countenance of Quarmal was obscured, only his pale irises gleamed phosphorescent from the shadows like two minute moons in a dark bloody sky.

As if he were measuring Flindach, or as if he saw him for the first time, Quarmal slowly raised his glance from foot to forehead of the figure before him, and looking direct into the shaded eyes of Flindach so like his own, he spoke. "O Master of Magicians, it is within your power to grant me a boon this night."

He raised a hand as Flindach would have spoken and swiftly continued: "I have watched you grow from boy to youth and from youth to man; I have nurtured your knowledge of the Art until it is only second to my own. The same mother carried us, though I her first-born and you the child of her last fertile year—that kinship helped. Your influence within Quarmall is almost equal to mine. So I feel that some reward is due your diligence and faithfulness."

Again Flindach would have spoken, but was dissuaded by a gesture. Quarmal spoke more slowly now, and accompanied his words with staccato taps on the parchment roll. "We both well know, from hearsay and direct knowledge, that my sons plot my death. And it is also true that in some manner they must be thwarted, for neither of the twain is fit to become the Lord of Quarmall; nor does it seem probable that either will ever reach wisdom. Under their warring, Quarmall would die of inanition and neglect, as has died the Ghost Hall. Furthermore, each of them, to buttress his sorceries, has secretly hired a sworded champion from afar—you've seen Gwaay's—and this is the beginning of the bringing of free mercenaries into Quarmall and the sure doom of our power." He stretched a hand toward the dark close-crowded rows of mummied and waxen masks and he asked rhetorically, "Did the Lords of Quarmall guard and preserve our hidden realm that its councils might be entered, crowded, and at last be captured by foreign captains?

"Now a far more secret matter," he continued, his voice sinking. "The concubine Kewissa carries my seed: male-growing, by all omens and oracles—though this is known only to Kewissa and myself, and now to you, Flindach. Should this unborn sprout reach but boyhood brotherless, I might die content, leaving to you his tutelage in all confidence and trust."

Quarmal paused and sat impassive as an effigy. "Yet to forestall

Hasjarl and Gwaay becomes more difficult each day, for they increase in power and in scope. Their own innate wickedness gives them access to regions and demons heretofore but imagined by their predecessors. Even I, well versed in necromancy, am often appalled." He paused and quizzically looked at Flindach.

For the first time since he had entered Flindach spoke. His voice was that of one trained in the recitation of incantations, deep and resonant. "Master, what you speak is true. Yet how will you encompass their plots? You know, as well as I, the custom that forbids what is perhaps the only means of thwarting them."

Flindach paused as if he would say more, but Quarmal quickly intervened. "I have concocted a scheme, which may or may not succeed. The success of it depends almost entirely upon your cooperation." He lowered his voice almost to a whisper, beckoning for Flindach to step closer. "The very stones may carry tales, O Flindach, and I would that this plan were kept entirely secret." Quarmal beckoned again, and Flindach stepped still nearer until he was within arm's reach of his master. Half stooping, he placed himself in such a position that his ear was close to Quarmal's mouth. This was closer than ever he remembered approaching Quarmal, and strange qualms filled his mind, recrudescences of childish old wives' tales. This ancient ageless man with eyes pearl-irised as his own seemed to Flindach not like half brother at all, but like some strange, merciless half father. His burgeoning terror was intensified when he felt the sinewy fingers of Quarmal close on his wrist and gently urge him closer, almost to his knees, beside the chair.

Quarmal's lips moved swiftly, and Flindach controlled his urge to rise and flee as the plan was unfolded to him. With a sibilant phrase, the final phrase, Quarmal finished and Flindach realized the full enormity of that plan. Even as he comprehended it, the single taper guttered and was extinguished. There was darkness absolute.

The chess game progressed swiftly; the only sounds, except the ceaseless shuffle of naked feet and the hiss of lamp wicks, were the dull click of the chessmen and the staccato cough of Hasjarl. The low table off which the twain had eaten was placed opposite the broad arched door which was the only apparent entrance to the council chamber.

There was another entrance. It led to the Keep of Quarmall; and it was toward this arras-concealed door that Gwaay glanced most often. He was positive that the news of the casting would be as usual, but a certain curiosity whelmed him this evening; he felt a faint foreshadowing of some untoward event, even as wind blows gusty before a storm.

An omen had been vouchsafed Gwaay by the gods today; an omen that neither his necromancers nor his own skill could interpret to his complete satisfaction. So he felt that it would be wise to await the development of events prepared and expectant.

Even as he watched the tapestry behind which he knew was the door whence would step Flindach to announce the consequences of the casting, that hanging bellied and trembled as if some breeze blew on it, or some hand pushed against it lightly.

Hasjarl abruptly threw himself back in his chair and cried in his high-pitched voice, "Check with my rook to your king, and mate in three!" He drooped one eyelid evilly and peered triumphantly at Gwaay.

Gwaay, without removing his eyes from the still swaying tapestry, said in precise, mellow words, "The knight interposes, Brother, discovering check. I mate in two. You are wrong again, my comrade."

But even as Hasjarl swept the men with a crash to the floor, the arras was more violently disturbed. It was parted by two slaves and the harsh gong-note, announcing the entrance of some high official, sounded.

Silently from betwixt the hangings stepped the tall lean form of Flindach. His shadowed face, despite the disfiguring wine mark and the treble mole, had a great and solemn dignity. And in its somber expressionlessness—an expressionlessness curiously mocked by a knowing glitter deep in the black pupils of the pearl-irised crimson-balled eyes—it seemed to forebode some evil tiding.

All motion ceased in that long hall as Flindach, standing in the archway framed in rich tapestries, raised one arm in a gesticulation demanding silence. The attendant well-trained slaves stood at their posts, heads bowed submissively; Gwaay remained as he was, looking directly at Flindach; and Hasjarl, who had half-turned at the gong note, likewise awaited the announcement. In a moment, they knew, Quarmal their father would step from behind Flindach and smiling evilly would announce his horoscope. Always this had been the procedure; and always, since each could remember, Gwaay and Hasjarl had at this moment wished for Quarmal's death.

Flindach, arm lifted in dramatic gesture, began to speak.

"The casting of the horoscope has been completed and the finding has been made. Even as the Heavens foretell is the fate of man fulfilled. I bring this news to Hasjarl and Gwaay, the sons of Quarmal."

With a swift motion Flindach plucked a slender parchment tube from his belt and, breaking it with hands, dropped it crumpled at his feet. In almost the same gesture he reached behind his left shoulder and stepping from the shadow of the arch drew a peaked cowl over his head.

Throwing wide both arms, Flindach spoke, his voice seeming to come from afar:

"Quarmal, Lord of Quarmall, rules no more. The casting is fulfilled. Let all within the walls of Quarmall mourn. For three days the place of the Lord of Quarmall will be vacant. So custom demands and so shall it be. On the morrow, when the sun enters his courtyard, that which remains of what was once a great and puissant lord will be given to the flames. Now I go to mourn my Master and oversee the obsequies and prepare myself with fasting and with prayer for his passing. Do you likewise."

Flindach slowly turned and disappeared into the darkness from which he had come.

For the space of ten full heartbeats Gwaay and Hasjarl sat motionless. The announcement came as a thunderclap to both. Gwaay for a second felt an impulse to giggle and smirk like a child who has unexpectedly escaped punishment and is instead rewarded; but in the back of his mind he was half-convinced that he had known all along the outcome of the casting. However, he controlled his childish glee and sat silent, staring.

On the other hand Hasjarl reacted as might be expected of him. He went through a series of outlandish grimaces and ended with an obscene half-smothered titter. Then he frowned, and turning said to Gwaay, "Heard you not what said Flindach? I must go and prepare myself!" and he lurched to his feet and paced silently across the room, out the broad-arched door.

Gwaay remained sitting for another few moments, frowning eyes narrowed in concentration, as if he were puzzling over some abstruse problems which required all his powers to solve. Suddenly he snapped his fingers and, motioning for his slaves to preceed him, made ready for his return to the Lower Levels, whence he had come.

Fafhrd had barely left the Ghost Hall when he heard the faint rattle and clink of armed men moving cautiously. His bemusement with Friska's charms vanished as if he had been soused with ice water. He shrank into the deeper darkness and eavesdropped long enough to learn that these were pickets of Hasjarl, guarding against an invasion from Gwaay's Lower Levels—and not tracking down Friska and himself as he'd first feared. Then he made off swiftly for Hasjarl's Hall of

Sorcery, grimly pleased that his memory for landmarks and turnings seemed to work as well for mazy tunnels as for forest trails and steep zigzag mountain escalades.

The bizarre sight that greeted him when he reached his goal stopped him on the stony threshold. Standing shin-deep and stark naked in a steaming marble tub shaped like a ridgy seashell, Hasjarl was berating and haranguing the great roomful around him. And every man jack of them—sorcerers, officers, overseers, pages bearing great fringy towels and dark red robes and other apparel—was standing quakingly still with cringing eyes, except for the three slaves soaping and laving their Lord with tremulous dexterity.

Fafhrd had to admit that Hasjarl naked was somehow more consistent—ugly everywhere—a kobold birthed from a hot-spring. And although his grotesque child-pink torso and mismated arms were a-writhe and a-twitch in a frenzy of apprehension, he had dignity of a sort.

He was snarling, "Speak, all of you, is there a precaution I have forgotten, a rite omitted, a rat-hole overlooked that Gwaay might creep through? Oh, that on this night when demons lurk and I must mind a thousand things and dress me for my father's obsequies, I should be served by wittols! Are you all deaf and dumb? Where's my great champion, who should ward me now? Where are my scarlet grommets? Less soap there, you—take that! You, Essem, are we guarded well above?—I don't trust Flindach. And Yissim, have we guards enough below?—Gwaay is a snake who'll strike through any gap. Dark Gods, defend me! Go to the barracks, Yissim, get more men, and reinforce our downward guards—and while you're there, I mind me now, bid them continue Friska's torture. Wring the truth from her! She's in Gwaay's plots—this night has made me certain. Gwaay knew my father's death was imminent and laid invasion plans long weeks agone. Any of you may be his purchased spies! Oh where's my champion? *Where are my scarlet grommets?*"

Fafhrd, who'd been striding forward, quickened his pace at mention of Friska. A simple inquiry at the torture chamber would reveal her escape and his part in it. He must create diversions. So he halted close in front of pink wet steaming Hasjarl and said boldly, "Here is your champion, Lord. And he counsels not sluggy defense, but some swift stroke at Gwaay! Surely your mighty mind has fashioned many a shrewd attacking stratagem. Launch you a thunderbolt!"

It was all Fafhrd could do to keep speaking forcefully to the end and not let his voice trail off as his attention became engrossed in the strange operation now going on. While Hasjarl crouched stock-still with head a-twist, an ashen-faced bath-slave had drawn out Hasjarl's left upper eyelid by its lashes and was inserting into the hole in it a tiny flanged scarlet ring or grommet no bigger than a lentil. The grommet was carried on the tip of an ivory wand as thin as a straw and the whole deed was being done by the slave with the anxiety of a man refilling the poison pouches of an untethered rattlesnake—if such an action might be imagined for purposes of comparison.

However, the operation was quickly completed, and then on the right eye too—and evidently with perfect satisfaction, since Hasjarl did not slash the slave with the soapy wet lash still dangling from his wrist—and when Hasjarl straightened up he was grinning broadly at Fafhrd.

"You counsel me well, champion," he cried. "These other fools could do nothing but shake. There *is* a stroke long-planned that I'll try now, one that won't violate the obsequies. Essem, take slaves and fetch the dust—you know the stuff I mean—and meet me at the vents! Girls, sluice these suds off with tepid water. Boy, give me my slippers and my toweling robe!—those other clothes can wait. Follow me, Fafhrd!"

But just then his red-grommeted gaze lit on his four-and-twenty bearded and hooded sorcerers standing apprehensive by their chairs.

"Back to your charms at once, you ignoramuses!" he roared at them. "I did not tell you to stop because I bathed! Back to your charms and send your plagues at Gwaay—red, black and green, nose drip and bloody rot—or I will burn your beards off to the eyelashes as prelude to more dire torturings! Haste, Essem! Come, Fafhrd!"

The Gray Mouser at that same moment was returning from his closet with Ivivis when Gwaay, velvet-shod and followed by barefoot slaves, came around a turn in the dim corridor so swiftly there was no evading him.

The young Lord of the Lower Levels seemed preternaturally calm and controlled, yet with the impression that under the calm was naught but quivering excitement and darting thought—so much so that it would hardly have surprised the Mouser if there had shone forth from Gwaay an aura of Blue Essence of Thunderbolt. Indeed, the Mouser felt his skin begin to prickle and sting as if just such an influence were invisibly streaming from his employer.

Gwaay scanned the Mouser and the pretty slavegirl in a flicker and spoke, his voice dancing rapid and gaysome.

"Well, Mouser, I can see you've sampled your reward ahead of time. Ah, youth and dim retreats and pillowed dreams and amorous hostessings—what else gilds life or makes it worth the guttering sooty candle? Was the girl skillful? Good! Ivivis, dear, I must reward your zeal. I gave Divis a necklace—would you one? Or I've a brooch shaped like a scorpion, ruby-eyed—"

The Mouser felt the girl's hand quiver and chill in his and he cut in quickly with, "My demon speaks to me, Lord Gwaay, and tells me it's a night when the Fates walk."

Gwaay laughed. "Your demon has been listening behind the arras. He's heard tales of my father's swift departure." As he spoke a drop formed at the end of his nose, between his nostrils. Fascinated, the Mouser watched it grow. Gwaay started to lift the back of his hand to it, then shook it off instead. For an instant he frowned, then laughed again.

"Aye, the Fates trod on Quarmall Keep tonight," Gwaay said, only now his gay rapid voice was a shade hoarse.

"My demon whispers me further that there are dangerous powers abroad this night," the Mouser continued.

"Aye, brother love and such," Gwaay quipped in reply, but now his voice was a croak. A look of great startlement widened his eyes. He shivered as with a chill and drops pattered from his nose. Three hairs came loose from his scalp and fell across his eyes. His slaves shrank back from him.

"My demon warns me we'd best use my Great Spell quickly against those powers," the Mouser went on, his mind returning as always to Sheelba's untested rune. "It destroys only sorcerers of the Second Rank and lower. Yours, being of the First Rank, will be untouched. But Hasjarl's will perish."

Gwaay opened his mouth to reply, but no words came forth, only a moaning nightmarish groan like that of a mute. Hectic spots shone forth high on his cheeks, and now it seemed to the Mouser that a reddish blotch was crawling up the right side of his chin, while on the left black spots were forming. A hideous stench became apparent. Gwaay staggered and his eyes brimmed with a greenish ichor. He lifted his hand to them and its back was yellowish crusted and red-cracked. His slaves ran.

"Hasjarl's sendings!" the Mouser hissed. "Gwaay's sorcerers still sleep! I'll rouse 'em! Support him, Ivivis!" And turning he sped like the wind down corridor and up ramp until he reached Gwaay's Hall of Sorcery. He entered it, clapping and whistling harshly between his teeth, for true enough the twelve scrawny loinclothed magi were still curled snoring on their wide high-backed chairs. The Mouser darted to each in turn, righting and shaking him with no gentle hands and shouting in his ear, "To your work! Anti-venom! Guard Gwaay!"

Eleven of the sorcerers roused quickly enough and were soon staring wide-eyed at nothingness, though with their bodies rocking and their heads bobbing for a while from the Mouser's shaking—like eleven small ships just overpassed by a squall.

He was having a little more trouble with the twelfth, though this one was coming awake, soon would be doing his share, when Gwaay appeared of a sudden in the archway with Ivivis at his side, though not supporting him. The young Lord's face gleamed as silvery clear in the dimness as the massy silver mask of him that hung in the niche above the arch.

"Stand aside, Gray Mouser, I'll jog the sluggard," he cried in a rippingly bright voice and snatching up a small obsidian jar tossed it toward the drowsy sorcerer.

It should have fallen no more than halfway between them. Did he mean to wake the ancient by its shattering? the Mouser wondered. But then Gwaay stared at it in the air and it quickened its speed fearfully. It was as if he had tossed up a ball, then batted it. Shooting forward like a bolt fired point-blank from a sinewy catapult it shattered the ancient's skull and spattered the chair and the Mouser with his brains.

Gwaay laughed, a shade high-pitched, and cried lightly, "I must curb my excitement! I must! I must! Sudden recovery from two dozen deaths—or twenty-three and the Nose Drip—is no reason for a philosopher to lose control. Oh, I'm a giddy fellow!"

Ivivis cried suddenly, "The room swims! I see silver fish!"

The Mouser felt dizzy himself then and saw a phosphorescent green hand reach through the archway toward Gwaay—reach out on a thin arm that lengthened to yards. He blinked hard and the hand was gone—but now there were swimmings of purple vapor.

He looked at Gwaay and that one, frowny-eyed now, was sniffling hard and then sniffling again, though no new drop could be seen to have formed on his nose-end.

Fafhrd stood three paces behind Hasjarl, who looked in his bunched and high-collared robe of earth-brown toweling rather like an ape.

Beyond Hasjarl on the right there trotted on a thick wide roller-riding leather belt three slaves of monstrous aspect: great splayed feet, legs like an elephant's, huge furnace-bellows chests, dwarfy arms, pinheads with wide toothy mouths and with nostrils bigger than their eyes or ears—creatures bred to run ponderously and nothing else. The moving belt disappeared with a half twist into a vertical cylinder of masonry five yards across and reemerged just below itself, but moving in the opposite direction, to pass under the rollers and complete its loop. From within the cylinder came the groaning of the great wooden fan which the belt whirled and which drove life-sustaining air downward to the Lower Levels.

Beyond Hasjarl on the left was a small door as high as Fafhrd's head in the cylinder. To it there mounted one by one, up four narrow masonry steps, a line of dusky, great-headed dwarves. Each bore on his shoulder a dark bag which when he reached the window he untied and emptied into the clamorous shaft, shaking it out most thoroughly while he held it inside, then folding it and leaping down to give place to the next bag-bearer.

Hasjarl leered over his shoulder at Fafhrd. "A nosegay for Gwaay!" he cried. " 'Tis a king's ransom I strew on the downward gale: powder of poppy, dust of lotus and mandragora, crumble of hemp. A million lewdly pleasant dreams, and all for Gwaay! Three ways this conquers him: he'll sleep a day and miss my father's funeral, then Quarmall's mine by right of sole appearance yet with no bloodshed, which would mar the rites; his sorcerers will sleep and my infectious spells burst through and strike him down in stinking jellied death; his realm will sleep, each slave and cursed page, so we'll conquer all merely by marching down after the business of the funeral. Ho, swifter there!" And seizing a long whip from an overseer, he began to crack it over the squat cones of the tread-slaves' heads and sting their broad backs with it. Their trot changed to a ponderous gallop, the moan of the fan rose in pitch, and Fafhrd waited to hear it shatter cracklingly, or see the belt snap, or the rollers break on their axles.

The dwarf at the shaft-window took advantage of Hasjarl's attention being elsewhere to snatch a pinch of powder from his bag and bring it to his nostrils and sniff it down, leering ecstatically. But Hasjarl saw and whipped him about the legs most cruelly. The dwarf dutifully emptied his bag and shook it out while making little hops of agony. However he did not seem much chastened or troubled by his whipping, for as he left the chamber Fafhrd saw him pull his empty bag over his head and waddle off breathing deeply through it.

Hasjarl went on whip-cracking and calling, "Swifter, I say! For Gwaay a drugged hurricane!"

The officer Yissim raced into the room and darted to his master.

"The girl Friska's escaped!" he cried. "Your torturers say your champion came with your seal, telling them you had ordered her release—and snatched her off! All this occurred a quarter day ago."

"Guards!" Hasjarl squealed. "Seize the Northerner! Disarm and bind the traitor!"

But Fafhrd was gone.

The Mouser, in company with Ivivis, Gwaay and a colorful rabble of drug-induced hallucinations, reeled into a chamber similar to the one from which Fafhrd had just disappeared. Here the great cylindrical shaft ended in a half turn. The fan that sucked down the air and blew it out to refresh the Lower Levels was set vertically in the mouth of the shaft and was visible as it whirled.

By the shaft-mouth hung a large cage of white birds, all lying on its floor with their feet in the air. Besides these telltales, there was stretched on the floor of the chamber its overseer, also overcome by the drugs whirlwinding from Hasjarl.

By contrast, the three pillar-legged slaves ponderously trotting their belt seemed not affected at all. Presumably their tiny brains and monstrous bodies were beyond the reach of any drug, short of its lethal dose.

Gwaay staggered up to them, slapped each in turn, and commanded, "Stop!" Then he himself dropped to the floor.

The groaning of the fan died away, its seven wooden vanes became clearly visible as it stopped (though for the Mouser they were interwoven with scaly hallucinations), and the only real sound was the slow gasping of the tread-slaves.

Gwaay smiled weirdly at them from where he sprawled and he raised an arm drunkenly and cried, "Reverse! About face!" Slowly the tread-slaves turned, taking a dozen tiny steps to do it, until they all three faced the opposite direction on the belt.

"Trot!" Gwaay commanded them quickly. Slowly they obeyed and slowly the fan took up again its groaning, but now it was blowing air up the shaft against Hasjarl's downward fanning.

Gwaay and Ivivis rested on the floor for a space, until their brains began to clear and the last hallucinations were chased from view. To the Mouser they seemed to be sucked up the shaft through the fan blades: a filmy horde of blue and purple wraiths armed with transparent saw-toothed spears and cutlasses.

Then Gwaay, smiling in highest excitement with his eyes, said softly and still a bit breathlessly, "My sorcerers . . . were not overcome . . . I think. Else I'd be dying . . . Hasjarl's two dozen deaths. Another moment . . . and I'll send across the level . . . to reverse the exhaust fan. We'll get fresh air through it. And put more slaves on this belt here—perchance I'll blow my brother's nightmares back to him. Then lave and robe me for my father's fiery funeral and mount to give Hasjarl a nasty shock. Ivivis, as soon as you can walk, rouse my bath girls. Bid them make all ready."

He reached across the floor and grasped the Mouser strongly at the elbow. "You, Gray One," he whispered, "prepare to work this mighty rune of yours which will smite down Hasjarl's warlocks. Gather your simples, pray your demonic prayers—consulting first with my twelve arch-magi . . . if you can rouse the twelfth from his dark hell. As soon as Quarmal's lich is in the flames, I'll send you word to speak your deadly spell." He paused and his eyes gleamed with a witchy glare in the dimness. "The time has come for sorcery and swords!"

There was a tiny scrabbling as one of the white birds staggered to its feet on the cage-bottom. It gave a chirrup that was rather like a hiccup, yet still had a note of challenge in it.

All that night through, all Quarmall was awake. Into the Ordering Room of the Keep, a magician came crying, "Lord Flindach! The mind-casters have incontrovertible advertisements that the two brothers war against each other. Hasjarl sends sleepy resins down the shafts, while Gwaay blows them back."

The warty and purple-blotched face of the Master of Magicians looked up from where he sat busy at a table surrounded by a small host awaiting orders.

"Have they shed blood?" he asked.

"Not yet."

"It is well. Keep enchanted eyes on them."

Then, gazing sternly in turn from under his hood at those whom he addressed, the Master of Magicians gave his other orders:

To two magicians robed as his deputies: "Go on the instant to Hasjarl and Gwaay. Remind them of the obsequies and stay with them until they and their companies reach the funeral courtyard."

To a eunuch: "Hasten to your master Brilla. Learn if he requires further materials or assistance building the funeral pyre. Help will be furnished him at once and without stint."

To a captain of slingers: "Double the guard on the walls. Yourself make the rounds. Quarmall must be entirely secure from outward assaults and escapes from within on this coming morn."

To a richly-clad woman of middle years: "To Quarmal's harem. See that his concubines are perfectly groomed and clad, as if their Lord

himself meant to visit them at dawn. Quiet their apprehensions. Send
to me the Ilthmarix Kewissa."

In Hasjarl's Hall of Sorcery, that Lord let his slaves robe him for
the obsequies, while not neglecting to direct the search for his traitorous champion Fafhrd, to instruct the shaft-watchers in the precautions they must take against Gwaay's attempts to return the poppy
dust, perchance with interest, and to tutor his sorcerers in the exact
spells they must use against Gwaay once Quarmal's body was devoured by the flames.

In the Ghost Hall, Fafhrd munched and drank with Friska a small
feast he'd brought. He told her how he'd fallen into disfavor with
Hasjarl, and he mulled plans for his escape with her from the realm
of Quarmall.

In Gwaay's Hall of Sorcery, the Gray Mouser conferred in turn
with the eleven skinny wizards in their white loincloths, telling them
nothing of Sheelba's spell, but securing from each the firm assurance
that he was a magus of the First Rank.

In the steam room of Gwaay's bath, that Lord recuperated his flesh
and faculties shaken by disease spells and drugs. His girls, supervised
by Ivivis, brought him fragrant oils and elixirs, and scrubbed and
laved him as he directed languidly yet precisely. The slender forms,
blurred and silvered by the clouds of steam, moved and posed as in a
languorous ballet.

The huge pyre was finally completed, and Brilla heaved a sigh of
relief and contentment with the knowledge of work well done. He
relaxed his fat, massive frame onto a bench against the wall and spoke
to one of his companions in a high-pitched feminine voice:

"Such short notice, and at such a time, but the gods are not to be
denied and no man can cheat his stars. It is shameful, though, to think
that Quarmal will go so poorly attended: only a half dozen
Lankhmarts, an Ilthmarix, and three Mingols—and one of those
blemished. I always told him he should keep a better harem. However
the male slaves are in fine fettle and will perhaps make up for the rest.
Ah! but it's a fine flame the Lord will have to light his way!" Brilla
wagged his head dolefully and, snuffling, blinked a tear from his
piggy eye; he was one of the few who really regretted the passing of
Quarmal.

As High Eunuch to the Lord, Brilla's position was a sinecure and,
besides, he had always been fond of Quarmal since he could remember. Once when a small chubby boy Brilla had been rescued from the

torments of a group of larger, more virile slaves who had freed him at the mere passing-by of Quarmal. It was this small incident, unwotted or long forgotten by Quarmal, which had provoked a life-long devotion in Brilla.

Now only the gods knew what the future held. Today the body of Quarmal would be burned and what would happen after that was better left unpondered, even in the innermost thoughts of a man. Brilla looked once more at his handiwork, the funeral pyre. Achieving it in six short hours, even with hosts of slaves at his command had taxed his powers. It towered in the center of the courtyard, even higher than the arch of the great gate thrice the stature of a tall man. It was built in the form of a square pyramid, truncated midway; and the inflammable woods that composed it were completely hidden by somber-hued drapes.

A runway was built from the ground across the vast courtyard to the topmost tier on each of the four sides; and at the top was a sizable square platform. It was here that the litter containing the body of Quarmal would be placed, and here the sacrificial victims be immolated. Only those slaves of proper age and talents were permitted to accompany their Lord on his long journey beyond the stars.

Brilla approved of what he saw and, rubbing his hands, looked about curiously. It was only on such occasions as this that one realized the immensity of Quarmall, and these occasions were rare; perhaps once in his life a man would see such an event. As far as Brilla could see small bands of slaves were lined, rank on rank, against the walls of the courtyard, even as was his own band of eunuchs and carpenters. There were the craftsmen from the Upper Levels, skilled workmen all in metal and in wood; there were the workers from the fields and vineyards all brown and gnarled from their labors; there were the slaves from the Lower Levels, blinking in the unaccustomed daylight, pallid and curiously deformed; and all the rest who served in the bowels of Quarmall, a representative group from each level.

The size of the turnout seemed to contradict the dawn's frightening rumors of secret war last night between the Levels, and Brilla felt reassured.

Most important and best placed were the two bands of henchmen of Hasjarl and Gwaay, one group on each side of the pyre. Only the sorcerers of the twain were absent, Brilla noted with a pang of unease, though refusing to speculate why.

High above all this mass of mixed humanity, atop the towering walls, were the ever silent, ever alert guards; standing quietly at their posts, slings dangling ready to hand. Never yet had the walls of

Quarmall been stormed and never had a slave once within those close-watched walls passed into the outer world alive.

Brilla was admirably placed to observe all that occurred. To his right, projecting from the wall of the courtyard, was the balcony from which Hasjarl and Gwaay would watch the consuming of their father's body; to his left, likewise projecting, was the platform from which Flindach would direct the rituals. Brilla sat almost next to the door whence the prepared and purified body of Quarmal would be borne for its final fiery cleansing. He wiped the sweat from his flabby jowls with the hem of his tunic and wondered how much longer it would be before things started. The sun could not be far from the top of the wall now, and with its first beams the rites began.

Even as he wondered there came the tremendous, muffled vibration of the huge gong. There was a craning of necks and a rustling as many bodies shifted; then silence. On the left balcony the figure of Flindach appeared.

Flindach was cowled with the Cowl of Death and his garments were of heavy woven brocades, somber and dull. At his waist glittered the circular fan-bladed Golden Symbol of Power, which while the Chair of Quarmall was vacant, Flindach as High Steward must keep inviolate.

He lifted his arms toward the place where the sun would in a moment appear and intoned the Hymn of Greeting; even as he chanted, the first tawny rays struck into the eyes of those across the courtyard. Again that muffled vibration, which shook the very bones of those closest it, and opposite Flindach, on the other balcony, appeared Gwaay and Hasjarl. Both were garbed alike but for their diadems and scepters. Hasjarl wore a sapphire-jeweled silver band on his forehead and in his hand was the scepter of the Upper Levels, crested with a clenched fist; Gwaay wore a diadem inlaid with rubies and in his hand was his scepter surmounted by a worm, dagger-transfixed. Otherwise the twain were dressed identically in ceremonial robes of darkest red, belted with broad leather girdles of black; they wore no weapons nor were any other ornaments permissable.

As they seated themselves upon the high stools provided, Flindach turned toward the gate nearest Brilla and began to chant. His sonorous voice was answered by a hidden chorus and reechoed by certain of the bands in the courtyard. For the third time the monstrous gong was sounded and as the last echoes faded the body of Quarmal, litter-borne, appeared. It was carried by the six Lankhmar slavegirls and followed by the Mingols; this small band was all that remained of the many who had slept in the bed of Quarmal.

But where, Brilla asked himself with a heart-bounding start, was Kewissa the Ilthmarix, the old Lord's favorite? Brilla had ordered the marshaling of the girls himself. She could not—

Slowly through a lane of prostrate bodies the litter progressed toward the pyre. The carcass of Quarmal was propped in a sitting posture, and it swayed in a manner horribly suggestive of life as the slavewomen staggered under their unaccustomed load. He was garbed in robes of purple silk and his brow bore the golden bands of Quarmall's Lord. Those lean hands, once so active in the practice of necromancy and incantations, were folded stiffly over the Grammarie which had been his bible during life. On his wrist, hooded and chained was a great gyrfalcon, and at the feet of its dead master lay his favorite coursing leopard, quiet in the quietness of death. Even as was the falcon hooded, so with wax-like lids were the once awesome eyes of Quarmal covered; those eyes which had seen so much of death were now forever dead.

Although Brilla's mind was still agitated about Kewissa, he spoke a word of encouragement to the other girls as they passed, and one of them flung him a wistful smile; they all knew it was an honor to accompany their master into the future, but none of them desired it particularly; however there was little they could do about it except follow directions. Brilla felt sorry for them all; they were so young, had such luscious bodies and were capable of giving so much pleasure to a man, for he had trained them well. But custom must be fulfilled. Yet how then had Kewissa—? Brilla shut off that speculation.

The litter moved on up the ramp. The chanting grew in volume and tempo as the top of the pyre was reached, and the rays of the sun, now shining full onto the dead countenance of Quarmal, as the litter turned toward it, reflected from the bright hair and white skin of the Lankhmar slavegirls, who had with their companions thrown themselves at the feet of Quarmal.

Suddenly Flindach dropped his arms and there was silence, a complete and total silence startling in its contrast to the measured chant and clashing gongs.

Gwaay and Hasjarl sat motionless, staring intently at the figure that had once been the Lord of Quarmall.

Flindach again raised his arms and from the gate opposite to that from whence had come the body of Quarmal, there leaped eight men. Each bore a flambeau and was naked but for a purple cowl which obscured his face. To the accompaniment of harsh gong notes they ran swiftly to the pyre, two on each side and, thrusting their torches

into the prepared wood, cast themselves over the flames they created
and clambering up the pyramid embraced the slavegirls wantonly.

Almost at once the flames ate into the resinous and oil-impregnated
wood. For a moment through the thick smoke the interlocking writhing forms of the slaves could be perceived, and the lean figure of dead
Quarmal staring through closed lids directly into the face of the sun.
Then, incensed by the heat and acrid fumes, the great falcon
screamed in vicious anger and wing-flapping rose from the wrist of
its master. The chains held fast; but all could see the arm of Quarmal
lifted high in a gesture of sublime dismissal before the smoke obscured. The chanting reached crescendo and abruptly ended as
Flindach gave the sign that the rites were finished.

As the eager flames swiftly consumed the pyre and the burden it
bore, Hasjarl broke the silence which custom had enjoined. He
turned toward Gwaay and, fingering the knuckly knob of his scepter,
with an evil grin he spoke.

"Ha! Gwaay, it would have been a merry thing to have seen you
leching in the flames. Almost as merry as to see our sire gesticulating
after death. Go quickly, Brother! There's yet a chance to immolate
yourself and so win fame and immortality." And he giggled, slobber-
ing.

Gwaay had just made an unapparent sign to a page nearby and the
lad was hurrying away. The young Lord of the Lower Levels was in
no manner amused by his brother's ill-timed jesting, but with a smile
and shrug he replied sarcastically, "I choose to seek death in less
painful paths. Yet the idea is a good one; I'll treasure it." Then suddenly in a deeper voice: "It had been better that we were both still-
born than to fritter our lives away in futile hatreds. I'll overlook your
dream-dust and your poppy hurricanes, and e'en your noisome sorceries, and make a pact with you, O Hasjarl! By the somber gods who
rule under Quarmall's Hill and by the Worm which is my sign I
swear that from my hand your life is sacrosanct; with neither spells
nor steel nor venoms will I slay thee!" Gwaay rose to his feet as he
finished and looked directly at Hasjarl.

Taken unaware, Hasjarl for a second sat in silence; a puzzled expression crossed his face; then a sneer distorted his thin lips and he
spat at Gwaay:

"So! You fear me more even than I thought. Aye! And rightly so!
Yet the blood of yon old cinder runs in both our bodies, and there is a
tender spot within me for my brother. Yes, I'll pact with thee,
Gwaay! By the Elder Ones who swim in lightless deeps and by the

Fist that is my token, I'll swear your life is sacrosanct—until I crush it out!" And with a final evil titter Hasjarl, like a malformed stoat, slid from stool and out of sight.

Gwaay stood quietly listening, gazing at the space where Hasjarl had sat; then, sure his brother was well gone, he slapped his thighs mightily and, convulsed with silent laughter, gasped to no one in particular, "Even the wiliest hares are caught in simple snares," and still smiling he turned to watch the dancing flames.

Slowly the variegated groups were herded into the passageways whence they had come and the courtyard was cleared once again, except for those slaves and priests whose duties kept them there.

Gwaay remained watching for a time, then he too slipped off the balcony into the inner rooms. And a faint smile yet clung to his mouth corners as if some jest were lingering in his mind pleasantly.

". . . And by the blood of that one whom it is death to look upon . . ."

So sonorously invoked the Mouser, as with eyes closed and arms outstretched he cast the rune given him by Sheelba of the Eyeless Face which would destroy all sorcerers of less than First Rank for an undetermined distance around the casting point—surely for a few miles, one might hope, so smiting Hasjarl's warlocks to dust.

Whether his Great Spell worked or not—and in his inmost heart he strongly mistrusted that it would—the Mouser was very pleased with the performance he was giving. He doubted Sheelba himself could have done better. What magnificent deep chest tones!—even Fafhrd had never heard him declaim so.

He wished he could open his eyes for just a moment to note the effect his performance was having on Gwaay's magicians—they'd be staring open-mouthed for all their supercilious boasting, he was sure —but on this point Sheelba's instructions had been adamant: eyes tightly shut while the last sentences of the rune were being recited and the great forbidden words spoken; even the tiniest blink would nullify the Great Spell. Evidently magicians were supposed to be without vanity or curiosity—what a bore!

Of a sudden in the dark of his head, he felt contact with another and a larger darkness, a malefic and puissant darkness, of which light itself is only the absence. He shivered. His hair stirred. Cold sweat prickled his face. He almost stuttered midway through the word "slewerisophnak." But concentrating his will, he finished without flaw.

When the last echoing notes of his voice had ceased to rebound between the domed ceiling and floor, the Mouser slit open one eye and glanced surreptitiously around him.

One glance and the other eye flew open to fullness. He was too surprised to speak.

And whom he would have spoken to, had he not been too surprised, was also a question.

The long table at the foot of which he stood was empty of occupants. Where but moments before had sat eleven of the very greatest magicians of Quarmall—sorcerers of the First Rank, each had sworn on his black Grammarie—was only space.

The Mouser called it softly. It was possible that these provincial fellows had been frightened at the majesty of his dark Lankhmarian delivery and had crawled under the table. But there was no answer.

He spoke louder. Only the ceaseless groan of the fans could be sensed, though hardly more noticeable after four days hearing them than the coursing of his blood. With a shrug the Mouser relaxed into his chair. He murmured to himself, "If those slick-faced old fools run off, what next? Suppose all Gwaay's henchmen flee?"

As he began to plan out in his mind what strategy of airy nothing to adopt if that should come to pass, he glanced somberly at the wide high-backed chair nearest his place, where had sat the boldest-seeming of Gwaay's arch-magi. There was only a loosely crumpled white loincloth—but in it was what gave the Mouser pause. A small pile of flocculent gray dust was all.

The Mouser whistled softly between his teeth and raised himself the better to see the rest of the seats. On each of them was the same: a clean loincloth, somewhat crumpled as if it had been worn for a little while, and within the cloth that small heap of grayish powder.

At the other end of the long table, one of the black counters, which had been standing on its edge, slowly rolled off the board of the thought-game and struck the floor with a tiny *tick*. It sounded to the Mouser rather like the last noise in the world.

Very quietly he stood up and silently walked in his ratskin moccasins to the nearest archway, across which he had drawn thick curtains for the Great Spell. He was wondering just what the range of the spell had been, *where* it had stopped, if it had stopped at all. Suppose, for instance, that Sheelba had underestimated its power and it disintegrated not only sorcerers, but . . .

He paused in front of the curtain and gave one last over-the-shoulder glance. Then he shrugged, adjusted his swordbelt, and, grinning far more bravely than he felt, said to no one in particular, "But they assured me that they were the *very* greatest sorcerers."

As he reached toward the curtain, heavy with embroidery, it wavered and shook. He froze, his heart leaping wildly. Then the curtains parted a little and there was thrust in the saucy face of Ivivis, wide-eyed with excited curiosity.

"Did your Great Spell work, Mouser?" she asked him breathlessly.

He let out his own breath in a sigh of relief. "You survived it, at all events," he said and reaching out pulled her against him. Her slim body pressing his felt very good. True, the presence of almost any living being would have been welcome to the Mouser at this moment, but that it should be Ivivis was a bonus he could not help but appreciate.

"Dearest," he said sincerely, "I was feeling that I was perchance the last man on Earth. But now—"

"And acting as if I were the last girl, lost a year," she retorted tartly. "This is neither the place nor the time for amorous consolations and intimate pleasantries," she continued, half mistaking his motives and pushing back from him.

"Did you slay Hasjarl's wizards?" she demanded, gazing up with some awe into his eyes.

"I slew *some* sorcerers," the Mouser admitted judiciously. "Just how many is a moot question."

"Where are Gwaay's?" she asked, looking past the Mouser at the empty chairs. "Did he take them all with him?"

"Isn't Gwaay back from his father's funeral yet?" the Mouser countered, evading her question, but as she continued to look into his eyes, he added lightly, "His sorcerers are in some congenial spot—I hope."

Ivivis looked at him queerly, pushed past, hurried to the long table, and gazed up and down the chair seats.

"Oh, *Mouser!*" she said reprovingly, but there was real awe in the gaze she shot him.

He shrugged. "They swore to me they were of First Rank," he defended himself.

"Not even a fingerbone or skullshard left," Ivivis said solemnly, peering closely at the nearest tiny gray dust pile and shaking her head.

"Not even a gallstone," the Mouser echoed harshly. "My rune was dire."

"Not even a tooth," Ivivis reechoed, rubbing curiously if somewhat callously through the pile. "Nothing to send their mothers."

"Their mothers can have their diapers to fold away with their baby ones," the Mouser said irascibly though somewhat uncomfortably. "Oh, Ivivis, sorcerers don't have mothers!"

"But what happens to our Lord Gwaay now his protectors are gone?" Ivivis demanded more practically. "You saw how Hasjarl's sendings struck him last night when they but dozed. And if anything happens to Gwaay, then what happens to us?"

Again the Mouser shrugged. "If my rune reached Hasjarl's twenty-four wizards and blasted them too, then no harm's been done—except to sorcerers, and they all take their chances, sign their death warrants when they speak their first spells—'tis a dangerous trade.

"In fact," he went on with argumentative enthusiasm, "we've gained. Twenty-four enemies slain at cost of but a dozen—no, eleven total casualties on our side—why, that's a bargain any warlord would jump at! Then with the sorcerers all out of the way—except for the Brothers themselves, and Flindach—that warty blotchy one is some-one to be reckoned with!—I'll meet and slay this champion of Has-jarl's and we'll carry all before us. And if . . ."

His voice trailed off. It had occurred to him to wonder why he himself hadn't been blasted by his own spell. He had never suspected, until now, that he might be a sorcerer of the First Rank—having despite a youthful training in country-sorceries only dabbled in magic since. Perhaps some metaphysical trick or logical fallacy was involved. . . . If a sorcerer casts a rune that midway of the casting blasts *all* sorcerers, *provided the casting be finished*, then does he blast himself, or . . . ? Or perhaps indeed, the Mouser began to think boastfully, he was unknown to himself a magus of the First Rank, or even higher, or—

In the silence of his thinking, he and Ivivis became aware of ap-proaching footsteps, first a multitudinous patter but swiftly a tumult. The gray-clad man and the slavegirl had hardly time to exchange a questioning apprehensive look when there burst through the draper-ies, tearing them down, eight or nine of Gwaay's chiefest henchmen, their faces death-pale, their eyes staring like madmen's. They raced across the chamber and out the opposite archway almost before the Mouser could recover from where he'd dodged out of their way.

But that was not the end of the footsteps. There was a last pair coming down the black corridor and at a strange unequal gallop, like a cripple sprinting, and with a squushy slap at each tread. The Mouser crossed quickly to Ivivis and put an arm around her. He did not want to be standing alone at this moment, either.

Ivivis said, "If your Great Spell missed Hasjarl's sorcerers, and their disease-spells struck through to Gwaay, now undefended . . ."

Her whisper trailed off fearfully as a monstrous figure clad in dark scarlet robes lurched by swift convulsive stages into view. At first the

Mouser thought it must be Hasjarl of the Mismated Arms, from what he'd heard of that one. Then he saw that its neck was collared by gray fungus, its right cheek crimson, its left black, its eyes dripping green ichor and its nose spattering clear drops. As the loathy creature took a last great stride into the chamber, its left leg went boneless like a pillar of jelly and its right leg, striking down stiffly though with a heel splash, broke in midshin and the jagged bones thrust through the flesh. Its yellow-crusted, red-cracked scurfy hands snatched futilely at the air for support and its right arm brushing its head carried away half the hair on that side.

Ivivis began to mewl and yelp faintly with horror and she clung to the Mouser, who himself felt as if a nightmare were lifting its hooves to trample him.

In such manner did Prince Gwaay, Lord of the Lower Levels of Quarmall, come home from his father's funeral, falling in a stenchful, scabrous, ichorous heap upon the torn-down richly embroidered curtains immediately beneath the pristine-handsome silver bust of himself in the niche above the arch.

The funeral pyre smoldered for a long time, but of all the inhabitants in that huge and ramified castle-kingdom Brilla the High Eunuch was the only one who watched it out. Then he collected a few representative pinches of ashes to preserve; he kept them with some dim idea that they might perhaps act as some protection, now that the living protector was forever gone.

Yet the fluffy-gritty gray tokens did not much cheer Brilla as he wandered desolately into the inner rooms. He was troubled and eunuch-like be-twittered by thoughts of the war between brothers that must now ensue before Quarmall had again a single master. Oh, what a tragedy that Lord Quarmal should have been snatched so suddenly by the Fates with no chance to make arrangement for the succession! —though what that arrangement might have been, considering custom's strictures in Quarmall, Brilla could not say. Still, Quarmal had always seemed able to achieve the impossible.

Brilla was troubled too, and rather more acutely, by his guilty knowledge that Quarmal's concubine Kewissa had evaded the flames. He might be blamed for that, though he could not see where he had omitted any customary precaution. And burning would have been small pain indeed to what the poor girl must suffer now for her transgression. He rather hoped she had slain herself by knife or poison, though that would doom her spirit to eternal wandering in the winds between the stars that make them twinkle.

Brilla realized his steps were taking him to the harem and he halted a-quake. He might well find Kewissa there and he did not want to be the one to turn her in.

Yet if he stayed in this central section of the Keep, he would momentarily run into Flindach and he knew he would hold back nothing when gimleted by that arch-sorcerer's stern witchy gaze. He would have to remind him of Kewissa's defection.

So Brilla bethought him of an errand that would take him to the nethermost sections of the Keep, just above Hasjarl's realm. There was a storeroom there, his responsibility, which he had not inventoried for a month. Brilla did not like the Dark Levels of Quarmall—it was his pride that he was one of the elite who worked in or at least near sunlight—but now, by reason of his anxieties, the Dark Levels began to seem attractive.

This decision made, Brilla felt slightly cheered. He set off at once, moving quite swiftly, with a eunuch's peculiar energy, despite his elephantine bulk.

He reached the storeroom without incident. When he had kindled a torch there, the first thing he saw was a small girl-like woman cowering among the bales of drapery. She wore a lustrous loose yellow robe and had the winsome triangular face, moss-green hair, and bright blue eyes of an Ilthmarix.

"Kewissa," he whispered shudderingly yet with motherly warmth. "Sweet chick . . ."

She ran to him. "Oh Brilla, I'm so frightened," she cried softly as she pressed against his paunch and hid herself in his great-sleeved arms.

"I know, I know," he murmured, making little clucking noises as he smoothed her hair and petted her. "You were always frightened of flames, I remember now. Never mind, Quarmal will forgive when you meet beyond the stars. Look you, little duck, it's a great risk I run, but because you were the old Lord's favorite I cherish you dearly. I carry a painless poison . . . only a few drops on the tongue, then darkness and the windy gulfs. . . . A long leap, true, but better far than what Flindach must order when he discovers—"

She pushed back from him. "It was Flindach who commanded me not to follow My Lord to his last hearth!" she revealed wide-eyed and reproachful. "He told me the stars directed otherwise and also that this was Quarmal's dying wish. I doubted and feared Flindach—he with face so hideous and eyes so horridly like My Dear Lord's—yet could not but obey . . . with some small thankfulness, I must confess, dear Brilla."

"But what reason earthly or unearthly . . . ?" Brilla stammered, his mind a-whirl.

Kewissa looked to either side. Then, "I bear Quarmal's quickening seed," she whispered.

For a bit this only increased Brilla's confusion. How could Quarmal have hoped to get a concubine's child accepted as Lord of All when there were two grown legitimate heirs? Or cared so little for the land's security as to leave alive even an unborn bastard? Then it occurred to him—and his heart shook at the thought—that Flindach might be seeking to seize supreme power, using Kewissa's babe and an invented death wish of Quarmal as his pretext along with those Quarmal-eyes of his. Palace revolutions were not entirely unknown in Quarmall. Indeed, there was a legend that the present line had generations ago clambered dagger-fisted to power by that route, though it was death to repeat the legend.

Kewissa continued, "I stayed hidden in the harem. Flindach said I'd be safe. But then Hasjarl's henchmen came searching in Flindach's absence and in defiance of all customs and decencies. I fled here."

This continued to make a dreadful sort of sense, Brilla thought. If Hasjarl suspected Flindach's impious snatch at power, he would instinctively strike at him, turning the fraternal strife into a three-sided one involving even—woe of woes!—the sunlit apex of Quarmall, which until this moment had seemed so safe from war's alarums. . . .

At that very instant, as if Brilla's fears had conjured up their fruition, the door of the storeroom opened wide and there loomed in it an uncouth man who seemed the very embodiment of battle's barbarous horrors. He was so tall his head brushed the lintel; his face was handsome yet stern and searching-eyed; his red-gold hair hung tangledly to his shoulders; his garment was a bronze-studded wolfskin tunic; longsword and massy short-handled ax, swung from his belt, and on the longest finger of his right hand Brilla's gaze—trained to miss no detail of decor and now fear-sharpened—noted a ring with Hasjarl's clenched-fist sigil.

The eunuch and the girl huddled against each other, quivering.

Having assured himself that these two were all he faced, the newcomer's countenance broke into a smile that might have been reassuring on a smaller man or one less fiercely accoutered. Then Fafhrd said, "Greetings, Grandfather. I require only that you and your chick help me find the sunlight and the stables of this benighted realm. Come, we'll plot it out so you may satisfy me with least danger to yourselves." And he swiftly stepped toward them, silently for all his size, his gaze returning with interest to Kewissa as he noted she was not child but woman.

Kewissa felt that and although her heart was a-flutter, piped up bravely, "You dare not rape me! I'm with child by a dead man!"

Fafhrd's smile soured somewhat. Perhaps, he told himself, he should feel complimented that girls started thinking about rape the instant they saw him, still he was a little irked. Did they deem him incapable of civilized seduction because he wore furs and was no dwarf? Oh well, they quickly learned. But what a horrid way to try to daunt him!

Meanwhile tubby-fat Grandfather, who Fafhrd now realized was hardly equipped to be that or father either, said fearful-mincing, "She speaks only the truth, oh Captain. But I will be o'erjoyed to aid you in any—"

There were rapid steps in the passage and the harsh slither of steel against stone. Fafhrd turned like a tiger. Two guards in the dark-linked hauberks of Hasjarl's guards were pressing into the room. The fresh-drawn sword of one had scraped the door-side, while a third behind them cried sharply now. "Take the Northern turncoat! Slay him if he shows fight. I'll secure old Quarmal's concubine."

The two guards started to run at Fafhrd, but he, counterfeiting even more the tiger, sprang at them twice as suddenly. Graywand coming out of his scabbard swept sideways up, fending off the sword of the foremost even as Fafhrd's foot came crushing down on that one's instep. Then Graywand's hilt crashed backhand into his jaw, so that he lurched against his fellow. Meanwhile Fafhrd's ax had come into his left hand and at close quarters he stroked it into their brains, then shouldering them off as they fell, he drew back the ax and cast it at the third, so that it lodged in his forehead between the eyes as he turned to see what was amiss, and he dropped down dead.

But the footsteps of a fourth and perhaps a fifth could be heard racing away. Fafhrd sprang toward the door with a growl, stopped with a foot-stamp and returned as swiftly, stabbing a bloody finger at Kewissa cowering into the great bulk of blanching Brilla.

"Old Quarmal's girl? With child by him?" he rapped out and when she nodded rapidly, swallowing hard, he continued, "Then you come with me. Now! The castrado too."

He sheathed Graywand, wrenched his ax from the sergeant's skull, grabbed Kewissa by the upper arm and strode toward the door with a devilish snarling head-wave to Brilla to follow.

Kewissa cried, "Oh mercy, sir! You'll make me lose the child."

Brilla obeyed, yet twittered as he did, "Kind Captain, we'll be no use to you, only encumber you in your—"

Fafhrd, turning suddenly again, spared him one rapid speech, shaking the bloody ax for emphasis: "If you think I don't understand the bargaining value or hostage-worth of even an unborn claimant to a throne, then your skull is as empty of brains as your loins are of seed —and I doubt that's the case. As for you, girl," he added harshly to Kewissa, "if there's anything but bleat under your green ringlets, you know you're safer with a stranger than with Hasjarl's hellions and that better your child miscarry than fall into their hands. Come, I'll carry you." He swept her up. "Follow, eunuch; work those great thighs of yours if you love living."

And he made off down the corridor, Brilla trotting ponderously after and wisely taking great gasping breaths in anticipation of exertions to come. Kewissa laid her arms around Fafhrd's neck and glanced up at him with qualified admiration. He himself now gave vent to two remarks which he'd evidently been saving for an unoccupied moment.

The first, bitterly sarcastic: ". . . if he shows fight!"

The second, self-angry: "Those cursed fans must be deafening me, that I didn't hear 'em coming!"

Forty loping paces down the corridor he passed a ramp leading upward and turned toward a narrower darker corridor.

From just behind, Brilla called softly yet rapidly, penurious of breath. "That ramp led to the stables. Where are you taking us, My Captain?"

"Down!" Fafhrd retorted without pausing in his lope. "Don't panic, I've a hidey-hole for the two of you—and even a girl-mate for little Prince-mother Greenilocks here." Then to Kewissa, gruffly, "You're not the only girl in Quarmall who wants rescuing, nor yet the dearest."

The Mouser, steeling himself for it, knelt and surveyed the noisome heap that was Prince Gwaay. The stench was abominably strong despite the perfumes the Mouser had sprinkled and the incense he had burned but an hour ago. The Mouser had covered with silken sheets and fur robes all the loathsomeness of Gwaay except for his plagues-stricken pillowed-up face. The sole feature of this face that had escaped obvious extreme contagion was the narrow handsome nose, from the end of which there dripped clear fluid, drop by slow drop, like the ticking of a water clock, while from below the nose proceeded a continual small nasty retching which was the only reasonably sure sign that Gwaay was not wholly moribund. For a while Gwaay had made faint straining moanings like the whispers of a mute, but now even those had ceased.

The Mouser reflected that it was very difficult indeed to serve a master who could neither speak, write, nor gesticulate—particularly when fighting enemies who now began to seem neither dull nor contemptible. By all counts Gwaay should have died hours since. Presumably only his steely sorcerous will and consuming hatred of Hasjarl kept his spirit from fleeing the horrid torment that housed it.

The Mouser rose and turned with a questioning shrug toward Ivivis, who sat now at the long table hemming up two hooded black voluminous sorcerer's robes, which she had cut down at the Mouser's direction to fit him and herself. The Mouser had thought that since he now seemed to be Gwaay's sole remaining sorcerer as well as champion, he should be prepared to appear dressed as the former and to boast at least one acolyte.

In answer to the shrug, Ivivis merely wrinkled her nostrils, pinched them with two dainty fingertips, and shrugged back. True, the Mouser thought, the stench was growing stronger despite all his attempts to mask it. He stepped to the table and poured himself a half cup of the thick blood-red wine, which he'd begun unwillingly to relish a little, although he'd learned it was indeed fermented from scarlet toadstools. He took a small swallow and summed up:

"Here's a pretty witch's kettle of problems. Gwaay's sorcerers blasted—all right, yes, by me, I admit it. His henchmen and soldiery fled—to the lowest loathy dank dim tunnels, I think, or else gone over to Hasjarl. His girls vanished save for you. Even his doctors fearful to come nigh him—the one I dragged here fainting dead away. His slaves useless with dread—only the tread-beasts at the fans keep their heads, and they because they haven't any! No answer to our message to Flindach suggesting that we league against Hasjarl. No page to send another message by—and not even a single picket to warn us if Hasjarl assaults."

"You could go over to Hasjarl yourself," Ivivis pointed out.

The Mouser considered that. "No," he decided, "there's something too fascinating about a forlorn hope like this. I've always wanted to command one. And it's only fun to betray the wealthy and victorious. Yet what strategy can I employ without even a skeleton army?"

Ivivis frowned. "Gwaay used to say that just as sword-war is but another means of carrying out diplomacy, so sorcery is but another means of carrying out sword-war. Spell-war. So you could try your Great Spell again," she concluded without vast conviction.

"Not I!" the Mouser repudiated. "It never touched Hasjarl's twenty-four or it would have stopped their disease-spells against Gwaay. Either they are of First Rank or else I'm doing the spell backwards—in which case the tunnels would probably collapse on me if I tried it again."

"Then use a different spell," Ivivis suggested brightly. "Raise an army of veritable skeletons. Drive Hasjarl mad, or put a hex on him so he stubs his toe at every step. Or turn his soldiers' swords to cheese. Or vanish their bones. Or transmew all his maids to cats and set their tails afire. Or—"

"I'm sorry, Ivivis," the Mouser interposed hurriedly to her mounting enthusiasm. "I would not confess this to another, but . . . that was my only spell. We must depend on wit and weapons alone. Again I ask you, Ivivis, what strategy does a general employ when his left is o'erwhelmed, his right takes flight, and his center is ten times decimated?"

A slight sweet sound like a silver bell chinked once, or a silver string plucked high in the harp, interrupted him. Although so faint, it seemed for a moment to fill the chamber with auditory light. The Mouser and Ivivis gazed around wonderingly and then at the same moment looked up at the silver mask of Gwaay in the niche above the arch before which Gwaay's mortal remains festered silken-wrapped.

The shimmering metal lips of the statua smiled and parted—so far as one might tell in the gloom—and faintly there came Gwaay's brightest voice, saying: "Your answer: he attacks!"

The Mouser blinked. Ivivis dropped her needle. The statua continued, its eyes seeming to twinkle, "Greetings, hostless captain mine! Greetings, dear girl. I'm sorry my stink offends you—yes, yes, Ivivis, I've observed you pinching your nose at my poor carcass this last hour through—but then the world teems with loathiness. Is that not a black death-adder gliding now through the black robe you stitch?"

With a gasp of horror Ivivis sprang cat-swift up and aside from the material and brushed frantically at her legs. The statua gave a naturally silver laugh, then quickly said, "Your pardon, gentle girl, I did but jest. My spirits are too high, too high—perchance because my body is so low. Plotting will curb my feyness. Hist now, hist!"

In Hasjarl's Hall of Sorcery his four-and-twenty wizards stared desperately at a huge magic screen set up parallel to their long table, trying with all their might to make the picture on it come clear. Hasjarl himself, dire in his dark red funeral robes, gazing alternately with open eyes and through the grommeted holes in his upper lids, as

if that perchance might make the picture sharper, stutteringly be-
rated them for their clumsiness and at intervals conferred staccato
with his military.

The screen was dark gray, the picture appearing on it in pale green
witch-light. It stood twelve feet high and eighteen feet long. Each
wizard was responsible for a particular square yard of it, projecting
on it his share of the clairvoyant picture.

This picture was of Gwaay's Hall of Sorcery, but the best effect
achieved so far was a generally blurred image showing the table, the
empty chairs, a low mound on the floor, a high point of silver light,
and two figures moving about—these last mere salamander-like blobs
with arms and legs attached, so that not even the sex could be determined, if indeed they were human at all or even male or female.

Sometimes a yard of the picture would come clear as a flowerbed
on a bright day, but it would always be a yard with neither of the
figures in it or anything of more interest than an empty chair. Then
Hasjarl would bark sudden for the other wizards to do likewise, or for
the successful wizard to trade squares with someone whose square
had a figure in it, and the picture would invariably get worse and
Hasjarl would screech and spray spittle, and then the picture would
go completely bad, swimming everywhere or with squares all jum-
bled and overlapping like an unsolved puzzle, and the twenty-four
sorcerers would have to count off squares and start over again while
Hasjarl disciplined them with fearful threats.

Interpretations of the picture by Hasjarl and his aides differed considerably. The absence of Gwaay's sorcerers seemed to be a good
thing, until someone suggested they might have been sent to infiltrate
Hasjarl's Upper Levels for a close-range thaumaturgic attack. One
lieutenant got fearfully tongue-lashed for suggesting the two blob-
figures might be demons seen unblurred in their true guise—though
even after Hasjarl had discharged his anger, he seemed a little frightened by the idea. The hopeful notion that all Gwaay's sorcerers had
been wiped out was rejected when it was ascertained that no sorcerous spells had been directed at them recently by Hasjarl or any of his
wizards.

One of the blob-figures now left the picture entirely and the point
of silvery light faded. This touched off further speculation, which was
interrupted by the entry of several of Hasjarl's torturers looking
rather battered and a dozen of his guards. The guards were surrounding—with naked swords aimed at his chest and back—the figure of an
unarmed man in a wolfskin tunic with arms bound tight behind him.

He was masked with a red silk eye-holed sack pulled down over his head and hair, and a black robe trailed behind him.

"We've taken the Northerner, Lord Hasjarl!" the leader of the dozen guards reported joyously. "We cornered him in your torture room. He disguised himself as one of those and tried to lie his way through our lines, humped and going on his knees, but his height still betrayed him."

"Good, Yissim—I'll reward you," Hasjarl approved. "But what of my father's treacherous concubine and the great castrado who were with him when he slew three of your fellows?"

"They were still with him when we glimpsed him near Gwaay's realm and gave chase. We lost 'em when he doubled back to the torture room, but the hunt goes on."

"Find 'em, you were best," Hasjarl ordered grimly, "or the sweets of my reward will be soured entire by the pains of my displeasure." Then to Fafhrd, "So, traitor! Now I will play with you the wrist game—aye, and a hundred others too, until you are wearied of sport."

Fafhrd answered loudly and clearly through his red mask, "I'm no traitor, Hasjarl. I was only tired of your twitching and of your torturing of girls."

There came a sibilant cry from the sorcerers. Turning, Hasjarl saw that one of them had made the low mound on the floor come clear, so that it was clearly seen as a stricken man covered to his pillowed head.

"Closer!" Hasjarl cried—all eagerness, no threat—and perhaps because they were neither startled nor threatened, each wizard did his work perfectly, so that there came green-pale onto the screen Gwaay's face, wide as an oxcart and team, the plagues visible by the huge pustules and crustings and fungoid growths if not by their colors, the eyes like great vats stewing with ichor, the mouth a quaking bog-hole, while each drop that fell from the nose-tip looked a gallon.

Hasjarl cried thickly, like a man choking with strong drink, "Joy, oh joy! My heart will break!"

The screen went black, the room dead silent, and into it from the further archway there came gliding noiselessly through the air a tiny bone-gray shape. It soared on unflapping wings like a hawk searching its prey, high above the swords that struck at it. Then turning in a smooth silent curve, it swooped straight at Hasjarl and, evading his hands that snatched at it too late, tapped him on the breast and fell to the floor at his feet.

It was a dart folded from parchment on which lines of characters showed at angles. Nothing more deadly than that.

Hasjarl snatched it up, pulled it crackingly open, and read aloud:

"Dear Brother. Let us meet on the instant in the Ghost Hall to settle the succession. Bring your four-and-twenty sorcerers. I'll bring one. Bring your champion. I'll bring mine. Bring your henchmen and guards. Bring yourself. I'll be brought. Or perhaps you'd prefer to spend the evening torturing girls. Signed (by direction) Gwaay."

Hasjarl crumpled the parchment in his fist and peering over it thoughtful-evil, rapped out staccato: "We'll go! He means to play on my brotherly pity—that would be sweet. Or else to trap us, but I'll out-trick him!"

Fafhrd called boldly, "You may be able to best your death-rotten brother, oh Hasjarl, but what of his champion?—cunninger than Zobold, more battle-fierce than a rogue elephant! Such an one can cut through your cheesy guards as easy as I bested 'em one-to-five in the Keep, and be at your noisy throat! You'll need me!"

Hasjarl thought for a heartbeat, then turning toward Fafhrd said, "I'm not mind-proud. I'll take advice from a dead dog. Bring him with us. Keep him bound, but bring his weapons."

Along a wide low tunnel that trended slowly upward and was lit by wall-set torches flaming no bluer-bright than marsh gas and as distant-seeming each from the next as coastal beacons, the Mouser striding swiftly yet most warily led a strange short cortege.

He wore a black robe with peaked black hood that thrown forward would hide his face entirely. Under it he carried at his belt his sword and dagger and also a skin of the blood-red toadstool wine, but in his fingers he bore a thin black wand tipped with a silver star, to remind him that his primary current role was Sorcerer Extraordinary to Gwaay.

Behind him trotted two-abreast four of the great-legged tiny-headed tread-slaves, looking almost like dark walking cones, especially when silhouetted by a torch just passed. They bore between them, each clutching a pole-end in both dwarfish hands, a litter of blood wood and ebony ornately carved, whereon rested mattressed and covered by furs and silks and richly embroidered fabrics the stenchful, helpless flesh and dauntless spirit of the young Lord of the Lower Levels.

Close behind Gwaay's litter followed what seemed a slightly smaller version of the Mouser. It was Ivivis, masquerading as his acolyte. She held a fold of her hood as a sort of windbreak in front of her mouth and nose, and frequently she sniffed a handkerchief steeped in spirits of camphor and ammonia. Under her arm she carried a silver gong in a woolen sack and a strange thin wooden mask in another.

The splayed calloused feet of the tread-slaves struck the stony floor with a faint *brush*, over which came at long regular intervals Gwaay's gargly retching. Other sound there was none.

The walls and low ceiling teemed with pictures, mostly in yellow ocher, of demons, strange beasts, bat-winged girls, and other infernal beauties. Their slow looming and fading was nightmarish, yet gently so. All in all, it was one of the pleasantest journeys the Mouser could recall, equal of a trip he had once made by moonlight across the roofs of Lankhmar to hang a wilting wreath on a forgotten tower-top statue of the God of Thieves, and light a small blue fire of brandy to him.

"Attack!" he murmured humorously and wholly to himself. "Forward, my big-foot phalanx! Forward, my terror-striking war-car! Forward, my dainty rearguard! Forward, my host!"

Brilla and Kewissa and Friska sat quiet as mice in the Ghost Hall beside the dried-up fountain pool yet near the open door of the chamber that was their appointed hiding place. The girls were whispering together, head leaned to head, yet that was no noisier than the squeaking of mice, nor was the occasional high sigh Brilla let slip.

Beyond the fountain was the great half open door through which the sole faint light came questing and through which Fafhrd had brought them before doubling back to draw off the pursuit. Some of the cobwebs stretching across it had been torn away by Brilla's ponderous passage.

Taking that door and the one to their hiding place as two opposite corners of the room, the two remaining opposite corners were occupied by a wide black archway and a narrow one, each opening on a large section of stony floor raised three steps above the still larger floor section around the dried-up pool. Elsewhere in the wall were many small doors, all shut, doubtless leading to onetime bed chambers. Over all hung the pale mortared great black slabs of the shallowly domed ceiling. So much their eyes, long accustomed to the darkness, could readily distinguish.

Brilla, who recognized that this place had once housed a harem, was musing melancholically that now it had become a kind of tiniest harem again, with eunuch—himself—and pregnant girl—Kewissa—gossiping with restless high-spirited girl—Friska—who was fretting for the safety of her tall barbarian lover. Old times! He had wanted to sweep up a bit and find some draperies, even if rotten ones, to hang and spread, but Friska had pointed out that they mustn't leave clues to their presence.

There came a faint sound through the great door. The girls quit their whispering and Brilla his sighs and musings, and they listened with all their beings. Then more noises came—footsteps and the knock of a sheathed sword against the wall of a tunnel—and they sprang silently up and scurried back into their hiding chamber and silently shut the door behind them, and the Ghost Hall was briefly alone with its ghosts once more.

A helmeted guard in the hauberk of Hasjarl's guards appeared in the great door and stood peering about with arrow nocked to the taut string of a short bow he held crosswise. Then he motioned with his shoulder and came sneaking in followed by three of his fellows and by four slaves holding aloft yellowly flaming torches, which cast the monstrous shadows of the guardsmen across the dusty floor, and the shadows of their heads against the curving far wall, as they spied about for signs of trap or ambush.

Some bats swooped about and fled the torchlight through the archways.

The first guardsman whistled then down the corridor behind him and waved an arm and there came two parties of slaves, who applied themselves each to a side of the great door, so that it groaned and creaked loudly at its hinges, and they pushed it open wide, though one of them leaped convulsively as a spider fell on him from the disturbed cobwebs, or he thought it did.

Then more guards came, each with a torch-slave, and moved about calling softly back and forth, and tried all the shut doors and peered long and suspiciously into the black spaces beyond the narrow archway and the wide one, but all returned quite swiftly to form a protective semicircle around the great door and enclosing most of the floor space of the central section of the Ghost Hall.

Then into that shielded space Hasjarl came striding, surrounded by his henchmen and followed at heel by his two dozen sorcerers closely ranked. With Hasjarl too came Fafhrd, still arm-bound and wearing his red bag-mask and menaced by the drawn swords of his guards. More torch-slaves came too, so that the Ghost Hall was flaringly lit around the great door, though elsewhere a mixture of glare and black shadow.

Since Hasjarl wasn't speaking, no one else was. Not that the Lord of the Upper Levels was altogether silent—he was coughing constantly, a hacking bark, and spitting gobbets of phlegm into a finely embroidered kerchief. After each small convulsion he would glare suspiciously around him, drooping evilly one pierced eyelid to emphasize his wariness.

Then there was a tiny scurrying and one called, "A rat!" Another loosed an arrow into the shadows around the pool where it rasped stone, and Hasjarl demanded loudly why his ferrets had been forgotten—and his great hounds too, for that matter, and his owls to protect him against poison-toothed bats Gwaay might launch at him—and swore to flay the right hands of the neglectful ones.

It came again, that swift-traveling rattle of tiny claws on smooth stone, and more arrows were loosed futilely to skitter across the floor, and guards shifted position nervously, and in the midst of all that Fafhrd cried, "Up shields, some of you, and make walls to either side of Hasjarl! Have you not thought that a dart, and not a paper one this time, might silently wing from either archway and drive through your dear Lord's throat and stop his precious coughing forever?"

Several leaped guiltily to obey that order and Hasjarl did not wave them away and Fafhrd laughed and remarked, "Masking a champion makes him more dreadsome, oh Hasjarl, but tying his hands behind him is not so apt to impress the enemy—and has other drawbacks. If there should now come suddenly a-rush that one wilier than Zobold, weightier than a mad elephant to tumble and hurl aside your panicky guards—"

"Cut his bonds!" Hasjarl barked and someone began to saw with a dagger behind Fafhrd's back. "But don't give him his sword or ax! Yet hold them ready for him!"

Fafhrd writhed his shoulders and flexed his great forearms and began to massage them and laughed again through his mask.

Hasjarl fumed and then ordered all the shut doors tried once more. Fafhrd readied himself for action as they came to the one behind which Friska and the two others were hidden, for he knew it had no bolt or bar. But it held firm against all shoving. Fafhrd could imagine Brilla's great back braced against it, with the girls perhaps pushing at his stomach, and he smiled under the red silk.

Hasjarl fumed a while longer and cursed his brother for his delay and swore he had intended mercy to his brother's minions and girls, but now no longer. Then one of Hasjarl's henchmen suggested Gwaay's dart-message might have been a ruse to get them out of the way while an attack was launched from below through other tunnels or even by way of the air-shafts, and Hasjarl seized that henchman by the throat and shook him and demanded why, if he had suspected that, he hadn't spoken earlier.

At that moment a gong sounded, high and silver-sweet, and Hasjarl loosed his henchman and looked around wonderingly. Again the silvery gong-note, then through the wider black archway there slowly stepped two monstrous figures each bearing a forward pole of an ornately carved black and red litter.

All of those in the Ghost Hall were familiar with the tread-slaves, but to see them anywhere except on their belts was almost as great and grotesque a wonder as to see them for the first time. It seemed to portend unsettlements of custom and dire upheavals, and so there was much murmuring and some shrinking.

The tread-slaves continued to step ponderously forward and their mates came into view behind them. The four advanced almost to the edge of the raised section of floor and set the litter down and folded their dwarfed arms as well as they could, hooking fingers to fingers across their gigantic chests, and stood motionless.

Then through the same archway there swiftly paced the figure of a rather small sorcerer in black robe and hood that hid his features, and close behind him like his shadow a slightly smaller figure identically clad.

The Black Sorcerer took his stand to one side of the litter and a little ahead of it, his acolyte behind him to his right, and he lifted alongside his cowl a wand tipped with glittering silver and said loudly and impressively, "I speak for Gwaay, Master of Demons and Lord of All Quarmall—as we will prove!"

The Mouser was using his deepest thaumaturgic voice, which none but himself had ever heard, except for the occasion on which he had blasted Gwaay's sorcerers—and come to think of it, that had ended with no one else having heard either. He was enjoying himself hugely, marveling greatly at his own audacity.

He paused just long enough, then slowly pointed his wand at the low mound on the litter, threw up his other arm in an imperious gesture, palm forward, and commanded, "On your knees, vermin, all of you, and do obeisance to your sole rightful ruler, Lord Gwaay, at whose name demons blench!"

A few of the foremost fools actually obeyed him—evidently Hasjarl had cowed them all too well—while most of the others in the front rank goggled apprehensively at the muffled figure in the litter—truly, it was an advantage having Gwaay motionless and supine, looking like Death's horridest self: it made him a more mysterious threat.

Searching over their heads from the cavern of his cowl, the Mouser spotted one he guessed to be Hasjarl's champion—gods, he was a whopper, big as Fafhrd!—and knowledgeable in psychology if that red silk bag-mask were his own idea. The Mouser didn't relish the idea of battling such a one, but with luck it wouldn't come to that.

Then there burst through the ranks of the awed guards, whipping them aside with a short lash, a hunch-shouldered figure in dark scarlet robes—Hasjarl at last! and coming to the fore just as the plot demanded.

Hasjarl's ugliness and frenzy surpassed the Mouser's expectations. The Lord of the Upper Levels drew himself up facing the litter and for a suspenseful moment did naught but twitch, stutter, and spray spittle like the veriest idiot. Then suddenly he got his voice and barked most impressively and surely louder than any of his great hounds:

"By right of death—suffered lately or soon—lately by my father, star-smitten and burned to ash—soon by my impious brother, stricken by my sorceries—and who dare not speak for himself, but must fee charlatans—I, Hasjarl, do proclaim myself sole Lord of Quarmall—and of all within it—demon or man!"

Then Hasjarl started to turn, most likely to order forward some of his guards to seize Gwaay's party, or perhaps to wave an order to his sorcerers to strike them down magically, but in that instant the Mouser clapped his hands together loudly. At that signal, Ivivis, who'd stepped between him and the litter, threw back her cowl and opened her robe and let them fall behind her almost in one continuous gesture—and the sight revealed held everyone spellbound, even Hasjarl, as the Mouser had known it would.

Ivivis was dressed in a transparent black silk tunic—the merest blackly opal gleaming over her pale flesh and slimly youthful figure—but on her face she wore the white mask of a hag, female yet with mouth a-grin showing fangs and with fiercely staring eyes red-balled and white-irised, as the Mouser had swiftly repainted them at the direction of Gwaay, speaking from his silver statua. Long green hair mixed with white fell from the mask behind Ivivis and some thin strands of it before her shoulders. Upright before her in her right hand she held ritualistically a large pruning knife.

The Mouser pointed straight at Hasjarl, on whom the eyes of the mask were already fixed, and he commanded in his deepest voice. "Bring that one here to me, oh Witch-Mother!" and Ivivis stepped swiftly forward.

Hasjarl took a backward step and stared horror-enchanted at his approaching nemesis, all motherly-cannibalistic above, all elfin-maidenly below, with his father's eyes to daunt him and with the cruel knife to suggest judgment upon himself for the girls he had lustingly done to death or lifelong crippledness.

The Mouser knew he had success within his grasp and there remained only the closing of the fingers.

At that instant there sounded from the other end of the chamber a great muffled gong-note deep as Gwaay's had been silvery-high, shuddering the bones by its vibrancy. Then from either side of the narrow black archway at the opposite end of the hall from Gwaay's litter, there rose to the ceiling with a hollow roar twin pillars of white fire, commanding all eyes and shattering the Mouser's spell.

The Mouser's most instant reaction was inwardly to curse such superior stage-management.

Smoke billowed out against the great black squares of the ceiling, the pillars sank to white jets, man-high, and there strode forward between them the figure of Flindach in his heavily embroidered robes and with the Golden Symbol of Power at his waist, but with the Cowl of Death thrown back to show his blotched warty face and his eyes like those in Ivivis' mask. The High Steward threw wide his arms in a proud imploring gesture and in his deep and resonant voice that filled the Ghost Hall recited thus:

"Oh Gwaay! Oh Hasjarl! In the name of your father burned and beyond the stars, and in the name of your grandmother whose eyes I too bear, think of Quarmall! Think of the security of this your kingdom and of how your wars ravage her. Forego your enmities, abjure your brotherly hates, and cast your lots now to settle the succession— the winner to be Lord Paramount here, the loser instantly to depart with great escort and coffers of treasure, and journey across the Mountains of Hunger and the desert and the Sea of the East and live out his life in the Eastern Lands in all comfort and high dignity. Or if not by customary lot, then let your champions battle to the death to decide it—all else to follow the same. Oh Hasjarl, oh Gwaay, I have spoken." And he folded his arms and stood there between the two pale flame pillars still burning high as he.

Fafhrd had taken advantage of the shocks to seize his sword and ax from the ones holding them nervelessly, and to push forward by Hasjarl as if properly to ward him standing alone and unshielded in front of his men. Now Fafhrd lightly nudged Hasjarl and whispered through his bag-mask, "Take him up on it, you were best. I'll win your stuffy loathy catacomb kingdom for you—aye, and once rewarded depart from it swifter ever than Gwaay!"

Hasjarl grimaced angrily at him and turning toward Flindach shouted, "*I* am Lord Paramount here, and no need of lots to deter-

mine it! Yes, and I have my arch-magi to strike down any who sorcerously challenge me!—and my great champion to smite to mincemeat
any who challenge me with swords!"

Fafhrd threw out his chest and glared about through red-ringed
eyeholes to back him up.

The silence that followed Hasjarl's boast was cut as if by keenest
knife when a voice came piercingly dulcet from the unstirring low
mound on the litter, cornered by its four impassive tread-slaves, or
from a point just above it.

"I, Gwaay of the Lower Levels, am Lord Paramount of Quarmall,
and not my poor brother there, for whose damned soul I grieve. And
I have sorceries which have saved my life from the evilest of his
sorceries and I have a champion who will smite his champion to
chaff!"

All were somewhat daunted at that seemingly magical speaking
except Hasjarl, who giggled sputteringly, twitching a-main, and then
as if he and his brother were children alone in a playroom, cried out,
"Liar and squeaker of lies! Effeminate boaster! Puny charlatan! *Where*
is this great champion of yours? Call him forth! Bid him appear! Oh
confess it now, he's but a figment of your dying thoughts! Oh, ho, ho,
ho!"

All began to look around wonderingly at that, some thoughtful,
some apprehensive. But as no figure appeared, certainly not a warlike
one, some of Hasjarl's men began to snigger with him. Others of
them took it up.

The Gray Mouser had no wish to risk his skin—not with Hasjarl's
champion looking a meaner foe every moment, side-armed with ax
like Fafhrd and now apparently even acting as counselor to his lord—
perhaps a sort of captain-general behind the curtain, as he was behind
Gwaay's—yet the Mouser was almost irresistibly tempted by this opportunity to cap all surprises with a master surprise.

And in that instant there sounded forth again Gwaay's eerie bell-
voice, coming not from his vocal cords, for they were rotted away,
but created by the force of his deathless will marshaling the unseen
atomies of the air:

"From the blackest depths, unseen by all, in very center of the Hall
—Appear, my champion!"

That was too much for the Mouser. Ivivis had reassumed her
hooded black robe while Flindach had been speaking, knowing that
the terror of her hag-mask and maiden-form was a fleeting thing, and
she again stood beside the Mouser as his acolyte. He handed her his
wand in one stiff gesture, not looking at her, and lifting his hands to

the throat of his robe, he threw it and his hood back and dropped them behind him, and drawing Scalpel whistling from her sheath leaped forward with a heel-stamp to the top of the three steps and crouched glaring with sword raised above head, looking in his gray silks and silver a figure of menace, albeit a rather small one and carrying at his belt a wineskin as well as a dagger.

Meanwhile Fafhrd, who had been facing Hasjarl to have a last word with him, now ripped off his red bag-mask, whipped Graywand screaming from his sheath, and leaped forward likewise with an intimidating stamp.

Then they saw and recognized each other.

The pause that ensued was to the spectators more testimony to the fearsomeness of each—the one so dreadful-tall, the other metamorphosed from sorcerer. Evidently they daunted each other greatly.

Fafhrd was the first to react, perhaps because there had been something hauntingly familiar to him all along about the manner and speech of the Black Sorcerer. He started a gargantuan laugh and managed to change it in the nick into a screaming snarl of, "Trickster! Chatterer! Player at magic! Sniffer after spells. Wart! *Little Toad!*"

The Mouser, mayhap the more amazed because he had noted and discounted the resemblance of the masked champion to Fafhrd, now took his comrade's cue—and just in time, for he was about to laugh too—and boomed back, "Boaster! Bumptious brawler! Bumbling fumbler after girls! Oaf! Lout! *Big Feet!*"

The taut spectators thought these taunts a shade mild, but the spiritedness of their delivery more than made up for that.

Fafhrd advanced another stamp, crying, "Oh, I have dreamed of this moment. I will mince you from your thickening toenails to your cheesy brain!"

The Mouser bounced for his stamp, so as not to lose height going down the steps, and skirled out the while, "All my rages find happy vent. I will gut you of each lie, especially those about your northern travels!"

Then Fafhrd cried, "Remember Ool Hrusp!" and the Mouser responded. "Remember Lithquil!" and they were at it.

Now for all most of the Quarmallians knew, Lithquil and Ool Hrusp might be and doubtless were places where the two heroes had earlier met in fight, or battlefields where they warred on opposing sides, or even girls they had fought over. But in actuality Lithquil was the Mad Duke of the city of Ool Hrusp, to humor whom Fafhrd and the Mouser had once staged a most realistic and carefully rehearsed duel lasting a full half hour. So those Quarmallians who anticipated a long and spectacular battle were in no wise disappointed.

First Fafhrd aimed three mighty slashing blows, any one enough to cleave the Mouser in twain, but the Mouser deflected each at the last moment strongly and cunningly with Scalpel, so that they whished an inch above his head, singing the harsh chromatic song of steel on steel.

Next the Mouser thrust thrice at Fafhrd, leaping skimmingly like a flying fish and disengaging his sword each time from Graywand's parry. But Fafhrd always managed to slip his body aside, with nearly incredible swiftness for one so big, and the thin blade would go hurtlessly by him.

This interchange of slash and thrust was but the merest prologue to the duel, which now carried into the area of the dried-up fountain pool and became very wild-seeming indeed forcing the spectators back more than once, while the Mouser improvised by gushing out some of his thick blood-red toadstool wine when they were momentarily pressed body-to-body in a fierce exchange, so that they both appeared sorely wounded.

There were three in the Ghost Hall who took no interest in this seeming masterpiece of duels and hardly watched it. Ivivis was not one of them—she soon threw back her hood, tore off her hag-mask, and came following the fight close, cheering on the Mouser. Nor were they Brilla, Kewissa and Friska—for at the sound of swords the two girls had insisted on opening their door a crack despite the eunuch's solicitous apprehensions and now they were all peering through, head above head, Friska in the midst agonizing at Fafhrd's perils.

Gwaay's eyes were clotted and the lids glued with ichor, and the tendons were dissolved whereby he might have lifted his head. Nor did he seek to explore with his sorcerous senses in the direction of the fight. He clung to existence solely by the thread of his great hatred for his brother, all else of life was to him less than a shadow-show; yet his hate held for him all of life's wonder and sweetness and high excitement—it was enough.

The mirror image of that hate in Hasjarl was at this moment strong enough too to dominate wholly his healthy body's instincts and hungers and all the plots and images in his crackling thoughts. He saw the first stroke of the fight, he saw Gwaay's litter unguarded, and then as if he had seen entire a winning combination of chess and been hypnotized by it, he made his move without another cogitation.

Widely circling the fight and moving swiftly in the shadows like a weasel, he mounted the three steps by the wall and headed straight for the litter.

There were no ideas in his mind at all, but there were some shadowy images distortedly seen as from a great distance—one of himself as a tiny child toddling by night along a wall to Gwaay's crib, to scratch him with a pin.

He did not spare a glance for the tread-slave and it is doubtful if they even saw, or at least took note of him, so rudimentary were their minds.

He leaned eagerly between two of them and curiously surveyed his brother. His nostrils drew in at the stench and his mouth contracted to its tightest sphincter yet still smiled.

He plucked a wide dagger of blued steel from a sheath at his belt and poised it above his brother's face, which by its plagues was almost unrecognizable as such. The honed edges of the dagger were tiny hooks directed back from the point.

The sword-clashing below reached one of its climaxes, but Hasjarl did not mark it.

He said softly, "Open your eyes, Brother. I want you to speak once before I slay you."

There was no reply from Gwaay—not a motion, not a whisper, not a bubble of retching.

"Very well," Hasjarl said harshly, "then die a prim shut-mouth," and he drove down the dagger.

It stopped violently a hairbreadth above Gwaay's upper cheek and the muscles of Hasjarl's arm driving it were stabbingly numbed by the jolt they got.

Gwaay did open his eyes then, which was not very pleasant to behold since there was nothing in them but green ichor.

Hasjarl instantly closed his own eyes, but continued to peer down through the holes of his upper lids.

Then he heard Gwaay's voice like a silver mosquito by his ear saying, "You have made a slight oversight, dear brother. You have chosen the wrong weapon. After our father's burning you swore to me my life was sacrosanct—until you killed me by crushing. 'Until I crush it out,' you said. The gods hear only our words, Brother, not our intentions. Had you come lugging a boulder, like the curious gnome you are, you might have accomplished your aim."

"Then I'll have you crushed!" Hasjarl retorted angrily, leaning his face closer and almost shouting. "Aye, and I'll sit by and listen to your bones crunch—what bones you have left! You're as great a fool as I, Gwaay, for you too after our father's funeral promised not to slay me. Aye, and you're a greater fool, for now you've spilled to me your little secret of how you may be slain."

"I swore not to slay you with spells or steel or venom or with my hand," the bright insect voice of Gwaay replied. "Unlike you, I said nothing at all of crushing."

Hasjarl felt a strange tingling in his flesh while in his nostrils there was an acrid odor like that of lightning mingling with the stink of corruption.

Suddenly Gwaay's hands thrust up to the palms out of his overly rich bedclothes. The flesh was shredding from the finger bones which pointed straight up, invokingly.

Hasjarl almost started back, but caught himself. He'd die, he told himself, before he'd cringe from his brother. He was aware of strong forces all about him.

There was a muffled grating noise and then an odd faintly pattering snowfall on the coverlet and on Hasjarl's neck . . . a thin snowfall of pale gritty stuff . . . grains of mortar. . . .

"Yes, you will crush me, dear brother," Gwaay admitted tranquilly. "But if you would know *how* you will crush me, recall my small special powers . . . or else *look up!*"

Hasjarl turned his head, and there was the great black basalt slab big as the litter rushing down, and the one moment of life left Hasjarl was consumed in hearing Gwaay say, "You are wrong, again, my comrade."

Fafhrd stopped a sword-slash in midcourse when he heard the crash and the Mouser almost nicked him with his rehearsed parry. They lowered their blades and looked, as did all others in the central section of the Ghost Hall.

Where the litter had been was now only the thick basalt slab mortar-streaked with the litter-poles sticking out from under, and above in the ceiling the rectangular white hole whence the slab had been dislodged. The Mouser thought, *That's a larger thing to move by thinking than a checker or jar, yet the same black substance.*

Fafhrd thought, *Why didn't the whole roof fall?—there's the strangeness.*

Perhaps the greatest wonder of the moment was the four tread-slaves still standing at the four corners, eyes forward, fingers locked across their chests, although the slab had missed them only by inches in its falling.

Then some of Hasjarl's henchmen and sorcerers who had seen their Lord sneak to the litter now hurried up to it, but fell back when they beheld how closely the slab approached the floor and marked the tiny rivulet of blood that ran from under it. Their minds quailed at the thought of those brothers who had hated each other so dearly, and now their bodies locked in an obscene interpenetrating and commingling embrace.

Meanwhile Ivivis came running to the Mouser and Friska to Fafhrd to bind up their wounds, and were astonished and mayhap a shade irked to be told there were none. Kewissa and Brilla came too and Fafhrd with one arm around Friska reached out the wine-bloody hand of the other and softly closed it around Kewissa's wrist, smiling at her friendlily.

Then the great muffled gong-note sounded again and the twin pillars of white flame briefly roared to the ceiling to either side of Flindach. They showed by their glare that many men had entered by the narrow archway behind Flindach and now stood around him: stout guardsmen from the companies of the Keep with weapons at the ready, and several of his own sorcerers.

As the flame-pillars swiftly shrank, Flindach imperiously raised hand and resonantly spoke:

"The stars which may not be cheated foretold the doom of the Lord of Quarmall. All of you heard those two"—he pointed toward the shattered litter—"proclaim themselves Lord of Quarmall. So the stars are twice satisfied. And the gods, who hear our words to each tiniest whisper, and order our fates by them, are content. It remains that I reveal to you the next Lord of Quarmall."

He pointed at Kewissa and intoned, "*The next Lord of Quarmall but one* sleeps and waxes in the womb of her, wife of the Quarmal so lately honored with burnings and immolations and ceremonious rites."

Kewissa shrank and her blue eyes went wide. Then she began to beam.

Flindach continued, "It still remains that I reveal to you *the next Lord of Quarmall*, who shall tutor Queen Kewissa's babe until he arrives at manhood a perfect king and all-wise sorcerer, under whom our buried realm will enjoy perpetual inward peace and outward-raiding prosperity."

Then Flindach reached behind his left shoulder. All thought he purposed to draw forward the Cowl of Death over his head and brows and hideous warty winy cheeks for some still more solemn speaking. But instead he grasped his neck by the short hairs of the nape and drew it upward and forward and his scalp and all his hair with it, and then the skin of his face came off with his scalp as he drew his hand down and to the side, and there was revealed, sweat-gleaming a little, the unblemished face and jutting nose and full mobile smiling lips of Quarmal, while his terrible blood-red white-irised eyes gazed at them all mildly.

"I was forced to visit Limbo for a space," he explained with a solemn yet genial fatherly familiarity, "while others were Lords of Quarmall in my stead and the stars sent down their spears. It was best so, though I lost two sons by it. Only so might our land be saved from ravenous self-war."

He held up for all to see the limp mask with empty lash-fringed eyeholes and purple-blotched left cheek and wart-triangled right. He said, "And now I bid you all honor great and puissant Flindach, the loyalest Master of Magicians a king ever had, who lent me his face for a necessary deception and his body to be burned for mine with waxen mask of mine to cover his poor head-front, which had sacrificed all. In solemnly supervising my own high flaming obsequies, I honored only Flindach. For him my women burned. This his face, well preserved by my own skills as flayer and swift tanner, will hang forever in place of honor in our halls, while the spirit of Flindach holds my chair for me in the Dark World beyond the stars, a Lord Paramount there until I come, and eternally a Hero of Quarmall."

Before my cheering or hailing could be started—which would have taken a little while, since all were much bemused—Fafhrd cried out, "Oh cunningest king, I honor you and your babe so highly and the Queen who carries him in her womb that I will guard her moment by moment, not moving a pace from her, until I and my small comrade here are well outside Quarmall—say a mile—together with horses for our conveyance and with the treasures promised us by those two late kings." And he gestured as Quarmal had toward the crushed litter.

The Mouser had been about to launch at Quarmal some subtly intimidating remarks about his own skills as a sorcerer in blasting Gwaay's eleven. But now he decided that Fafhrd's words were sufficient and well-spoken, save for the slighting reference to himself, and he held his peace.

Kewissa started to withdraw her hand from Fafhrd's, but he tightened his grip just a little and she looked at him with understanding. In fact, she called brightly to Quarmal, "Oh Lord Husband, this man saved my life and your son's from Hasjarl's fiends in a storeroom of the Keep. I trust him," while Brilla, dabbing tears of joy from his eyes with his undersleeve, seconded her with, "My very dear Lord, she speaks only nakedest truth, bare as a newborn babe or new-wed wife."

Quarmal raised his hand a little, reprovingly, as if such speaking

were unnecessary and somewhat out of place, and smiling thinly at
Fafhrd and the Mouser said, "It shall be as you have spoken. I am
neither ungenerous nor unperceptive. Know that it was not altogether by chance that my late sons unbeknown to each other hired
you two friends—also mutually unknowing—to be their champions.
Furthermore know that I am not altogether unaware of the curiosities
of Ningauble of the Seven Eyes or of the spells of Sheelba of the
Eyeless Face. We grandmaster sorcerers have a— But to speak more
were only to kindle the curiosity of the gods and alert the trolls and
attract the attention of the restless hungry Fates. Enough is enough."

Looking at Quarmal's slitted eyes, the Mouser was glad he had not
boasted and even Fafhrd shivered a little.

Fafhrd cracked whip above the four-horse team to set them pulling
the high-piled wagon more briskly through this black sticky stretch
of road deeply marked with cart tracks and the hoofprints of oxen, a
mile from Quarmall. Friska and Ivivis were turned around on the seat
beside him to wave as long a farewell as they might to Kewissa and
the eunuch Brilla, standing at the roadside with four impassive
guardsmen of Quarmall, to whom they had but now been released.

The Gray Mouser, sprawled on his stomach atop the load, waved
too, but only with his left hand—in his right he held a cocked crossbow while his eyes searched the trees about for sign of ambush.

Yet the Mouser was not truly apprehensive. He thought that
Quarmal would hardly be apt to try any tricks against such a proven
warrior and sorcerer as himself—or Fafhrd too, of course. The old
Lord had shown himself a most gracious host during the last few
hours, plying them with rare wines and loading them with rich gifts
beyond what they'd asked or what the Mouser had purloined in advance, and even offering them other girls in addition to Ivivis and
Friska—a benison which they'd rejected, with some inward regrets,
after noting the glares in the eyes of those two. Twice or thrice
Quarmal had smiled in too tiger-friendly a fashion, but at such times
Fafhrd had stood a little closer to Kewissa and emphasized his light
but inflexible grip on her, to remind the old Lord that she and the
prince she carried were hostages for his and the Mouser's safety.

As the mucky road curved up a little, the towers of Quarmall came
into view above the treetops. The Mouser's gaze drifted to them and
he studied the lacy pinnacles thoughtfully, wondering whether he'd
ever see them again. Suddenly the whim seized him to return to
Quarmall straightway—yes, to slip off the back of the load and run
there. What did the outer world hold half so fine as the wonders of

that subterranean kingdom?—it's mazy mural-pictured tunnelings a man might spend his life tracing . . . its buried delights . . . even its evils beautiful . . . its delicious infinitely varied blacks . . . its hidden fan-driven air. . . . Yes, suppose he dropped down soundlessly this very moment . . .

There was a flash, a brilliant scintillation from the tallest keep. It pricked the Mouser like a goad and he loosed his hold and let himself slide backward off the load. But just at that instant the road turned and grew firm and the trees moved higher, masking the towers, and the Mouser came to himself and grabbed hold again before his feet touched the road and he hung there while the wheels creaked merrily and cold sweat drenched him.

Then the wagon stopped and the Mouser dropped down and took three deep breaths and then hastened forward to where Fafhrd had descended too and was busy with the harness of the horses and their traces.

"Up again, Fafhrd, and whip up!" he cried. "This Quarmal is a cunninger witch than I guessed. If we waste time by the way, I fear for our freedom and our souls!"

"You're telling me?" Fafhrd retorted. "This road winds and there'll be more sticky stretches. Trust a wagon's speed?—pah! We'll uncouple the four horses and taking only simplest victuals and the smallest and most precious of the treasure, gallop across the moor away from Quarmall straight as the crow flies. That way we *should* dodge ambush and outrun ranging pursuit. Friska, Ivivis! Spring to it, all!"

THE SWORDS OF LANKHMAR

AUTHOR'S NOTE

Fafhrd and the Mouser are rogues through and through, though each has in him a lot of humanity and at least a diamond chip of the spirit of true adventure. They drink, they feast, they wench, they brawl, they steal, they gamble, and surely they hire out their swords to powers that are only a shade better, if that, than the villains. It strikes me (and something might be made of this) that Fafhrd and the Gray Mouser are almost at the opposite extreme from the heroes of Tolkien. My stuff is at least equally as fantastic as his, but it's an earthier sort of fantasy with a strong seasoning of "black fantasy"—or of black humor, to use the current phrase for something that was once called gallows' humor and goes back a long, long way. Though with their vitality, appetites, warm sympathies, and imagination, Fafhrd and the Mouser are anything but "sick" heroes.

One of the original motives for conceiving Fafhrd and the Mouser was to have a couple of fantasy heroes closer to true human stature than supermen like Conan and Tarzan and many another. In a way they're a mixture of Cabell and Eddison, if we must look for literary ancestors. Fafhrd and the Mouser have a touch of Jurgen's cynicism and anti-romanticism, but they go on boldly having adventures—one more roll of the dice with destiny and death. While the characters they most parallel in *The Worm Ouroboros* are Corund and Gro, yet I don't think they're touched with evil as those two, rather they're rogues in a decadent world where you have to be a rogue to survive; perhaps, in legendry, Robin Hood comes closest to them, though they're certainly a pair of lone-wolf Robin Hoods. . . .

FRITZ LEIBER

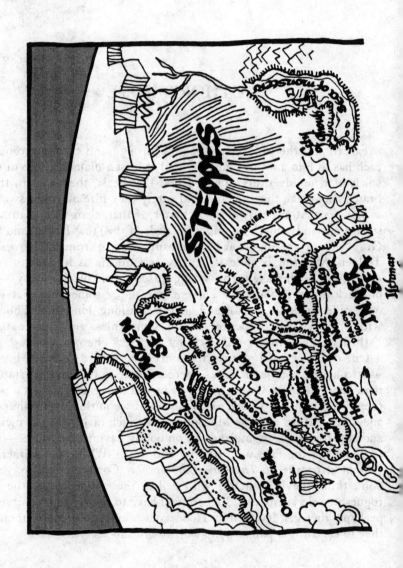

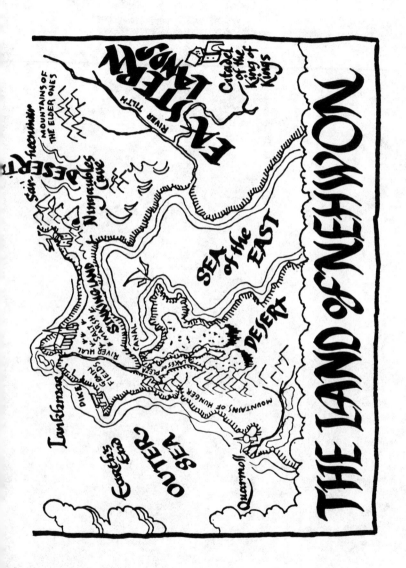

I

"I SEE WE'RE expected," the small man said, continuing to stroll to-ward the large open gate in the long, high, ancient wall. As if by chance, his hand brushed the hilt of his long, slim rapier.

"At over a bowshot distance how can you—" the big man began. "I get it. Bashabeck's orange headcloth. Stands out like a whore in church. And where Bashabeck is, his bullies are. You should have kept your dues to the Thieves Guild paid up."

"It's not so much the dues," the small man said. "It slipped my mind to split with them after the last job, when I lifted those eight diamonds from the Spider God's temple."

The big man sucked his tongue in disapproval. "I sometimes won-der why I associate with a faithless rogue like you."

The small man shrugged. "I was in a hurry. The Spider God was after me."

"Yes, I seem to recall he sucked the blood of your lookout man. You've got the diamonds to make the payoff now, of course?"

"My purse is as bulging as yours," the small man asserted. "Which is exactly as much as a drunk's wineskin the morning after. Unless you're holding out on me, which I've long suspected. Incidentally, isn't that grossly fat man—the one between the two big-shouldered bravos—the keeper of the Silver Eel tavern?"

The big man squinted, nodded, then rocked his head disgustedly. "To make such a to-do over a brandy tab."

"Especially when it couldn't have been much more than a yard long," the small man agreed. "Of course there were those two full casks of brandy you smashed and set afire the last night you were brawling at the Eel."

"When the odds are ten to one against you in a tavern fight, you have to win by whatever methods come easiest to hand," the big man protested. "Which I'll grant you are apt at times to be a bit bizarre."

He squinted ahead again at the small crowd ranged around the square inside the open gate. After a while he said, "I also make out Rivis Rightby the swordsmith . . . and just about all the other creditors any two men could have in Lankhmar. And each with his hired thug or three." He casually loosened in its scabbard his somewhat huge weapon, shaped like a rapier, but heavy almost as a broadsword. "Didn't you settle *any* of our bills before we left Lankhmar the last time? I was dead broke, of course, but you must have had money from all those earlier jobs for the Thieves Guild."

"I paid Nattick Nimblefingers in full for mending my cloak and for a new gray silk jerkin," the small man answered at once. He frowned. "There must have been others I paid—oh, I'm sure there were, but I can't recall them at the moment. By the by, isn't that tall rangy wench—half behind the dainty man in black—one you were in trouble with? Her red hair stands out like a . . . like a bit of Hell. And those three other girls—each peering over her besworded pimp's shoulder like the first—weren't you in trouble with them also when we last left Lankhmar?"

"I don't know what you mean by trouble," the big man complained. "I rescued them from their protectors, who were abusing them dreadfully. Believe me, I trounced those protectors and the girls laughed. Thereafter I treated them like princesses."

"You did indeed—and spent all your cash and jewels on them, which is why you were broke. But one thing you didn't do for them: you didn't become their protector in turn. So they had to go back to their former protectors, which has made them justifiably angry at you."

"I should have become a pimp?" the big man objected. "Women!" Then, "I see a few of *your* girls in the crowd. Neglect to pay them off?"

"No, borrowed from them and forgot to return the money," the small man explained. "Hi-ho, it certainly appears that the welcoming committee is out in force."

"I told you we should have entered the city by the Grand Gate, where we'd have been lost in the numbers," the big man grumbled. "But no, I listened to you and came to this godforsaken End Gate."

"Wrong," the other said. "At the Grand Gate we wouldn't have been able to tell our foes from the bystanders. Here at least we know that everyone is against us, except for the Overlord's gate watch, and I'm not too sure of them—at the least they'll have been bribed to take no notice of our slaying."

"Why should they all be so hot to slay us?" the big man argued. "For all they know we may be coming home laden with rich treasures garnered from many a high adventure at the ends of the earth. Oh, I'll admit that three or four of them may also have a private grudge, but—"

"They can see we haven't a train of porters or heavily-laden mules," the small man interrupted reasonably. "In any case they know that after slaying us, they can pay themselves off from any treasure we may have and split the remainder. It's the rational procedure, which all civilized men follow."

"Civilization!" the big man snorted. "I sometimes wonder—"

"—why you ever climbed south over the Trollstep Mountains and got your beard trimmed and discovered that there were girls without hair on their chests," the small man finished for him. "Hey, I think our creditors and other haters have hired a third S besides swords and staves against us."

"Sorcery?"

The small man drew a coil of thin yellow wire from his pouch. He said, "Well, if those two graybeards in the second-story windows aren't wizards, they shouldn't scowl so ferociously. Besides, I can make out astrological symbols on the one's robe and see the glint of the other's wand."

They were close enough now to the End Gate that a sharp eye could guess at such details. The guardsmen in browned-iron mail leaned on their pikes impassively. The faces of those lining the small square beyond the gateway were impassive too, but grimly so, except for the girls, who smiled with venom and glee.

The big man said grumpily, "So they'll slay us by spells and incantations. Failing which, they'll resort to cudgels and gizzard-cutters." He shook his head. "So much hate over a little cash. Lankhmarts are ingrates. They don't realize the tone we give their city, the excitement we provide."

The small man shrugged. "This time they're providing the excitement for us. Playing host, after a fashion." His fingers were deftly making a slipknot in one end of the pliant wire. His steps slowed a trifle. "Of course," he mused, "we don't have to return to Lankhmar."

The big man bristled. "Nonsense, we must! To turn back now would be cowardly. Besides, we've done everything else."

"There must be a few adventures left outside Lankhmar," the small man objected mildly, "if only little ones, suitable for cowards."

"Perhaps," the big man agreed, "but big or little, they all have a way of beginning in Lankhmar. Whatever are you up to with that wire?"

The small man had tightened the slipknot around the pommel of his rapier and let the wire trail behind him, flexible as a whip. "I've grounded my sword," he said. "Now any death-spell launched against me, striking my drawn sword first, will be discharged into the ground."

"Giving Mother Earth a tickle, eh? Watch out you don't trip over it." The warning seemed well-advised—the wire was fully a half score yards long.

"And don't you step on it. 'Tis a device Sheelba taught me."

"You and your swamp-rat wizard!" the big man mocked. "Why isn't he at your side now, making some spells for us?"

"Why isn't Ningauble at your side, doing the same?" the small man counter-asked.

"He's too fat to travel." They were passing the blank-faced guardsmen. The atmosphere of menace in the square beyond thickened like a storm. Suddenly the big man grinned broadly at his comrade. "Let's not hurt any of them too seriously," he said in a somewhat loud voice. "We don't want our return to Lankhmar beclouded."

As they stepped into the open space walled by hostile faces, the storm broke without delay. The wizard in the star-symboled robe howled like a wolf and lifting his arms high above his head, threw them toward the small man with such force that one expected his hands to come off and fly through the air. They didn't, but a bolt of bluish fire, wraithlike in the sunlight, streamed from his out-flung fingers. The small man had drawn his rapier and pointed it at the wizard. The blue bolt crackled along the slim blade and then evidently did discharge itself into the ground, for he only felt a stinging thrill in his hand.

Rather unimaginatively the wizard repeated his tactics, with the same result, and then lifted his hands for a third bolt-hurling. By this time the small man had got the rhythm of the wizard's actions and just as the hands came down, he flipped the long wire so that it curled against the chests and faces of the bullies around the orange-turbaned

Bashabeck. The blue stuff, whatever it was, went crackling into them from the wire and with a single screech each they fell down writhing.

Meanwhile the other sorcerer threw his wand at the big man, quickly following it with two more which he plucked from the air. The big man, his own out-size rapier drawn with surprising speed, awaited the first wand's arrival. Somewhat to his surprise, it had in flight the appearance of a silver-feathered hawk stooping with silver talons forward-pointing to strike. As he continued to watch it closely, its appearance changed to that of a silvery, long knife with this addition: that it had a silvery wing to either side.

Undaunted by this prodigy and playing the point of his great rapier as lightly as a fencing foil, the big man deftly deflected the first flying dagger so that it transfixed the shoulder of one of the bullies flanking the keeper of the Silver Eel. He treated the second and third flying dagger in the same fashion, so that two other of his foes were skewered painfully though unfatally.

They screeched too and collapsed, more from terror of such supernatural weapons than the actual severity of their wounds. Before they hit the cobbles, the big man had snatched a knife from his belt and hurled it left-handed at his sorcerous foe. Whether the graybeard was struck or barely managed to dodge, he at any rate dropped out of sight.

Meanwhile the other wizard, with continuing lack of imagination or perhaps mere stubbornness, directed a fourth bolt at the small man, who this time whipped upward the wire grounding his sword so that it snapped at the very window from which the blue bolt came. Whether it actually struck the wizard or only the window frame, there was a great crackling there and a bleating cry and that wizard dropped out of sight also.

It is to the credit of the assembled bullies and bravos that they hesitated hardly a heartbeat at this display of reflected death-spells, but urged on by their employers—and the pimps by their whores— they rushed in, lustily trampling the wounded and thrusting and slashing and clubbing with their various weapons. Of course, they had something of a fifty-to-two advantage; still, it took a certain courage.

The small man and the big man instantly placed themselves back to back and with lightning-like strokes stood off the first onset, seeking to jab as many faces and arms as they could rather than make the blows deep and mortal. The big man now had in his left hand a short-handled axe, with whose flat he rapped some skulls for variety, while the small man was supplementing his fiendishly pricking rapier with a long knife whose dartings were as swift as those of a cat's paw.

At first the greater number of the assaulters was a positive hindrance to them—they got into each other's way—while the greatest danger to the two fighting back-to-back was that they might be overwhelmed by the mere mass of their wounded foes, pushed forward enthusiastically by comrades behind. Then the battling got straightened out somewhat, and for a while it looked as if the small and big man would have to use more deadly strokes—and perhaps nevertheless be cut down. The clash of tempered iron, the stamp of boots, the fighting-snarls from twisted lips, and the excited screeches of the girls added up to a great din, which made the gate guard look about nervously.

But then the lordly Bashabeck, who had at last deigned to take a hand, had an ear taken off and his collarbone on that side severed by a gentle swipe of the big man's axe, while the girls—their sense of romance touched—began to cheer on the outnumbered two, at which their pimps and bullies lost heart.

The attackers wavered on the verge of panic. There was a sudden blast of six trumpets from the widest street leading into the square. The great skirling sound was enough to shatter nerves already frayed. The attackers and their employers scattered in all other directions, the pimps dragging their fickle whores, while those who had been stricken by the blue lightning and the winged daggers went crawling after them.

In a short time the square was empty, save for the two victors, the line of trumpeters in the street mouth, the line of guards outside the gateway now facing away from the square as if nothing at all had happened—and a hundred and more pairs of eyes as tiny and red-glinting black as wild cherries, which peered intently from between the grills of street drains and from various small holes in the walls and even from the rooftops. But who counts or even notices rats?—especially in a city as old and vermin-infested as Lankhmar.

The big man and the small man gazed about fiercely a bit longer. Then, regaining their breaths, they laughed uproariously, sheathed their weapons, and faced the trumpeters with a guarded yet relaxed curiosity.

The trumpeters wheeled to either side. A line of pikemen behind them executed the same movement, and there strode forward a venerable, clean-shaven, stern-visaged man in a black toga narrowly bordered with silver.

He raised his hand in a dignified salute. He said gravely, "I am chamberlain of Glipkerio Kistomerces, Overlord of Lankhmar, and here is my wand of authority." He produced a small silver wand tipped with a five-pointed bronze emblem in the form of a starfish.

The two men nodded slightly, as though to say, "We accept your statement for what it's worth."

The chamberlain faced the big man. He drew a scroll from his toga, unrolled, it, scanned it briefly, then looked up. "Are you Fafhrd the northern barbarian and brawler?"

The big man considered that for a bit, then said, "And if I am—"

The chamberlain turned toward the small man. He once more consulted his parchment. "And are you—your pardon, but it's written here—that mongrel and long-suspected burglar, cutpurse, swindler and assassin, the Gray Mouser?"

The small man fluffed his gray cape and said, "If it's any business of yours—well, he and I might be connected in some way."

As if those vaguest answers settled everything, the chamberlain rolled up his parchment with a snap and tucked it inside his toga. "Then my master wishes to see you. There is a service which you can render him, to your own considerable profit."

The Gray Mouser inquired, "If the all-powerful Glipkerio Kistomerces has need of us, why did he allow us to be assaulted and for all he might know slain by that company of hooligans who but now fled this place?"

The chamberlain answered, "If you were the sort of men who would allow yourselves to be murdered by such a mob, then you would not be the right men to handle the assignment, or fulfill the commission, which my master has in mind. But time presses. Follow me."

Fafhrd and the Gray Mouser looked at each other and after a moment they simultaneously shrugged, then nodded. Swaggering just a little, they fell in beside the chamberlain, the pikemen and trumpeters fell in behind them, and the cortege moved off the way it had come, leaving the square quite empty.

Except, of course, for the rats.

II

WITH THE MOTHERLY-generous west wind filling their brown triangular sails, the slim war galley and the five broad-beamed grain ships, two nights out of Lankhmar, coursed north in line ahead across the Inner Sea of the ancient world of Nehwon.

It was late afternoon of one of those mild blue days when sea and sky are the same hue, providing irrefutable evidence for the hypothesis currently favored by Lankhmar philosophers: that Nehwon is a giant bubble rising through the waters of eternity with continents, islands, and the great jewels that at night are the stars all orderly afloat on the bubble's inner surface.

On the afterdeck of the last grain ship, which was also the largest, the Gray Mouser spat a plum skin to leeward and boasted luxuriously, "Fat times in Lankhmar! Not one day returned to the City of the Black Toga after months away adventuring and we get this cushy job from the Overlord himself—and with an advance on pay too."

"I have an old distrust of cushy jobs," Fafhrd replied, yawning and pulling his fur-trimmed jerkin open wider so that the mild wind might trickle more fully through the tangled hair-field of his chest. "And we were rushed out of Lankhmar so quickly that we had not even time to pay our respects to the ladies. Nevertheless I must confess that we might have done worse. A full purse is the best ballast for any manship, especially one bearing letters of marque against ladies."

Ship's Master Slinoor looked back with hooded appraising eyes at the small lithe gray-clad man and his tall, more gaudily accoutered barbarian comrade. The master of *Squid* was a sleek black-robed man of middle years. He stood beside the two stocky black-tunicked bare-legged sailors who held steady the great high-arching tiller that guided *Squid*.

"How much do you two rogues really know of your cushy job?" Slinoor asked softly. "Or rather, how much did the arch-noble Glipkerio choose to tell you of the purpose and dark antecedents of this voyaging?" Two days of fortunate sailing seemed at last to have put the closed-mouthed ship's master in a mood to exchange confidences, or at least trade queries and lies.

From a bag of netted cord that hung by the taffrail, the Mouser speared a night-purple plum with the dirk he called Cat's Claw. Then he answered lightly, "This fleet bears a gift of grain from Overlord Glipkerio to Movarl of the Eight Cities in gratitude for Movarl's sweeping the Mingol pirates from the Inner Sea and mayhap divert-ing the steppe-dwelling Mingols from assaulting Lankhmar across the Sinking Land. Movarl needs grain for his hunter-farmers turned city-man-soldiers and especially to supply his army relieving his border city of Klelg Nar, which the Mingols besiege. Fafhrd and I are, you might say, a small but mighty rearguard for the grain and for certain more delicate items of Glipkerio's gift."

"You mean those?" Slinoor bent a thumb toward the larboard rail.

Those were twelve large white rats distributed among four silver-barred cages. With their silky coats, pale-rimmed blue eyes and espe-cially their short, arched upper lips and two huge upper incisors, they looked like a clique of haughty, bored, inbred aristocrats, and it was in a bored aristocratic fashion that they were staring at a scrawny black kitten which was perched with dug-in claws on the starboard rail, as if to get as far away from the rats as possible, and staring back at them most worriedly.

Fafhrd reached out and ran a finger down the black kitten's back. The kitten arched its spine, losing itself for a moment in sensuous delight, but then edged away and resumed its worried rat-peering— an activity shared by the two black-tunicked helmsmen, who seemed both resentful and fearful of the silver-caged afterdeck passengers.

The Mouser sucked plum juice from his fingers and flicked out his tongue-tip to neatly capture a drop that threatened to run down his chin. Then, "No, I mean not chiefly those high-bred gift-rats," he

replied to Slinoor and kneeling lightly and unexpectedly and touching two fingers significantly to the scrubbed oak deck, he said, "I
mean chiefly *she* who is below, who ousts you from your master's
cabin, and who now insists that the gift-rats require sunlight and
fresh air—which strikes me as a strange way of cosseting burrow-and
shadow-dwelling vermin."

Slinoor's cropped eyebrows rose. He came close and whispered,
"You think the Demoiselle Hisvet may not be merely the conductress
of the rat-gift, but also herself part of Glipkerio's gift to Movarl?
Why, she's the daughter of the greatest grain-merchant in Lankhmar,
who's grown rich selling tawny corn to Glipkerio."

The Mouser smiled cryptically but said nothing.

Slinoor frowned, then whispered even lower, "True, I've heard the
story that Hisvet has already been her father Hisvin's gift to
Glipkerio to buy his patronage."

Fafhrd, who'd been trying to stroke the kitten again with no more
success than to chase it up the aftermast, turned around at that.
"Why, Hisvet's but a child," he said almost reprovingly. "A most
prim and proper miss. I know not of Glipkerio, he seems decadent"—
the word was not an insult in Lankhmar—"but surely Movarl, a
Northerner albeit a forest man, likes only strong-beamed, ripe, complete women."

"Your own tastes, no doubt?" the Mouser remarked, gazing at
Fafhrd with half-closed eyes. "No traffic with childlike women?"

Fafhrd blinked as if the Mouser had dug fingers in his side. Then
he shrugged and said loudly, "What's so special about these rats? Do
they do tricks?"

"Aye," Slinoor said distastefully. "They play at being men. They've
been trained by Hisvet to dance to music, to drink from cups, hold
tiny spears and swords, even fence. I've not seen it—nor would care
to."

The picture struck the Mouser's fancy. He visioned himself small
as a rat, dueling with rats who wore lace at their throats and wrists,
slipping through the mazy tunnels of their underground cities, becoming a great connoisseur of cheese and smoked meats, perchance
wooing a slim rat-queen and being surprised by her rat-king husband
and having to dagger-fight him in the dark. Then he noted one of the
white rats looking at him intently through the silver bars with a cold
inhuman blue eye and suddenly his idea didn't seem amusing at all.
He shivered in the sunlight.

Slinoor was saying, "It is not good for animals to try to be men."
Squid's skipper gazed somberly at the silent white aristos. "Have you

ever heard tell of the legend of—" he began, hesitated, then broke off, shaking his head as if deciding he had been about to say too much.

"A sail!" The call winged down thinly from the crow's nest. "A black sail to windward!"

"What manner of ship?" Slinoor shouted up.

"I know not, master. I see only sail top."

"Keep her under view, boy," Slinoor commanded.

"Under view it is, master."

Slinoor paced to the starboard rail and back.

"Movarl's sails are green," Fafhrd said thoughtfully.

Slinoor nodded. "Ilthmar's are white. The pirates' were red, mostly. Lankhmar's sails once were black, but now that color's only for funeral barges and they never venture out of sight of land. At least I've never known . . ."

The Mouser broke in with, "You spoke of dark antecedents of this voyaging. Why dark?"

Slinoor drew them back against the taffrail, away from the stocky helmsmen. Fafhrd ducked a little, passing under the arching tiller. They looked all three into the twisting wake, their heads bent together.

Slinoor said, "You've been out of Lankhmar. Did you know this is not the first gift-fleet of grain to Movarl?"

The Mouser nodded. "We'd been told there was another. Somehow lost. In a storm, I think. Glipkerio glossed over it."

"There were two," Slinoor said tersely. "Both lost. Without a living trace. There was no storm."

"What then?" Fafhrd asked, looking around as the rats chittered a little. "Pirates?"

"Movarl had already whipped the pirates east. Each of the two fleets was galley-guarded like ours. And each sailed off into fair weather with a good west wind." Slinoor smiled thinly. "Doubtless Glipkerio did not tell you of these matters for fear you might beg off. We sailors and the Lankhmarines obey for duty and the honor of the City, but of late Glipkerio's had trouble hiring the sort of special agents he likes to use for second bowstrings. He has brains of a sort, our overlord has, though he employs them mostly to dream of visiting other world bubbles in a great diving-bell or sealed metallic diving-ship, while he sits with trained girls watching trained rats and buys off Lankhmar's enemies with gold and repays Lankhmar's evermore-greedy friends with grain, not soldiers." Slinoor grunted. "Movarl grows most impatient, you know. He threatens, if the grain comes not, to recall his pirate patrol, league with the land-Mingols and set them at Lankhmar.

"Northerners, even though not snow-dwelling, league with Mingols?" Fafhrd objected. "Impossible!"

Slinoor looked at him. "I'll say just this, ice-eating Northerner. If I did not believe such a league both possible and likely—and Lankhmar thereby in dire danger—I would never have sailed with this fleet, honor and duty or no. Same's true of Lukeen, who commands the galley. Nor do I think Glipkerio would otherwise be sending to Movarl at Kvarch Nar his noblest performing rats and dainty Hisvet."

Fafhrd growled a little. "You say both fleets were lost without a trace?" he asked incredulously.

Slinoor shook his head. "The first was. Of the second, some wreckage was sighted by an Ilthmar trader Lankhmar-bound. The deck of only one grain ship. It had been ripped off its hull, splinteringly— how or by what, the Ilthmart dared not guess. Tied to a fractured stretch of railing was the ship's master, only hours dead. His face had been nibbled, his body gnawed."

"Fish?" the Mouser asked.

"Seabirds?" Fafhrd inquired.

"Dragons?" a third voice suggested, high, breathless, and as merry as a schoolgirl's. The three men turned around, Slinoor with guilty swiftness.

The Demoiselle Hisvet stood as tall as the Mouser, but judging by her face, wrists, and ankles was considerably slenderer. Her face was delicate and taper-chinned with small mouth and pouty upper lip that lifted just enough to show a double dash of pearly tooth. Her complexion was creamy pale except for two spots of color high on her cheeks. Her straight fine hair, which grew low on her forehead, was pure white touched with silver and all drawn back through a silver ring behind her neck, whence it hung unbraided like a unicorn's tail. Her eyes had china whites but darkly pink irises around the large black pupils. Her body was enveloped and hidden by a loose robe of violet silk except when the wind briefly molded a flat curve of her girlish anatomy. There was a violet hood, half thrown back. The sleeves were puffed but snug at the wrists. She was barefoot, her skin showing as creamy there as on her face, except for a tinge of pink about the toes.

She looked them all three one after another quickly in the eye. "You were whispering of the fleets that failed," she said accusingly. "Fie, Master Slinoor. We must all have courage."

"Aye," Fafhrd agreed, finding that a cue to his liking. "Even dragons need not daunt a brave man. I've often watched the sea monsters, crested, horned, and some two-headed, playing in the waves of outer ocean as they broke around the rocks sailors call the Claws. They were not to be feared, if a man remembered always to fix them with a commanding eye. They sported lustily together, the man dragons pursuing the woman dragons and going—" Here Fafhrd took a tremendous breath and then roared out so loudly and wailingly that the two helmsmen jumped—"*Hoongk! Hoongk!*"

"Fie, Swordsman Fafhrd," Hisvet said primly, a blush mantling her cheeks and forehead. "You are most indelicate. The sex of dragons—"

But Slinoor had whirled on Fafhrd, gripping his wrist and now crying, "Quiet, you monster-fool! Know you not we sail tonight by moonlight past the Dragon Rocks? You'll call them down on us!"

"There are no dragons in the Inner Sea," Fafhrd laughingly assured him.

"There's something that tears ships," Slinoor asserted stubbornly.

The Mouser took advantage of this brief interchange to move in on Hisvet, rapidly bowing thrice as he approached.

"We have missed the great pleasure of your company on deck, Demoiselle," he said suavely.

"Alas, sir, the sun mislikes me," she answered prettily. "Now his rays are mellowed as he prepares to submerge. Then too," she added with an equally pretty shudder, "these rough sailors—" She broke off as she saw that Fafhrd and the master of *Squid* had stopped their argument and returned to her. "Oh, I meant not you, dear Master Slinoor," she assured him, reaching out and almost touching his black robe.

"Would the Demoiselle fancy a sun-warmed, wind-cooled black plum of Sarheenmar?" the Mouser suggested, delicately sketching in the air with Cat's Claw.

"I know not." Hisvet said, eyeing the dirk's needlelike point. "I must be thinking of getting the White Shadows below before the evening's chill is upon us."

"True," Fafhrd agreed with a flattering laugh, realizing she must mean the white rats. "But 'twas most wise of you, Little Mistress, to let them spend the day on deck, where they surely cannot hanker so much to sport with the Black Shadows—I mean, of course, their black free commoner brothers, and slim delightful sisters, to be sure, hiding here and there in the hold."

"There are no rats on my ship, sportive or otherwise," Slinoor asserted instantly, his voice loud and angry. "Think you I run a rat-brothel? Your pardon, Demoiselle," he added quickly to Hisvet. "I mean, there are no common rats aboard *Squid*."

"Then yours is surely the first grain ship so blessed," Fafhrd told him with indulgent reasonableness.

The sun's vermilion disk touched the sea to the west and flattened like a tangerine. Hisvet leaned back against the taffrail under the arching tiller. Fafhrd was to her right, the Mouser to her left with the plums hanging just beyond him, near the silver cages. Slinoor had moved haughtily forward to speak to the helmsmen, or pretend to.

"I'll take that plum now, Dirksman Mouser," Hisvet said softly.

As the Mouser turned away in happy obedience and with many a graceful gesture, delicately palpating the net bag to find the most tender fruit, Hisvet stretched her right arm out sideways and without looking once at Fafhrd slowly ran her spread-fingered hand through the hair on his chest, paused when she reached the other side to grasp a fistful and tweak it sharply, then trailed her fingers lightly back across the hair she had ruffled.

Her hand came back to her just as the Mouser turned around. She kissed the palm lingeringly, then reached it across her body to take the black fruit from the point of the Mouser's dirk. She sucked delicately at the prick Cat's Claw had made and shivered.

"Fie, sir," she pouted. "You told me 'twould be sun-warmed and 'tis not. Already all things grow chilly with evening." She looked around her thoughtfully. "Why, Swordsman Fafhrd is all gooseflesh," she announced, then blushed and tapped her lips reprovingly. "Close your jerkin, sir. 'Twill save you from catarrh and perchance from further embarrassment a girl who is unused to any sight of manflesh save in slaves."

"Here is a toastier plum," the Mouser called from beside the bag. Hisvet smiled at him and lightly tossed him back-handed the plum she'd sampled. He dropped that overboard and tossed her the second plum. She caught it deftly, lightly squeezed it, touched it to her lips, shook her head sadly though still smiling, and tossed back the plum. The Mouser, smiling gently too, caught it, dropped it overboard and tossed her a third. They played that way for some time. A shark following in the wake of the *Squid* got a stomachache.

The black kitten came single-footing back along the starboard rail with a sharp eye to larboard. Fafhrd seized it instantly as any good general does opportunity in the heat of battle.

"Have you seen the ship's catling, Little Mistress?" he called, crossing to Hisvet, the kitten almost hidden in his big hands. "Or perhaps we should call the *Squid* the catling's ship, for she adopted it, skipping by herself aboard just as we sailed. Here, Little Mistress. It feels sun-toasted now, warmer than any plum," and he reached the kitten out sitting on the palm of his right hand.

But Fafhrd had been forgetting the kitten's point of view. Its fur stood on end as it saw itself being carried toward the rats and now, as Hisvet stretched out her hand toward it, showing her upper teeth in a tiny smile and saying, "Poor little waif," the kitten hissed fiercely and raked out stiff armed with spread claws.

Hisvet drew back her hand with a gasp. Before Fafhrd could drop the kitten or bat it aside, it sprang to the top of his head and from there onto the highest point of the tiller.

The Mouser darted to Hisvet, crying meanwhile at Fafhrd, "Dolt! Lout! You knew the beast was half wild!" Then, to Hisvet, "Demoiselle! Are you hurt?"

Fafhrd struck angrily at the kitten and one of the helmsmen came back to bat at it too, perhaps because he thought it improper for kittens to walk on the tiller. The kitten made a long leap to the starboard rail, slipped over it, and dangled by two claws above the curving water.

Hisvet was holding her hand away from the Mouser and he was saying, "Better let me examine it, Demoiselle. Even the slightest scratch from a filthy ship's cat can be dangerous," and she was saying, almost playfully, "No, Dirksman, I tell you it's nothing."

Fafhrd strode to the starboard rail, fully intending to flick the kitten overboard, but somehow when he came to do it he found he had instead cupped the kitten's rear in his hand and lifted it back on the rail. The kitten instantly sank its teeth deeply in the root of his thumb and fled up the aftermast. Fafhrd with difficulty suppressed a great yowl. Slinoor laughed.

"Nevertheless, I will examine it," the Mouser said masterfully and took Hisvet's hand by force. She let him hold it for a moment, then snatched it back and drawing herself up said frostily, "Dirksman, you forget yourself. Not even her own physician touches a Demoiselle of Lankhmar, he touches only the body of her maid, on which the Demoiselle points out her pains and symptoms. Leave me, Dirksman."

The Mouser stood huffily back against the taffrail. Fafhrd sucked the root of his thumb. Hisvet went and stood beside the Mouser. Without looking at him, she said softly, "You should have asked me to call my maid. She's quite pretty."

Only a fingernail clipping of red sun was left on the horizon. Slinoor addressed the crow's nest: "What of the black sail, boy?"

"She holds her distance, master," the cry came back. "She courses on abreast of us."

The sun went under with a faint green flash. Hisvet bent her head sideways and kissed the Mouser on the neck, just under the ear. Her tongue tickled.

"Now I lose her, master," the crow's nest called. "There's mist to the northwest. And to the northeast . . . a small black cloud . . . like a black ship specked with light . . . that moves through the air. And now that fades too. All gone, master."

Hisvet straightened her head. Slinoor came toward them muttering, "The crow's nest sees too much." Hisvet shivered and said, "The White Shadows will take a chill. They're delicate, Dirksman." The Mouser breathed, "You are Ecstacy's White Shadow, Demoiselle," then strolled toward the silver cages, saying loudly for Slinoor's benefit, "Might we not be privileged to have a show of them, Demoiselle, tomorrow here on the afterdeck? 'Twould be wondrous instructive to watch you control them." He caressed the air over the cages and said, lying mightily, "My, they're fine handsome fellows." Actually he was peering apprehensively for any of the little spears and swords Slinoor had mentioned. The twelve rats looked up at him incuriously. One even seemed to yawn.

Slinoor said curtly, "I would advise against it, Demoiselle. The sailors have a mad fear and hatred of all rats. 'Twere best not to arouse it."

"But these are aristos," the Mouser objected, while Hisvet only repeated, "They'll take a chill."

Fafhrd, hearing this, took his hand out of his mouth and came hurrying to Hisvet, saying, "Little Mistress, may I carry them below? I'll be gentle as a Kleshite nurse." He lifted between thumb and third finger a cage with two rats in it. Hisvet rewarded him with a smile, saying, "I wish you would, gallant Swordsman. The common sailors handle them too roughly. But two cages are all you may safely carry. You'll need proper help." She gazed at the Mouser and Slinoor.

So Slinoor and the Mouser, the latter much to his distaste and apprehension, must each gingerly take up a silver cage, and Fafhrd two, and follow Hisvet to her cabin below the afterdeck. The Mouser could not forbear whispering privily to Fafhrd, "Oaf! To make rat-grooms of us! May you get rat-bites to match your cat-bite!" At the cabin door Hisvet's dark maid Frix received the cages, Hisvet thanked her three gallants most briefly and distantly and Frix closed the door against them. There was the muffled thud of a bar dropping across it and the jangle of a chain locking down the bar.

Darkness grew on the waters. A yellow lantern was lit and hoisted to the crow's nest. The black war galley *Shark*, its brown sail temporarily furled, came rowing back to fuss at *Clam*, next ahead of *Squid* in line, for being slow in getting up its masthead light, then dropped back by *Squid* while Lukeen and Slinoor exchanged shouts about a black sail and mist and ship-shaped small black clouds and the Dragon Rocks. Finally the galley went bustling ahead again with its Lankhmarines in browned-iron chain mail to take up its sailing station at the head of the column. The first stars twinkled, proof that the sun had not deserted through the waters of eternity to some other world bubble, but was swimming as he should back to the east under the ocean of the sky, errant rays from him lighting the floating star-jewels in his passage.

After moonrise that night Fafhrd and the Mouser each found private occasion to go rapping at Hisvet's door, but neither profited greatly thereby. At Fafhrd's knock Hisvet herself opened the small grille set in the larger door, said swiftly, "Fie, for shame, Swordsman! Can't you see I'm undressing?" and closed it instantly. While when the Mouser asked softly for a moment with "Ecstacy's White Shadow," the merry face of the dark maid Frix appeared at the grille, saying, "My mistress bid me kiss my hand good night to you." Which she did and closed the grille.

Fafhrd, who had been spying, greeted the crestfallen Mouser with a sardonic, "Ecstacy's White Shadow!"

"Little Mistress!" the Mouser retorted scathingly.

"Black Plum of Sarheenmar!"

"Kleshite Nurse!"

Neither hero slept restfully that night and two-thirds through it the *Squid*'s gong began to sound at intervals, with the other ships' gongs replying or calling faintly. When at dawn's first blink the two came on deck, *Squid* was creeping through fog that hid the small sail top. The two helmsmen were peering about jumpily, as if they expected to see ghosts. The sails were barely filled. Slinoor, his eyes dark-circled by fatigue and big with anxiety, explained tersely that the fog had not only slowed but disordered the grain fleet.

"That's *Tunny* next ahead of us. I can tell by her gong note. And beyond *Tunny*, *Carp*. Where's *Clam*? What's *Shark* about? And still not certainly past the Dragon Rocks! Not that I want to see 'em!"

"Do not some captains call them the Rat Rocks?" Fafhrd interposed. "From a rat-colony started there from a wreck?"

"Aye," Slinoor allowed and then grinning sourly at the Mouser, observed, "Not the best day for a rat-show on the afterdeck, is it?

Which is some good from this fog. I can't abide the lolling white brutes. Though but a dozen in number they remind me too much of the Thirteen. Have you ever heard tell of the legend of the Thirteen?"

"I have," Fafhrd said somberly. "A wise woman of the Cold Waste once told me that for each animal kind—wolves, bats, whales, it holds for all and each—there are always thirteen individuals having almost manlike (or demonlike!) wisdom and skill. Can you but find and master this inner circle, the Wise Woman said, then through them you can control all animals of that kind."

Slinoor looked narrowly at Fafhrd and said, "She was not an altogether stupid woman."

The Mouser wondered if for men also there was an inner circle of Thirteen.

The black kitten came ghosting along the deck out of the fog forward. It made toward Fafhrd with an eager mew, then hesitated, studying him dubiously.

"Take for example, cats," Fafhrd said with a grin. "Somewhere in Nehwon today, mayhap scattered but more likely banded together, are thirteen cats of superfeline sagacity, somehow sensing and controlling the destiny of all catkind."

"What's this one sensing now?" Slinoor demanded softly.

The black kitten was staring to larboard, sniffing. Suddenly its scrawny body stiffened, the hair rising along its back and its skimpy tail a-bush.

"Hoongk!"

Slinoor turned to Fafhrd with a curse, only to see the Northerner staring about shut-mouthed and startled. Clearly *he* had not bellowed.

III

Out of the fog to larboard came a green serpent's head big as a horse's, with white dagger teeth fencing red mouth horrendously agape. With dreadful swiftness it lunged low past Fafhrd on its endless yellow neck, its lower jaw loudly scraping the deck, and the white daggers clashed on the black kitten.

Or rather, on where the kitten had just been. For the latter seemed not so much to leap as to lift itself, by its tail perhaps, onto the starboard rail and thence vanished into the fog at the top of the aftermast in at most three more bounds.

The helmsmen raced each other forward. Slinoor and the Mouser threw themselves against the starboard taffrail, the unmanned tiller swinging slowly above them affording some sense of protection against the monster, which now lifted its nightmare head and swayed it this way and that, each time avoiding Fafhrd by inches. Apparently it was searching for the black kitten or more like it.

Fafhrd stood frozen, at first by sheer shock, then by the thought that whatever part of him moved first would get snapped off.

Nevertheless he was about to jump for it—besides all else the monster's mere stench was horrible—when a second green dragon's head, four times as big as the first with teeth like scimitars, came looming out of the fog. Sitting commandingly atop this second head was a man

dressed in orange and purple, like a herald of the Eastern Lands, with
red boots, cape and helmet, the last with a blue window in it, seemingly of opaque glass.

There is a point of grotesquerie beyond which horror cannot go,
but slips into delirium. Fafhrd had reached that point. He began to
feel as if he were in an opium dream. Everything was unquestionably
real, yet it had lost its power to horrify him acutely.

He noticed as the merest of quaint details that the two greenish
yellow necks forked from a common trunk.

Besides, the gaudily garbed man or demon riding the larger head
seemed very sure of himself, which might or might not be a good
thing. Just now he was belaboring the smaller head, seemingly in
rebuke, with a blunt-pointed, blunt-hooked pike he carried, and roaring out, either under or through his blue red helmet, a gibberish that
might be rendered as:

*"Gottverdammter Ungeheuer!"**

The smaller head cringed away, whimpering like seventeen pup-
pies. The man-demon whipped out a small book of pages and after
consulting it twice (apparently he could see *out* through his blue window) called down in broken, outlandishly accented Lankhmarese,
"What world is this, friend?"

Fafhrd had never before in his life heard that question asked, even
by an awakening brandy guzzler. Nevertheless in his opium-dream
mood he answered easily enough, "The world of Nehwon, oh sorcerer!"

*"Got set dank!"*** the man-demon gibbered.

Fafhrd asked, "What world do *you* hail from?"

The question seemed to confound the man-demon. Hurriedly consulting his book, he replied, "Do you know about other worlds? Don't
you believe the stars are only huge jewels?"

Fafhrd responded, "Any fool can see that the lights in the sky are
jewels, but we are not simpletons, we know of other worlds. The
Lankhmarts think they're bubbles in infinite waters. *I* believe we live
in the jewel-ceilinged skull of a dead god. But doubtless there are
other such skulls, the universe of universes being a great frosty battle-
field."

The tiller, swinging as *Squid* wallowed with sail a-flap, bumped the
lesser head, which twisted around and snapped at it, then shook
splinters from its teeth.

---

* "Goddam monster!" German is a language completely unknown in Nehwon.
** Thank God!"

"Tell the sorcerer to keep it off!" Slinoor shouted, cringing.

After more hurried page-flipping the man-demon called down, "Don't worry, the monster seems to eat only rats. I captured it by a small rocky island where many rats live. It mistook your small black ship's cat for a rat."

Still in his mood of opium-lucidity, Fafhrd called up, "Oh sorcerer, do you plan to conjure the monster to your own skull-world, or world-bubble?"

This question seemed doubly to confound and excite the man-demon. He appeared to think Fafhrd must be a mind reader. With much frantic book-consulting, he explained that he came from a world called simply Tomorrow and that he was visiting many worlds to collect monsters for some sort of museum or zoo, which he called in his gibberish *Hagenbeck's Zietgarten.** On this particular expedition he had been seeking a monster that would be a reasonable facsimile of a wholly mythical six-headed sea-monster that devoured men off the decks of ships and was called Scylla by an ancient fantasy writer named Homer.

"There never was a Lankhmar poet named Homer," muttered Slinoor.

"Doubtless he was a minor scribe of Quarmall or the Eastern Lands," the Mouser told Slinoor reassuringly. Then, grown less fearful of the two heads and somewhat jealous of Fafhrd holding the center of the stage, the Mouser leapt atop the taffrail and cried, "Oh, sorcerer, with what spells will you conjure your Little Scylla back to, or perhaps I should say ahead to your Tomorrow bubble? I myself know somewhat of witchcraft. Desist, vermin!" This last remark was directed with a gesture of lordly contempt toward the lesser head, which came questing curiously toward the Mouser. Slinoor gripped the Mouser's ankle.

The man-demon reacted to the Mouser's question by slapping himself on the side of his red helmet, as though he'd forgotten something most important. He hurriedly began to explain that he traveled between worlds in a ship (or space-time engine, whatever that might mean) that tended to float just above the water—"a black ship with little lights and masts"—and that the ship had floated away from him in another fog a day ago while he'd been absorbed in taming the newly captured sea-monster. Since then the man-demon, mounted on

---

* Literally, in German, "Hagenbeck's Time garden," apparently derived from *Tiergarten*, which means animal-garden, or zoo.

his now-docile monster, had been fruitlessly searching for his lost vehicle.

The description awakened a memory in Slinoor, who managed to nerve himself to explain audibly that last sunset *Squid*'s crow's nest had sighted just such a ship floating or flying to the northeast.

The man-demon was voluble in his thanks and after questioning Slinoor closely announced (rather to everyone's relief) that he was now ready to turn his search eastward with new hope.

"Probably I will never have the opportunity to repay your courtesies," he said in parting. "But as you drift through the waters of eternity at least carry with you my name: Karl Treuherz of Hagenbeck's."

Hisvet, who had been listening from the middeck, chose that moment to climb the short ladder that led up to the afterdeck. She was wearing an ermine smock and hood against the chilly fog.

As her silvery hair and pale lovely features rose above the level of the afterdeck the smaller dragon's head, which had been withdrawing decorously, darted at her with the speed of a serpent striking. Hisvet dropped. Woodwork rended loudly.

Backing off into the fog atop the larger and rather benign-eyed head, Karl Treuherz gibbered as never before and belabored the lesser head mercilessly as it withdrew.

Then the two-headed monster with its orange-and-purple mahout could be dimly seen moving around *Squid*'s stern eastward into thicker fog, the man-demon gibbering gentlier what might have been an excuse and farewell: *"Es tut mir sehr leid! Aber dankeschoen, dankeschoen!"*[*]

With a last gentle *"Hoongk!"* the man-demon dragon-dragon assemblage faded into the fog.

Fafhrd and the Mouser raced a tie to Hisvet's side, vaulting down over the splintered rail, only to have her scornfully reject their solicitude as she lifted herself from the oaken middeck, delicately rubbing her hip and limping for a step or two.

"Come not near me, Spoonmen," she said bitterly. "Shame it is when a Demoiselle must save herself from toothy perdition only by falling helter-skelter on that part of her which I would almost shame to show you on Frix. You are no gentle knights, else dragons' heads had littered the afterdeck. Fie, fie!"

Meanwhile patches of clear sky and water began to show to the west and the wind to freshen from the same quarter. Slinoor dashed

---

[*] It was: "I am so very sorry! But thank you, thank you so nicely!"

forward, bawling for his bosun to chase the monster-scared sailors up from the forecastle before *Squid* did herself an injury.

Although there was yet little real danger of that, the Mouser stood by the tiller, Fafhrd looked to the mainsheet. Then Slinoor, hurrying back aft followed by a few pale sailors, sprang to the taffrail with a cry.

The fogbank was slowly rolling eastward. Clear water stretched to the western horizon. Two bowshots north of *Squid* four other ships were emerging in a disordered cluster from the white wall: the war galley *Shark* and the grain ships *Tunny, Carp* and *Grouper*. The galley, moving rapidly under oars, was headed toward *Squid*.

But Slinoor was staring south. There, a scant bowshot away, were two ships, the one standing clear of the fogbank, the other half hid in it.

The one in the clear was *Clam*, about to sink by the head, its gunwales awash. Its mainsail, somehow carried away, trailed brownly in the water. The empty deck was weirdly arched upward.

The fog-shrouded ship appeared to be a black cutter with a black sail.

Between the two ships, from *Clam* toward the cutter, moved a multitude of tiny, dark-headed ripples.

Fafhrd joined Slinoor. Without looking away, the latter said simply, "Rats!" Fafhrd's eyebrows rose.

The Mouser joined them, saying, "*Clam*'s holed. The water swells the grain, which mightily forces up the deck."

Slinoor nodded and pointed toward the cutter. It was possible dimly to see tiny dark forms—rats surely!—climbing over its side from out of the water. "There's what gnawed holes in *Clam*," Slinoor said.

Then Slinoor pointed between the ships, near the cutter. Among the last of the ripple-army was a white-headed one. A second later a small white form could be seen swiftly mounting the cutter's side. Slinoor said, "There's what commanded the hole-gnawers."

With a dull splintering rumble the arched deck of *Clam* burst upward, spewing brown.

"The grain!" Slinoor cried hollowly.

"Now you know what tears ships," the Mouser said.

The black cutter grew ghostlier, moving west now into the retreating fog.

The galley *Shark* went boiling past *Squid*'s stern, its oars moving like the legs of a leaping centipede. Lukeen shouted up, "Here's foul trickery! *Clam* was lured off in the night!"

The black cutter, winning its race with the eastward-rolling fog, vanished in whiteness.

The split-decked *Clam* nosed under with hardly a ripple and angled down into the black and salty depths, dragged by its leaden keel.

With war trumpet skirling, *Shark* drove into the white wall after the cutter.

Clam's masthead, cutting a little furrow in the swell, went under. All that was to be seen now on the waters south of *Squid* was a great spreading stain of tawny grain.

Slinoor turned grim-faced to his mate. "Enter the Demoiselle Hisvet's cabin, by force if need be," he commanded. "Count her white rats!"

Fafhrd and the Mouser looked at each other.

Three hours later the same four persons were assembled in Hisvet's cabin with the Demoiselle, Frix and Lukeen.

The cabin, low-ceilinged enough so that Fafhrd, Lukeen and the mate must move bent and tended to sit hunch-shouldered, was spacious for a grain ship, yet crowded by this company together with the caged rats and Hisvet's perfumed, silver-bound baggage piled on Slinoor's dark furniture and locked sea chests.

Three horn windows to the stern and louver slits to starboard and larboard let in a muted light.

Slinoor and Lukeen sat against the horn windows, behind a narrow table. Fafhrd occupied a cleared sea chest, the Mouser an upended cask. Between them were racked the four rat-cages, whose white-furred occupants seemed as quietly intent on the proceedings as any of the men. The Mouser amused himself by imagining what it would be like if the white rats were trying the men instead of the other way round. A row of blue-eyed white rats would make most formidable judges, already robed in ermine. He pictured them staring down mercilessly from very high seats at a tiny cringing Lukeen and Slinoor, round whom scuttled mouse pages and mouse clerks and behind whom stood rat pikemen in half armor holding fantastically barbed and curvy-bladed weapons.

The mate stood stooping by the open grille of the closed door, in part to see that no other sailors eavesdropped.

The Demoiselle Hisvet sat cross-legged on the swung-down seabed, her ermine smock decorously tucked under her knees, managing to look most distant and courtly even in this attitude. Now and again her right hand played with the dark wavy hair of Frix, who crouched on the deck at her knees.

Timbers creaked as *Squid* bowled north. Now and then the bare feet of the helmsmen could be heard faintly slithering on the after-deck overhead. Around the small trapdoor-like hatches leading below and through the very crevices of the planking came the astringent, toastlike, all-pervasive odor of the grain.

Lukeen spoke. He was a lean, slant-shouldered, cordily muscled man almost as big as Fafhrd. His short coat of browned-iron mail over his simple black tunic was of the finest links. A golden band confined his dark hair and bound to his forehead the browned-iron five-pointed curvy-edged starfish emblem of Lankhmar.

"How do I know *Clam* was lured away? Two hours before dawn I twice thought I heard *Shark*'s own gong-note in the distance, although I stood then beside *Shark*'s muffled gong. Three of my crew heard it too. 'Twas most eerie. Gentlemen, I know the gong-notes of Lankhmar war galleys and merchantmen better than I know my chil-dren's voices. This that we heard was so like *Shark*'s I never dreamed it might be that of another ship—I deemed it some ominous ghost-echo or trick of our minds and I thought no more about it as a matter for action. If I had only had the faintest suspicion. . . ."

Lukeen scowled bitterly, shaking his head, and continued, "Now I know the black cutter must carry a gong shaped to duplicate *Shark*'s note precisely. They used it, likely with someone mimicking my voice, to draw *Clam* out of line in the fog and get her far enough off so that the rat-horde, officered by the white one, could work its will on her without the crew's screams being heard. They must have gnawed twenty holes in her bottom for *Clam* to take on water so fast and the grain to swell so. Oh, they're far shrewder and more persevering than men, the little spade toothed fiends!"

"Midsea madness!" Fafhrd snorted in interruption. "Rats make men scream? And do away with them? Rats seize a ship and sink it? Rats officered and accepting discipline? Why this is the rankest super-stition!"

"You're a fine one to talk of superstition and the impossible, Fafhrd," Slinoor shot at him, "when only this morning you talked with a masked and gibbering demon who rode a two-headed dragon."

Lukeen lifted his eyebrows at Slinoor. This was the first he'd heard of the Hagenbeck episode.

Fafhrd said, "That was travel between worlds. Another matter al-together. No superstition in it."

Slinoor responded skeptically. "I suppose there was no superstition in it either when you told me that you'd heard from the Wise Woman about the Thirteen?"

Fafhrd laughed. "Why, I never believed one word the Wise Woman ever told me. She was a witchy old fool. I recounted her nonsense merely as a curiosity."

Slinoor eyed Fafhrd with slit-eyed incredulity, then said to Lukeen, "Continue."

"There's little more to tell," the latter said. "I saw the rat-battalions swimming from *Clam* to the black cutter. I saw, as you did, their white officer." This with a glare at Fafhrd. "Thereafter I fruitlessly hunted the black cutter two hours in the fog until cramp took my rowers. If I'd found her, I'd not boarded her but thrown fire into her! Aye, and stood off the rats with burning oil on the waters if they tried again to change ships! Aye, and laughed as the furred murderers fried!"

"Just so," Slinoor said with finality. "And what, in your judgment, Commander Lukeen, should we do now?"

"Sink the white archfiends in their cages," Lukeen answered instantly, "before they officer the rape of more ships, or our sailors go mad with fear."

This brought an instant icy retort from Hisvet. "You'll have to sink me first, silver-weighted, oh Commander!"

Lukeen's gaze moved past her to a scatter of big-eared silver unguent jars and several looped heavy silver chains on a shelf by the bed. "That too is not impossible, Demoiselle," he said, smiling hardly.

"There's not one shred of proof against her!" Fafhrd exploded. "Little Mistress, the man is mad."

"No proof?" Lukeen roared. "There were twelve white rats yesterday. Now there are eleven." He waved a hand at the stacked cages and their blue-eyed haughty occupants. "You've all counted them. Who else but this devilish Demoiselle sent the white officer to direct the sharp-toothed gnawers and killers that destroyed *Clam?* What more proof do you want?"

"Yes, indeed!" the Mouser interjected in a high vibrant voice that commanded attention. "There is proof aplenty . . . *if* there were twelve rats in the four cages yesterday." Then he added casually but very clearly, "It is my recollection that there were eleven."

Slinoor stared at the Mouser as though he couldn't believe his ears. "You lie!" he said. "What's more, you lie senselessly. Why, you and Fafhrd and I all spoke of there being twelve white rats!"

The Mouser shook his head. "Fafhrd and I said no word about the exact number of rats. *You* said there were a dozen," he informed Slinoor. "Not twelve, but . . . a dozen. I assumed you were using the expression as a round number, an approximation." The Mouser snapped his fingers. "Now I remember that when you said a dozen I became idly curious and counted the rats. And got eleven. But it seemed to me too trifling a matter to dispute."

"No, there were twelve rats yesterday," Slinoor asserted solemnly and with great conviction. "You're mistaken, Gray Mouser."

"I'll believe my friend Slinoor before a dozen of you," Lukeen put in.

"True, friends should stick together," the Mouser said with an approving smile. "Yesterday I counted Glipkerio's gift-rats and got eleven. Ship's Master Slinoor, any man may be mistaken in his recollections from time to time. Let's analyze this. Twelve white rats divided by four silver cages equals three to a cage. Now let me see . . . I have it! There was a time yesterday when between us, we surely counted the rats—when we carried them down to this cabin. How many were in the cage you carried, Slinoor?"

"Three," the latter said instantly.

"And three in mine," the Mouser said.

"And three in each of the other two," Lukeen put in impatiently. "We waste time!"

"We certainly do," Slinoor agreed strongly, nodding.

"Wait!" said the Mouser, lifting a point-fingered hand. "There was a moment when all of us must have noticed how many rats there were in one of the cages Fafhrd carried—when he first lifted it up, speaking the while to Hisvet. Visualize it. He lifted it like this." The Mouser touched his thumb to his third finger. "How many rats were in that cage, Slinoor?"

Slinoor frowned deeply. "Two," he said, adding instantly, "and four in the other."

"You said three in each just now," the Mouser reminded him.

"I did not!" Slinoor denied. "Lukeen said that, not I."

"Yes, but you nodded, agreeing with him," the Mouser said, his raised eyebrows the very emblem of innocent truthseeking.

"I agreed with him only that we wasted time," Slinoor said. "And we do." Just the same a little of the frown lingered between his eyes and his voice had lost its edge of utter certainty.

"I see," the Mouser said doubtfully. By stages he had begun to play the part of an attorney elucidating a case in court, striding about and frowning most professionally. Now he shot a sudden question: "Fafhrd, how many rats did you carry?"

"Five," boldly answered the Northerner, whose mathematics were not of the sharpest, but who'd had plenty time to count surreptitiously on his fingers and to think about what the Mouser was up to. "Two in one cage, three in the other."

"A feeble falsehood!" Lukeen scoffed. "The base barbarian would swear to anything to win a smile from the Demoiselle, who has him fawning."

"That's a foul lie!" Fafhrd roared, springing up and fetching his head such a great hollow thump on a deck beam that he clapped both hands to it and crouched in dizzy agony.

"Sit down, Fafhrd, before I ask you to apologize to the deck!" the Mouser commanded with heartless harshness. "This is solemn civilized court, no barbarous brawling session! Let's see—three and three and five make . . . eleven. Demoiselle Hisvet!" He pointed an accusing finger straight between her red-irised eyes and demanded most sternly, "How many white rats did you bring aboard *Squid?* The truth now and nothing but the truth!"

"Eleven," she answered demurely. "La, but I'm joyed someone at last had the wit to ask me."

"That I know's not true!" Slinoor said abruptly, his brow once more clear. "Why didn't I think of it before?—'twould have saved us all this bother of questions and counting. I have in this very cabin Glipkerio's letter of commission to me. In it he speaks verbatim of entrusting to me the Demoiselle Hisvet, daughter of Hisvin, and twelve witty white rats. Wait, I'll get it out and prove it to your faces!"

"No need, Ship's Master," Hisvet interposed. "I saw the letter writ and can testify to the perfect truth of your quotations. But most sadly, between the sending of the letter and my boarding of *Squid,* poor Tchy was gobbled up by Glippy's giant boarhound Bimbat." She touched a slim finger to the corner of her eye and sniffed. "Poor Tchy, he was the most winsome of the twelve. 'Twas why I kept to my cabin the first two days." Each time she spoke the name Tchy, the eleven caged rats chittered mournfully.

"Is it Glippy you call our overlord?" Slinoor ejaculated, genuinely shocked. "Oh shameless one!"

"Aye, watch your language, Demoiselle," the Mouser warned severely, maintaining to the hilt his new role of austere inquisitor. "Any familiar relationship between you and our overlord the archnoble Glipkerio Kistomerces does not come within the province of this court."

"She lies like a shrewd subtle witch!" Lukeen asserted angrily. "Thumbscrew or rack, or perchance just a pale arm twisted high behind her back would get the truth from her fast enough!"

Hisvet turned and looked at him proudly. "I accept your challenge, Commander," she said evenly, laying her right hand on her maid's dark head. "Frix, reach out your naked hand, or whatever other part of you the brave gentleman wishes to torture." The dark maid straightened her back. Her face was impassive, lips firmly pressed together, though her eyes searched around wildly. Hisvet continued to Slinoor and Lukeen, "If you know any Lankhmar law at all, you know that a virgin of the rank of Demoiselle is tortured only in the person of her maid, who proves by her steadfastness under extreme pain the innocence of her mistress."

"What did I tell you about her?" Lukeen demanded of them all. "Subtle is too gross a term for her spiderwebby sleights!" He glared at Hisvet and said scornfully, his mouth a-twist, "Virgin!"

Hisvet smiled with cold long-suffering. Fafhrd flushed and although still holding his battered head, barely refrained from leaping up again. Lukeen looked at him with amusement, secure in his knowledge that he could bait Fafhrd at will and that the barbarian lacked the civilized wit to insult him deeply in return.

Fafhrd stared thoughtfully at Lukeen from under his capping hands. Then he said, "Yes, you're brave enough in armor, with your threats against girls and your hot imaginings of torture, but if you were without armor and had to prove your manhood with just one brave girl alone, you'd fall like a worm!"

Lukeen shot up enraged and got himself such a clout from a deck beam that he squeaked shudderingly and swayed. Nevertheless he gripped blindly for his sword at his side. Slinoor grasped that wrist and pulled him down into his seat.

"Govern yourself, Commander," Slinoor implored sternly, seeming to grow in resolution as the rest quarreled and quibbled. "Fafhrd, no more dagger words. Gray Mouser, this is not your court but mine and we are not met to split the hairs of high law but to meet a present peril. Here and now this grain fleet is in grave danger. Our very lives are risked. Much more than that, Lankhmar's in danger if Movarl gets not his gift-grain at this third sending. Last night *Clam* was foully murdered. Tonight it may be *Grouper* or *Squid*, *Shark* even, or no less than all our ships. The first two fleets went warned and well guarded, yet suffered only total perdition."

He paused to let that sink in. Then, "Mouser, you've roused some small doubts in my mind by your eleven-twelving. But small doubts are nothing where home lives and home cities are in peril. For the safety of the fleet and of Lankhmar we'll sink the white rats forthwith and keep close watch on the Demoiselle Hisvet to the very docks of Kvarch Nar."

"Right!" the Mouser cried approvingly, getting in ahead of Hisvet. But then he instantly added, with the air of sudden brilliant inspiration, "*Or* . . . better yet . . . appoint Fafhrd and myself to keep unending watch not only on Hisvet but also on the eleven white rats. That way we don't spoil Glipkerio's gift and risk offending Movarl."

"I'd trust no one's mere watching of the rats. They're too tricksy," Slinoor informed him. "The Demoiselle I intend to put on *Shark*, where she'll be more closely guarded. The grain is what Movarl wants, not the rats. He doesn't know about them, so can't be angered at not getting them."

"But he does know about them," Hisvet interjected. "Glipkerio and Movarl exchange weekly letters by albatross-post. La, but Nehwon grows smaller each year, Ship's Master—ships are snails compared to the great winging mail-birds. Glipkerio wrote of the rats to Movarl, who expressed great delight at the prospective gift and intense anticipation of watching the White Shadows perform. Along with myself," she added, demurely bending her head.

"Also," the Mouser put in rapidly, "I must firmly oppose—most regretfully, Slinoor—the transfer of Hisvet to another ship. Fafhrd's and my commission from Glipkerio, which I can produce at any time, states in clearest words that we are to attend the Demoiselle at all times outside her private quarters. He makes us wholly responsible for her safety—and also for that of the White Shadows, which creatures our overlord states, again in clearest writing, that he prizes beyond their weight in jewels."

"You can attend her in *Shark*," Slinoor told the Mouser curtly.

"I'll not have the barbarian on my ship!" Lukeen rasped, still squinting from the pain of his clout.

"I'd scorn to board such a tricked-out rowboat or oar-worm," Fafhrd shot back at him, voicing the common barbarian contempt for galleys.

"*Also,*" the Mouser cut in again, loudly, with an admonitory gesture at Fafhrd, "it is my duty as a friend to warn you, Slinoor, that in your reckless threats against the White Shadows and the Demoiselle herself, you risk incurring the heaviest displeasure not only of our overlord but also of the most powerful grain-merchant in Lankhmar."

Slinoor answered most simply, "I think only of the City and the grain fleet. You know that," but Lukeen, fuming, spat out a "Hah!" and said scornfully, "The Gray Fool has not grasped that it is Hisvet's very father Hisvin who is behind the rat-sinkings, since he thereby grows rich with the extra nation's-ransoms of grain he sells Glipkerio!"

"Quiet, Lukeen!" Slinoor commanded apprehensively. "This dubious guesswork of yours has no place here."

"Guesswork? Mine?" Lukeen exploded. "It was *your* suggestion, Slinoor—Yes, and that Hisvin plots Glipkerio's overthrow—Aye, and even that he's in league with the Mingols! Let's speak truth for once!"

"Then speak it for yourself alone, Commander," Slinoor said most sober-sharply. "I fear the blow's disordered your brain. Gray Mouser, you're a man of sense," he appealed. "Can you not understand my one overriding concern? We're alone with mass murder on the high seas. We must take measures against it. Oh, will none of you show some simple wit?"

"La, and I will, Ship's Master, since you ask it," Hisvet said brightly, rising to her knees on the seabed as she turned toward Slinoor. Sunlight striking through a louver shimmered on her silver hair and gleamed from the silver ring confining it. "I'm but a girl, unused to problems of war and rapine, yet I have an all-explaining simple thought that I have waited in vain to hear voiced by one of you gentlemen, wise in the ways of violence.

"Last night a ship was slain. You hang the crime on rats—small beasties which would leave a sinking ship in any case, which often have a few whites among them, and which only by the wildest stretch of imagination are picturable as killing an entire crew and vanishing their bodies. To fill the great gaps in this weird theory you make me a sinister rat-queen, who can work black miracles, and now even, it seems, create my poor doting daddy an all-powerful rat-emperor.

"Yet this morning you met a ship's murderer if there ever was one and let him go honking off unchallenged. La, but the man-demon even confessed he'd been seeking a multi-headed monster that would snatch living men from a ship's deck and devour them. Surely he lied when he said his this-world foundling ate small fry only, for it struck at me to devour me—and might earlier have snapped up any of you, except it was sated!

"For what is more likely than that the two-head long-neck dragon ate all *Clam*'s sailors off her deck, snaking them out of the forecastle and hold, if they fled there, like sweetmeats from a compartmented comfit-box, and then scratched holes in *Clam*'s planking? Or perhaps more likely still, that *Clam* tore out her bottom on the Dragon Rocks in the fog and at the same time met the sea-dragon? These are sober possibilities, gentlemen, apparent even to a soft girl and asking no mind-stretch at all."

This startling speech brought forth an excited medley of reactions. Simultaneously the Mouser applauded, "A gem of princess-wit, Demoiselle; oh you'd make a rare strategist." Fafhrd said stoutly, "Most lucid, Little Mistress, yet Karl Treuherz seemed to me an honest demon." Frix told them proudly, "My mistress outthinks you all." The mate at the door goggled at Hisvet and made the sign of the starfish. Lukeen snarled, "She conveniently forgets the black cutter," while Slinoor cried them all down with, "Rat-queen you say jestingly? Rat-queen you are!"

As the others grew silent at that dire accusation, Slinoor gazing grimly fearful at Hisvet, continued rapidly, "The Demoiselle has recalled to me by her speech the worst point against her. Karl Treuherz said his dragon, living by the Rat Rocks, ate only rats. It made no move to gobble us several men, though it had every chance, yet when Hisvet appeared it struck at her at once. It knew her true race."

Slinoor's voice went shudderingly low. "Thirteen rats with the minds of men rule the whole rat race. That's ancient wisdom from Lankhmar's wisest seers. Eleven are these silver-furred silent sharpies, hearing our every word. The twelfth celebrates in the black cutter his conquest of *Clam*. The thirteenth"—and he pointed finger—"is the silver-haired, red-eyed Demoiselle herself!"

Lukeen slithered to his feet at that, crying, "Oh most shrewdly reasoned, Slinoor! And why does she wear such modest shrouding garb except to hide further evidence of the dread kinship? Let me but strip off that cloaking ermine smock and I'll show you a white-furred body and ten small black dugs instead of proper maiden breasts!"

As he came snaking around the table toward Hisvet, Fafhrd sprang up, also cautiously, and pinned Lukeen's arms to his sides in a bear-hug, calling, "Nay, and you touch her, you die!"

Meantime Frix cried, "The dragon was sated with *Clam*'s crew, as my mistress told you. It wanted no more coarse-fibered men, but eagerly seized at my dainty-fleshed darling for a dessert mouthful!"

Lukeen wrenched around until his black eyes glared into Fafhrd's green ones inches away. "Oh most foul barbarian!" he grated. "I forego rank and dignity and challenge you this instant to a bout of quarterstaves on middeck. I'll prove Hisvet's taint on you by trial of battle. That is, if you dare face civilized combat, you great stinking ape!" And he spat full in Fafhrd's taunting face.

Fafhrd's only reaction was to smile a great smile through the spittle running gummily down his cheek, while maintaining his grip of Lukeen and wary lookout for a bite at his own nose.

Thereafter, challenge having been given and accepted, there was naught for even the head-shaking, heaven-glancing Slinoor to do but hurry preparation for the combat or duel, so that it might be fought before sunset and leave some daylight for taking sober measures for the fleet's safety in the approaching dark of night.

As Slinoor, the Mouser and mate came around them, Fafhrd released Lukeen, who scornfully averting his gaze instantly went on deck to summon a squad of his marines from *Shark* to second him and see fair play. Slinoor conferred with his mate and other officers. The Mouser, after a word with Fafhrd, slipped forward and could be seen gossiping industriously with *Squid*'s bosun and the common members of her crew down to cook and cabin boy. Occasionally something might have passed rapidly from the Mouser's hand to that of the sailor with whom he spoke.

IV

Despite Slinoor's urging, the sun was dropping down the western sky before *Squid*'s gongsman beat the rapid brassy tattoo that signalized the imminence of combat. The sky was clear to the west and overhead, but the sinister fogbank still rested a Lankhmar league (twenty bowshots) to the east, paralleling the northward course of the fleet and looking almost as solid and dazzling as a glacier wall in the sun's crosswise rays. Most mysteriously neither hot sun nor west wind dissipated it.

Black-suited, brown-mailed and brown-helmeted marines facing aft made a wall across *Squid* to either side of the mainmast. They held their spears horizontal and crosswise at arm's-length down, making an additional low fence. Black-tunicked sailors peered between their shoulders and boots, or sat with their own brown legs a-dangle on the larboard side of the foredeck, where the great sail did not cut off their view. A few perched in the rigging.

The damaged rail had been stripped away from the break in the afterdeck and there around the bare aftermast sat the three judges: Slinoor, the Mouser, and Lukeen's sergeant. Around them, mostly to larboard of the two helmsmen, were grouped *Squid*'s officers and certain officers of the other ship on whose presence the Mouser had stubbornly insisted, though it had meant time-consuming ferrying by ship's boat.

Hisvet and Frix were in the cabin with the door shut. The Demoiselle had wanted to watch the duel through the open door or even from the afterdeck, but Lukeen had protested that this would make it easier for her to work an evil spell on him, and the judges had ruled for Lukeen. However the grille was open and now and again the sun's rays twinkled on a peering eye or silvered fingernail.

Between the dark spear-wall of marines and the afterdeck stretched a great square of white oaken deck, empty save for the crane-fittings and like fixed gear and level except for the main hatch, which made a central square of deck a hand's span above the rest. Each corner of the larger square was marked off by a black-chalked quarter circle. Either contestant stepping inside a quarter circle after the duel began (or springing on the rail or grasping the rigging or falling over the side) would at once forfeit the match.

In the forward larboard quarter circle stood Lukeen in black shirt and hose, still wearing his gold-banded starfish emblem. By him was his second, his own hawkfaced lieutenant. With his right hand Lukeen gripped his quarterstaff, a heavy wand of close-grained oak as tall as himself and thick as Hisvet's wrist. Raising it above his head he twirled it till it hummed. He smiled fiendishly.

In the after starboard quarter circle, next to the cabin door, were Fafhrd and his second, the mate of *Carp*, a grossly fat man with a touch of the Mingol in his sallow features. The Mouser could not be judge and second both, and he and Fafhrd had diced more than once with *Carp*'s mate in the old days at Lankhmar—losing money to him, too, which at least indicated that he might be resourceful.

Fafhrd took from him now his own quarterstaff, gripping it cross-handed near one end. He made a few slow practice passes with it through the air, then handed it back to *Carp*'s mate and stripped off his jerkin.

Lukeen's marines sniggered to each other at the Northerner handling a quarterstaff as if it were a two-handed broadsword, but when Fafhrd bared his hairy chest *Squid*'s sailors set up a rousing cheer and when Lukeen commented loudly to his second, "What did I tell you? A great hairy-pelted ape, beyond question," and spun his staff again, the sailors booed him lustily.

"Strange," Slinoor commented in a low voice. "I had thought Lukeen to be popular among the sailors."

Lukeen's sergeant looked around incredulously at that remark. The Mouser only shrugged. Slinoor continued to him, "If the sailors knew

your comrade fought on the side of rats, they'd not cheer him." The
Mouser only smiled.

The gong sounded again.

Slinoor rose and spoke loudly: "A bout at quarterstaves with no
breathing spells! Commander Lukeen seeks to prove on the overlord's
mercenary Fafhrd certain allegations against a Demoiselle of
Lankhmar. First man struck senseless or at mercy of his foe loses.
Prepare!"

Two ship's boys went skipping across the middeck, scattering
handfuls of white sand.

Sitting, Slinoor remarked to the Mouser, "A pox on this footling
duel! It delays our action against Hisvet and the rats. Lukeen was a
fool to bridle at the barbarian. Still, when he's drubbed him, there'll
be time enough."

The Mouser lifted an eyebrow. Slinoor said lightly, "Oh didn't you
know? Lukeen will win; that's certain," while the sergeant, nodding
soberly, confirmed, "The Commander's a master of staves. 'Tis no
game for barbarians."

The gong sounded a third time.

Lukeen sprang nimbly across the chalk and onto the hatch, crying,
"Ho, hairy ape! Art ready to double-kiss the oak?—first my staff, then
the deck?"

Fafhrd came shambling out, gripping his wand most awkwardly
and responding, "Your spit has poisoned my left eye, Lukeen, but I
see some civilized target with my right."

Lukeen dashed at him joyously then, feinting at elbow and head,
then rapidly striking with the other end of his staff at Fafhrd's knee
to tumble or lame him.

Fafhrd, abruptly switching to conventional stance and grip, parried the blow and swung a lightning riposte at Lukeen's jaw.

Lukeen got his staff up in time so that the blow hit only his cheek
glancingly, but he was unsettled by it and thereafter Fafhrd was upon
him, driving him back in a hail of barely-parried blows while the
sailors cheered.

Slinoor and the sergeant gaped wide-eyed, but the Mouser only
knotted his fingers, muttering, "Not so fast, Fafhrd."

Then, as Fafhrd prepared to end it all, he stumbled stepping off the
hatch, which changed his swift blow to the head into a slow blow at
the ankles. Lukeen leaped up so that Fafhrd's staff passed under his
feet, and while he was still in the air rapped Fafhrd on the head.

The sailors groaned. The marines cheered once, growlingly.

The unfooted blow was not of the heaviest, nonetheless it three-

quarters stunned Fafhrd and now it was his turn to be driven back
under a pelting shower of swipes. For several moments there was no
sound but the rutch of soft-soled boots on sanded oak and the rapid
dry musical *bong* of staff meeting staff.

When Fafhrd came suddenly to his full senses he was falling away
from a wicked swing. A glimpse of black by his heel told him that his
next inevitable backward step would carry him inside his own quarter circle.

Swift as thought he thrust far behind him with his staff. Its end
struck deck, then stopped against the cabin wall, and Fafhrd heaved
himself forward with it, away from the chalk line, ducking and lunging to the side to escape Lukeen's blows while his staff could not
protect him.

The sailors screamed with excitement. The judges and officers on
the afterdeck kneeled like dice-players, peering over the edge.

Fafhrd had to lift his left arm to guard his head. He took a blow on
the elbow and his left arm dropped limp to his side. Thereafter he
had to handle his staff like a broadsword indeed, swinging it one-
handed in whistling parries and strokes.

Lukeen hung back, playing more cautiously now, knowing
Fafhrd's one wrist must tire sooner than his two. He'd aim a few
rapid blows at Fafhrd, then prance back.

Barely parrying the third of these attacks, Fafhrd riposted recklessly, not with a proper swinging blow, but simply gripping the end
of his staff and lunging. The combined length of Fafhrd and his staff
overtook Lukeen's retreat and the tip of Fafhrd's staff poked him low
in the chest, just on the nerve spot.

Lukeen's jaw dropped, his mouth stayed open wide, and he wavered. Fafhrd smartly rapped his staff out of his fingers and as it
clattered down, toppled Lukeen to the deck with a second almost
casual prod.

The sailors cheered themselves hoarse. The marines growled sur-
lily and one cried, "Foul!" Lukeen's second knelt by him, glaring at
Fafhrd. *Carp*'s mate danced a ponderous jig up to Fafhrd and wafted
the wand out of his hands. On the afterdeck *Squid*'s officers were
glum, though those of the other grain ships seemed strangely jubilant.
The Mouser gripped Slinoor's elbow, urging, "Cry Fafhrd victor,"
while the sergeant frowned prodigiously, hand to temple, saying,
"Well, there's nothing I know of in the *rules* . . ."

At that moment the cabin door opened and Hisvet stepped out,
wearing a long scarlet, scarlet-hooded silk robe.

The Mouser, sensing climax, sprang to starboard, where *Squid*'s gong hung, snatched the striker from the gongsman and clanged it wildly.

Squid grew silent. Then there were pointings and questioning cries as Hisvet was seen. She put a silver recorder to her lips and began to dance dreamily toward Fafhrd, softly whistling with her recorder a high haunting tune of seven notes in a minor key. From somewhere tiny tuned bells accompanied it tinklingly. Then Hisvet swung to one side, facing Fafhrd as she moved around him, and the questioning cries changed to ones of wonder and astonishment and the sailors came crowding as far aft as they could and swinging through the rigging, as the procession became visible that Hisvet headed.

It consisted of eleven white rats walking in single file on their hind legs and wearing little scarlet robes and caps. The first four carried in each forepaw clusters of tiny silver bells which they shook rhythmically. The next five bore on their shoulders, hanging down between them a little, a double length of looped gleaming silver chain—they were very like five sailors lugging an anchor chain. The last two each bore slantwise a slim silver wand as tall as himself as he walked erect, tail curving high.

The first four halted side by side in rank facing Fafhrd and tinkling their bells to Hisvet's piping.

The next five marched on steadily to Fafhrd's right foot. There their leader paused, looked up at Fafhrd's face with upraised paw, and squeaked three times. Then, gripping his end of the chain in one paw, he used his other three to climb Fafhrd's boot. Imitated by his four fellows, he then carefully climbed Fafhrd's trousers and hairy chest.

Fafhrd stared down at the mounting chain and scarlet-robed rats without moving a muscle, except to frown faintly as tiny paws unavoidably tweaked clumps of his chest-hair.

The first rat mounted to Fafhrd's right shoulder and moved behind his back to his left shoulder, the four other rats following in order and never letting slip the chain.

When all five rats were standing on Fafhrd's shoulders, they lifted one strand of the silver chain and brought it forward over his head, most dexterously. Meanwhile he was looking straight ahead at Hisvet, who had completely circled him and now stood piping behind the bell-tinklers.

The five rats dropped the strand, so that the chain hung in a gleaming oval down Fafhrd's chest. At the same instant each rat lifted his scarlet cap as high above his head as his foreleg would reach. Someone cried, "Victor!"

The five rats swung down their caps and again lifted them high, and as if from one throat all the sailors and most of the marines and officers cried in a great shout: "*Victor!*"

The five rats led two more cheers for Fafhrd, the men aboard *Squid* obeying as if hypnotized—though whether by some magic power or simply by the wonder and appropriateness of the rats' behavior, it was hard to tell.

Hisvet finished her piping with a merry flourish and the two rats with silver wands scurried up onto the afterdeck and standing at the foot of the aftermast where all might see, began to drub away at each other in most authentic quarterstaff style, their wands flashing in the sunlight and chiming sweetly when they clashed. The silence broke in rounds of exclamation and laughter. The five rats scampered down Fafhrd and returned with the bell-tinklers to cluster around the hem of Hisvet's skirt. Mouser and several officers were leaping down from the afterdeck to wring Fafhrd's good hand or clap his back. The marines had much ado to hold back the sailors, who were offering each other bets on which rat would be the winner in this new bout.

Fafhrd, fingering his chain, remarked to the Mouser, "Strange that the sailors were with me from the start," and under cover of the hubbub the Mouser smilingly explained, "I gave them money to bet on you against the marines. Likewise I dropped some hints and made some loans for the same purpose to the officers of the other ships—a fighter can't have too big a claque. Also I started the story going round that the whiteys are anti-rat rats, trained exterminators of their own kind, sample of Glipkerio's latest device for the safety of the grain fleets—sailors eat up such tosh."

"Did you first cry victor?" Fafhrd asked.

The Mouser grinned. "A judge take sides? In *civilized* combat? Oh, I was prepared to, but 'twasn't needful."

At that moment Fafhrd felt a small tug at his trousers and looking down saw that the black kitten had bravely approached through the forest of legs and was now climbing him purposefully. Touched at this further display of animal homage, Fafhrd rumbled gently as the kitten reached his belt, "Decided to heal our quarrel, eh, small black one?" At that the kitten sprang up his chest, sunk his little claws in Fafhrd's bare shoulder and, glaring like a black hangman, raked Fafhrd bloodily across the jaw, then sprang by way of a couple of startled heads to the mainsail and rapidly climbed its concave taut brown curve. Someone threw a belaying pin at the small black blot, but it was negligently aimed and the kitten safely reached the masttop.

"I forswear all cats!" Fafhrd cried angrily, dabbling at his chin. "Henceforth rats are my favored beasties."

"Most properly spoken, Swordsman!" Hisvet called gaily from her own circle of admirers, continuing, "I will be pleased by your company and the Dirksman's at dinner in my cabin an hour past sunset. We'll conform to the very letter of Slinoor's stricture that I be closely watched and the White Shadows too." She whistled a little call on her silver recorder and swept back into her cabin with the nine rats close at her heels. The quarterstaving scarlet-robed pair on the afterdeck broke off their drubbing with neither victorious and scampered after her, the crowd parting to make way for them admiringly.

Slinoor, hurrying forward, paused to watch. *Squid*'s skipper was a man deeply bemused. Somewhere in the last half hour the white rats had been transformed from eerie poison-toothed monsters threatening the fleet into popular, clever, harmless animal-mountebanks, whom *Squid*'s sailors appeared to regard as a band of white mascots. Slinoor seemed to be seeking unsuccessfully but unceasingly to decipher how and why.

Lukeen, still looking very pale, followed the last of his disgruntled marines (their purses lighter by many a silver smerduk, for they had been coaxed into offering odds) over the side into *Shark*'s long dinghy, brushing off Slinoor when *Squid*'s skipper would have conferred with him.

Slinoor vented his chagrin by harshly commanding his sailors to leave off their disorderly milling and frisking, but they obeyed him right cheerily, skipping to their proper stations with the happiest of sailor smirks. Those passing the Mouser winked at him and surreptitiously touched their forelocks. *Squid* bowled smartly northward a half bowshot astern of *Tunny*, as she'd been doing throughout the duel, only now she began to cleave the blue water a little more swiftly yet as the west wind freshened and her after sail was broken out. In fact, the fleet began to sail so swiftly now that *Shark*'s dinghy couldn't make the head of the line, although Lukeen could be noted bullying his marine-oarsmen into back-cracking efforts, and the dinghy had finally come to signal *Shark* herself to come back and pick her up— which the war galley achieved only with difficulty, rolling dangerously in the mounting seas and taking until sunset, oars helping sails, to return to the head of the line.

"*He*'ll not be eager to come to *Squid*'s help tonight, or much able to either," Fafhrd commented to the Mouser where they stood by the larboard middeck rail. There had been no open break between them and Slinoor, but they were inclined to leave him the afterdeck, where he stood beyond the helmsmen in bent-head converse with his three officers, who had all lost money on Lukeen and had been sticking close to their skipper ever since.

"Not still expecting *that* sort of peril tonight, are you, Fafhrd?" the Mouser asked with a soft laugh. "We're far past the Rat Rocks."

Fafhrd shrugged and said frowningly, "Perhaps we've gone just a shade too far in endorsing the rats."

"Perhaps," the Mouser agreed. "But then their charming mistress is worth a fib and false stamp or two, aye and more than that, eh, Fafhrd?"

"She's a brave sweet lass," Fafhrd said carefully.

"Aye, and her maid too," the Mouser said brightly. "I noted Frix peering at you adoringly from the cabin entryway after your victory. A most voluptuous wench. Some men might well prefer the maid to the mistress in this instance. Fafhrd?"

Without looking around at the Mouser, the Northerner shook his head.

The Mouser studied Fafhrd, wondering if it were politic to make a certain proposal he had in mind. He was not quite certain of the full nature of Fafhrd's feelings toward Hisvet. He knew the Northerner was a goatish man enough and had yesterday seemed quite obsessed with the love-making they'd missed in Lankhmar, yet he also knew that his comrade had a variable romantic streak that was sometimes thin as a thread yet sometimes grew into a silken ribbon leagues wide in which armies might stumble and be lost.

On the afterdeck Slinoor was now conferring most earnestly with the cook, presumably (the Mouser decided) about Hisvet's (and his own and Fafhrd's) dinner. The thought of Slinoor having to go to so much trouble about the pleasures of three persons who today had thoroughly thwarted him made the Mouser grin and somehow also nerved him to take the uncertain step he'd been contemplating.

"Fafhrd," he whispered, "I'll dice you for Hisvet's favors."

"Why, Hisvet's but a girl—" Fafhrd began in accents of rebuke, then cut off abruptly and closed his eyes in thought. When he opened them, they were regarding the Mouser with a large smile.

"No," Fafhrd said softly, "for truly I think this Hisvet is so balky and fantastic a miss it will take both our most heartfelt and cunning efforts to persuade her to aught. And, after that, who knows? Dicing for such a girl's favors were like betting when a Lankhmar night-lily will open and whether to north or south."

The Mouser chuckled and lovingly dug Fafhrd in the ribs, saying, "There's my shrewd true comrade!"

Fafhrd looked at the Mouser with sudden dark suspicions. "Now don't go trying to get me drunk tonight," he warned, "or sifting opium in my drink."

"Hah, you know me better than that, Fafhrd," the Mouser said with laughing reproach.

"I certainly do," Fafhrd agreed sardonically.

Again the sun went under with a green flash, indicating crystal clear air to the west, though the strange fogbank, now an ominous dark wall, still paralleled their course a league or so to the east.

The cook, crying, "My mutton!" went racing forward past them toward the galley, whence a deliciously spicy aroma was wafting.

"We've an hour to kill," the Mouser said. "Come on, Fafhrd. On our way to board *Squid* I bought a little jar of wine of Quarmall at the Silver Eel. It's still sealed."

From just overhead in the rat-lines, the black kitten hissed down at them in angry menace or perhaps warning.

V

Two hours later the Demoiselle Hisvet offered to the Mouser, "A golden rilk for your thoughts, Dirksman."

She was on the swung-down sea-bed once more, half reclining. The long table, now laden with tempting viands and tall silver wine cups, had been placed against the bed. Fafhrd sat across from Hisvet, the empty silver cages behind him, while the Mouser was at the stern end of the table. Frix served them all from the door forward, where she took the trays from the cook's boys without giving them so much as a peep inside. She had a small brazier there for keeping hot such items as required it and she tasted each dish and set it aside for a while before serving it. Thick dark pink candles in silver sconces shed a pale light.

The white rats crouched in rather disorderly fashion around a little table of their own set on the floor near the wall between the sea-bed and the door, just aft of one of the trapdoors opening down into the grain-redolent hold. They wore little black jackets open at the front and little black belts around their middles. They seemed more to play with than eat the bits of food Frix set before them on their three or four little silver plates and they did not lift their small bowls to drink their wine-tinted water but rather lapped at them and that not very industriously. One or two would always be scampering up onto the bed to be with Hisvet, which made them most difficult to count, even for Fafhrd, who had the best view. Sometimes he got eleven, sometimes ten. At intervals one of them would stand up on the pink coverlet by Hisvet's knees and chitter at her in cadences so like those of human speech that Fafhrd and the Mouser would have to chuckle.

"Dreamy Dirksman, two rilks for your thoughts!" Hisvet repeated, upping her offer. "And most immodestly I'll wager a third rilk they are of me."

The Mouser smiled and lifted his eyebrows. He was feeling very light-headed and a bit uneasy, chiefly because contrary to his intentions he had been drinking much more than Fafhrd. Frix had just served them the main dish, a masterly yellow curry heavy with dark-tasting spices and originally appearing with "Victor" pricked on it with black capers. Fafhrd was devouring it manfully, though not voraciously, the Mouser was going at it more slowly, while Hisvet all evening had merely toyed with her food.

"I'll take your two rilks, White Princess," the Mouser replied airily, "for I'll need one to pay the wager you've just won and the other to fee you for telling me *what* I was thinking of you."

"You'll not keep my second rilk long, Dirksman," Hisvet said merrily, "for as you thought of me you were looking not at my face, but most impudently somewhat lower. You were thinking of those somewhat nasty suspicions Lukeen voiced this day about my secretest person. Confess it now, you were!"

The Mouser could only hang his head a little and shrug helplessly, for she had most truly divined his thoughts. Hisvet laughed and frowned at him in mock anger, saying, "Oh, you are most indelicate minded, Dirksman. Yet at least you can see that Frix, though indubitably mammalian, is not fronted like a she-rat."

This statement was undeniably true, for Hisvet's maid was all dark smooth skin except where black silk scarves narrowly circled her slim body at breasts and hips. Silver net tightly confined her black hair and there were many plain silver bracelets on each wrist. Yet although garbed like a slave, Frix did not seem one tonight, but rather a lady-companion who expertly played at being slave, serving them all with perfect yet laughing, wholly unservile obedience.

Hisvet, by contrast, was wearing another of her long smocks, this of black silk edged with black lace, with a lace-edged hood half thrown back. Her silvery white hair was dressed high on her head in great smooth swelling sweeps. Regarding her across the table, Fafhrd said, "I am certain that the Demoiselle would be no less than completely beautiful to us in whatever shape she chose to present herself to the world—wholly human or somewhat otherwise."

"Now that was most gallantly spoken, Swordsman," Hisvet said with a somewhat breathless laugh. "I must reward you for it. Come to me, Frix." As the slim maid bent close to her, Hisvet yet twined her white hands round the dark waist and imprinted a sweet slow kiss on Frix's lips. Then she looked up and gave a little tap on the shoulder to Frix, who moved smiling around the table and, half kneeling by Fafhrd, kissed him as she had been kissed. He received the token graciously, without unmannerly excitement, yet when Frix would have drawn back, prolonged the kiss, explaining a bit thickly when he released her: "Somewhat extra to return to the sender, perchance." She grinned at him saucily and went to her serving table by the door, saying, "I must first chop the rats their meat, naughty barbarian." While Hisvet discoursed, "Don't seek too much, Bold Swordsman. That was in any case but a small proxy reward for a small gallant speech. A reward with the mouth for words spoken with the mouth. To reward you for drubbing Lukeen and vindicating my honor were a more serious matter altogether, not to be entered on lightly. I'll think of it."

At this point the Mouser, who just had to be saying something but whose fuddled brain was momentarily empty of suitably venturesome yet courteous wit, called out to Frix, "Why chop you the rats their mutton, dusky minx? 'Twould be rare sport to see them slice it for themselves." Frix only wrinkled her nose at him, but Hisvet expounded gravely, "Only Skwee carves with any great skill. The others might hurt themselves, particularly with the meat shifting about in the slippery curry. Frix, reserve a single chunk for Skwee to display us his ability. Chop the rest fine. Skwee!" she called, setting her voice high. "Skwee-skwee-skwee!"

A tall rat sprang onto the bed and stood dutifully before her with forelegs folded across his chest. Hisvet instructed him, then took from a silver box behind her a most tiny carving set of knife, steel and fork in joined treble scabbard and tied it carefully to his belt. Then Skwee bowed low to her and sprang nimbly down to the rats' table.

The Mouser watched the little scene with clouded and heavy-lidded wonder, feeling that he was falling under some sort of spell. At times thick shadows crossed the cabin; at times Skwee grew tall as Hisvet or perhaps it was Hisvet tiny as Skwee. And then the Mouser grew small as Skwee, too, and ran under the bed and fell into a chute that darkly swiftly slid him, not into a dark hold of sacked or loose delicious grain, but into the dark spacious low-ceilinged pleasance of a subterranean rat-metropolis, lit by phosphorus, where robed and long-skirted rats whose hoods hid their long faces moved about mysteriously, where rat-swords clashed behind the next pillar and rat-money chinked, where lewd female rats danced in their fur for a fee, where masked rat-spies and rat-informers lurked, where everyone—every-furry-one—was cringingly conscious of the omniscient overlordship of a supernally powerful Council of Thirteen, and where a rat-Mouser sought everywhere a slim rat-princess named Hisvet-sur-Hisvin.

The Mouser woke from his dinnerdream with a jerk. Somehow he'd surely drunk even more cups than he'd counted, he told himself haltingly. Skwee, he saw, had returned to the rats' table and was standing before the yellow chunk Frix had set on the silver platter at Skwee's end. With the other rats watching him, Skwee drew forth knife and steel with a flourish. The Mouser roused himself more fully with another jerk and shake and was inspired to say, "Ah, were I but a rat, White Princess, so that I might come as close to you, serving you!"

The Demoiselle Hisvet cried, "A tribute indeed!" and laughed with delight, showing—it appeared to the Mouser—a slim pink tongue half splotched with blue and an inner mouth similarly pied. Then she said rather soberly, "Have a care what you wish, for some wishes have been granted," but at once continued gaily, "nevertheless, 'twas most gallantly said, Dirksman. I must reward you. Frix, sit at my right side here."

The Mouser could not see what passed between them, for Hisvet's loosely smocked form hid Frix from him, but the merry eyes of the maid peered steadily at him over Hisvet's shoulder, twinkling like the black silk. Hisvet seemed to be whispering into Frix's ear while nuzzling it playfully.

Meanwhile there commenced the faintest of high *skirrings* as Skwee rapidly clashed steel and knife together, sharpening the latter. The Mouser could barely see the rat's head and shoulders and the tiny glimmer of flashing metal over the larger table intervening. He felt the urge to stand and move closer to observe the prodigy—and perchance glimpse something of the interesting activities of Hisvet and Frix—but he was held fast by a great lethargy, whether of wine or sensuous anticipation or pure magic he could not tell.

He had one great worry—that Fafhrd would out with a cleverer compliment than his own, one so much cleverer that it might even divert Frix's mission to him. But then he noted that Fafhrd's chin had

fallen to his chest, and there came to his ears along with the silvery
klirring the barbarian's gently rumbling snores.

The Mouser's first reaction was pure wicked relief. He remembered gloatingly past times he'd gamboled with generous, gay girls
while his comrade snored sodden. Fafhrd must after all have been
sneaking many extra swigs or whole drinks!

Frix jerked and giggled immoderately. Hisvet continued to whisper
in her ear while Frix giggled and cooed again from time to time,
continuing to watch the Mouser impishly.

Skwee scabbarded the steel with a tiny *clash*, drew the fork with a
flourish, plunged it into the yellow-coated meat-chunk, big as a roast
for him, and began to carve most dexterously.

Frix rose at last, received her tap from Hisvet, and headed around
the table, smiling the while at the Mouser.

Skwee came up with a paper-thin tiny slice of mutton on his fork
and flapped it this way and that for all to see, then brought it close to
his muzzle for a sniff and a taste.

The Mouser in his dreamy slump felt a sudden twinge of apprehension. It had occurred to him that Fafhrd simply couldn't have sneaked
that much extra wine. Why, the Northerner hadn't been out of his
sight the past two hours. Of course blows on the head sometimes had
a delayed effect.

All the same his first reaction was pure angry jealousy when Frix
paused beside Fafhrd and leaned over his shoulder and looked in his
forward-tipped face.

Just then there came a great squeak of outrage and alarm from
Skwee and the white rat sprang up onto the bed, still holding carving
knife and fork with the mutton slice dangling from it.

From under eyelids that persisted in drooping lower and lower, the
Mouser watched Skwee gesticulate with his tiny implements, as he
chittered dramatically to Hisvet in most man-like cadences, and finally lift the petal of mutton to her lips with an accusing squeak.

Then, coming faintly through the chittering, the Mouser heard a
host of stealthy footsteps crossing the middeck, converging on the
cabin. He tried to call Hisvet's attention to it, but found his lips and
tongue numb and unobedient to his will.

Frix suddenly grasped the hair of Fafhrd's forehead and jerked his
head up and back. The Northerner's jaw hung slackly, his eyes fell
open, showing only whites.

There was a gentle rapping at the door, exactly the same as the
cook's boys had made delivering the earlier courses.

A look passed between Hisvet and Frix. The latter dropped

Fafhrd's head, darted to the door, slammed the bar across it and locked the bar with the chain (the grille already being shut) just as something (a man's shoulder, it sounded) thudded heavily against the thick panels.

That thudding continued and a few heartbeats later became much more sharply ponderous, as if a spare mast-section were being swung like a battering ram against the door, which yielded visibly at each blow.

The Mouser realized at last, much against his will, that something was happening that he ought to do something about. He made a great effort to shake off his lethargy and spring up.

He found he could not even twitch a finger. In fact it was all he could do to keep his eyes from closing altogether and watch through lash-blurred slits as Hisvet, Frix and the rats spun into a whirlwind of silent activity.

Frix jammed her serving table against the jolting door and began to pile other furniture against it.

Hisvet dragged out from behind the sea-bed various dark long boxes and began to unlock them. As fast as she threw them open the white rats helped themselves to the small blued-iron weapons they contained: swords, spears, even most wicked-looking blued-iron crossbows with belted cannisters of darts. They took more weapons than they could effectively use themselves. Skwee hurriedly put on a black-plumed helmet that fitted down over his furry cheeks. The number of rats busy around the boxes was ten—that much the Mouser noted clearly.

A split appeared in the middle of the piled door. Nevertheless Frix sprang away from there to the starboard trapdoor leading to the hold and heaved it up. Hisvet threw herself on the floor toward it and thrust her head down into the dark square hole.

There was something terribly animal-like about the movements of the two women. It may have been only the cramped quarters and the low ceiling, but it seemed to the Mouser that they moved by preference on all fours.

All the while Fafhrd's chest-sunk head kept lifting very slowly and then falling with a jerk as he went on snoring.

Hisvet sprang up and waved on the ten white rats. Led by Skwee, they trooped down through the hatch, their blued-iron weapons flashing and once or twice clashing, and were gone in a twinkling. Frix grabbed dark garments out of a curtained niche. Hisvet caught her by the wrist and thrust the maid ahead of her down the trap and then descended herself. Before pulling the hatch down above her, she took a last look around the cabin. As her red eyes gazed briefly at the Mouser, it seemed to him that her forehead and cheeks were grown over with silky white hair, but that may well have been a combination of eyelash-blur and her own disordered hair streaming and streaking down across her face.

The cabin door split and a man's length of thick mast boomed through, overturning the bolstering table and scattering the furniture set on and against it. After the mast-end came piling in three apprehensive sailors followed by Slinoor, holding a cutlass low, and Slinoor's starsman (navigation officer) with a crossbow at the cock.

Slinoor pressed ahead a little and surveyed the scene swiftly yet intently, then said, "Our poppy-dust curry has taken Glipkerio's two lust-besotted rogues, but Hisvet's hid with her nymphy slave-girl. The rats are out of their cages. Search, sailors! Starsman, cover us!"

Gingerly at first, but soon in a rush, the sailors searched the cabin, tumbling the empty boxes and jerking the quilts and mattress off the sea-bed and swinging it up to see beneath, heaving chests away from walls and flinging open the unlocked ones, sweeping Hisvet's wardrobe in great silken armfuls out of the curtained niches in which it had been hanging.

The Mouser again made a mighty effort to speak or move, with no more success than to widen his blurred eye-slits a little. A sailor louted into him and he helplessly collapsed sideways against an arm of his chair without quite falling out of it. Fafhrd got a shove behind and slumped face-down on the table in a dish of stewed plums, his great arms outsweeping unconsciously, upsetting cups and scattering plates.

The starsman kept crossbow trained on each new space uncovered. Slinoor watched with eagle eye, flipping aside silken fripperies with his cutlass point and using it to overset the rats' table, peering the while narrowly.

"There's where the vermin feasted like men," he observed disgustedly. "The curry was set before them. Would they had gorged themselves senseless on it."

"Likely they were the ones to note the drug even through the masking spices of the curry, and warn the women," the starsman put in. "Rats are prodigiously wise to poisons."

As it became apparent neither girls nor rats were in the cabin, Slinoor cried with angry anxiety, "They can't have escaped to the deck—there's the sky-trap locked below besides our guard above. The mate's party bars the after hold. Perchance the stern-lights—"

But just then the Mouser heard one of the horn windows behind him being opened and *Squid*'s arms-master call from there, "Naught came this way. Where are they, captain?"

"Ask someone wittier than I," Slinoor tossed him sourly. "Certain they're not here."

"Would that these two could speak," the starsman wished, indicating the Mouser and Fafhrd.

"No," Slinoor said dourly. "They'd just lie. Cover the larboard trap to the hold. I'll have it up and speak to the mate."

Just then footsteps came hurrying across the middeck and *Squid*'s mate with blood-streaked face entered by the broken door, half dragging and half supporting a sailor who seemed to be holding a thin stick to his own bloody cheek.

"Why have you left the hold?" Slinoor demanded of the first. "You should be with your party below."

"Rats ambushed us on our way to the after hold," the mate gasped. "There were dozens of blacks led by a white, some armed like men. The sword of a beam-hanger almost cut my eye across. Two foamy-mouthed springers dashed out our lamp. 'Twere pure folly to have gone on in the dark. There's scarce a man of my party not bitten, slashed or jabbed. I left them guarding the foreway to the hold. They say their wounds are poisoned and talk of nailing down the hatch."

"Oh monstrous cowardice!" Slinoor cried. "You've spoiled my trap that would have scotched them at the start. Now all's to do and difficult. Oh scarelings! Daunted by rats!"

"I tell you they were armed!" the mate protested and then, swinging the sailor forward, "Here's my proof with a spearlet in his cheek."

"Don't drag her out, captain, sir," the sailor begged as Slinoor moved to examine his face. " 'Tis poisoned too, I wot."

"Hold still, boy," Slinoor commanded. "And take your hands away —I've got it firm. The point's near the skin. I'll drive it out forward so the barbs don't catch. Pinion his arms, mate. Don't move your face, boy, or you'll be hurt worse. If it's poisoned, it must come out the faster. There!"

The sailor squeaked. Fresh blood rilled down his cheek.

" 'Tis a nasty needle indeed," Slinoor commended, inspecting the bloody point. "Doesn't look poisoned. Mate, gently cut off the shaft aft of the wound, draw out the rest forward."

"Here's further proof, most wicked," said the starsman, who'd been picking about in the litter. He handed Slinoor a tiny crossbow.

Slinoor held it up before him. In the pale candlelight it gleamed bluely, while the skipper's dark-circled eyes were like agates.

"Here's evil's soul," he cried. "Perchance 'twas well you were ambushed in the hold. 'Twill teach each mariner to hate and fear all rats again, like a good grain-sailor should. And now by a swift certain killing of all rats on *Squid* wipe out today's traitorous foolery, when you clapped for rats and let rats lead your cheers, seduced by a scarlet girl and bribed by that most misnamed Mouser."

The Mouser, still paralyzed and perforce watching Slinoor aslant as Slinoor pointed at him, had to admit it was a well-turned reference to himself.

"First off," Slinoor said, "drag those two rogues on deck. Truss them to mast or rail. I'll not have them waking to botch my victory."

"Shall I up with a trap and loose a dart in the after hold?" the starsman asked eagerly.

"You should know better," was all Slinoor answered.

"Shall I gong for the galley and run up a red lamp?" the mate suggested.

Slinoor was silent two heartbeats, then said, "No. This is *Squid*'s fight to wipe out today's shame. Besides, Lukeen's a hothead butcher. Forget I said that, gentlemen, but it is so."

"Yet we'd be safer with the galley standing by," the mate ventured to continue. "Even now the rats may be gnawing holes in us."

"That's unlikely with the Rat-Queen below," Slinoor retorted. "Speed's what will save us and not standby ships. Now hearken close. Guard well all ways to the hold. Keep traps and hatches shut. Rouse the off watch. Arm every man. Gather on middeck all we can spare from sailing. Move!"

The Mouser wished Slinoor hadn't said "Move!" quite so vehemently, for the two sailors instantly grabbed his ankles and dragged him most enthusiastically out of the littered cabin and across the middeck, his head bumping a bit. True, he couldn't feel the bumps, only hear them.

To the west the sky was a quarter globe of stars, to the east a mass of fog below the thinner mist above, with the gibbous moon shining through the latter like a pale misshapen silver ghost-lamp. The wind had slackened. *Squid* sailed smoothly.

One sailor held the Mouser against the mainmast, facing aft, while the other looped rope around him. As the sailors bound him with his arms flat to his sides, the Mouser felt a tickle in his throat and life returning to his tongue, but he decided not to try to speak just yet. Slinoor in his present mood might order him gagged.

The Mouser's next divertisement was watching Fafhrd dragged out by four sailors and bound lengthwise, facing inboard with head aft

and higher than feet, to the larboard rail. It was quite a comic performance, but the Northerner snored through it.

Sailors began to gather then on middeck, some palely silent but
most quipping in low voices. Pikes and cutlasses gave them courage.
Some carried nets and long sharp-tined forks. Even the cook came
with a great cleaver, which he hefted playfully at the Mouser.

"Struck dumb with admiration of my sleepy curry, eh?"

Meanwhile the Mouser found he could move his fingers. No one
had bothered to disarm him, but Cat's Claw was unfortunately fixed
far too high on his left side for either hand to touch, let alone get out
of its scabbard. He felt the hem of his tunic until he touched, through
the cloth, a rather small flat round object thinner along one edge than
the other. Gripping it by the thick edge through the cloth, he began
to scrape with the thin edge at the fabric confining it.

The sailors crowded aft as Slinoor emerged from the cabin with his
officers and began to issue low-voiced orders. The Mouser caught,
"Slay Hisvet or her maid on sight. They're not women but were-rats
or worse," and then the last of Slinoor's orders: "Poise your parties
below the hatch or trap by which you enter. When you hear the
bosun's whistle, move!"

The effect of this "Move!" was rather spoiled by a tiny *twing* and
the arms-master clapping his hand to his eye and screaming. There
was a flurry of movement among the sailors. Cutlasses struck at a pale
form that scurried along the deck. For an instant a rat with a crossbow in his forepaws was silhouetted on the starboard rail against the
moon-pale mist. Then the starsman's crossbow twanged and the dart
winging with exceptional accuracy or luck knocked the rat off the rail
into the sea.

"That was a whitey, lads!" Slinoor cried. "A good omen!"

Thereafter there was some confusion, but it was quickly settled,
especially when it was discovered that the arm's-master had not been
struck in the eye but only near it, and the beweaponed parties moved
off, one into the cabin, two forward past the mainmast, leaving on
deck a skeleton crew of four.

The fabric the Mouser had been scraping parted and he most carefully eased out of the shredded hem an iron tik (the Lankhmar coin of
least value) with half its edge honed to razor sharpness and began to
slice with it in tiny strokes at the nearest loop of the line binding him.
He looked hopefully toward Fafhrd, but the latter's head still hung at
a senseless angle.

A whistle sounded faintly, followed some ten breaths later by a
louder one from another part of the hold, it seemed. Then muffled

shouts began to come in flurries, there were two screams, something thumped the deck from below, and a sailor swinging a rat squeaking in a net dashed past the Mouser.

The Mouser's fingers told him he was almost through the first loop. Leaving it joined by a few threads, he began to slice at the next loop, bending his wrist acutely to do it.

An explosion shook the deck, stinging the Mouser's feet. He could not conjecture its nature and sawed furiously with his sharpened coin. The skeleton crew cried out and one of the helmsmen fled forward but the other stuck by the tiller. Somehow the gong clanged once, though no one was by it.

Then *Squid*'s sailors began to pour up out of the hold, half of them without weapons and frantic with fear. They milled about. The Mouser could hear sailors dragging *Squid*'s boats, which were forward of the mainmast, to the ship's side. The Mouser gathered that the sailors had fared most evilly below, assaulted by battalions of black rats, confused by false whistles, slashed and jabbed from dark corners, stung by darts, two struck in the eye and blinded. What had completed their rout was that, coming to a hold of unsacked grain, they'd found the air above it choked with grain dust from the recent churnings and scatterings of a horde of rats, and Frix had thrown in fire from beyond, exploding the stuff and knocking them off their feet though not setting fire to the ship.

At the same time as the panic-stricken sailors, there also came on deck another group, noted only by the Mouser—a most quiet and orderly file of black rats that went climbing around him up the mainmast. The Mouser weighed crying an alarm, although he wouldn't have wagered a tik on his chances of survival with hysterical becutlassed sailors rat-slashing all around him.

In any case his decision was made for him in the negative by Skwee, who climbed on his left shoulder just then. Holding on by a lock of the Mouser's hair, Skwee leaned out in front of him, staring into the Mouser's left eye with his own two wally blue ones under his black-plumed silver helmet. Skwee touched pale paw to his bucktoothed lips, enjoining silence, then patted the little sword at his side and jerked his rat-thumb across his rat-throat to indicate the penalty for silence broken. Thereafter he retired into the shadows by the Mouser's ear, presumably to watch the routed sailors and wave on and command his own company—and keep close to the Mouser's jugular vein. The Mouser kept sawing with his coin.

The starsman came aft followed by three sailors with two white lanterns apiece. Skwee crowded back closer between the Mouser and the mast, but touched the cold flat of his sword to the Mouser's neck, just under the ear, as a reminder. The Mouser remembered Hisvet's kiss. With a frown at the Mouser the starsman avoided the mainmast and had the sailors hang their lanterns to the aftermast and the crane fittings and the forward range of the afterdeck, fussing about the exact positions. He asserted in a high babble that light was the perfect military defense and counter-weapon, and talked wildly of light-entrenchments and light palisades, and was just about to set the sailors hunting more lamps, when Slinoor limped out of the cabin bloody-foreheaded and looked around.

"Courage, lads," Slinoor shouted hoarsely. "On deck we're still masters. Let down the boats orderly, lads, we'll need 'em to fetch the marines. Run up the red lamp! You there, gong the alarm!"

Someone responded, "The gong's gone overboard. The ropes that hung it—gnawed!"

At the same time thickening waves of fog came out of the east, shrouding Squid in deadly moonlit silver. A sailor moaned. It was a strange fog that seemed to increase rather than diminish the amount of light cast by the moon and the starsman's lantern. Colors stood out, yet soon there were only white walls beyond the Squid's rails.

Slinoor ordered, "Get up the spare gong! Cook, let's have your biggest kettles, lids and pots—anything to beat an alarm!"

There were two splashing thumps as Squid's boats hit the water.

Someone screamed agonizingly in the cabin.

Then two things happened together. The mainsail parted from the mast, falling to starboard like a cathedral ceiling in a gale, its lines and ties to the mast gnawed loose or sawed by tiny swords. It floated darkly on the water, dragging the boom wide. Squid lurched to starboard.

At the same time a horde of black rats spewed out of the cabin door and came pouring over the taffrail, the latter presumably by way of the stern lights. They rushed at the humans in waves, springing with equal force and resolution whether they landed on pike points or tooth-clinging to noses and throats.

The sailors broke and made for the boats, rats landing on their backs and nipping at their heels. The officers fled too. Slinoor was carried along, crying for a last stand. Skwee out with his sword on the Mouser's shoulder and bravely waved on his suicidal soldiery, chittering high, then leaped down to follow in their rear. Four white rats armed with crossbows knelt on the crane fittings and began to crank, load and fire with great efficiency.

Splashings began, first two and three, then what sounded like a half dozen together, mixed with screams. The Mouser twisted his head around and from the corner of his eye saw the last two of *Squid's* sailors leap over the side. Straining a little further around yet, he saw Slinoor clutch to his chest two rats that worried him and follow the sailors. The four white-furred arbalesters leaped down from the crane fittings and raced toward a new firing position on the prow. Hoarse human cries came up from the water and faded off. Silence fell on *Squid* like the fog, broken only by the inevitable chitterings—and those few now.

When the Mouser turned his head aft again, Hisvet was standing before him. She was dressed in close-fitting black leather from neck to elbows and knees, looking most like a slim boy, and she wore a black leather helmet fitting down over her temples and cheeks like Skwee's silver one, her white hair streaming down in a tail behind making her plume. A slim dagger was scabbarded on her left hip.

"Dear, dear Dirksman," she said softly, smiling with her little mouth, "you at least do not desert me," and she reached out and almost brushed his cheek with her fingers. Then, "Bound!" she said, seeming to see the rope for the first time and drawing back her hand. "We must remedy that, Dirksman."

"I would be most grateful, White Princess," the Mouser said humbly. Nevertheless, he did not let go his sharpened coin, which although somewhat dulled had now sliced almost halfway through a third loop.

"We must remedy that," Hisvet repeated a little absently, her gaze straying beyond the Mouser. "But my fingers are too soft and unskilled to deal with such mighty knots as I see. Frix will release you. Now I must hear Skwee's report on the afterdeck. Skwee-skwee-skwee!"

As she turned and walked aft the Mouser saw that her hair all went through a silver-ringed hole in the back top of her black helmet. Skwee came running past the Mouser and when he had almost caught up with Hisvet he took position to her right and three rat-paces behind her, strutting with forepaw on sword-hilt and head held high, like a captain-general behind his empress.

As the Mouser resumed his weary sawing of the third loop, he looked at Fafhrd bound to the rail and saw that the black kitten was crouched fur-on-end on Fafhrd's neck and slowly raking his cheek with the spread claws of a forepaw while the Northerner still snored garglingly. The kitten dipped its head and bit Fafhrd's ear. Fafhrd groaned piteously, but then came another of the gargling snores. The kitten resumed its cheek-raking. Two rats, one white, one black, walked by and the kitten wailed at them softly yet direly. The rats stopped and stared, then scurried straight toward the afterdeck, presumably to report the unwholesome condition to Skwee or Hisvet.

The Mouser decided to burst loose without more ado, but just then the four white arbalesters came back dragging a brass cage of frightened cheeping wrens the Mouser remembered seeing hanging by a sailor's bunk in the forecastle. They stopped by the crane fittings again and started a wren-shoot. They'd release one of the tiny terrified flutters, then as it winged off bring it down with a well-aimed dart—at distances up to five and six yards, never missing. Once or twice one of them would glance at the Mouser narrowly and touch the dart's point.

Frix stepped down the ladder from the afterdeck. She was now dressed like her mistress, except she had no helmet, only the tight silver hairnet, though the silver rings were gone from her wrists.

"Lady Frix!" the Mouser called in a light voice, almost gaily. It was hard to say how one should speak on a ship manned by rats, but a high voice seemed indicated.

She came toward him smiling, but, "Frix will do better," she said. "Lady is such a corset title."

"Frix then," the Mouser called, "on your way would you scare that black witch cat from our poppy-sodden friend? He'll rake out my comrade's eye."

Frix looked sideways to see what the Mouser meant, but still kept stepping toward him.

"I never interfere with another person's pleasures or pains, since it's hard to be certain which are which," she informed him, coming close. "I only carry out my mistress' directives. Now she bids me tell you be patient and of good cheer. Your trials will soon be over. And this withal she sends you as a remembrancer." Lifting her mouth, she kissed the Mouser softly on each upper eyelid.

The Mouser said, "That's the kiss with which the green priestess of Djil seals the eyes of those departing this world."

"Is it?" Frix asked softly.

"Aye, 'tis," the Mouser said with a little shudder, continuing briskly, "So now undo me these knots, Frix, which is something your mistress has directed. And then perchance give me a livelier smack—after I've looked to Fafhrd."

"I only carry out the directives of my mistress' own mouth," Frix said, shaking her head a little sadly. "She said nothing to me about untying knots. But doubtless she will direct me to loose you shortly."

"Doubtless," the Mouser agreed, a little glumly, forbearing to saw with his coin at the third loop while Frix watched him. If he could but sever at once three loops, he told himself, he might be able to shake off the remaining ones in a not impossibly large number of heartbeats.

As if on cue, Hisvet stepped lightly down from the afterdeck and hastened to them.

"Dear mistress, do you bid me undo the Dirksman his knots?" Frix asked at once, almost as if she wanted to be told to.

"I will attend to matters here," Hisvet replied hurriedly. "Go you to the afterdeck, Frix, and harken and watch for my father. He delays overlong this night." She also ordered the white crossbow-rats, who'd winged their last wren, to retire to the afterdeck.

VI

After Frix and the rats had gone, Hisvet gazed at the Mouser for the space of a score of heartbeats, frowning just a little, studying him deeply with her red-irised eyes.

Finally she said with a sigh, "I wish I could be certain."

"Certain of what, White Princessship?" the Mouser asked.

"Certain that you love me truly," she answered softly yet downrightly, as if he surely knew. "Many men—aye and women too and demons and beasts—have told me they loved me truly, but truly I think none of them loved me for myself (save Frix, whose happiness is in being a shadow) but only because I was young or beautiful or a Demoiselle of Lankhmar or dreadfully clever or had a rich father or was dowered with power, being blood-related to the rats, which is a certain sign of power in more worlds than Nehwon. Do you truly love me for myself, Gray Mouser?"

"I love you most truly indeed, Shadow Princess," the Mouser said with hardly an instant's hesitation. "Truly I love you for yourself alone, Hisvet. I love you more dearly than aught else in Nehwon—aye, and in all other worlds too and heaven and hell besides."

Just then Fafhrd, cruelly clawed or bit by the kitten, let off a most piteous groan indeed with a dreadful high note in it, and the Mouser said impulsively, "Dear Princess, first chase me that were-cat from my large friend, for I fear it will be blinding and death's bane, and then we shall discourse of our great loves to the end of eternity."

"*That* is what I mean," Hisvet said softly and reproachfully. "If you loved me truly for myself, Gray Mouser, you would not care a feather if your closest friend or your wife or mother or child were tortured and done to death before your eyes, so long as my eyes were upon you and I touched you with my fingertips. With my kisses on your lips and my slim hands playing about you, my whole person accepting and welcoming you, you could watch your large friend there scratched to blindness and death by a cat—or mayhap eaten alive by rats—and be utterly content. I have touched few things in this world, Gray Mouser. I have touched no man, or male demon or larger male beast, save by the proxy of Frix. Remember that, Gray Mouser."

"To be sure, Dear Light of my Life!" the Mouser replied most spiritedly, certain now of the sort of self-adoring madness with which he had to deal, since he had a touch of the same mania and so was well-acquainted with it. "Let the barbarian bleed to death by pinpricks! Let the cat have his eyes! Let the rats banquet on him to his bones! What skills it while we trade sweet words and caresses, discoursing to each other with our entire bodies and our whole souls!"

Meanwhile, however, he had started to saw again most fiercely with his now-dulled coin, unmindful of Hisvet's eyes upon him. It joyed him to feel Cat's Claw lying against his ribs.

"That's spoken like my own true Mouser," Hisvet said with most melting tenderness, brushing her fingers so close to his cheek that he could feel the tiny chill zephyr of their passage. Then, turning, she called, "Holla, Frix! Send to me Skwee and the White Company. Each may bring with him two black comrades of his own choice. I have somewhat of a reward for them, somewhat of a special treat. Skwee! Skwee-skwee-skwee!"

What would have happened then, both instantly and ultimately, is impossible to say, for at that moment Frix hailed, "Ahoy!" into the fog and called happily down, "A black sail! Oh Blessed Demoiselle, it is your father!"

Out of the pearly fog to starboard came the shark's-fin triangle of the upper portion of a black sail, running alongside *Squid* aft of the dragging brown mainsail. Two boathooks, a small ship's length apart, came up and clamped down on the starboard middeck rail while the black sail flapped. Frix came running lightly forward and secured to the rail midway between the boathooks the top of a rope ladder next heaved up from the black cutter (for surely this must be that dire craft, the Mouser thought).

Then up the ladder and over the rail came nimbly an old man of Lankhmar dressed all in black leather and on his left shoulder a white rat clinging with right forepaw to a cheekflap of his black leather cap. He was followed swiftly by two lean bald Mingols with faces yellow-brown as old lemons, each shoulder bearing a large black rat that steadied itself by a yellow ear.

At that moment, most coincidentally, Fafhrd groaned again, more loudly, and opened his eyes and cried out in the faraway moan of an opium-dreamer, "Millions of black monkeys! Take him off, I say! 'Tis a black fiend of hell torments me! Take him off!"

At that the black kitten raised up, stretched out its small evil face, and bit Fafhrd on the nose. Disregarding this interruption, Hisvet threw up her hand at the newcomers and cried clearly, "Greetings, oh Co-commander my Father! Greetings, peerless rat-captain Grig! *Clam* is conquered by you, now *Squid* by me, and this very night, after small business of my own attended to, shall see the perdition of all this final fleet. Then it's Movarl estranged, the Mingols across the Sinking Land, Glipkerio hurled down, and the rats ruling Lankhmar under my overlordship and yours!"

The Mouser, sawing ceaselessly at the third loop, chanced to note Skwee's muzzle at that moment. The small white captain had come down from the afterdeck at Hisvet's summoning along with eight white comrades, two bandaged, and now he shot Hisvet a silent look that seemed to say there might be doubts about the last item of her boast, once the rats ruled Lankhmar.

Hisvet's father Hisvin had a long-nosed, much wrinkled face patched by a week of white, old-man's beard, and he seemed permanently stooped far over, yet he moved most briskly for all that, taking very rapid little shuffling steps.

Now he answered his daughter's bragging speech with a petulant sideways flirt of his black glove close to his chest and a little impatient "Tsk-tsk!" of disapproval, then went circling the deck at his odd scuttling gait while the Mingols waited by the ladder-top. Hisvin circled by Fafhrd and his black tormenter ("Tsk-tsk!") and by the Mouser (another "Tsk!") and stopping in front of Hisvet said rapid and fumingly, still crouched over, jogging a bit from foot to foot, "Here's confusion indeed tonight! You catsing and romancing with bound men!—I know, I know! The moon coming through too much! (I'll have my astrologer's liver!) *Shark* oaring like a mad cuttlefish through the foggy white! A black balloon with little lights scudding above the waves! And but now ere we found you, a vast sea monster swimming about in circles with a gibbering demon on his head—it came sniffing at us as if we were dinner, but we evaded it!

"Daughter, you and your maid and your little people must into the cutter at once with us, pausing only to slay these two and leave a suicide squad of gnawers to sink *Squid!*"

"Yeth, think *Thquid!*" the Mouser could have sworn he heard the rat on Hisvin's shoulder lisp shrilly in Lankhmarese.

"Sink *Squid?*" Hisvet questioned. "The plan was to slip her to Ilthmar with a Mingol skeleton crew and there sell her cargo."

"Plans change!" Hisvin snapped. "Daughter, if we're not off this ship in forty breaths, *Shark* will ram us by pure excess of blundering energy or the monster with the clown-clad mad mahout will eat us up as we drift here helpless. Give orders to Skwee! Then out with your knife and cut me those two fools' throats! Quick, quick!"

"But, Daddy," Hisvet objected, "I had something quite different in mind for them. Not death, at least not altogether. Something far more artistic, even loving—"

"I give you thirty breaths each to torture ere you slay them!" Hisvin conceded. "Thirty breaths and not one more, mind you! I know your somethings!"

"Dad, don't be crude! Among new friends! *Why* must you always give people a wrong impression of me? I won't endure it longer!"

"Chat-chat-chat! You pother and pose more than your rat-mother."

"But I tell you I won't endure it. This time we're going to do things *my* way for a change!"

"Hist-hist!" her father commanded, stooping still lower and cupping hand to left ear, while his white rat Grig imitated his gesture on the other side.

Faintly through the fog came a gibbering. *"Gottverdammter Nebel! Freunde, wo sind Sie?"*＊

"'Tis the gibberer!" Hisvin cried under his breath. "The monster will be upon us! Quick, daughter, out with your knife and slay, or I'll have my Mingols dispatch them!"

Hisvet lifted her hand against that villainous possibility. Her proudly plumed head literally bent to the inevitable.

"I'll do it," she said. "Skwee, give me your crossbow. Load with silver."

The white rat-captain folded his forelegs across his chest and chittered at her with a note of demand.

＊ "Goddam fog! Friends, where are you?" Evidently Karl Treuherz Lankhmarese dictionary was unavailable to him at the moment.

"No, you can't have him," she said sharply. "You can't have either of them. They're mine now."

Another curt chitter from Skwee.

"Very well, your people may have the small black one. Now quick with your crossbow or I'll curse you! Remember, only a smooth silver dart."

Hisvin had scuttled to his Mingols and now he went around in a little circle, almost spitting. Frix, smiling, glided to him and touched his arm but he shook away from her with an angry flirt.

Skwee was fumbling into his cannister rat-frantically. His eight comrades were fanning out across the deck toward Fafhrd and the black kitten, which leaped down now in front of Fafhrd, snarling defiance.

Fafhrd himself was looking about bloody-faced but at last lucid-eyed, drinking in the desperate situation, poppy-languor banished by nose-bite.

Just then there came another gibber through the fog, "*Gottverdammter Nirgendswelt!*"*

Fafhrd's bloodshot eyes widened and brightened with a great inspiration. Bracing himself against his bonds, he inflated his mighty chest.

"*Hoongk!*" he bellowed. "*Hoongk!*"

Out of the fog came eager answer, growing each time louder: "Hoongk! *Hoongk! Hoongk!*"

Seven of the eight white rats that had crossed the deck now returned carrying stretched between them the still-snarling black kitten, spread-eagled on its back, one to each paw and ear while the seventh tried to master but was shaken from side to side by the whipping tail. The eighth came hobbling behind on three legs, shoulder paralyzed by a deep-stabbing cat-bite.

From cabin and forecastle and all corners of the deck, the black rats scurried in to watch gloatingly their traditional enemy mastered and delivered to torment, until the middeck was thick with their bloaty dark forms.

Hisvin cracked a command at his Mingols. Each drew a wavy-edged knife. One headed for Fafhrd, the other for the Mouser. Black rats hid their feet.

Skwee dumped his tiny darts on the deck. His paw closed on a palely gleaming one and he slapped it in his crossbow, which he hurriedly handed up toward his mistress. She lifted it in her right

---

* "Goddam Nowhere-World!"

hand toward Fafhrd, but just then the Mingol moving toward the Mouser crossed in front of her, his kreese point-first before him. She shifted crossbow to left hand, whipped out her dagger and darted ahead of the Mingol.

Meanwhile the Mouser had snapped the three cut loops with one surge. The others still confined him loosely at ankles and throat, but he reached across his body, drew Cat's Claw and slashed out at the Mingol as Hisvet shouldered the yellow man aside.

The dirk sliced her pale cheek from jaw to nose.

The other Mingol, advancing his kreese toward Fafhrd's throat, abruptly dropped to the deck and began to roll back across it, the black rats squeaking and snapping at him in surprise.

"Hoongk!"

A great green dragon's head had loomed from the moon-mist over the larboard rail just at the spot where Fafhrd was tied. Strings of slaver trailed on the Northerner from the dagger-toothed jaws.

Like a ponderous jack-in-the-box, the red-mawed head dipped and drove forward, lower jaw rasping the oaken deck and sweeping up from a swath of black rats three rats wide. The jaws crunched together on their great squealing mouthful inches from the rolling Mingol's head. Then the green head swayed aloft and a horrid swelling traveled down the greenish yellow neck.

But even as it poised there for a second strike, it shrank in size by comparison with what now appeared out of the mist after it—a second green dragon's head fourfold larger and fantastically crested in red, orange and purple (for at first sight the rider seemed to be part of the monster). This head now drove forward as if it were that of the father of all dragons, sweeping up a black-rat swath twice as wide as had the first and topping off its monster gobble with the two white rats behind the rat-carried black kitten.

It ended its first strike so suddenly (perhaps to avoid eating the kitten) that its parti-colored rider, who'd been waving his pike futilely, was hurled forward off its green head. The rider sailed low past the mainmast, knocking aside the Mingol striking at the Mouser, and skidded across the deck into the starboard rail.

The white rats let go of the kitten, which raced for the mainmast.

Then the two green heads, famished by their two days of small fishy pickings since their last real meal at the Rat Rocks, began methodically to sweep *Squid's* deck clean of rats, avoiding humans for the most part, though not very carefully. And the rats, huddled in their mobs, did little to evade this dreadful mowing. Perhaps in their straining toward world-dominion they had grown just human and civilized enough to experience imaginative, unhelpful, freezing panic and to have acquired something of humanity's talent for inviting and enduring destruction. Perhaps they looked on the dragons' heads as the twin red maws of war and hell, into which they must throw themselves willy-nilly. At all events they were swept up by dozens and scores. All but three of the white rats were among those engulfed.

Meanwhile the larger people aboard *Squid* faced up variously to the drastically altered situation.

Old Hisvin shook his fist and spat in the larger dragon's face when after its first gargantuan swallow it came questing toward him, as if trying to decide whether this bent black thing were (ugh!) a very queer man or (yum!) a very large rat. But when the stinking apparition kept coming on, Hisvin rolled deftly over the rail as if into bed and swiftly climbed down the rope ladder, fairly chittering in consternation, while Grig clung for dear life to the back of the black leather collar.

Hisvin's two Mingols picked themselves up and followed him, vowing to get back to their cozy cold steppes as soon as Mingolly possible.

Fafhrd and Karl Treuherz watched the melee from opposite sides of the middeck, the one bound by ropes, the other by out-wearied astonishment.

Skwee and a white rat named Siss ran over the heads of their packed apathetic black fellows and hopped on the starboard rail. There they looked back. Siss blinked in horror. But Skwee, his black-plumed helmet pushed down over his left eye, menaced with his little sword and chittered defiance.

Frix ran to Hisvet and urged her to the starboard rail. As they neared the head of the rope ladder, Skwee went down it to make way for his empress, dragging Siss with him. Just then Hisvet turned like someone in a dream. The smaller dragon's head drove toward her viciously. Frix sprang in the way, arms wide, smiling, a little like a ballet dancer taking a curtain call. Perhaps it was the suddenness or seeming aggressiveness of her move that made the dragon sheer off, fangs clashing. The two girls climbed the rail.

Hisvet turned again, Cat's Claw's cut a bold red line across her face, and sighted her crossbow at the Mouser. There was the faintest silvery flash. Hisvet tossed the crossbow in the black sea and followed Frix down the ladder. The boathooks let go, the flapping black sail filled, and the black cutter faded into the mist.

The Mouser felt a little sting in his left temple, but he forgot it while whirling the last loops from his shoulders and ankles. Then he ran across the deck, disregarding the green heads lazily searching for last rat morsels, and cut Fafhrd's bonds.

All the rest of that night the two adventurers conversed with Karl Treuherz, telling each other fabulous things about each other's worlds, while Scylla's sated daughter slowly circled *Squid*, first one head sleeping and then the other. Talking was slow and uncertain work, even with the aid of the little Lankhmarese-German German-Lankhmarese Dictionary for Space-Time and Inter-Cosmic Travelers, and neither party really believed a great deal of the other's tales, yet pretended to for friendship's sake.

"Do all men dress as grandly as you do in Tomorrow?" Fafhrd once asked, admiring the German's purple and orange garb.

"No, Hagenbeck just has his employees do it, to spread his time zoo's fame," Karl Treuherz explained.

The last of the mist vanished just before dawn and they saw, silhouetted against the sea silvered by the sinking gibbous moon, the black ship of Karl Treuherz hovering not a bowshot west of *Squid*, its little lights twinkling softly.

The German shouted for joy, summoned his sleepy monster by thwacking his pike against the rail, swung astride the larger head, and swam off calling after him, *"Auf Wiedersehen!"*

Fafhrd had learned just enough Gibberish during the night to know this meant, "Until we meet again."

When the monster and the German had swum below it, the space-time engine descended, somehow engulfing them. Then a little later the black ship vanished.

"It dove into the infinite waters toward Karl's Tomorrow bubble," the Gray Mouser affirmed confidently. "By Ning and by Sheel, the German's a master magician!"

Fafhrd blinked, frowned, and then simply shrugged.

The black kitten rubbed his ankle. Fafhrd lifted it gently to eye level, saying, "I wonder, kitten, if you're one of the Cat's Thirteen or else their small agent, sent to wake me when waking was needful?" The kitten smiled solemnly into Fafhrd's cruelly scratched and bitten face and purred.

Clear gray dawn spread across the waters of the Inner Sea, showing them first *Squid*'s two boats crowded with men and Slinoor sitting dejected in the stern of the nearer but standing with uplifted hand as he recognized the figures of the Mouser and Fafhrd; next Lukeen's war galley *Shark* and the three other grain ships *Tunny, Carp* and

Grouper; lastly, small on the northern horizon, the green sails of two dragonships of Movarl.

The Mouser, running his left hand back through his hair, felt a short, straight, rounded ridge in his temple under the skin. He knew it was Hisvet's smooth silver dart, there to stay.

VII

FAFHRD AWOKE CONSUMED by thirst and amorous yearning, and with a certainty that it was late afternoon. He knew where he was and, in a general way, what had been happening, but his memory for the past half day or so was at the moment foggy. His situation was that of a man who stands on a patch of ground with mountains sharp-etched all around, but the middle distance hidden by a white sea of ground-mist.

He was in leafy Kvarch Nar, chief of the Eight so-called Cities—truly, none of them could compare with Lankhmar, the only city worth the name on the Inner Sea. And he was in his room in the straggling, low, unwalled, yet shapely wooden palace of Movarl. Four days ago the Mouser had sailed for Lankhmar aboard *Squid* with a cargo of lumber which the thrifty Slinoor had shipped, to report to Glipkerio the safe delivery of four-fifths of the grain, the eerie treacheries of Hisvin and Hisvet, and the whole mad adventure. Fafhrd, however, had chosen to remain a while in Kvarch Nar, for to him it was a fun-place, not least because he had found a fun-loving, handsome girl there, one Hrenlet.

More particularly, Fafhrd was snug abed but feeling somewhat constricted—clearly he had not taken off his boots or any other of his clothing or even unbelted his short-ax, the blade of which, fortu-

nately covered by its thick leather sheath, stuck into his side. Yet he
was also filled with a sense of glorious achievement—why, he wasn't
yet sure, but it was a grand feeling.

Without opening his eyes or moving any part of him the thickness
of a Lankhmar penny a century old, he oriented himself. To his left,
within easy arm-reach on a stout night table would be a large pewter
flagon of light wine. Even now he could sense, he thought, its coolth.
Good.

To his right, within even easier reach, Hrenlet. He could feel her
radiant warmth and hear her snoring—very loudly, in fact.

Or was it Hrenlet for certain?—or at any rate *only* Hrenlet? She
had been very merry last night before he went to the gaming table,
playfully threatening to introduce him intimately to a red-haired and
hot-blooded female cousin of hers from Ool Hrusp, where they had
great wealth in cattle. Could it be that . . . ? At any rate, good too, or
even better.

While under his downy thick pillows— Ah, there was the explanation for his ever-mounting sense of glory! Late last night he had
cleaned them all out of every golden Lankhmarian rilk, every golden
Kvarch Nar gront, every golden coin from the Eastern Lands,
Quarmall, or elsewhere! Yes, he remembered it well now: he had
taken them all—and at the simple game of sixes and seven, where the
banker wins if he matches the number of coins the player holds in his
fist; those Eight-City fools didn't realize they tried to make their fists
big when they held six golden coins and tightened them when they
held seven. Yes, he had turned all their pockets and pouches inside
out—and at the end he had crazily matched a quarter of his winnings
against an oddly engraved slim tin whistle supposed to have magical
properties . . . and won that too! And then saluted them all and
reeled off happily, well-ballasted by gold like a treasure galleon, to
bed and Hrenlet. Had he had Hrenlet? He wasn't sure.

Fafhrd permitted himself a dry-throated, raspy yawn. Was ever
man so fortunate? At his left hand, wine. At his right a beauteous girl,
or more likely two, since there was a sweet strong farm-smell coming
to him under the sheets; and what is juicier than a farmer's (or cattle-
man's) redhead daughter? While under his pillows— He twisted his
head and neck luxuriously; he couldn't quite feel the tight-bulging
bag of golden coins—the pillows were many and thick—but he could
imagine it.

He tried to recall why he had made that last harebrained successful
wager. The curly-bearded braggart had claimed he had the slim tin
whistle of a wise woman and that it summoned thirteen helpful

beasts of some sort—and this had recalled to Fafhrd the wise woman who had told him in his youth that each sort of animal has its governing thirteen—and so his sentimentality had been awakened—and he had wanted to get the whistle as a present for the Gray Mouser, who doted on the little props of magic—yes, that was it!

Eyes still shut, Fafhrd plotted his course of action. He suddenly stretched out his left arm blind and without any groping fastened it on the pewter flagon—it was even bedewed!—and drained half of it—nectar!—and set it back.

Then with his right hand he stroked the girl—Hrenlet, or her cousin?—from shoulder to haunch.

She was covered with short bristly fur and, at his amorous touch, she mooed!

Fafhrd wide-popped his eyes and jackknifed up in the bed, so that sunlight, striking low through the small unglazed window, drenched him yellowly and made a myriad wonder of the hand-polished woods paneling the room, their grains an infinitely varied arabesque. Beside him, pillowed as thickly as he was—and possibly drugged—was a large, long-eared, pink-nostriled auburn calf. Suddenly he could feel her hooves through his boots, and drew the latter abruptly back. Beyond her was no girl—or even other calf—at all.

He dove his right hand under his pillows. His fingers touched the familiar double-stitched leather of his pouch, but instead of being ridgy and taut with gold pieces, it was, except for one thin cylinder—that tin whistle—flat as an unleavened Sarheenmar pancake.

He flung back the bedclothes so that they bellied high and wild in the air, like a sail torn loose in a squall. Thrusting the burgled purse under his belt, he vaulted out of bed, snatched up his long-sword by its furry scabbard—he intended it for spanking purposes—and dashed through the heavy double drapes out the door, pausing only to dump down his throat the last of the wine.

Despite his fury at Hrenlet, he had to admit, as he hurriedly quaffed, that she had dealt honestly with him up to a point: his bed-comrade was female, red-haired, indubitably from the farm and—for a calf—beauteous, while her now-alarmed mooing had nevertheless a throaty amorous quality.

The common-room was another wonder of polished wood—Movarl's kingdom was so young that its forests were still its chief wealth. Most of the windows showed green leaves close beyond. From walls and ceiling jutted fantastic demons and winged warrior-maidens all wood-carved. Here and there against the wall leaned beautifully polished bows and spears. A wide doorway led out to a narrow courtyard where a bay stallion moved restlessly under an irregular green roof. The city of Kvarch Nar had twenty times as many mighty trees as homes.

About the common-room lounged a dozen men clad in green and brown, drinking wine, playing at board-games, and conversing. They were dark-bearded brawny fellows, a little shorter—though not much —than Fafhrd.

Fafhrd instantly noted that they were the identical fellows whom he had stripped of their gold-pieces at last night's play. And this tempted him—hot with rage and fired by gulped wine—into a near-fatal indiscretion.

"Where is that thieving, misbegotten Hrenlet?" he roared, shaking his scabbarded sword above his head. "She's stolen from under my pillows all my winnings!"

Instantly the twelve sprang to their feet, hands gripping sword hilts. The burliest took a step toward Fafhrd, saying icily, "You dare suggest that a noble maiden of Kvarch Nar shared your bed, barbarian?"

Fafhrd realized his mistake. His liaison with Hrenlet, though obvious to all, had never before been remarked on, because the women of the Eight Cities are revered by their men and may do what they wish, no matter how licentious. But woe betide the outlander who puts this into words.

Yet Fafhrd's rage still drove him beyond reason. "Noble?" he cried. "She's a liar and a whore! Her arms are two white snakes, a-crawl 'neath the blankets—for gold, not man-flesh! Despite which, she's also a shepherd of lusts and pastures her flock between my sheets!"

A dozen swords came screeching out of their scabbards at that and there was a rush. Fafhrd grew logical, almost too late. There seemed only one chance of survival left. He sprinted straight for the big door, parrying with his still-scabbarded sword the hasty blows of Movarl's henchmen, raced across the courtyard, vaulted into the saddle of the bay, and kicked him into a gallop.

He risked one backward look as the bay's iron-shod hooves began to strike sparks from the flinty narrow forest road. He was rewarded by a vivid glimpse of his yellow-haired Hrenlet leaning bare-armed in her shift from an upper window and laughing heartily.

A half-dozen arrows whirred viciously around him and he devoted himself to getting more speed from the bay. He was three leagues along the winding road to Klelg Nar, which runs east through the thick forest close to the coast of the Inner Sea, when he decided that the whole business had been a trick, worked by last night's losers in league with Hrenlet, to regain their gold—and perhaps one of them his girl—and that the arrows had been deliberately winged to miss.

He drew up the bay and listened. He could hear no pursuit. That pretty well confirmed it.

Yet there was no turning back now. Even Movarl could hardly protect him after he had spoken the words he had of a Kvarch Nar lady.

There were no ports between Kvarch Nar and Klelg Nar. He would have to ride at least that far around the Inner Sea, somehow evading the Mingols beseiging Klelg Nar, if he were to get back to Lankhmar and his share of Glipkerio's reward for bringing all the grain ships save *Clam* safe to port. It was most irksome.

Yet he still could not really hate Hrenlet. This horse was a stout one and there was a big saddlebag of food balancing a large canteen of wine. Besides, its reddish hue delightfully echoed that of the calf. A rough joke, but a good one.

Also, he couldn't deny that Hrenlet had been magnificent between the sheets—a superior sort of slim unfurred cow, and witty too.

He dipped in his pancake-flat pouch and examined the tin whistle, which aside from memories was now his sole spoil from Kvarch Nar. It had down one side of it a string of undecipherable characters and down the other the figure of a slim feline beast couchant. He grinned widely, shaking his head. What a fool was a drunken gambler! He made to toss it away, then remembered the Mouser and returned it to his pouch.

He touched the bay with his heels and cantered on toward Klelg Nar, whistling an eerie but quickening Mingol march.

Nehwon—a vast bubble leaping up forever through the waters of eternity. Like airy champagne . . . or, to certain moralists, like a globe of stinking gas from the slimiest, most worm-infested marsh.

Lankhmar—a continent firm-seated on the solid watery inside of the bubble called Nehwon. With mountains, hills, towns, plains, a crooked coastline, deserts, lakes, marshes too, and grainfields—especially grainfields, source of the continent's wealth, to either side of the Hlal, greatest of rivers.

And on the continent's northern tip, on the east bank of the Hlal, mistress of the grainfields and their wealth, the City of Lankhmar, oldest in the world. Lankhmar, thick-walled against barbarians and beasts, thick-floored against creepers and crawlers and gnawers.

At the south of the City of Lankhmar, the Grain Gate, its twenty-foot thickness and thirty-foot width often echoing with the creak of

ox-drawn wagons bringing in Lankhmar's tawny, dry, edible trea-
sure. Also the Grand Gate, larger still and more glorious, and the
smaller End Gate. Then the South Barracks with its black-clad soldiery, the Rich Men's Quarter, the Park of Pleasure and the Plaza of
Dark Delights. Next Whore Street and the streets of other crafts.
Beyond those, crossing the city from the Marsh Gate to the docks, the
Street of the Gods, with its many flamboyantly soaring fanes of the
Gods *in* Lankhmar and its single squat black temple of the Gods *of*
Lankhmar—more like an ancient tomb except for its tall, square, eternally silent bell-tower. Then the slums and the windowless homes of
the nobles; the great grain-towers, like a giant's forest of house-thick
tree-trunks chopped off evenly. Finally, facing the Inner Sea to the
north and the Hlal to the west, the North Barracks, and on a hill of
solid, sea-sculptured rock, the Citadel and the Rainbow Palace of
Glipkerio Kistomerces.

An adolescent serving maid balancing on her close-shaven head
with aid of a silver coronet-ring a large tray of sweetmeats and brimming silver goblets, strode like a tightrope walker into a green-tiled
antechamber of the Blue Audience Chamber of that palace. She wore
black leather collars around her neck, wrists, and slender waist. Light
silver chains a little shorter than her forearms tied her wrist-collars to
her waist-collar—it was Glipkerio's whim that no maid's finger
should touch his food or even its tray and that every maid's balance
be perfect. Aside from her collars she was unclothed, while aside
from her short-clipped eyelashes, she was entirely shaven—another of
the fantastic monarch's dainty whims, that no hair should drop in his
soup. She looked like a doll before it is dressed, its wig affixed, and its
eyebrows painted on.

The sea-hued tiles lining the chamber were hexagonal and big as
the palm of a large hand. Most were plain, but here and there were
ones figured with sea creatures: a mollusk, a cod, an octopus, a sea
horse.

The maid was almost halfway to the narrow, curtained archway
leading to the Blue Audience Chamber when her gaze became fixed
on a tile in the floor a long stride from the archway ahead but somewhat to the left. It was figured with a sea lion. It lifted the breadth of
a thumb, like a little trapdoor, and eyes with a jetty gleam a finger-
joint apart peered out at her.

She shook from toes to head, but her tight-bitten lips uttered no
sound. The goblets chinked faintly, the tray began to slide, but she
got her head under its center again with a swift sidewise ducking
movement, and then began to go with long fearful steps around the

horrid tile as far as she could to the right, so that the edge of the tray was hardly a finger's-breadth from the wall.

Just under the edge of the tray, as if that were a porch-roof, a plain green tile in the wall opened like a door and a rat's black face thrust out with spade-teeth bared.

The maid leaped convulsively away, still in utter silence. The tray left her head. She tried to get under it. The floortile clattered open wide and a long-bodied black rat came undulating out. The tray struck the dodging maid's shoulder, she strained toward it futilely with her short-chained hands, then it struck the floor with a nerve-shattering clangor and all the spilled goblets rang.

As the silver reverberations died, there was else only the rapid soft *thump* of her bare feet running back the way she had come. One goblet rolled a last turn. Then there was desert stillness in the green antechamber.

Two hundred heartbeats later, it was broken by another muted thudding of bare feet, this time those of a party returning the way the maid had run. There entered first, watchful-eyed, two shaven-headed white-smocked, browny cooks, each armed with a cleaver in one hand and a long toasting-fork in the other. Second, two naked and shaven kitchen boys, bearing many wet and dry rags and a broom of black feathers. After them, the maid, her silver chains gathered in her hands, so that they would not chink from her trembling. Behind her, a monstrously fat woman in a dress of thick black wool that went to her redoubled chins and plump knuckles and hid her surely monstrous feet and ankles. Her black hair was dressed in a great round beehive stuck through and through with long black-headed pins, so that it was as if she bore a prickly planet on her head. This appeared to be the case, for her puffed face was weighted with a world of sullenness and hate. Her black eyes peered stern and all-distrustful from between folds of fat, while a sparse black moustache, like the ghost of a black centipede, crossed her upper lip. Around her vast belly, she wore a broad leather belt from which hung at intervals keys, thongs, chains, and whips. The kitchen boys believed she had deliberately grown mountain-fat to keep them from clinking together and so warn them when she came a-spying.

Now the fat kitchen-queen and palace mistress stared shrewdly around the antechamber, then spread her humpy palms, glaring at the maid. Not one green tile was displaced.

In like dumb-show, the maid nodded vehemently, pointing from her waist at the tile figured with a sea lion, then threaded tremblingly forward between the spilled stuff and touched it with her toe.

One of the cooks quickly knelt and gently thumped it and the surrounding tiles with a knuckle. Each time the faint sound was equally
solid. He tried to get the tines of his fork under the sea lion tile from
every side and failed.

The maid ran to the wall where the other glazed door had opened
and searched the bare tiles frantically, her slim hands tugging use-
lessly. The other cook thumped the tiles she indicated without getting
a hollow sound.

The glare of the palace mistress changed from suspicion to certainty. She advanced on the maid like a storm cloud, her eyes its
lightning, and suddenly thrusting out her two ham-like arms,
snapped a thong to a silver ring in the maid's collar. That snap was
the loudest sound yet.

The maid shook her head wildly three times. Her trembling increased, then suddenly stopped altogether. As the palace mistress led
her back the way they had come, she drooped her head and shoulders,
and at the first vindictive downward jerk dropped to her hands and
knees and padded rapidly, dog-fashion.

Under the watchful eyes of one of the cooks, the kitchen boys began swiftly to clean up the mess, wrapping each goblet in a rag ere
they laid it on the platter, lest it chink. Their gazes kept darting
fearfully about at the myriad tiles.

The Gray Mouser, standing on *Squid*'s gently-dipping prow,
sighted the soaring Citadel of Lankhmar through the dispersing fog.
Beyond it to the east there soon came into view the square-topped
minarets of the Overlord's palace, each finished in stone of different
hue, and to the south the dun granaries like vast smokestacks. He
hailed the first sea-wherry he saw to *Squid*'s side. With the black kitten spitting at him reproachfully, and against Slinoor's command—
but before Slinoor could decide to have him forcibly restrained—he
slid down the long boathook with which the prow wherryman had
caught hold of *Squid*'s rail. Landing lightly in the wherry, he gave an
approving shoulder-pat to the astonished hook-holder, then commanded, promising a fat fee, that he be rowed with all speed to the
palace dock. The hook was shipped, the Mouser wove his way to the
slender craft's stern, the three wherrymen out-oared and the craft
raced east over the silty water, brown with mud from the Hlal.

The Mouser called consolingly back to Slinoor, "Never fear, I will
make a marvelous report to Glipkerio, praising you to the skies—and
even Lukeen to the height of a low raincloud!"

Then he faced forward, faintly smiling and frowning at once in thought. He was somewhat sorry he had had to desert Fafhrd, who had been immersed in an apparently endless drinking and dicing bout with Movarl's toughest henchmen when *Squid* had sailed from Kvarch Nar—the great oafs died of wine and their losses each dawn, but were reborn in the late afternoon with thirst restored and money-pouches miraculously refilled.

But he was even more pleased that now he alone would bear to Glipkerio Movarl's thanks for the four shiploads of grain and be able all by himself to tell the wondrous tale of the dragon, the rats, and their human masters—or colleagues. By the time Fafhrd got back from Kvarch Nar, broken-pursed and likely broken-pated too, the Mouser would be occupying a fine apartment in Glipkerio's palace and be able subtly to irk his large comrade by offering him hospitalities and favors.

He wondered idly where Hisvin and Hisvet and their small entourage were now. Perhaps in Sarheenmar, or more likely Ilthmar, or already lurching by camel-train from that city to some retreat in the Eastern Lands, to be well away from Glipkerio's and Movarl's vengeance. Unwilled, his left hand rose to his temple, gently fingering the tiny straight ridge there. Truly, at this already dreamy distance, he could not hate Hisvet or the brave proxy-creature Frix. Surely Hisvet's vicious threats had been in part a kind of love-play. He did not doubt that some part of her yearned for him. Besides, he had marked her far worse than she had marked him. Well, perhaps he would meet her again some year in some far corner of the world.

These foolishly forgiving and forgetting thoughts of the Mouser were in part due, he knew himself, to his present taut yearning for any acceptable girl. Kvarch Nar under Movarl had proved a strait-laced city, by the Mouser's standards, and during his brief stay the one erring girl encountered—one Hrenlet—had chosen to err with Fafhrd. Well, Hrenlet had been something of a giantess, albeit slender, and now he was in Lankhmar, where he knew a dozen score spots to ease his tautness.

The silty-brown water gave way abruptly to deep green. The sea-wherry passed beyond the outflow of the Hlal and was darting along atop the Lankhmar Deep, which dove down sheer-walled and bottomless at the very foot of the wave-pitted great rock on which stood the citadel and the palace. And now the wherrymen had to row out around a strange obstruction: a copper chute wide as a man is tall that, braced by great brazen beams, angled down from a porch of the palace almost to the surface of the sea. The Mouser wondered if the whimmy Glipkerio had taken up aquatic sports during his absence.

Or perhaps this was a new way of disposing of unsatisfactory servants and slaves—sliding them suitably weighted into the sea. Then
he noted a spindle-shaped vehicle (if it was that) thrice as long as a
man and made of some dull gray metal poised at the top of the chute.
A puzzle.

The Mouser dearly loved puzzles, if only to elaborate on them
rather than solve them, but he had no time for this one. The wherry
had drawn up at the royal wharf, and he was haughtily exhibiting to
the clamoring eunuchs and guards his starfish-emblemed courier's
ring from Glipkerio and his parchment sealed with the cross-sworded
seal of Movarl.

The latter seemed to impress the palace-fry most. He was swiftly
bowed across the dock, mounted a dizzily tall, gaily-painted wooden
stair, and found himself in Glipkerio's audience chamber—a glorious
sea-fronting blue-tiled room, each large triangular tile bearing a fishy
emblem in bas-relief.

The room was huge despite the blue curtains dividing it now into
two halves. A pair of naked and shaven pages bowed to the Mouser
and parted the curtains for him. Their sinuous silent movements
against that blue background made him think of mermen. He stepped
through the narrow triangular opening—to be greeted by a rather
distant but imperious "Hush!"

Since the hissing command came from the puckered lips of
Glipkerio himself and since one of the beanpole monarch's hand-long
skinny fingers now rose and crossed those lips, the Mouser stopped
dead. With a fainter hiss the blue curtains fell together behind him.

It was a strange and most startling scene that presented itself. The
Mouser's heart missed a beat—mostly in self-outrage that his imagination had completely missed the weird possibility that was not staged
before him.

Three broad archways led out onto a porch on which rested the
pointy-ended gray vehicle he had noted balanced at the top of the
chute. Now he could see a hinged manhole toward its out-jutting
bow.

At the near end of the room was a large, thick-bottomed, close-
barred cage containing at least a score of black rats, which chittered
and wove around each other ceaselessly and sometimes clattered the
bars menacingly.

At the far end of the sea-blue room, near the circular stair leading
up into the palace's tallest minaret, Glipkerio had risen in excitement
from his golden audience couch shaped like a seashell. The fantastic
overlord stood a head higher than Fafhrd, but was thin as a starved

Mingol. His black toga made him look like a funeral cypress. Perhaps to offset this dismal effect, he wore a wreath of small violet flowers around his blond head, the hair of which clustered in golden ringlets.

Close beside him, scarce half his height, hanging weightlessly on his arm like an elf and dressed in a loose robe of pale blonde silk, was Hisvet. The Mouser's dagger-cut, stretching from her left nostril to her jaw, was still a pink line and would have given her a sardonic expression, except that now as her gaze swung to the Mouser she smiled most prettily.

Standing almost midway between the audience couch and the caged rats was Hisvet's father Hisvin. His skinny frame was wrapped in a black toga, but he still wore his tight black leather cap with its long cheek-flaps. His gaze was fixed fiercely on the caged rats and he was weaving his bony fingers at them hypnotically.

"Gnawers dark from deep below . . ." he began to incant in a voice that whistled with age yet was authoritatively strident.

At that instant a naked young servant maid appeared through a narrow archway near the audience couch, bearing on her shaven head a great silver tray laden with goblets and temptingly-mounded silver plates. Her wrists were chained to her waist, while a fine silver chain between her narrow black anklets prevented her from taking steps more than twice as long as her narrow pink-toed feet.

Without a "Hush!" this time, Glipkerio raised a narrow long palm to her and once again put a long, skinny finger to his lips. The slim maid's movements ceased imperceptibly and she stood silent as a birch tree on a windless day.

The Mouser was about to say, "Puissant Overlord, this is evilest enchantment. You are consorting with your dearest enemies!"—but at that instant Hisvet smiled at him again and he felt a frighteningly delicious tingling run down his cheek and gums from the silver dart in his left temple to his tongue, inhibiting speech.

Hisvin recommenced in his commanding Lankhmarese that bore the faintest trace of an Ilthmar lisp and reminded the Mouser of the lisping rat Grig:

> "Gnawers dark from deep below,
>   To ratty grave you now must go!
> Blear each eye and drag each tail!
>   Fur fall off and heartbeat fail!"

All the black rats crowded to the farthest side of their cage from Hisvin, chittering and squeaking as if in maddest terror. Most of them were on their hind feet, clawing toward the bars like a panicky human crowd.

The old man, now swiftly weaving his fingers in a most complex, mysterious pattern, continued relentlessly:

> "Blur your eyesight, stop your breath!—
> By corrupting spell of Death!
> Your brains are cheese, your life is fled!
> Spin once around and drop down dead!"

And the black rats did just that—spinning like amateur actors both to ease and dramatize their falls, yet falling most convincingly all the same with varying *plops* onto the cage floor or each other and lying stiff and still with furry eyelids a-droop and hairless tails slack and sharp-nailed feet thrust stiffly up.

There was a curious slow-paced slappy clapping as Glipkerio applauded with his narrow hands which were long as human feet. Then the beanpole monarch hurried to the cage with strides so lengthy that the lower two-thirds of his toga looked like the silhouette of a tent. Hisvet skipped merrily at his side, while Hisvin came circling swiftly.

"Didst see that wonder, Gray Mouser?" Glipkerio demanded in piping voice, waving his courier closer. "There is a plague of rats in Lankhmar. You, who might from your name be expected to protect us, have returned somewhat tardily. But—bless the Black-Boned Gods!—my redoubtable servant Hisvin and his incomparable sorcerer-apprentice daughter Hisvet, having conquered the rats which menaced the grain fleet, hastened back in good time to take measures against our local rat-plague—magical measures which will surely be successful, as has now been fully demonstrated."

At this point the fantastical overlord reached a long thin naked arm from under his toga and chucked the Mouser under the chin, much to the latter's distaste, though he concealed it. "Hisvin and Hisvet even tell me," Glipkerio remarked with a fluty chuckle, "that they suspected *you* for a while of being in league with the rats—as who would not from your gray garb and small crouchy figure?—and kept you tied. But all's well that ends well and I forgive you."

The Mouser began a most polemical refutation and accusation—but only in his mind, for he heard himself saying, "Here, Milord, is an urgent missive from the King of the Eight Cities. By the by, there was a dragon—"

"Oh, that two-headed dragon!" Glipkerio interrupted with another piping chuckle and a roguish finger-wave. He thrust the parchment into the breast of his toga without even glancing at the seal. "Movarl has informed me by albatross post of the strange mass delusion in my fleet. Hisvin and Hisvet, master psychologists both, confirm this. Sailors are a woefully superstitious lot, Gray Mouser, and 'tis evident their fancies are more furiously contagious than I suspected—for even you were infected! I would have expected it of your barbarian mate—Favner? Fafrah?—or even of Slinoor and Lukeen—for what are captains but jumped-up sailors?—but you, who are at least sleazily civilized . . . However, I forgive you that too! Oh, what a mercy that wise Hisvin here thought to keep watch on the fleet in his cutter!"

The Mouser realized he was nodding—and that Hisvet and, in his wrinkle-lipped fashion, Hisvin were smiling archly. He looked down at the piled stiff rats in their theatrical death-throes. Issek take 'em, but their droopy-lidded eyes even looked whitely glazed!

"Their fur hasn't fallen off," he criticized mildly.

"You are too literal," Glipkerio told him with a laugh. "You don't comprehend poetic license."

"Or the devices of humano-animal suggestion," Hisvin added solemnly.

The Mouser trod hard—and, he thought, surreptitiously—on a long tail that drooped from the cage bottom to the tiled floor. There was no atom of response.

But Hisvin noted and lightly clicked a fingernail. The Mouser fancied there was a slight stirring deep in the ratpile. Suddenly a nauseous stink sprang from the cage. Glipkerio gulped. Hisvet delicately pinched her pale nostrils between thumb and ring-finger.

"You had some question about the efficacy of my spell?" Hisvin asked the Mouser most civilly.

"Aren't the rats corrupting rather fast?" the Mouser asked. It occurred to him that there might have been a tight-sealed sliding door in the floor of the cage and a dozen long-dead rats or merely a well-rotted steak in the thick bottom beneath.

"Hisvin kills 'em doubly dead," Glipkerio asserted somewhat feebly, pressing his long hand to his narrow stomach. "All processes of decay are accelerated!"

Hisvin waved hurriedly and pointed toward an open window beyond the archways to the porch. A brawny yellow Mingol in black loincloth sprang from where he squatted in a corner, heaved up the cage, and ran with it to dump it in the sea. The Mouser followed him. Elbowing the Mingol aside with a shrewd dig at the short ribs and leaning far out, supporting himself with his other hand reaching up and gripping the tiled window-side, the Mouser saw the cage tumbling down the sheer wall and sea-eaten rock, the stiff rats tumbling about in it, and fall with a white splash into the blue waters.

At the same instant he felt Hisvet, who had rapidly followed him, press closely with her silken side against his from armpit to ankle bone.

The Mouser thought he made out small dark shapes leaving the cage and swimming strongly underwater toward the rock as the iron rat-prison sank down and down.

Hisvet breathed in his ear, "Tonight when the evening star goes to bed. The Plaza of Dark Delight. The grove of closet trees."

Turning swiftly back, Hisvin's delicate daughter commanded the black-collared, silver-chained maid, "Light wine of Ilthmar for his Majesty! Then serve us others."

Glipkerio gulped down a goblet of sparkling colorless ferment and turned a shade less green. The Mouser selected a goblet of darker, more potent stuff and also a black-edged tender beef cutlet from the great silver tray as the maid dropped gracefully to both knees while keeping her slender upper body perfectly erect.

As she rose with an effortless-seeming undulation and moved mincingly toward Hisvin, the short steps enforced by her silver ankles-chain, the Mouser noted that although her front had been innocent of both raiment and ornamentation, her naked back was crisscrossed diamond-wise by a design of evenly-spaced pink lines from nape to heels.

Then he realized that these were not narrow strokes painted on, but the weals of a whiplashing. So stout Samanda was maintaining her artistic disciplines! The unspoken torment-conspiracy between the lath-thin effeminate Glipkerio and the bladder-fat palace mistress was both psychologically instructive and disgusting. The Mouser wondered what the maid's offense had been. He also pictured Samanda sputtering through her singing black woolen garb in a huge white-hot oven—or sliding with a leaden weight on her knee-thick ankles down the copper chute outside the porch.

Glipkerio was saying to Hisvin, "So it is only needful to lure out all the rats into the streets and speak your spell at them?"

"Most true, O sapient Majesty," Hisvin assured him, "though we must delay a little, until the stars have sailed to their most potent stations in the ocean of the sky. Only then will my magic slay rats at a distance. I'll speak my spell from the blue minaret and slay them all."

"I hope those stars will set all canvas and make best speed,"

Glipkerio said, worry momentarily clouding the childish delight in his long, low-browed face. "My people have begun to fret at me to do something to disperse the rats or fight 'em back into their holes. Which will interfere with luring them forth, don't you think?"

"Don't trouble your mighty brain with that worry," Hisvin reassured him. "The rats are not easily scared. Take measures against them in so far as you're urged to. Meanwhile, tell your council you have an all-powerful weapon in reserve."

The Mouser suggested, "Why not have a thousand pages memorize Hisvin's deadly incantation and shout it down the ratholes? The rats, being underground, won't be able to tell that the stars are in the wrong place."

Glipkerio objected, "Ah, but it is necessary that the tiny beasts also see Hisvin's finger-weaving. You do not understand these refinements, Mouser. You have delivered Movarl's missive. Leave us.

"But mark this," he added, fluttering his black toga, his yellow-irised eyes like angry gold coins in his narrow head. "I have forgiven you once your delays, Small Gray Man, and your dragon-delusions and your doubts of Hisvin's magical might. But I shall not forgive a second time. Never mention such matters again."

The Mouser bowed and made his way out. As he passed the statuesque maid with crisscrossed back, he whispered, "Your name?"

"Reetha," she breathed.

Hisvet came rustling past to dip up a silver forkful of caviar, Reetha automatically dropping to her knees.

"Dark delights," Hisvin's daughter murmured and rolled the tiny black fish eggs between her bee-stung upper lip and pink and blue tongue.

When the Mouser was gone, Glipkerio bent down to Hisvin, until his figure somewhat resembled a black gibbet. "A word in your ear," he whispered. "The rats sometimes make even me . . . well, nervous."

"They are most fearsome beasties," Hisvin agreed somberly, "who might daunt even the gods."

Fafhrd spurred south along the stony sea-road that led from Klelg Nar to Sarheenmar and which was squeezed between steep, rocky mountains and the Inner Sea. The sea's dark swells peaked up blackly as they neared shore and burst with unending crashes a few yards below the road, which was dank and slippery with their spray. Overhead pressed low dark clouds which seemed less water vapor than the smoke of volcanoes or burning cities.

The Northerner was leaner—he had sweated and burned away weight—and his face was grim, his eyes red-shot and red-rimmed from dust, his hair dulled with it. He rode a tall, powerful, gaunt-ribbed gray mare with dangerous eyes, also red-shot—a beast looking as cursed as the landscape they traversed.

He had traded the bay with the Mingols for this mount, and despite its ill temper got the best of the bargain, for the bay had been redly gasping out its life from a lance thrust at the time of the trade. Approaching Klelg Nar along the forest road, he had spied three spider-thin Mingols preparing to rape slender twin sisters. He had managed to thwart this cruel and unaesthetic enterprise because he had given the Mingols no time to use their bows, only the lance, while their short narrow scimitars had been no match for Gray-wand. When the last of the three had gone down, sputtering curses and blood, Fafhrd had turned to the identically-clad girls, only to discover that he had rescued but one—a Mingol had mean-heartedly cut the other's throat before turning his scimitar on Fafhrd. Thereafter Fafhrd had mastered one of the tethered Mingol horses despite its fiendish biting and kicking. The surviving girl had revealed among her other shriekings that her family might still be alive among the defenders of Klelg Nar, so Fafhrd had swung her up on his saddlebow despite her frantic struggles and efforts to bite. When she quieted somewhat, he had been stirred by her slim sprawly limbs so close and her lemur-large eyes and her repeated assertion, reinforced by horrendous maidenly curses and quaint childhood slang, that all men without exception were hairy beasts, this with a sneer at Fafhrd's luxuriously furred chest. But although tempted to amorousness he had restrained himself out of consideration for her coltish youth—she seemed scarce twelve, though tall for her age—and recent bereavement. Yet when he had returned her to her not very grateful and strangely suspicious family, she had replied to his courteous promise to return in a year or two with a wrinkling of her snub nose and a sardonic flirt of her blue eyes and slim shoulders, leaving Fafhrd somewhat doubtful of his wisdom in sparing her his wooing and also saving her in the first place. Yet he had gained a fresh mount and a tough Mingol bow with its quiver of darts.

Klelg Nar was the scene of bitter house-to-house and tree-to-tree street fighting, while Mingol campfires glowed in a semicircle to the east every night. To his dismay Fafhrd had learned that for weeks there had not been a ship in Klelg Nar's harbor, of which the Mingols held half the perimeter. They had not fired the city because wood was wealth to the lean dwellers of the treeless steppes—in fact, their slaves dismantled and plucked apart houses as soon as won and the precious planks and lovely carvings were instantly carted off east, or more often dragged on travoises.

So despite the rumor that a branch of the Mingol horde had bent south, Fafhrd had set off in that direction on his vicious-tempered mount, somewhat tamed by the whip and morsels of honeycomb. And now it seemed from the smoke adrift above the sea-road that the Mingols might not have spared Sarheenmar from the torch as they had Klelg Nar. It also began to seem certain that the Mingols had taken Sarheenmar, from the evidence of the wild-eyed, desperate, ragged, dust-caked refugees who began to crowd the road in their flight north, forcing Fafhrd to tour now and again up the hillside, to save them from his new mount's savage hooves. He questioned a few of the refugees, but they were incoherent with terror, babbling as wildly as if he sought to waken them from nightmare. Fafhrd nodded to himself—he knew the Mingol penchant for torture.

But then a disordered troop of Mingol cavalry had come galloping along in the same direction as the escaping Sarheenmarts. Their horses were lathered with sweat and their skinny faces contorted by terror. They appeared not to see Fafhrd, let alone consider attacking him, while it seemed not from malice but panic that they rode down such refugees as got in their way.

Fafhrd's face grew grim and frowning as he cantered on, still against the gibbering stream, wondering what horror would daunt Mingol and Sarheenmart alike.

Black rats kept showing themselves in Lankhmar by day—not stealing or biting, squealing or scurrying, but only showing themselves. They peered from drains and new-gnawed holes, they sat in window slits, they crouched indoors as calmly and confident-eyed as cats—and as often, proportionately, in milady's boudoir as in the tenement-cells of the poor.

Whenever they were noted, there was a gasping and thin shrieking, a rush of footsteps, and a hurling of black pots, begemmed bracelets, knives, rocks, chessmen, or whatever else might be handy. But often it was a time before the rats were noted, so serene and at home they seemed.

Some trotted sedately amidst the ankles and swaying black togas of the crowds on the tiled or cobbled streets, like pet dwarf dogs, causing sharp human eddies when they were recognized. Five sat like black, bright-eyed bottles on a top shelf in the store of the wealthiest grocer in Lankhmar, until they were spied for what they were and hysterically pelted with clumpy spice-roots, weighty Hrusp nuts, and even jars of caviar, whereupon they made their leisurely exit through a splinter-edged rat doorway which had not been in the back of the shelf the day before. Among the black marble sculptures lining the walls of the Temple of the Beasts, another dozen posed two-legged like carvings until the climax of the ritual, when they took up a fife-like squeaking and began a slow, sure-foot weaving through the niches. Beside the blind beggar Naph, three curled on the curb, mistaken for his soot-dirty rucksack, until a thief tried to steal it. Another reposed on the jeweled cushion of the pet black marmoset of Elakeria, niece of the overlord and a most lush devourer of lovers, until she absently reached out a plump hand to stroke the beastie and her nail-gilded fingers encountered not velvet fur, but short and bristly.

During floods and outbreaks of the dread Black Sickness, rats had in remembered times invaded the streets and dwellings of Lankhmar, but then they had raced and dodged or staggered in curves, never moved with their present impudent deliberation.

Their behavior made old folks and storytellers and thin-bearded squinting scholars fearfully recall the fables that there had once been a humped city of rats large as men where imperial Lankhmar had now stood for three-score centuries; that rats had once had a language and government of their own and a single empire stretching to the borders of the unknown world, coexistent with man's cities but more unified; and that beneath the stoutly mortared stones of Lankhmar, far below their customary burrowings and any delvings of man, there was a low-ceilinged rodent metropolis with streets and homes and glow-lights all its own and granaries stuffed with stolen grain.

Now it seemed as if the rats owned not only that legendary sub-metropolitan rodent Lankhmar, but Lankhmar above ground as well, they stood and sat and moved so arrogantly.

The sailors from *Squid,* prepared to awe their sea-tavern cronies and get many free drinks with their tales of the horrid rat-attack on their ship, found Lankhmar interested only in its own rat plague. They were filled with chagrin and fear. Some of them returned for refuge to *Squid,* where the starsman's light-defenses had been renewed and both Slinoor and the black kitten worriedly paced the poop.

VIII

GLIPKERIO KISTOMERCES ORDERED tapers lit while the sunset glow still flared in his lofty sea-footed banquet hall. Yet the beanpole monarch seemed very merry as with many a giggle and whinnying laugh he assured his grave, nervous councillors that he had a secret weapon to scotch the rats at the peak of their insolent invasion and that Lankhmar would be rid of them well before the next full moon. He scoffed at his wrinkle-faced Captain General, Olegnya Mingolsbane, who would have him summon troops from the outlying cities and towns to deal with the furry attackers. He seemed unmindful of the faint patterings that came from behind the gorgeously figured draperies whenever a lull in the conversation and clink of eating tools let it be heard, or of the occasional small, hunchbacked, four-footed shadow cast by the tapers' light. As the long banquet went its bibulous course, he seemed to grow more merry and carefree yet—*fey*, some whispered in their partners' ears. But twice his right hand shook as he lifted his tall-stemmed wine glass, while beneath the table his ropy left fingers quivered continuously, and he had doubled his long skinny legs and hooked the heels of his gilded boots over a silver rung of his chair to keep his feet off the floor.

Outdoors the rising moon, gibbous and waning, showed small, low, humped shapes moving along each roof-ridge of the city, except those on the Street of the Gods, both the many temples of the Gods *in* Lankhmar and the grimy cornices of the temple of the Gods *of* Lankhmar and its tall, square bell-tower which never issued chimes.

The Gray Mouser scuffed moodily up and down the pale sandy path that curved around the grove of perfumy closet trees. Each tree was like a huge, upended, hemispherical basket, its bottom and sides formed by the thin, resilient, closely-spaced branches which, weighted with dark green leaves and pure white blooms, curved widely out and down, so that the interior was a single bell-shaped, leaf-and-flower-walled room, most private. Fire-beetles and glow-wasps and night-bees supping at the closet flowers dimly outlined each natural tent with their pale, winking, golden and violet and pinkish lights.

From within two or three of the softly iridescent bowers already came the faint murmurings of lovers, or perhaps, the Mouser thought with a vicious stab of the mind, of thieves who had chosen one of these innocent and traditionally hallowed privacies to plot the night's maraudings. Younger or on another night, the Mouser would have eavesdropped on the second class of privacy-seekers, in order to loot their chosen victims ahead of them. But now he had other rats to roast.

High tenements to the east hid the moon, so that beyond the twinkling twilight of the closet trees, the rest of the Plaza of Dark Delights was almost gropingly black, except where some small dim sheen marked store or stand, or ghostly flames and charcoal glow showed hot food and drink available, or where some courtesan rhythmically swung her tiny scarlet lantern as she sauntered.

Those last lights mightily irked the Mouser at the moment, though there had been times when they had drawn him as the closet bloom does the night-bee and twice they had jogged redly through his dreams as he had sailed home in *Squid*. But several most embarrassing visits this afternoon—first to fashionable female friendlets, then to the city's most titillating brothels—had demonstrated to him that his manhood, which he had felt so ravenously a-leap in Kvarch Nar and aboard *Squid*, was limply dead except—he first surmised, now rather desperately hoped—where Hisvet was concerned. Every time he had embraced a girl this disastrous half-day, the slim triangular face of Hisvin's daughter had got ghostily in the way, making the visage of his companion of the moment dull and gross by comparison, while from the tiny silver dart in his temple a feeling of sick boredom and unjoyful satiety had radiated through all his flesh.

Reflected from his flesh, this feeling filled his mind. He was dully aware that the rats, despite the great losses they had suffered aboard *Squid*, threatened Lankhmar. Rats were deterred even less than men by numerical losses and made them up more readily. And Lankhmar was a city for which he felt some small affection, as of a man for a very large pet. Yet the rats menacing it had, whether from Hisvet's training or some deeper source, an intelligence and organization that was eerily frightening. Even now he could imagine troops of black rats footing it unseen across the lawns and along the paths of the Plaza beyond the closet trees' glow, encircling him in a great ambush, rank on black rank.

He was aware too that he had lost whatever small trust the fickle Glipkerio had ever had in him and that Hisvin and Hisvet, after their seemingly total defeat, had turned the tables on him and must be opposed and defeated once again, just as Glipkerio's favor must be re-won.

But Hisvet, far from being an enemy to be beaten, was the girl to whom he was in thrall, the only being who could restore him to his rightful, calculating, selfish self. He touched with his fingertips the little ridge the silver dart made in his temple. It would be the work of a moment to squeeze it out point-first through its thin covering of skin. But he had a dread of what would happen then: he might not lose only his bored satiety, but the juice of all feeling, or even life itself. Besides, he didn't want to give up his silver link with Hisvet.

A tiny treading on the gravel of the path, a very faint rutching that was nevertheless more than that of one pair of footsteps, made him look up. Two slim nuns in the black robes of the Gods *of* Lankhmar and in the customary narrow, jutting hoods which left faces totally shadowed were approaching him, long-sleeved arm in arm.

He had known courtesans in the Plaza of Dark Delights to adopt almost any garb to inflame the senses of their customers, new or old, and capture or recapture their interest: the torn smock of a beggar girl, the hose and short jerkin and close-cropped hair of a page, the beads and bangles of a slave-girl of the Eastern Lands, the fine chain mail and visored helmet and slim sword of a fighting prince from those same areas of Nehwon, the rustling greenery of a wood nymph, the green or purplish weeds of a sea nymph, the prim dress of a schoolgirl, the embroidered garb of a priestess of any of the Gods *in* Lankhmar—the folk of the City of the Black Toga are rarely or never disturbed by blasphemies committed against such gods, since there are thousands of them, and easily replaced.

But there was one dress that no courtesan would dare counterfeit:

the simple, straight-falling black robes and hood of a nun of the Gods
of Lankhmar.

And yet . . .

A dozen yards short of him, the two slim black figures turned off
the path toward the nearest closet tree. One parted its rustling, pendant branches, black sleeve hanging from her arm like a bat's wing.
The other slipped inside. The first swiftly followed her, but not before her hood had slipped back a little, showing for an instant by a
wasp's violet pulse the smiling face of Frix.

The Mouser's heart leaped. So did he.

As the Mouser arrived inside the bower amid an explosion of dislodged white blooms, as if the tree herself were throwing flowers to
welcome him, the two slim black figures faced around toward him,
and dropped back their hoods. The same as he had last seen it aboard
Squid, Frix's hair was confined by a silver net. The smile still curved
her lips, though her gaze was distant and grave. But Hisvet's hair was
itself a silver-blonde wonder, her lips pouted enticingly, as if blowing
him a kiss, while her gaze danced all over his person with naughty
merriment.

She moved toward him a step.

With a happy roaring shout only he could hear, blood rushed
through the Mouser's arteries toward his center, reviving his limp
manhood in a mere moment, as a magically summoned genie offhandedly builds a tower.

The Mouser imitated his blood, rushing blindly to Hisvet and clapping his arms around her.

But with a concerted movement like a half circling in a swift dance,
the two girls had changed places, so that it was Frix he found himself
embracing, and with cheek pressed to cheek, for at the last moment
she had swayed her head aside.

The Mouser would have disengaged himself then, murmuring
courteous and indeed almost sincere excuses, for through her robe
Frix's body felt slimly enticing and most interestingly embossed, except that at that instant Hisvet leaned her head over Frix's shoulder
and tipping her elfin face sideways, planted her half-parted lips on
the Mouser's mouth, which instantly began to imitate that of the
industrious bee sipping nectar.

It seemed to him that he was in the Seventh Heaven, which is
reserved for only the most youthful and beauteous of the gods.

When at last Hisvet removed her lips from his, keeping her face so
close that the fresh scar Cat's Claw had made was a blue-edged pink
ribbon from magnificent nostril to velvet-rounded slender jaw, it was

instantly to murmur to him, "Rejoice, delicious Dirksman, for you have kissed with your own the actual lips of a Demoiselle of Lankhmar, which is a familiarity almost beyond imagining, and you have kissed *my* lips, an intimacy which passeth all understanding. And now, Dirksman, embrace Frix closely whilst I preoccupy your eyes and solace your face, which is truly the noblest area of the skin, the very soul's vizard. It is demeaning work for me, to be sure, as if a goddess should scrub and anoint with oil a common soldier's dirty boot, yet know that I do it right gladly."

Meanwhile Frix's slim fingers were unbuckling his ratskin belt. With the faintest slither and tiniest double *thunk*, it slipped with Scalpel and Cat's Claw to the springy close-cropped turf bleached almost white by the closet tree's perpetual shade.

"Remember, your eyes on *me* only," Hisvet whispered with the faintest yet firmest note of reproach. "I remain unjealous of Frix only so long as you disregard her utterly."

Though the light was still velvet soft, it seemed brighter inside the closet tree's bower than without. Perhaps the gibbous moon had risen. Perhaps the glimmer of the nectar-supping fire-beetles and glow-wasps and night-bees was concentrated here. A few of them circled lazily inside the bower, winking on and off like flirtatious gem moons.

The Mouser clapped his arms more tightly around Frix's slim waist, meanwhile murmuring to Hisvet, "Oh, White Princess . . . Oh, icy directress of desire . . . Oh, frosty goddess of the erotic . . . Oh, satanic virgin . . ." as she all the while planted tiny kisses on his eyelids and cheeks and free ear, and raked them with the long silvery lashes of her blinking eyes, so that the plant of love was tenderly cultivated and grew and grew. The Mouser sought to return these favors, but she stopped his mouth with hers. As his tongue caressed her teeth, he noted that her two center front incisors were somewhat overlarge, but in his infatuated state this difference seemed only one more point of beauty. Why even if Hisvet turned out to have some of the appurtenances of a dragon or a giant white spider—or a rat, for that matter—he would love and cosset them each and all. Even if there lifted over her head from behind the joint-masted white moist sting of a scorpion, he would honor it with a loving kiss—well, he mightn't go quite so far as that, he decided abruptly . . . still and on the other hand, he almost might, for at that instant Hisvet's eyelashes tickled the ridge of skin over the silver dart in his temple.

This was ecstacy indeed, he assured himself. It seemed to him that he was now in the Ninth and topmost Heaven, where a few select heroes luxuriate and dream and submit themselves to almost unendurable pleasures, at whiles glancing down with lazy amusement at all the gods toiling at their sparrow-watching and incense-sniffing and destiny-directing on the many tiers below.

The Mouser might never have known what happened next—and it might have been a direly different happening too—if it had not been that, never satisfied even with the most supreme ecstacy, he decided once more to disobey Hisvet's explicit injunction and steal a glance at Frix. Up to this moment he had been obediently disregarding her with eye and ear, but now it occurred to him that it would twist the launching cords of the catapult of pleasure a notch tighter if he observed both faces of his—after a fashion—two-headed light-of-love.

So when Hisvet once again nuzzled his outside ear with her slender pink and blue tongue and while he encouraged her to keep at it with small twistings of his head and moanings of delight, he rolled his eyes in the other direction, gazing surreptitiously at the face of Frix.

His first thought was that she had her neck bent at an angle that could hardly be anything but uncomfortable, to keep her head quite out of the way of the Mouser's and her mistress'. His second thought was that although her cheeks were passionately inflamed and her perfumy breath was panting through her yawn-slack lips, her gaze was coolly sad, distantly melancholy, and fixed on something worlds away, perhaps a chess game in which she and the Mouser and even Hisvet were less than pawns, perhaps a scene from an unimaginably remote childhood, perhaps—

Or perhaps she was watching something a little closer than that, something behind him and not quite worlds away—

Although it discourteously took his ear away from Hisvet's maddening tongue, he rolled his whole head in the direction he had his eyeballs and glancing over shoulder saw, blackly outlined against the pale pulsating wall of closet-blooms, the edge of a crouching silhouette with half-outstretched arm and something gleaming blue-gray at the end of that.

Instantly the Mouser crouched himself, rudely drawing back from Frix, and then half spun around, flailing out backhanded with his left hand, which had an instant earlier embraced Hisvet's maid.

It was a blow barely in time and of necessity imperfectly aimed. As the back of his left fist crashed against the lean wrist of the ocher hand holding the knife, he felt the sting of its point in his forearm. But then his right fist smashed into the Mingol's face, stirring it at least for a moment from its taut-skinned impassiveness.

As the snugly black-clad figure staggered backward under the impact, it seemed to divide in two, like some creature of slime reproducing itself, as a second dagger-armed Mingol circled from behind the first and moved toward the Mouser, who was snatching up his belt and its pendant scabbards with a curse, drawing his dirk Cat's Claw, because the pommel of that weapon came first to his hand.

Frix, who still stood dreamily in her black draperies, was saying in a husky, faraway voice, "Alarums and excursions. Enter two Mingols," while behind her Hisvet was exclaiming petulantly, "Oh, my accursed, spoilsport father! He always ruins my most aesthetic creations in the realms of delight, whether from some vile and most unfatherly jealousy, or from—"

By now the first Mingol had recovered and the two rushed warily toward the Mouser, flickering their knives ahead of their slit-eyed yellow faces as they came in. The Mouser, Cat's Claw poised a little ahead of his chest, drove them back with a sudden swishing swing of his belt held in his other hand. The weighted scabbard of his sword Scalpel took one of them in the ear, so that he winced in pain. Now would be the time to leap forward and finish them—with a single dagger-thrust apiece if he were lucky.

But the Mouser didn't. He had no way of knowing that these Mingols were the only two, or whether Hisvet and Frix might not leave off their playacting—if it had been altogether that—and leap upon him with knives of their own as he attacked his lean black assassins. Moreover, his left arm was dripping blood and he could not yet tell how bad that wound was. Finally, it was being borne in reluctantly on his proud mind that he was faced with dangers which might be a mite too much for even his great cunning, that he was blundering about in a situation he did not wholly understand, that he had even now, drunken-sensed, risked his very life against an admittedly unusual ecstacy, that he dared not depend longer on fickle luck, and that—especially in the absence of brawny Fafhrd—he badly needed wise counsel.

In two heartbeats he had turned his back on his assailants, darted past a somewhat startled-looking Frix and Hisvet, and burst out through the branchy wall of the closet-bower amidst a second and even larger explosion of white blooms.

Five heartbeats more and as he scurried north across the Plaza of Dark Delights in the light of the new-risen moon, he had buckled on his belt and withdrawn from a small pouch pendant on it a bandage which he began deftly to wrap tightly about his wound.

Five more heartbeats and he was hastening through a narrow cobbled alleyway that led in the direction of the Marsh Gate.

For he had decided that, much as he hated to admit it to himself, the time had come when he must venture across the treacherous, malodorous Great Salt Marsh and seek the advice of his sorcerous mentor, Sheelba of the Eyeless Face.

Fafhrd spurred his tall gray mare south through the burning streets of Sarheenmar, since no road led around that city fronted by the Inner Sea and backed by desert mountains. Through those latter dry, craggy hills the only trail led east to the land-locked desert-grit Sea of Monsters, by which stood the lonely City of Ghouls, avoided by all other men.

It was smoke-clouded night and the sole light was that of the flames gushing in streamers and roaring sheets from the roofs, doors, and windows of buildings once noted for their coolness, firing their thick walls of dried-clay bricks to red heat and a beauteous, rippling porcelain-like gloss where they did not melt and topple entirely.

Though the wide street was empty, Fafhrd's bloodshot eyes were watchful in his haggard, smoke-stained, sweat-riveted face. He had loosened his sword in its scabbard and his short-ax in its wide sheath, strung his Mingol bow and held it ready in his left hand, and slung the quiver of its arrows high behind his right shoulder. His lightened saddlebag and half-full canteen thumped against his mount's ribs, while his flat pouch, still empty except for the ridiculous tin whistle, flapped about.

For a wonder the mare was not panicked by the fire all around. Fafhrd had heard that the Mingols, by stark-real tests, inured their horses to all manner of horrors almost as sternly as they did themselves, slaying without mercy those who still quailed on the seventh attempt of a beast or the second of a man.

Yet now Fafhrd's mount suddenly stopped dead, just short of a narrow side street, snorting her lathered nostrils and glaring her great eyes more wild and bloodshot than Fafhrd's. Heel-thuds on her ribs would not put her in motion again, so Fafhrd dismounted and began to drag her forward by brute force down the center of the smoke-swirled, flame-walled street.

Then there came rushing from around the burning corner ahead what looked at first glance to be a gang of exceptionally tall and skinny red-litten skeletons, each wearing a skimpy harness and brandishing in either bony hand a short tapering double-edged needle-pointed sword.

After an instant's shock, Fafhrd realized these must be Ghouls, whose flesh and inner organs, he had heard—with much skepticism, but now no longer—were transparent except where the skin became sallowly or rosily translucent on the genital organs and on the lips and small breasts of their women.

It was said also that they ate only flesh, human by preference, and that it was strange indeed to watch the raw gobbets they gulped course down and churn within the bars of their ribs, gradually turning to mush and fading from sight as their sightless blood assimilated and transformed the food—granting that a mere normal man might ever have opportunity to watch Ghouls feast without becoming a supply of gobbets himself.

Fafhrd was filled with dread, but also indignation, that he, clearly a neutral in a Ghoul-Sarheenmart-Mingol war, should be thus ambushed—for now the leading skeleton hurled his right-hand sword and Fafhrd had to weave swiftly aside as it came cartwheeling through the smoky air.

Whipping his hand over shoulder, he set arrow to bow and dropped the foremost Ghoul with a shot that transfixed his ribs just to the left of his breastbone. Somewhat to his surprise, he discovered that having a skeleton for foe and target made it easier to aim for a vital part. Now as the Ghouls approached closer, uttering horrendous warshrieks, he noted the flame-light glinting here and there from their glassy hides and realized that even counting their flesh as solid, they were an exceptionally skinny, though rangy, folk.

He brought down two more of his charging foes, the last with a dart into a black eye socket, then dropped his bow, whirled out short-ax and sword, and made a long lunge with the latter as the four remaining Ghouls, their speed unchecked, were upon him.

Graywand took a Ghoul under the chin, jolting him to a dying stop. It was weird to see the skeleton collapse without rattle of bone. The short-ax next licked out, decapitating another enemy, whose glassy-fleshed skull went spinning off, but whose torso, louting forward, drenched the Northerner's ax-hand with invisible, warm, silky fluid.

These grisly events gave the third Ghoul time to run around his stricken comrades and get in on Fafhrd a thrust which, fortunately coming from above, glanced off his left ribs without wounding him deeply.

The long smarting sword-slice, however, turned Fafhrd's indignation wholly to fury and he smote that Ghoul so deeply in the skull that the short-ax stuck and was jerked from Fafhrd's hand. His fury became an almost blinding red rage, not lacking sexual undertones, so that when he noted that the fourth and last Ghoul carried pale breasts on her white ribs like two roses pinned there, he knocked the weapons from her hands with short disarming sword-swipes as she came darting toward him; then as she faltered stretched her full-length on the road with a left-handed punch to her jaw.

He stood panting, closely eyeing the scattered skeletons for sign of movement—there was none—and glaring all about for evidence of other parties of Ghouls. None also.

The horror-inured gray mare had hardly shifted an ironshod hoof during the melee. Now she tossed her gaunt head, writhed back her black lips from her huge teeth and whinnied snickeringly.

Sheathing Graywand, Fafhrd knelt warily by the female skeleton and pressed two fingers into the invisible flesh under the hinges of her jaw. He felt a slow pulse. Without ceremony he hoisted her by the waist. She weighed a little more than he anticipated so that her slenderness surprised him as did also the resilience and smooth texture of her invisible skin. Cold-headedly leashing his hot vengeful impulses, he dumped her over his saddlebow so that her legs dangled on one side and her trunk on the other. The mare glared back over shoulder and again lip-writhingly bared her yellowish teeth, but did no more than that.

Fafhrd bandaged his wound, rocked his hand-ax from its bony trap and sheathed it, gathered up his bow, mounted the mare and cantered on down the fire-fenced street through the wreaths of smoke and swirls of stinging sparks. He was constantly peering for more ambushes, yet glancing down once he found himself disconcerted that there should appear to be a bare white pelvic girdle on his saddlebow, just a fantastically-finned large loose bony knot to the eyes, even though hitched on either side by misty sinews and other cloudy gristle to the balance of a skeleton. After a bit he slung his strung bow over her left shoulder and rested his left hand on the slim warm invisible buttocks, to reassure himself there was a woman there.

The rats were looting by night in Lankhmar. Everywhere in the age-old city they were pilfering, and not only food. They filched the greenish bent brass coins off a dead carter's eyes and the platinum-set nose, ear and lip jewels from the triply locked gem chest of Glipkerio's wraith-thin aunt, gnawing in the thick oak a postern door neat as a fairy tale. The wealthiest grocer lost all his husked Hrusp nuts, gray caviar from sea-sundered Ool Plerns, dried larks' hearts, strength-imparting tiger meal, sugar-dusted ghostfingers, and ambrosia wafers, while less costly dainties were untouched. Rare parchments were taken from the Great Library, including original deeds to the sewerage and tunneling rights under the most ancient parts of the city. Sweetmeats vanished from beside tables, toys from princes' nurseries, tidbits from gold-inlaid silver appetizer trays, and flinty grain from horses' feedbags. Bracelets were unhooked from the wrists of embracing lovers, the pouches and snugly-flapped pockets of crossbow-armed rat watchers were picked, and from under the noses of cats and ferrets their food was stolen.

Ominous touch, the rats gnawed nothing except where it was needful to make entries, they left no dirty, clawed tracks or fluted tooth-marks, and they befouled nothing, but left their dark droppings in neat pyramids, as if taking an absent owner's care for a house they might decide to occupy permanently.

The most cunning traps were set, subtle poisons laid out invitingly, ratholes stoppered with leaden plugs and brazen plates, candles lit in dark corners, unwinking watch kept in every likely spot. All to no avail.

Shiversomely, the rats showed a human sagacity in many of their actions. Of their few doorways discovered, some looked sawed rather than gnawed, the sawed-out part being replaced like a little door. They swung by cords of their own to dainties hung from ceilings for safety, and a few terrified witnesses claimed to have seen them hurling such cords over their hanging places like bolas, or even shooting them there attached to the darts of tiny crossbows. They seemed to practice a division of labor, some acting as lookouts, others as leaders and guards, others as skilled breakers and mechanics, still others as mere burden-bearers docile to the squeak of command.

Worst of all, the humans who heard their rare squeakings and chitterings claimed they were not mere animal noises, but the language of Lankhmar, though spoken so swiftly and pitched so high that it was generally impossible to follow.

Lankhmar's fears grew. Prophecies were recalled that a dark conqueror commanding a countless horde of cruel followers who aped the manners of civilization but were brutes *and wore dirty furs*, would some day seize the city. This had been thought to refer to the Mingols, but it could be construed as designating the rats.

Even fat Samanda was inwardly terrorized by the depredation of the overlord's pantries and food lockers, and by a ceaseless invisible pattering. She had all the maids and pages routed from their cots two hours before dawn and in the cavernous kitchen and before the roaring fireplace, big enough to roast two beefs and heat two dozen ovens, she conducted a mass interrogation and whipping to quiet her nerves

and divert her thoughts from the real culprits. Looking like slim copper statues in the orange light each shaven victim stood, bent, knelt or
lay flat before Samanda, as directed, and endured her or his artisti-
cally laid-on welting, afterwards kissing the black hem of Samanda's
skirt or gently patting her face and neck with a lily-white towel,
chilled with ice water and wrung out, for the ogress plied her whip
until the sweat trickled down from the black sphere of her hair and
dripped in beads from her moustache. Slender Reetha was lashed
once more, but she had a revenge by slipping a fistful of finely ground
white pepper into the icy basin when she returned the towel to it;
true, this resulted in a quadrupling of the next victim's punishment,
but when one achieves revenge, the innocent perforce suffer.

The spectacle was watched by a select audience of white-smocked
cooks and grinning barbers, of whom not a few were needed to shave
the palace's army of servants. They guffawed and giggled appreciatively. It was also observed by Glipkerio from behind curtains in a
gallery. The beanpole overlord was entranced and his aristocratically
long nerves as much soothed as Samanda's—until he noted in the
kitchen's topmost gloomy shelves the hundreds of paired pinpoints of
the eyes of uninvited onlookers. He raced back to his well-guarded
private chambers with his black toga flapping like a sail torn loose in
a squall from a tall-masted yacht. Oh, he thought, if only Hisvin
would work his master spell! But the old grain-merchant and sorcerer
had told him that one planet was not quite yet in the proper configu-
ration to reinforce his magic. Events in Lankhmar had begun to look
like a race between some star and the rats. Well, if worse came to
worst, Glipkerio told himself, at once giggling and panting in his
swirly flight, he had an infallible way of escaping from Lankhmar
and Nehwon too, and winning his way to some other world, where
he would doubtless quickly be proclaimed monarch of all or at any
rate an ample principality to begin with—he was a very reasonable
overlord, Glipkerio felt—and thereby have some small solace for the
loss of Lankhmar.

IX

SHEELBA OF THE Eyeless Face reached into the hut without turning his hooded head and swiftly found a small object and held it forth.

"Here is your answer to Lankhmar's Rat Plague," he said in a voice deep, hollow, rapid and grating as round stones thudding together in a moderate surf. "Solve that problem, you solve all."

Gazing from more than a yard below, the Gray Mouser saw silhouetted against the paling sky a small squat bottle pinched between the black fabric of the overlong sleeve of Sheelba, who chose never to show his fingers, if they were that. Silvery dawnlight shivered through the bottle's crystal stopper.

The Mouser was not impressed. He was bone-weary and be-mired from armpit to boots, which were now sunk ankle-deep in sucking muck and sinking deeper all the time. His coarse gray silks were beslimed and ripped, he feared, beyond the most cunning tailor's repair. His scratched skin, where it was dry, was scaled with the Marsh's itching muddy salt. The bandaged wound in his left arm ached and burned. And now his neck had begun to ache too, from having to peer craningly upward.

All around him stretched the dismal reaches of the Great Salt Marsh, acres of knife-edged sea grass hiding treacherous creeks and deadly sink-holes and pimpled with low hummocks crowded with twisted, dwarfed thorn trees and bloated prickly cactuses. While its animal population ran a noxious gamut from sea leeches, giant worms, poison eels and water cobras to saw-beaked, low-flapping cadaver birds and far-leaping, claw-footed salt-spiders.

Sheelba's hut was a black dome about as big as the closet-tree bower in which the Mouser had last evening endured ecstacy and attempted assassination. It stood above the Marsh on five crooked poles or legs, four spaced evenly around its rim, the fifth central. Each leg was footed with a round plate big as a cutlassman's shield, concave upward, and apparently envenomed, for ringing each was a small collection of corpses of the Marsh's deadly fauna.

The hut had a single doorway, low and top-rounded as a burrow entrance. In it now Sheelba lay, chin on bent left elbow, if either of those were those, stretching out the squat bottle and seeming to peer down at the Mouser, unmindful of the illogicality of one called the Eyeless peering. Yet despite the sky-rim now pinkening to the east, the Mouser could see no hint of face of any sort in the deep hood, only midnight dark. Wearily and for perhaps the thousandth time, the Mouser wondered if Sheelba were called the Eyeless because he was blind in the ordinary way, or had only leathery skin between nostrils and pate, or was skull-headed, or perhaps had quivering antennae where eyes should be. The speculation gave him no shiver of fear, he was too angry and fatigued—and the squat bottle still didn't impress him.

Batting aside a springing salt-spider with the back of his gauntleted hand, the Mouser called upward, "That's a mighty small jug to hold poison for all the rats of Lankhmar. Hola, you in the black bag there, aren't you going to invite me up for a drink, a bite, and a dry-out? I'll curse you otherwise with spells I've unbeknownst stolen from you!"

"I'm not your mother, mistress, or nurse, but your wizard!" Sheelba retorted in his harsh hollow sea-voice. "Cease your childish threats and stiffen your back, small gray one!"

That last seemed the ultimate and crushing indignity to the Mouser with his stiff neck and straining spine. He thought bitterly of the sinew-punishing, skin-smarting night he'd just spent. He'd left Lankhmar by the Marsh Gate, to the frightened amazement of the guards, who had strongly advised against solo Marsh sorties even by day. Then he'd followed the twisty causeway by moonlight to the lightning-blasted but still towering gray Seahawk Tree. There after long peering he'd spotted Sheelba's hut by a pulsing blue glow coming from its low doorway, and plunged boldly toward it through the swordish sea grass. Then had come nightmare. Deep creeks and thorny hummocks had appeared where he didn't expect them and he had speedily lost his usually infallible sense of direction. The small blue glow had winked out and finally reappeared far to his right, then seemed to draw near and recede bafflingly time after time. He had realized he must be walking in circles around it and guessed that Sheelba had cast a dizzying enchantment on the area, perhaps to ensure against interruption while working some particularly toilsome and heinous magic. Only after twice almost perishing in quicksands and being stalked by a long-legged marsh leopard with blue-glinting eyes which the Mouser once mistook for the hut, because the beast seemed to have a habit of winking, had he at last reached his destination as the stars were dimming.

Thereafter he had poured out, or rather up, to Sheelba all his recent vexations, suggesting suitable solutions for each problem: a love potion for Hisvet, friendship potions for Frix and Hisvin, a patron potion for Glipkerio, a Mingol-repellent ointment, a black albatross to seek out Fafhrd and tell him to hurry home, and perhaps something to use against the rats, too. Now he was being offered only the last.

He rotated his head writhingly to unkink his neck, flicked a sea cobra away with Scalpel's scabbard-tip, then gazed up sourly at the little bottle.

"How am I supposed to administer it?" he demanded. "A drop down each rathole? Or do I spoon it into selected rats and release them? I warn you that if it contains seeds of the Black Sickness, I will send all Lankhmar to extirpate you from the Marsh."

"None of those," Sheelba grated contemptuously. "You find a spot where rats are foregathered. Then you drink it yourself."

The Mouser's eyebrows lifted. After a bit he asked, "What will that do? Give me an evil eye for rats, so my glance strikes them dead? Make me clairvoyant, so I can spy out their chief nests through solid earth and rock? Or wondrously increase my cunning and mental powers?" he added, though truth to tell, he somewhat doubted if the last were possible to any great degree.

"Something like all those," Sheelba retorted carelessly, nodding his hood. "It will put you on the right footing to cope with the situation. It will give you a power to deal with rats and deal death to them too, which no complete man has ever possessed on earth before. Here." He let go the bottle. The Mouser caught it. Sheelba added instantly, "The effects of the potion last but nine hours, to the exact pulse-beat, which I reckon at a tenth of a million to the day, so see that all your work be finished in three-eighths that time. Do not fail to report to me at once thereafter all the circumstances of your adventure. And now farewell. Do not follow me."

Sheelba withdrew inside his hut, which instantly bent its legs and by ones and twos lifted its shield-like feet with sucking *plops* and walked away—somewhat ponderously at first, but then more swiftly, footing it like a great black beetle or water bug, its platters fairly skidding on the mashed-down sea grass.

The Mouser gazed after it with fury and amazement. Now he understood why the hut had been so elusive, and what had *not* gone wrong with his sense of direction, and why the tall Seahawk Tree was no longer anywhere in sight. The wizard had led him a long chase last night, and doubtless a merry one from Sheelba's viewpoint.

And when it occurred to the bone-tired, be-mired Mouser that Sheelba could readily now have transported him to the vicinity of the Marsh Gate in his traveling hut, he was minded to peg at the departing vehicular dwelling the lousy little bottle he'd got.

Instead he knotted a length of bandage tightly around the small black container, top to bottom, to make sure the stopper didn't come out, put the bottle in the midst of his pouch, and carefully retightened and tied the pouch's thong. He promised himself that if the potion did not solve his problems, he would make Sheelba feel that the whole city of Lankhmar had lifted up on myriad stout legs and come trampling across the Great Salt Marsh to pash the wizard in his hut. Then with a great effort he pulled his feet one after the other out of the muck into which he'd sunk almost knee-deep, pried a couple of pulsing sea slugs off his left boot with Cat's Claw, used the same dagger to slay by slashing a giant worm tightening around his right ankle, drank the last stinging sup of wine in his wine-flask, tossed that away, and set out toward the tiny towers of Lankhmar, now dimly visible in the smoky west, directly under the sinking, fading gibbous moon.

The rats were harming in Lankhmar, inflicting pain and wounds. Dogs came howling to their masters to have needle-like darts taken out of their faces. Cats crawled into hiding to wait it out while rat-bites festered and healed. Ferrets were found squealing in rat-traps that bruised flesh and broke bones. Elakeria's black marmoset almost drowned in the oiled and perfumed water of his mistress' deep, slippery-sided silver bathtub, into which the spidery-armed pet had somehow been driven, befouling the water in his fear.

Rat-nips on the face brought sleepers screamingly awake, sometimes to see a small black form scuttling across the blanket and leaping from the bed. Beautiful or merely terrified women took to wearing while they slept full masks of silver filigree or tough leather. Most households, highest to humblest, slept by candlelight and in shifts, so that there were always watchers. A shortage of candles developed, while lamps and lanterns were priced almost out of sight. Strollers had their ankles bitten; most streets showed only a few hurrying figures, while alleys were deserted. Only the Street of the Gods, which stretched from the Marsh Gate to the granaries on the Hlal, was free of rats, in consequence of which it and its temples were crammed with worshipers rich and poor, credulous and hitherto atheist, praying for relief from the Rat Plague to the ten hundred and one Gods *in* Lankhmar and even to the dire and aloof Gods *of* Lankhmar, whose bell-towered, ever-locked temple stood at the granaries-end of the street, opposite the narrow house of Hisvin the grain-merchant.

In frantic reprisal, ratholes were flooded, sometimes with poisoned water. Fumes of burning phosphorous and sulfur were pumped down them with bellows. By order of the Supreme Council and with the oddly ambivalent approval of Glipkerio, who kept chattering about his secret weapons, professional rat-catchers were summoned en masse from the grainfields to the south and from those to the west, across the river Hlal. By command of Olegnya Mingolsbane, acting without consultation with his overlord, regiments of black-clad soldiers were rushed at the double from Tovilyis, Kartishla, even Land's End, and issued on the way weapons and items of uniform which puzzled them mightily and made them sneer more than ever at their quartermasters and at the effete and fantasy-minded Lankhmar military bureaucracy: long-handled three-tined forks, throwing balls pierced with many double-ended slim spikes, lead-weighted throwing nets, sickles, heavy leather gauntlets and bag-masks of the same material.

Where *Squid* was docked at the towering granaries near the end of the Street of the Gods, waiting fresh cargo, Slinoor paced the deck nervously and ordered smooth copper disks more than a yard across set midway up each mooring cable, to baffle any rat creeping up them. The black kitten stayed mostly at the mast-top, worriedly a-peer at the city and descending only to scavenge meals. No wharf-cats came sniffing aboard *Squid* or were to be seen prowling the docks.

In a green-tiled room in the Rainbow Palace of Glipkerio Kistomerces, and in the midst of a circle of fork-armed pages and guardsmen officers with bared dirks and small one-hand crossbows at the cock, Hisvin sought to cope with the hysteria of Lankhmar's beanpole monarch, whom a half-dozen slim naked serving maids were simultaneously brow-stroking, finger-fondling, toe-kissing, plying with wine and black opium pills tiny as poppy seeds, and otherwise hopefully soothing.

Twisting away from his delightful ministrants, who moderated but did not cease their attentions, Glipkerio bleated petulantly, "Hisvin, Hisvin, you must hurry things. My people mutter at me. My Council and Captain General take measures over my head. There are even slavering mad-dog whispers of supplanting me on my seashell throne, as by my idiot cousin Radomix Kistomerces-Null. Hisvin, you've got your rats in the streets by day and night now, all set to be blasted by your incantations. When, oh when, is that planet of yours going to reach its proper spot on the starry stage so you can recite and finger-weave your rat-deadly magic? What's delaying it, Hisvin? I command that planet to move faster! Else I will send a naval expedition across the unknown Outer Sea to sink it!"

The skinny, round-shouldered grain-merchant sorrowfully sucked in his cheeks beneath the flaps of his black leather cap, raised his beady eyes ceilingward, and in general made a most pious face.

"Alas, my brave overlord," he said, "that star's course may not yet be predicted with absolute certainty. It will soon arrive at its spot, never fear, but exactly how soon the most learned astrologer cannot foretell. Benign waves urge it forward, then a malign sky-swell drives it back. It is in the eye of a celestial storm. As an iceberg-huge jewel floating in the blue waters of the heavens, it is subject to their currents and ragings. Recall also that I've told you of your traitorous courier, the Gray Mouser, who it now appears is in league with powerful witch doctors and fetish-men working against us."

Nervously plucking at his black toga and slapping away with his long flappy fingers the pink hand of a maid who sought to rearrange the garment, Glipkerio spat out peevishly, "Now the Mouser. Now the stars. What sort of impotent sorcerer are you? Methinks the rats rule the stars as well as the streets and corridors of Lankhmar."

Reetha, who was the rebuffed maid, uttered a soundless philosophic sigh and softly as a mouse inserted her slapped hand under her overlord's toga and began most gently to scratch his stomach, meanwhile occupying her mind with a vision of herself girdled in three leather loops with Samanda's keys, thongs, chains, and whips, while the blubbery palace mistress knelt naked and quaking before her.

Hisvin intoned, "Against that pernicious thought, I present you with a most powerful palindrome: Rats live on no evil star. Recite it with lips and mind when your warlike eagerness to come to final grips with your furry foes makes you melancholy, oh most courageous commander in chief."

"You give me words; I ask for action," Glipkerio complained.

"I will send my daughter Hisvet to attend you. She has now disciplined into instructive erotic capers a new dozen of silver-caged white rats."

"Rats, rats, rats! Do you seek to drive me mad?" Glipkerio squeaked angrily.

"I will at once order her to destroy her harmless pets, good scholars though they be," Hisvin answered smoothly, bowing very low so that he could make a nasty face unseen. "Then, your overlordship wishing, she shall come to soothe your battle-strung nerves with mystic rhythms learned in the Eastern Lands. While her maid Frix is skilled in subtle massages known only to her and to certain practitioners in Quarmall, Kokgnab, and Klesh."

Glipkerio lifted his shoulders, pouted his lips and uttered a little grunt midway between indifference and unwilling satisfaction.

At that instant, a half-dozen of the officers and pages crouched together and directed their gazes and weapons at a doorway in which had appeared a little low shadow.

At the same moment, her mind overly absorbed and excited by the imagined squeals and groans of Samanda forced to crawl about the kitchen floor by jerks of her globe-dressed black hair and by jabs of the long pins taken from it, Reetha inadvertently tweaked a tuft of body hair which her gently scratching fingers had encountered.

Her monarch writhed as if stabbed and uttered a thin, piercing shriek.

A dwarf white cat had trotted nervously into the doorway, looking back over shoulder with nervous pink eyes, and now when Glipkerio screamed, disappeared as if batted by an unseen broom.

Glipkerio gasped, then shook a pointing finger under Reetha's nose. It was all she could do not to snap with her teeth at the soft, perfumed object, which looked as long and loathsome to her as the white caterpillar of a giant moon moth.

"Report yourself to Samanda!" he commanded. "Describe to her in full detail your offense. Tell her to inform me beforehand of your hour of punishment."

Against his own rule, Hisvin permitted himself a small, veiled expression of his contempt for his overlord's wits. In his solemn professional voice he said, "For best effect, recite my palindrome backwards, letter by letter."

The Mouser snored peacefully on a thick mattress in a small bedroom above the shop of Nattick Nimblefingers the tailor, who was furiously at work below cleaning and mending the Mouser's clothing and accouterments. One full and one half-empty wine-jug rested on the floor by the mattress, while under the Mouser's pillow, clenched in his left fist for greater security, was the small black bottle he'd got from Sheelba.

It had been high noon when he had finally climbed out of the Great Salt Marsh and trudged through the Marsh Gate, utterly spent. Nattick had provided him with a bath, wine and a bed—and what sense of security the Mouser could get from harboring with an old slum friend.

Now he slept the sleep of exhaustion, his mind just beginning to be tickled by dreams of the glory that would be his when, under the eyes of Glipkerio, he would prove himself Hisvin's superior at blasting rats. His dreams did not take account of the fact that Hisvin could hardly be counted a blaster of rats, but rather their ally—unless the wily grain-merchant had decided it was time to change sides.

Fafhrd, stretched out in a grassy hilltop hollow lit by moonlight and campfire, was conversing with a long-limbed recumbent skeleton named Kreeshkra, but whom he now mostly addressed by the pet name Bonny Bones. It was a moderately strange sight, yet one to touch the hearts of imaginative lovers and enemies of racial discrimination in all the many universes.

The somewhat oddly-matched pair regarded each other tenderly. Fafhrd's curly, rather abundant body hair against his pale skin, where his loosened jerkin revealed it, was charmingly counterpointed by the curving glints of campfire reflected here and there from Kreeshkra's skin against the background of her ivory bones. Like two scarlet minnows joined head and tail, her mobile lips played or lay quivering side by side, alternately revealing and hiding her pearly front teeth. Her breasts mounted on her rib cage were like the stem-halves of pears, shading from palest pink to scarlet.

Fafhrd thoughtfully gazed back and forth between these colorful adornments.

"Why?" he asked finally.

Her laughter rippled like glass chimes. "Dear stupid Mud Man!" she said in her outlandishly-accented Lankhmarese. "Girls who are not Ghouls—all your previous women, I suppose, may they be chopped to still-sentient raw bits in Hell!—draw attention to their points of attraction by concealing them with rich fabric or precious metals. We, who are transparent-fleshed and scorn all raiment, must go about it another way, employing cosmetics."

Fafhrd chuckled lazily in answer. He was now looking back and forth between his dear white-ribbed companion and the moon seen through the smooth, pale gray branches of the dead thorn tree on the rim of the hollow, and finding a wondrous content in *that* counterpoint. He thought how strange it was, though really not so much, that his feelings toward Kreeshkra had changed so swiftly. Last night, when she had revived from her knockout a mile or so beyond burning Sarheenmar, he had been ready to ravage and slay her, but she had comported herself with such courage and later proven herself such a spirited and sympathetic companion, and possessed of a ready wit, though somewhat dry, as befitted a skeleton, that when the pink rim of dawn had added itself to and then drunk the city's flames, it had seemed the natural thing that she should ride pillion behind him as he resumed his journey south. Indeed, he'd thought, such a comrade might daunt without fight the brigands who swarmed around Ilthmar and thought Ghouls a myth. He had offered her bread, which she refused, and wine, which she drank sparingly. Toward evening his arrow had brought down a desert antelope and they had feasted well, she devouring her portion raw. It was true what they said about Ghoulish digestion. Fafhrd had at first been bothered because she seemed to hold no grudge on behalf of her slain fellows and he suspected that she might be employing her extreme amiability to put him off guard and then slay him, but he had later decided that life or its loss was likely accounted no great matter by Ghouls, who looked so much like skeletons to begin with.

The gray Mingol mare, tethered to the thorn tree on the hollow's rim, threw up her head and nickered.

A mile or more overhead in the windy dark, a bat slipped from the back of a strongly winging black albatross and fluttered earthward like an animate large black leaf.

Fafhrd reached out an arm and ran his fingers through Kreeshkra's invisible, shoulder-length hair. "Bonny Bones," he asked, "why do you call me Mud Man?"

She answered tranquilly, "All your kind seem mud to us, whose flesh is as sparkling clear as running water in a brook untroubled by man or rains. Bones are beautiful. They are made to be seen." She reached out skeleton-seeming soft-touching hand and played with the hair on his chest, then went on seriously, staring toward the stars. "We Ghouls have such an aesthetic distaste for mud-flesh that we consider it a sacred duty to transform it to crystal-flesh by devouring it. Not yours, at least not tonight, Mud Man," she added, sharply tweaking a copper ringlet.

He lightly captured her wrist. "So your love for me is most unnatural, at least by Ghoulish standards," he said with a touch of argumen-
tiveness.

"If you say so, master," she answered with a sardonic, mock-sub-
missive note.

"I stand, or rather lie, corrected," Fafhrd murmured. "I'm the
lucky one, whatever your motives and whatever name we give them."
His voice became clearer again. "Tell me, Bonny Bones, how in the
world did you ever come to learn Lankhmarese?"

"Stupid, *stupid* Mud Man," she replied indulgently. "Why, 'tis our
native tongue"—and here her voice grew dreamy—"deriving from
those ages a millennium and more ago when Lankhmar's empire
stretched from Quarmall to the Trollstep Mountains and from
Earth's End to the Sea of Monsters, when Kvarch Nar was
Hwarshmar and we lonely Ghouls alley-and-graveyard thieves only.
We had another language, but Lankhmarese was easier."

He returned her hand to her side, to plant his own beyond her and
stare down into her black eye sockets. She whimpered faintly and ran
her fingers lightly down his sides. Fighting impulse for the moment,
he said, "Tell me, Bonny Bones, how do you manage to *see* anything
when light goes right through you? Do you see with the inside of the
back of your skull?"

"Questions, questions, questions," she complained moaningly.

"I only want to become less stupid," he explained humbly.

"But I *like* you to be stupid," she answered with a sigh. Then raising up on her elbow so that she faced the still blazing campfire—the
thorn tree's dense wood burnt slowly and fiercely—she said, "Look
closely into my eyes. No, without getting between them and the fire.
Can you see a small rainbow in each? That's where light is refracted
to the seeing part of my brain, and a very tiny real image formed
there."

Fafhrd agreed he could see twin rainbows, then went on eagerly,
"Don't stop looking at the fire yet; I want to show you something."
He made a cylinder of one hand and held an end of the cylinder to
her nearest eye, then clapped his fingers, held tightly together,
against the other end. "There!" he said. "You can see the fire glow
through the edges of my fingers, can't you? So I'm part transparent.
I'm part crystal, at least."

"I can, I can," she assured him with singsong weariness. She looked
away from his hands and the fire at his face and hairy chest. "But I
like you to be mud," she said. She put her hands on his shoulders.
"Come, darling, be dirtiest mud."

He gazed down at the moonlit pearl-toothed skull and blackest eye sockets in each of which a faint opalescent moonbow showed, and he remembered how a wisewoman of the North had once told him and the Mouser that they were both in love with Death. Well, she'd been right, at least about himself, Fafhrd had to confess now, as Kreesh-kra's arms began to tug at him.

At that instant there sounded a thin whistle, so high as to be almost inaudible, yet piercing the ear like a needle finer than a hair. Fafhrd jerked around. Kreeshkra swiftly lifted her head, and they noted that they were being watched not only by the Mingol mare, but also with upside-down eyes by a black bat which hung from a high gray twig of the thorn tree.

Filled with premonition, Fafhrd pointed a forefinger at the dangling black flier, which instantly fluttered down to the fleshly perch presented. Fafhrd drew off its leg a tiny black roll of parchment springy as thinnest tempered iron, waved the flutterer back to its first perch, and unrolling the black parchment and holding it close to the firelight and his eyes close to it, read the following missive writ in a white script:

> Mouser in direst danger. Also Lankhmar. Consult Ningauble of the Seven Eyes. Speed of the essence. Don't lose the tin whistle.

The signature was a tiny unfeatured oval, which Fafhrd knew to be one of the sigils of Sheelba of the Eyeless Face.

White jaw resting on folded white knuckles, Kreeshkra watched the Northerner from her inscrutable black eye pits as he buckled on his sword.

"You're leaving me," she asserted in a flat voice.

"Yes, Bonny Bones, I must ride south like the wind," Fafhrd admitted hurriedly. "A lifelong comrade's in immense peril."

"A man, of course," she divined with the same tonelessness. "Even Ghoulish men save their greatest love for their male swordmates."

"It's a different sort of love," Fafhrd started to argue as he untied the mare from the thorn tree, feeling at the flat pouch hanging from the saddlebow, to make sure it still held the thin tin cylinder. Then, more practically, "There's still half the antelope to give you strength for your trudge home—and it's uncooked too."

"So you assume my people are eaters of carrion, and that half a dead antelope is a proper measure of what I mean to you?"

"Well, I'd always heard that Ghouls . . . and no, of course, I'm not trying to *pay* you. . . . Look here, Bonny Bones—I won't argue with you, you're much too good at it. Suffice it that I must course like the lonely thunderbolt to Lankhmar, pausing only to consult my master sorcerer. I couldn't take you—or anyone!—on that journey."

Kreeshkra looked around curiously. "Who asked to go? The bat?"

Fafhrd bit his lip, then said, "Here, take my hunting knife," and when she made no reply, laid it by her hand. "Can you shoot an arrow?"

The skeleton girl observed to some invisible listener, "Next the Mud Man will be asking if I can slice a liver. Oh well, I should doubtless have tired of him in another night and on pretext of kissing his neck, bit through the great artery under his ear, and drunk his blood and devoured his carrion mud-flesh, leaving only his stupid brain, for fear of contaminating and making imbecilic my own."

Abstaining from speech, Fafhrd laid the Mingol bow and its quiver of arrows beside the hunting knife. Then he knelt for a farewell kiss, but at the last instant the Ghoul turned her head so that his lips found only her cold cheek.

As he stood up, he said, "Believe it or not, I'll come back and find you."

"You won't do either," she assured him, "and I shan't be anywhere."

"Nevertheless I will hunt you down," he said. He had untethered the mare and stood beside it. "For you have given me the weirdest and most wondrous ecstacy of any woman in the world."

Looking out into the night, the Ghoulish girl said, "Congratulations, Kreeshkra. Your gift to humanity: freakish thrills. Make like a thunderbolt, Mud Man. I dote on thrills too."

Fafhrd shut his lips, gazed at her a moment longer. Then as he whirled about him his cloak, the bat fluttered to it and hung there.

Kreeshkra nodded her head. "I said the bat." Fafhrd mounted the mare and cantered down the hillside.

Kreeshkra sprang up, snatched the bow and arrow, ran to the rim of the grassy saucer and drew a bead on Fafhrd's back, held it for three heartbeats, then turned abruptly and winged the arrow at the thorn tree. It lodged quivering in the center of the gray trunk.

Fafhrd glanced quickly around at the *snap, whir, tchunk!* A skeleton arm was waving him goodbye and continued to do so until he reached the road at the foot of the slope, where he urged the mare into a long-striding lope.

On the hilltop Kreeshkra stood in thought for two breaths. Then from her belt she detached something invisible, which she dropped in the center of the dying campfire.

There was a sputtering and a shower of sparks, when a bright blue flame shot straight up a dozen yards and burnt for as many heartbeats before it died. Kreeshkra's bones looked like blued iron, her glinting glassy flesh like scraps of tropic night-sky, but there was none to see this beauty.

Fafhrd watched the needlelike flare over shoulder as he sped rockingly along and he frowned into the wind.

The rats were murdering in Lankhmar that night. Cats died by swiftly sped crossbow darts that punctured slit-pupiled eye to lodge in brain. Poison set out for rats was cunningly secreted in gobbets of dogs' dinners. Elakeria's marmoset died crucified to the head of the sandalwood bed of that plump wanton, just opposite her ceiling-tall mirror of daily-polished silver. Babies were bitten to death in their cradles. A few big folk were stung by deep-burrowing darts smeared with a black stuff and died in convulsions after hours of agony. Many drank to still their fears, but the unwatched dead-drunk bled to death from neat cuts that tapped arteries. Glipkerio's aunt, who was also Elakeria's mother, strangled in a noose hung over a dark steep stairs made slippery by spilled oil. A venturesome harlot was overrun in the Plaza of Dark Delights and eaten alive while no one heeded her screams.

So tricky were some of the traps the rats set and by circumstantial evidence so deft their wielding of their weapons, that many folk began to insist that some of them, especially the rare and elusive albinos, had on their forelegs tiny clawed hands rather than paws, while there were many reports of rats running on their hind legs.

Ferrets were driven in droves down ratholes. None returned. Eerily bag-headed, brown-uniformed soldiers rushed about in squads, searching in vain for targets for their new and much-touted weapons. The deepest wells in the city were deliberately poisoned, on the assumption that the city of rats went as deep and tapped those wells for its water supply. Burning brimstone was recklessly poured into ratholes and soldiers had to be detached from their primary duty to fight the resultant fires.

An exodus begun by day continued by night from the city, by yacht, barge, rowboat, and raft, also south by cart, carriage, or afoot through the Grain Gate and even east through the Marsh Gate, until bloodily checked by command of Glipkerio, advised by Hisvin and by the city's stiff-necked and ancient Captain General, Olegnya Mingolsbane. Lukeen's war galley was one of the several which rounded up the fleeing civilian vessels and returned them to their docks—that is, all but the most gold-heavy, bribe-capable yachts. Shortly afterwards, rumor spread fast as news of a new sin, that there was a conspiracy to assassinate Glipkerio and set on his throne his widely-admired and studious pauper cousin, Radomix Kistomerces-Null, who was known to keep seventeen pet cats. A striking force of plainclothes constables and Lankhmarines was sent from the Rainbow Palace through the torchlit dark to seize Radomix, but he was warned in time and lost himself and his cats in the slums, where he and they had many friends, both human and feline.

As the night of terror grew older at snail's pace, the streets emptied of civilian human traffic and grew peculiarly silent and dark, since all cellars and many ground floors had been abandoned and locked, barred, and barricaded from above. Only the Street of the Gods was still crowded, where the rats still had made no assault and where comfort of a sort was to be had against fears. Elsewhere the only sounds were the quick, nervous tramp of squads of constables and soldiers on night guard and patterings and chitterings that grew ever more bold and numerous.

Reetha lay stretched before the great kitchen fire, trying to ignore Samanda sitting in her huge palace mistress' chair and inspecting her whips, rods, paddles, and other instruments of correction, sometimes suddenly whishing one through the air. A very long thin chain confined Reetha by her neck collar to a large, recessed, iron ring-bolt in the kitchen's tiled floor near the center of the room. Occasionally Samanda would eye her thoughtfully, and whenever the bell tolled the half hour, she'd order the girl to stand to attention and perhaps perform some trifling chore, such as filling Samanda's wine-tankard. Yet still she never struck the girl, nor so far as Reetha knew, had sent message to Glipkerio apprising him of the time of his maid's correction.

Reetha realized that she was being deliberately subjected to the torment of punishment deferred and tried to lose her mind in sleep and fantasies. But sleep, the few times she achieved it, brought nightmares and made more shockful the half-hourly wakenings, while fantasies of lording it cruelly over Samanda rang too hollow in her present situation. She tried to romance, but the material she had to work with was thin. Among other scraps, there was the smallish, gray-clad swordsman who had asked her her name the day she had been whipped for being scared by rats into dropping her tray. He at least had been courteous and had seemed to regard her as more than an animated serving tray, but surely he had long since forgotten her.

Without warning, the thought flashed across her mind that if she could lure Samanda close, she might if she were swift enough be able to strangle her with the slack of her chain—but this thought only set her trembling. In the end she was driven to a count of her blessings, such as that at least she had no hair to be pulled or set afire.

The Gray Mouser woke an hour past midnight feeling fit and ready for action. His bandaged wound didn't bother him, though his left forearm was still somewhat stiff. But since he could not favorably contact Glipkerio before daylight, and having no mind to work Sheelba's anti-rat magic except in the overlord's admiring presence, he decided to put himself to sleep again with the remaining wine.

Operating silently, so as not to disturb Nattick Nimblefingers, whom he heard snoring tiredly on a pallet near him, he rather rapidly finished off the half jug and then began more meditatively to suck on the full one. Yet drowsiness, let alone sleep, perversely refused to come. Instead the more that he drank, the more tinglingly alive he became, until at last with a shrug and a smile he took up Scalpel and Cat's Claw with never a clink and stole downstairs.

There a horn-shielded lamp burning low showed his clothes and accouterments all orderly lying on Nattick's clean worktable. His boots and other leather had been brushed and scrubbed and then resuppled with neat's-foot oil, and his gray silk tunic and cloak washed, dried, and neatly mended, each new seam and patch interlocked and double-stitched. With a little wave of thanks at the ceiling, he rapidly dressed himself, lifted one of the two large oil-filmed identical keys from their secret hook, unlocked the door, drew it open on its well-greased hinges, slipped into the night and locked the door behind him.

He stood in deep shadow. Moonlight impartially silvered the ageworn walls opposite and their stains and the tight-shuttered little windows and the low, shut doors above the footstep-hollowed stone thresholds and the worn-down cobbles and the bronze-edged drainslits and the scattered garbage and trash. The street was silent and empty either way to where it curved out of sight. So, he thought, must look the City of Ghouls by night, except that there, there were supposed to be skeletons slipping about on narrow ridgy ivory feet with somehow never a *clack* or *click*.

Moving like a great cat, he stepped out of the shadows. The swollen but deformed moon peered down at him almost blindingly over Nattick's scolloped roof-ridge. Then he was himself part of the silvered world, padding at a swift, long-striding walk on his spongy-soled boots along Cheap Street's center toward its curve-hidden intersections with the Street of the Thinkers and the Street of the Gods. Whore Street paralleled Cheap Street to the left and Carter Street and Wall Street to the right, all four following the curving Marsh Wall beyond Wall Street.

At first the silence was unbroken. When the Mouser moved like a cat, he made no more noise. Then he began to hear it—a tiny pattering, almost like a first flurry of small raindrops, or the first breath of a storm through a small-leafed tree. He paused and looked around. The pattering stopped. His eyes searched the shadows and discerned nothing except two close-set glints in the trash that might have been water-drops or rubies—or something.

He set out again. At once the pattering was resumed, only now there was more of it, as if the storm were about to break. He quickened his stride a little, and then all of a sudden they were upon him: two ragged lines of small low silvered shapes rushing out of the shadows to his right and from behind the trash-heaps and out of the drain-slits to his left and a few even squeezing under the scoop-thresholded doors.

He began to run skippingly and much faster than his foes, Scalpel striking out like a silver toad's tongue to pink one after another of them in a vital part, as if he were some fantastic trash collector and the rats animate small rubbish. They continued to close on him from ahead, but most he outran and the rest he skewered. The wine he'd bibbed giving him complete confidence, it became almost a dance—a dance of death with the rats figuring as humanity and he their grisly gray overlord, armed with rapier instead of scythe.

Shadows and silvered wall switched sides as the street curved. A larger rat got past Scalpel and sprang for his waist, but he deftly flicked it past him on Cat's Claw's point while his sword thrust through two more. Never in his life, he told himself gleefully, had he been so truly and literally the Gray Mouser, decimating a mouser's natural prey.

Then something whirred past his nose like an angry wasp, and everything changed. He recalled in a vivid flash the supremely strange night of decision aboard *Squid*, which had become almost a fantasy-memory to him, and the crossbow rats and Skwee with sword at his jugular, and he realized fully for the first time in Lankhmar that he was not dealing with ordinary or even extraordinary rats, but with an alien and hostile culture of intelligent beings, small to be sure, but perhaps more clever and surely more prolific and murder-bent than even men.

Leaving off skipping, he ran as fast as he could, slashing out repeat-edly with Scalpel, but thrusting his dirk in his belt and grabbing in his pouch for Sheelba's black bottle.

It wasn't there. With sinking heart and a self-curse, he remembered that, wine-bemused, he'd left it under his pillow at Nattick's.

He shot past the black Street of the Thinkers with its taller build-ings shutting out the moon. More rats poured out. His boot squished down on one and he almost slipped. Two more steel wasps buzzed past his face and—he'd never have believed it from another's lips—a small blue-flaming arrow. He raced past the lightless long wall of the building housing the Thieves' Guild, thinking chiefly of making more speed and hardly at all of rat-slashing.

Then almost at once, Cheap Street curving more sharply, there were bright lights ahead of him and many people, and a few strides later he was among them and the rats all gone.

He bought from a street vendor a small tankard of charcoal-heated ale to occupy the time while his dread and gasping faded. When his dry throat had been warmly and bitterly wetted, he gazed east two squares down the Street of the Gods to the Marsh Gate and then west more glittering blocks than he could clearly see.

It seemed to him that all Lankhmar was gathered here tonight by light of flaring torch and lamp and horn-shielded candle—and pole-lofted flare—praying and strolling, moaning and drinking, munch-ing, and whispering fearful gossip. He wondered why the rats had spared this street only. Were they even more afraid of men's gods than men were?

At the Marsh Gate end of the Street of the Gods were only the hutments of the newest, poorest, and most slum-suited Gods *in* Lankhmar. Indeed most of the congregation here were mere curb-side gatherings about some scrawny hermit or leather-skinned death-skinny priest come from the deserts of the Eastern Lands.

The Mouser turned the other way and began a slow and twisty stroll through the hush-voiced mob, here greeting an old acquain-tance, there purchasing a cup of wine or a noggin of spirits from a street seller, for the Lankhmarts believe that religion and minds half-fuddled, or at least drink-soothed, go nicely together.

Despite momentary temptation, he successfully got by the intersec-tion with Whore Street, tapping the dart in his temple to remind himself that erotic experience would end in futility. Although Whore Street itself was dark, the girls young and old were out in force to-night, doing their business in the shadowed porticos, workmanlike providing man's third most potent banishment of fears after prayers and wine.

The farther he got from the Marsh Gate, the wealthier and more richly served became the Gods *in* Lankhmar whose establishments he passed—churches and temples now, some even with silver-chased pillars and priests with golden chains and gold-worked vestments. From the open doors came rich yellow light and heady incense and the drone of chanted curses and prayers—all against the rats, so far as the Mouser could make them out.

Yet the rats were not altogether absent from the Street of the Gods, he began to note. Tiny black heads peered down from the roofs now and again, while more than once he saw close-set amber-red eyes behind the grill of a drain in the curb.

But by now he had taken aboard enough wine and spirits not to be troubled by such trifles, despite his recent fright, and his memory wandered off to the strange season, years ago, when Fafhrd had been the penniless, shaven acolyte of Bwadres, sole priest of Issek of the Jug, and he himself had been lieutenant to the racketeer Pulg, who preyed on all priests and prayerful folk.

He returned to his complete senses near the Hlal end of the Street of the Gods, where the temples are all golden-doored and their spires shoot sky-high and the priests' robes are rainbow expanses of jewels. Around him was a throng of folk almost as richly clad, and now through a break in it he suddenly perceived, under green velvet hood and high-piled, silver-woven black hair, the merry-melancholy face of Frix with dark eyes upon him. Something pale brown and small and irregularly shaped dropped noiselessly from her hand to the pavement, here of ceramic bricks morticed with brass. Then she turned and was gone. He rushed after her, snatching up the small square of ball-crumpled parchment she'd dropped, but two aristos and their courtesans and a merchant in cloth of gold got shoulderingly in his way, and when he had broken free of them, resolutely curbing his wine-fired temper to avoid a duel, and got out of the press, no hooded green velvet robe was to be seen, or any woman in any guise looking remotely like Frix.

He smoothed the crumpled parchment and read it by the light of a low-swinging, horn-paned oil street lamp.

> *Be of hero-like patience and courage.*
> *Your dearest desire will be fulfilled*

beyond your daringest expectations,
and all enchantments lifted.
                                    Hisvet

He looked up and discovered he was past the last luxuriously gleaming, soaring temple of the Gods *in* Lankhmar and facing the lightless low square fane with its silent square bell-tower of the Gods *of* Lankhmar, those brown-boned, black-togaed ancestor-deities, whom the Lankhmarts never gather to worship, yet fear and revere in their inmost sleeping minds beyond the sum of all the other gods and devils in Nehwon.

The excitement engendered in him by Hisvet's note momentarily extinguished by that sight, the Mouser moved forward from the last street lamp until he stood in the lightless street facing the lightless low temple. There crowded into his liquored compassless mind all he had ever heard of the dread Gods *of* Lankhmar: They cared not for priests, or wealth, or even worshipers. They were content with their dingy temple *so long as they were not disturbed.* And in a world where practically all other gods, including all the Gods *in* Lankhmar, seemed to desire naught but more worshipers, more wealth, more news of themselves to be dissipated to the ends of the world, this was most unusual and even sinister. They emerged only when Lankhmar was in direct peril—and even then not always—they rescued and then they chastised—not Lankhmar's foes but her folks—and after that they retired as swiftly as possible to their dismal fane and rotting beds.

There were no rat-shapes on the roof of *that* temple, or in the shadows crowding thick around it.

With a shudder the Mouser turned his back on it, and there across the street, shouldered by the great dim cylinders of the granaries and backgrounded by Glipkerio's palace with its rainbow minarets pastel in the moonlight, was the narrow, dark-stoned house of Hisvin the grain-merchant. Only one window in the top floor showed light.

The wild desires roused in the Mouser by Hisvet's note flared up again and he was mightily tempted to climb that window, however smooth and holdless looked the unadorned sooty stone wall, but common sense got the better of wild desire in him despite the fire of wine. After all, Hisvet had writ "patience" before "courage."

With a sigh and a shrug he turned back toward the brightly lit section of the Street of the Gods, gave most of the coins in his pouch to a mincing, bejeweled slave-girl for a small crystal flask of rare white brandy from the walled tray hung from her shoulders just below her naked breasts, took one swig of the icily fiery stuff, and was by that swig emboldened to cut down pitch-black Nun Street, intending to go a square beyond the Street of the Thinkers and by way of Crafts Street, weave home to Cheap Street and Nattick's.

Aboard *Squid*, curled up in the crow's nest, the black kitten writhed and whimpered in his sleep as though racked by the nightmares of a full-grown cat, or even a tiger.

X

FAFHRD STOLE A lamb at dawn and broke into a cornfield north of Ilthmar to provide breakfast for himself and his mount. The thick chops, broiled or at least well-scorched on a thick green twig over a small fire, were delicious, but the mare as she chomped grimly eyed her new master with what seemed to him qualified approval, as if to say, "I'll eat this corn, though it is soft, milky, and effeminate truck compared to the flinty Mingol grain on which they raised me and grew my stern courage, which comes of grinding the teeth."

They finished their repast, but made off hurriedly when outraged shepherds and farmers came hooting at them through the tall green field. A stone slung by a shepherd who'd probably brained a few dozen wolves in his day, whizzed close above Fafhrd's ducked head. He attempted no reprisal, but galloped out of range, then reined in to an amble to give himself time to think before passing through Ilthmar, around which no roads led, and the squatty towers of which were already visible ahead, glinting deceptively golden in the new-minted rays of the fresh sun.

Ilthmar, fronting the Inner Sea somewhat north of the Sinking Land which led west to Lankhmar, was an ill, treacherous, money-minded city. Though nearest Lankhmar, it stood at the crossroads of the known world, roughly equidistant from the desert-guarded Eastern Lands, the forested Land of the Eight Cities, and the steppes, where traveled about the great tent-city of the merciless Mingols. And being so situated, it forever sought by guile or secret force to levy toll on all travelers. Its land-pirates and sea-brigands, who split their take with its unruly governing barons, were widely feared, yet the great powers could never permit one of themselves to dominate such a strategic point, so Ilthmar maintained the independence of a middleman, albeit a most thievish and untrustworthy one.

Central location, where the gossip of all Nehwon crossed tracks along with the world's travelers, was surely also the reason why Nigauble of the Seven Eyes had located himself in a mazy, enchantment-guarded cave at the foot of the little mountains south of Ilthmar.

Fafhrd saw no signs of Mingol raiding, which did not entirely please him. An alarmed Ilthmar would be easier to slip through than an Ilthmar pretending to laze in the sun, but with pig-eyes ever a-watch for booty. He wished now he'd brought Kreeshkra with him, as he'd earlier planned. Her terrifying bones would have been a surer guarantee of safe transit than a passport from the King of the East stamped in gold-sifted wax with his famed Behemoth Seal. What a fool, either to dote or to flee, a man was about a woman new-bedded! He wished also that he had not given her his bow, or rather that he'd had two bows.

However, he was three-quarters of the way through the trash-paved city with its bedbug inns and smiling little taverns of resinous wine, more often than not laced with opium for the unwary, before trouble pounced. A great gaudy caravan rousing itself for its homeward journey to the Eastern Lands doubtless attracted attention from him. The only decor of the mean buildings around him was the emblem of Ilthmar's rat-god, endlessly repeated.

The trouble came two blocks beyond the caravan and consisted of seven scarred and pockmarked rogues, all clad in black boots, tight black trousers and jerkins and black cloaks with hoods thrown back to show close-fitting black skullcaps. One moment the street seemed clear, the next all seven were around him, menacing with their wickedly saw-toothed swords and other weapons, and demanding he dismount.

One made to seize the mare's bridle near the bit. That was definitely a mistake. She reared and put an iron-shod hoof past his guard and into his skull as neatly as a duelist. Fafhrd drew Graywand and at the end of the drawing stroke slashed through the throat of the nearest black brigand. Coming down on her forehooves the mare lashed out a hind one and ruined the guts of an unchivalrous fellow preparing to launch a short javelin at Fafhrd's back. Then horse and rider were galloping away at a pace that at the southern outskirts of the city took them past Ilthmar's baronial guard before those slightly more respectable, iron-clad brigands could get set to stop them.

A half league beyond, Fafhrd looked back. There was no sign as yet of pursuit, but he was hardly reassured. He knew his Ilthmar brigands. They were stickers. Fired now by revenge-lust as well as loot-hunger, the four remaining black rogues would doubtless soon be on his trail. And this time they'd have arrows or at least more javelins, and use them at a respectful distance. He began to scan the slopes ahead for the tricky, almost unmarked path leading to Ningauble's underground dwelling.

Glipkerio Kistomerces found the meeting of the Council of Emergency almost more than he could bear. It was nothing more than the Inner Council plus the War Council, which overlapped in membership, these two being augmented by a few additional notables, including Hisvin, who had said nothing so far, though his small black-irised eyes were watchful. But all the others, waving their toga-winged arms for emphasis, did nothing but talk, talk, talk about the rats, rats, rats!

The beanpole overlord, who did not look tall when seated, since all his height was in his legs, had long since dropped his hands below the tabletop to hide the jittery way they were weaving like a nest of nervous white snakes, but perhaps because of this he had now developed a violent facial tic which jolted his wreath of daffodils down over his eyes every thirteenth breath he drew—he had been counting and found the number decidedly ominous.

Besides this, he had lunched only hurriedly and meagerly and—worse—not watched a page or maid being whipped or even slapped since before breakfast, so that his long nerves, finer drawn than those of other men by reason of his superior aristocracy and great length of limb, were in a most wretched state. It was all of yesterday, he recalled, that he had sent that one mincing maid to Samanda for punishment and still had got no word from his overbearing palace mistress. Glipkerio knew well enough the torment of punishment deferred, but in this case it seemed to have turned into a torment of pleasure deferred—for himself. The beastly fat woman should have more imagination! Why, oh why, he asked himself, was it only that watching a whipping could soothe him? He was a man greatly abused by destiny.

Now some black-togaed idiot was listing out nine arguments for feeing the entire priesthood of Ilthmar's rat-god to come to Lankhmar and make propitiating prayers. Glipkerio had grown so nervously impatient that he was exasperated even by the fulsome compliments to himself with which each speaker lengthily prefaced his speech, and whenever a speaker paused more than a moment for breath or effect, he had taken to quickly saying "Yes," or "No," at random, hoping this would speed things up, but it appeared to be working out the other way. Olegnya Mingolsbane had still to speak and he was the most boring, lengthiest, and self-infatuated talker of them all.

A page approached him and kneeled, holding respectfully out a scrap of dirty parchment twice folded and sealed with candle grease. He snatched it, glancing at Samanda's unmistakably large and thick-whorled thumbprint in the sooty grease, and tore it open and read the black scrawl.

She shall be lashed with white-hot wires on the stroke of three. Do not be tardy, little overlord, for I shall not wait for you.

Glipkerio sprang up, his thoughts for the moment concerned only with whether it was the half-hour or three-quarter hour after two o'clock he had last heard strike.

Waving the refolded note at his council—or perhaps it was only that his hand was wildly a-twitch—he said in one breath, glaring defiantly as he did so, "Important news of my secret weapon! I must closet me at once with its sender," and without waiting for reactions, but with a final tic so violent it jolted his daffodil wreath forward to rest on his nose, Lankhmar's overlord dashed through a silver-chased purple-wood arch out of the Council Chamber.

Hisvin slid out of his chair with a curt, thin-lipped bow to the council and went scuttling after him as fast as if he had wheels under his toga rather than feet. He caught up with Glipkerio in the corridor, laid firm hand on the skinny elbow high as his black-capped skull and after a quick glance ahead and back for eavesdroppers, called up softly yet stirringly, "Rejoice, oh mighty mind that is Lankhmar's very brain, for the lagging planet has at last arrived at his proper station, made rendezvous with his starry fleet, and tonight I speak my spell that shall save your city from the rats!"

"What's that? Oh yes. Good, oh good," the other responded, seeking chiefly to break loose from Hisvin's grasp, though meanwhile pushing back his yellow wreath so it was once more atop his blond-ringleted narrow skull. "But now I must rush me to—"

"She will stand and wait for her thrashing," Hisvin hissed with naked contempt. "I said that tonight at the stroke of twelve I speak my spell that shall save Lankhmar from the rats, and save your overlord's throne too, which you must certainly lose before dawn if we beat not the rats tonight."

"But that's just the point, she *won't* wait," Glipkerio responded with agonizing agitation. "It's *twelve*, you say? But that can't be. It's not yet three!—surely?"

"Oh wisest and most patient one, master of time and the waters of space," Hisvin growled obsequiously, a-tiptoe. Then he dug his nails into Glipkerio's arm and said slowly, marking each word, "I said that tonight's the night. My demonic intelligencers assure me the rats plan to hold off this evening, to lull the city's wariness, then make a grand assault at midnight. To make sure they're all in the streets and stay there while I recite my noxious spell from this palace's tallest minaret, you must an hour beforehand order all soldiers to the South Barracks and your constables too. Tell Captain General Olegnya you wish him to deliver them a morale-building address—the old fool won't be able to resist that bait. Do . . . you . . . understand . . . me . . . my . . . overlord?"

"Yes, yes, oh yes!" Glipkerio babbled eagerly, grimacing at the pain of Hisvin's grip, yet not angered but thinking only of getting loose. "Eleven o'clock tonight . . . all soldiers and constables off streets . . . oration by Olegnya. And now, please, Hisvin, I must rush me to—"

"—to see a maid thrashed," Hisvin finished for him flatly. Again the fingernails dug. "Expect me infallibly at a quarter to midnight in your Blue Audience Chamber, whence I shall climb the Blue Minaret to speak my spell. You yourself *must* be there—and with a corps of your pages to carry a message of reassurance to your people. See that they are provided with wands of authority. I will bring my daughter and her maid to mollify you—and also a company of my Mingol slaves to supplement your pages if need be. There'd best be wands for them too. Also—"

"Yes, yes, dear Hisvin," Glipkerio cut in, his babbling growing desperate. "I'm very grateful . . . Frix and Hisvet, they're good ones . . . I'll remember all . . . quarter to midnight . . . Blue Chamber . . . pages . . . wands . . . wands for Mingols. And now I must rush me—"

"*Also,*" Hisvin continued implacably, his fingernails like a spiked trap. "*Beware of the Gray Mouser!* Set your guards on the watch for him! And now . . . be off to your flagellatory pastimes," he added lightly, loosing his horny nails from Glipkerio's arm.

Massaging the dents they'd made, hardly yet realizing he was free, Glipkerio babbled on, "Ah yes, the Mouser—bad, bad! But the rest . . . good, good! Enormous thanks, Hisvin! And now I *must* rush me —" And he turned away with a lunging, improbably long step.

"—to see a maid—" Hisvin couldn't resist repeating.

As if the words stung him between the shoulders, Glipkerio turned back at that and interrupted with some spirit. "To attend to business of highest importance! I have other secret weapons than yours, old man—and other sorcerers too!" And then he was swift-striding off again, black toga at extremest stretch.

Cupping bony hand to wrinkled lips, Hisvin cried after him sweetly, "I hope your business writhes prettily and screams most soothingly, brave overlord!"

The Gray Mouser showed his courier's ring to the guards at the opal-tiled land entry of the palace. He half expected it not to work. Hisvin had had two days to poison silly Glip's mind against him. And indeed there were sidewise glances and a wait long enough for the Mouser to feel the full strength of his hangover and to swear he'd never drink so much, so mixed again. And to marvel too at his stupidity and good luck in venturing last night into the dark, rat-infested streets and getting back silly-drunk to Nattick's through some of the darkest of them without staggering into a second rat-ambush. Ah well, at least he'd found Sheelba's black vial safe at Nattick's, resisted the impulse to drink it while tipsy, and he'd got that heartening, titillating note from Hisvet. As soon as his business was finished here, he must hie himself straight to Hisvin's house and—

A guard returned from somewhere and nodded sourly. He was passed inside.

From the sneer-lipped third butler, who was an old gossip friend of the Mouser, he learned that Lankhmar's overlord was with his Emergency Council, which now included Hisvin. He resisted the grandiose impulse to show off his Sheelban rat-magic before the notables of Lankhmar and in the presence of his chief sorcerous rival, though he did confidently pat the black vial in his pouch. After all, he needed a spot where rats were foregathered for the thing to work and he needed Glipkerio alone best to work on *him*. So he strolled into the dim mazy lower corridors of the palace to waste an hour and eavesdrop or chat as opportunity afforded.

As generally happened when he killed time, the Mouser soon found himself headed for the kitchen. Though he dearly detested Samanda, he made a point of slyly courting her, because he knew her power in the palace and liked her stuffed mushrooms and mulled wine.

The plain-tiled yet spotless corridors he now traversed were empty. It was the slack half hour when dinner has been washed up and supper mostly not begun, and every weary servitor who can flops on a cot or the floor. Also, the menace of the rats doubtless discouraged wanderings of servant and master alike. Once he thought he heard a faint boot-tramp behind him, but it faded when he looked back, and no one appeared. By the time he had begun to smell foods and fire and pots and soap and dishwater and floorwater, the silence had become almost eerie. Then somewhere a bell harshly knelled three times and from ahead, "Get out!" was suddenly roared in Samanda's harsh voice. The Mouser shrank back despite himself. A leather curtain bellied a score of paces ahead of him and three kitchen boys and a maid came hurrying silently into the corridor, their bare feet making no sound on the tiles. In the light filtering down from the tiny, high windows they looked like waxen mannikins as they filed swiftly past him. Though they avoided him, they seemed not to see him. Or perhaps that was only some whip-ingrained "Eyes front!" discipline.

As silently as they—who couldn't even make the noise of a hair dropping, since this morning's barbering had left them none—the Mouser hurried forward and put his eye to the slit in the leather curtains.

The four other doorways to the kitchen, even the one in the gallery, also had their curtains drawn. The great hot room had only two occupants. Fat Samanda, perspiring in her black wool dress and under the prickly plum pudding of her piled black hair, was heating in the whitely blazing fireplace the seven wire lashes of a long-handled whip. She drew it forth a little. The strands glowed dull red. She thrust it back. Her sparse, sweat-beaded black moustache lengthened and shed its salt rain in a smile as her tiny, fat-pillowed eyes fed on Reetha, who stood with arms straight down her sides and chin high, almost in the room's center, half faced away from the blaze. The serving maid wore only her black leather collar. The diamond stripe patterns of her last whippings still showed faintly down her back.

"Stand straighter, my pet," Samanda cooed like a cow. "Or would it be easier if your wrists were roped to a beam and your ankles to the ring-bolt in the cellar door?"

Now the dry stink of dirty floorwater was strongest in the Mouser's nostrils. Glancing down and to one side through his slit, he noted a large wooden pail filled almost to the brim with a mop's huge soggy head, lapped around by gray, soap-foamy water.

Samanda inspected the seven wires again. They glowed bright red. "Now," she said. "Brace yourself, my poppet."

Slipping through the curtain and snatching up the mop by its thick, splintery handle, the Mouser raced at Samanda, holding the mop's huge, dripping Medusa-head between their faces in hopes that she would not be able to identify her assailant. As the fiery wires hissed faintly through the air, he took her square in the face with a big smack and a gray splash, so that she was driven back a yard before she tripped on a long grilling-fork and fell backwards on her hinder fat-cushions.

Leaving the mop lying on her face with its handle neatly down her front, the Mouser whirled around, noting as he did a watery yellow eye in the nearest curtain slit and also the last red winking out of the wires lying midway between the fireplace and Reetha, still stiffly erect and with eyes squeezed shut and muscles taut against the red-hot blow.

He grabbed her arm at its pit, she screamed with amazement and pent tension, but he ignored this and hurried her toward the doorway by which he had entered, then stopped short at the tramp of many boots just beyond it. He rushed the girl in turn toward the two other leather-curtained doorways that hadn't an eye in their slits. More boots tramping. He sped back to the room's center, still firmly gripping Reetha.

Samanda, still on her back, had pushed the mop away and was frantically wiping her eyes with her pudgy fingers and squealing from soap-smart and rage.

The watery yellow eye was joined by its partner as Glipkerio strode in, daffodil wreath awry, black toga a-flap, and to either side of him a guardsman presenting toward the Mouser the gleaming brown-steel blade of a pike, while close behind came more guardsmen. Still others, pikes ready, filled the other three doorways and even appeared in the gallery.

Waving long white fingers at the Mouser, Glipkerio hissed, "Oh, most false Gray Mouser! Hisvin has hinted you work against me and now I catch you at it!"

The Mouser squatted suddenly on his hams and heaved muscle-crackingly with both hands on a big recessed iron ring-bolt. A thick square trapdoor made of heavy wood topped with tile, came up on its hinges. "Down!" he commanded Reetha, who obeyed with commendably cool-headed alacrity. The Mouser followed hunched at her heels, and let drop the trapdoor. It slammed down just in time to catch the blades of two pikes thrust at him, and presumably lever them with a jerk from their wielders' hands. Admirable wedges those tapering browned-iron blades would make to keep the trapdoor shut, the Mouser told himself.

Now he was in absolute darkness, but an earlier glance had shown him the shape and length of the stone stairs and an empty flagstoned area below abutting a niter-stained wall. Once again grasping Reetha's upper arm, he guided her down the stairs and across the gritty floor to within a couple of yards of the unseen wall. Then he let go the girl and felt in his pouch for flint, steel, his tinderbox, and a short thick-wicked candle.

From above came a muffled crack. Doubtless a pike-pole breaking as someone sought to rock out the trapped blade. Then someone commanded a muffled, "Heave!" The Mouser grinned in the dark, thinking how that would wedge the browned-iron wedges tighter.

Tiny sparks showered, a ghostly flame rose from a corner of the tinderbox, a tiny round flame like a golden pillbug with a sapphire center appeared at the tip of the candle's wick and began to swell. The Mouser snapped shut the tinderbox and held up the candle beside his head. Its flame suddenly flared big and bright. The next instant Reetha's arms were clamped around his neck and she was gasping in dry-mouthed terror against his ear.

Surrounding them on three sides and backing them against the ancient stone wall with its pale crystalline splotches, were a dozen ranks of silent rats formed in a semicircle about a spear-length away —hundreds, nay thousands of blackest long-tails, and more pouring out to join them from a score of ratholes in the base of the walls in the long cellar, which was piled here and there with barrels, casks, and grain-sacks.

The Mouser suddenly grinned, thrust tinderbox, steel, and flint back in his pouch and felt there for something else.

Meanwhile he noted a tall, narrow rathole just by them, newly gnawed—or perhaps chiseled and pick-axed, to judge from the fragments of mortar and tiny shards of stone scattered in front of it. No rats came from it, but he kept a wary eye on it.

The Mouser found Sheelba's squat black bottle, pried the bandage off it, and withdrew its crystal stopper.

The dull-brained louts in the kitchen overhead were pounding on the trapdoor now—another useless assault!

The rats still poured from the holes and in such numbers that they threatened to become a humpy black carpet covering the whole floor of the cellar except for the tiny area where Reetha clung to the Mouser.

His grin widened. He set the bottle to his lips, took an experimental sip, thoughtfully rolled it on his tongue, then upended the vial and let its faintly bitter contents gurgle into his mouth and down his throat.

Reetha, unlinking her arms, said a little reproachfully, "I could use some wine too."

The Mouser raised his eyebrows happily at her and explained, "Not wine. Magic!" Had not her own eyebrows been shaven, they would have risen in puzzlement. He gave her a wink, tossed the bottle aside, and confidently awaited the emergence of his anti-rat powers, whatever they might be.

From above came the groan of metal and the slow cracking of tough wood. Now they were going about it the right way, with pry-bars. Likely the trap would open just in time for Glipkerio to witness the Mouser vanquishing the rat army. Everything was timing itself perfectly.

The black sea of hitherto silent rats began to toss and wave and from it came an angry chittering and a clashing of tiny teeth. Better and better!—this warlike show would put some life into their defeat.

He idly noted that he was standing in the center of a large, gray-bordered splotch of pinkish slime he must have overlooked before in his haste and excitement. He had never seen a cellar-mold quite like it.

His eyeballs seemed to him to swell and burn a little and suddenly he felt in himself the powers of a god. He looked up at Reetha to warn her not to be frightened at anything that might happen—say his flesh glowing with a golden light or two bright scarlet beams flashing from his eyes to shrivel rats or heat them to popping.

Then he was asking himself, "*Up* at Reetha?"

The pinkish splotch had become a large puddle lapping slimily over the soles of his boots.

There was a splintering. Light spilled down from the kitchen on the crowded rats.

The Mouser gawked at them horror-struck. They were as big as cats! No, black wolves! No, furry black men on all fours! He clutched at Reetha . . . and found himself vainly seeking to encircle with his arms a smooth white calf thick as a temple pillar. He gazed up at Reetha's amazed and fear-struck giant face two stories above. There echoed evilly in his ears Sheelba's carelessly spoken, fiendishly ambiguous: ". . . put you on the right footing to cope with the situation . . ." Oh yes indeed!

The slime-puddle and its gray border had grown wider still and he was in it up to his ankles.

He clung to Reetha's leg a moment longer with the faint and ungracious hope that since his weapons and his clothing, which touched him, had shrunk with him, she might shrink too at his touch. He would at least have a companion. Perhaps to his credit, it did not occur to him to yell, "Pick me up!"

The only thing that happened was that an almost inaudibly deep voice thundered down at him from Reetha's mouth, big as a red-edged shield, "What are you doing? I'm scared. Start the magic!"

The Mouser jumped away from the fleshly pillar, splashing the nasty pink stuff and almost slipping in it, and whipped out his sword Scalpel. It was just a shade bigger than a needle for mending sails. While the candle, which he still held in his left hand, was the proper size to light a small room in a doll's house.

There was loud, confused, multiple padding and claw-clicking, chittering war cries blasted his ears, and he saw the huge black rats stampeding him from three sides, kicking up the gray border in puffs as if it were a powder and then splashing the pink slime and sending ripples across it.

Reetha, terror-struck, watched her inexplicably diminished rescuer spin around, leap over a shard of rock, land in a pink splash, and brandishing his tiny sword before him, shielding his doll's candle with his cloak, and ducking his head, rush into the rathole behind her and so vanish. Racing rats brushed her ankles and snapped at each other, to be first down the hole after the Mouser. Elsewhere the rat horde was swiftly disappearing down the other holes. But one rat stayed long enough to nip her foot.

Her nerve snapped. Her first footsteps splattering pink slime and gray dust, she shrieked and ran, rats dodging from under her feet, and dashed up the steps, clawed her way past several wide-eyed guardsmen into the kitchen, and sank sobbing and panting on the tiles. Samanda snapped a chain on her collar.

Fafhrd, his arms joined in a circle above and before his head to avoid skull-bump from rocky outcrops and also the unexpected brushings on face of cobwebs and wraithlike fingers and filmy wings, at last saw a jaggedly circular green glow ahead. Soon he emerged from the black tunnel into a large and many entranced cavern somewhat lit at the center of its rocky floor by a green fire which was being replenished with thin blood-red logs by two skinny, raggedy-tunicked, sharp-eyed boys, who looked like typical street urchins of Lankhmar or Ilthmar, or any other decadent city. One had a puckered scar under his left eye. On the other side of the fire from them sat on low wide stone an obscenely fat figure so well cloaked and hooded that not a speck of his face or hands were visible. He was sorting out a large pile of parchment scraps and potsherds, pinching hold of them through the dark fabric of his overlong, dangling sleeves, and scanning them close-sightedly, almost putting them inside his hood.

"Welcome, my Gentle Son," he called to Fafhrd in a voice like a quavering sweet flute. "What happy chance brings you here?"

"*You* know!" Fafhrd said harshly, striding forward until he was glaring across the leaping green flames at the black oval defined by the forward edge of the hood. "How am I to save the Mouser? What's with Lankhmar? And why, in the name of all the gods of death and destruction, is the tin whistle so important?"

"You speak in riddles, Gentle Son," the fluty voice responded soothingly, as its owner went on sorting his scraps. "What tin whistle? What peril's the Mouser in now?—reckless youth! And what *is* with Lankhmar?"

Fafhrd let loose a flood of curses, which rattled impotently among the stalactites overhead. Then he jerked free from his pouch the tiny black oblong of Sheelba's message and held it forward between finger and thumb that shook with rage. "Look, Know-nothing One: I dumped a lovely girl to answer this and now—"

But the hooded figure had whistled warblingly and at that signal the black bat, which Fafhrd had forgot, launched itself from his shoulder, snatched with sharp teeth the black note from his finger-grip, and fluttered past the green flames to land on the paunchy one's sleeve-hidden hand, or tentacle, or whatever it was. The whatever-it-was conveyed to hood-mouth the bat, who obligingly fluttered inside and vanished in the coally dark there.

There followed a squeaky, unintelligible, hood-muffled dialogue while Fafhrd sat his fists on his hips and fumed. The two skinny boys gave him sly grins and whispered together impudently, their bright eyes never leaving him. At last the fluty voice called, "Now it's crystal clear to me, Oh Patient Son. Sheelba of the Eyeless Face and I have been on the outs—a bit of a wizardly bicker—and now he seeks to mend fences with this. Well, well, well, first advances by Sheelba. Ho-ho-ho!"

"Very funny," Fafhrd growled. "Haste's the marrow of our confab.

The Sinking Land came up, shedding its waters, as I entered your caves. My swift but jaded mount crops your stingy grass outside. I must leave within the half hour if I am to cross the Sinking Land before it resubmerges. *What do I do about the Mouser, Lankhmar, and the tin whistle?*"

"But, Gentle Son, I know nothing about those things," the other replied artlessly. " 'Tis only Sheelba's motives are air-clear to me. Oh, ho, to think that he— Wait, wait now, Fafhrd! Don't rattle the stalactites again. I've ensorcled them against falling, but there are no spells in the universe which a big fellow can't sometimes break through. I'll advise you, never fear. But I must first clairvoy. Scatter on the golden dust, boys—thriftily now, don't waste it, 'tis worth ten times its weight in diamond unpowdered."

The two urchins each dipped into a bag beside them and threw into the feet of the green flames a glittering golden swirl. Instantly the flames darkened, though leaping high as ever and sending off no soot. Watching them in the now almost night-dark cavern, Fafhrd thought he could make out the transitory, ever-distorting shadows of twisty towers, ugly trees, tall hunchbacked men, low-shouldered beasts, beautiful wax women melting, and the like, but nothing was clear or even hinted at a story.

Then from the obese warlock's hood came toward the darkened fire two greenish ovals, each with a vertical black streak like the jewel cat's eye. A half yard out of the hood they paused and held steady. They were speedily joined by two more which both diverged and went farther. Then came a single one arching up over the fire until one would have thought it was in great danger of sizzling. Lastly, two which floated in opposite directions almost impossibly far around the fire and then hooked in to observe it from points near Fafhrd.

The voice fluted sagely: "It is always best to look at a problem from all sides."

Fafhrd drew his shoulders together and repressed a shudder. It never failed to be disconcerting to watch Ningauble send forth his Seven Eyes on their apparently indefinitely extensible eyestalks. Especially on occasions when he'd been coy as a virgin in a bathrobe about keeping them hidden.

So much time passed that Fafhrd began to snap his fingers with impatience, softly at first, then more cracklingly. He'd given up looking at the flames. They never held anything but the tantalizing, churning shadows.

At last the green eyes floated back into the hood, like a mystic fleet returning to port. The flames turned bright green again, and Ningauble said, "Gentle Son, I now understand your problem and its answer. In part, I have seen much, yet cannot explain all. The Gray Mouser, now. He's exactly twenty-five feet below the deepest cellar in the palace of Glipkerio Kistomerces. But he's not buried there, or even dead—though about twenty-four parts in twenty-five of him *are* dead, in the cellar I mentioned. But *he* is alive."

"But *how?*" Fafhrd almost gawked, spreading his spread-fingered hands.

"I haven't the faintest idea. He's surrounded by enemies but near him are two friends—of a sort. Now about Lankhmar, that's clearer. She's been invaded, her walls breached everywhere and desperate fighting going on in the streets, by a fierce host which outnumbers Lankhmar's inhabitants by . . . my goodness . . . fifty to one—and equipped with all modern weapons.

"Yet you can save the city, you can turn the tide of battle—this part came through very clearly—if you only hasten to the temple of the Gods *of* Lankhmar and climb its bell-tower and ring the chimes there, which have been silent for uncounted centuries. Presumably to rouse those gods. But that's only my guess."

"I don't like the idea of having anything to do with that dusty crew," Fafhrd complained. "From what I've heard of them, they're more like walking mummies than true gods—and even more dry-spirited and unloving, being sifted through like sand with poisonous senile whims."

Ningauble shrugged his cloaked, bulbous shoulders. "I thought you were a brave man, addicted to deeds of derring-do."

Fafhrd cursed sardonically, then demanded, "But even if I should go clang those rusty bells, how can Lankhmar hold out until then with her walls breached and the odds fifty to one against her?"

"I'd like to know that myself," Ningauble assured him.

"And how do I get to the temple when the streets are crammed with warfare?"

Ningauble shrugged once again. "You're a hero. You should know."

"Well then, the tin whistle?" Fafhrd grated.

"You know, I didn't get a thing on the tin whistle. Sorry about that. Do you have it with you? Might I look at it?"

Grumbling, Fafhrd extracted it from his flat pouch, and brought it around the fire.

"Have you ever blown it?" Ningauble asked.

"No," Fafhrd said with surprise, lifting it to his lips.

"Don't!" Ningauble squeaked. "Not on any account! Never blow a strange whistle. It might summon things far worse even than savage mastiffs or the police. Here, give it to me."

He pinched it away from Fafhrd with a double fold of animated sleeve and held it close to his hood, revolving it clockwise and counterclockwise, finally serpentinely gliding out four of his eyes and subjecting it to their massed scrutiny at thumbnail distance.

At last he withdrew his eyes, sighed, and said, "Well . . . I'm not sure. But there are thirteen characters in the inscription—I couldn't decipher 'em, mind you, but there *are* thirteen. Now if you take that fact in conjunction with the slim couchant feline figure on the other side . . . Well, I think you blow this whistle to summon the War Cats. Mind you, that's only a deduction, and one of several steps, each uncertain."

"Who are the War Cats?" Fafhrd asked.

Ningauble writhed his fat shoulders and neck under their garments. "I've never been quite certain. But putting together various rumors and legends—oh yes, and some cave drawings north of the Cold Waste and south of Quarmall—I have arrived at the tentative conclusion that they are a military aristocracy of all the feline tribes, a bloodthirsty Inner Circle of thirteen members—in short, a dozen and one ailuric berserkers. I would assume—provisionally only, mind you—that they would appear when summoned, as perhaps by this whistle, and instantly assault whatever creature or creatures, beast or man, that seemed to threaten the feline tribes. So I would advise you not to blow it except in the presence of enemies of cats more worthy of attack than yourself, for I suppose you have slain a few tigers and leopards in your day. Here, take it."

Fafhrd snatched and pouched it, demanding, "But by God's ice-rimmed skull, when *am* I to blow it? How can the Mouser be two parts in fifty alive when buried eight yards deep? What vast, fifty-to-one host can have assaulted Lankhmar without months of rumors and reports of their approach? What fleets could carry—"

"No more questions!" Ningauble interposed shrilly. "Your half hour is up. If you are to beat the Sinking Land and be in time to save the city, you must gallop at once for Lankhmar. Now no more words."

Fafhrd raved for a while longer, but Ningauble maintained a stubborn silence, so Fafhrd gave him a last thundering curse, which brought down a small stalactite that narrowly missed bashing his brains out, and departed, ignoring the urchins' maddening grins.

Outside the caves, he mounted the Mingol mare and cantered, followed by hoof-raised dust-cloud, down the sun-yellowed, dryly rustling slope toward the mile-wide westward-leading isthmus of dark brown rock, salt-filmed and here and there sea-puddled, that was the Sinking Land. Southward gleamed the placid blue waters of the Sea of the East, northward the restless gray waters of the Inner Sea and the glinting squat towers of Ilthmar. Also northward he noted four small dust-clouds like his own coming down the Ilthmar road, which he had earlier traveled himself. Almost surely and just as he'd guessed, the four black brigands were after him at last, hot to revenge their three slain or at least woefully damaged fellow-rogues. He narrowed his eyes and nudged the gray mare to a lively lope.

XI

THE MOUSER WAS hurrying against a marked moist cool draft through a vast, low-ceilinged concourse close-pillared like a mine with up-ended bricks and sections of pike-haft and broom-handle, and lit by caged fire-beetles and glow-worms and an occasional sputtering torch held by a rat-page in jacket and short trews lighting the way for some masked person or persons of quality. A few jewel-decked or mon-strously fat rat-folk, likewise masked, traveled in litters carried by two or four squat, muscular, nearly naked rats. A limping, aged rat carrying two sacks which twitched a little from the inside was remov-ing dim, weary fire-beetles from their cages and replacing them with fresh bright ones. The Mouser hastened along on tiptoe with knees permanently bent, body hunched forward, and chin out-thrust. It made his legs in particular ache abominably, but it gave him, he hoped, the general silhouette and gait of a rat walking two-legged. His entire head was covered by a cylindrical mask cut from the bot-tom of his cloak, provided with eye-holes only, and which, stiffened by a wire which had previously stiffened the scabbard of Scalpel, thrust down several inches below his chin to give the impression that it covered a rat's long snout.

He worried what would happen if someone came close enough and were sufficiently observant to note that his mask and cloak too of course were made of tiny ratskins closely stitched together. He hoped that rats were plagued by proportionately tinier rats, though he hadn't noted any tiny ratholes so far; after all, there was the proverb about little bugs having littler bugs, and so on; at any rate he could claim in a pinch that he came from a distant rat-city where such was the case. To keep the curious and watchful at a distance he hovered his gauntleted hands a-twitch above the pommels of Scalpel and Cat's Claw, and chittered angrily or muttered such odd oaths as "All rat-catchers fry!" or "By candle-fat and bacon-rind!" In Lankhmarese, for now that he had ears small and quick enough to hear, he knew that the language was spoken underground, and especially well by the aristos of these lower levels. And what more natural than that rats, who were parasites on man's farms and ships and cities, should copy his language along with many other items of his habits and culture? He had already noted other solitary armed rats—bravos or berserkers, presumably—who behaved in the irritable and dangerous manner he now put on.

His escape from the cellar-rats had been achieved by his own cool-headedness and his pursuers' blundering eagerness, which had made them fight to be first, so that the tunnel had been briefly blocked behind him. His candle had been most helpful in his descent of the first sharply down-angling, rough-hewn, then rough-digged passages, where he had made his way by sliding and leaping, checking himself on a rocky outcropping or by digging heel into dirt only when his speed became so great as to threaten a disastrous fall. The first rough-pillared concourse had also been pitchdark, almost. There he had quickly thrown his cloak over his face to the eyes, for his candle had shown him numerous rats, most of them going naked on all fours, but a few of them hunchedly erect and wearing rough dark clothing, if only a pair of trews or a jacket or slouch hat or smock, or a belt for a short-bladed hanger. Some of these had carried pickax or shovel or pry-bar over shoulder. And there had been one rat fully clothed in black, armed with sword and dagger and wearing a silver-edged full-face vizard—at least the Mouser had assumed it was a rat.

He had taken the first passage leading down—there had been regular steps now, hewn in rock or cut in gravel—and had paused at a turn in the stairs by a curious though stenchful alcove. It contained the first he had seen of the fire-beetle lamps and also a half-dozen small compartments, each closed by a door that left space below and above. After a moment's hesitation he had darted into one which showed no black hind paws or boots below and securely hooking the door behind him, had instantly and rapidly begun to fabricate his ratskin mask. His instinctive assumption about the function of the compartments was confirmed by a large two-handled basket half full of rat droppings and a bucket of stinking urine. After his long-chinned vizard had been made and donned, he had shaken out his candle, pouched it, and then relieved himself, at least permitting himself to wonder in amazement that all his clothes and belongings had been reduced in size proportionately with his body. Ah, he told himself, that would account for the wide gray border of the pink puddle which had appeared around his boots in the cellar above. When he'd been sorcerously shrunken, the excess motes or atomies of his flesh, blood, and bones had been shed downward to make the pink pool, while those of his gray clothing and tempered iron weapons had sifted away to make up the pool's gray border, which had been powdery rather than slimy, of course, because metal or fabric contains little or no liquid compared to flesh. It had occurred to him that there must be twenty times as much of the Mouser by weight in that poor abused pink pool overhead as there was in his present rat-small form, and for a moment he had felt a sentimental sadness.

Finishing his business, he had prepared to continue his downward course when there had come the descending clatter of paw- and boot-steps, quickly followed by a banging on the door of his compartment.

Without hesitation he had unhooked the door and opened it with a jerk. Facing him close there had been the black-clad, black-and-silver-masked rat he had seen on the level above, and behind him three bare-faced rats with drawn hangers that looked and probably were sharper than gross human fingers could ever hone.

After the first glance, the Mouser had looked lower than his pursuers' faces, for fear the color and shape and especially the placings of his eyes might give him away.

The vizarded one had said swiftly and clearly in excellent Lankhmarese, "Have you seen or heard anyone come down the stairs? —in particular an armed human magically reduced to decent and normal size?"

Again without hesitation the Mouser had chittered most angrily, and roughly shouldering his questioner and the others aside, had spat out, "Idiots! Opium-chewers! Nibblers of hemp! Out of my way!"

On the stairs he had paused to look back briefly, snarl loudly and contemptuously, "No, of course not!" and then gone down the stairs with dignity, though taking them two at a time.

The next level had shown no rats in sight and been redolent of grain. He had noted bins of wheat, barley, millet, kombo, and wild rice from the River Tilth. A good place to hide—perhaps. But what could he gain by hiding?

The next level—the third down—had been full of military clatter and rank with rat-stink. He had noted rat pikemen drilling in bronze cuirasses and helmets and another squad being instructed in the crossbow, while still others crowded around a table where routes on a great map were being pointed out. He had lingered even a shorter time there.

Midway down each stairs had been a compartmented nook like the first he'd used. He had docketed away in his mind this information.

Refreshingly clean, moist air had poured out of the fourth level, it had been more brightly lit, and most of the rats strolling in it had been richly dressed and masked. He had turned into it at once, walking against the moist breeze, since that might well come from the outer world and mark a route of escape, and he had continued with angry chitters and curses to play his impulsively assumed role of crotchety, half-mad rat-bravo or rogue-rat.

In fact, he found himself trying so hard to be a convincing rat that without volition his eyes now followed with leering interest a small mincing she-rat in pink silk and pearls—mask as well as dress—who led on a leash what he took at first to be a baby rat and then realized was a dwarfish, well-groomed, fear-eyed mouse; and also an imperiously tall ratess in dark green silk sewn over with ruby chips and holding in one hand a whip and in the other the short leashes of two fierce-eyed, quick-breathing shrews that looked as big as mastiffs and were doubtless even more bloodthirsty.

Still looking lustfully at this striking proud creature as she passed him with green, be-rubied mask tilted high, he ran into a slow-gaited, portly rat robed and masked in ermine, which looked extremely coarse-haired now, and wearing about his neck a long gold chain and about his aldermanic waist a gold-studded belt, from which hung a heavy bag that chinked dulcetly at the Mouser's jolting impact.

Snapping a "Your pardon, merchant!" at the wheezingly chittering fellow, the Mouser strode on without backward glance. He grinned conceitedly under his mask. These rats were easy to befool!—and perhaps reduction in size had sharpened finer his own sharp wits.

He was tempted for an instant to turn back and lure off and rob the fat fellow, but realized at once that in the human world the chinking goldpieces would be smaller than sequins.

This thought set his mind on a problem which had been obscurely terrifying him ever since he had plunged into the rat-world. Sheelba had said the effects of the potion would last for nine hours. Then presumably the Mouser would resume his normal size as swiftly as he had lost it. To have that happen in a burrow or even in the foot-and-a-half-high, pillar-studden concourse would be disastrous—it made him wince to think of it.

Now, the Mouser had no intention of staying anything like nine hours in the rat-world. On the other hand, he didn't exactly want to escape at once. Dodging around in Lankhmar like a nimbly animate gray doll for half a night didn't appeal to him—it would be shame-making even if, or perhaps especially if while doll-size he had to report his important intelligences about the rat-world to Glipkerio and Olegnya Mingolsbane—with Hisvet watching perhaps. Besides, his mind was already afire with schemes to assassinate the rats' king, if they had one, or foil their obvious project of conquest in some even more spectacular fashion on their home ground. He felt a peculiarly great self-confidence and had not realized yet that it was because he was fully as tall as the taller rats around, as tall as Fafhrd, relatively, and no longer the smallish man he had been all his life.

However, there was always the possibility that by some unforeseeable ill fortune he might be unmasked, captured, and imprisoned in a tiny cell. A panicking thought.

But even more unnerving was the basic problem of time. Did it move faster for the rats, or slower? He had the impression that life and all its processes moved at a quicker tempo down here. But was that true? Did he now clearly hear the rat-Lankhmarese, which had previously sounded like squeaks, because his ears were quicker, or merely smaller, or because most of a rat's voice was pitched too high for human ears to hear, or even because rats spoke Lankhmarese only in their burrows? He surreptitiously felt his pulse. It seemed the same as always. But mightn't it be greatly speeded up equally, so that he noted no difference? Sheelba had said something about a day being a tenth of a million pulsebeats. Was that rat or human pulse? Were rat-hours so short that nine of them might pass in a hundred or so human minutes? Almost he was tempted to rush up the first stairs he saw. No, wait . . . if the timing was by pulse and his pulse seemed normal, then wouldn't he have one normal Mouser-sleep to work on down here? It was truly most confusing. "Out upon it all, by cat-gut sausages and roasted dog's eyes!" he heard himself curse with sincerity.

Several things at any rate were clear. Before he dared idle or nap, let alone sleep, he must discover some way of measuring down here the passage of time in the aboveground world. Also, to get at the truth about rat-night and day, he must swiftly learn about rodent sleeping habits. For some reason his mind jumped back to the tall ratess with the brace of straining shrews. But that was ridiculous, he told himself. There was sleeping and sleeping, and that one had very little if anything to do with the other.

He came out of his thought-trance to realize fully what his senses had for some time been telling him: that the strollers had become fewer, the breeze more damp and cool and fresh, and sea-odorous too, and the pillars ahead natural rock, while through the doorways chiseled between them shone a yellowish light, not bright yet twinkling and quite unlike that of the fire-beetles, glow-wasps, and tiny torches.

He passed a marble doorway and noted white marble steps going down from it. Then he stepped between two of the rocky pillars and halted on the rim of a wonder-place.

It was a roughly circular natural rock cave many rats high and many more long and wide, and filled with faintly rippling seawater which transmitted a mild flood of yellowish light that came through a great wide hole, underwater by about the length of a rat's-pike, in the other end of the glitter-ceilinged cavern. All around this sea lake, about two rat-pikes above the water, went the rather narrow rock road, looking in part natural, in part chiseled and pick-axed, on which he now stood. At its distant end, in the shadows above the great underwater hole, he could dimly make out the forms and gleaming weapons of a half-dozen or so motionless rats, evidently on guard duty.

As the Mouser watched, the yellow light became yellower still, and he realized it must be the light of later afternoon, surely the afternoon of the day in which he had entered the rat-world. Since sunset was at six o'clock and he had entered the rat-world after three, he had spent fewer than three of his nine hours. Most important, he had linked the passage of time in the rat-world with that in the big world—and was somewhat startled at the relief he felt.

He recalled too the "dead" rats which had seemed to swim away from the cage dropped from the palace window into the Inner Sea after Hisvin's demonstration of his deathspell. They might very well have swum underwater into this very cavern, or another like it.

It also came to him that he had discovered the secret of the damp breeze. He knew the tide was rising now, an hour or so short of full, and in rising it drove the cave-trapped air through the concourse. At low tide the great hole would be in part above water, allowing the cavern air to be refreshed from outside. A rather clever if intermittent ventilation system. Perhaps some of these rats were a bit more ingenious than he had given them credit for.

At that instant there came a light, inhuman touch on his right shoulder. Turning around, he saw stepping back from him with naked rapier held a little to one side the black-masked black-clad rat who had disturbed him in the privy.

"What's the meaning of this?" he chitteringly blustered. "By God's hairless tail, why am I catted and ferreted?—you black dog!"

In far less ratlike Lankhmarese than the Mouser's, the other asked quietly, "What are you doing in a restricted area? I must ask you to unmask, sir."

"Unmask? I'll see the color of your liver first, mousling!" the Mouser ranted wildly. It would never do, he knew, to change character now.

"Must I call in my underlings to unmask you by force?" the other inquired in the same soft, deadly voice. "But it is not necessary. Your reluctance to unmask is final confirmation of my deduction that you are indeed the magically shrunken human come as a spy into Lankhmar Below."

"That opium specter again?" the Mouser raved, dropping his hand to Scalpel's hilt. "Begone, mad mouse dipped in ink, before I cut you to collops!"

"Your threats and brags are alike useless, sir," the other answered with a low and humorous laugh. "You wonder how I became certain of your identity? I suppose you think you were very clever Actually you gave yourself away more than once. First, by relieving yourself in that jakes where I first encountered you. Your dung was of a different shape, color, consistency, and odor than that of my compatriots. You should have sought out a water-privy. Second, although you did try to shadow your eyes, the eye-holes in your mask are too squintingly close together, as are all human eyes. Third, your boots are clearly made to fit human rather than rodent feet, though you have the small sense to walk on your toes to ape our legs and gait."

The Mouser noted that the other's black boots had far tinier soles than his own and were of soft leather both below and above the big ankle-bend.

The other continued, "And from the very first I knew you must be an utter stranger, else you would never have dared shoulder aside and insult the many times proven greatest duelist and fastest sword in all Lankhmar Below."

With black-gloved left paw the other whipped off his silver-trimmed mask, revealing upstanding oval ears and long furry black face and huge, protuberant, wide-spaced black eyes. Baring his great white incisors in a lordly smirk and bringing his mask across his chest in a curt, sardonic bow, he finished, "Svivomilo, at your service."

At least now the Mouser understood the vast vanity—great almost as his own!—which had led his pursuer to leave his underlings behind in the concourse while he came on alone to make the arrest. Whipping out simultaneously Scalpel and Cat's Claw, purposely not pausing to unmask, the Mouser made his most rapid advance, ending in a tremendous lunge at the neck. It seemed to him that he had never before in his life moved as swiftly—small size certainly had its points.

There was a flash and a clash and Scalpel was deflected—by Svivomilo's dagger drawn with lightning speed. And then Svivomilo's rapier was on the offensive and the Mouser barely avoided it by rapid parries with both his weapons and by backing off perilously along the water's brink. Now his involuntary thought was that his opponent had had a much longer time than he of being small and practicing the swiftness it allowed, while his mask interfered with his vision and if it slipped a little would blind him altogether. Yet Svivomilo's incessant attacks gave him no time to whip it off. With sudden desperation he lunged forward himself, managing to get a bind with Scalpel on the rapier that momentarily took both weapons out of the fight, and an instant later lashed out with Cat's Claw at Svivomilo's dagger-stabbing wrist, and by accurate eye and good fortune cut its inner tendons.

Then as Svivomilo hesitated and sprang back, the Mouser disengaged Scalpel and launched it in another sinew-straining, long lunge, thrice dipping his point just under Svivomilo's double and then circle parries, and finally drove its point on in a slicing thrust that went through the rat's neck and ended grating against the vertebra there.

Scarlet blood pouring over the black lace at Svivomilo's throat and down his chest, and with only one short, bubbling suffocated gasp, for the Mouser's thrust had severed windpipe as well as arteries, the rightly boastful but foolishly reckless duelist pitched forward on his face and lay writhing.

The Mouser made the mistake of trying to sheathe his bloodied sword, forgetting that Scalpel's scabbard was no longer wire-stiffened, which made the action difficult. He cursed the scabbard, limp as Svivomilo's now nerveless tail.

Four cuirassed and helmeted rats with pikes at the ready appeared at two of the rocky doorways. Brandishing his red-dripping sword and gleaming dirk, the Mouser raced through an untenanted doorway and with a chittering scream to clear the way ahead of him, sprinted across the concourse to the marble doorway he'd noted earlier, and plunged down the white stairway.

The usual nook in the turn of the stairs held only three compartments, each with a silver-fitted door of ivory. Into the central one there was going a white-booted rat wearing a voluminous white cloak and hood and bearing in his white-gloved right hand an ivory staff with a large sapphire set in its top.

Without an instant's pause the Mouser ended his plunging descent with a dash into the nook. He hurled ahead of him the white-cloaked rat and slammed and hooked fast behind them the ivory door.

Recovering himself, the Mouser's victim turned and with outraged dignity and brandished staff demanded through his white mask set with diamonds, "Who dareth dithturb with rude thcufflingth Counthillor Grig of the Inner Thircle of Thirteen? Mithcreant!"

While a part of the Mouser's brain was realizing that this was the lisping white rat he had seen aboard *Squid* sitting on Hisvin's shoulder, his eyes were informing him that this compartment held not a box for droppings, but a raised silver toilet seat, up through which came the sound and odor of rushing seawater. It must be one of the water-privies Svivomilo had mentioned.

Dropping Scalpel, the Mouser threw back Grig's hood, dragged off his mask over his head, tripped the sputtering councillor and forced his head down against the far side of the privy's silver rim, and then with Cat's Claw cut Grig's furry white throat almost from ratty ear to ear, so that his blood gushed down into the rushing water below. As soon as his victim's writhings stilled, the Mouser drew off Grig's white cloak and hood, taking great care that no blood got on them.

At that moment he heard the booted footsteps of several persons coming down the stairs. Operating with demonic speed, the Mouser placed Scalpel, the ivory staff, and the white mask and hood and cloak behind the seat of the privy, then hoisted the dead body so that it sat on the same, and himself stood crouching on the silver rim, facing the hooked door and holding the limp trunk erect. Then he silently prayed with great sincerity to Issek of the Jug, the first god he could think of, the one whom Fafhrd had once served.

Wavy and hooked brown-iron pike-blades gleamed above the doorways. The two to either side were slammed open. Then after a pause, during which he hoped someone had peered under the central door just enough to note the white boots, there came a light rapping, and then a respectful voice inquiring, "Your pardon, Nobility, but have you recently seen anything of a person in gray with cloak and mask of finest gray fur, and armed with rapier and dagger?"

The Mouser answered in a voice which he tried to make calm and dignifiedly benign, "I have theen nothing, thir. About thicty breathth ago I heard thomeone clattering at thpeed down the thtairth."

"Our humblest thanks, Nobility," the questioner responded, and the booted footsteps continued rapidly down toward the fifth level.

The Mouser let off a long soft sigh and chopped short his prayer. Then he set swiftly to work, for he knew he had a considerable task ahead of him, some of it most grisly. He wiped off and scabbarded Scalpel and Cat's Claw. Then he examined his victim's cloak, hood, and mask, discovering almost no blood on them, and set them aside. He noted that the cloak could be fastened down the front with ivory buttons. Then he dragged off Grig's tall boots of whitest suede and tried them on his own legs. Though their softness helped, they fitted abominably, the sole covering little more than the area under his toes. Still, this would keep him reminded to maintain a rat's gait at all times. He also tried on Grig's long white gloves, which fitted worse, if that were possible. Still, he could wear them. His own boots and gauntlets he tucked securely over his gray belt.

Next he undressed Grig and dropped his garments one by one into the water, retaining only a razor-sharp ivory-and-gold-fitted dagger, a number of small parchment scrolls, Grig's undershirt, and a double-ended purse filled with gold coins struck with a rat's head on one side, circled by a wreath of wheat, and on the other a complex maze (tunnels?) and a numeral followed by the initials *S. F. L. B.* "Since the Founding of Lankhmar Below?" he hazarded brilliantly. He hung the purse over his belt, fixed the dagger to it by a gold hook on its ivory sheath, and thrust the scrolls unscanned into his own pouch.

Then with a grunt of distaste he rolled up his sleeves and using the ivory-handled dagger, proceeded to dismember the furry corpse into pieces small enough to force through the silver rim so that they splashed into the water and were carried away.

This horrid task at last accomplished, he made a careful search for blood splatters, wiped them up with Grig's undershirt, used it to polish the silver rim, then dropped it after the other stuff.

Still not giving himself a pause, he pulled on again the white suede boots, donned the white cloak, which was of finest wool, and buttoned it all the way down the front, thrusting his arms through the slits in the cloak to either side. Then he put on the mask, discovered that he had to use the dagger to extend narrowly the eye-slits at their inner ends to be able to see at all with his own close-set human eyes. After that he tied on the hood, throwing it as far forward as practicable to hide the mask's mutilations and his lack of befurred rat ears. Finally he drew on the long, ill-fitting white gloves.

It was well that he had worked as speedily as he had, allowing himself no time for rest, for now there came booted footsteps up the stairs and the nastily hooked pike-blades a-wave again, while below the door of his compartment there appeared typically crooked rat-boots of fine black leather embossed with golden scroll-work.

There was a sharper knocking and a grating voice, polite yet peremptory, said, "Your pardon, Councillor. This is Hreest. As Lieutenant Warden of the Fifth Level, I must ask you to open the door. You have been closeted a long while in there, and I must assure myself that the spy we seek is not holding a knife at your throat."

The Mouser coughed, took up the sapphire-headed ivory staff, drew wide the door and majestically strode forth with a slight hobble. Resuming with tired legs the aching, tip-toe rat-gait had given him a sudden torturing cramp in his left calf.

The pike-rats knelt. The fancy-booted rat, whose black clothes, mask, gauntlets and rapier-scabbard were also covered with fine-lined golden arabesques, dropped back two steps.

Directing only a brief gaze at him, the Mouser said coolly, "You dare dithturb and hathten Counthillor Grig at hith eliminationth? Well, perhapth your reathonth are good enough. Perhapth."

Hreest swept off his wide-brimmed hat plumed with the breast-feathers of black canaries. "I am certain they are, Nobility. There is loose in Lankhmar Below a human spy, magically changed to our size. He has already murdered that skillful if unruly and conceited swordsman Svivomilo."

"Thorry newth indeed!" the Mouser lisped. "Thearch out thith thpy at onthe! Thpare no ecthpenthe in men or effort. I will inform the Counthil, Hreetht, if you have not."

And while Hreest's voice followed him with ratly apologies, thanks, and reassurances, the Mouser stepped regally down the white marble stairs, his limp hardly noticeable due to the grateful support afforded by his ivory staff. The sapphire in its top twinkled like the blue star Ashsha. He felt like a king.

Fafhrd rode west through the gathering twilight, the iron-shod hooves of the Mingol mare striking sparks from the flinty substance of the Sinking Land. The sparks were becoming faintly visible, just as were a few of the largest stars. The road, mere hoof dints, was becoming hard to discern. To north and south, the Inner Sea and the Sea of the East were sullen gray expanses, the former wave-flecked. And now finally, against the last dirty pink ribbon of sunset fringing the west, he made out the wavery black line of squat trees and towering cactuses that marked the beginning of the Great Salt Marsh.

It was a welcome sight, yet Fafhrd was frowning deeply—two vertical furrows springing up from the inside end of either eyebrow.

The left furrow, you might say, was for what followed him. Taking an unhurried look over shoulder, he saw that the four riders whom he had first glimpsed coming down the Sarheenmar road were now only a bowshot and a half behind him. Their horses were black and they wore great black cloaks and hoods. He knew now to a certainty they were his four black Ilthmar brigands. And Ilthmar land-pirates hungry only for loot, let alone vengeance, had been known to pursue their prey to the very Marsh Gate of Lankhmar.

The right furrow, which was deepest, was for an almost imperceptible tilt, south lifting above north, in the ragged black horizon ahead. That this was actually a slight tilting of the Sinking Land in the opposite direction was proven when the Mingol mare took a lurch to the left. Fafhrd harshly kicked his mount into a gallop. It would be a near thing whether he reached the Marsh causeway before he was engulfed.

Lankhmar philosophers believe that the Sinking land is a vast long shield, concave underneath, of hard-topped rock so porous below that it is exactly the same weight as water. Volcanic gases from the roots of the Ilthmar Mountains and also mephitic vapors from the incredibly deep-rooted and yeasty Great Salt Marsh gradually fill the concavity and lift the huge shield above the surface of the seas. But then an instability develops, due to the greater density of the shield's topping. The shield begins to rock. The supporting gasses and vapors escape in great alternate belches through the waters to north and south. Then the shield sinks somewhat below the waves and the whole slow, rhythmic process begins again.

So it was that the tilting told Fafhrd that the Sinking Land was once more about to submerge. And now the tilt had increased so much that he had to pull a little on the mare's right bridle to keep her to the road. Looking back over right shoulder, he saw that the four black horsemen were also coming on faster, in fact somewhat faster than he.

As his gaze returned to his goal of safety, the Marsh, he saw the near waters of the Inner Sea shoot upward in a line of gray, foamy geysers—the first escape of vapors—while the waters of the Sea of the East drew suddenly closer.

Then very slowly the rock beneath him began to tilt in the opposite direction, until at last he was pulling on the mare's left bridle to keep her to the road. He was very glad she was a Mingol beast, trained to ignore any and all unnaturalness, even earthquake.

And now it was the still waters of the Sea of the East that exploded upward in a long, dirty, bubbling fence of escaping gas, while the waters of the Inner Sea came foaming almost to the road.

Yet the Marsh was very close. He could make out individual thorn trees and cactuses and thickets of giant sea-grass outlined against the now utterly bled west. And then he saw straight ahead a gap that—pray Issek!—would be the causeway.

Sparks sped whitely from under the mare's iron shoes. The beast's breath rasped.

But now there was a new disquieting change in the landscape, though a very slight one. Almost imperceptibly, the whole Great Salt Marsh was beginning to rise.

The Sinking Land was beginning its periodic submergence.

From either side, from north and south, gray walls were converging on him—the foam-fronted raging waters of the Inner Sea and the Sea of the East rushing to sink the great stone shield now its gaseous support was gone.

A black barrier a yard high loomed just ahead. Fafhrd leaned low in the saddle, nudging the mare's flanks with his heels, and with a great long leap the mare lifted them the needed yard and found them firm footing again, and with never a pause galloped on unchangingly, except that now instead of clashing sharply against rock, the iron shoes struck mutedly on the tight-packed gravel of the causeway.

From behind them came a mounting, rumbling, snarling roar that suddenly rose to a crashing climax. Fafhrd looked back and saw a great starburst of waters—not gray now, but ghostly white in the remaining light from the west—where the waves of the Inner Sea had met the rollers of the Sea of the East exactly at the road.

He was about to look forward again and slow his mount, when out of that pale, churny explosion there appeared a black horse and rider, then another, then a third. But no more—the fourth had evidently been engulfed. The hair lifted on his back at the thought of the leaps the three other beasts had made with their black riders, and he cursed the Mingol mare to make more speed, knowing that kind words went unheard by her.

XII

LANKHMAR READIED HERSELF for another night of terror as shadows lengthened toward infinity and the sunlight turned deep orange. Her inhabitants were not reassured by the lessening number of murderous rats in the streets; they smelled the electric calm before the storm and they barricaded themselves in upper stories as they had the night gone by. Soldiers and constables, according to their individual characters, grinned with relief or griped at bureaucracy's inanities when they got the news that they were to repair to the Southern Barracks one hour before midnight to be harangued by Olegnya Mingolsbane, who was reputed to make the longest and most tedious spittle-spraying speeches of any Captain General in Nehwon's history, and to stink with the sourness of near-senility besides that.

Aboard *Squid*, Slinoor gave orders for lights to burn all night and an all-hands watch to be kept. While the black kitten, forsaking the crow's nest, paced the rail nearest the docks, from time to time uttering an anxious mew and eyeing the dark streets as if with mingled temptation and dread.

For a while Glipkerio soothed his nerves by observing the subtle torturing of Reetha, designed chiefly to fray her nerves rather than her flesh, and by auditing her hours-long questioning by well-trained inquisitors, who sought to hammer from her the admission that the

Gray Mouser was leader of the rats—as his shrinking to rat-size seemed surely to prove—and also force her to divulge a veritable handbook of information on the Mouser's magical methods and sorcerous strategems. The girl truly entranced Glipkerio: she reacted to threats, evil teasings, and relatively minor pain in such a lively, unwearying way.

But after a while he nonetheless grew bored and had a light supper served him in the sunset's red glow on his seaporch outside the Blue Audience Chamber and beside the head of the great copper chute where balanced the great leaden spindle, which he reached out and touched from time to time for reassurance. He hadn't lied to Hisvin, he told himself smugly; he *did* have at least one other secret weapon, albeit it wasn't a weapon of offense, but rather the ultimate opposite. Pray, though, he wouldn't have to use it! Hisvin had promised that at midnight he would work his spell against the assaulting rats, and thus far Hisvin had never failed—had he not conquered the rats of the grain fleet?—while his daughter and her maid had ways of soothing Glipkerio that amazingly did not involve whippings. He had seen with his own eyes Hisvin slay rats with his spell—while on his own part he had arranged for all soldiers and police to be in the South Barracks at midnight listening to that tiresome Olegnya Mingolsbane. He had done his part, he told himself; Hisvin would do his; and at midnight his troubles and vexations would be done.

But it was such a long time until midnight! Once more boredom engulfed the black-togaed, purple-pansy coroneted, beanpole monarch, and he began to think wistfully of whips and Reetha. Beyond all other men, he mused, an overlord, burdened by administration and ceremonies, had no time for even the most homely hobbies and innocent diversions.

Reetha's questioners, meanwhile, gave up for the day and left her in Samanda's charge, who from time to time described gloatingly to the girl the various all-out thrashings and other torments the palace mistress would visit on her as soon as her namby-pamby inquisitors were through with her. The much-abused maid sought to comfort herself with the thought that her madcap gray rescuer might somehow regain his proper size and return to work again her escape. Surely, and despite all the nasty insinuations she had endured, the Gray Mouser was rat-size against his will. She recalled the many fairy tales she had heard of lizard- and frog-princes restored to handsomeness and proper height by a maiden's loving kiss, and despite her miseries, her eyebrowless eyes grew dreamy.

The Mouser squinted through Grig's notched mask at the glorious Council Chamber and the other members of the Supreme Thirteen. Already the scene had become oppressively familiar to him, and he was damnably tired of lisping. Nevertheless, he gathered himself for a supreme effort, which at least was one that tickled his wits.

His coming here had been simplicity itself, and inevitability too. Upon reaching the Fifth Level after parting with Hreest and his pike-rats, rat-pages had fallen in beside him at the foot of the white marble stairs, and a rat-chamberlain had gone solemnly before him, ringing an engraved silver bell which probably once had tinkled from the ankle of a temple dancer in the Street of the Gods in the world above. Thus, footing it grandly himself with the aid of his sapphire-topped ivory staff, though still hobbling a little, he had been wordlessly conducted into the Council Chamber and to the very chair which he now occupied.

The chamber was low but vast, pillared by golden and silver candlesticks doubtless pilfered from palaces and churches overhead. Among them were a few of what looked like jeweled scepters of office and maces of command. In the background, toward the distant walls and half hid by the pillars, were grouped rat-pikemen, waiters, and other servants, litter-bearers with their vehicles, and the like.

The chamber was lit by golden and silver cages of fire-beetles and night-bees and glow-wasps large as eagles, and so many of them that the pulsing of their light was barely apparent. The Mouser had decided that if it became necessary to create a diversion, he would loose some of the glow-wasps.

Within a central circle of particularly costly pillars was set a great round table, about which sat evenly spaced the Thirteen, all masked and clad in white hoods and robes, from which white-gloved rat-hands emerged.

Opposite the Mouser and on a slightly higher chair sat Skwee, well remembered from the time he had crouched on the Mouser's shoulder threatening to sever the artery under his ear. On Skwee's right sat Siss, while on his left was a taciturn rat whom the rest addressed as Lord Null. Alone of the Thirteen, this grumpy Lord Null was clad in robe, hood, mask, and gloves of black. There was something hauntingly familiar about him, perhaps because the hue of his garb recalled to the Mouser Svivomilo and also Hreest.

The remaining nine rats were clearly apprentice members, promoted to fill the gaps in the Circle of Thirteen left by the white rats slain aboard *Squid*, for they never spoke and when questions were voted, only bobbingly agreed with the majority opinion among

Skwee, Siss, Lord Null, and Grig—that is, the Mouser—or if that opinion were split two to two, abstained.

The entire tabletop was hidden by a circular map of what appeared to be well-tanned and buffed human skin, the most delicate and finely pored. The map itself was nothing but innumerable dots: golden, silver, red and black, and thick as fly-specks in the stall of a slum fruit-merchant. At first the Mouser had been able to think of nothing but some eerie, dense starfield. Then it had been revealed to him, by the references the others made to it, that it was nothing more or less than a map of all the ratholes in Lankhmar!

At first this knowledge hadn't made the map come to life for the Mouser. But then gradually he had begun to see in the apparently randomly clustered and twisty-trailed dots the outlines of at least the principal buildings and streets of Lankhmar. Of course, the whole plot of the city was reversed, because viewed from below instead of above.

The golden dots, it had turned out, stood for ratholes unknown to humans and used by rats; the red, for holes known to humans yet still used by rats; the silver, for holes unknown to humans, but not currently employed by the dwellers underneath; while the black dots designated the holes known to humans and avoided by the rodents of Lankhmar Below.

During the entire council session, three slim female rat-pages silently went about, changing the color of ratholes and even dotting in new ones, according to information whispered them by rat-pages, who ceaselessly came and went on equally silent paws. For this purpose, the three females used rat-tail brushes each made of a single, stiffened horsehair frayed at the tip, which they employed most dexterously, and each had slung in a rack at the waist four ink-pots of the appropriate colors.

What the Mouser had learned during the council session had been, simply yet horribly, the all-over plan for the grand assault on Lankhmar Above, which was to take place a half-hour before this very midnight: detailed information about the disposition of pike companies, crossbow detachments, dagger groups, poison-weapon brigades, incendiaries, lone assassins, child-killers, panic-rats, stink-rats, genital-snappers and breast-biters and other berserkers, setters of man-traps such as trip-cords and needle-sharp caltrops and strangling nooses, artillery brigades which would carry up piecemeal larger weapons to be assembled above ground, until his brain could no longer hold all the data.

He had also learned that the principal attacks were to be made on

the South Barracks and especially on the Street of the Gods, hitherto
spared.

Finally he learned that the aim of the rats was not to exterminate
humans or drive them from Lankhmar, but to force an unconditional
surrender from Glipkerio and enslave the overlord's subjects by that
agreement and a continuing terror so that Lankhmar would go on as
always about its pleasures and business, buying and selling, birthing
and dying, sending out of ships and caravans, gathering of grain—
especially grain!—but ruled by the rats.

Fortunately all this briefing had been done by Skwee and Siss.
Nothing had been asked of the Mouser—that is, Grig—or of Lord
Null, except to supply opinions on knotty problems and lead in the
voting. This had also provided the Mouser with time to devise ways
and means of throwing a cat into the rats' plans.

Finally the briefing was done and Skwee asked around the table for
ideas to improve the grand assault—not as if he expected to get any.

But at this point the Mouser rose up—somewhat crippled, since
Grig's damnably ill-fitting rat-boots were still giving him the cramp
—and taking up his ivory staff laid its tip unerringly on a cluster of
silver dots at the west end of the Street of Gods.

"Why ith no aththault made here?" he demanded. "I thuggetht that
at the height of the battle, a party of ratth clad in black togath iththue
from the temple of the Godth *of* Lankhmar. Thith will convinthe the
humanth ath nothing elthe that their very godth—the godth of their
thity—have turned againtht them—been tranthformed, in fact, to
ratth!"

He swallowed hard down his raw, wearied throat. Why the devil
had Grig had to have a lisp?

His suggestion appeared for a moment to stupify the other members of the Council. Then Siss said, wonderingly, admiringly, envi-
ously, and as if against his will, "I never thought of that."

Skwee said, "The temple of the gods *of* Lankhmar has long been
avoided by man and rat alike, as you well know, Grig. Nevertheless . . ."

Lord Null said peevishly, "I am against it. Why meddle with the
unknown? The humans of Lankhmar fear and avoid the temple of
their city's gods. So should we."

The Mouser glared at the black-robed rat through his mask slits.
"Are we mithe or ratth?" he demanded. "Or are we even cowardly,
thuperthtitiouth men? Where ith your ratly courage, Lord Null? Or
thovereign, thkeptical, ratly reathon? My thratagem will cow the

humanth and prove forever the thuperior bravery of ratth! Thkwee! Thith! Ith it not tho?"

The matter was put to a vote. Lord Null voted nay, Siss and the Mouser and—after a pause—Skwee voted aye, the other nine bobbed, and so Operation Black Toga, as Skwee christened it, was hastily added to the battle plans.

"We have over four hours in which to organize it," Skwee reminded his nervous colleagues.

The Mouser grinned behind his mask. He had a feeling that the Gods *of* Lankhmar, if ever roused, would side with the city's human inhabitants. Or would they!—he wondered belatedly.

In any case, his business and desire now was to get out of the Council Chamber as soon as possible. A stratagem instantly suggested itself to him. He waved to a page.

"Thummon a litter," he commanded. "Thith deliberathion hath tired me. I feel faint and am troubled by leg cramp. I will go for a thhort while to my home and wife to retht me."

Skwee looked around at him. "Wife?" the white rat asked incredulously.

Instantly the Mouser answered, "Ith it any buthineth of yourth if it ith my whim to call my mithtreth my wife?"

Skwee still eyed him for a bit, then shrugged.

The litter arrived almost immediately, borne by two very brawny, half-naked rats. The Mouser rolled into it gratefully, laying his ivory staff beside him, commanded "To my home!" and waved a gentle goodbye to Skwee and Lord Null as he was carried joggingly off. He felt himself at the moment to be the most brilliant mind in the whole universe and thoroughly deserving of a rest, even in a rat burrow. He reminded himself he had at least four hours to go before Sheelba's spell wore off and he became once more human size. He'd done his best for Lankhmar, now he must think of himself. He lazily wondered what the comforts of a rat home would be like. He must sample them before escaping above ground. It really had been a damnably tiring council session after all that had gone before.

Skwee turned to Lord Null as the litter disappeared by stages beyond the pillars and said through his be-diamonded white mask, "So Grig has a mistress, the old misogynist! Perhaps it's she who has quickened his mind to such new brilliancies as Operation Black Toga."

"I still don't like that one, though you outvoted me and I must go along," chittered the other irritably from behind his black vizard.

"There's too much uncertainty tonight. The final battle about to be joined. A magically transformed human spy reported in Lankhmar Below. The change in Grig's character. That rabid mouse running widdershins a-foam at the jaws, outside the Council Chamber, and which squeaked thrice when you slew him. The uncustomary buzzing of the night-bees in Siss' chambers. And now this new operation adopted on the spur of the moment—"

Skwee clapped Lord Null on the shoulder in friendly fashion. "You're distraught tonight, comrade, and see omens in every night-bug," he said. "Grig at all events had one most sound notion. We all could do with a little rest and refreshment. Especially you before your all-important mission. Come."

And turning the table over to Siss, he and Lord Null went to a curtained alcove just off the Council Chamber, Skwee ordering on the way that food and drink be brought them.

When the curtains were closed behind them, Skwee seated himself in one of the two chairs beside the small table there and took off his mask. In the pulsing violet light of the three silver-caged glow-wasps illuminating the alcove, his long, white-furred, blue-eyed snout looked remarkably sinister.

"To think," he said, "that tomorrow my people will be masters of Lankhmar Above. For millennia we rats have planned and built, tunneled and studied and striven, and now in less than six hours—it's worth a drink! Which reminds me, comrade, isn't it time for your medicinal draught?"

Lord Null hissed with consternation, prepared to lift his black mask distractedly, dipped his black-gloved right fore-member into his pouch, and came up with a tiny white vial.

"Stop!" Skwee commanded with some horror, capturing the black-gloved wrist with a sudden grab. "If you should drink *that one* now—!"

"I *am* nervous tonight, nervous to flusteration," the other admitted, returning the white vial to his pouch and coming up with a black one. Before draining its contents, he lifted his black mask entirely. The face behind was not a rat's, but the seamed and beady-eyed visage, rat-small, of Hisvin the grain-merchant.

The black draught swallowed, he appeared to experience relief and easement of tension. The worry lines in his face were replaced by those of thought.

"Who is Grig's mistress, Skwee?" he speculated suddenly. "No common slut, I'll swear, or vanity-puffed courtesan."

Skwee shrugged his hunchy shoulders and said cynically, "The more brilliant the enchanted male, the stupider the enchanting female."

"No!" Hisvin said impatiently. "I sense a brilliant and rapacious mind here that is not Grig's. He was ambitious once, you know, sought your position, then his fires sank to coals glowing through wintery ash."

"That's true," Skwee agreed thoughtfully.

"Who has blown him alight again?" Hisvin demanded, now with anxious suspicion. "*Who* is his mistress, Skwee?"

Fafhrd pulled up the Mingol mare before that iron-hearted beast should topple from exhaustion—and had trouble doing it, so resolute unto death was the grim creature. Yet once stopped, he felt her legs giving under her and he dropped quickly from the saddle lest she collapse from his weight. She was lathered with sweat, her head hung between her trembling forelegs, and her slatted ribs worked like a bellows as she gasped whistlingly.

He rested his hand lightly on her shaking shoulders. She never could have made Lankhmar, he knew. They were less than halfway across the Great Salt Marsh.

Low moonlight, striking from behind, washed with a faint gold the gravel of the causeway road and yellowly touched the tops of thorn tree and cactus, but could not yet slant down to the Marsh's seagrassed floor and black bottoms.

Save for the hum and crackle of insects and the calls of night birds, the moonlight-brushed area was silent—yet would not be so for long, Fafhrd knew with a shudder.

Ever since the preternatural emergence of the three black riders from the crash of waves over the Sinking Land and their drumming unshakable pursuit of him through the deepening night, he had been less and less able to think of them as mere vengeful Ilthmar brigands, and more and more conceived them as a supernatural black trinity of death. For miles now, besides, something huge and long-legged and lurching, though never distinctly seen, had been pursuing him through the Marsh, keeping pace with him at the distance of a spear cast. Some giant familiar or obedient djinn of the black horsemen seemed most likely.

His fears had so worked on him that Fafhrd had finally put the mare to her extremest gallop, outdistancing the hoof-noise of the pursuit, though with no effect on the lurching shape and with the inevitable present result. He drew Graywand and faced back toward the new-risen gibbous moon.

Then very faintly he began to hear it: the muted rhythmic drumming of hooves on gravel. They were coming.

At the same moment, from the deep shadows where the giant familiar should be, he heard the Gray Mouser call hoarsely, "This way, Fafhrd! Toward the blue light. Lead your mount. Make it swift!"

Grinning even as the hairs lifted on his neck, Fafhrd looked south and saw a shaped blue glow, like a round-topped, smallish, blue-lit window in the blackness of the Marsh. He plunged down the causeway's slanting south side toward it, pulling the mare after him, and found underfoot a low ridge of firm ground rather than mud. He moved ahead eagerly through the dark, digging in his heels and leaning forward as he dragged his spent mount. The blue window looked a little above his head now. The drumming coming up from the east was louder.

"Shake a leg, Lazybones!" he heard the Mouser call in the same rasping tones. The Gray One must have caught a cold from the Marsh's damp or—the Fates forfend!—a fever from its miasmas.

"Tether your mount to the thorn stump," the Mouser continued gruffly. "There's food for her there and a water pool. Then come up. Speed, speed!"

Fafhrd obeyed without word or waste motion, for the drumming had become very loud.

As he leaped and caught hold of the blue window's bottom and drew himself up to it, the blue glow went out. He scrambled inside onto the reed-carpeted floor of whatever it was and swiftly squirmed around so he was looking back the way he'd come.

The Mingol mare was invisible in the dark below. The causeway's top glowed faintly in the moonlight.

Then round a cluster of thorn trees came speeding the three black riders, the drumming of the twelve hooves thunderous now. Fafhrd thought he could make out a fiendish phosphorescent glow around the nostrils and eyes of the tall black horses and he could faintly discern the black cloaks and hoods of the riders streaming in the wind of their speed. With never a pause they passed the point where he'd left the causeway and vanished behind another thorn grove to the west. He let out a long-held breath.

"Now get away from the door and brace yourself," a voice that wasn't the Mouser's at all grated over his shoulder. "I've got to be there to pilot this rig."

The hairs that had just lain down on Fafhrd's neck erected themselves again. He had more than once heard the rock-harsh voice of Sheelba of the Eyeless Face, though never seen, let alone entered, his fabulous hut. He swiftly hitched himself to one side, back against wall. Something smooth and round and cool touched the back of his neck. A wall-hung skull, it almost had to be.

A black figure crawled into the space he'd just vacated. Dimly silhouetted in the doorway, its edge touched by moonlight, he saw a black cowl.

"Where's the Mouser?" Fafhrd asked with a wheeze in his voice.

The hut gave a violent lurch. Fafhrd grabbed gropingly for and luckily found two wall posts.

"In trouble. *Deep*-down trouble," Sheelba answered curtly. "I did his voice to make you jump lively. As soon as you've fulfilled whatever geas Ningauble has laid upon you—bells, isn't it?—you must go instantly to his aid."

The hut gave a second lurch and a third, then began to rock and pitch somewhat like a ship, but in a swift rhythm and more joltingly, as if one were in a howdah on the slant back of a drunken giant giraffe.

"Go instantly where?" Fafhrd demanded, somewhat humbly.

"How should I know and why should I tell you if I did? I'm not your wizard. I'm just taking you to Lankhmar by secret ways as a favor to that paunchy, seven-eyed, billion-worded dilettante in sorcery who thinks himself my colleague and has gulled you into taking him as mentor," the harsh voice responded from the hood. Then, relenting somewhat, though growing gruffer, "Overlord's palace, most likely. Now shut up."

The rocking of the hut and also its speed increased. Wind pushed in, flapping the edge of Sheelba's hood. Flashes of moon-dappled marsh shot by.

"Who were those riders after me?" Fafhrd asked, clinging to his wall posts. "Ilthmar brigands? Acolytes of the grisly, scythe-armed lord?"

No reply.

"What *is* it all about?" Fafhrd persisted. "Grand assault by a near numberless yet nameless host on Lankhmar. Nameless black riders. The Mouser deep-buried and woefully shrunk, yet alive. A tin whistle maybe summoning War Cats who are dangerous to the blower. None of it makes sense."

The hut gave a particularly vicious lurch. Sheelba still said not a word. Fafhrd grew seasick and devoted himself to hanging on.

Glipkerio, nerving himself, poked his pansy-wreathed, gold-ringleted head on its long neck through the kitchen door's leather curtains and blinking his weak yellow-irised eyes at the fire's glare, grinned an archly amiable, foolish grin.

Reetha, chained once more by the neck, sat cross-legged in front of the fire, head a-droop. Surrounded by four other maids squatting on their heels, Samanda nodded in her great chair. Yet now, though no noise had been made, her snores broke off, she opened her pig-eyes toward Glipkerio, and said familiarly, "Come in, little overlord, don't stand there like a bashful giraffe. Have the rats got you scared too? Be off to your cots, girls."

Three maids instantly rose. Samanda snatched a long pin from her sphere-dressed hair and lightly jabbed awake the fourth, who had been asleep on her heels.

Silently, except for a single swift-stifled squeal from the pricked one, the four maids bobbed a bow at Glipkerio, two at Samanda, and hurried out like so many wax mannequins. Reetha looked around wearily. Glipkerio wandered about, looking anywhere but at her, his chin a-twitch, his long fingers jittery, twining and untwining.

"The restless bug bite you, little overlord?" Samanda asked him. "Shall I make you a hot poppy-posset? Or would you like to see her whipped?" she asked, jerking a thick thumb toward Reetha. "The inquisitors ordered me not to, but of course if you should command me—"

"Oh, no, no, no, no, of course not," Glipkerio protested. "But speaking of whips, I've some new ones in my private collection I'd like to show you, dear Samanda, including one reputedly from Far Kiraay coated with rough-ground glass, if only you'd come with me. Also a handsomely embossed six-tined silver bull prod from—"

"Oh, so it's company you want, like all the other scared ones," Samanda told him. "Well, I'd be willing to oblige you, little overlord, but the 'quisitors told me I must keep an eye all night on this wicked girl, who's in league with the rats' leader."

Glipkerio hemmed and hawed, finally said, "Well, you could bring her along, I suppose, if you really have to."

"So I could," Samanda agreed heartily, at last levering her black-dressed bulk from her chair. "We can test your new whips on her."

"Oh, no, no, *no*," Glipkerio once more protested. Then frowning and also writhing his narrow shoulders, he added thoughtfully, "Though there are times when to get the hang of a new instrument of pain one simply must . . ."

". . . simply must," Samanda agreed, unsnapping the silver chain from Reetha's collar and snapping on a short leash. "Lead the way, little overlord."

"Come first to my bedroom," he told her. "I'll go ahead to get my guardsmen out of the way." And he made off at his longest, toga-stretching stride.

"No need to, little overlord, they know all about your habits," Samanda called after him, then jerked Reetha to her feet. "Come, girl!—you're being mightily honored. Be glad I'm not Glipkerio, or you'd be rubbed with cheese and shoved down-cellar for the rats to nibble."

When they finally arrived through empty silk-hung corridors at Glipkerio's bed-chamber, he was standing in mingled agitation and irritation before its open, jewel-studded, thick oaken door, his black toga a-rustle from his nervous jerking.

"There weren't any guardsmen for me to warn off," he complained. "It seems my orders were stupidly misinterpreted, extended farther than I'd intended, and my guardsmen have all gone off with the soldiers and constables to the South Barracks."

"What need you of guardsmen when you have *me* to protect you, little overlord?" Samanda answered boisterously, slapping a truncheon hanging from her belt.

"That's true," he agreed, only a shade doubtfully, and twitched a large and complex golden key from a fold of his toga. "Now let's lock the girl in here, Samanda, if you please, while we go to inspect my new acquisitions."

"And decide which to use on her?" Samanda asked in her loud coarse voice.

Glipkerio shook his head as if in shocked disapproval, and looking at last at Reetha said in grave fatherly tones, "No, of course not, it is only that I imagine the poor child would be bored at our expertise."

Yet he couldn't quite keep a sudden eagerness from his tones, nor a furtive gleam from his eyes.

Samanda unsnapped the leash and pushed Reetha inside.

Glipkerio warned her in last-minute apprehension, "Don't touch my night-draught now," pointing at a golden tray on a silver night table. Crystal flagons sat on the tray and also a long-stemmed goblet filled with pale apricot-hued wine.

"*Don't touch one thing*, or I'll make you beg for death," Samanda amplified, suddenly all unhumorously brutal. "Kneel at the foot of the bed on knees and heels with head bent—service posture three—and don't move a muscle until we return."

As soon as the thick door was closed and its lock softly thudded shut and the golden key chinkingly withdrawn on the other side, Reetha walked straight to the night table, worked her cheeks a bit, spat into the night-draught, and watched the bubbly scum slowly revolve. Oh if she only had some hairs to drop in it, she yearned fiercely, but there seemed to be no fur or wool in the room and she had been shaved this very morning.

She unstoppered the most tempting of the crystal flagons and carried it about with her, swigging daintily, as she examined the room, paneled with rare woods from the Eight Cities, and its ever rarer treasures, pausing longest at a heavy golden casket full of cut but unset jewels—amethysts, aquamarines, sapphires, jades, topazes, fire opals, rubies, gimpels, and ice emeralds—which glittered and gleamed like the shards of a shattered rainbow.

She also noted a rack of women's clothes, cut for someone very tall and thin, and—surprising beside these evidences of effeminacy—a rack of browned-iron weapons.

She glanced over several shelves of blown-glass figurines long enough to decide that the most delicate and costly-looking was, almost needless to say, that of a slim girl in boots and scanty jacket wielding a long whip. She flicked it off its shelf, so that it shattered on the polished floor and the whip went to powder.

What could they do to her that they weren't planning to do already?—she asked herself with a tight smile.

She climbed into the bed, where she stretched and writhed luxuriously, enjoying to the full the feel of the fine linen sheets against her barbered limbs, body, and head, and now and again trickling from the crystal flagon a few nectarous drops between her playfully haughty-shaped lips. She'd be damned, she told herself, if she'd drink enough to get dead drunk before the last possible instant. Thereafter Samanda and Glipkerio might find themselves hard-put to torment a limp body and blacked-out mind with any great pleasure to themselves.

XIII

THE MOUSER, RECLINING on his side in his litter, the tail of one of the fore-rats swaying a respectful arm's length from his head, noted that, without leaving the Fifth Level, they had arrived at a wide corridor stationed with pike-rats stiffly on guard and having thirteen heavily curtained doorways. The first nine curtains were of white and silver, the next of black and gold, the last three of white and gold.

Despite his weariness and grandiose feeling of security, the Mouser had been fairly watchful along the trip suspecting though not very seriously that Skwee or Lord Null might have him followed—and then there was Hreest to be reckoned with, who might have discovered some clue at the water-privy despite the highly artistic job the Mouser felt he had done. From time to time there had been rats who might have been following his litter, but all these had eventually taken other turns in the mazy corridors. The last to engage his lazy suspicions had been two slim rats clad in black silken cloaks, hoods, masks, and gloves, but these without a glance toward him now disappeared arm-in-arm through the black-and-gold curtains, whispering together in a gossipy way.

His litter stopped at the next doorway, the third from the end. So Skwee and Siss outranked Grig, but he outranked Lord Null. This might be useful to know, though it merely confirmed the impression he had got at the council.

He sat, then stood up with the aid of his staff, rather exaggerating his leg cramp now, and tossed the fore-rat a corn-wreathed silver coin he had selected from Grig's purse. He assumed that tips would be the custom of any species of being whatever, in particular rats. Then without a backward look he hobbled through the heavy curtains, noting in passing that they were woven of fine soft gold wire and braided fine white silk threads. There was a short, dim passageway similarly curtained at the other end. He pushed through the second set of curtains and found himself alone in a cozy-feeling but rather shabby square room with curtained doorways in each of the other three walls and lit by a bronze-caged fire-beetle over each doorway. There were two closed cupboards, a writing desk with stool, many scrolls in silver containers that looked suspiciously like thimbles from the human world, crossed swords and a battle-ax fixed to the dingy walls, and a fireplace in which a single giant coal glowed redly through its coat of white ash. Above the fireplace, or rather brazier-nook, emerged from the wall a bronze-ringed hemisphere about as big as the Mouser's own rat-size head. The hemisphere was yellowish, with a large greenish-brown circle on it, and centered in this circle a black one. With a qualm of horror, the Mouser recognized it as a mummified human eye.

In the center of the room was a pillowed couch with the high back support of one who does a lot of reading lying down, and beside the couch a sizable low table with nothing on it but three bells, one copper, one silver, and one gold.

Putting his horror out of mind, for it is a singularly useless emotion, the Mouser took up the silver bell and rang it vigorously, deciding to see what taking the middle course would bring.

He had little more time than to decide that the room was that of a crusty bachelor with studious inclinations when there came backing through the curtains in the rear wall a fat old rat in spotless long white smock with a white cap on his head. This one turned and showed his silver snout and bleared eyes, and also the silver tray he was carrying, on which were steaming plates and a large steaming silver jug.

The Mouser pointed curtly at the table. The cook, for so he seemed to be, set the tray there and then came hesitantly toward the Mouser, as if to help him off with his robe. The Mouser waved him away and pointed sternly at the rear doorway. He'd be damned if he'd go to the trouble of lisping in Grig's own home. Besides, servants might have a sharper ear than colleagues for a false voice. The cook bowed bumblingly and departed.

The Mouser settled himself gratefully on the couch, deciding against removing as yet his gloves or boots. Now that he was reclining, the latter bothered him hardly at all. However, he did remove his mask and place it close by—it was good to get more than a squinty view of things—and set to at Grig's dinner.

The steaming jug turned out to contain mulled wine. It was most soothing to his raw, dry throat and wearied nerves, though excessively aromatic—the single black clove bobbing in the jug was large as a lime and the cinnamon stick big as one of the parchment scrolls. Then, using Cat's Claw and the two-tined fork provided, he began cutting up and devouring the steaming cutlets of beef—for his nose told him it was that and not, for instance, baby. From another steaming plate he sampled one of the objects that looked like small sweet potatoes. It turned out to be a single grain of boiled wheat. Likewise, one of the yellowish cubes about as big as dice proved a grain of coarse sugar, while the black balls big as the end joint of his thumb were caviar. He speared them one at a time with his fork and munched, alternating this with mouthfuls of the beef. It was very strange to eat good tender beef, the fibers of which were thick as his fingers.

Having consumed the meaty portions of Grig's dinner and drunk all the mulled wine, the Mouser resumed his mask and settled back to plot his escape to Lankhmar Above. But the golden bell kept teasing his thoughts away from practical matters, so he reached out and rang it. Yield to curiosity without giving the mind time to get roiled, was one of his mottoes.

Hardly had the sweet *chinks* died away when the heavy curtains of one of the side doors parted and there appeared a slim straight rat—or ratess, rather, he judged—dressed in robe, hood, mask, slippers and gloves all of fine lemon yellow.

This one, holding the curtains parted, looked toward him and said softly, "Lord Grig, your mistress awaits you."

The Mouser's first reaction was one of gratified conceit. So Grig did have a mistress, and his spur-of-the-moment answer to Skwee's "Wife?" question at the council had been a brilliant stroke of intuition. Whether human-large or rat-small, he could outsmart anyone. He possessed Mouser-mind, unequaled in the universe.

Then the Mouser stood up and approached the slender, yellow-clad figure. There was something cursedly familiar about her. He wondered if she were the ratess in green he'd seen leading short-leashed the brace of shrews. She had a pride and poise about her.

Using the same strategem he had with the cook, he silently pointed from her to the doorway that she should precede him. She acquiesced and he followed close behind her down a dim twisty corridor.

And cursedly attractive too, he decided, eyeing her slender silhouette and sniffing her musky perfume. Rather belatedly, he reminded himself that she was a rat and so should waken his extremest repugnance. But was she necessarily a rat? He had been transformed in size, why not others? And if this were merely the maid, what would the mistress be? Doubtless lard-fat or hag-hairy, he told himself cynically. Still his excitement grew.

Sparing a moment's thought to orient himself, he discovered that the side door they'd gone out by led toward the black-curtained apartments of Lord Null—presumably—rather than to those of Siss and Skwee.

At last the yellow-clad ratess parted gold-heavy black drapes, then light violet silken ones. The Mouser passed her and found himself staring about through the notched eye-holes of Grig's mask at a large bedroom, beautifully and delicately furnished in many ways, yet the weirdest and perhaps the most frightening he had ever seen.

It was draped and carpeted and ceilinged and upholstered all in silver and violet, the latter color the exact complement of the yellow of his conductress's gowning. It was lit indirectly from below by narrow deep tanks of slimy glow-worms big as eels, set against the walls. Against these tanks were several vanity tables, each backed by its large silver mirror, so that the Mouser saw more than one reflection of his white-robed self and his slim cicerone, who had just let the silken violet curtains waft together again. The tabletops were strewn with cosmetics and the tools of beauty, variously colored elixirs and tiny cups—all except one, near a second silver-draped door, which held nothing but two score or so black and white vials.

But between the vanity tables there hung on silver chains, close to the walls and brightly lit by the glow-worm's up-jutting effulgence, large silver cages of scorpions, spiders, mantises, and suchlike glittering vermin, all large as puppy dogs or baby kangaroos. In one spacious cage coiled a Quarmall pocket-viper huge as a python. These clashed their fangs or hissed, according to their kind, while one scorpion angrily clattered its sting across the gleaming bars of its cage, and the viper darted its trebly forked tongue between those of its own.

One short wall, however, was bare except for two pictures tall and wide as doors, the one depicting against a dusky background a girl and crocodile amorously intertwined, the other a man and a leopardess similarly preoccupied.

Almost central in the room was a large bed covered only by a tight-drawn white linen sheet, the woven threads looking coarse as burlap, yet inviting nonetheless, and with one fat white pillow.

Lying supine and at ease on this bed, her head propped against the pillow to survey the Mouser through the eyeholes of her mask, was a figure somewhat slighter than that of his guide, yet otherwise identical and identically clad, except that the silk of her garb was finer still and violet instead of yellow.

"Well met below ground. Sweet Greetings, Gray Mouser," this one called softly in a familiar silvery voice. Then, looking beyond him, "Sweetest slave, make our guest comfortable."

Softest footsteps approached. The Mouser turned a little and saw that his conductress had removed her yellow mask, revealing the merry yet melancholy-eyed dark face of Frix. Her black hair this time hung in two long plaits, braided with fine copper wire.

Without more ado than a smile, she began deftly to unbutton Grig's long white robe. The Mouser lifted his arms a little and let himself be undressed as effortlessly as in a dream, and with even less attention paid for the process, for he was most eagerly scanning the violet-masked figure on the bed. He knew to a certainty who it must be, beyond all contributing evidence, for the silver dart was throbbing in his temple and the hunger which had haunted him for days returned redoubled.

The situation was strange almost beyond comprehension. Although guessing that Frix and the other must have used an elixir like Sheelba's, the Mouser could have sworn they were all three human size, except for the presence of the familiar vermin, scuttlers and slitherers, so huge.

It was a great relief to have his cramping rat-boots deftly drawn off, as he lifted first one leg, then the other. Yet although he submitted so docilely to Frix's ministrations, he kept hold of his sword Scalpel and of the belt it hung from and also, on some cloudy impulse, of Grig's mask. He felt the smaller scabbard empty on the belt and realized with a pang of apprehension that he had left Cat's Claw behind in Grig's apartment along with the latter's ivory staff.

But these worries vanished like the last snowflake in spring when the one on the bed asked cajolingly, "Will you partake of refreshment, dearest guest?" and when he said, "I will most gladly," lifted a violet-gloved hand and ordered, "Dear Frix, fetch sweetmeats and wine."

While Frix busied herself at a far table, the Mouser whispered, his heart a-thump. "Ah, most delectable Hisvet—For I deem you are she?"

"As to that, you must judge for yourself," the tinkling voice responded coquettishly.

"Then I shall call you Hisvet," the Mouser answered boldly, "recognizing you as my queen of queens and princess of princesses. Know, delicious Demoiselle, that ever since our raptures 'neath the closet tree were so rudely broken off by an interruption of Mingols, my mind, nay, my mania has been fixed solely on you."

"That were some small compliment—" the other allowed, lolling back luxuriously, "if I could believe it."

"Believe it you must," the Mouser asserted masterfully, stepping forward. "Know, moreover, that it is my intention that on this occasion our converse not be conducted over Frix's shoulder, dear companion that she is, but at the closest range. I am fixedly desirous of all refreshments, omitting none."

"You cannot think I am Hisvet!" the other countered, starting up in what the Mouser hoped was mock indignation. "Else you would never dare such blasphemy!"

"I dare far more!" the Mouser declared with a soft amorous growl, stepping forward more swiftly. The vermin hanging round about moved angrily, striking against their silver bars and setting their cages a little a-swing, and clashing, clattering, and hissing more. Nevertheless the Mouser, dropping his belt and sword by the edge of the bed and setting a knee thereon, would have thrust himself directly upon Hisvet, had not Frix come bustling up at that moment and set between them on the coarse linen a great silver tray with slim decanters of sweet wine and crystal cups for its drinking and plates of sugary tidbits.

Not entirely to be balked, the Mouser darted his hand across and snatched away the vizard of violet silk from the visage it hid. Violet-gloved hand instantly snatched the mask back from him, but did not replace it, and there confronting him was indeed the slim triangular face of Hisvet, cheeks flushed, red-irised eyes glaring, but pouty lips grinning enough to show the slightly overlarge pearly upper incisors, the whole being framed by silver-blonde hair interwoven like that of Frix, but with even finer wire of silver, into two braids that reached to her waist.

"Nay," she said laughingly, "I see you are most wickedly presumptuous and that I must protect myself." Reaching down on her side of the bed, she procured a long slender-bladed gold-hilted dagger. Waving it playfully at the Mouser, she said, "Now refresh yourself from the cups and plates before you, but have a care of sampling other sweetmeats, dear guest."

The Mouser complied, pouring for himself and Hisvet. He noted from a corner of his eye that Frix, moving silently in her silken robe, had rolled up Grig's white boots and gloves in his white hood and robe and set them on a stool near the floor-to-ceiling painting of the man and the leopardess and that she had made as neat a bundle of all the rest of the Mouser's garb—his own garb, mostly—and set them on a stool next the first. A most efficient and foresighted maid, he thought, and most devoted to her mistress—in fact altogether too devoted: he wished at this moment she would take herself off and leave him private with Hisvet.

But she showed no sign of so doing, nor Hisvet of ordering her away, so without more ado the Mouser began a mild love-play, catching at the violet-gloved fingers of Hisvet's left hand as they dipped toward the sweetmeats or plucking at the ribbons and edges of her violet robe, in the latter case reminding her of the discrepancy in their degree of undress and suggesting that it be corrected by the subtraction of an item or two from her outfit. Hisvet in turn would deftly jab with her dagger at his snatching hand, as if to pin it to tray or bed, and he would whip it back barely in time. It was an amusing game, this dance of hand and needle-sharp dagger—or at least it seemed amusing to the Mouser, especially after he had drained a cup or two of fiery colorless wine—and so when Hisvet asked him how he had come into the rat-world, he merrily told her the story of Sheelba's black potion and how he had first thought its effects a most damnably unfair wizardly joke, but now blessed them as the greatest good ever done him in his life—for he twisted the tale somewhat to make it appear that his sole objective all along had been to win to her side and bed.

He ended by asking, as he parted two fingers to let Hisvet's dagger strike between them, "How ever did you and dear Frix guess that I was impersonating Grig?"

She replied, "Most simply, gracious gamesman. We went to fetch my father from the council, for there is still an important journey he, Frix, and I must make tonight. At a distance we heard you speak and I divined your true voice despite your clever lispings. Thereafter we followed you."

"Ah, surely I may hope you love me as dearly, since you trouble to know me so well," the Mouser warbled infatuatedly, slipping hand aside from a cunning slash. "But tell me, divine one, how comes it that you and Frix and your father are able to live and hold great power in the rat-world?"

With her dagger she pointed somewhat languidly toward the vanity table holding the black and white vials, informing him, "My family has used the same potion as Sheelba's for countless centuries, and also the white potion, which restores us at once to human-size. During those same centuries we have interbred with the rats, resulting in divinely beautiful monsters such as I am, but also in monsters most ugly, at least by human standards. Those latter of my family stay always below ground, but the rest of us enjoy the advantages and delights of living in two worlds. The interbreeding has also resulted in many rats with human-like hands and minds. The spreading of civilization to the rats is largely our doing, and we shall rule as chiefs and chieftesses paramount, or even goddesses and gods, when the rats rule men."

This talk of interbreeding and monsters startled the Mouser somewhat and gave him to think, despite his ever more firmly gyved ensorcelment by Hisvet. He recalled Lukeen's old suggestion, made aboard *Squid*, that Hisvet concealed a she-rat's body under her maiden robes and he wondered—somewhat fearfully yet most curiously—just what form Hisvet's slim body did take. For instance, did she have a tail? But on the whole he was certain that whatever he discovered under her violet robe would please him mightily, since now his infatuation with the grain-merchant's daughter had grown almost beyond all bounds.

However, he outwardly showed none of this wondering, but merely asked, as if idly, "So your father is also Lord Null, and you and he and Frix regularly travel back and forth between the big and little worlds?"

"Show him, dear Frix," Hisvet commanded lazily, lifting slim fingers to mask a yawn, as though the hand-and-dagger game had begun to bore her.

Frix moved back against the wall until her head with its natural jet-black sheath and copper-gleaming plaits, for she had thrown back her hood, was between the cages of the pocket-viper and the most enraged scorpion. Her dark eyes were a sleep-walker's, fixed on things infinitely remote. The scorpion darted his moist white sting between the bars rat-inches from her ear, the viper's trifid tongue vibrated angrily against her cheek, while his fangs struck the silver rounds and dripped venom that wetted oilily her yellow silken shoulder, but she seemed to take no note whatever of these matters. The fingers of her right hand, however, moved along a row of medallions decorating the glow-worm tank behind her, and without looking down, she pressed two at once.

The painting of the girl and crocodile moved swiftly upward, revealing the foot of a dark steep stairway.

"That leads without branchings to my father's and my house," Hisvet explained.

The painting descended. Frix pressed two other medallions and the companion painting of man and leopardess rose, revealing a like stairway.

"While that one ascends directly by way of a golden rathole to the private apartments of whoever is Lankhmar's seeming overlord, now Glipkerio Kistomerces," Hisvet told the Mouser as the second painting slid down into place. "So you see, beloved, our power goes everywhere." And she lifted her dagger and touched it lightly to his throat. The Mouser let it rest there a space before taking its tip between fingers and thumb and moving it aside. Then he as gently caught hold of the tip of one of Hisvet's braids, she offering no resistance, and began to unweave the fine silver wires from the finer silver-blonde hairs.

Frix still stood like a statue between fang and sting, seeming to see things beyond reality.

"Is Frix one of your breed?—combining in some fashion the finest of human and ratly qualities," the Mouser asked quietly, keeping up with the task which, he told himself, would eventually and after an admittedly weary amount of unbraiding, allow him to arrive at his heart's desire.

Hisvet shook her head languorously, laying aside her dagger. "Frix is my dearest slave and almost sister, but not by blood. Indeed she is the dearest slave in all Nehwon, for she is a princess and perchance by now a queen in her own world. While a-travel between worlds, she was ship-wrecked here and beset by demons, from whom my father rescued her, at the price that she serve me forever."

At this, Frix spoke at last, though without moving else but her lips and tongue, not even her eyes to look at them. "Or until, sweetest mistress, I three times save your life at entire peril of my own. That has happened once now, aboard *Squid*, when the dragon would have gobbled you."

"You would never leave me, dear Frix," Hisvet said confidently.

"I love you dearly and serve you faithfully," Frix replied. "Yet all things come to an end. O blessed Demoiselle."

"Then I shall have the Gray Mouser to protect me, and you unneeded," Hisvet countered somewhat pettishly, lifting on an elbow. "Leave us for the nonce, Frix, for I would speak privately with him."

With merriest smile Frix came from between the deadly cages, made a curtsy toward the bed, resumed her yellow mask and swiftly went off through the second unsecret doorway, curtained with filmy silver.

Still lifted on her elbow, Hisvet turned toward the Mouser her slender form and her taper-face alight with beauty. He reached toward her eagerly, but she captured his questing hands in her cool fingers and fondling them asked, or rather stated, her eyes feeding on his, "You will love me forever, will you not, who dared the dark and fearsome tunnels of the rat-world to win me?"

"That will I surely, O Empress of Endless Delights," the Mouser answered fervently, maddened by desire and believing his words to the ends of the universe of his feelings—almost.

"Then I think it proper to relieve you of *this*," Hisvet said, putting the fingers of her two hands to his temple, "for it would be an offense against myself and my supreme beauty to depend on a charm when I may now wholly depend on *you*."

And with only the tiniest tweak of pain inflicted, she deftly squeezed with her fingernails the silver dart from under the Mouser's skin, as any woman might squeeze out a blackhead or whitehead from the visage of her lover. She showed him the dart gleaming on her palm. He for his part felt no change in his feelings whatever. He still adored her as divinity—and the fact that previously in his life he had never put any but momentary trust in any divinity whatever seemed of no importance at all, at least at this moment.

Hisvet laid a cool hand on the Mouser's side, but her red eyes were no longer languorously misty; they were sparklingly bright. And when he would have touched her similarly she prevented him, saying in most businesslike fashion, "No, no, not quite yet! First we must plan, my sweet—for you can serve me in ways which even Frix will not. To begin, you must slay me my father, who thwarts me and confines my life unbearably, so that I may be imperatrix of all and you my most favored consort. There will be no end to our powers. Tonight, Lankhmar! Tomorrow, all Nehwon! Then . . . the conquest of other universes beyond the waters of space! The subjugation of the angels and demons of heaven itself and hell! At first it may be well that you impersonate my father, as you have Grig—and done most cleverly, by my own witnessing, pet. You are of men the most like me in the world for deceptions, darling. Then—"

She broke off at something she saw in the Mouser's face. "You will of course obey me in all things?" she asked sharply, or rather asserted. "Well . . ." the Mouser began.

The silver drape billowed to the ceiling and Frix dashed in on silent silken slippers, her yellow robe and hood flying behind her. "Your masks! Your masks!" she cried. " 'Ware! 'Ware!" And she whirled over them to their necks an opaque violet coverlet, hiding Hisvet's violet-robed form, the Mouser's unclad body, and the tray between them. "Your father comes with armed attendants, lady!" And she knelt by the head of the bed nearest Hisvet and bowed her yellow-masked head, assuming a servile posture.

Hardly were the white and violet masks in place and the silver curtains settled to the floor than the latter were jerked rudely aside. Hisvin and Skwee appeared, both unmasked, followed by three pike-rats. Despite the presence of the huge vermin in their cages, the Mouser found it hard to banish the illusion that all the rats were actually five feet and more tall.

Hisvin's face grew dusky red as he surveyed the scene. "Oh, most monstrous!" he cried at Hisvet. "Shameless filth! Loose with my own colleague!"

"Don't be dramatic, Daddy," Hisvet countered, while to the Mouser she whispered tersely, "Slay him now. I'll clear you with Skwee and the rest."

The Mouser, fumbling under the coverlet over the side of the bed for Scalpel, while presenting a steady white be-diamonded mask at Hisvin, said blandly, "Calm yourthelf, counthillor. If your divine daughter chootheth me above all other ratth and men, ith it my fault, Hithvin? Or herth either? Love knowth no ruleth."

"I'll have your head for this, Grig," Hisvin screeched at him, advancing toward the bed.

"Daddy, you've become a puritanical dodderer," Hisvet said sharply, almost primly, "to indulge in antique tantrums on this night of our great conquest. Your day is done. I must take your place on the Council. Tell him so, Skwee. Daddy darling, I think you're just madly jealous of Grig because you're not where he is."

Hisvin screamed, "O dirt that was my daughter!" and snatching with youthful speed a stiletto from his waist, drove it at Hisvet's neck betwixt violet mask and coverlet—except that Frix, lunging suddenly on her knees, swung her open left hand hard between, as one bats a ball.

The needlelike blade drove through her palm to the slim dagger's hilt and was wrenched from Hisvin's grasp.

Still on one knee, the bright blade transfixing her outstretched left palm and dripping red a little, Frix turned toward Hisvin and advancing her other hand graciously, she said in clear, winning tones, "Govern your rage for all our sakes, dear my dear mistress' father. These matters can be composed by quiet reason, surely. You must not quarrel together on this night of all nights."

Hisvin paled and retreated a step, daunted most likely by Frix's preternatural composure, which indeed was enough to send shivers up a man's or even a rat's spine.

The Mouser's fumbling hand closed around Scalpel's hilt. He prepared to spring out and dash back to Grig's apartment, snatching up his bundle of clothes on the way. At some point during the last score or so heartbeats, his great undying love for Hisvet had quietly perished and was now beginning to stink in his nostrils.

But at that instant the violet drapes were torn apart and there rushed from the Mouser's chosen escape route the rat Hreest in his gold-embellished black garb and brandishing rapier and dirk. He was followed by three guardsmen-rats in green uniforms, each with a like naked sword. The Mouser recognized the dirk Hreest held—it was his own Cat's Claw.

Frix moved swiftly behind the head of the bed to the post she'd earlier taken between viper and scorpion cage, the stiletto still transfixing her left hand like a great pin. The Mouser heard her murmur rapidly, "The plot thickens. Enter armed rats at all portals. A climax nears."

Hreest came to a sudden halt and cried ringingly at Skwee and Hisvin, "The dismembered remains of Councillor Grig have been discovered lodged against the Fifth Level sewer's exit-grill! The human spy is impersonating him in Grig's own clothes!"

Not at the moment, except for mask, the Mouser thought, and making one last effort cried out, "Nonthenthe! Thithe ith midthummer madneth! I am Grig! It wath thome other white rat got tho foully thlain!"

Holding up Cat's Claw and eyeing the Mouser, Hreest continued, "I discovered this dagger of human device in Grig's apartment. The spy is clearly here."

"Kill him in the bed," Skwee commanded harshly, but the Mouser, anticipating a little the inevitable, had rolled out from under his sheets and now took up guard position naked, the white mask cast aside, Scalpel gleaming long and deadly in his right hand, while his left, in lieu of his dirk, held his belt and Scalpel's limp scabbard, both doubled.

With a weird laugh Hreest lunged at him, rapier a-flicker, while Skwee drew sword and came leaping across the foot of the bed, his boot crunching glass against tray beneath the coverlet.

Hreest got a bind on Scalpel, carrying both long swords out to the side, and stepping in close stabbed with Cat's Claw. The Mouser struck his own dirk aside with his doubled belt and drove his left shoulder into Hreest's chest, slamming him back against two of his green-uniformed sword-rats, who were thereby forced to give ground too.

At almost the same instant the Mouser parried high to the side with Scalpel, deflecting Skwee's rapier when its point was inches from his neck. Then swiftly changing fronts, he fenced a moment with Skwee, beat the rat's blade aside, and lunged strongly. The white-clad rat was already in retreat across the foot of the bed, from the head of which Hisvet, now unmasked, watched critically, albeit a little sulkily, but the Mouser's point nevertheless reached Skwee's sword-wrist and pinked it halfway through.

By this time the third green-clad rat, a giant relatively seven feet tall, who had to duck through the doorway, came lunging fiercely, though a little slowly. Meanwhile Hreest was picking himself up from the floor, while Skwee dropped his dagger and switched his rapier to his unwounded hand.

The Mouser parried the giant's lunge, a hair's-breadth from his naked chest, and riposted. The giant counter-parried in time, but the Mouser dropped Scalpel's tip under the other's blade and continuing his riposte, skewered him through the heart.

The giant's jaw gaped, showing his great incisors. His eyes filmed. Even his fur seemed to dull. His weapons dropped from his nerveless hands and he stood dead on his feet a moment before starting to fall. In that moment the Mouser, squatting a little on his right leg, kicked out forcefully with his left. His heel took the giant in the breastbone, pushing his corpse off Scalpel and sending it careening back against Hreest and his two green-clad sword-rats.

One of the pike-rats leveled his weapon for a run at the Mouser, but at that moment Skwee commanded loudly, "No more single attacks! Form we a circle around him!"

The others were swift to obey, but in that brief pause Frix dropped open the silver-barred door that was one end of the scorpion's cage, and despite her dagger-transfixed hand lifted the cage and heaved it sharply, sending its fearsome occupant flying to land on the foot of the bed, where it jigged about, big by comparison as a large cat, clashing its claws, rattling its chelicerae, and menacing with its sting over its head.

Most of the rats directed their weapons at it. Snatching up her dagger, Hisvet crouched at the opposite corner from it, preparing to defend herself from her pet. Hisvin dodged in back of Skwee.

At the same time Frix dropped her good hand to the medallions on the glow-worm tank. The painting of man and leopardess rose. The Mouser didn't need the prompting of her wild smile and over-bright eyes. Snatching up the gray bundle of his clothes, he dashed up the dark steep stairs three at a time. Something hissed past his head and struck with a *zing* the riser of a stone step above and clattered down. It was Hisvet's long dagger and it had struck point-first. The stairway grew dark and he began taking its steps only two at a time, crouching low as he could and peering wide-eyed ahead. Faintly he heard Skwee's shrill command, "After him!"

Frix with a grimace drew Hisvin's stiletto from her palm, lightly kissed the bleeding wound, and with a curtsey presented the weapon to its owner.

The bedroom was empty save for those two and Hisvet, who was drawing her violet robe around her, and Skwee, who was knotting with spade teeth and good hand a bandage round his injured wrist.

Pierced by a dozen thrusts and oozing dark blood on the violet carpet, the scorpion still writhed on its back, its walking legs and great claws a-tremble, its sting sliding a little back and forth.

Hreest, the two green sword-rats, and the three pike-rats had gone in pursuit of the Mouser and the clatter of their boots up the steep stairs had died away.

Frowning darkly, Hisvin said to Hisvet, "I still should slay you."

"Oh Daddy dear, you don't understand at all what happened," Hisvet said tremulously. "The Gray Mouser forced me at sword's point. It was a rape. And at sword's point under the coverlet he compelled me to say those dreadful things to you. You saw I did my best to kill him at the end."

"Pah!" Hisvin spat, turning half aside.

"*She's* the one should be slain," Skwee asserted, indicating Frix. "She worked the spy's escape."

"Most true, oh mighty councillor," Frix agreed. "Else he would have killed at least half of you, and your brains are greatly needed—in fact, indispensable, are they not?—to direct tonight's grand assault on

Lankhmar Above?" She held out her red-dripping palm to Hisvet and said softly, "That's twice, dear mistress."

"For that you shall be rewarded," Hisvet said, setting her lips primly. "And for helping the spy escape—and not preventing my rape!—you shall be whipped until you can no longer scream—tomorrow."

"Right joyfully, milady—tomorrow," Frix responded with a return of something of her merry tones. "But tonight there is work must be done. At Glipkerio's palace in the Blue Audience Chamber. Work for all three of us. And at once, I believe, milord," she added deferentially, turning to Hisvin.

"That's true," Hisvin said with a start. He scowled back and forth between his daughter and her maid three times, then with a shrug, said, "Come."

"How can you trust them?" Skwee demanded.

"I must," Hisvin said. "They're needful if I am properly to control Glipkerio. Meanwhile your place is that of supreme command, at the council table. Siss will be needing you. Come!" he repeated to the two girls. Frix worked the medallions. The second painting rose. They went all three up the stairs.

Skwee paced the bed-chamber alone, head bowed in angry thought, automatically overstepping the corpse of the giant sword-rat and circling the still-writhing scorpion. When he at last stopped and lifted his gaze, it was to rest it on the vanity table bearing the black and white bottles of the size-change magic. He approached that table with the gait of a sleepwalker or one who walks through water. For a space he played aimlessly with the vials, rolling them this way and that. Then he said aloud to himself, "Oh why is it that one can be wise and command a vast host and strive unceasingly and reason with diamond brilliance, and still be low as a silverfish, blind as a cutworm? The obvious is in front of our toothy muzzles and we never see it—because we rats have accepted our littleness, hypnotized ourselves with our dwarfishness, our incapacity, and our inability to burst from our cramping prison-tunnels, to leap from the shallow but deadly jail-rut, whose low walls lead us only to the stinking rubbish heap or narrow burial crypt."

He lifted his ice-blue eyes and glared coldly at his silver-furred image in the silver mirror. "For all your greatness, Skwee," he told himself, "you have thought small all your rat's life. Now for once, Skwee, think big!" And with that fierce self-command, he picked up one of the white vials and pouched it, hesitated, swept all the white vials into his pouch, hesitated again, then with a shrug and a sardonic grimace swept the black vials after them and hurried from the room.

On its back on the violet carpet, the scorpion still vibrated its legs feebly.

XIV

FAFHRD SWIFTLY CLIMBED, by the low moonlight, the high Marsh Wall of Lankhmar at the point to which Sheelba had delivered him, a good bowshot south of the Marsh Gate. "At the gate you might run into your black pursuers," Sheelba had told him. Fafhrd had doubted it. True, the black riders had been moving like a storm wind, but Sheelba's hut had raced across the sea-grass like a low-scudding pocket hurricane; surely he had arrived ahead of them. Yet he had put up no argument. Wizards were above all else persuasive salesmen, whether they flooded you off your feet with words, like Ningauble, or manipulated you with meaningful silences, like Sheelba. For the swamp wizard had otherwise maintained his cranky quiet throughout the entire rocking, pitching, swift-skidding trip, from which Fafhrd's stomach was still queasy.

He found plenty of good holds for hand and foot in the ancient wall. Climbing it was truly child's play to one who had scaled in his youth Obelisk Polaris in the frosty Mountains of the Giants. He was far more concerned with what he might meet at the top of the wall, where he would be briefly helpless against a foe footed above him.

But more than all else—and increasingly so—he was puzzled by the darkness and silence with which the city was wrapped. Where was the battle-din; where were the flames? Or if Lankhmar had already been subdued, which despite Ningauble's optimism seemed most likely from the fifty-to-one odds against her, where were the screams of the tortured, the shrieks of the raped, and all the gleeful clatter and shout of the victors?

He reached the wall's top and suddenly drew himself up and vaulted through a wide embrasure down onto the wide parapet, ready to draw Graywand and his ax. But the parapet was empty as far as he could see in either direction.

Wall Street below was dark, and empty too as far as he could tell. Cash Street, stretching west and flooded with pale moonlight from behind him, was visibly bare of figures. While the silence was even more marked than when he'd been climbing. It seemed to fill the great, walled city, like water brimming a cup.

Fafhrd felt spooked. Had the conquerors of Lankhmar already departed?—carrying off all its treasure and inhabitants in some unimaginably huge fleet or caravan? Had they shut up themselves and their gagged victims in the silent houses for some rite of mass torture in darkness? Was it a demon, not human army which had beset the city and vanished its inhabitants? Had the very earth gaped for victor and vanquished alike and then shut again? Or was Ningauble's whole tale wizardly flimflam?—yet even that least unlikely explanation still left unexplained the city's ghostly desolation.

Or was there a fierce battle going on under his eyes at this very moment, and he by some spell of Ningauble or Sheelba unable to see, hear, or even scent it?—until, perchance, he had fulfilled the geas of the bells which Ningauble had laid on him.

He still did not like the idea of his bells-mission. His imagination pictured the Gods *of* Lankhmar resting in their brown mummy-wrappings and their rotted black togas, their bright black eyes peeping from between resin-impregnated bandages and their deadly black staves of office beside them, waiting another call from the city that forgot yet feared them and which they in turn hated yet guarded. Waking with naked hand a clutch of spiders in a hole in desert rocks seemed wiser than waking such. Yet a geas was a geas and must be fulfilled.

He hurried down the nearest dark stone stairs three steps at a time and headed west on Cash Street, which paralleled Crafts Street a block to the south. He half imagined he brushed unseen figures. Crossing curvy Cheap Street, dark and untenanted as the others, he thought he heard a murmuring and chanting from the north, so faint that it must come from at least as far away as the Street of Gods. But he held to his predetermined course, which was to follow Cash Street to Nun Street, then three blocks north to the accursed bell-tower.

Whore Street, which was even more twisty than Cheap Street, looked tenantless too, but he was hardly half a block beyond it when he heard the tramp of boots and the clink of armor behind him. Ducking into the narrow shadows, he watched a double squad of guardsmen cross hurriedly through the moonlight, going south on Whore Street in the direction of the South Barracks. They were crowded close together, watched every way, and carried their weapons at the ready, despite the apparent absence of foe. This seemed to confirm Fafhrd's notion of an army of invisibles. Feeling more spooked than ever, he continued rapidly on his way.

And now he began to note, here and there, light leaking out from around the edges of a shuttered upper window. These dim-drawn oblongs only increased his feeling of supernatural dread. Anything, he told himself, would be better than this locked-in silence, now broken only by the faint echoing tread of his own boots on the moonlit cobbles. And at the end of his trip: mummies!

Somewhere, faintly, muffled, eleven o'clock knelled. Then of a sudden, crossing narrow, black-brimming Silver Street, he heard a multitudinous pattering, like rain—save that the stars were bright overhead except for the moon's dimming of them, and he felt no drops. He began to run.

Aboard *Squid*, the kitten, as if he had received a call which he might not disregard despite all dreads, made the long leap from the scuppers to the docks, clawed his way up onto the latter and hurried off into the dark, his black hair on end and his eyes emerald bright with fear and danger-readiness.

Glipkerio and Samanda sat in his Whip Room, reminiscing and getting a tipsy glow on, to put them in the right mood for Reetha's thrashing. The fat palace mistress had swilled tankards of dark wine of Tovilyis until her black wool dress was soaked with sweat and salty beads stood on each hair of her ghostly black moustache. While her overlord sipped violet wine of Kiraay, which she had fetched from the upper pantry when no butler or page answered the ring of the silver and even the brazen summoning-bell. She'd said, "They're scared to stir since your guardsmen went off. I'll welt them properly —but only when you've had your special fun, little master."

Now, for the nonce neglecting all the rare and begemmed instruments of pain around them and blessedly forgetting the rodent menace to Lankhmar, their thoughts had returned to simpler and happier days. Glipkerio, his pansy wreath awry and somewhat wilted, was saying with a tittering eagerness, "Do you recall when I brought you my first kitten to throw in the kitchen fire?"

"Do I?" Samanda retorted with affectionate scorn. "Why, little master, I remember when you brought me your first fly, to show me how neatly you could pluck off his wings and legs. You were only a toddler, but already skinny-tall."

"Yes, but about that kitten," Glipkerio persisted, violet wine dribbling down his chin as he took a hasty and tremble-handed swallow. "It was black with blue eyes newly unfilmed. Radomix was trying to stop me—he lived at the palace then—but you sent him away bawling."

"I did indeed," Samanda concurred. "The cotton-hearted brat! And I remember how the kitten screamed and frizzled, and how you cried afterwards because you hadn't him to throw in again. To divert your mind and cheer you, I stripped and whipped an apprentice maid as skinny-tall as yourself and with long blonde braids. That was before you got your thing about hairs"—she wiped her moustache—"and had all the girls and boys shaved. I thought it was time you graduated to manlier pleasures, and sure enough you showed your excitement in no uncertain fashion!" And with a whoop of laughter she reached across and thumbed him indelicately.

Excited by this tickling and his thoughts, Lankhmar's overlord stood up cypress-tall-and-black in his toga, though no cypress ever twitched as he did, except perhaps in an earthquake or under most potent witchcraft. "Come," he cried. "Eleven's struck. We've barely time before I must haste me to the Blue Audience Chamber to meet with Hisvin and save the city."

"Right," Samanda affirmed, levering herself up with her brawny forearms pulling at her knees and then pushing the pinching armchair off her large rear. "Which whips was it you'd picked now for the naughty and traitorous minx?"

"None, none," Glipkerio cried with impatient glee. "In the end that well-oiled old black dog-whip hanging from your belt always seems best. Hurry we, dear Samanda, hurry!"

Reetha shot up in crispy-linened bed as she heard hinges creak. Shaking nightmares from her smooth-shaven head, she fumbled frantically about for the bottle whose draining would bring her protective oblivion.

She put it to her lips, but paused a moment before upending it. The door still hadn't opened and the creaking had been strangely tiny and shrill. Glancing over the edge of the bed, she saw that another door not quite a foot high had opened outward at floor level in the seamless-seeming wood paneling. Through it there stepped swiftly and silently, ducking his head a trifle, a well-formed and leanly muscular little man, carrying in one hand a gray bundle and in the other what seemed to be a long toy sword as naked as himself.

He closed the door behind him, so that it once more seemed not to be there, and gazed about piercingly.

"Gray Mouser!" Reetha yelled, springing from bed and throwing herself down on her knees beside him. "You've come back to me!"

He winced, lifting his burdened tiny hands to his ears.

"Reetha," he begged, "don't shout like that again. It blasts my brain." He spoke slowly and as deep-pitched as he could, but to her his voice was shrill and rapid, though intelligible.

"I'm sorry," she whispered contritely, restraining the impulse to pick him up and cuddle him to her bosom.

"You'd better be," he told her brusquely. "Now find something heavy and put it against this door. There's those coming after, whom you wouldn't want to meet. Quick about it, girl!"

She didn't stir from her knees, but eagerly suggested, "Why not work your magic and make yourself big again?"

"I haven't the stuff to work that magic," he told her exasperatedly. "I had a chance at a vial of it and like any other sex-besotted fool didn't think to swipe it. Now jump to it, Reetha!"

Suddenly realizing the strength of her bargaining position, she merely leaned closer to him and smiling archly though lovingly, asked, "With what doll-tiny bitch have you been consorting now? No, you needn't answer that, but before I stir me to help you, you must give me six hairs from your darling head. I have good reason for my request."

The Mouser started to argue insanely with her, then thought better of it and snicked off with Scalpel a small switch of his locks and laid them in her huge, crisscross furrowed, gleaming palm, where they were fine as baby hairs, though slightly longer and darker than most.

She stood up briskly, marched to the night table, and dropped them in Glipkerio's night draught. Then dusting off her hands above the goblet, she looked around. The most suitable object she could see for the Mouser's purpose was the golden casket of unset jewels. She lugged it into place against the small door, taking the Mouser's word as to where the small door exactly was.

"That should hold them for a bit," he said, greedily noting for

future reference the rainbow gems bigger than his fists, "but 'twere
best you also fetch—"

Dropping to her knees, she asked somewhat wistfully, "Aren't you
ever going to be big again?"

"Don't boom the floor! Yes, of course! In an hour or less, if I can
trust my tricksy, treacherous wizard. Now, Reetha, while I dress me,
please fetch—"

A key chinked dulcetly and a bolt thudded softly in its channel.
The Mouser felt himself whirled through the air by and with Reetha
onto the soft springy white bed, and a white translucent sheet
whirled over them.

He heard the door open.

At that moment a hand on his head pressed him firmly down into a
squat and as he was about to protest, Reetha whispered—it was a
growl like light surf—"Don't make a bump in the sheet. Whatever
happens, hold still and hide for your dear life's sake."

A voice like battle trumpets blared then, making the Mouser glad
of what shielding the sheet gave his ears. "The nasty girl's crawled in
my bed! Oh, the disgust of it! I feel faint. Wine! Ah! *Aaarrrggghhh!*"
There came ear-shaking chokings, spewings, and spittings, and then
the battle trumpets again, somewhat muffled, as if stuffed with flan-
nel, though even more enraged: "The filthy and demonic slut has put
hairs in my drink! Oh whip her, Samanda, until she's everywhere
welted like a bamboo screen! Lash her until she licks my feet and
kisses each toe for mercy!"

Then another voice, this one like a dozen huge kettledrums, thundering through the sheet and pounding the Mouser's tinied goldleaf-
thin eardrums. "That will I, little master. Nor heed you, if you ask I
desist. Come out of there, girl, or must I whip you out?"

Reetha scrambled toward the head of the bed, away from that
voice. The Mouser followed crouching after her, though the mattress
heaved like a white-decked ship in a storm, the sheet figuring as an
almost deck-low ceiling of fog. Then suddenly that fog was whirled
away, as if by a supernal wind, and there glared down the gigantic
double red-and-black sun of Samanda's face, inflamed by liquor and
anger, and of her globe-dressed, pin-transfixed black hair. And the
sun had a black tail—Samanda's raised whip.

The Mouser bounded toward her across the disordered bed, brandishing Scalpel and still lugging under his other arm the gray bundle
of his clothes.

The whip, which had been aimed at Reetha, changed direction and
came whistling toward him. He sprang straight up with all his

strength and it passed just under his naked feet like a black dragon's tail, the whistling abruptly lowering in pitch. By good luck keeping his footing as he came down, he leaped again toward Samanda, stabbed her with Scalpel in her black-wool-draped huge kneecap, and sprang down to the parquet floor.

Like a browned-iron thunderbolt, a great ax-head bit into the wood close by him, jarring him to his teeth. Glipkerio had snatched a light battle-ax from his weapon-rack with surprising speed and wielded it with unlikely accuracy.

The Mouser darted under the bed, raced across that—to him—low-ceilinged dark wide portico, emerged on the other side and doubled swiftly back around the foot of the bed to slash at the back of Glipkerio's ankle.

But this ham-stringing stroke failed when Glipkerio turned around. Samanda, limping just a little, came to her overlord's side. Gigantic ax and whip were again lifted at the Mouser.

With a rather happy hysterical scream that almost ruined the Mouser's eardrums for good, Reetha hurled her crystal wine-flagon. It passed close between Samanda's and Glipkerio's heads, hitting neither of them, but staying their strokes at the Mouser.

All this while, unnoticed in the racket and turmoil, the golden jewel-box had been moving away, jolt by tiny jolt, from the wall. Now the door behind it was open wide enough for a rat to get through, and Hreest emerged followed by his armed band—three masked sword-rats in all, the other two green-uniformed, and three naked-faced pike-rats in browned-iron helmets and mail.

Utterly terrified by this eruption, Glipkerio raced from the room, followed only less slowly by Samanda, whose heavy treadings shook the wooden floor like earthquake shocks.

Mad for battle and also greatly relieved to face foes his own size, the Mouser went on guard, using his clothes bundle as a sort of shield and crying out fearsomely, "Come and be killed, Hreest!"

But at that instant he felt himself snatched up with stomach-wrenching speed to Reetha's breasts.

"Put me down! Put me down!" he yelled, still in a battle-rage, but futilely, for the drunken girl carried him reelingly out the door and slammed it behind her—once more the Mouser's eardrums were assaulted—slammed it on a rat-pike.

Samanda and Glipkerio were running toward a distant, wide, blue curtain, but Reetha ran the other way, toward the kitchen and the servants' quarters, and the Mouser was perforce carried with her—his gray bundle bouncing about, his pin-sword useless, and despite his shrill protests and tears of wrath.

The rats everywhere launched their grand assault on Lankhmar Above a half hour before midnight, striking chiefly by way of golden ratholes. There were a few premature sorties, as on Silver Street, and elsewhere a few delays, as at ratholes discovered and blocked by humans at the last moment, but on the whole the attack was simultaneous.

First to emerge from Lankhmar Below were wild troops of four-foot goers, a fierce riderless cavalry, savage rats from the stinking tunnels and warrens under the slums of Lankhmar, rodents knowing few if any civilized amenities and speaking at most a pidgin-Lankhmarese helped out with chitters and squeals. Some fought only with tooth and claw like the veriest primitives. Among them went berserkers and special-mission groups.

Then came the assassins and the incendiaries with their torches, resins, and oils—for the weapon of fire, hitherto unused, was part of the grand plan, even though the rats' upper-level tunnels were menaced thereby. It was calculated that victory would be gained swiftly enough for the humans to be enforced to put out the blazes.

Finally came the armed and armored rats, all going biped except for those packing extra missiles and parts of light-artillery pieces to be assembled above ground.

Previous forays had been made almost entirely through ratholes in cellars and ground floors and by way of street-drains and the like. But tonight's grand assault was delivered whenever possible through ratholes on upper floors and through rat-ways that emerged in attics, surprising the humans in the supposedly safe chambers in which they had shut themselves and driving them in panic into the streets.

It was turn-about from previous nights and days, when the rats had risen in black waves and streams. Now they dropped like a black indoor rain and leaked in rat-big gushes from walls thought sound, bringing turmoil and terror. Here and there, chiefly under eaves, flames began to flicker.

The rats emerged inside almost every temple and cultish hovel lining the Street of the Gods, driving out the worshippers until that wide avenue was milling with humans too terrified to dare the dark side streets or create more than a few pockets of organized resistance.

In the high-windowed assembly hall of the South Barracks, Olegnya Mingolsbane loudly sputter-quavered to a weary audience which following custom had left their weapons outside—the soldiers

of Lankhmar had been known to use them on irritating or merely
boresome speakers. As he perorated, "You who have fought the black
behemoth and leviathan, you who have stood firm against Mingol and
Mirphian, you who have broken the spear-squares of King Krimaxius
and routed his fortressed elephants, that *you* should be daunted by
dirty vermin—" eight large ratholes opened high in the back wall and
from these sinister orifices a masked battery of crossbow artillery
launched their whirring missiles at the aged and impassioned general.
Five struck home, one down his gullet, and gargling horridly he fell
from the rostrum.

Then the fire of the crossbows was turned on the startled yet le-
thargic audience, some of whom had been applauding Olegnya's de-
mise as if it had been a carnival turn. From other high ratholes actual
fire was tossed down in the forms of white phosphorus and flaming,
oil-soaked, resin-hearted bundles of rags, while from various low
golden ratholes, noxious vapors brewed in the sewers were bellows-
driven.

Groups of soldiers and constables broke for the doors and found
them barred from the outside—one of the most striking achievements
of the special-missions groups, made possible by Lankhmar having
things arranged so that she could massacre her own soldiers in times
of mutiny. With smuggled weapons and those of officers, a counter-
fire was turned on the ratholes, but they were difficult targets and for
the most part the men of war milled about as helplessly as the worshipers in the Street of the Gods, coughing and crying out, more
troubled for the present by the stinking vapors and the choking
fumes of little flames here and there than by the larger fire-danger.

Meanwhile the black kitten was flattening himself on top of a cask
in the granaries area while a party of armed rats trooped by. The
small beast shivered with fear, yet was drawn on deeper and deeper
into the city by a mysterious urging which he did not understand, yet
could not ignore.

Hisvin's house had in its top floor a small room, the door and window shutters of which were all tightly barred from the inside so that
a witness, if there could have been one, would have wondered how
this barring had been accomplished in such fashion as to leave the
room empty.

A single thick, blue-burning candle, which had somewhat fouled
the air, revealed no furniture whatsoever in the room. It showed six
wide, shallow basins that were part of the tiled floor. Three of these
basins were filled with a thick pinkish liquid across which ever and

anon a slow quivering ran. Each pink pool had a border of black dust with which it did not commingle. Along one wall were shelves of small vials, the white ones near the floor, the black ones higher.

A tiny door opened at floor level. Hisvin, Hisvet, and Frix filed silently out. Each took a white vial and walked to a pink pool and then unhesitatingly down into it. The dark dust and pinkish liquid slowed but did not stop their steps. It moved out in sluggish ripples from their knees. Soon each stood thigh-deep at a pool's center. Then each drained his vial.

For a long instant there was no change, only the ripples intersecting and dying by the candle's feeble gleam.

Then each figure began to grow while soon the pools were visibly diminished. In a dozen heartbeats they were empty of liquid and dust alike, while in them Hisvin, Hisvet, and Frix stood human-high, dry-shod, and clad all in black.

Hisvin unbarred a window opening on the Street of the Gods, threw wide the shutters, drew a deep breath, stooped to peer out briefly and cautiously, then turned him crouching to the girls.

"It has begun," he said somberly. "Haste we now to the Blue Audience Chamber. Time presses. I will alert our Mingols to assemble and follow us." He scuttled past them to the door. "Come!"

Fafhrd drew himself up onto the roof of the temple of the Gods *of* Lankhmar and paused for a backward and downward look before tackling the belfry, although so far this climb had been easier even than that of the city's wall.

He wanted to know what all the screaming was about.

Across the street were several dark houses, first among them Hisvin's, while beyond them rose Glipkerio's Rainbow Palace with its moonlit, pastel-hued minarets, tallest of them the blue, like a troup of tall, slender dancing girls behind a phalanx of black-robed squat priests.

Immediately below him was the temple's unroofed yet dark front porch and low, wide steps leading up to it from the street. Fafhrd had not even tried the verdigrised, copper-bound, worm-eaten doors below him. He had had no mind to go stumbling around hunting for a stairs in the inner dark and dust, where his groping hands might touch mummy-wrapped, black-togaed forms which might not lie still like other dead earth, but stir with crotchety limitless anger, like ancient yet not quite senile kings who did not relish their sleep disturbed at midnight. On both counts, an outside climb had seemed healthier and likewise the awakening of the Gods *of* Lankhmar, if they were to be wakened, better by a distant bell than by a touch on a skeletal shoulder wrapped in crumbling linen or on a bony foot.

When Fafhrd had begun his short climb, the Street of the Gods had been empty at this end, though from the open doors of its gorgeous temples—the temples of the Gods *in* Lankhmar—had spilled yellow light and come the mournful sound of many litanies, mixed with the sharper accents of impromptu prayers and beseechings.

But now the street was churning with white-faced folk, while others were still rushing screaming from temple doorways. Fafhrd still couldn't see what they were running from, and once more he thought of an army of invisibles—after all, he had only to imagine Ghouls with invisible bones—but then he noted that most of the shriekers and churners were looking downward toward their feet and the cobbles. He recollected the eerie pattering which had sent him running away from Silver Street. He remembered what Ningauble had asserted about the huge numbers and hidden source of the army besieging Lankhmar. And he recalled that *Clam* had been sunk and *Squid* captured by rats working chiefly alone. A wild suspicion swiftly bloomed in him.

Meanwhile some of the temple refugees had thrown themselves to their knees in front of the dingy fane on which he stood, and were bumping their heads on the cobbles and lower steps and uttering frenzied petitions for aid. As usual, Lankhmar was appealing to her own grim, private gods only in a moment of direst need, when all else failed. While a bold few directly below Fafhrd had mounted the dark porch and were beating on and dragging at the ancient portals.

There came a loud creaking and groaning and a sound of rending. For a moment Fafhrd thought that those below him, having broken in, were going to rush inside. But then he saw them hurrying back down the steps in attitudes of dread and prostrating themselves like the others.

The great doors had opened until there was a hand's breadth between them. Then through that narrow gap there issued from the temple a torchlit procession of tiny figures which advanced and ranged themselves along the forward edge of the porch.

They were two score or so of large rats walking erect and wearing black togas. Four of them carried lance-tall torches flaming brightly white-blue at their tips. The others each carried something that Fafhrd, staring down eagle-eyed, could not quite discern—a little black staff? There were three whites among them, the rest black.

A hush fell on the Street of the Gods, as if at some secret signal the humans' tormentors had ceased their persecutions.

The black-togaed rats cried out shrilly in unison, so that even
Fafhrd heard them clearly, "We have slain your gods, O Lankhmarts!
We are your gods now, O folk of Lankhmar. Submit yourselves to our
worldly brothers and you will not be harmed. Hark to their commands. Your gods are dead, O Lankhmarts! We are your gods!"

The humans who had abased themselves continued to do so and to
bump their heads. Others of the crowd imitated them.

Fafhrd thought for a moment of seeking something to hurl down
on that dreadful little black-clad line which had cowed humanity. But
the nasty notion came to him that if the Mouser had been reduced to
a fraction of himself and able to live far under the deepest cellar, what
could it mean but that the Mouser had been transformed into a rat by
wicked magic, Hisvin's most likely? In slaying any rat, he might slay
his comrade.

He decided to stick to Ningauble's instructions. He began to climb
the belfry with great reaches and pulls of his long arms and doublings
and straightenings of his still longer legs.

The black kitten, coming around a far corner of the same temple,
bugged his little eyes at the horrid tableaux of black-togaed rats. He
was tempted to flee, yet moved never a muscle, as a soldier who
knows he has a duty to perform, though he has forgotten or not yet
learned the nature of that duty.

XV

GLIPKERIO SAT FIDGETING on the edge of his seashell-shaped couch of gold. His light battle-ax lay forgot on the blue floor beside him. From a low table he took up a delicate silver wand of authority tipped with a bronze starfish—it was one of several dozen lying there—and sought to play with it nervously. But he was too nervous for that. Within moments it shot out of his hands and clattered musically on the blue floor-tiles a dozen feet away. He knotted his wand-long fingers together tightly, and rocked in agitation.

The Blue Audience Chamber was lit only by a few guttering, soot-runneled candles. The central curtains had been raised, but this doubling of the room's length only added to its gloom. The stairway going up into the blue minaret was a spiral of shadows. Beyond the dark archways leading to the porch, the great gray spindle balancing atop the copper chute gleamed mysteriously in the moonlight. A narrow silver ladder led up to its manhole, which stood open.

The candles cast on the blue-tiled inner wall several monstrous shadows of a bulbous figure seeming to bear two heads, the one atop the other. It was made by Samanda, who stood watching Glipkerio with stolid intentness, as one watches a lunatic up to tricks.

Finally Glipkerio, whose own gaze never ceased to twitch about at floor level, especially at the foot of blue curtains masking arched blue doorways, began to mumble, softly at first, then louder and louder, "I can't stand it any more. Armed rats loose in the palace. Guardsmen gone. Hairs in my throat. That horrid girl. That indecent hairy jumping jack with the Mouser's face. No butler or maid to answer my bell. Not even a page to trim the candles. And Hisvin hasn't come. Hisvin's not coming! I've no one. All's lost! *I can't stand it. I'm leaving! World, adieu! Nehwon, goodbye! I seek a happier universe!*"

And with that warning, he dashed toward the porch—a streak of black toga from which a lone pansy petal fluttered down.

Samanda, clumping after him heavily, caught him before he could climb the silver ladder, largely because he couldn't get his hands unknotted to grip the rungs. She grasped him round with a huge arm and led him back toward the audience couch, meanwhile straightening and unslipping his fingers for him and saying, "Now, now, no boat trips tonight, little master. It's on dry land we stay, your own dear palace. Only think: tomorrow, when this nonsense is past, we'll have such lovely whippings. Meanwhile to guard you, pet, you've me, who am worth a regiment. Stick to Samanda!"

As if taking her at her literal word, Glipkerio, who had been confusedly pulling away, suddenly threw his arms around her neck and almost managed to seat himself upon her great belly.

A blue curtain had billowed wide, but it was only Glipkerio's niece Elakeria in a gray silk dress that threatened momently to burst at the seams. The plump and lascivious girl had grown fatter than ever the past few days from stuffing herself with sweets to assuage her grief at her mother's broken neck and the crucifixion of her pet marmoset, and even more to still her fears for herself. But at the moment a weak anger seemed to be doing the work of honey and sugar.

"Uncle!" she cried. "You must do something at once! The guardsmen are gone. Neither my maid nor page answered my bell, and when I went to fetch them, I found that insolent Reetha—wasn't she to be whipped?—inciting all the pages to revolt against you, or do something equally violent. And in the crook of her left arm sat a living gray-clad doll waving a cruel little sword—surely it was he who crucified Kwe-Kwe!—urging further enormities. I stole away unseen."

"Revolt, eh?" Samanda growled, setting Glipkerio aside and unsnapping whip and truncheon from her belt. "Elakeria, look out for Uncle here. You know, boat trips," she added in a hoarse whisper, tapping her temple significantly. "Meanwhile I'll give those naked sluts and minions a counter-revolution they'll not forget."

"Don't leave me!" Glipkerio implored, throwing himself at her neck and lap again. "Now that Hisvin's forgot me, you're my only protection."

A clock struck the quarter hour. Blue drapes parted and Hisvin came in with measured steps instead of his customary scuttling. "For good or ill, I come upon my instant," he said. He wore his black cap and toga and over the latter a belt from which hung ink-pot, quill-case, and a pouch of scrolls. Hisvet and Frix came close after him, in sober silken black robes and stoles. The blue drapes closed behind them. All three black-framed faces were grave.

Hisvan paced toward Glipkerio, who somewhat shamed into composure by the orderly behavior of the newcomers was standing beanpole tall on his own two gold-sandaled feet, had adjusted a little the disordered folds of his toga, and straightened around his golden ringlets the string of limp vegetable matter which was all that was left of his pansy wreath.

"Oh most glorious overlord," Hisvin intoned solemnly, "I bring you the worst news"—Glipkerio paled and began again to shake—"and the best." Glipkerio recovered somewhat. "The worst first. The star whose coming made the heavens right has winked out, like a candle puffed on by a black demon, its fires extinguished by the black swells of the ocean of the sky. In short, she's sunk without a trace and so I cannot speak my spell against the rats. Furthermore, it is my sad duty to inform you that the rats have already, for all practical purposes, conquered Lankhmar. All your soldiery is being decimated in the South Barracks. All the temples have been invaded and the very Gods *of* Lankhmar slain without warning in their dry, spicy beds. The rats only pause, out of a certain courtesy which I will explain, before capturing your palace over your head."

"Then all's lost," Glipkerio quavered chalk-pale and turning his head added peevishly, "I *told* you so, Samanda! Naught remains for me but the last voyage. World, adieu! Nehwon, farewell! I seek a happier—"

But this time his lunge toward the porch was stopped at once by his plump niece and stout palace mistress, hemming him close on either side.

"Now hear the best," Hisvin continued in livelier accents. "At great personal peril I have put myself in touch with the rats. It transpires that they have an excellent civilization, finer in many respects than man's—in fact, they have been secretly guiding the interests and growth of man for some time—oh 'tis a cozy, sweet civilization these wise rodents enjoy and 'twill delight your sense of fitness when you know it better! At all events the rats, now loving me well—ah, what

rare diplomacies I've worked for you, dear master!—have entrusted
me with their surrender terms, which are unexpectedly generous!"

He snatched from his pouch one of the scrolls in it, and saying, "I'll
summarize," read: ". . . hostilities to cease at once . . . by Glipkerio's command transmitted by his agents bearing his wands of authority . . . Fires to be extinguished and damage to Lankhmar repaired
by Lankhmarts under direction of . . . et cetera. Damage to ratly
tunnels, arcades, pleasances, privies, and other rooms to be repaired
by humans, 'Suitably reduced in size' should go in there. All soldiers
disarmed, bound, confined . . . and so forth. All cats, dogs, ferrets,
and other vermin . . . well, naturally. All ships and all Lankhmarts
aboard . . . that's clear enough. Ah, here's the spot! Listen now.
Thereafter each Lankhmart to go about his customary business, free
in all his actions and possessions—*free*, you hear that?—subject only
to the commands of his personal rat or rats, who shall crouch upon
his shoulder or otherwise dispose themselves on or within his clothing, as they shall see fit, and share his bed. But *your* rats," he went on
swiftly, pointing to Glipkerio, who had gone very pale and whose
body and limbs had begun again their twitchings and his features
their tics, "*your* rats shall, out of deference to your high position, not
be rats at all—but rather my daughter Hisvet and, temporarily, her
maid Frix, who shall attend you day and night, watch and watch,
granting your every wish on the trifling condition that you obey their
every command. What could be fairer, my dear master?"

But Glipkerio had already gone once more into his, "World, adieu!
Nehwon, farewell! I seek a—" meanwhile straining toward the porch
and convulsing up and down in his efforts to be free of Samanda's and
Elakeria's restraining arms. Of a sudden, however, he stopped still,
cried, "Of course I'll sign!" and grabbed for the parchment. Hisvin
eagerly led him to his audience couch and the table, meanwhile ready-
ing his writing equipment.

But here a difficulty developed. Glipkerio was shaking so that he
could hardly hold pen, let alone write. His first effort with the quill
sent a comet's tail of inkdrops across the clothing of those around him
and Hisvin's leathery face. All efforts to guide his hand, first by gen-
tleness, then by main force, failed.

Hisvin snapped his fingers in desperate impatience, then pointed a
sudden finger at his daughter. She produced a flute from her black
silken robe and began to pipe a sweet yet drowsy melody. Samanda
and Elakeria held Glipkerio face down on his couch, the one at his
shoulders, the other at his ankles, while Frix, kneeling with one knee
on the small of his back began with her fingertips to stroke his spine

from skull to tail in time to Hisvet's music, favoring her left hand with its bandaged palm.

Glipkerio continued to convulse upward at regular intervals, but gradually the violence of these earthquakes of the body decreased and Frix was able to transfer some of her rhythmic strokings to his flailing arms.

Hisvin, hard a-pace and snapping his fingers again, his shadows marching like those of giant rats moving confusedly and size-changingly against each other across the blue tiles, demanded suddenly on noting the wands of authority, "Where are your pages you promised to have here?"

Glipkerio responded dully, "In their quarters. In revolt. You stole my guards who would have controlled them. Where are your Mingols?"

Hisvin stopped dead in his pacing and frowned. His gaze went questioningly toward the unmoving blue door-drapes through which he had entered.

Fafhrd, breathing a little heavily, drew himself up into one of the belfry's eight windows and sat on its sill and scanned the bells.

There were eight in all and all large: five of bronze, three of browned-iron, coated with the sea-pale vertigris and earth-dark rust of eons. Any ropes had rotted away, centuries ago for all he knew. Below them was dark emptiness spanned by four narrow flat-topped stone arches. He tried one of them with his foot. It held.

He set the smallest bell, a bronze one, swinging. There was no sound except for a dismal creaking.

He first peered, then felt up inside the bell. The clapper was gone, its supporting link rusted away.

All the other bells' clappers were likewise gone, presumably fallen to the bottom of the tower.

He prepared to use his ax to beat out the alarum, but then he saw one of the fallen clappers lying on a stone arch.

He lifted it with both hands, like a somewhat ponderous club, and moving about recklessly on the arches, struck each bell in turn. Rust showered him from the iron ones.

Their massed clangor sounded louder than mountainside thunder when lightning strikes from a cloud close by. The bells were the least musical Fafhrd had ever heard. Some made swelling beats together, which periodically tortured the ear. They must have been shaped and cast by a master of discord. The brazen bells shrieked, clanged, clashed, roared, twanged, jangled, and screamingly wrangled. The iron bells groaned rusty-throated, sobbed like leviathan, throbbed as the heart of universal death, and rolled like a black swell striking a smooth rock coast. They exactly suited the Gods *of* Lankhmar, from what Fafhrd had heard of the latter.

The metallic uproar began to fade somewhat and he realized that he was becoming deafened. Nevertheless he kept on until he had struck each bell three times. Then he peered out the window by which he had entered.

His first impression was that half the human crowd was looking straight at *him*. Then he realized it must be the noise of the bells which had turned upward those moonlit faces.

There were many more kneelers before the temple now. Other Lankhmarts were pouring up the Street of the Gods from the east, as if being driven.

The erect, black-togaed rats still stood in the same tiny line below him, auraed by grim authority despite their size, and now they were flanked by two squads of armored rats, each bearing a small weapon which puzzled Fafhrd, straining his eyes, until he recalled the tiny crossbows which had been used aboard *Squid*.

The reverberations of the bells had died away, or sunk too low for his deafened ears to note, but then he began to hear, faintly at first, murmurings and cries of hopeless horror from below.

Gazing across the crowd again, he saw black rats climbing unresisting up some of the kneeling figures, while many of the others already had something black squatting on their right shoulders.

There came from directly below a creaking and groaning and rending. The ancient doors of the temple of the Gods *of* Lankhmar were thrust wide open.

The white faces that had been gazing upward now stared at the porch.

The black-togaed rats and their soldiery faced around.

There strode four abreast from the wide-open doorway a company of fearfully thin brown figures, black-togaed too. Each bore a black staff. The brown was of three sorts: aged linen mummy-banding, brittle parchment-like skin stretched tight over naught but skeleton, and naked old brown bones themselves.

The crossbow-rats loosed a volley. The skeletal brown striders came on without pause. The black-togaed rats stood their ground, squeaking imperiously. Another useless volley from the tiny crossbows. Then, like so many rapiers, black staffs thrust out. Each rat they touched shriveled where he stood, nor moved again. Other rats came scurrying in from the crowd and were similarly slain. The brown company advanced at an even pace, like doom on the march. There were screams then and the human crowd before the temple began to melt, racing down side streets and even dashing back into the temples from which they had fled. Predictably, the folk of Lankhmar were more afraid of their own gods come to their rescue than of their foes.

Himself somewhat aghast at what his ringing had roused, Fafhrd climbed down the belfry, telling himself that he must dodge the eerie battle below and seek out the Mouser in Glipkerio's vast palace.

At the corner of the temple's foot, the black kitten became aware of the climber high above, recognized him as the huge man he had scratched and loved, and realized that the force holding him here had something to do with that man.

The Gray Mouser loped purposefully out of the palace kitchen and up a corridor leading toward the royal dwelling quarters. Though still tiny, he was at last dressed. Beside him strode Reetha, armed with a long and needle-pointed skewer for broiling cutlets in a row. Close behind them marched a disorderly-ranked host of pages armed with cleavers and mallets, and maids with knives and toasting forks.

The Mouser had insisted that Reetha not carry him on this foray and the girl had let him have his way. And truly it made him feel more manly again to be going on his own two feet and from time to time swishing Scalpel menacingly through the air.

Still, he had to admit, he would feel a lot better were he his rightful size again, and Fafhrd at his side. Sheelba had told him the effects of the black potion would last for nine hours. He had drunk it a few minutes at most past three. So he should regain his true size a little after midnight, if Sheelba had not lied.

He glanced up at Reetha, more huge than any giantess and bearing a gleaming steel weapon tall as a catboat's mast, and felt further reassured.

"Onward!" he squeaked to his naked army, though he tried to pitch his voice as low as possible. "Onward to save Lankhmar and her overlord from the rats!"

Fafhrd dropped the last few feet to the temple's roof and faced around. The situation below had altered considerably.

The human folk were gone—that is, the living human folk.

The skeletal brown striders had all emerged through the door below and were marching west down the Street of the Gods—a procession of ugly ghosts, except these wraiths were opaque and their bony feet clicked harshly on the cobbles. The moonlit porch, steps, and flagstones behind them were blackly freckled with dead rats.

But the striders were moving more slowly now and were surrounded by shadows blacker than the moon could throw—a veritable sea of black rats lapping the striders and being augmented faster from all sides than the deadly staves could strike them down.

From two areas ahead, to either side of the Street of the Gods, flaming darts came arching and struck in the foreranks of the striders. These missiles, unlike the crossbow darts, took effect. Wherever they struck, old linen and resin-impregnated skin began to flicker and flame. The striders came to a halt, ceased slaying rats, and devoted themselves to plucking out the flaming darts sticking in them and beating out the flames on their persons.

Another wave of rats came racing down the Street of the Gods from the Marsh Gate end, and behind them on three great horses three riders leaning low in their saddles and sword-slashing at the small beasts. The horses and the cloaks and hoods of the riders were inky black. Fafhrd, who thought himself incapable of more shivers, felt another. It was as if Death itself, in three persons, had entered the scene.

The rodent fire-artillery, slewed partly around, let off at the black riders a few flaming darts which missed.

In return the black riders charged hoof-stamping and sword-slashing into the two artillery areas. Then they faced toward the brown skeletal striders, several of whom still smoldered and flickered, and doffed their black hoods and mantles.

Fafhrd's face broke into a grin that would have seemed most inappropriate to one knowing he feared an apparition of Death, but not knowing his experiences of the last few days.

Seated on the three black horses were three tall skeletons gleaming white in the moonlight, and with a lover's certainty he recognized the first as being Kreeshkra's.

She might, of course, be seeking him out to slay him for his faithlessness. Nevertheless, as almost any other lover in like circumstances —though seldom, true, near the midst of a natural-supernatural battle —he grinned a rather egotistic grin.

He lost not a moment in beginning his descent.

Meanwhile Kreeshkra, for it was indeed she, was thinking as she gazed at the Gods *of Lankhmar, Well, I suppose brown bones are better than none at all. Still, they seem a poor fire risk. Ho, here come more rats! What a filthy city! And where oh where is my abominable Mud Man?*

The black kitten mewed anxiously at the temple's foot where he awaited Fafhrd's arrival.

Glipkerio, calm as a cushion now, completely soothed by Frix's massage and Hisvet's piping, was halfway through signing his name, forming the letters more ornately and surely than he ever had in his life, when the blue drapes in the largest archway were torn down and there pressed into the chamber on silent naked feet the Mouser's and Reetha's forces.

Glipkerio gave a great twitch, upsetting the ink bottle on the parchment of the surrender terms, and sending his quill winging off like an arrow.

Hisvin, Hisvet, and even Samanda backed away from him toward the porch, daunted at least momentarily by the newcomers—and indeed there was something dire about that naked, shaven youthful army be-weaponed with kitchen tools, their eyes wild, their lips a-snarl or pressed tightly together. Hisvin had been expecting his Mingols at last and so got a double shock.

Elakeria hurried after them, crying, "They've come to slay us all! It's the revolution!"

Frix held her ground, smiling excitedly.

The Mouser raced across the blue-tiled floor, sprang up on Glipkerio's couch and balanced himself on its golden back. Reetha followed rapidly and stood beside him, menacing around with her skewer.

Unmindful that Glipkerio was flinching away, pale yellow eyes peering affrightedly from a coarse fabric of crisscrossed fingers, the Mouser squeaked loudly, "Oh mighty overlord, no revolution this! Instead, we have come to save you from your enemies! That one"—he pointed at Hisvin—"is in league with the rats. Indeed, he is by blood more rat than man. Under his toga you'll find a tail. I saw him in the tunnels below, member of the Rat Council of Thirteen, plotting your overthrow. It is he—"

Meanwhile Samanda had been regaining her courage. Now she charged her underlings like a black rhinoceros, her globe-shaped, pin-skewered coiffure more than enough horn. Laying about with her black whip, she roared fearsomely, "Revolt, will you? On your knees, scullions and sluts! Say your prayers!"

Taken by surprise and readily falling back into an ingrained habit, their fiery hopes quenched by familiar abuse, the naked slim figures flinched away from her to either side.

Reetha, however, grew pink with anger. Forgetting the Mouser and all else but her rage, envenomed by many injuries, she ran after Samanda, crying to her fellow-slaves, "Up, and at her, you cowards! We're fifty to one against her!" And with that she thrust out mightily with her skewer and jabbed Samanda from behind.

The palace mistress leaped ponderously forward, her keys and chains swinging wildly from her black leather belt. She lashed the last maids out of her way and pounded off at a thumping run toward the servants' quarters.

Reetha cried over shoulder, "After her, all—before she rouses the cooks and barbers to her aid!" and was off in sprinting pursuit.

The maids and pages hardly hesitated at all. Reetha had refired their hot hatreds as readily as Samanda had quenched them. To play heroes and heroines rescuing Lankhmar was moonshine. To have vengeance on their old tormenter was blazing sunlight. They all raced after Reetha.

The Mouser, still balancing on the fluted golden back of Glipkerio's couch and mounting his dramatic oration, realized somewhat belatedly that he had lost his army and was still only doll size. Hisvin and Hisvet, drawing long knives from under their black togas, rapidly circled between him and the doorway through which his forces had fled. Hisvin looked vicious and Hisvet unpleasantly like her father—the Mouser had never before noted the striking family resemblance. They began to close in.

To his left Elakeria snatched up a handful of the wands of office and raised them threateningly. To the Mouser, even those flimsy rods were huge as pikes.

To his right Glipkerio, still cringing away, reached down surreptitiously for his light battle-ax. Evidently the Mouser's loyal squeaks had gone unheard, or not been believed.

The Mouser wondered which way to jump.

Behind him Frix murmured softly, though to the Mouser's ears still somewhat boomingly, "Exit kitchen tyrant pursued by pages unclad and maids in a state of nature, leaving our hero beset by an ogre and two—or is it three?—ogresses."

XVI

FAFHRD, ALTHOUGH HE came down the temple's wall fast, found the battle once more considerably changed when he reached the bottom.

The Gods *of* Lankhmar, though not exactly in panicky rout, were withdrawing toward the open door of their temple, thrusting their staves from time to time at the horde of rats which still beset them. Wisps of smoke still trailed from a few of them—ghostly moonlit pennons. They were coughing, or more likely cursing and it sounded like coughs. Their brown skull-faces were dire—the expression of elders defeated and trying to cloak their impotent, gibbering rage with dignity.

Fafhrd moved rapidly out of their way.

Kreeshkra and her two male Ghouls were slashing and stabbing from their saddles at another flood of rats in front of Hisvin's house, while their black horses crunched rats under their hooves.

Fafhrd made toward them, but at that moment there was a rush of rats at him and he had to unsheathe Graywand. Using the great sword as a scythe, he cleared a space around him with three strokes, then started again toward the Ghouls.

The doors of Hisvin's house burst open and there fled out down the short steps a crowd of Mingol slaves. Their faces grimaced with terror, but even more striking was the fact that they were thin almost beyond emaciation. Their once-tight black liveries hung loosely on them. Their hands were skeletal. Their faces were skulls covered with yellow skin.

Three groups of skeletons: brown, ivory and yellow—*It is a prodigy of prodigies,* Fafhrd thought, *the beginning of a dark spectrum of bones.*

Behind the Mingols and driving them, not so much to kill them as to get them out of the way, came a company of crouchy but stalwart masked men, some wearing armor, all brandishing weapons—swords and crossbows. There was something horribly familiar about their scuttling, hobble-legged gait. Then came some with pikes and helmets, but without masks. The faces, or muzzles rather, were those of rats. All the newcomers, masked or nakedly fur-faced, made for the three Ghoulish riders.

Fafhrd sprang forward, Graywand singing about his head, unmindful of the new surge of ordinary rats coming against him—and came to a skidding halt.

The man-sized and man-armed rats were still pouring from Hisvin's house. Hero or no, he couldn't kill *that* many of them.

At that instant he felt claws sink into his leg. He raised his crook-fingered big left hand to sweep away from him whatever now attacked him . . . and saw climbing his thigh the black kitten from *Squid.*

That scatterbrain mustn't be in this dread battle, he thought . . . and opened his empty pouch to thrust in the kitten . . . and saw gleaming dully at its bottom the tin whistle . . . and realized that here was a metal straw to cling to.

He snatched it out and set it to his lips and blew it.

When one taps with idle finger a toy drum, one does not expect a peal of thunder. Fafhrd gasped and almost swallowed the whistle. Then he made to hurl it away from him. Instead he set it to his lips once more, put his hands to his ears, for some reason closed his eyes tight, and once more blew it.

Once again the horrendous noise went shuddering up toward the moon and down the shadowed streets of Lankhmar.

Imagine the scream of a leopard, the snarl of a tiger, and the roaring of a lion commingled, and one will have some faint suggestion of the sound the tin whistle produced.

Everywhere the little rats held still in their hordes. The skeletal Mingols paused in their shaking, staggering flight. The big armed rats, masked or helmeted, halted in their attack upon the Ghouls. Even the Ghouls and their horses held still. The fur on the black kitten fluffed out as it still clung to Fafhrd's crouching thigh, and its green eyes became enormous.

Then the awesome sound had died away, a distant bell was tolling midnight, and all the battlers fell to action again.

But black shapes were forming in the moonlight around Fafhrd. Shapes that were at first no more than shadows with a sheen to them. Then darker, like translucent polished black horn. Then solid and velvet black, their pads resting on the moonlit flagstones. They had the slender, long-legged forms of cheetahs, but the mass of tigers or lions. They stood almost as high at the shoulder as horses. Their somewhat small and prick-eared heads swayed slowly, as did their long tails. Their fangs were like needles of faintly green ice. Their eyes, which were like frozen emeralds, stared all twenty-six at Fafhrd —for there were thirteen of the beasts.

Then Fafhrd realized that they were staring not at his head but at his waist.

The black kitten there gave a shrill, wailing cry that was at once a young cat's first battle call and also a greeting.

With a screaming, snarling roar, like thirteen of the tin whistles blown at once, the War Cats bounded outward. With preternatural agility, the black kitten leaped after a group of four of them.

The small rats fled toward walls and gutters and doors—wherever holes might be. The Mingols threw themselves down. The half-splintered doors of the temple of the Gods *of* Lankhmar could be heard to screech shut rather rapidly.

The four War Cats to whom the kitten had attached himself raced toward the man-size rats coming from Hisvin's house. Two of the Ghouls had been struck from their saddles by pikes or swords. The third—it was Kreeshkra—parried a blow from a rapier, then kicked her horse into a gallop past Hisvin's house toward the Rainbow Palace. The two riderless black horses followed her.

Fafhrd prepared to follow her, but at that instant a black parrot swooped down in front of him, beating its wings, and a small skinny boy with a puckered scar under his left eye was tugging at his waist.

"Mouser-Mouser!" the parrot squawked. "Danger-danger! Blue-Blue-Blue Blue Audience Chamber!"

"Same message, big man," the urchin rasped with a grin.

So Fafhrd, running around the battle of armed rats and War Cats— a whirling melee of silvery swords and flashing claws, of cold green and hot red eyes—set out after Kreeshkra anyhow, since she had been going in the same direction.

Long pikes struck down a War Cat, but the kitten sprang like a shining black comet at the face of the foremost of the giant rodent pike-wielders as the other three War Cats closed in beside him.

The Gray Mouser lightly dropped off the back of the golden couch the instant Hisvin and Hisvet got within stabbing distance. Then, since they were both coming around the couch, he ran under it and from thence under the low table. During his short passage through the open, Glipkerio's ax crashed on the tiles to one side of him, while Elakeria's bundle of wands smashed clatteringly down on the other. He paused under the center of the table, plotting his next action.

Glipkerio darted prudently away, leaving his ax where he had let go of it from the sting of the blow. Plump Elakeria, however, slipped and fell with the force of her clumsy thwack and for the moment both her sprawled form and the ax were quite close to the Mouser.

Then—well, one moment the table was a roof a comfortable rat's-span or so above the Mouser's head. The next moment he had, without moving, bumped his head on it and very shortly afterward somehow overturned it to one side without touching it with his hands and despite the fact that he had sat down rather hard on the floor.

While Elakeria was no longer an obese wanton bulging out a gray dress, but a slender nymph totally unclad. And the head of Glipkerio's ax, which Scalpel's slim blade now touched, had shrunk to a ragged sliver of metal, as if eaten away by invisible acid.

The Mouser realized that he had regained his original size, even as Sheelba had foretold. The thought flashed through his mind that, since nothing can come of nothing, the atomies shed from Scalpel in the cellar had now been made up from those in the ax-head, while to replace his flesh and clothing he had stolen somewhat of that of Elakeria. She certainly had benefited from the transaction, he decided.

But this was not the time for metaphysics or for moralizing, he told himself. He scrambled to his feet and advanced on his shrunken-seeming tormenters, menacing with Scalpel.

"Drop your weapons!" he commanded.

Neither Glipkerio, Elakeria, or Frix held any. Hisvet let go of her long dagger at once, probably recalling that the Mouser knew she had some skill in hurling it. But Hisvin, foaming now with rage and frustration, held onto his. The Mouser advanced Scalpel flickeringly toward his scrawny throat.

"Call off your rats, Lord Null," he ordered, "or you die!"

"Shan't!" Hisvin spat at him, stabbing futilely at Scalpel. Then, reason returning to him a little, he added, "And even if I wished to, I couldn't!"

The Mouser, knowing from his session at the Council of Thirteen that this was the truth, hesitated.

Elakeria, seeing her nakedness, snatched a light coverlet from the golden couch and huddled it around her, then immediately drew it aside again to admire her slender new body.

Frix continued to smile excitedly but somehow composedly, as if all this were a play and she its audience.

Glipkerio, although seeking to firm himself by tightly embracing a spirally fluted pillar between candlelit chamber and moonlit porch, clearly had the grand, rather than merely the petty twitches again. His narrow face, between its periodic convulsions, was a study in consternation and nervous exhaustion.

Hisvet called out, "Gray lover, kill the old fool my father! Slay Glip and the rest too, unless you desire Frix as a concubine. Then rule all Lankhmar Above and Below with my willingest aid. You've won the game, dear one. I confess myself beaten. I'll be your humblest slave-girl, my only hope that some day I'll be your most favorite too."

And so ringingly sincere was her voice and so dulcet-sweet in making its promises, that despite his experiences of her treacheries and cruelties and despite the cold murderousness of some of her words, the Mouser was truly tempted. He looked toward her—her expression was that of a gambler playing for the highest stakes—and in that instant Hisvin lunged.

The Mouser beat the dagger aside and retreated a double step, cursing only himself for the wavering of his attention. Hisvin continued to lunge desperately, only desisting when Scalpel pricked his throat swollen with curses.

"Keep your promise and show your courage," Hisvet cried to the Mouser. "Kill him!"

Hisvin began to gabble his curses at her too.

The Mouser was never afterwards quite certain as to what he would have done next, for the nearest blue curtains were jerked away to either side and there stood Skwee and Hreest, both man-size, both unmasked and with rapiers drawn, both of lordly, cool, assured, and dire mien—the white and the black of rat aristocracy.

Without a word Skwee advanced a pace and pointed his sword at the Mouser. Hreest copied him so swiftly it was impossible to be sure it was a copy. The two green-uniformed sword-rats moved out from behind them and went on guard to either side. From behind *them*, the three pike-rats, man-size like the rest, moved out still farther on the flank, two toward the far end of the room, one toward the golden couch, beside which Hisvet now stood near Frix.

His hand clutching his scrawny throat, Hisvin mastered his astonishment and pointing at his daughter, croaked commandingly, "kill her too!"

The lone pike-rat obediently leveled his weapon and ran with it. As the great wavy blade passed close by her, Frix cast herself at the weapon, hugging its pole. The blade missed Hisvet by a finger's breadth and Frix fell. The pike-rat jerked back his weapon and raised it to skewer Frix to the floor, but, "Stop!" Skwee cried. "Kill none—as yet—except the one in gray. All now, advance!"

The pike-rat obediently swiveled round, re-leveling his weapon at the Mouser.

Frix picked herself up and casually murmuring in Hisvet's ear, "That's three times, dear mistress," turned to watch the rest of the drama.

The Mouser thought of diving off the porch, but instead broke for the far end of the room. It was perhaps a mistake. The two pike-rats were at the far door ahead of him, while the sword-rats at his heels gave him no time to feint around the pike-blades, kill the pike-rats and get around them. He dodged behind a heavy table and turning abruptly, managed to wound lightly in the thigh a green-uniformed rat who had run a bit ahead of the rest. But that rat dodged back and the Mouser found himself faced by four rapiers and two pikes—and just conceivably by death too, he had to admit to himself as he noted the sureness with which Skwee was directing and controlling the attack. So—slash, jump, slash, thrust, parry, kick the table—he must attack Skwee—thrust, parry, riposte, counter-riposte, retreat—but Skwee had anticipated that, so—slash, jump, thrust, jump, jump again, bump the wall, thrust—whatever he was going to do, he'd have to do it very soon!

A rat's head, detached from its rat, spun across the edge of his field of vision and he heard a happy, familiar shout.

Fafhrd had just entered the room, beheaded from behind the third pike-rat, who had been acting as a sort of reserve, and was rushing the others from behind.

At Skwee's swift signal, the lesser sword-rats and the two remaining pike-rats turned. The latter were slow in shifting their long weapons. Fafhrd beheaded the blade of one pike and then its owner, parried the second pike and thrust home through the throat of the rat wielding it, then met the attack of the two lesser sword-rats, while Skwee and Hreest redoubled their assault on the Mouser. Their snarl-twisted bristles, snarl-bared incisors, long flat furry faces and huge eyes blue and black were almost as daunting as their swift swords, while Fafhrd found equal menace in his pair.

At Fafhrd's entry, Glipkerio had said very softly to himself, "No, I cannot bear it longer," run out onto the porch and up the silver ladder, and sprung down through the manhole of the spindle-shaped gray vehicle. His weight overbalanced it, so that it slowly nosed down in the copper chute. He called out, somewhat more loudly, "World, adieu! Nehwon, goodbye! I go to seek a happier universe. Oh, you'll regret me, Lankhmar! Weep, oh City!" Then the gray vehicle was sliding down the chute, faster and faster. He dropped inside and jerked shut the hatch after him. With a small, sullen splash the vehicle vanished beneath the dark, moon-fretted waters.

Only Elakeria and Frix, whose eyes and ears missed nothing, saw Glipkerio go or heard his valedictory.

With a sudden concerted effort Skwee and Hreest rammed the table, across which they'd been fencing, against the Mouser, to pin him to the wall. Barely in time, he sprang atop it, dodged Skwee's thrust, parried Hreest's, and on a lucky riposte sent Scalpel's tip into Hreest's right eye and brain, whipping his sword out just soon enough to parry Skwee's next thrust.

Skwee retreated a double step. By virtue of the almost panoramic vision of his wide-spaced blue eyes, he noted that Fafhrd was finishing off the second of his two sword-rats, beating through by brute force the parries of their lighter swords, and himself suffering only a few scratches and minor pricks in the process.

Skwee turned and ran. The Mouser leaped from the table after him. Midway down the room something was falling in blue folds from the ceiling. Hisvet, midway along the wall, had slashed with her dagger the cords supporting the curtains that could divide the room in two. Skwee ran a-crouch under them, but the Mouser almost ran into them, dodging swiftly back as Skwee's rapier thrust through the heavy fabric inches from his throat.

Moments later the Mouser and Fafhrd located the central split in the drapes and suddenly parted them with the tips of their swords, closely a-watch for another rapier-thrust or even a thrown dagger.

Instead they saw Hisvin, Hisvet, and Skwee standing in front of the audience couch in attitudes of defiance, but grown small as children—if that can be said of a rat. The Mouser started toward them, but before he was halfway there, they became small as rats and swiftly tumbled down a tile-size trapdoor. Skwee, who went last, turned for one more angry chitter at the Mouser, one more shake of toy-size rapier, before he pulled the tile shut over his head.

The Mouser cursed, then burst into laughter. Fafhrd joined him, but his eyes were warily on Frix, still standing human-size behind the couch. Nor did he miss Elakeria on the couch, peering with one affrighted eye from under the coverlet while also thrusting out, inadvertently or no, one slender leg.

Still laughing wildly, the Mouser reeled over to Fafhrd, threw an arm up around his shoulders, and pummeled him playfully in the chest, demanding, "Why did you have to turn up, you great lout? I was about to die heroically, or else slay in mass combat the seven greatest sword-rats in Lankhmar Below! You're a scene-stealer!"

Eyes still on Frix, Fafhrd roughed the Mouser's chin affectionately with his fist, then gave him an elbow-dig sharp enough to take half his breath away and stop his laughter. "Three of them were only pikemen, or pike-rats, as I suppose you call them," he corrected, then complained gruffly, "I gallop two nights and a day—halfway around the Inner Sea—to save your undersized hide. And do so! Only to be told I'm an actor."

The Mouser gasped out, still with a snickering whoop, "You don't know how undersized! Halfway around the Inner Sea, you say . . . and nevertheless time your entrance perfectly! Why, you're the greatest actor of them all!" He dropped to his knees in front of the tile that had served as trapdoor and said in tones compounded equally of philosophy, humor, and hysteria, "While I must lose—forever, I suppose —the greatest love of my life." He rapped the tile—it sounded very solid—and thrusting down his face called out softly, "Yoo-hoo! Hisvet!" Fafhrd jerked him to his feet.

Frix raised a hand. The Mouser looked at her, while Fafhrd had never taken his eyes off her.

"Here, little man, catch!" Smiling, she called to the Mouser and tossed him a small black vial, which he caught and goggled at foolishly. "Use it if you are ever again so silly as to wish to seek out my late mistress. I have no need of it. I have worked out my bondage in this world. I have done the diabolic Demoiselle her three services. I am free!"

As she said that last word, her eyes lit up like lamps. She threw back her black hood and took a breath so deep it seemed almost to lift her from the floor. Her eyes fixed on infinity. Her dark hair lifted on her head. Lightning crackled in her hair, formed itself in a blue nimbus, and streamed like a blue cloak down her body, over and through her black silk dress.

She turned and ran swiftly out onto the porch, Fafhrd and the Mouser after her. Glowing still more bluely and crying, "Free! Free! *Free!* Back to Arilia! Back to the World of Air," she dove off the edge.

She did not seem to enter the waves, but skimmed just along their crests like a small, faint blue comet and then mounting toward the sky, higher and higher, became a faint blue star and vanished.

"Where is Arilia?" the Mouser asked.

"I thought this was the World of Air," Fafhrd mused.

XVII

THE RATS ALL over Lankhmar, after suffering huge losses, dove back everywhere into their holes and pulled tight shut the doors of such as had them. This happened also in the rooms of pink pools in the third floor of Hisvin's house, where the War Cats had driven back the last of the rats who had gained their human size by drinking the white vials there and at the expense of the flesh of Hisvin's Mingols. Now they guzzled the black vials even more eagerly, to escape back into their tunnels.

The rats also suffered total defeat in the South Barracks, where the War Cats ravaged after clawing and crashing open the doors with preternatural strength.

Their work done, the War Cats regathered at the place where Fafhrd had summoned them and there faded away even as they had earlier materialized. They were still thirteen, although they had lost one of their company, for the black kitten faded away with them, comporting himself like an apprentice member of their company. It was ever afterwards believed, by most Lankhmarts, that the War Cats and the white skeletons as well had been summoned by the Gods *of* Lankhmar, whose reputation for horrid powers and dire activities was thereby bolstered, despite some guilty recollections of their temporary defeat by the rats.

By twos and threes and sixes, the people of Lankhmar emerged from their places of hiding, learned that the Rat Plague was over, and wept, prayed, and rejoiced. Gentle Radomix Kistomerces-Null was plucked from his retreat in the slums and with his seventeen cats carried in triumph to the Rainbow Palace.

Glipkerio, his leaden craft tightly collapsed around him by weight of water, until it had become a second leaden skin molded to his form —truly a handsome coffin—continued to sink in the Lankhmar Deep, but whether to reach a solid bottom, or only a balancing place between world bubbles in the waters of infinity, who may say?

The Gray Mouser recovered Cat's Claw from Hreest's belt, marveling somewhat that all the rat-corpses were yet human size. Likely enough death froze all magics.

Fafhrd noted with distaste the three pools of pink slime in front of the gold audience couch and looked for something to throw over them. Elakeria coyly clutched her coverlet around her. He dragged from a corner a colorful rug that was a duke's ransom and made that do.

There was the noise of hooves on tiles. In the high, wide archway from which the drapes had been torn there appeared Kreeshkra, still on horseback and leading the other two Ghoulish mounts, empty saddled. Fafhrd swung the skeleton girl down and embraced her heartily, somewhat to the Mouser's and Elakeria's shock, but soon said, "Dearest love, I think it best you put on again your black cloak and hood. Your naked bones are to me the acme of beauty, but here come others they may disturb."

"Already ashamed of me, aren't you? Oh, you dirty-minded puritanical Mud Folk!" Kreeshkra commented with a sour laugh, yet complied, while the rainbows in her eye sockets twinkled.

The others Fafhrd had referred to consisted of the councillors, soldiers, and various relatives of the late overlord, including the gentle Radomix Kistomerces-Null and his seventeen cats, each now carried and cosseted by some noble hoping to gain favor from Lankhmar's most likely next overlord.

Not all the new arrivals were so commonplace. One, heralded by more hoof-cloppings on tile, was Fafhrd's Mingol mare, her tether bitten through. She stopped by Fafhrd and glared her bloodshot eyes at him, as if to say, "I am not so easily got rid of. Why did you cheat me of a battle?"

Kreeshkra patted the grim beast's nose and observed to Fafhrd,

"You are clearly a man who awakens deep loyalty in others. I trust you have the same quality yourself."

"Never doubt me, dearest," Fafhrd answered with fond sincerity.

Also among the newcomers and returners was Reetha, looking suavely happy as a cat who has licked cream, or a panther some even more vital fluid, and naked as ever except for three broad black leather loops around her waist. She threw her arms about the Mouser. "You're big again!" she rejoiced. "And you beat them all!"

The Mouser accepted her embrace, though he purposely put on a dissatisfied face and said sourly, "You were a big help!—you and your naked army, deserting me when I most needed help. I suppose you finished off Samanda?"

"Indeed we did!" Reetha smirked like a sated leopardess. "What a sizzling she made! Look, doll, her belt of office *does* go three times round my waist. Oh yes, we cornered her in the kitchen and brought her down. Each of us took a pin from her hair. Then—"

"Spare me the details, darling," the Mouser cut her short. "This night for nine hours I've been a rat, with all of a rat's nasty feelings, and that's quite long enough. Come with me, pet; there's something we must attend to ere the crowd gets too thick."

When they returned after a short space, the Mouser was carrying a box wrapped in his cloak, while Reetha wore a violet robe, around which was still triply looped, however, Samanda's belt. And the crowd had thickened indeed. Radomix Kistomerces-no-longer-Null had already been informally vested with Lankhmar's overlordship and was sitting somewhat bemused on the golden seashell audience couch along with his seventeen cats and also a smiling Elakeria, who had wrapped her coverlet like a sari around her sylphlike figure.

The Mouser drew Fafhrd aside. "That's quite a girl you've got," he remarked, rather inadequately, of Kreeshkra.

"Yes, isn't she," Fafhrd agreed blandly.

"You should have seen mine," the Mouser boasted. "I don't mean Reetha there, I mean my *weird* one. She had—"

"Don't let Kreeshkra hear you use that word," Fafhrd warned sharply though *sub voce.*

"Well, anyhow, whenever I want to see her again," the Mouser continued conspiratorially, "I have only to swallow the contents of this black vial and—"

"I'll take charge of that," Reetha announced crisply, snatching it out of his hand from behind him. She glanced at it, then expertly pitched it through a window into the Inner Sea.

The Mouser started a glare at her which turned into an ingratiating smile.

Flapping her black robe to cool her, Kreeshkra came up behind Fafhrd. "Introduce me to your friends, dear," she directed.

Meanwhile around the golden couch was an ever-thickening press of courtiers, nobles, councillors, and officers. New titles were being awarded by the dozen to all first-comers. Sentences of perpetual banishment and confiscation of property were being laid on Hisvin and all others absent, guilty or guiltless. Reports were coming in of the successful fighting of all fires in the city and the complete vanishment of rats from its streets. Plans were being laid for the complete extirpation from under the city of the entire rat-metropolis of Lankhmar Below—subtle and complex plans which did not sound to the Mouser entirely practical. It was becoming clear that under saintly Radomix Kistomerces, Lankhmar would more than ever be ruled by foolish fantasy and shameless greed. At moments like these it was easy to understand why the Gods *of* Lankhmar were so furiously exasperated by their city.

Various lukewarm thanks were extended to the Mouser and Fafhrd, although most of the newcomers seemed not at all clear as to what part the two heroes had played in conquering the rats, despite Elakeria's repeated accounts of the final fighting and of Glipkerio's sea-plunge. Soon, clearly, seeds would be planted against the Mouser and Fafhrd in Radomix's saintly-vague mind, and their bright heroic roles imperceptibly darkened to blackest villainy.

At the same time it became evident that the new court was disturbed by the restless tramping of the four ominous war-horses, three Ghoulish and one Mingol, and that the presence of an animated skeleton was becoming more and more disquieting, for Kreeshkra continued to wear her black robe and hood like a loose garment. Fafhrd and the Mouser looked at one another, and then at Kreeshkra and Reetha, and they realized that there was agreement between them. The Northerner mounted the Mingol mare, and the Mouser and Reetha the two leftover Ghoulish horses, and they all four made their way out of the Rainbow Palace as quietly as is possible when hooves clop on tile.

Thereafter there swiftly grew in Lankhmar a new legend of the Gray Mouser and Fafhrd: how as rat-small midget and bell-tower-tall giant they had saved Lankhmar from the rats, but at the price of being personally summoned and escorted to the Afterworld by Death himself, for the black-robed ivory skeleton was remembered as male, which would doubtless have irked Kreeshkra greatly.

However, as next morning the four rode under the fading stars toward the paling east along the twisty causeway across the Great Salt Marsh, they were all merry enough in their own fashions. They had commandeered three donkeys and laden them with the box of jewels the Mouser had abstracted from Glipkerio's bed-chamber and with food and drink for a long journey, though exactly where that journey would lead they had not yet agreed. Fafhrd argued for a trip to his beloved Cold Waste, with a long stopover on the way at the City of Ghouls. The Mouser was equally enthusiastic for the Eastern Lands, slyly pointing out to Reetha what an ideal place it would be for sunbathing unclad.

Yanking up her violet robe to make herself more comfortable, Reetha nodded her agreement. "Clothes are so itchy," she said. "I can hardly bear them. I like to ride bareback—my back, not the horse's. While hair is even itchier—I can feel mine growing. You will have to shave me every day, dear," she added to the Mouser.

He agreed to take on that chore, but added, "However, I can't concur with you altogether, sweet. Besides protecting from brambles and dust, clothes give one a certain dignity."

Reetha retorted tartly, "I think there's far more dignity in the naked body."

"Pish, girl," Kreeshkra told her, "what can compare with the dignity of naked bones?" But glancing toward Fafhrd's red beard and red, curled chest, she added, "However, there is something to be said for hair."

SWORDS AND ICE MAGIC

ACKNOWLEDGMENTS

I
THE SADNESS OF THE EXECUTIONER

THERE WAS A sky that was always gray.

There was a place that was always far away.

There was a being who was always sad.

Sitting on his dark-cushioned, modest throne in his low, rambling castle in the heart of the Shadowland, Death shook his pale head and pommeled a little his opalescent temples and slightly pursed his lips, which were the color of violet grapes with the silvery bloom still on, above his slender figure armored in chain mail and his black belt, studded with silver skulls tarnished almost as black, from which hung his naked, irresistible sword.

He was a relatively minor death, only the Death of the World of Nehwon, but he had his problems. Tenscore flickering or flaring human lives to have their wicks pinched in the next twenty heartbeats. And although the heartbeats of Death resound like a leaden bell far underground and each has a little of eternity in it, yet they do finally pass. Only nineteen left now. And the Lords of Necessity, who outrank Death, still to be satisfied.

Let's see, thought Death with a vast coolness that yet had a tiny seething in it, one hundred sixty peasants and savages, twenty nomads, ten warriors, two beggars, a whore, a merchant, a priest, an aristocrat, a craftsman, a king, and two heroes. That would keep his books straight.

Within three heartbeats he had chosen one hundred and ninety-six of the tenscore and unleashed their banes upon them: chiefly invisible, poisonous creatures within their flesh which suddenly gan multiply into resistless hordes, here a dark and bulky bloodclot set loose with feather touch to glide through a vein and block a vital portal, there a long-eroded artery wall tunneled through at last; sometimes slippery slime oozing purposefully onto the next footrest of a climber, sometimes an adder told where to wriggle and when to strike, or a spider where to lurk.

Death, by his own strict code known only to himself, had cheated just a little on the king. For some time in one of the deepest and darkest corners of his mind he had been fashioning the doom of the current overlord of Lankhmar, chiefest city and land in the World of Nehwon. This overlord was a gentle and tenderhearted scholar, who truly loved only his seventeen cats, yet wished no other being in Nehwon ill, and who was forever making things difficult for Death by pardoning felons, reconciling battling brothers and feuding families, hurrying barges or wains of grain to regions of starvation, rescuing distressed small animals, feeding pigeons, fostering the study of medicine and kindred arts, and most simply of all by always having about him, like finest fountain spray on hottest day, an atmosphere of sweet and wise calm which kept swords in scabbards, brows unknotted, and teeth unclenched. But now, at this very instant, by Death's crooked, dark-alleyed plotting hidden almost but not quite from himself, the thin wrists of the benign monarch of Lankhmar were being pricked in innocent play by his favoritest cat's needle-sharp claws, which had by a jealous, thin-nosed nephew of the royal ailurophile been late last night envenomed with the wind-swift poison of the rare emperor snake of tropical Klesh.

Yet on the remaining four and especially the two heroes—Death assured himself a shade guiltily—he would work solely by improvisation. In no time at all he had a vision of Lithquil, the Mad Duke of Ool Hrusp, watching from high balcony by torchlight three northern berserks wielding saw-edged scimitars joined in mortal combat with four transparent-fleshed, pink-skeletoned ghouls armed with poniards and battle-axes. It was the sort of heavy experiment Lithquil never tired of setting up and witnessing to the slaughterhouse end, and incidentally it was getting rid of the majority of the ten warriors Death had ticketed for destruction.

Death felt a less than momentary qualm recalling how well Lithquil had served him for many years. Even the best of servants must some day be pensioned off and put to grass, and in none of the worlds Death had heard of, certainly not Nehwon, was there a dearth of willing executioners, including passionately devoted, incredibly untiring, and exquisitely fantastic-minded ones. So even as the vision came to Death, he sent his thought at it and the rearmost ghoul looked up with his invisible eyes, so that his pink-broidered black skull-sockets rested upon Lithquil, and before the two guards flanking the Mad Duke could quite swing in their ponderous shields to protect their master, the ghoul's short-handled ax, already poised overshoulder, had flown through the narrowing gap and buried itself in Lithquil's nose and forehead.

Before Lithquil could gin crumple, before any of the watchers around him could nock an arrow to dispatch or menace the assassin, before the naked slavegirl who was the promised but seldom-delivered prize for the surviving gladiator could start to draw breath for a squealing scream, Death's magic gaze was fixed on Horborixen, citadel-city of the King of Kings. But not on the interior of the Great Golden Palace, though Death got a fleeting glimpse of that, but on the inwardness of a dingy workshop where a very old man looked straight up from his rude pallet and truly wished that the cool dawn light, which was glimmering through window- and lower-crack, would never more trouble the cobwebs that made ghostly arches and buttresses overhead.

This ancient, who bore the name of Gorex, was Horborixen's and perhaps all Nehwon's skillfulest worker in precious and military metals and deviser of cunningest engines, but he had lost all zest in his work or any other aspect of life for the last weary twelve-month, in fact ever since his great granddaughter Eesafem, who was his last surviving kin and most gifted apprentice in his difficult craft, a slim, beauteous, and barely nubile girl with almond eyes sharp as needles, had been summarily abducted by the harem scouts of the King of Kings. His furnace was ice cold, his tools gathered dust, he had given himself up entirely to sorrow.

He was so sad in fact that Death had but to add a drop of his own melancholy humor to the black bile coursing slowly and miserably through the tired veins of Gorex, and the latter painlessly and instantly expired, becoming one with his cobwebs.

So!—the aristocrat and the craftsman were disposed of in no more than two snaps of Death's long, slender, pearly midfinger and thumb, leaving only the two heroes.

Twelve heartbeats to go.

Death most strongly felt that, if only for artistry's sake, heroes should be made to make their exits from the stage of life in the highest melodramatic style, with only one in fifty score let to die of old age and in the bed of sleep for the object of irony. This necessity was incidentally so great that it permitted, he believed as part of his self-set rules, the use of outwardly perceptible and testifiable magic and need not be puttied over with realism, as in the case of more humdrum beings. So now for two whole heartbeats he listened only to the faint simmer of his cool mind, while lightly massaging his temples again with nacreous knuckles. Then his thoughts shot toward one Fafhrd, a largely couth and most romantical barbarian, the soles of whose feet and mind were nonetheless firmly set in fact, particularly when he was either very sober, or very drunk, and toward this one's lifelong comrade, the Gray Mouser, perhaps the cleverest and wittiest thief in all Nehwon and certainly the one with either the bonniest or bitterest self-conceit.

The still less than momentary qualm which Death experienced at this point was far deeper and stronger than that which he had felt in the case of Lithquil. Fafhrd and the Mouser had served him well and in vastly more varied fashion than the Mad Duke, whose eyes had been fixed on death to the point of crossedness, making his particular form of ax-dispatch most appropriate. Yes, the large vagabond Northerner and the small, wry-smiling, eyebrow-arching cutpurse had been most useful pawns in some of Death's finest games.

Yet without exception every pawn must eventually be snapped up and tossed in box in the course of the greatest game, even if it have advanced to the ultimate rank and become king or queen. So Death reminded himself, who knew that even he himself must ultimately die, and so he set to his intuitively creative task relentlessly and swifter than ever arrow or rocket or falling star flew.

After the fleetingest glance southwest toward the vast, dawn-pink city of Lankhmar, to reassure himself that Fafhrd and the Mouser still occupied a rickety penthouse atop an inn which catered to the poorer sort of merchants and faced on Wall Street near the Marsh Gate, Death looked back at the late Lithquil's slaughter pen. In his improvisations he regularly made a practice of using materials closest at hand, as any good artist will.

Lithquil was in mid-crumple. The slavegirl was screaming. The mightiest of the berserks, his big face contorted by a fighting fury that would never fade till sheer exhaustion forced it, had just slashed off the bonily pink, invisibly fleshed head of Lithquil's assassin. And quite unjustly and even idiotically—but most of Death's lesser banes outwardly appear to work in such wise—a halfscore arrows were winging from the gallery toward Lithquil's avenger. Death magicked and the berserk was no longer there. The ten arrows transfixed empty air, but by that time Death, again following the practice of economy in materials, was peering once more at Horborixen and into a rather large cell lit by high, barred windows in the midst of the harem of the King of Kings. Rather oddly, there was a small furnace in the cell, a quenching bath, two small anvils, several hammers, many other tools for working metals, as well as a small store of precious and workaday metals themselves.

In the center of the cell, examining herself in a burnished silver mirror with almond eyes sharp as needles and now also quite as mad as the berserk's, there stood a deliciously slender girl of no more than sixteen, unclad save for four ornaments of silver filigree. She was, in fact, unclad in extremest degree, since except for her eyelashes, her every last hair had been removed and wherever such hair had been she was now tattooed in fine patterns of green and blue.

For seven moons now Eesafem had suffered solitary confinement for mutilating in a harem fight the faces of the King of Kings' favoritest concubines, twin Ilthmarts. Secretly the King of Kings had not been at all displeased by this event. Truth to tell, the facial mutilations of his special darlings slightly increased their attractiveness to his jaded appetite. Still, harem discipline had to be kept, hence Eesafem's confinement, loss of all hairs—most carefully one at a time —and tattooing.

The King of Kings was a thrifty soul and unlike many monarchs expected all his wives and concubines to perform useful work rather than be forever lolling, bathing, gossiping and brawling. So, it being the work she was uncontestably best trained for and the one most apt to bring profit, Eesafem had been permitted her forge and her metals.

But despite her regular working of these and her consequent production of numerous beauteous and ingenious objects, Eesafem's young mind had become viciously unhinged from her twelve harem moons, seven of those in lonely cell, and from the galling fact that the King of Kings had yet to visit her once for amorous or any other reason, even despite the charming metal gifts she had fashioned for him. Nor had any other man visited her, excepting eunuchs who had lectured her on the erotic arts—while she was securely trussed up, else she would have flown at their pudgy faces like a wildcat, and even at that she spat at them whenever able—and gave her detailed and patronizing advice on her metalworking, which she ignored as haughtily as she did their other fluting words.

Instead, her creativity, now fired by insane jealousies as well as racklike aches for freedom, had taken a new and secret turn.

Scanning the silver mirror, she carefully inspected the four ornaments adorning her slender yet wirey-strong figure. They were two breast cups and two shin-greaves, all chiefly of a delicate silver filigree, which set off nicely her green and blue tattooing.

Once her gaze in the mirror wandered overshoulder, past her naked pate with its finely patterned, fantastical skullcap, to a silver cage in which perched a green and blue parrot with eye as icily malevolent as her own—perpetual reminder of her own imprisonment.

The only oddity about the filigree ornaments was that the breast cups, jutting outward over the nipples, ended in short spikes trained straight forward, while the greaves were topped, just at the knee, with vertical ebony lozenges about as big as a man's thumb.

These bits of decor were not very obtrusive, the spikes being stained a greenish blue, as though to match her tattooing.

So Eesafem gazed at herself with a crafty, approving smile. And so Death gazed at her with a more crafty one, and one far more coldly approving than any eunuch's. And so she vanished in a flash from her cell. And before the blue-green parrot could gin squawk his startlement, Death's eyes and ears were elsewhere also.

Only seven heartbeats left.

Now it may be that in the world of Nehwon there are gods of whom even Death does not know and who from time to time take pleasure in putting obstacles in his path. Or it may be that Chance is quite as great a power as Necessity. At any rate, on this particular morning Fafhrd the Northerner, who customarily snoozed till noon, waked with the first dull silvery shaft of dawn and took up his dear weapon Graywand, naked as he, and blearily made his way from his penthouse pallet out onto the roof, where he gan practice all manner of swordstrokes, stamping his feet in his advances and from time to time uttering battleshouts, unmindful of the weary merchants he waked below him into groaning, cursing, or fright-quivering life. He shivered at first from the chill, fishy dawnmist from the Great Salt Marsh, but soon was sweating from his exercise, while his thrusts and parries, perfunctory to begin with, grew lightning-swift and most authoritative.

Except for Fafhrd, it was a quiet morning in Lankhmar. The bells had not yet begun to toll, nor the deep-throated gongs resound for the passage of the city's gentle overlord, nor the news been bruited about of his seventeen cats netted and hustled to the Great Gaol, there in separate cages to await trial.

It also happened that on this same day the Gray Mouser had waked till dawn, which usually found him an hour or so asleep. He curled in penthouse corner on a pile of pillows behind a low table, chin in hand, a woolly gray robe huddled around him. From time to time he wryly sipped sour wine and thought even sourer thoughts, chiefly about the evil and untrustworthy folk he had known during his mazily crooked lifetime. He ignored Fafhrd's exit and shut his ears to his noisy prancings, but the more he wooed sleep, the further she drew away.

The foamy-mouthed, red-eyed berserk materialized in front of Fafhrd just as the latter assumed the guard of low tierce, swordhand thrust forward, down, and a little to the right, sword slanting upward. He was astounded by the apparition, who, untroubled by sanity's strictures, instantly aimed at the naked Northerner's neck a great swipe with his saw-edged scimitar, which looked rather like a row of short, broad-bladed daggers forged side to side and freshly dipped in blood—so that it was pure automatism made Fafhrd shift his guard to a well-braced high carte which deflected the berserk's sword so that it whished over Fafhrd's head with something of the sound of a steel rod very swiftly dragged along a fence of steel pickets, as each razor-edged tooth in turn met the Northerner's blade.

Then reason took a hand in the game and before the berserk could begin a back-handed return swipe, Graywand's tip made a neat, swift counter-clockwise circle and flicked upward at the berserk's sword-wrist, so that his weapon and hand went flying harmlessly off. Far safer, Fafhrd knew, to disarm—or dishand?—such a frenziedly fell opponent before thrusting him through the heart, something Fafhrd now proceeded to do.

Meantime the Mouser was likewise astounded by the abrupt, entirely non sequitur appearance of Eesafem in the center of the penthouse. It was as if one of his more lurid erotic dreams had suddenly come to solid life. He could only goggle as she took a smiling step toward him, knelt a little, carefully faced her front at him, and then drew her upper arms close to her sides so that the filigree band which supported her breast cups was compressed. Her almond eyes flashed sinister green.

What saved the Mouser then was simply his lifelong antipathy to having anything sharp pointed at him, be it only the tiniest needle— or the playfully menacing spikes on exquisite silver breast cups doubtless enclosing exquisite breasts. He hurled himself to one side just as with simultaneous *zings* small but powerful springs loosed the envenomed spikes as though they were crossbow quarrels and buried them with twin *zaps* in the wall against which he had but now been resting.

He was scrambling to his feet in an instant and hurled himself at the girl. Now reason, or perhaps intuition, told him the significance of her grasping toward the two black lozenges topping her silver greaves. Tackling her, he managed to get to them before her, withdraw the twin, black-handled stilettos, and toss them beyond Fafhrd's tousled pallet.

Thereafter, twining his legs about hers in such fashion that she could not knee him in the groin, and holding her snapping, spitting head in the crook of his left arm and by an ear—after futilely grasping for hair—and finally mastering with his right hand the wrists of her two sharp-nailed, flailing ones, he proceeded by gradual and not unnecessarily brutal steps to ravage her. As she ran out of spit, she quieted. Her breasts proved to be very small, but doubly delicious.

Fafhrd, returning mightily puzzled from the roof, goggled in turn at what he saw. How the devil had the Mouser managed to smuggle in that winsome bit? Oh, well, no business of his. With a courteous "Pardon me. Pray continue," he shut the door behind him and tackled the problem of disposing of the berserk's corpse. This was readily achieved by heaving him up and dropping him four storeys onto the vast garbage heap that almost blocked Specter Alley. Next Fafhrd picked up the saw-edged scimitar, pried from it the still-clenched hand, and tossed that after. Then frowning down at the encrimsoned weapon, which he intended to keep as a souvenir, he futilely wondered, "Whose blood?"

(Disposing of Eesafem was hardly a problem capable of any such instant, hand-brushing solution. Suffice it that she gradually lost much of her madness and a little of her hatred of humanity, learned to speak Lankhmarese fluently, and ended up quite happily running a tiny smithy of her own on Copper Court behind Silver Street, where she made beautiful jewelry and sold under the counter such oddments as the finest poison-fanged rings in all Nehwon.)

Meanwhile Death, for whom time moves in a somewhat different fashion than for men, recognized that there remained to him only two heartbeats in which to fill his quota. The extremely faint thrill of excitement he had felt at seeing his two chosen heroes foil his brilliant improvisations—and at the thought that there *might* be powers in the universe unknown to him and subtler even than his—was replaced by a wry disgust at the realization that there was no longer time enough left for artistry and for indirection and that he must personally take a hand in the business—something he thoroughly detested, since the deus ex machina had always struck him as fiction's— or life's—feeblest device.

Should he slay Fafhrd and the Mouser direct? No, they had somehow outwitted him, which ought in all justice (if there be any such thing) give them immunity for a space. Besides, it would smack now almost of anger, or even resentment. And after his fashion and despite his occasional and almost unavoidable cheating, Death was a sportsman.

With the faintest yet weariest of sighs, Death magicked himself into the royal guardroom in the Great Golden Palace in Horborixen, where with two almost sightlessly swift, mercifully near-instantaneous thrusts, he let the life out of two most noble and blameless heroes whom he had barely glimpsed there earlier, yet ticketed in his boundless and infallible memory, two brothers sworn to perpetual celibacy and also to the rescue of at least one damsel in distress per moon. And so now they were released from this difficult destiny and Death returned to brood sadly on his low throne in his modest castle in the Shadowland and to await his next mission.

The twentieth heartbeat knelled.

II
BEAUTY AND THE BEASTS

SHE WAS UNDOUBTEDLY the most beautiful girl in Lankhmar, or all Nehwon, or any other world. So Fafhrd, the red-haired Northerner, and the Gray Mouser, that swarthy, cat-faced Southerner, were naturally following her.

Her name, most strangely, was Slenya Akkiba Magus, the most witching brunette in all the worlds, and also, most oddly, the most sorcerous blonde. They knew Slenya Akkiba Magus was her name because someone had called it out as she glided ahead of them up Pinchbeck Alley, which parallels Gold Street, and she hesitated for an instant in that drawing-together fashion one only does when one's name is unexpectedly called out, before gliding on without looking around.

They never saw who called. Perhaps someone on a roof. They looked into Sequin Court as they passed, but it was empty. So was Fools Gold Court.

Slenya was two inches taller than the Gray Mouser and ten shorter than Fafhrd—a nice height for a girl.

"She's mine," the Gray Mouser whispered with great authority.

"No, she's mine," Fafhrd murmured back with crushing casualness.

"We *could* split her," the Mouser hissed judiciously.

There was a zany logic to this suggestion for, quite amazingly, she was completely black on the right side and completely fair on the left side. You could see the dividing line down her back very distinctly. This was because of the extreme thinness of the dress of beige silk she was wearing. Her two colors split exactly at her buttocks.

On the fair side her hair was completely blonde. On the black side it was brunette.

At this moment an ebony-black warrior appeared from nowhere and attacked Fafhrd with a brass scimitar.

Drawing his sword Graywand in a rush, Fafhrd parried at a square angle. The scimitar shattered, and the brazen fragments flew about. Fafhrd's wrist whipped Graywand in a circle and struck off his foe's head.

Meanwhile the Mouser was suddenly faced by an ivory-white warrior sprung from another nowhere and armed with a steel rapier, silver-plated. The Mouser whisked out Scalpel, laid a bind on the other's blade, and thrust him through the heart.

The two friends congratulated each other.

Then they looked around. Save for the corpses, Pinchbeck Alley was empty.

Slenya Akkiba Magus had disappeared.

The twain pondered this for five heartbeats and two inhalations. Then Fafhrd's frown vanished and his eyes widened.

"Mouser," he said, "the girl divided into the two villains! That explains all. They came from the same nowhere."

"The same somewhere, you mean," the Mouser quibbled. "A most exotic mode of reproduction, or fission rather."

"And one with a sex alternation," Fafhrd added. "Perhaps if we examined the corpses—"

They looked down to find Pinchbeck Alley emptier still. The two liches had vanished from the cobbles. Even the chopped-off head was gone from the foot of the wall against which it had rolled.

"An excellent way of disposing of bodies," Fafhrd said with approval. His ears had caught the tramp and brazen clank of the approaching watch.

"They might have lingered long enough for us to search their pouches and seams for jewels and precious metal," the Mouser demurred.

"But what was behind it all?" Fafhrd puzzled. "A black-and-white magician—?"

"It's bootless to make bricks without straw," said the Mouser, cutting him short. "Let us hie to the Golden Lamprey and there drink a health to the girl, who was surely a stunner."

"Agreed. And we will drink to her appropriately in blackest stout laced with the palest bubbly wine of Ilthmar."

III
TRAPPED IN THE SHADOWLAND

FAFHRD AND THE Gray Mouser were almost dead from thirst. Their horses had died from the same Hell-throated ailment at the last waterhole, which had proved dry. Even the last contents of their waterbags, augmented by water of their own bodies, had not been enough to keep alive the dear dumb equine beasts. As all men know, camels are the only creatures who can carry men for more than a day or two across the almost supernaturally hot arid deserts of the World of Nehwon.

They tramped on south-westward under the blinding sun and over the burning sand. Despite their desperate plight and heat-fevered minds and bodies, they were steering a canny course. Too far south and they would fall into the cruel hands of the emperor of the Eastern Lands, who would find rare delight in torturing them before killing them. Too far east and they would encounter the merciless Mingols of the Steppes and other horrors. West and northwest were those who were pursuing them now. While north and northeast lay the Shadowland, the home of Death himself. So much they well knew of the geography of Nehwon.

Meanwhile, Death grinned faintly in his low castle in the heart of the Shadowland, certain that he had at last got the two elusive heroes in his bony grip. They had years ago had the nerve to enter his do-

main, visiting their first loves, Ivrian and Vlana, and even stealing
from his very castle Death's favorite mask. Now they would pay for
their temerity.

Death had the appearance of a tall, handsome young man, though
somewhat cadaverous and of opalescent complexion. He was staring
now at a large map of the Shadowland and its environs set in a dark
wall of his dwelling. On this map Fafhrd and the Mouser were a
gleaming speck, like an errant star or fire beetle, south of the Shadowland.

Death writhed his thin, smiling lips and moved his bony fingertips
in tiny, cabalistic curves, as he worked a small but difficult magic.

His incantation done, he noted with approval that on the map a
southern tongue of the Shadowland was visibly extending itself in
pursuit of the dazzling speck that was his victims.

Fafhrd and the Mouser tramped on south, staggering and reeling
now, their feet and minds aflame, their faces a-drip with precious
sweat. They had been seeking, near the Sea of Monsters and the City
of Ghouls, their strayed newest girls, Mouser's Reetha and Fafhrd's
Kreeshkra, the latter a Ghoul herself, all her blood and flesh invisible,
which made her bonny pink bones stand out the more, while Reetha
believed in going naked and shaven from head to toe, a taste which
gave the girls a mutual similarity and sympathy.

But the Mouser and Fafhrd had found nothing but a horde of fierce
male Ghouls, mounted on equally skeletal horses, who had chased
them east and south, either to slay them, or to cause them to die of
thirst in the desert or of torture in the dungeons of the King of Kings.

It was high noon and the sun was hottest. Fafhrd's left hand
touched in the dry heat a cool fence about two feet high, invisible at
first though not for long.

"Escape to damp coolth," he said in a cracked voice.

They eagerly clambered over the fence and threw themselves down
on a blessed thick turf of dark grass two inches high, over which a
fine mist was falling. They slept about ten hours.

In his castle Death permitted himself a thin grin, as on his map the
south-trending tongue of the Shadowland touched the diamond spark
and dimmed it.

Nehwon's greatest star, Astorian, was mounting the eastern sky,
precursor of the moon, as the two adventurers awoke, greatly refreshed by their long nap. The mist had almost ceased, but the only
star visible was vast Astorian.

The Mouser sprang up agitatedly in his gray hood, tunic, and ratskin shoes. "We must escape backward to hot dryth," he said, "for this is the Shadowland, Death's homeland."

"A very comfortable place," Fafhrd replied, stretching his huge muscles luxuriously on the thick greensward. "Return to the briny, granular, rasping, fiery land-sea? Not I."

"But if we stay here," the Mouser countered, "we will be will-lessly drawn by devilish and delusive will-o'-the-wisps to the low-walled Castle of Death, whom we defied by stealing his mask and giving its two halves to our wizards Sheelba and Ningauble, an action for which Death is not likely to love us. Besides, here we might well meet our two first girls, Ivrian and Vlana, now concubines of Death, and that would not be a pleasant experience."

Fafhrd winced, yet stubbornly repeated, "But it is comfortable here." Rather self-consciously he writhed his great shoulders and restretched his seven feet on the deliciously damp turf. (The "seven feet" refers to his height. He was by no means an octopus missing one limb, but a handsome, red-bearded, very tall barbarian.)

The Mouser persisted, "But what *if* your Vlana should appear, blue-faced and unloving? Or my Ivrian in like state, for that matter?"

That dire image did it. Fafhrd sprang up, grabbing for the low fence. But—lo and behold—there was no fence at hand. In all directions stretched out the damp, dark green turf of the Shadowland. While the soft drizzle had thickened again, hiding Astorian. There was no way to tell directions.

The Mouser searched in his ratskin pouch and drew out a blue bone needle. He pricked himself finding it, and cursed. It was wickedly sharp at one end, round and pierced at the other.

"We need a pool or puddle," he said.

"Where did you get that toy?" Fafhrd quizzed. "Magic, eh?"

"From Nattick Nimblefingers the Tailor in vasty Lankhmar," the Mouser replied. "Magic, nay! Hast heard of compass needles, oh wise one?"

Not far off they found a shallow puddle atop the turf. The Mouser carefully floated his needle on the small mirror of clear, placid water. It spun about slowly and eventually settled itself.

"We go that way," Fafhrd said, pointing out from the pierced end of the needle. "South." For he realized the pricking end must point toward the heart of the Shadowland—Nehwon's Death Pole, one might call it. For an instant he wondered if there were another such pole at the antipodes—perhaps a Life Pole.

"And we'll still need the needle," the Mouser added, pricking himself again and cursing as he pouched it, "for future guidance."

"Hah! Wah-wah-wah-*hah*!" yelled three berserks, emerging like fleet statues from the mist. They had been long marooned in the skirts of the Shadowland, reluctant either to advance to the Castle of Death and find their Hell or Valhalla, or to seek escape, but always ready for a fight. They rushed at Fafhrd and the Mouser, bareskinned and naked-bladed.

It took the Twain ten heartbeats of clashing sword-fight to kill them, though killing in the domain of Death must be at least a misdemeanor, it occurred to the Mouser—like poaching. Fafhrd got a shallow slash wound across his biceps, which the Mouser carefully bound up.

"Wow!" said Fafhrd. "Where did the needle point? I've got turned around."

They located the same or another puddle-mirror, floated the needle, again found South, and then took up their trek.

They twice tried to escape from the Shadowland by changing course, once east, once west. It was no use. Whatever way they went, they found only soft-turfed earth and bemisted sky. So they kept on south, trusting Nattick's needle.

For food they cut out black lambs from the black flocks they encountered, slew, bled, skinned, dressed, and roasted the tender meat over fires from wood of the squat black trees and bushes here and there. The young flesh was succulent. They drank dew.

Death in his low-walled keep continued to grin from time to time at his map, as the dark tongue of his territory kept magically extending southwest, the dimmed spark of his doomed victims in its margin.

He noted that the Ghoulish cavalry originally pursuing the Twain had halted at the boundary of his marchland.

But now there was the faintest trace of anxiety in Death's smile. And now and again a tiny vertical frown creased his opalescent, unwrinkled forehead, as he exerted his faculties to keep his geographical sorcery going.

The black tongue kept on down the map, past Sarheenmar and thievish Ilthmar to the Sinking Land. Both cities on the shore of the Inner Sea were scared unto death by the dark invasion of damp turf and misty sky, and they thanked their degenerate gods that it narrowly bypassed them.

And now the black tongue crossed the Sinking Land, moving due west. The little frown in Death's forehead had become quite deep. At the Swamp Gate of Lankhmar the Mouser and Fafhrd found their magical mentors waiting, Sheelba of the Eyeless Face and Ningauble of the Seven Eyes.

"What have you been up to?" Sheelba sternly asked the Mouser.

"And what have *you* been doing?" Ningauble demanded of Fafhrd.

The Mouser and Fafhrd were still in the Shadowland, and the two wizards outside it, with the boundary midway between. So their conversation was like that of two pairs of people on opposite sides of a narrow street, on the one side of which it is raining cats and dogs, the other side dry and sunny, though in this instance stinking with the smog of Lankhmar.

"Seeking Reetha," the Mouser replied, honestly for once.

"Seeking Kreeshkra," Fafhrd said boldly, "but a mounted Ghoul troop harried us back."

From his hood Ningauble writhed out six of his seven eyes and regarded Fafhrd searchingly. He said severely, "Kreeshkra, tired of your untameable waywardness, has gone back to the Ghouls for good, taking Reetha with her. I would advise you instead to seek Frix," naming a remarkable female who had played no small part in the adventure of the rathordes, the same affair in which Kreeshkra the Ghoul girl had been involved.

"Frix is a brave, handsome, remarkably cool woman," Fafhrd temporized, "but how to reach her? She's in another world, a world of air."

"While I counsel that *you* seek Hisvet," Sheelba of the Eyeless Face told the Mouser grimly. The unfeatured blackness in *his* mood grew yet blacker (with concentration) if that were possible. He was referring to yet another female involved in the rat-adventure, in which Reetha also had been a leading character.

"A great idea, Father," responded the Mouser, who made no bones about preferring Hisvet to all other girls, particularly since he had never once enjoyed her favors, though on the verge of doing so several times. "But she is likely deep in the earth and in her rat-size persona. How would I do it? How, how?"

If Sheel and Ning could have smiled, they would have.

However, Sheelba said only, "It is bothersome to see you both bemisted, like heroes in smoke."

He and Ning, without conference, collaborated in working a small but very difficult magic. After resisting most tenaciously, the Shadowland and its drizzle retreated east, leaving the Twain in the same sunshine as their mentors. Though two invisible patches of dark mist remained, entering into the flesh of the Mouser and Fafhrd and closing forever around their hearts.

Far eastaways, Death permitted himself a small curse which would have scandalized the high gods, had they heard it. He looked daggers at his map and its shortening black tongue. For Death, he was in a most bitter temper. Foiled again!

Ning and Sheel worked another diminutive wizardry.

Without warning, Fafhrd shot upwards in the air, growing tinier and tinier, until at last he was lost to sight.

Without moving from where he stood, the Mouser also grew tiny, until he was somewhat less than a foot high, of a size to cope with Hisvet, in or out of bed. He dove into the nearest rathole.

Neither feat was as remarkable as it sounds, since Nehwon is only a bubble rising through the waters of infinity.

The two heroes each spent a delightful weekend with his lady of the week.

"I don't know why I do things like this," Hisvet said, lisping faintly and touching the Mouser intimately as they lay side by side supine on silken sheets. "It must be because I loathe you."

"A pleasant and even worthy encounter," Frix confessed to Fafhrd in similar situation. "It is my hang-up to enjoy playing, now and then, with the lower animals. Which some would say is a weakness in a queen of the air."

Their weekend done, Fafhrd and the Mouser were automatically magicked back to Lankhmar, encountering one another in Cheap Street near Nattick Nimblefinger's narrow and dirty-looking dwelling. The Mouser was his right size again.

"You look sunburned," he observed to his comrade.

"Space-burned, it is," Fafhrd corrected. "Frix lives in a remarkably distant land. But you, old friend, look paler than your wont."

"Shows what three days underground will do to a man's complexion," the Mouser responded. "Come, let's have a drink at the Silver Eel."

Ningauble in his cave near Ilthmar and Sheelba in his mobile hut in the Great Salt Marsh each smiled, though lacking the equipment for that facial expression. They knew they had laid one more obligation on their protégés.

IV
THE BAIT

Fafhrd the northerner was dreaming of a great mound of gold.

The Gray Mouser the Southerner, ever cleverer in his forever competitive fashion, was dreaming of a heap of diamonds. He hadn't tossed out all of the yellowish ones yet, but he guessed that already his glistening pile must be worth more than Fafhrd's glowing one.

How he knew in his dream what Fafhrd was dreaming was a mystery to all beings in Nehwon, except perhaps Sheelba of the Eyeless Face and Ningauble of the Seven Eyes, respectively the Mouser's and Fafhrd's sorcerer-mentors. Maybe, a vast, black basement mind shared by the two was involved.

Simultaneously they awoke, Fafhrd a shade more slowly, and sat up in bed.

Standing midway between the feet of their cots was an object that fixed their attention. It weighed about eighty pounds, was about four feet eight inches tall, had long straight black hair pendant from head, had ivory-white skin, and was as exquisitely formed as a slim chesspiece of the King of Kings carved from a single moonstone. It looked thirteen, but the lips smiled a cool self-infatuated seventeen, while the gleaming deep eye-pools were first blue melt of the Ice Age. Naturally, she was naked.

"She's mine!" the Gray Mouser said, always quick from the scabbard.

"No, she's mine!" Fafhrd said almost simultaneously, but conceding by that initial "No" that the Mouser had been first, or at least he had expected the Mouser to be first.

"I belong to myself and to no one else, save two or three virile demidevils," the small naked girl said, though giving them each in turn a most nymphish lascivious look.

"I'll fight you for her," the Mouser proposed.

"And I you," Fafhrd confirmed, slowly drawing Graywand from its sheath beside his cot.

The Mouser likewise slipped Scalpel from its ratskin container. The two heroes rose from their cots.

At this moment, two personages appeared a little behind the girl—from thin air, to all appearances. Both were at least nine feet tall. They had to bend, not to bump the ceiling. Cobwebs tickled their pointed ears. The one on the Mouser's side was black as wrought iron. He swiftly drew a sword that looked forged from the same material.

At the same time, the other newcomer—bone-white, this one—produced a silver-seeming sword, likely steel plated with tin.

The nine-footer opposing the Mouser aimed a skull-splitting blow at the top of his head. The Mouser parried in prime and his opponent's weapon shrieked off to the left. Whereupon, smartly swinging his rapier widdershins, the Mouser slashed off the black fiend's head, which struck the floor with a horrid clank.

The white afreet opposing Fafhrd trusted to a downward thrust. But the Northerner, catching his blade in a counterclockwise bind, thrust him through, the silvery sword missing Fafhrd's right temple by the thinness of a hair.

With a petulant stamp of her naked heel, the nymphet vanished into thin air, or perhaps Limbo.

The Mouser made to wipe off his blade on the cotclothes, but discovered there was no need. He shrugged. "What a misfortune for you, comrade," he said in a voice of mocking woe. "Now you will not be able to enjoy the delicious chit as she disports herself on your heap of gold."

Fafhrd moved to cleanse Graywand on *his* sheets, only to note that it too was altogether unbloodied. He frowned. "Too bad for you, best of friends," he sympathized. "Now you won't be able to possess her as she writhes with girlish abandon on your couch of diamonds, their glitter striking opalescent tones from her pale flesh."

"Mauger that effeminate artistic garbage, how did you know that I was dreaming diamonds?" the Mouser demanded.

"How did I?" Fafhrd asked himself wonderingly. At last he begged the question with, "The same way, I suppose, that you knew I was dreaming of gold."

The two excessively long corpses chose that moment to vanish, and the severed head with them.

Fafhrd said sagely, "Mouser, I begin to believe that supernatural forces were involved in this morning's haps."

"Or else hallucinations, oh great philosopher," the Mouser countered somewhat peevishly.

"Not so," Fafhrd corrected, "for see, they've left their weapons behind."

"True enough," the Mouser conceded, rapaciously eyeing the wrought-iron and tin-plated blades on the floor. "Those will fetch a fancy price on Curio Court."

The Great Gong of Lankhmar, sounding distantly through the walls, boomed out the twelve funereal strokes of noon, when burial parties plunge spade into earth.

"An after-omen," Fafhrd pronounced. "Now we know the source of the supernal force. The Shadowland, terminus of all funerals."

"Yes," the Mouser agreed. "Prince Death, that eager boy, has had another go at us."

Fafhrd splashed cool water onto his face from a great bowl set against the wall. "Ah well," he spoke through the splashes, "Twas a pretty bait at least. Truly, there's nothing like a nubile girl, enjoyed or merely glimpsed naked, to give one an appetite for breakfast."

"Indeed yes," the Mouser replied, as he tightly shut his eyes and briskly rubbed his face with a palm full of white brandy. "She was just the sort of immature dish to kindle your satyrish taste for maids newly budded."

In the silence that came as the splashing stopped, Fafhrd inquired innocently, "*Whose* satyrish taste?"

V

UNDER THE THUMBS OF THE GODS

Dʀɪɴᴋɪɴɢ sᴛʀᴏɴɢ ᴅʀɪɴᴋ one night at the Silver Eel, the Gray Mouser and Fafhrd became complacently, even luxuriously, nostalgic about their past loves and amorous exploits. They even boasted a little to each other about their most recent erotic solacings (although it is always very unwise to boast of such matters, especially out loud; one never knows who may be listening).

"Despite her vast talent for evil," the Mouser said, "Hisvet remains always a child. Why should that surprise me?—evil comes naturally to children, it is a game to them, they feel no shame. Her breasts are no bigger than walnuts, or limes, or at most small tangerines topped by hazelnuts—all eight of them."

Fafhrd said, "Frix is the very soul of the dramatic. You should have seen her poised on the battlement later that night, her eyes raptly agleam, seeking the stars. Naked save for some ornaments of copper fresh as rosy dawn. She looked as if she were about to fly—which she can do, as you know."

In the Land of the Gods, in short in Godsland and near Nehwon's Life Pole there, which lies in the southron hemisphere at the antipodes from the Shadowland (abode of Death), three gods sitting together cross-legged in a circle picked out Fafhrd's and the Mouser's voices from the general mutter of their worshippers, both loyal and lapsed, which resounds eternally in any god's ear, as if he held a seashell to it.

One of the three gods was Issek, whom Fafhrd had once faithfully served as acolyte for three months. Issek had the appearance of a delicate youth with wrists and ankles broken, or rather permanently bent at right angles. During his Passion he had been severely racked. Another was Kos, whom Fafhrd had revered during his childhood in the Cold Waste, rather a squat, brawny god bundled up in furs, with a grim, not to say surly, heavily bearded visage.

The third god was Mog, who resembled a four-limbed spider with a quite handsome, though not entirely human face. Once the girl Ivrian, the Mouser's first love, had taken a fancy to a jet statuette of Mog he had stolen for her and decided, perhaps roguishly, that Mog and the Mouser looked alike.

Now the Gray Mouser is generally believed to be and have always been complete atheist, but this is not true. Partly to humor Ivrian, whom he spoiled fantastically, but partly because it tickled his vanity that a god should choose to look like him, he made a game for several weeks of firmly believing in Mog.

So the Mouser and Fafhrd were clearly worshippers, though lapsed, and the three gods singled out their voices because of that and because they were the most noteworthy worshippers these three gods had ever had and because they were boasting. For the gods have very sharp ears for boasts, or for declarations of happiness and self-satisfaction, or for assertions of a firm intention to do this or that, or for statements that this or that must surely happen, or any other words hinting that a man is in the slightest control of his own destiny. And the gods are jealous, easily angered, perverse, and swift to thwart.

"It's them, all right—the haughty bastards!" Kos grunted, sweating under his furs—for Godsland is paradisial.

"They haven't called on me for years—the ingrates!" Issek said with a toss of his delicate chin. "We'd be dead for all they care, except we've our other worshippers. But they don't know that—they're heartless."

"They have not even taken our names in vain," said Mog. "I believe, gentlemen, it is time they suffered the divine displeasure. Agreed?"

In the meanwhile, by speaking privily of Frix and Hisvet, the Mouser and Fafhrd had aroused certain immediate desires in themselves without seriously disturbing their mood of complacent nostalgia.

"What say you, Mouser," Fafhrd mused lazily, "should we now seek excitement? The night is young."

His comrade replied grandly, "We have but to stir a little, to signify our interest, and excitement will seek us. We've loved and been forever adored by so many girls that we're bound to run into a pair of 'em. Or even two pair. They'll catch our present thoughts on the wing and come running. We will hunt girls—ourselves the bait!"

"So let's be on our way," said Fafhrd, drinking up and rising with a lurch.

"Ach, the lewd dogs!" Kos growled, shaking sweat from his brow, for Godsland is balmy (and quite crowded). "But how to punish 'em?"

Mog said, smiling lopsidedly because of his partially arachnid jaw structure, "They seem to have chosen their punishment."

"The torture of hope!" Issek chimed eagerly, catching on. "We grant them their wishes—"

"—and then leave the rest to the girls," Mog finished.

"You can't trust women," Kos asserted darkly.

"On the contrary, my dear fellow," Mog said, "when a god's in good form, he can safely trust his worshippers, female and male alike, to do all the work. And now, gentlemen, on with our thinking caps!"

Kos scratched his thickly matted head vigorously, dislodging a louse or two.

Whimsically, and perhaps to put a few obstacles between themselves and the girls presumably now rushing toward them, Fafhrd and the Gray Mouser chose to leave the Silver Eel by its kitchen door, something they'd never done once before in all their years of patronage.

The door was low and heavily bolted, and when those were shot still wouldn't budge. And the new cook, who was deaf and dumb, left off his stuffing of a calf's stomach and came over to make gobbling noises and flap his arms in gestures of protest or warning. But the Mouser pressed two bronze agols into his greasy palm while Fafhrd kicked the door open. They prepared to stride out into the dismal lot covered by the eroded ashes of the tenement where the Mouser had dwelt with Ivrian (and she and Fafhrd's equally dear Vlana had burned) and also the ashes of the wooden garden house of mad Duke Danius, which they'd once stolen and occupied for a space—the dismal and ill-omened lot which they'd never heard of anyone building on since.

But when they'd ducked their heads and gone through the doorway, they discovered that construction of a sort *had* been going on (or else that they'd always seriously underestimated the depth of the Silver Eel) for instead of on empty ground open to the sky, they found themselves in a corridor lit by torches held in brazen hands along each wall.

Undaunted, they strode forward past two closed doors.

"That's Lankhmar City for you," the Mouser observed. "You turn your back and they've put up a new secret temple."

"Good ventilation, though," Fafhrd commented on the absence of smoke.

They followed the corridor around a sharp turn . . . and stopped dead. The split-level chamber facing them had surprising features. The sunken half was close-ceilinged and otherwise gave the impression of being far underground, as if its floor were not eight finger-joints deeper than the raised section but eighty yards. Its furniture was a bed with a coverlet of violet silk. A thick yellow silk cord hung through a hole in the low ceiling.

The chamber's raised half seemed the balcony or battlement of a tower thrust high above Lankhmar's smog, for stars were visible in the black upper background and ceiling.

On the bed, silver-blonde head to its foot, slim Hisvet lay prone but upthrust on her straightened arms. Her robe of fine silk, yellow as desert sunlight, was outdented by her pair of small high breasts, but depended freely from the nipples of those, leaving unanswered the question of whether there were three more pairs arranged symmetrically below.

While against starry night (or its counterfeit), her dark hair braided with scrubbed copper wire, Frix stood magnificently tall and light-footed (though motionless) in her silken robe violet as a desert's twilight before dawn.

Fafhrd was about to say, "You know, we were just talking about you," and the Mouser was about to tread on his instep for being so guileless, when Hisvet cried to the latter, "You again!—intemperate dirksman. I told you never even to *think* of another rendezvous with me for two years' space."

Frix said to Fafhrd, "Beast! I told you I played with a member of the lower orders only on *rare* occasions."

Hisvet tugged sharply on the silken cord. A heavy door dropped down in the men's faces from above and struck its sill with a great and conclusive jar.

Fafhrd lifted a finger to his nose, explaining ruefully, "I thought the door had taken off the tip. Not exactly a loving reception."

The Mouser said bravely, "I'm glad they turned us off. Truly, it would have been too soon, and so a bore. On with our girl hunt!"

They returned past the mute flames held in bronze hands to the second of the two closed doors. It opened at a touch to reveal another dual chamber and in it their loves Reetha and Kreeshkra, whom only short months ago they'd been seeking near the Sea of Monsters, until they were trapped in the Shadowland and barely escaped back to Lankhmar. To the left, in muted sunlight on a couch of exquisitely smoothed dark wood, Reetha reclined quite naked. Indeed, extremely naked, for as the Mouser noted, she'd kept up her habit, inculcated when she'd been slave of a finicky overlord, of regularly shaving all of herself, even her eyebrows. Her totally bare head, held at a pert angle, was perfectly shaped and the Mouser felt a surge of sweet desire. She was cuddling to her tender bosom a very emaciated-seeming but tranquil animal, which the Mouser suddenly realized was a cat, hairless save for its score of whiskers bristling from its mask.

To the right, in dark night a-dance with the light of campfire and on a smooth shale shore of what Fafhrd recognized to be, by the large white-bearded serpents sporting in it, the Sea of Monsters, sat his beloved Kreeshkra, more naked even than Reetha. She might have been a disquieting sight to some (naught but an aristocratically handsome skeleton), except that the flames near which she sat struck dark blue gleams from the sweetly curved surfaces of her transparent flesh casing her distinguished bones.

"Mouser, why have you come?" Reetha cried out somewhat reproachfully. "I'm happy here in Eevamarensee, where all men are as hairless by nature (our household animals too) as I am by my daily industry. I love you dearly still, but we can't live together and must not meet again. This is my proper place."

Likewise, bold Kreeshkra challenged Fafhrd with "Mud Man, avaunt! I loved you once. Now I'm a Ghoul again. Perhaps in future time . . . But now, begone!"

It was well neither Fafhrd nor Mouser had stepped across the threshold, for at those words this door slammed in their faces too, and this time stuck fast. Fafhrd forbore to kick it.

"You know, Mouser," he said thoughtfully, "We've been enamored of some strange ones in our time. But always most intensely interesting," he hastened to add.

"Come on, come on," the Mouser enjoined gruffly. "There are other fish in the sea."

The remaining door opened easily too, though Fafhrd pushed it somewhat gingerly. Nothing startling, however, came into view this time, only a long dark room, empty of persons and furniture, with a second door at the other end. Its only novel feature was that the right-hand wall glowed green. They walked in with returning confidence. After a few steps they became aware that the glowing wall was thick crystal enclosing pale green, faintly clouded water. As they watched, continuing to stroll, there swam into view with lazy undulations two beautiful mermaids, the one with long golden hair trailing behind her and a sheathlike garb of wide-meshed golden fishnet, the other with short dark hair parted by a ridgy and serrated silver crest. They came close enough for one to see the slowly pulsing gills scoring their necks where they merged into their sloping, faintly scaled shoulders, and farther down their bodies those discrete organs which contradict the contention, subject of many a crude jest, that a man is unable fully to enjoy an unbifurcated woman (though any pair of snakes in love tell us otherwise). They swam closer still, their dreamy eyes now wide and peering, and the Mouser and Fafhrd recognized the two queens of the sea they had embraced some years past while deep diving from their sloop *Black Treasurer.*

What the wide-peering fishy eyes saw evidently did not please the mermaids, for they made faces and with powerful flirts of their long finny tails retreated away from the crystal wall through the greenish water, whose cloudiness was increased by their rapid movements, until they could no longer be seen.

Turning to the Mouser, Fafhrd inquired, eyebrows alift, "You mentioned other fish in the sea?"

With a quick frown the Mouser strode on. Trailing him, Fafhrd mused puzzledly, "You said this might be a secret temple, friend. But if so, where are its porters, priests, and patrons other than ourselves?"

"More like a museum—scenes of distant life. And a piscesium, or piscatorium," his comrade answered curtly over shoulder.

"I've also been thinking," Fafhrd continued, quickening his steps, "there's too much space here we've been walking through for the lot behind the Silver Eel to hold. What *has* been builded here?—or there?"

The Mouser went through the far door. Fafhrd was close behind.

In Godsland Kos snarled, "The rogues are taking it too easily. Oh, for a thunderbolt!"

Mog told him rapidly, "Never you fear, my friend, we have them on the run. They're only putting up appearances. We'll wear them down by slow degrees until they pray to us for mercy, groveling on their knees. That way our pleasure's greater."

"Quieter, you two," Issek shrilled, waving his bent wrists, "I'm getting another girl pair!"

It was clear from these and other quick gesticulations and injunctions—and from their rapt yet tense expressions—that the three gods in close inward-facing circle were busy with something interesting. From all around other divinities large and small, baroque and classical, noisome and beautiful, came drifting up to comment and observe. Godsland *is* overcrowded, a veritable slum, all because of man's perverse thirst for variety. There are rumors among the packed gods there of other and (perish the thought!) superior gods, perhaps invisible, who enjoy roomier quarters on another and (oh woe!) higher level and who (abysmal deviltry!) even hear thoughts, but nothing certain.

Issek cried out in ecstasy, "There, there, the stage is set! Now to search out the next teasing pair. Kos and Mog, help me. Do your rightful share."

The Gray Mouser and Fafhrd felt they'd been transported to the mysterious realm of Quarmall, where they'd had one of their most fantastic adventures. For the next chamber seemed a cave in solid rock, given room-shape by laborious chipping. And behind a table piled with parchments and scrolls, inkwells and quills, sat the two saucy, seductive slavegirls they'd rescued from the cavern-world's monotonies and tortures: slender Ivivis, supple as a snake, and pleasantly plump Friska, light of foot. The two men felt relief and joy that they'd come home to the familiar and beloved.

Then they saw the room had windows, with sunlight suddenly striking in (as if a cloud had lifted), and was not solid rock but morticed stone, and that the girls wore not the scanty garb of slaves but rich and sober robes, while their faces were grave and self-reliant.

Ivivis looked up at the Mouser with inquiry but instant disapproval. "What dost here, figment of my servile past? Tis true, you rescued me from Quarmall foul. For which I paid you with my body's love. Which ended at Tovilysis when we split. We're quits, dear Mouser, yes by Mog, we are!" (She wondered why she used that particular oath.)

Likewise Friska looked at Fafhrd and said, "That goes for you too, bold barbarian. You also killed my lover Hovis, you'll recall—as Mouser did Ivivis' Klevis. We are no longer simple-minded slaves, playthings of men, but subtile secretary and present treasurer of the Guild of Free Women at Tovilysis. We'll never love again unless I choose—which I do not today! And so, by Kos and Issek, now begone!" (She wondered likewise why she invoked those particular deities, for whom she had no respect whatever.)

These rebuffs hurt the two heroes sorely, so that they had not the spirit to respond with denials, jests, or patient gallantries. Their tongues clove to their hard palates, their hearts and privates grew chilly, they almost cringed—and they rather swiftly stole from that chamber by the open door ahead . . . into a large room shaped of bluish ice, or rock of the same hue and translucence and as cold, so that the flames dancing in the large fireplace were welcome. Before this was spread a rug looking wondrously thick and soft, about which were set scatteredly jars of unguents, small bottles of perfume (which made themselves known by their ranging scents), and other cosmetic containers and tools. Furthermore, the invitingly textured rug showed indentations as if made by two recumbent human forms, while about a cubit above it floated two living masks as thin as silk or paper or more thin, holding the form of wickedly pretty, pert girl faces, the one rosy mauvette, the other turquoise green.

Others would have deemed it a prodigy, but the Mouser and Fafhrd at once recognized Keyaira and Hirriwi, the invisible frost princesses with whom they'd once been separately paired for one long, long night in Stardock, tallest of Nehwon's northron peaks, and knew that the two gaysome girls were reclining unclad in front of the fire and had been playfully anointing each other's faces with pigmented salves.

Then the turquoise mask leapt up betwixt Fafhrd and the fire, so that dancing orange flames only shone through its staring eye holes and between its now cruel and amused lips as it spoke to him, saying, "In what frowsty bed are you now dead asleep, gross one-time lover, that your squeaking soul can be blown halfway across the world to gape at me? Some day again climb Stardock and in your solid form importune me. I might hark. But now, phantom, depart!"

The mallow mask likewise spoke scornfully to the Mouser, saying in tones as stinging and impelling as the flames seen through its facial orifices, "And you remove too, wraith most pitiful. By Khahkht of the Black Ice and Gara of the Blue—and e'en Kos of the Green—I enjoin it! Blow winds! and out lights all!"

Fafhrd and the Mouser were hurt even more sorely by these new rebuffs. Their very souls were shriveled by the feeling that they were indeed the phantoms, and the speaking masks the solid reality. Nevertheless, they might have summoned the courage to attempt to answer the challenge (though 'tis doubtful), except that at Keyaira's last commands they were plunged into darkness absolute and manhandled by great winds and then dumped in a lighted area. A wind-slammed door crashed shut behind them.

They saw with considerable relief that they were not confronting yet another pair of girls *(that* would have been unendurable) but were in another stretch of corridor lit by clear-flaming torches held in brazen wall brackets in the form of gripping bird-talons, coiling squid-tentacles, and pinching crabclaws. Grateful for the respite, they took deep breaths.

Then Fafhrd frowned deeply and said, "Mark me, Mouser, there's magic somewhere in all this. Or else the hand of a god."

The Mouser commented bitterly, "If it's a god, he's a thumb-fingered one, the way he sets us up to be turned down."

Fafhrd's thoughts took a new tack, as shown by the changing furrows in his forehead. "Mouser, I never squeaked," he protested. "Hirriwi said I squeaked."

"Manner of speaking only, I suppose," his comrade consoled. "But gods! what misery I felt myself, as if I were no longer man at all, and *this* no more than broomstick." He indicated his sword Scalpel at his side and gazed with a shake of his head at Fafhrd's scabbarded Graywand.

"Perchance we dream—" Fafhrd began doubtfully.

"Well, if we're dreaming, let's get on with it," the Mouser said and, clapping his friend around the shoulders, started them down the corridor. Yet despite these cheerful words and actions, both men felt they were getting more and more into the toils of nightmare, drawing them on will-lessly.

They rounded a turn. For some yards the right-hand wall became a row of slender dark pillars, irregularly spaced, and between them they could see more random dusky slim shafts and at middle distance a long altar on which light showered softly down, revealing a tall, naked woman stretched on it, and by her a priestess in purple robes with dagger bared in one hand and large silver chalice in the other, who was intoning a litany.

Fafhrd whispered, "Mouser! the sacrifice is the courtesan Lessnya, with whom I had some dealings when I was acolyte of Issek, years ago."

"While the other is Ilala, priestess of the like-named goddess, with whom I had some commerce when I was lieutenant to Pulg the extortioner," the Mouser whispered back.

Fafhrd protested, "But we *can't* have already come all the way to the temple of Ilala, though this looks like it. It's halfway across Lankhmar from the Eel," while the Mouser recalled tales he'd heard of secret passages in Lankhmar that connected points by distances shorter than the shortest distance between.

Ilala turned toward them in her purple robes and said with eyebrows raised, "Quiet back there! You are committing sacrilege, trespassing on most holy ritual of the great goddess of all shes. Impious intruders, depart!" While Lessnya lifted on an elbow and looked at them haughtily. Then she lay back again and regarded the ceiling while Ilala plunged her dagger deep into her chalice and then with it flicked sprinkles of wine (or whatever other fluid the chalice held) on Lessnya's naked shape, wielding the blade as if it were an aspergillum. She aspersed her thrice—on bosom, loins, and knees—and then resumed her muttered litany, while Lessnya echoed her (or else snored) and the Mouser and Fafhrd stole on along the torchlit corridor.

But they had little time to ponder on the strange geometries and stranger religiosities of their nightmare progress, for now the left-hand wall gave way for a space to a fabulously decorated, large, dim chamber, which they recognized as the official residence room of the Grandmaster of the Thieves' Guild in Thieves' House, half Lankhmar City back again from Ilala's fane. The foreground was filled with figures kneeling away from them in devout supplication toward a thick-topped ebony table, behind which there stood queenly tall a handsome red-haired woman dressed in jewels and behind her a trim second female in maid's black tunic collared and cuffed with white.

" 'Tis Ivlis in her beauty from the past, for whom I stole Ohmphal's erubescent fingertips," the Mouser whispered in stupefaction. "And now she's got herself a peck more gems."

"And that is Freg, her maid, looking no older," Fafhrd whispered back hoarsely in dream-drugged wonderment.

"But what's she doing here in Thieves' House?" the Mouser pressed, his whisper feverish, "where women are forbidden and contemned. As if *she* were grandmaster of the Guild . . . grand-mistress . . . goddess . . . worshipped . . . Is Thieves' Guild upside down? . . . all Nehwon turvy-topsy . . . ?"

Ivlis looked up at them across the heads of her kneeling followers. Her green eyes narrowed. She casually lifted her fingers to her lips, then flicked them sideways twice, indicating to the Mouser that he should silently keep going in that direction and not return.

With a slow unloving smile, Freg made exactly the same gesture to Fafhrd, but even more idly seeming, as if humming a chorus. The two men obeyed, but with their gazes trailing behind them, so that it was with complete surprise, almost with starts of fear, that they found they had walked blindly into a room of rare woods embellished with intricate carvings, with a door before them and doors to either side, and in the one of the latter nearest the Mouser a freshly nubile girl with wicked eyes, in a green robe of shaggy toweling cloth, her black hair moist, and in the one nearest Fafhrd two slim blondes a-smile with dubious merriment and wearing loosely the black hoods and robes of nuns of Lankhmar. In nightmare's fullest grip they realized that this was the very same garden house of Duke Danius, haunted by their earliest deepest loves, impiously reconstituted from the ashes to which the sorcerer Sheelba had burned it and profanely refurbished with all the trinkets wizard Ningauble had magicked from it and scattered to the four winds; and that these three nightfillies were Ivmiss Ovartamortes, niece of Karstak like-named, Lankhmar's then overlord, and Fralek and Fro, mirror-twin daughters of the death-crazed duke, the three she-colts of the dark to whom they'd madly turned after losing even the ghosts of their true loves in Shadowland. Fafhrd was wildly thinking in unvoiced sound, "Fralek and Fro, and Freg, Friska and Frix—what is this Fr'-charm on me?" while through the Mouser's mind was skipping likewise, "Ivlis, Ivmiss, Ivivis (two Iv's—and there's e'en an Iv in Hisvet)—who are these girl-lets of the Iv . . . .?"

(Near the Life Pole, the gods Mog, Issek, and Kos were working at the top of their bent, crying out to each other new girl-discoveries with which to torment their lapsed worshippers. The crowd of spectator gods around them was now large.)

And then the Mouser bethought him with a shiver that he had not listed amongst his girl-lings of the Iv the archgirl of them all, fair Ivrian, forever lost in Death's demesne. And Fafhrd likewise shook. And the nightfillies flanking them pouted and made moues at them, and they were fairly catapulted into the midst of a pavilion of wine-dark silk, beyond whose unstirring folds showed the flat black horizons of the Shadowland.

Beauteous, slate-visaged Vlana spat full in Fafhrd's face, saying, "I told you I'd do that if you came back," but fair Ivrian only eyed the Mouser with never a sign or word.

And then they were back in the betorched corridor, more hurried along it than hurrying, and the Mouser envied Fafhrd death's spittle inching down his cheek. And girls were flashing by like ghosts, unheedingly—Mara of Fafhrd's youth, Atya who worshipped Tyaa, bovine-eyed Hrenlet, Ahura of Seleucia, and many many more—until they were feeling the utter despair that comes with being rejected not

by one or a few loves, but by all. The unfairness of it alone was
enough to make a man die.

Then in the rush one scene lingered awhile: Alyx the Picklock
garbed in the scarlet robes and golden tiara a-swarm with rubies of
the archpriest of an eastern faith, and kneeling before her costumed
as clerk Lilyblack, the Mouser's girlish leman from his criminous
days, intoning, "Papa, the heathen rage, the civilized decay," and the
transvestite archpriestess pronouncing, "All men are enemies . . ."

Almost Fafhrd and the Mouser dropped to their knees and prayed
to whatever gods may be for surcease from their torment. But somehow they didn't, and of a sudden they found themselves on Cheap
Street near where it crosses Crafts and turning in at a drab doorway
after two females, whose backs were teasingly familiar, and following
them up a narrow flight of stairs that stretched up so far in one flight
that its crazy warpage was magnified.

In Godsland Mog threw himself back, blowing out his breath and
saying, "There! that gets them all," while Issek likewise stretched
himself out (so far as his permanently bent ankles and wrists would
permit), observing, "Lord, people don't appreciate how we gods
work, what toil in sparrow-watching!" and the spectator gods began
to disperse.

But Kos, still frowningly immersed in his task to such a degree that
he wasn't aware of the pain in his short burly thighs from sitting
cross-legged so long, cried out, "Hold on! here's another pair: to wit,
one Nemia of the Dusk, one Eyes of Ogo, woman of lax morals and,
to boot, receivers of stolen property—oh, that's vile!"

Issek laughed wearily and said, "Quit now, dear Kos. I crossed
those two off at the very start. They're our men's dearest enemies,
swindled them out of a precious loot of jewels, as almost any god
around could tell you. Sooner than seek them out (to be rebuffed in
any case, of course) our boys would rot in hell," while Mog yawned
and added, "Don't you ever know, dear Kos, when the game's done?"

So the befurred short god shrugged and gave over, cursing as he
tried to straighten his legs.

Meanwhile, the Eyes of Ogo and Nemia of the Dusk reached the
summit of the endless stairs and tiredly entered their pad, eyeing it
with disfavor. (It *was* an impoverished, dingy, even noissome place—
the two best thieves in Lankhmar had fallen on hard times, as even
the best of thieves and receivers will in the course of long careers.)

Nemia turned round and said, "Look what the cat dragged in."
Hardship had drastically straightened her lush curves. Her comrade
Ogo-Eyes still looked somewhat like a child, but a very old and ill-

used one. "Wow," she said wearily, "you two look miserable, as if you'd just 'scaped death and sorry you had. Do yourselves a favor— fall down the stairs, breaking your necks."

When Fafhrd and the Mouser didn't move, or change their woebe-gone expressions, she laughed shortly, cropped into a broken-seated chair, poked out a leg at the Mouser, and said, "Well, if you're not leaving, make yourself useful. Remove my sandals, wash my feet," while Nemia sat down before a rickety dressing table and, while sur-veying herself in the broken mirror, held out a broken-toothed instru-ment in Fafhrd's direction, saying, "Comb my hair, barbarian. Watch out for snarls and knots."

Fafhrd and the Mouser (the later preparing and fetching warm water) began solemn-faced to do those very things most carefully.

After quite a long time (and several other menial services rendered, or servile penances done) the two women could no longer keep from smiling. Misery, *after* it's comforted, loves company. "That's enough for now," Eyes told the Mouser. "Come, make yourself comfortable." Nemia spoke likewise to Fafhrd, adding, "Later you men can make the dinner and go out for wine."

After a while the Mouser said, "By Mog, this is more like it." Fafhrd agreed. "By Issek, yes. Kos damn all spooked adventures."

The three gods, hearing their names taken in vain as they rested in paradise from their toils, were content.

VI
TRAPPED IN THE SEA OF STARS

FAFHRD THE EDUCATED barbarian and his constant comrade the Gray (Grey?) Mouser, city-born but wizard-tutored in the wilds, had in their leopard-boat *Black Racer* sailed farther south in the Outer Sea along the Quarmallian or west coast of Lankhmar continent than they had ever ventured before, or any other honest mariner they knew.

They were lured on by a pair of shimmer-sprights, as they are called, a breed of will-o'-the-wisps which men deem infallible guides to lodgements of precious metals, if only one have a master hunter's patience and craft to track them down, by reason of which they are also called treasure-flies, silver-moths, and gold-bugs. This pair had a coppery pink seeming by day and a silvery black gleam by night, promising by those hues a trove of elektrum and still dearer, because massier, white gold. They most resembled restlessly flowing, small bedsheets of gossamer. They fluttered ceaselessly about the single mast, darting ahead, drifting behind. Sometimes they were almost invisible, faintest heat-blurs in the pelting fire of the near vertical sun, ghostliest shimmers in the dark of night and easily mistaken for reflections of the White Huntress' light on sea and sail, the moon now being near full. Sometimes they moved as sprightly as their name, sometimes they drooped and lagged, but ever moved on. At such times they seemed sad (or melancholy, Fafhrd said, one of his favorite moods). On other occasions, they became (if ears could be trusted) vocal with joy, filling the air about the leopard-boat with faint sweet jargonings, whispers 'twixt wind and speech, and long ecstatic purrs.

By the Gray Mouser's and Fafhrd's calculations, *Black Racer* had now left behind Lankhmar continent to loadside, and the hypothetical Western continent far, far to steerside, and struck out due south into the Great Equatorial Ocean (sometimes called—but why?—the Sea of Stars) that girdles Nehwon and is deemed wholly dire and quite uncrossable by Lankhmarts and Easterners alike, who in their sailings hug the southern coasts of the northern continents, so that one would have thought the doughtiest sailors would have ere this turned back.

But there was, you see, another reason besides the hope of vast riches—and not chiefly their great courage either, by any means— that Fafhrd and the Mouser kept sailing on in the face of unknown perils and horrid legendry of monsters that crunched ships, and currents swifter than the hurricane, and craterous maelstroms that swallowed vastest vessels in one gulp and even sucked down venturesome islands. It was a reason they spoke of seldom to each other and then only most guardedly, in low tones after long silence in the long silent watches of the night. It was this: that on the edge of darkest sleep, or sluggishly rousing from sail-shadowed nap by day, they briefly saw the shimmer-sprights as beautiful, slim, translucent girls, mirror-image twins, with loving faces and great, glimmering wings. Girls with fine hair like gold or silver clouds and distant eyes that yet brimmed with thought and witchery, girls slim almost beyond belief yet not too slim for the act of love, if only they might wax sufficiently substantial, which was something their smiles and gazes seemed to promise might come to pass. And the two adventurers felt a yearning for these shimmer-girls such as they had never felt for mortal woman, so that they could no more turn back than men wholly ensorceled or stark lockjawed mad.

That morning as their treasure-sprights led them on, looking like rays of rainbow in the sun, the Mouser and Fafhrd were each lost in his secret thoughts of girls and gold, so that neither noted the subtle changes in the ocean surface ahead, from ripply to half smooth with odd little long lines of foam racing east. Suddenly the gold-bugs darted east and the next instant something seized the leopard-boat's keel so that she veered strongly east with a bound like that of the lithe beast for which her class of craft was named. The tall mast was almost snapped and the two heroes were nearly thrown to the deck, and by the time they had recovered from their surprise the *Black Racer* was speeding east, the twin shimmer-sprights winging ahead exultantly, and the two heroes knew that they were in the grip of the Great Eastward Equatorial Current and that it was no fable.

Momentarily forgetting their aerial maybe-girls, they moved to steer north out of it, Fafhrd leaning on the tiller while the Mouser saw to the large single sail, but at that moment a northwest wind struck from astern with gale force, almost driving the *Black Racer* under as it drove her deeper and deeper south into the current. This wind was no mere gust but steadily mounted to storm force, so that it would infallibly have torn their sail away ere they could furl it save that the current below was carrying them east almost as fast as the wind harried them on above.

Then a league to the south they saw three waterspouts traveling east together, gray pillars stretching halfway from earth to sky, at thrice *Black Racer*'s speed at least, indicating that the current was still swifter there. As the two still-astonished sailormen perforce accepted their plight—helpless in the twin grasp of furiously speeding water and air as if their craft were frozen to the sea—the Gray Mouser cried out, "O Fafhrd, now I can well believe that metaphysical fancy that the whole universe is water and our world but one wind-haunted bubble in it."

From where white-knuckled he gripped the tiller, Faf replied, "I'll grant, what with those 'spouts and all this flying foam, it seems right now there's water everywhere. Yet still I can't believe that philosopher's dream of Nehwon-world a bubble, when any fool can see the sun and moon are massy orbs like Nehwon thousands of leagues distant in the high air, which must be very thin out there, by the by.

"But man, this is no time for sophistries. I'll tie the tiller, and while this weird calm lasts (born of near equal speeds of current and wind, and as if the air were cut away before and closing in behind) let's triple-reef the sail and make all snug."

As they worked, the three waterspouts vanished in the distance ahead, to be replaced by a group of five more coming up fast from astern—somewhat nearer this time, for all the while *Black Racer* was being driven gradually but relentlessly south. From almost overhead the midday sun beat down fiercely, for the storm wind blowing near hurricane force had brought no clouds or opaque air with it—in itself a prodigy unparalleled in the recollection of the Mouser or even Fafhrd, a widely sailed man. After several futile efforts to steer north out of the mighty current (which resulted only in the following storm wind shifting perversely north a point or two, driving them deeper south) the two men gave over, thereby admitting their complete inability at present to influence their leopard boat's course.

"At this rate," Fafhrd opined, "we'll cross the Great Equatorial Ocean in a matter of month or two. Lucky we're well provisioned."

The Mouser replied dolefully, "If *Racer* holds together a day amidst those 'spouts and speeds, I'll be surprised."

"She's a stout craft," Fafhrd said lightly. "Just think, Small Gloomy One, the southern continents, unknown to man! We'll be the first to visit 'em!"

"If there are any such. And our planks don't split. Continents?—I'd give my soul for one small isle."

"The first to reach Nehwon's south pole!" Fafhrd daydreamed on. "The first to climb the southern Stardocks! The first to loot the treasures of the south! The first to find what land lies at antipodes from Shadowland, realm of Death! The first—"

The Mouser quietly removed himself to the other side of the shortened sail from Fafhrd and cautiously made his way to the prow, where he wearily threw himself down in a narrow angle of shadow. He was dazed by wind, spray, exertion, the needling sun, and sheer velocity. He dully watched the coppery pinkish shimmer-sprights, which were holding position with remarkable steadiness for them at mast height a ship's length ahead.

After a while he slept and dreamed that one of them detached itself from the other, and came down and hovered above him like a long rosy spectrum and then became a fond- and narrow-visaged green-eyed girl in his arms, who loosened his clothing with slim fingers cool as milk kept in a well, so that looking down closely he saw the nipples of her dainty breasts pressing like fresh-scoured copper thimbles into the curly dark hair on his chest. And she was saying softly and sweetly, head bent forward like his, lips and tongue brushing his ear, "Press on, press on. This is the only way to Life and immortality and paradise." And he replied, "My dearest love, I will."

He woke to Fafhrd's shout and to a fugitive but clear, though almost blinding vision of a female face that was narrow and beautiful, but otherwise totally unlike that of the douce girl of his dream. A sharp, imperious face, wildly alive, made all of red-gold light, the irises of her wide eyes vermilion.

He lifted up sluggishly. His jerkin was unlaced to his waist and pushed back off his shoulders.

"Mouser," Fafhrd said urgently, "when I first glimpsed you but now, you were all bathed in fire!"

Gazing stupidly down, the Mouser saw twin threads of smoke rising from his matted chest where the nipples of his dream had pressed into it. And as he stared at the gray threads, they died. He smelled the stink of burning hair.

He shook his head, blinked, and pushed himself to his feet. "What a strange fancy," he said to Fafhrd. "The sun must have got in your eye. Say, look there!"

The five waterspouts had drawn far ahead and had been replaced by two groups (of three and four respectively) swiftly overtaking *Black Racer* from astern, the four rather distant, the three appallingly close, so that they could see clearly the structure of each: pillars of wild gray water almost a ship's length thick and towering up to thrice mast height, where each broke off abruptly.

And in the distance they could now see still more groups of speeding spouts, and most distant-dim yet speediest of all a gigantic single one that looked leagues thick. A-prow the twin shimmer-sprights led on.

" 'Tis passing strange," Fafhrd averred.

"Does one speak of a covey of waterspouts?" the Mouser wanted to know. "Or a pride? A congeries? A fountain? Or—yes!—a tower! A tower of waterspouts!"

The day passed and half the night, and their weird situation of eastward speeding held—and *Black Racer* held together. The sea was slick and moving in long low swells across which blew thin, long, pale lines of foam. The wind was hurricane force at very least, but the velocity of the Great Equatorial Current had increased to match it.

Overhead, nearly at mast-top, the full moon shone down, scantily scattered about with stars. Her White Huntress light showed the smooth surface of the racing sea to be outdinted near and far by towers of waterspouts racing by in majestical array and yet with fantastical celerity, as if they somehow profited far more from the speed of the current than did *Black Racer*. At mast height and ship's length ahead, the twin shimmer-sprights flew on like flags of silver lace against the dark. All almost silently.

"Fafhrd," the Gray Mouser spoke very softly, as if reluctant to break the silver moonlight's spectral spell, "Tonight I clearly see that Nehwon *is* a vast bubble rising through waters of eternity, with continents and isles afloat inside."

"Yes, and they'd move around—the continents, I mean—and bump each other," Fafhrd said, softly too, albeit a little gruffly. "That is, providing they'd float at all. Which I most strongly doubt."

"They move all orderly, in pre-established harmony," the Mouser replied. "And as for buoyancy, think of the Sinking Land."

"But then where'd be the sun and moon and stars and planets nine?" Fafhrd objected. "All in a jumble in the bubble's midst? That's quite impossible—and ridiculous."

"I'm getting to the stars," the Mouser said. "They're all afloat in even stricter pre-established harmony in the Great Equatorial Ocean, which as we've seen this day and night, speeds around Nehwon's waist once each day—that is, in its effects on the waterspouts, not on *Black Racer.* Why else, I ask you, is it also called the Sea of Stars?"

Fafhrd blinked, momentarily impressed against his will. Then he grinned. "But if this ocean's all afloat with stars," he demanded, "why can't we see 'em all about our ship? Riddle me that, O Sage!"

The Mouser smiled back at him, very composedly. "They're all of 'em inside the waterspouts," he said, "which are gray tubes of water pointing toward heaven—by which I mean, of course, the antipodes of Nehwon. Look up, bold comrade mine, at arching sky and heaven's top. You're looking at the same Great Equatorial Ocean we're afloat in, only halfway around Nehwon from *Black Racer.* You're looking *down* (or *up*, what skills it?) the tubes of the waterspouts there, so you can see the star at bottom of each."

"I'm looking at the full moon too," Fafhrd said. "Don't try to tell me *that's* at the bottom of a waterspout!"

"But I will," the Mouser responded gently. "Recall the gigantic spout like speeding mesa we briefly saw far south of us last noon? That was the moonspout, to invent a word. And now it's raced to sky ahead of us, in half day since."

"Fry me for a sardine!" Fafhrd said with great feeling. Then he sought to collect his comprehension. "And those folk on Nehwon's other side—up *there*—they're seeing a star at the bottom of each waterspout now around us here?"

"Of course not," the Mouser said patiently. "Sunlight drowns out their twinkles for those folk. It's *day* up there, you see." He pointed at the dark near the moon. "Up there, you see, they're bathed in highest noon, drenched in the light of sun, which now is somewhere near us, but hid from us by the thick walls of his sunspout, to coin a word wholly analogous to moonspout."

"Oh, monstrous!" Fafhrd cried. "For if it's day up there, you little fool, why can't we see it here? Why can't we see up there Nehwon lands bathed in light with bright blue sea around 'em? Answer me that!"

"Because there are two different kinds of light," the Mouser said with an almost celestial tranquility. "Seeming the same by every local test, yet utterly diverse. First, there's *direct* light, such as we're getting now from moon and stars up there. Second, there is *reflected* light, which cannot make the really longer journeys, and certainly can't recross—not one faint ray of it—Nehwon's central space to reach us here."

"Mouser," Fafhrd said in a very small voice, but with great certainty, "you're not just inventing words, you're inventing the whole business—on the spur of the moment as you go along."

"Invent the Laws of Nature?" the Mouser asked with a certain horror. "That were far worse than darkest blasphemy."

"Then in the name of all the gods at once!" Fafhrd demanded in a very large voice, "how can the sun be in a waterspout and not boil it all away in an instant in an explosion vast? Tell me at once."

"There are some things man was not meant to know," the Mouser said in a most portentous voice. Then, swiftly switching to the familiar, "or rather, since I am in no way superstitious, there are some things which have not yielded yet to our philosophy. An omission which in this instance I will remedy at once. There are, you see, two different kinds of *energy*, the one pure heat, the other purest light, which cannot boil the tiniest waterdrop—the direct light I've already told you of, which changes almost entirely to heat where e'er it hits, which in turn tells us why reflected light can't make the long trip back through Nehwon's midst. There, have I answered you?"

"Oh damn, damn, damn," Fafhrd said weakly. Then managing to rally himself, if only desperately for a last time, he asked somewhat sardonically, "All right, all right! But just where then is this floating sun you keep invoking, tucked in his vast adamantine-walled waterspout?"

"Look there," the Mouser said, pointing due south, steerside abeam.

Across the moon-silvered gray field of the sea pricked out with speeding towers of waterspouts, almost at the dim distant horizon, Fafhrd saw a solitary gigantic waterspout huge as an island, taller than tallest mesa, moving east at least as swiftly as the rest and as ponderous-relentlessly as a juggernaut of the emperor of the Eastern Lands. The hair rose on the back of Fafhrd's neck, he was harrowed with fear and wonder, and he said not a word, but only stared and stared as the horrendous thing forged ahead in its immensity.

After a while he began also to feel a great weariness. He looked ahead and a little up at the stiffly flapping silver lace of the twin shimmer-sprights before the prow, taking comfort from their nearness and steadiness as if they were *Black Racer's* flags. He slowly lowered himself until he lay prone on the narrow, snugly abutting planks of the deck, his head toward the prow, his chin propped on his hands, still observing the night-sprights.

"You know how groups of stars sometimes wink out mysteriously on clearest Nehwon nights?" the Mouser said lightly and bemusedly.

"That's true enough, they do," Fafhrd agreed, somewhat sleepily.

"That must be because the tubes of their waterspout-walls are bent enough, by a strong gale perchance, to hide their light, keep it from getting out."

Fafhrd mumbled, "If you say so."

After a considerable pause the Mouser asked in the same tones, "Is it not passing strange to think that in the heart of each dark, gray 'spout out there dotting the main, there burns (without any heat) a jewel of blinding, purest diamond light?"

Fafhrd managed what might have been a weighty sigh of agreement.

After another long pause the Mouser said reflectively, as one who tidies up loose ends, "It's easy now to see, isn't it, that the 'spouts small and great must all be tubes? For if they were solid water by some strange chance, they'd suck the oceans dry and fill the heavens with heaviest clouds—nay, with the sea! You get my point?"

But Fafhrd had gone to sleep. In his sleep he dreamed and in that dream he rolled over on his back and one of the shimmer-sprights parted from her sister and winged down to flutter close above him: a long and slender, black-haired form, moon pale, appareled in finest silver-shot black lace that witchingly enhanced her nakedness. She was gazing down at him tenderly yet appraisingly, with eyes that would have been violet had there been more light. He smiled at her. She slightly shook her head, her face grew grave, and she flowed down against him head to heel, her wraithlike fingers busy at the great bronze buckle of his heavy belt, while with one long, night-cool cheek pressed 'gainst his fevered one, she whispered softly and yet most clearly in his ear, each word a symbol finely drawn in blackest ink on moon-white paper, "Turn back, turn back, my dearest man, to Shadowland and Death, for that's the only way to stay alive. Trust only in the moon. Suspect all other prophesies but mine. So now, steer north, steer strongly strongly north."

In his dream, Fafhrd replied, "I can't steer north, I've tried. Love me, my dearest girl," and she answered huskily, "That's as may hap, my love. Seek Death to 'scape from him. Suspect all flaming youth and scarlet shes. Beware the sun. Trust in the moon. Wait for her certain sign."

At that instant Fafhrd's dream was snatched from him and he

roused numbly to the Mouser's sharp cries and to the chilling fugitive glimpse of a face narrow, beauteous, and of most melancholy mien, pale violet-blue of hue and with eyes like black holes. This above wraithlike, like-complected figure, and all receding swift as thought amidst a beating of black wings.

Then the Mouser was shaking him by the shoulders and crying out, "Wake up, wake up! Speak to me, man!"

Fafhrd brushed his face with the back of his hand and mumbled, "Wha' happ'n?"

Crouched beside him, the Mouser narrated rapidly and somewhat breathlessly, "The shimmer-sprights grew restless and 'gan play about the mast like corposants. One buzzed around me shrilly like a wasp, and when I'd driven it off, I saw the other nosing you from toe to waist to head, then nuzzling your neck. Your flesh grew silver-white, as white as death, the whiles the corposant became your glowing shroud. I greatly feared for you and drove it off."

Fafhrd's muddied eyes cleared somewhat whilst the Mouser spoke and when the latter was done, he nodded and said knowingly, "That would be right. She spoke me much of death and at the end she looked like it, poor sibyl."

"Who spoke?" the Mouser asked. "What sibyl?"

"The shimmer-girl, of course," Fafhrd told him. "You know what I mean."

He stood up. His belt began to slip. He stared down wide-eyed at the undone buckle, then drew it up and hooked it together swiftly.

"Fafhrd, I don't know what you're talking of," the Mouser denied, his expression suddenly hooded. "Girl? What girl? Art seeing mirages? Has lack of erotic exercise addled your wits? Have you turned moon-mad lunatic?"

At this point Fafhrd had to speak most sharply and shrewdly to the Mouser to get him to admit that he—the Mouser—had suspected for days that the shimmer-sprights were girls, albeit girls with a strong admixture of the supernatural, insofar as any admixture of anything is able to affect the essential girlness of any such being, which isn't much.

But the Mouser did eventually make the admission although his mind had not the edge-of-sleep honesty of Fafhrd's and tended to drift off to musings on his bubble-cosmos. Yet under strong prompting by Fafhrd he even confessed to his encounter with the sun-red vermilion-eyed shimmer-girl last noon, when he'd looked afire, and upon Fafhrd's insistence recalled the exact words she'd said to him in dream.

"Your red girl spoke of Life and pressing on south to immortality and paradise," Fafhrd summed up thoughtfully, "whilst my dark dear talked of Death and turning back north toward Shadowland and Lankhmar and Cold Waste." Then, with swift-growing excitement and utter amazement at his own insight, "Mouser, I see it all! There are two different pairs of shimmer-girls! The daytime ones (you spoke with one of those) are children of the sun and messengers from the fabled Land of Gods at Nehwon's Life Pole. While the nighttimers, replacing them from dusk to dawn, are minions of the moon, White Huntress' daughters, owing allegiance to the Shadowland, which lies across the world from the Life Pole."

"Fafhrd, hast thou thought," the Mouser spoke from a brown study, "how nicely calculated must be the height and diameter of each waterspout-tube, so that the star at its bottom is seen from every spot in other half of Nehwon (up there, when it's night there) but from no spot in our half down here?—which incidentally explains why stars are brightest at zenith, you see all of each, not just a lens or biconvex meniscus. It seems to argue that some divinity must—" At that point the impact of Fafhrd's words at last sank in and he said in tones less dreamy, "Two different sets of girls? Four girls in all? Fafhrd, I think you're overcomplicating things. By Ildritch's Scimitar—"

"There are two sets of girl twins," Fafhrd overrode him. "That much is certain though all else be lies. And mark you this, Small Man, your sun-girls mean us ill though seeming to promise good, for how reach immortality and paradise except by dying? How reach Godsland except by perishing? The whiles the sun, pure light or no, is baleful, hot, and deadly. But my moon-girls, seeming to mean us ill, intend good only—being at once as cool and lovely as the moon. She said to me in dream, 'Turn back to Death,' which sounds dire. But you and I have lived with Death for dozen years and ta'en no lasting hurt—just as she said herself, 'for that's the only way to stay alive. Seek Death to 'scape from him!' So steer we north at once!—as she directed. For if we keep on south, deeper and deeper into torrid realm of sun ('Beware the sun,' she said!) we'll die for sure, betrayed by your false, lying girls of fire. Recall, her merest touch made your chest smoke. While my girl said, 'Suspect all flaming youth and scarlet shes,' capping my argument."

"I don't see that at all," the Mouser said. "I *like* the sun myself, I always have. His searching warmth is best of medicines. It's you who love the cold and clammy dark, you Cold Waste savage! My girl was sweet and fiery pink with life, while yours was gloomy-spoken and as livid as a corpse, on your own admission. Take her word for things? Not I. Besides, by Ildritch's Scimitar—to get back to that—the simplest explanation is always the best as well as the most elegant. There are *two* shimmer-girls only, the one I spoke in dream and the one you spoke—not four buzzing about bewilderingly and changing guard at dawn and dusk, to our and their confusion. The two girls—only two! —look the same in outward seeming—copper by day, silver by night —but inwardly mine is angel, yours deadly valkyr. As was revealed in dream, your surest guide."

"Now you are quibbling," Fafhrd said decisively, "and are making my head spin, to boot, with 'wildering words. This much is clear to me: We now get ready, and ready *Black Racer*, to steer north, as my poor lovely moon-girl strongly advised me more than once."

"But Fafhrd," the Mouser protested, "we tried again and again to steer north yesterday and failed each time. What reason have you to suppose, you big lug—"

Fafhrd cut in with, " 'Trust only in the moon,' she said. 'Wait for her certain sign.' So wait we, for the nonce, and watch. Look at the sea and sky, idiot boy, and be amazed."

The Mouser was indeed. While they had been disputing, intent only on the cuts and thrusts and parries and ripostes of their word-duel, the smooth surface of the racing Sea of Stars had changed from sleek and slick to mat yet ripply. Great vibrations were speeding across it, making the leopard-boat quiver. The moon-silvered lines of foam were blowing over it less predictably—the hurricane itself, though diminished no whit, was getting flukey, the wind now hot, now cold about their necks. While in the sky were clouds at last, coming in swiftly from northwest and east at once and mounting toward the moon. All of nature seemed to cringe apprehensively, as if in anticipation of some dire event about to hap, heralding war in heaven. The two silvery shimmer-sprights appeared to share this foreboding or presentiment, for they 'gan fly about most erratically, their lace wildly aflow, uttering high cheeping cries and whistlings of alarm against the unnatural silence and at last parting so that one hovered agitatedly to the southeast above the prow, the other near the stern to the northwest.

The rapidly thickening clouds had blotted out most of the stars and mounted almost to the moon. The wind held still, exactly equalling the current's speed. *Black Racer* poised, as if at crest of a gigantic wave. For an instant the sea seemed to freeze. Silence was absolute.

The Mouser looked straight up and uttered from the back of his throat a half choked, high pitched, little scream that froze his comrade's blood. After mastering that shock, Fafhrd looked up too—at just which instant it grew very dark. The hungry clouds had blotted out the moon.

"Why did you so cry out?" he demanded angrily.

The Mouser answered with difficulty, his teeth chattering, "Just before the clouds closed on her, *the moon moved.*"

"How could you know that, you little fool, when the clouds were moving?—which always makes the moon seem to move."

"I don't know, but as sure as I stand firm-footed here, I saw it! *The moon began to move.*"

"Well, if the moon be in a waterspout, as you claim, she's subject to all whims of wind and wave. So what's so blood-curdling strange in her moving?" Fafhrd's frantic voice belied the reasonableness of his question.

"I don't know," the Mouser repeated in a curiously small, strained voice, his teeth still clinking together, "*but I didn't like it.*"

The shimmer-spright at the stern whistled thrice. Her nervously twisting, lacy, silver luminescence stood out plainly in the black night, as did her sister's at the prow.

"It is the sign!" Fafhrd cried hoarsely. "Ready to go about!" And he threw his full weight against the tiller, driving it steerside and so the rudder loadside, to steer them north. *Black Racer* responded most sluggishly, but did break the grip of current and wind to the extent of swinging north a point or two, no more.

A long flat lightning flash split the sky and showed the gray sea to the horizon's rim, where they now saw *two* giant waterspouts, the one due south, the other rushing in from the west. Thunder crashed like armies or armadas meeting at an iron-sonorous Armageddon.

Then all was wildfire and chaos in the night, great crashing waves, and winds that fought like giants whose heads scraped heaven. Whilst round about the ship the shimmer-sprights fought too, now two, now seeming four of them at least as they circled and dipped at and about each other. The frozen sea was ripped, great rags of it thrown skyward, pits opening that seemed to go down to the black, mucky seabottom unknown to man. Lightning and deafening thunderclaps became almost continuous, revealing all. And through that all, *Black Racer* somehow lived, a chip in chaos, Fafhrd and Mouser performing prodigies of seamanship.

And now from the southwest the second giant waterspout drove in like a moving mountain, sending great swells before it that mightily aided Fafhrd's tillering, driving them north, and north again, and again still north. While from the south the first giant 'spout turned back, or so it seemed, and those two (moonspout and sunspout?) battled.

And then of a sudden it was as if *Black Racer* had struck a wall. Fafhrd and Mouser were thrown to the deck and when they had madly struggled to their feet they found to their utter astonishment that their leopard-boat was floating in calm water, while in the distance lightning and thunder played, almost inaudible and unseen to their numbed ears and half-blinded eyes. There were no stars and moon, only thick night. There were no shimmer-sprights. Their sail was split to ribbons, the faint lightning showed. Under his hand Fafhrd felt a looseness in the tiller, as if the whole steering assemblage had been strained to breaking point and only survived by miracle.

The Mouser said, "She lists a little to stern and steerside, don't you think? She's taking water, I trow. Perhaps there's stuff shifted below. Man we the pump. Later we can bend on a new sail."

So they fell to and for some hours worked together silently as in many old times, nursing the leopard-boat and making all new, by light of two lanterns Fafhrd rigged from the mast that burned purest leviathan-oil, for the storm had entirely gone with its lightnings and the dark clouds pressed down.

As the cloud ceiling did, indeed, over all Nehwon that night (and day on other side). Over the subsequent months and years reports drifted in of the Great Dark, as it came mostly to be called, that had shrouded all Nehwon for a space of hours, so that it was never truly known whether the moon had monstrously traveled halfway round the world that time to battle with the sun and then back again to her appointed spot, or no, though there were scattered but persistent disquieting rumors of such a dread journeying glimpsed through fugitive gaps in the cloud-cover, and even that the sun himself had briefly moved to war with her.

After long while Fafhrd said quietly as they took a break from their labors. "It's lonely without the shimmer-sprights, don't you think?"

The Mouser said, "Agreed. I wonder if they'd ever have led us to treasure, or ever so intended? Or would have led us, or one of us, somewhere, either your spright, or mine?"

"I still firmly believe there were four sprights," Fafhrd said. "So either pair of twins might have led us somewhere together without parting us."

"No, there were only two sprights," the Mouser said, "and they were set on leading us in very different directions, antipodean, off from each other." And when Fafhrd did not reply he said after a time,

"Part of me wishes I'd gone with my fiery girl to find what's like to dwell in paradise bathed by the splendid sun."

Fafhrd said, "Part of me wishes I'd followed my melancholy maid to dwell in the pale moon, spending the summer months mayhap in Shadowland." Then, after a silent space, "But man was not meant for paradise, I trow, whether of warmth or coolth. No, never, never, never, never."

"Never shares a big bed with once," the Mouser said.

While they were speaking it had grown light. The clouds had all lifted. The new sail shone. The leviathan lamps burned wanly, their clear beam almost invisible against the paling sky. Then in the farthest distance north the two adventurers made out the loom of a great aurochs couchant, unmistakable sign of the southernmost headland of the Eastern Lands.

"We've weathered Lankhmar continent in a single day and night," the Mouser said.

A breeze sprang up from the south, stirring the still air. They set course north up the long Sea of the East.

VII
THE FROST MONSTREME

"I AM TIRED, Gray Mouser, of these these little brushes with Death," Fafhrd the Northerner said, lifting his dinted, livid goblet and taking a measured sup of sweet ferment of grape laced with bitter brandy.

"Want a big one?" His comrade scoffed, drinking likewise.

Fafhrd considered that, while his gaze traveled slowly yet without stop all the way round the tavern, whose sign was a tarnished and serpentine silver fish. "Perhaps," he said.

"It's a dull night," the other agreed.

True indeed, the interior of the Silver Eel presented a tavern visage as leaden-hued as its wine cups. The hour was halfway between midnight and dawn, the light dim without being murky, the air dank yet not chill, the other drinkers like moody statues, the faces of the barkeep and his bully and servers paralyzed in expressions of petulant discontent, as if Time herself had stopped.

Outside, the city of Lankhmar was silent as a necropolis, while beyond that the world of Nehwon had been at peace—unwar, rather —for a full year. Even the Mingols of the vasty Steppes weren't raiding south on their small, tough horses.

Yet the effect of all this was not calm, but an unfocused uneasiness, a restlessness that had not yet resulted in the least movement, as if it were the prelude to an excruciating flash of cold lightning transfixing every tiniest detail of life.

This atmosphere affected the feelings and thoughts of the tall, brown-tunicked barbarian and his short, gray-clad friend.

"Dull indeed," Fafhrd said. "I long for some grand emprise!"

"Those are the dreams of untutored youth. Is that why you've shaved your beard?—to match your dreams? Both barefaced lies!" the Mouser asked, and answered.

"Why have you let yours grow these three days?" Fafhrd countered.

"I am but resting the skin of my face for a full tweaking of its hairs. And you've lost weight. A wishfully youthful fever?"

"Not that, or any ill or care. Of late you're lighter, too. We are changing the luxuriant musculature of young manhood for a suppler, hardier, more enduring structure suited to great mid-life trials and venturings."

"We've had enough of those," the Mouser asserted. "Thrice around Nehwon, at the least."

Fafhrd shook his head morosely. "We've never really lived. We've not owned land. We've not led men."

"Fafhrd, you're gloomy-drunk!" the Mouser chortled. "Would you be a farmer? Have you forgot a captain is the prisoner of his command? Here, drink yourself sober, or at least glad."

The Northerner let his cup be refilled from two jars, but did not change his mood. Staring unhappily, he continued, "We've neither homes nor wives."

"Fafhrd, you need a wench!"

"Who spoke of wenches?" the other protested. "I mean women. I had brave Kreeshkra, but she's gone back to her beloved Ghouls. While your pert Reetha prefers the hairless land of Eevamarensee."

The Mouser interjected *sotto voce*, "I also had imperious, insolent Hisvet, and you her brave, dramatic queen-slave Frix."

Fafhrd went on, "Once, long ago, there were Friska and Ivivis, but they were Quarmall's slaves and then became free women at Tovilysis. Before them were Keyaira, Hirriwi, but they were princesses, invisibles, loves of one long, long night, daughters of dread Oomforafor and sib of murderous Faroomfar. Long before all of those, in Land of Youth, there were fair Ivrian and slender Vlana. But they were girls, those lovely in-betweens (or actresses, those mysteries), and now they dwell with Death in Shadowland. So I'm but half a man. I need a *mate*. And so do you, perchance."

"Fafhrd, you're mad! You prate of world-spanning wild adventures and then babble of what would make them impossible: wife, home, henchmen, duties. One dull night without girl or fight, and your brains go soft. Repeat, you're mad."

Fafhrd reinspected the tavern and its stodgy inmates. "It stays dull, doesn't it," he remarked, "as if not one nostril had twitched or ear wiggled since I last looked. And yet it is a calm I do not trust. I feel an icy chill. Mouser—"

That one was looking past him. With little sound, or none at all, two slender persons had just entered the Silver Eel and paused appraisingly inside the lead-weighted iron-woven curtains that kept out fog and could turn sword thrusts. The one was tall and rangy as a man, blue-eyed, thin-cheeked, wide-mouthed, clad in jerkin and trousers of blue and long cloak of gray. The other was wiry and supple-seeming as a cat, green-eyed, compact of feature, short thick lips compressed, clothed similarly save the hues were rust red and brown. They were neither young nor yet near middle age. Their smooth unridged brows, tranquil eyes, evenly curving jaws, and long cheek-molding hair—here silvery yellow, there black shot with darkest brown (in turn gold-shotten, or were those golden wires braided in?) —proclaimed them feminine.

That last attribute broke the congealed midnight trances of the assembled dullards, a half dozen of whom converged on the newcomers, calling low invitations and trailing throaty laughs. The two moved forward as if to hasten the encounter, with gaze unwaveringly ahead.

And then—and without an instant's pause or any collision, except someone recoiled slightly as if his instep had been trod on and someone else gasped faintly as if his short ribs had encountered a firm elbow—the two were past the six. If was as if they had simply walked through them, as a man would walk through smoke with no more fuss than the wrinkling of a nostril. Behind them, the ignored smoke fumed and wove a bit.

Now there were in their way the Gray Mouser and Fafhrd, who had both risen and whose hands still indicated the hilts of their scabbarded swords without touching them.

"Ladies—" the Mouser began.

"Will you take wine—?" Fafhrd continued.

"Strengthened against night's chill," the Mouser concluded, sketching a bow, while Fafhrd courteously indicated the four-chaired table from which they'd just risen.

The slender women halted and surveyed them without haste.

"We might—" the smaller purred.

"Provided you let Rime Isle pay for the drinks," the taller concluded in tones bright and swift as running snow water.

At the words "Rime Isle," the faces of the two men grew thoughtful and wondering, as if in another universe someone had said Atlan-
tis or El Dorado or Ultima Thule. Nevertheless they nodded agreement and drew back chairs for the women.

"Rime Isle," Fafhrd repeated conjuringly, as the Mouser did the
honors with cups and jars. "As a child in the Cold Waste and later in
my adolescent piratings, I've heard it and Salthaven City whispered
of. Legend says the Claws point at it—those thin, stony peninsulas
that tip Nehwonland's last northwest corner."

"For once legend speaks true," the electrum-haired woman in blue
and gray said softly yet crisply. "Rime Isle exists today. Salthaven,
too."

"Come," said the Mouser with a smile, ceremoniously handing her
her cup, "it's said Rime Isle's no more real than Simorgya."

"And is Simorgya unreal?" she asked, accepting it.

"No," he admitted with a somewhat startled, reminiscent look. "I
once watched it from a very small ship when it was briefly risen from
the deeps of the Outer Sea. My more venturesome friend"—he nodded toward Fafhrd—"trod its wet shale for a short space to see some
madmen dance with devilfish which had the aspect of black fur cloaks
awrithe."

"North of Simorgya, westward from the Claws," briskly said the
red- and brown-clad woman with black hair shot with glistening dark
bronze and gold. Her right hand holding steady in the air her brimming wine cup where she'd just received it, she dipped her left beneath the table and swiftly slapped it down on the arabesquery of
circle-stained oak, then lifted it abruptly to reveal four small rounds
gleaming pale as moons. "You agreed Rime Isle would play."

With nods abstracted yet polite, the Mouser and Fafhrd each took
up one of the coins and closely studied it.

"By the teats of Titchubi," the former breathed, "this is no *sou
marque*, black dog, no *chien noir*."

"Rime Isle silver?" Fafhrd asked softly, lifting his gaze, eyebrows
a-rise, from the face of the coin toward that of the taller woman.

Her gaze met his squarely. There was the hint of a smile at the ends
of her long lips, back in her cheeks. She said sincerely yet banter-
ingly, "Which never tarnishes."

He said, "The obverse shows a vast sea monster menacing out of
the depths."

She said, "Only a great whale blowing after a deep sound."

The Mouser said to the other woman, "Whilst the reverse depicts a ship-shaped, league-long square rock rising from miles-long swells."

She said, "Only an iceberg hardly half that size."

Fafhrd said, "Well, drink we what this bright, alien coinage has bought. I am Fafhrd, the Gray Mouser he."

The tall woman said, "And I Afreyt, my comrade Cif."

After deep draughts, they put down their cups, Afreyt with a sharp double tap of pewter on oak. "And now to business," she said cliptly, with the faintest of frowns at Fafhrd (it was arguable if there was any frown at all) as he reached for the wine jars. "We speak with the voice of Rime Isle—"

"And dispurse her golden monies," Cif added, her green eyes glinting with yellow flecks. Then, flatly, "Rime Isle is straitly menaced."

Her voice going low, Afreyt asked, "Hast ever heard of the Sea Mingols?" and, when Fafhrd nodded, shifted her gaze to the Mouser, saying, "Most Southrons misdoubt their sheer existence, deeming every Mingol a lubber when off his horse, whether on land or sea."

"Not I," he answered. "I've sailed with Mingol crew. There's one, now old, named Ourph—"

"And I've met Mingol pirates," Fafhrd said. "Their ships are few, each dire. Arrow-toothed water rats—Sea Mingols, as you say."

"That's good," Cif told them both. "Then you'll more like believe me when I tell you that in response to the eldritch prophecy, 'Who seizes Nehwon's crown, shall win her all—' "

"For crown, read north polar coasts," Afreyt interjected.

"And supremely abetted by the Wizard of Ice, Khahkht, whose very name's a frozen cough—"

"Perchance the evilest being ever to exist—" Afreyt supplemented, her eyes a sapphire moon shining frosty through two narrowed, crosswise window slits.

"The Mingols have ta'en ship to harry Nehwon's northmost coasts in two great fleets, one following the sun, the other—the Widdershin Mingols—going against it—"

"For a few dire ships, believe armadas," Afreyt put in, still gazing chiefly at Fafhrd (just as Cif favored the Mouser), and then took up the main tale with, "Till Sunwise and Widdershins meet at Rime Isle, overwhelm her, and fan out south to rape the world!"

"A dismal prospect," Fafhrd commented, setting down the brandy jar with which he'd laced the wine he'd poured for all.

"At least an overlively one," the Mouser chimed in. "Mingols are tireless raptors."

Cif leaned forward, chin up. Her green eyes flamed. "So Rime Isle is the chosen battleground. Chosen by Fate, by cold Khahkht, and the Gods. The place to stop the Steppe horde turned sea raiders."

Without moving, Afreyt grew taller in her chair, her blue gaze flashing back and forth between Fafhrd and his comrade, "So Rime Isle arms, and musters men, and hires mercenaries. The last's my work and Cif's. We need two heroes, each to find twelve men like himself and bring them to Rime Isle in the space of three short moons. You are the twain!"

"You mean there's any other one man in Nehwon like me—let alone a dozen?" the Mouser asked incredulously.

"It's an expensive task, at very least," Fafhrd said judiciously.

Her biceps swelling slightly under the close-fitting rust-red cloth, Cif brought up from beneath the table two tight-packed pouches big as oranges and set one down before each man. The small thuds and swiftly damped chinkings were most satisfying sounds.

"Here are your funds!"

The Mouser's eyes widened, though he did not yet touch his globular sack. "Rime Isle must need heroes sorely. And heroines?—if I might make suggestion."

"That has been taken care of," Cif said firmly.

Fafhrd's middle finger feather-brushed his bag and came away.

Afreyt said, "Drink we."

As the goblets lifted, there came from all around a tiny tinkling as of faery bells; a minute draft, icy chill, stole past from the door; and the air itself grew very faintly translucent, very slightly softening and pearling all things seen—all of which portents grew light-swift by incredible tiger leaps into a stunning, sense-raping clangor of bells big as temple domes and thick as battlements, an ear-splittingly roaring and whining polar wind that robbed away all heat in a trice and blew out flat the iron-and-lead-weighted door drapes and sent the inhabitants of the Silver Eel sailing and tumbling, and an ice fog thick as milk, through which Cif could be heard to cry, " 'Tis icy breath of Khahkht!" and Afreyt, "It's tracked us down!" before pandemonium drowned out all else.

Fafhrd and the Mouser each desperately gripped money bag with one hand and with the other, table, glad it was bolted down to stop its use in brawls.

The gale and the tumult died and the fog faded, not quite as swiftly as it all had come. They unclenched their hands, wiped ice crystals from brows and eyes, lit lamps, and looked around.

The place was a bloodless shambles, silent too as death until the frightened moaning began, the cries of pain and wonder. They scanned the long room, first from their tables, then afoot. Their slender tablemates were not among the slowly recovering victims.

The Mouser intoned, somewhat airily, "were such folk here as we've been searching for? Or have we drunk some drug that—"

He broke off. Fafhrd had taken up his fat little moneybag and headed for the door. "Where away?" Mouser called.

Fafhrd stopped and turned. He called back unsmiling, "North of the Trollsteps, to hire my twelve berserks. Doubtless you'll find your dozen swordsmen-thieves in warmer clime. In three moons less three days, we rendezvous at sea midway between Simorgya and Rime Isle. Till then, fare well."

The Mouser watched him out, shrugged, rummaged up a cup and the brandy jar overset but unbroken, bedewed by the magic blast. The liquor that hadn't spilled made a gratifying large slug. He fingered his moneybag a moment, then teased open the hard knot in its thong. Inside, the leather had a faint amber glow. "A golden orange indeed," he said happily, unmindful of the forms mewling and crawling and otherwise crippling around him, and plucked out one of the packed yellow coins. Reverse, a smoking volcano, possibly snow-clad; obverse, a great cliff rising from the sea and looking not quite like ice or any ordinary rock. What drollery! He gazed again at the iron-curtained doorway. What a huge fool, he thought, to take seriously a quite impossible task set by vanished females most likely dead or at best sorceled beyond reach! Or to make rendezvous at distant date in uncharted ocean betwixt a sunken land and a fabulous one—Fafhrd's geography was even more hopeful than his usual highly imaginative wont.

And just think what rare delights—nay, what whole sets of ecstasies and blisses—this much gold would buy. How fortunate that metal was mindless slave of the man who held it!

He returned the coin, thonged shut the gold and its glow, stood up decisively, then looked back at the table top, near an edge of which the four silver coins still lay cozily flat.

While he regarded them, the grubby hand of a fat server who'd been wedged under the table by the indoor blizzard reached up and whisked them down.

With another shrug, the Mouser ambled rather grandly toward the doorway, whistling between his teeth a Mingol march.

Inside a sphere half again as tall as a man, a skinny old being was busy. On the interior of the sphere was depicted a world map of Nehwon, the seas in blackest blues, the lands in blackest greens and browns, yet all darkly agleam like blued, greened, and browned iron, creating the illusion that the sphere was a giant bubble rising forever through infinite murky, oily waters—as some Lankhmar philosophers assert is veriest truth about Nehwonworld itself. South of the Eastern Lands in the Great Equatorial Ocean there was even depicted a ring-shaped water wall a span across and three fingers high, such as those same philosophers say hides the sun from the half of Nehwon it is floating across, though no blinding solar disk now lay in the bottom of the liquid crater, but only a pale glow sufficient to light the sphere's interior.

Where they were not hid by a loose, light robe, the old being's four long, ever-active limbs were covered by short, stiff black hairs either grizzled or filmed with ice, while Its narrow face was nasty as a spider's. Now It lifted Its leathery lips and nervously questing long-nailed fingers toward an area of the map where a tiny, gleaming black blotch south of blue and amidst brown signified Lankhmar City on the southron coast of the Inner Sea. Was it Its breath that showed frosty, or did Its will conjure up the white wisp that streaked across the black blotch? Whichever, the vapor vanished.

It muttered high-pitched in Mingolish, "They're gone, the bitches. Khahkht sees each fly die, and sends Its shriveling breath where'er It will. Mingols harry, world unwary. Harlots fumble, heroes stumble. And now 'tis time, 'tis time, 'tis time to gin to build the frost mon-streme."

It opened a circular trap door in the South Polar Regions and lowered Itself out on a thin line.

Three days short of three moons later, the Mouser was thoroughly disgusted, bone weary, and very cold. His feet and toes were very, very cold inside fine, fur-lined boots, which slowly rose and fell under his soles as the frosty deck lifted and sank with the long, low swell. He stood by the short mainmast, from the long yard of which (longer than the boom) the loosely furled mainsail hung in frozen festoons. Beyond dimly discerned low prow and stern and mainyard top, vision was utterly blotted out by a fog of tiniest ice crystals, like cirrus cloud come down from Stardock heights, through which the light of an unseen gibbous moon, still almost full swollen, seeped out dark pearl gray. The windlessness and general stillness, contrary to all experience, seemed to make the cold bite deeper.

Yet the silence was not absolute. There was the faint wash and drip —perhaps even tiniest crackling of thinnest ice film—as the hull yielded to the swell. There were the resultant small creakings of the timbers and rigging of *Flotsam.* And beneath or beyond these, still fainter sounds lurked in the fringes of the inaudible. A part of the Mouser's mind that worked without being paid attention strained ceaselessly to hear those last. He was of no mind to be surprised by a Mingol flotilla, or single craft even. *Flotsam* was transport, not warship, he repeatedly warned himself. Very strange some of those last real or fancied sounds were that came out of the frigid fog—shatterings of massive ice leagues away, the thump and splash of mighty oars even farther off, distant doleful shriekings, still more distant deep minatory growlings, and a laughter as of fiends beyond the rim of Nehwon. He thought of the invisible fliers that had troubled the snowy air halfway up Stardock when Fafhrd and he had climbed her, Nehwon's loftiest peak.

The cold snapped that thought chain. The Mouser longed to stamp his feet, flail his hands cross-front against his sides, or—best!—warm himself with a great burst of anger, but he perversely held off, perhaps so ultimately relief would be greater, and set to analyze his disgusted weariness.

First off, there'd been the work of finding, winning, and mastering twelve fighter-thieves—a rare breed to begin with. And training 'em! —half of 'em had to be taught the art of the sling, and two (Mog help him!) swordsmanship. And the choosing of the likeliest two for corporals—Pshawri and Mikkidu, who were now sleeping snug below with their double squad, damn their hides!

Concurrent with that, there'd been the searching out of Old Ourph and gathering of his Mingol crew of four. A calculated risk, that. Would Mingol mariners fight fiercely 'gainst their own in the pinch? Mingols were ever deemed treacherous. Yet 'twas always good to have some of the enemy on your side, the better to understand 'em. And from them he might even get wider insight into the motives behind the present Mingol excursions naval.

Concurrent with *that,* the selection, hire, patching, and provisioning of *Flotsam* for its voyage.

And then the study needed! Beginning with poring over ancient charts filched from the library of the Lankhmar Starsmen and Navigators Guild, the refreshing of his knowledge of wind, waves, and celestial bodies. And the responsibility!!for no fewer than seventeen men, with no Fafhrd to share it and spell him while he slept—to lick 'em into shape, doctor their scurvies, probe under water for 'em with boathook when they tumbled overboard (he'd almost lost thumb-footed Mikkidu that way the first day out), keep 'em in good spirits but in their places too, discipline 'em as required. (Come to think of it, that last was sometimes delight as well as duty. How quaintly Pshawri squealed when shrewedly thwacked with Cat's-Claw's scabbard!—and soon would again, by Mog!)

Lastly, the near moon-long perilous voyage itself!!!Northwest from Lankhmar across the Inner Sea. Through a treacherous gap in the Curtain Wall (where Fafhrd had once sought sequined sea-queens) into the Outer Sea. Then a swift, broad reach north with the wind on their load side until they sighted the black ramparts of No-Ombrulsk, which shared the latitude of sunken Simorgya. There he had nosed *Flotsam* due west, away from all land and almost into the teeth of the west wind, which blew a little on their steer side. After four days of that weary, close reach, they had arrived at the undistinguished patch of troubled ocean that marked Simorgya's grave, according to the independent cipherings of the Mouser and Ourph, the one working from his stolen charts, the other counting knots in grimy Mingol calculating cords. Then a swift two-day broad reach north again, while air and sea grew rapidly colder, until by their reckonings they were half-journey to the latitude of the Claws. And now two days of dismal beating about in one place await for Fafhrd, with the cold increasing steadily until, this midnight, clear skies had given way to the ice fog in which *Flotsam* lay becalmed. Two days in which to wonder if Fafhrd would manage to find this spot, or even come at all. Two days in which to get bored with and maddened by his sacred, rebellious crew and dozen soldier-thieves—all snoring warm below, Mog flog 'em! Two days to wonder *why* in Mog's name he'd spent all but four of his Rime Isle doubloons on this insane voyage, on *work* for himself, instead of on wine and women, rare books and art objects, in short on sweet bread and circuses for himself alone.

And finally, superlastly, the suspicion growing toward conviction that Fafhrd had never started out from Lankhmar at all!!!!that he'd strode so nobly, so carkingly high-minded, out of the Silver Eel with his bag of gold—and instantly begun to spend it on those very same delights which the Mouser (inspired by Fafhrd's seeming-good example) had denied himself.

In a pinnacle of exasperation, a mountaintop of rage, the Mouser seized the padded striker from its mainmast hook and smote the ship's gong a blow mighty enough to shatter the gelid bronze. In fact, he was mildly surprised that *Flotsam*'s frosty deck wasn't showered with sharp-edged frozen shards of brown metal. Whereupon he smote it again and again and again, so that the gong swung like a signboard in a hurricane, and meanwhile he jumped up and down, adding to the general alarm the resounding thuds of his feet (and haply warming them).

The forward hatch was flung back from below and Pshawri shot up out of it like a jack-in-the-box, to scurry to the Mouser and stand before him mad-eyed. The corporal major was followed in a pouring rush by Mikkidu and the rest of the two squads, most of them half-naked. After them—and far more leisurely—came Gavs and the other Mingol crewman off watch, thonging their black hoods closely under their yellow chins, while Ourph came ghosting up behind this captain, though the two other Mingols properly kept to their stations at tiller and prow. The Mouser was vastly surprised. So his scabbard thwackings had actually done some good!

Measuredly beating the padded striker head in the cupped palm of his right hand, the Mouser observed, "Well, my small stealers"—(all of the thieves were in fact at least a finger-breadth shorter than the Gray One)—"it appears you've missed a beating, *barely*," his face in a hideous grin as he closely surveyed the large areas of bare flesh exposed to the icy air.

He went on, "But now we must keep you warm—a sailorly necessity in this clime, for which each of you is responsible on pain of flogging, I'll have you know." His grin became more hideous still. "To evade night ramming attack, *man the sweeps!*"

The ragged dozen poured past him to snatch up the long, slender oars from their rack between mainmast and mizzen, and drop their looms into the ten proper locks, and stand facing prow at the ready, feet braced against sweeping studs, oar handles against chests, blades poised overside in the fog. Pshawri's squad was stationed steer-side, Mikkidu's load-side, while major and minor corporals supervised fore and aft.

After a quick glance at Pshawri, to assure himself every man was at his station, the Mouser cried, "Flotsamers! One, two, three—sweep!" and tapped the gong, which he steadied and damped by its edge gripped in his right hand. The ten sweepsmen dipped blades into the unseen salt water and thrust heavily forward against the tholes.

"Recover!" the Mouser growled slowly, then gave the gong another tap. The ship began to move forward and the wash of the swell became tiny slaps against the hull.

"And now keep to it, you clownish, ill-clad cut-purses!" he cried. "Master Mikkidu! Relieve me at the gong! Sir Pshawri, keep 'em sweepin' evener!" And as he handed the striker to the gasping corporal minor, he dipped his lips toward the cryptic wrinkled face of

Ourph and whispered, "Send Trenchi and Gib below to fetch 'em their warm duds on deck."

Then he allowed himself a sigh, generally pleased yet perversely dissatisfied because Pshawri hadn't given him excuse to thwack him. Well, one couldn't have everything. Odd to think of a Lankhmar second-story man and Thieves Guild malcontent turned promising soldier-sailor. Yet natural enough—there wasn't that much difference between climbing walls and rigging.

Feeling warmer now, he thought more kindly of Fafhrd. Truly, the Northerner had not yet missed rendezvous; it was *Flotsam*, rather, that'd been early. Now was the time appointed. His face grew somber as he permitted himself the coldly realistic thought (of the sort no one likes) that it would indeed be miracle if he and Fafhrd did find each other in this watery waste, not to mention the icy fog. Still, Fafhrd was resourceful.

The ship grew silent again except for the brush and drip of the sweeps, the clink of the gong, and the small commotions as Pshawri briefly relieved oarsmen hurrying into the clothes the Mingols had fetched. The Mouser turned his attention to the part of his mind that kept watch on the fog's hiddenmost sounds. Almost at once he turned questioningly toward Old Ourph. The dwarfish Mingol flapped his arms slowly up and down. Straining his ears, the Mouser nodded. Then the beat of approaching wings became generally audible. Something struck the icy rigging overhead and a white shape hurtled down. The Mouser threw up his right arm to fend it off and felt his wrist and forearm strongly gripped by something that heaved and twisted. After a moment of breathless fear, in which his left hand snatched at his dirk, he reached it out instead and touched the horny talons tight as gyves around his wrist, and found rolled around a scaly leg a small parchment, the threads of which he cut with sharpened thumbnail. Whereupon the large white hawk left his wrist and perched on the short, round rod from which the ship's gong hung.

Then by flame of fat candle a Mingol crewman fetched after lighting it from the firebox, the Mouser read in Fafhrd's huge script writ very small:

> *Ahoy, Little Man!—for 'tis unlike there's vessel closer in this wavy wilderness. Burn a red flare and I'll be there.*
>
> F.

And then in blacker but sloppier letters suggesting hurried afterthought:

Let's feign mutual attack when we meet, to train our crews.
Agreed!

The white flame, burning steady and bright in the still air, showed the Mouser's delighted grin and also the added expression of incredulous outrage as he read the postscript. Northerners as a breed were battle-mad, and Fafhrd the feyest.

"Gib, get quill and squid ink," he commanded. "Sir Pshawri, take slow-fire and a red flare to the mainmast top and burn it there. Yarely! But if you fire *Flotsam*, I'll nail you to the burning deck!"

Some moments later, as the Mouser-enlisted small cat-burglar steadily mounted the rigging, though additionally encumbered by a boathook, his captain reversed the small parchment, spread it flat against the mast, and neatly inscribed on its back by light of candle, which Gib held along with the inkhorn:

Madman Most Welcome!—I'll burn them one each bell. I do not
agree. My crew is trained already.

                                                              M.

He shook the note to dry it, then gingerly wrapped it closely around the glaring hawk's leg, just above talons and threaded it tight. As his fingers came away, the bird bated with a shriek and winged off into the fog without command. Fafhrd had at least his avian messengers well trained.

A red glare, surprisingly bright, sprang forth from the fog at the masthead and rose mysteriously a full ten cubits above the top. Then the Mouser saw that, for safety's sake, his own and his ship's, the little corporal major had fixed the flare to the boathook's end and thrust it aloft, thereby also increasing the distance at which it could be seen— by at least a Lankhmar league, the Mouser hurriedly calculated. A sound thought, he had to admit, almost a brilliancy. He had Mikkidu reverse *Flotsam*'s course for practice, the steerside sweepsman pulling water to swing the ship their way. He went to the prow to assure himself that the heavily muffled Mingol there was steadily scanning the fog ahead, next he returned to the stern, where Ourph stood by his tillerman, both equally thick-coated against the cold.

Then, as the red flare glowed on and the relative quiet of steady sweeping returned, the Mouser's ears unwilled resumed their work of searching the fog for strange sounds, and he said softly to Ourph without looking at him, "Tell me now, Old One, what you really

think about your restless nomad brotheren and why they've ta'en to
ship instead of horse."

"They rush like lemmings, seeking death . . . for others," the an-
cient croaked reflectively. "Gallop the waves instead of flinty steppes.
To strike down cities is their chiefest urge, whether by land or sea.
Perhaps they flee the People of the Ax."

"I've heard of those," the Mouser responded doubtfully. "Think
you they'd league with Stardock's viewless fliers, who ride the icy airs
above the world?"

"I do not know. They'll follow their clan wizards anywhere."

The red flare died. Pshawri came down rather jauntily from the top
and reported to his dread captain, who dismissed him with a glare
which was unexpectedly terminated by a broad wink and the command to burn another flare at the next bell, or demihour. Then turning once more to Ourph, the Mouser spoke low: "Talking of wizards,
do you know of Khahkht?"

The ancient let five heartbeats go by, then croaked, "Khahkht is
Khahkht. It is no tribal sorcerer, 'tis sure. It swells in farthest north
within a dome—some say a floating globe—of blackest ice, from
whence It watches the least deeds of men, devising evil every chance
It gets, as when the stars are right—better say wrong—and all the
Gods asleep. Mingols dread Khahkht and yet . . . whene'er they
reach a grand climacteric they turn to It, beseech It ride ahead before
their greatest, bloodiest centaurings. Ice is Its favored quarter, ice Its
tool, and icy breath Its surest sign save blink."

"Blink?" the Mouser asked uneasily.

"Sunlight or moonlight shining back from ice," the Mingol replied.
"Ice blink."

A soft white flash paled for an instant the dark, pearly fog, and
through it the Mouser heard the sound of oars—mightier strokes than
those of *Flotsam*'s sweeps and set in a more ponderous rhythm, yet
oars or sweeps indubitably, and swiftly growing louder. The Mouser's face grew gladsome. He peered about uncertainly. Ourph's pointing finger stabbed dead ahead. The Mouser nodded, and pitching his
voice trumpet-shrill to carry, he hailed forward, "Fafhrd! Ahoy!"

There was a brief silence, broken only by the beat of *Flotsam*'s
sweeps and of the oncoming oars, and then there came out of the fog
the heart-quickening though still eerie cry, "Ahoy, small man!
Mouser, well met in wildering waters! And now—on guard!"

The Mouser's glad grin grew frantic. Did Fafhrd seriously intend
to carry out *in fog* his fey suggestion of a feigned ships-battle? He

looked with a wild questioning at Ourph, who shrugged hugely for one so small.

A brighter white blink momentarily lightened the fog ahead. Without pausing an instant for thought, the Mouser shouted his commands. "Load-side sweeps! pull water! Yarely! Steer-side, push hard!" And unmindful of the Mingol manning it, he threw himself at the tiller and drove it steer-side so that *Flotsam*'s rudder would strengthen the turning power of the load-side sweeps.

It was well he acted as swiftly as he did. From out the fog ahead thrust a low, thick, sharp-tipped, glittering shaft that would otherwise have rammed *Flotsam*'s bow and split her in twain. As it was, the ram graced *Flotsam*'s side with shuddering rasp as the small ship veered abruptly load-side in response to the desperate sweeping of its soldier-thieves.

And now, following its ram, the white, sharp prow of Fafhrd's ship parted the gleam-shot fog. Almost incredibly lofty that prow was, high as a house and betokening ship as huge, so that *Flotsam*'s men had to crane necks up at it and even the Mouser gasped in fear and wonder. Fortunately it was yards to steerward as *Flotsam* continued to veer loadward, or else the smaller ship had been battered in.

Out of the fog dead ahead there appeared a flatness traveling sideways. A yard above the deck, it struck the mast, which might have snapped except that the flatness broke off first and there dropped with a clash at the Mousers feet something which further widened his eyes: the great ice-crusted blade and some of the loom of an oar twice the size of *Flotsam*'s sweeps, and looking for all the world like a dead giant's fingernail.

The next huge oar missed the mast, but struck Pshawri a glancing blow and sent him sprawling. The rest missed *Flotsam* by widening margins. From the vast and towering, white, glittering bulk already vanishing in the fog there came a mighty cry: "Oh coward! To turn aside from battle challenge! Oh, crafty coward! But go on guard again! I'll get you yet, small one, howe'er you dodge!"

Those huge, mad words were followed by an equally insane laughter. It was the sort of laughter the Mouser had heard before from Fafhrd in perilous battle plights, now madder than ever, fiendish even, but it was loud as if there were a dozen Fafhrds voicing it in unison. Had he trained his berserks to echo him?

A clawlike hand gripped the Mouser's elbow hard. Then Ourph was pointing at the big, broken oar end on the deck. "It's nought but ice." The old Mingol's voice resonated with superstitious awe. "Ice forged in Khahkht's chill smithy." He let go Mouser and, swiftly stooping, raised the thing in black-mitted hands widely spaced, as one might a wounded deadly serpent, and of a sudden hurled it overboard.

Beyond him, Mikkidu had lifted Pshawri's shoulders and bloodied head from the deck. But now he was peering up at his captain over his still, senseless comrade. In his wild eyes was a desperate questioning.

The Mouser hardened his face. "Sweep on, you sluggards," he commanded measuredly. "Push strongly. Mikkidu, let crewmen see to Pshawri, you chink gong for the sweeps. Swiftest beat! Ourph, arm your crew. Send down for arrows and your bows of horn—and for my soldiers their slings and ammunition. Leaden ball, not rock. Gavs, keep close watch astern, Trenchi at prow. Yarely all!"

The Gray One looked grimly dangerous and was thinking thoughts he hated. A thousand years ago in the Silver Eel, Fafhrd had announced he'd hire twelve berserkers, madmen in battle. But had his dear friend, now demon-possessed, guessed then just how mad his dozen dements would be, and that their craziness would be catching? and infect himself?

Above the ice fog, the stars glittered like frost candles, dimmed only by the competing light of the gibbous moon low in the southwest, where in the distance the front of an approaching gale was rolling up the thick carpet of ice crystals floating in air.

Not far above the pearly white surface, which stretched to all horizons save the southwest, the messenger hawk the Mouser had released was winging east. As far as eye could see, no other living thing shared its vast-arched loneliness, yet the bird suddenly veered as if attacked, then frantically beat its wings and came to a twisting stop in mid-air, as if it had been seized and held helpless. Only there was nothing to be seen sharing the clear air with the thrashing bird.

The scrap of parchment around its leg unrolled like magic, lay flat in the air for a space, then rolled itself around the scaly leg again. The white hawk shot off desperately to the east, zigzagging as if to dodge pursuit and flying very close to the white floor, as if ready at any moment to dive into it.

A voice came out of the empty air at the point where the bird had been released, soliloquizing, "There's profit enow and more in this leaguer of Oomforafor of Stardock and the Khahkht of the Black Ice, if my ruse works—and it will! Dear devilish sisters, weep!—your lovers who defiled you are dead men already, though they still breathe and walk awhile. Delayed revenge long savored and denied is sweeter than swift. And sweetest of all when the ones you hate love, but are forced to kill, each other. For if my notes effect not that mebliss, my name's not Faroomfar! And now, wing sound-swift! my flat steed of air, my viewless magic rug."

The strange, low fog stayed thick and bitter cold, but Fafhrd's garb of reversed snow-fawn fur was snug. Gauntleted hand on the low figurehead—a hissing snow serpent—he gazed back with satisfaction from *Sea Hawk*'s prow at his oarsmen, still rowing as strongly as when he'd first commanded them on sighting Mouser's red flare from the masthead. They were staunch lads, when kept busy and battered as needed. Nine of them tall as he, and three taller—his corporals Skullick and Mannimark and sergeant Skor, the last two hid by the fog where Skor clinked time at the stern. Each petty officer immediately commanded a squad of three men.

And *Sea Hawk* was a staunch sailing galley!—a little longer and narrower of beam and with much taller mast, rigged fore and aft, than the Gray Mouser's ship (though Fafhrd could not know that, never having seen *Flotsam*).

Yet he frowned slightly. Pelly should be back by now, provided Mouser had sent a return message, and the little gray man never lost chance to talk, whether by tongue or pen. It was time he visited the top anyhow—the Mouser might burn another flare, and Skullick wake-dream on watch. But as he neared the mast, a seven-foot ghost loomed up—a ghost in turned gray otter's fur.

"How now, Skullick?" Fafhrd rasped, looking up their half span's difference in height. "Why have you left your station? Speak swiftly, scum!" And without other warning or preparation, he struck his corporal major a short-traveling jolt in the midriff that jarred him back a step and (rather illogically) robbed him of most of the breath he had to speak with.

"It's cold . . . as witch's womb . . . up there," Skullick gasped with pain and difficulty. "And my relief's . . . o'erdue."

"From now on you'll wait on station for your relief until Hell freezes over, and haply you too. But you're relieved." And Fafhrd struck him again in the same crucial spot. "Now water the rowers, four measures of water to one of usquebaugh—and if you take more than two gulps of the last, I'll surely know!"

He turned away abruptly, reached the mast in two strides, and climbed it rhythmically by the pins of its bronze collars, past the mainyard, to which the big sail was snugly furled, past the peak, until his gloved hands gripped the short, horizontal bar of the crow's-perch. As he drew himself up by them, it was a wonder how the fog gave way without gradation to star-ceilinged air, as though a fine film, impalpable yet tough, confined the ice motes, held them down. When he stood on the bar and straightened himself, he was waist-deep in fog so thick he could barely see his feet. He and the mast top were scudding through a pearly sea, strongly propelled by the invisible rowers below. The stars told him *Sea Hawk* was still headed due west. His sense of direction had worked truly in the fog below. Good!

Also, the feckless Skullick had spoken true. It was cold indeed as a she-demon's privies, yet wonderfully bracing. He noted the new wind sweeping up the fog in the southwest, and north of that the spot where he'd picked up the Mouser's flare on the horizon's brim. The deformed fat moon was there now, almost touching it, yet still most bright. If the Mouser burned another flare, it ought to be higher, because Fafhrd's rowing should be bringing the ships together. He searched the west closely to make sure another red spark wasn't being drowned by Nehwon's strong moonlight.

He saw a black speck against the lopsided, bright pearl orb. As he watched, it rapidly increased in size, grew wings, and with a white beat of them landed with jolting twin-talon grip on Fafhrd's gauntleted wrist.

"You're ruffled, Pelly. Who has troubled you?" he asked as he snapped threads and unrolled from leg the parchment scrap. He recognized the start of his own note, flipped it over, and by the flat moonlight read the Mouser's.

> *Madman Most Welcome!—I'll burn them one each bell. I do* not
> *agree. My crew is trained already.*
>
> M.

> *No feigned attack, you cur once my friend, but earnest deadly. I*
> *want no less than your destruction, dog. To the death!*

Fafhrd read the salutation and first sentence with great relief and joy. The next two sentences made him frown in puzzlement. But with the dire postscript, his face fell, and his expression became one of deep dread and utter dolefulness. He hurriedly rescanned the script to see how the letters and words were formed. They were the Mouser's unquestionably, the postscript slightly scrawled 'cause writ more swift. Something he'd missed nagged briefly at his mind, then was forgot. He crumpled the parchment and thrust it deep in his pouch.

He said to himself in the naked, low tones of a man plunged into nightmare, "I can't believe and yet cannot deny. I know when Mouser jests and when speaks true. There must be swift-striking madness in these polar seas, perhaps loosed by that warlock Afreyt named . . . Ice Wizard . . . It . . . Khahkht. And yet . . . and yet I must ready *Sea Hawk* for total war, howe'er it grieve me. A man must be prepared for *all* events, no matter how they chill and tear his heart."

He gave the west a final glance. The front of the southwest gale was close now, sweeping up the ice crystals ahead of it. It was a chord that cut off a whole sector of the circular white fog-sea, replacing it with naked black ocean. From that came a fleeting white glow that made Fafhrd mutter, "Ice blink."

Then closer still, hardly a half-score bowshots away, still in the fog yet near its wind-smitten edge, a redness flared bright, then died.

Fafhrd sank swiftly into the fog, going down the mast in swift hand-over-hand drops, his boots hardly touching the bronze collar pins.

Inside the dark-mapped globular vacuity, It ceased Its dartings, held Itself rigidly erect, facing away from the water-walled equatorial sun disk, and intoned in voice like grinding ice floes, "Heed me, smallest atomies, that in rime seas seethe and freeze. Hear me, spirits of the cold, then do straightway what you're told. Ships are meeting, heroes greeting; gift to each, from each, of death. Monstreme lurk, in icy murk, picket of the Mingol work 'gainst each city, hearth, and kirk. If they 'scape the Viewless ruse, make yourself of direst use. Vessels shatter! Manbones scatter! Bloody flesh, bones darkness splatter!—every splinter, every tatter! Deeds of darkness, darkness merit—so, till's done, put out the sun!"

And with reptilian swiftness It whipped around and clapped a blacked-iron lid over the softly flaring, walled solar disk, which plunged the spherical cavity into an absolute blackness, wherein It whispered grindingly and chucklesome, ". . . and the Ghouls conjured the sun out of Heaven, quotha! Ghouls, indeed!—ever o'erboastful. Khahkht never boasts, but does!"

At the foot of *Flotsam*'s mainmast the Gray Mouser gripped Pshawri by the throat, but forbore to shake him. Beneath bloody head-circling bandage, his corporal major's white-circled pupils stared at him defiantly from bloodless face.

"Was one light battle-tap enough to make a crack for all your brains to leak out?" the Mouser demanded. "*Why did you fire that flare*, and so reveal us to our enemy?"

Pshawri winced but continued to oppose his gaze to the captain's glare. "You ordered it—and did not countermand," he stated stubbornly.

The Mouser sputtered, but had to allow the truth of that. The fool had been obedient, even if utterly lacking in judgment. Soldiers and their blind devotion to duty! especially spoken order! Most odd to think that this faithful idiot was yesterday a burglar-thief, child of treachery and lies and blinkered selfishness. The Mouser had also guiltily to admit he could have countermanded his command, paying lip service to logic and making allowance for stupidity, and particularly have noted what the fool was up to when he mounted the mast a second time. Pshawri was clearly still shaken from his head blow, poor devil, and at least he had been quick enough in casting boathook and flare into the sea when the Mouser'd roared at him from below.

"Very well," he said gruffly, releasing his grip. "Next time think too—if there's time—and there was!—as well as act. Ask Ourph for a noggin of white brandy. Then be forward lookout with Gavs—I'm doubling them bow and stern."

And with that, the Mouser himself took up the general work of trying to pierce the stilly fog with eyes and ears, wondering the while unhappy and uneasy about the nature of Fafhrd's madness and of the vast, fell vessel he'd built, bought, commandeered, or perchance got from Ningauble or other sorcerer. Or sorcerers?—it had surely been big and weird enough to be the chattel of several archimages! Conceivably a refitted prison hulk from rimy No-Ombrulsk. Or, illest thought of all (stemming from Ourph's fears 'bout the vanished oar shard), was the sorcerer Khahkht?—and some link 'twixt that warlock and mad Fafhrd?

Flotsam ghosted on, the sweepsmen pushing only enough to keep her under way. Mouser had early ordered slowest beat to conserve their strength.

"Three bells," Ourph softly called.

Dawn nighs, the Mouser thought.

Pshawri could not have been long at the bow when his cry came back, "Clear sea ahead! And wind!"

The fog thinned to wisps torn and tossed aft by the eddying, frosty air. The gibbous moon was firmly bedded on the western horizon, yet still sent an eerie white glare, while south of her a few lonely stars hung in the sky. That was uncanny, the Mouser thought, for the imminent dawn should already have extinguished them. He faced east—and almost gasped. Above the low, moonlit fog bank, the heavens were darker than ever, the night was starless, while due east on the fog bank there rested a sliver of blackness blacker than any night could be, as if a black sun were rising that shot out beams of a darkness powerful and active as light—not light's absence, but its enemy-opposite. And from that same thickening sliver, along with the potent darkness, there seemed to come a cold more intense and differing in kind from that of the bitter southwest wind striking behind his right ear.

"Ship on our load-side beam!" Pshawri cried shrilly.

At once the Mouser dropped his gaze and sighted the stranger vessel, about three bowshots distant, just emerged from the fog bank and equally illumined by the moon glare, and headed straight at *Flotsam*. At first he took it for Fafhrd's icy leviathan come again, then saw it was small as his own ship, maybe narrower of beam. His thoughts zigzagged wildly—did mad Fafhrd command a fleet? was it a Sea Mingol warcraft? or still other pirate? or from Rime Isle? He forced himself to think more to the purpose.

His heart pulsed twice. Then, "Make sail, my Mingols all!" he commanded. "Odd-numbered sweepsmen! rack your long tools, then arm! Pshawri! command 'em!" And he grasped the tiller as the steersman let it go.

Aboard *Sea Hawk*, Fafhrd saw *Flotsam*'s low hull and short masts and long, slantwise main and mizzen yards blackly silhouetted against the spectrally white, misshapen moon awash in the west. In the same instant he at last realized what it was that had nagged his mind at the mast top. He whipped gauntlet from his right hand, plunged the latter into his pouch, plucked out the parchment scrap, and this time reread his own note—and saw below it the damning postscript he knew he'd never written. Clearly both postscripts, penned in deceptive scrawls, were cunning forgeries, however done o'erhead in birds' realm.

So even as he felt the wind and commanded, "Skor! Take your squad. Prepare to make sail!" he drew a favorite arrow from the quiver ready beside him on the deck, threaded the note around it in studied haste, swiftly uncased and strung his great bow, and with a curt prayer to Kos bent it to its muscle-cracking extreme and sent the pet arrow winging high into the black sky toward the moon and the black two-master.

Aboard *Flotsam*, the Mouser felt the shiver of superadded apprehension which mounted while he watched his Mingols purposefully struggling with frozen lines and ties in the freshening chilly wind, until it culminated in the *chunk* of an arrow almost vertically into the deck scarce a cubit from his foot. So the small, moonlit sailing galley (for he had meanwhile identified it as such a craft) was signaling attack! Yet the range was still so great that he knew of only one bowman in Nehwon who could have made that miraculous shot. Not letting go the tiller, he stooped and severed the threads of the pale parchment wrapped tightly just behind the arrow's half-buried head, and read (or rather mostly reread) the two notes, his with the devilish postscript he'd never seen before. Even as he finished, the characters became unreadable from the black beams of antisun fighting down the moon rays and beginning to darken that orb. Yet he made the same deduction as had Fafhrd, and hot tears of joy were squeezed from his chilled eye sockets as he realized that whatever impossible-seeming sleights of ink and voice had been worked this night, his friend was sane and true.

There was a protracted sharp crackling as the last ties of the sails were loosed and wind filled them, breaking their frozen folds and festoons. The Mouser bore on the tiller, heading *Flotsam* into what was now a strengthening gale. But at the same time he sharply commanded, "Mikkidu! burn three flares, two red, one white!"

Aboard *Sea Hawk*, Fafhrd saw the blessed treble sign flare up in gathering unnatural murk, even as his reefed sails filled and he turned his own craft into the wind. He ordered, "Mannimark! answer those flares with like. Skullick, you dolt! slack your squad's bows. Those to the west are friends!" Then he said to Skor beside him, "Take the helm. My friend's ship is on close-hauled southron course like ours. Work over to her. Lay us alongside."

Aboard *Flotsam*, the Mouser was giving like directions to Ourph. He was cheered by sight of Fafhrd's flares matching his own, though he did not need their testimony. Now he longed for talk with Fafhrd. Which would be soon. The gap of black water between ships was narrowing rapidly. He wasted a moment musing whether mere chance or else some goddess had steered his comrade's arrow aside from his heart. He thought of Cif.

Aboard both ships, almost in unison, Pshawri and Mannimark cried out fearfully, "Ship close astern!"

Out of the torn and darkening fog bank, driving with preternatural rapidity into the teeth of the gale on a course to smash them both, there had silently come a craft monstrous in size and aspect. It might well have remained unseen until collision, save that the weird rays of the rising black sun striking its load side engendered there a horrid, pale reflection, not natural white light at all, but a loathy, colorless luminescence—a white to make the flesh crawl, a cave-toad, fish-belly white. And if the substance making the reflection had any texture at all, it was that of ridged and crinkled gray horn—dead men's finger-nails.

The leprous Hel-glow showed the demonic craft to have thrice the freeboard of any natural ship. Its towering prow and sides were craggy and jagged, as if it were cast entire of ice in a titanic rough mold left over from the Age of Chaos, or else hacked by jinn into crude ship-likeness from a giant berg broken off from glacier vast. And it was driven by banks of oars long and twitchy as insect legs or limbs of myriapod, yet big as jointed yards or masts, as they sent it scuttling monstrously across black ocean vast. And from its lofty deck, as if hurled by demon ballistas, catapults, and mangonels, there now came hurtling down around *Flotsam* and *Sea Hawk* great blocks of ice which sent up black, watery volcanoes. While from the jagged top of its foremast—pale, big, and twisted as a thunder-blasted pine long dead—there shot out two thin beams of blackest black, like rays of antisun but more intense, which smote the Gray Mouser and Fafhrd each in the chest with deep-striking chill and sick, spreading dizziness and weakening of will.

Nevertheless they each managed to give rapid, stinging commands, and the two ships turned away in time's nick from each other and the oared deathberg striking between them. *Flotsam* had had only to turn further into the wind and so come round smoothly and swiftly. But *Sea Hawk* perforce must jibe. Its sail shivered a space, then filled abruptly on the other side with noise like thunder crack, but the stout Ool Krut canvas did not split. Both ships scudded north before the gale.

Behind them the eldritch bergship slowed and turned with super-natural celerity, spider-walked by its strange oars, and came in mon-strous pursuit, gigantically oared on. And although no word was voiced or sign given by the pursued—almost as if by taking no notice of it, the menacing tangle of ghostly white evil astern could be made not to be—a collective shudder nevertheless went through the crews and captains of the sailing galley and the long-yarded two-master.

With that began a time of trial and tension, a Reign of Terror, an Eternal Night, such as no one amongst them had ever known before. First, there was the darkness, which grew greater the higher the an-tisun climbed in the black heavens. Even candle flames below and the cook fires sheltered from the blast grew blue and dim. While the pustulant white glow hunting them had this quality: that its light illumined nothing it fell on, but rather darkened it, as if it carried the essence of the antilight along with it, as if it existed solely to make visible the terror of the bergship. Although the bergship was real as death and ever inching nearer, that eerie light sometimes seemed to Fafhrd and the Mouser most akin to the glows seen crawling on the inside of closed eyelids in darkness absolute.

Second, there was the cold that was a part of the antisunlight and struck deep with it, that penetrated every cranny of *Sea Hawk* and *Flotsam*, that had to be fought with both protective huddlings and violent movement, and also with drink and food warmed very slowly and with difficulty over the enfeebled flames—a cold that could paralyze both mind and body, and then kill.

Third, there was the potent silence that came with the unnatural dark and cold, the silence that made almost inaudible the constant creakings of rigging and wood, that muffled all foot-stampings and side-flailings against the cold, that turned all speech to whispers and changed the pandemonium of the great gale itself driving them north to the soft roaring of a seashell held forever to the ear.

And then there was that great gale itself, no whit weaker that it had no great noise—the gale that blew icy spume over the stern, the murderous gale that had always to be struggled against and kept watch on (gripping with fingers and thumbs like gyves to hopefully firm handholds when a man was anywhere on deck or above), the gale near hurricane force that was driving them ever north at an unprecedented pace. None of them had ever before sailed before such a wind, even in the Mouser's and Fafhrd's and Ourph's first passage of the Outer Sea. Any of them would have long since hove to with bare masts and likely sea anchor, save for the menace of the bergship behind.

Last, there was that monstrous craft itself, deathberg or bergship, ever gaining on them, it's leggy oars ever more strongly plied. Rarely, a jagged ice block crashed in black sea beside them. Rarely, a black ray teased at hero's heart. But those were but cackling reminders. The monster craft's main menace: it did nothing (save close the distance to its fleeing foes). The monster craft's intent: grapple and board! (or so it seemed).

Each on his own ship, Fafhrd and Mouser fought weariness and chill; insane desire to sleep; strange, fleeting dreads. Once Fafhrd fancied unseen fliers battling overhead, as if in fabulous aerial extension of the sea war of his and Mouser's craft 'gainst iceship huge. Once Mouser seemed to see black sails of two great fleets. Both masters cheered their men, kept them alive.

Sometimes *Sea Hawk* and *Flotsam* were far apart in their parallel flight north, quite out of sight and hail. Sometimes they came together enough to see glints of each other. And once so close their captains could trade words.

Fafhrd hailed in bursts (they were whispers in Mouser's ears), "Ho, Small One! Heard you Stardock's fliers? Our mountain princess . . . fighting with Faroomfar?"

The Mouser shouted back, "My ears are frostbit. Have you sighted . . . other foe ships . . . besides monstreme?"

FAFHRD: Monstreme? What's that?
MOUSER: That ill astern. My word's analogous . . . to bireme . . . quadrireme. Monstreme!—rowed by monsters.
FAFHRD: A monstreme in full gale. An awful thought! (He looked astern at it.)
MOUSER: Monstreme in monsoon . . . would be awfuler.
FAFHRD: Let's not waste breath. When will we raise Rime Isle?
MOUSER: I had forgot we had a destination. What time think you?
FAFHRD: First bell in second dogwatch. Sunset season.
MOUSER: It should get lighter . . . when this black sun sets.
FAFHRD: It ought to. Damn the double dark!
MOUSER: Damn the dimidiate halved white astern! What's its game?
FAFHRD: Freeze fast to us, I wot. Then kill by cold, else board us.
MOUSER: That's great, I must say. They should hire you.

So their shouts trailed off—a joy at first, but soon a tiredness. And they had their men to care for. Besides, it was too risky, ships so close.

There passed a weary and nightmarish time. Then to the north, where nought had changed all the black day of plunging into it, Fafhrd marked a dark red glow. Long while he doubted it, deemed it some fever in his frozen skull. He noted Afreyt's slender face bobbing among his thoughts. At his side Skor asked him, "Captain, is that a distant fire dead ahead? Our lost sun about to rise in north?" At last Fafhrd believed in the red glow.

Aboard *Flotsam*, the Mouser, racked by the poisons of exhaustion and barely awake, heard Fafhrd whisper, "Mouser, ahoy. Look ahead. What do you see?" He realized it was a mighty shout diminished by black silence and the gale, and that *Sea Hawk* had come close again. He could see glints from the shields affixed along her side, while astern the monstreme was close too, looming like a leprously opalescent cliff arock. Then he looked ahead.

After a bit, "A red light," he wheezed, then forced himself to bellow the same words alee, adding, "Tell me what is it. And then let me sleep."

"Rime Isle, I trow," Fafhrd replied across the gap.

"Are they burning her down?" the Mouser asked.

The answer came back faintly and eerily, "Remember . . . on the gold pieces . . . a volcano?"

The Mouser didn't believe he'd heard aright his comrade's next cry after that one, until he'd made him repeat it. Then, "Sir Pshawri!" he called sharply, and when that one came limping up, hand to bandaged head, he ordered, "Heave bucket overside on line and haul it up. I want waves' sample. Swiftly, you repulsive cripple!"

Somewhat later, Pshawri's eyebrows rose as his captain took the sloshing bucket he proffered and set it to his lips and uptilted it, next handed it back to Pshawri, swished around his teeth the sample he'd taken into his mouth, made a face, and spat to lee.

The fluid was far less icy than the Mouser had expected, almost tepid—and saltier than the water of the Sea of Monsters, which lies just west of the Parched Mountains that hide the Shadowland. He wondered for a mad moment if they'd been magicked to that vast, dead lake. 'Twould fit with monstreme. He thought of Cif.

There was impact. The deck tilted and did not rock back. Pshawri dropped the bucket and screamed.

The monstreme had thrust between the smaller ships and instantly frozen to them with its figurehead (living or dead?) of sea monster hacked or born of ice, its jaws agape betwixt their masts, while from the lofty deck high overhead there pealed down Fafhrd's laughter, monstrously multiplied.

The monstreme visibly shrank.

At one side went the dark. From the low west the true sun burst forth, warmly lighting the bay in which they lay and striking an infinitude of golden gleams from the great, white, crystalline cliff to steerside, down which streaming water rushed in a thousand streams and runnels. A league or so beyond it rose a conical mountain down whose sides flowed glaring scarlet and from whose jaggedly truncated summit brilliant vermilion flames streamed toward the zenith, their dark smoke carried off northeastward by the wind.

Pointing at it with outthrown arm, Fafhrd called, "See, Mouser, the red glow."

Straight ahead, nearer than the cliff and drifting steadily still nearer, was a town or small unwalled city of low buildings hugging gentle hills, its waterfront one long low wharf, where a few ships were docked and a small crowd was assembled quietly. While to the

west, rounding out the bay, there were more cliffs, the nearer bare
dark rock, the farther robed in snow.

Facing the city, Fafhrd said, "Salthaven."

Studying the steaming, streaming, glittering white cliff and fiery
peak beyond, the Mouser remembered the two scenes on his golden
coins, all spent. This reminded him of the four silver coins he'd not
been able to spend because they'd been snatched from his table at the
Eel by the battered server, and of the two scenes on *their* faces: an
iceberg and a monster. He turned round.

The monstreme was gone. Or rather, its last dissolving shards were
sinking into the tranquil waters of the bay without sound or commo-
tion, save that a little steam was rising.

Half-hurled, half-self-magicked from the monstreme's bridge,
where It had been gazing out in triumph over the welter of dire,
frigid forms on the decks below, Its mind obsessed with evil, back
into Its cramped black sphere, Khahkht cursed in voice like Fafhrd's
which midway became again a croak, "Damn to the depths of Hell
Rime Isle's strange gods! Their day will come, their dooms! Which
now devise I whilst I snugly sleep. . . ." It whipped the lid off the
water-walled sun and spoke a spell that rotated the sphere until the
sun was topmost, the Great Subequatorial Desert nethermost. It
briefly fanned the former hot and then curled up in the latter and
closed Its eyes, muttering, ". . . for even Khahkht is cold."

While on tall Stardock, Great Oomforafor listened to the news of
the defeat, or setback rather, and of his dear daughters' further
treacheries, as told him by his furious, bedraggled son Prince Faroomfar, who'd been hurled back much as Khahkht.

As the Mouser turned back to the great white cliff, he realized that
it must be made entire of salt—hence the seaport's name—and that
the hot, volcanic waters coursing down it were dissolving it, which
did much to account for the warm saltiness of ocean hereabouts and
the swift melting of the frost monstreme. The last made all of magic
ice, he mused, both stronger and weaker than the ordinary—as magic
itself than life.

Fafhrd and he, looking toward the long wharf as they experienced
sweetest relief and their ships drew steadily closer to it, saw two
slender figures of different heights standing somewhat apart from the
other seaside welcomers, who by that token and their proud attitudes
and quietly rich garb—blue-gray the one, rust-red the other—must be
individuals high in the councils of Rime Isle.

VIII
RIME ISLE

FAFHRD AND THE Gray Mouser supervised the mooring of *Sea Hawk* and *Flotsam* by bow and stern lines made fast round great wooden bollards, then sprang nimbly ashore, feeling unutterably weary, yet knowing that as captains they should not show it. They made their way to each other, embraced, then turned to face the crowd of Rime Isle men who had witnessed their dramatic arrival standing in a semicircle around the length of dock where their battered and salt-crusted ships were now moored.

Beyond the crowd stretched the houses of Salthaven port—small, stout and earth-hugging, as befitted this most northerly clime—in hues of weathered blue and green and a violet that was almost gray, except for those in the immediate neighborhood, which seemed rather squalid, where they were all angry reds and plague yellow.

Beyond Salthaven the low rolling land went off, gray-green with moss and heather, until it met the gray-white wall of a great glacier, and beyond that the old ice stretched until it met in turn the abrupt slopes of an active and erupting volcano, although the red glow of its lava and the black volume of its flamy smoke seemed to have diminished since they first glimpsed it from their ships.

The foremost of the crowd were all large, burly, quiet-faced men, booted, trousered, and smocked as fishers. Most of them bore quarterstaves, handling them as if they knew well how to use these formidable weapons. They curiously yet composedly eyed the twain and their ships, the Mouser's broad-beamed and somewhat lubberly trader *Flotsam* with its small Mingol crew and squad of disciplined (a wonder!) thieves, Fafhrd's trimmer galley *Sea Hawk* with its contingent of disciplined (if that can be imagined at all) berserkers. On the dock near the bollards where they'd made fast were Fafhrd's lieutenant Skor, the Mouser's—Pshawri—and two other crew members.

It was the quietness and composure of the crowd that puzzled and now began even to nettle the Mouser and Fafhrd. Here they'd sailed all this distance and survived almost unimaginable black hurricane-dangers to help save Rime Isle from a vast invasion of maddened and piratical Sea-Mingols bent on world-conquest, and there was no gladness to be seen anywhere, only stolidly appraising looks. There should be cheering and dancing and some northerly equivalent of maidens throwing flowers! True, the two steaming cauldrons of chowder borne on a shoulder-yoke by one of the fishermen seemed to betoken thoughtful welcome—but they hadn't yet been offered any!

The mouth-watering aroma of the fish-stew now reached the nostrils of the crewmen lining the sides of the two vessels in various attitudes of extreme weariness and dejection—for they were at least half as spent as their captains and had no urge to conceal it—and their eyes slowly brightened and their jaws began to work sympathetically. Behind them the sun-dancing snug harbor, so recently black-skyed, was full of small ships riding at anchor, local fishing craft chiefly with the lovely lines of porpoises, but near at hand several that were clearly from afar, including a small trading galleon of the Eastern Lands and (wonder!) a Keshite junk, and one or two modest yet unfamiliar craft that had the disquieting look of coming from seas beyond Nehwon's. (Just as there was a scatter of sailors from far-off ports in the crowd, peering here and there from between the tall Rime Islanders.)

And now the Rime Isler nearest the Twain walked silently toward them, flanked a pace behind by two others. He stopped a bare yard away, but still did not speak. In fact, he still did not seem so much to be looking at them as past them at their ships and crews, while working out some abstruse reckoning in his head. All three men were quite as tall as Fafhrd and his berserkers.

Fafhrd and the Mouser retained their dignity with some difficulty. Never did to speak first when the other man was supposed to be your debtor.

Finally the other seemed to terminate his calculations and he spoke, using the Low Lankhmarese that is the trade jargon of the northern world.

"I am Groniger, harbor master of Salthaven. I estimate your ships will be a good week repairing and revictualling. We will feed and board your crew ashore in the traders' quarter." He gestured toward the squalid red and yellow buildings.

"Thank you," Fafhrd said gravely, while the Mouser echoed coolly, "Indeed, yes." Hardly an enthusiastic welcome, but still one.

Groniger thrust out his hand, palm uppermost. "The charge," he said loudly, "will be five gold pieces for the galley, seven for the tub. Payment in advance."

Fafhrd's and the Mouser's jaws dropped. The latter could not contain his indignation, captain's dignity or no.

"But we're your sworn allies," he protested, "come here as promised, through perils manifold, to be your mercenaries and help save you from the locust-swarm invasion of the raptorial Sea-Mingols counseled and led by evilest Khakht, the Wizard of Ice."

Groniger's eyebrows lifted. "What invasion?" he queried. "The Sea-Mingols are our friends. They buy our fish. They may be pirates to others, but never to Rime Isle ships. Khakht is an old wives' tale, not to be credited by men of sense."

"Old wives' tale?" the Mouser exploded. "When we were but now three endless nights harried by Khakht's monstrous galley and sank it at last on your very doorstep. His invasion came that close to success. Did you not observe the universal blackness and hell-wind when he conjured the sun out of heaven three days running?"

"We saw some dark clouds blowing up from the south," Groniger said, "under whose cover you approached Salthaven. They vanished when they touched Rime Isle—as all things superstitious are like to do. As for invasion, there were rumors of such an eruption some months back, but our council sifted 'em and found 'em idle gossip. Have any of you heard aught of a Sea-Mingol invasion since?" he asked loudly, looking from side to side at his fellow Rime Islers. They all shook their heads.

"So pay up!" he repeated, jogging his outthrust palm, while those behind him wagged their quarterstaves, firming their grips.

"Shameless ingratitude!" the Mouser rebuked, taking a moral tone as a leader of men. "What gods do you worship here on Rime Isle, to be so hard-hearted?"

Groniger's answer rang out distinct and cool. "We worship no gods at all, but do our business in the world clearheadedly, no misty dreams. We leave such fancies to the so-called civilized people—decadent cultures of the hothouse south. Pay up, I say."

At that moment Fafhrd, whose height permitted him to see over the crowd, cried out, "Here are those coming who hired us, harbor master, and will give the lie to your disclaimers."

The crowd parted respectfully to let through two slender, trousered women with long knives at their belts in jeweled scabbards. The taller was clad all in blue, with like eyes, and fair hair. Her comrade was garmented in dark red, with green eyes and black hair that seemed to have gold wires braided in it. Skor and Pshawri, still stupid with fatigue, took note of them and it was impossible to mistake the message in the sea-dogs' kindling eyes: Here were the northern angels come at last!

"The eminent councilwomen Afreyt and Cif," Groniger intoned. "We are honored by their presence."

They approached with queenly smiles and looks of amiable curiosity.

"Tell them, Lady Afreyt," said Fafhrd courteously to the one in blue, "how you commissioned me to bring Rime Isle twelve—" Suppressing the word "berserk," he smoothly made it, "—stout northern fighters of the fiercest temper."

"And I twelve . . . nimble and dextrous Lankhmar sworders and slingers, sweet Lady Cif," the Mouser chimed in airily, avoiding the word "thief."

Afreyt and Cif looked at them blankly. Then their gazes became at once anxious and solicitous.

Afreyt commented, "They've been tempest-tossed, poor lads, and doubtless it has disordered their memories. Our little northern gales come as a surprise to southerners. They seem gentle. Use them well, Groniger." Looking intently at Fafhrd, she lifted her hand to adjust her hair and in lowering it hesitated a finger for a moment crosswise to her tightly shut long lips.

Cif added, "Doubtless privation has temporarily addled their wits. Their ships have seen hard use. But what a tale! I wonder who they are? Nourish them with hot soup—after they've paid, of course." And she winked at the Mouser a green dark-lashed eye on the side away from Groniger. Then the two ladies wandered on.

It is a testimony to the fundamental level-headedness and growing self-control of the Mouser and Fafhrd (now having, as captains, to control others) that they did not expostulate at this astounding and barely-tempered rebuff, but actually each dug a hand into his purse—though they did look after the two strolling females somewhat won-

deringly. So they saw Skor and Pshawri, who had been dazedly following the two apparitions of northernly delight, now approach
these houris with the clear intent of establishing some sort of polite
amorous familiarity.

Afreyt struck Skor aside in no uncertain fashion, but only after
leaning her face close enough to his head to hiss a word or two into
his ear and grasp his wrist in a way that would have permitted her to
slip a token or note into his palm. Cif treated Pshawri's advances
likewise.

Groniger, pleased at the way the two captains were now dragging
gold pieces from their purses, nevertheless admonished them, "And
see to it that your crewmen offer no affront to our Salthaven women,
nor stray one step beyond the bounds of the traders' quarter."

Paying up took the last of the Rime Isle gold that Cif had given
them back at the Silver Eel in Lankhmar, while the Mouser had to
piece out his seven with two Lankhmar rilks and a Sarheenmar
dubloon.

Groniger's eyebrows rose as he scanned the take. "Rime Isle coinage! So you'd touched here before and knew our harbor rules and
were only seeking to bargain? But what made you invent such an
unbelievable story?"

Fafhrd shrugged and said shortly, "Not so. Had 'em off an Eastern
trading galley in these waters," while the Mouser only laughed.

Nevertheless, a thought struck Groniger, and he looked after the
two Rime Isle councilwomen speculatively as he said shortly, "Now
you may feed your men."

The Mouser called toward *Flotsam*, "Ho, lads! Fetch your bowls,
cups, and spoons. These most hostful Rime Islanders have provided a
feast for you. Orderly now! Pshawri, attend me."

While Fafhrd commanded likewise, adding, "Forget not they're our
friends. Do 'em courtesies. A word with you, Skor." Never do to
show resentment, though that "tub" still rankled with the Mouser,
despite it being a very fair description of the broad-beamed, sweep-
propelled *Flotsam*.

When the Mouser and Fafhrd had seen all their men eating and
served a measure of grog to celebrate safe arrival, they turned to their
somewhat doleful lieutenants, who with only a show of reluctance
yielded up the notes they'd been slipped—as the Twain had surmised
—along with the words, "For your master!"

Unfolded, Afreyt's read, "Another faction controls the Rime Isle
council, temporarily. You do not know me. At dusk tomorrow seek
me at the Hill of the Eight-Legged Horse," while Cif's message was,

"Cold Khahkht has sowed dissension in our council. We never met—play it that way. You'll find me tomorrow night at the Flame Den if you come alone."

"So she does not speak with the voice of Rime Isle after all," Fafhrd commented softly. "To what fiery female politicians have we joined our destinies?"

"Her gold was good," the Mouser answered gruffly. "And now we've two new riddles to solve."

"Flame Den and Eight-Legged Horse," Fafhrd echoed.

"Tub, he called her," the Mouser mused bitterly, his mind veering. "What godless literal-minded philosophers are we now supposed to succor in spite of themselves?"

"You're a godless man too," Fafhrd reminded him.

"Not so, there was once Mog," the Mouser protested with a touch of his old playful plaintiveness, referring to a youthful credulity, when he had briefly believed in the spider god to please a lover.

"Such questions can wait, along with the two riddles," Fafhrd decided. "Now let's curry favor with the atheist fishermen while we can."

And accompanied by the Mouser, he proceeded ceremoniously to offer Groniger white brandy fetched from *Flotsam* by old Ourph the renegade Mingol. The harbor master was prevailed upon to accept a drink, which he took in slow sips, and by way of talk of repair docks, watering, crew dormitories ashore, and the price of salt fish, the conversation became somewhat more general. With difficulty Fafhrd and the Mouser won license to venture outside the traders' quarter, but only by day, and not their men. Groniger refused a second drink.

Inside Its icy sphere, which would have cramped a taller being, Khahkht roused, muttering, "Rime Isle's new gods are treacherous—betray and re-betray—yet stronger than I guessed."

It began to study the dark map of the world of Nehwon depicted on the sphere's interior. Its attention moved to the northern tongue of the Outer Sea, where a long peninsula of the Western Continent reached toward the Cold Waste, with Rime Isle midway between. Leaning Its spidery face close to the tip of that peninsula, It made out on the northern side tiny specks in the dark blue waters.

"The armada of the Widdershins Sea-Mingols invests Sayend," It chuckled, referring to the easternmost city of the ancient Empire of Eevamarensee. "To work!"

It wove Its thickly black-bristled hands incantingly above the gathered specks and droned, "Harken to me, slaves of death. Hear my

word and feel my breath. Every least instruction learn. First of all,
Sayend must burn! Against Nehwon your horde be hurled, next
Rime Isle and then the world." One spider-hand drifted sideways
toward the small green island in ocean's midst. "Round Rime Isle let
fishes swarm, provisioning my Mingol storm." The hand drifted back
and the passes became swifter. "Blackness seize on Mingol mind,
bend it 'gainst all humankind. Madness redden Mingol ire, out of cold
come death by fire!"

It blew strongly as if on cold ashes and a tiny spot on the peninsula
tip glowed dark red like an uncovered ember.

"By will of Khahkht these weirds be locked!" It grated, sealing the
incantment.

The ships of the Widdershins Sea-Mingols rode at anchor in
Sayend harbor, packed close together as fish in a barrel, and as silvery
white. Their sails were furled. Their midships decks, abutting abeam,
made a rude roadway from the precipitous shore to the flagship,
where Edumir, their chief paramount, sat enthroned on the poop,
quaffing the mushroom wine of Quarmall that fosters visions. Cold
light from the full moon south in the wintry sky revealed the narrow
horse-cage that was the forecastle of each ship and picked out the mad
eyes and rawboned head of the ship's horse, a gaunt Steppe-stallion,
thrust forward through the wide-set irregular bars and all confronting the east.

The taken town, its sea-gate thrown wide, was dark. Before its
walls and in its sea-street its small scatter of defenders sprawled as
they'd fallen, soaked in their own blood and scurried over by the
looting Sea-Mingols, who did not, however, bother the chief doors
behind which the remaining inhabitants had locked and barred themselves. They'd already captured the five maidens ritual called for and
dispatched them to the flagship, and now they sought oil of whale,
porpoise, and scaly fish. Puzzlingly, they did not bring most of this
treasure-trove down to their ships, but wasted it, breaking the casks
with axes and smashing the jars, gushing the precious stuff over doors
and wooden walls and down the cobbled street.

The lofty poop of the great flagship was dark as the town in the
pouring moonlight. Beside Edumir his witchdoctor stood above a brazier of tinder, holding aloft a flint and a horseshoe in either hand, his
eyes wild as those of the ship-horses. Next him crouched a wiry-
threwed warrior naked to the waist, bearing the Mingol bow of
melded horn that is Nehwon's most feared, and five long arrows

winged with oily rags. While to the other side was an ax-man with five casks of the captured oil.

On the next level below, the five Sayend maidens cowered wide-eyed and silent, their pallor set off by their long dark braided hair, each in the close charge of two grim she-Mingols who flashed naked knives.

While on the main deck below that, there were ranked five young Mingol horsemen, chosen for this honor because of proven courage, each mounted on an iron-disciplined Steppe-mare, whose hoofs struck random low drum-notes from the hollow deck.

Edumir cast his wine cup into the sea and very deliberately turned his long-jawed, impassive face toward his witchdoctor and nodded once. The latter brought down horseshoe and flint, clashing them just above the brazier, and then nurtured the sparks so engendered until the tinder was all aflame.

The bowman laid his five arrows across the brazier and then, as they came alight, plucked them out and sent them winging successively toward Sayend with such miraculous swiftness that the fifth was painting its narrow orange curve upon the midnight air before the first had struck.

They lodged each in wood and with a preternatural rapidity the oil-drenched town flared up like a single torch, and the muffled, despairing cries of its trapped inhabitants rose like those of Hell's prisoners.

Meanwhile the she-Mingols guarding her had slashed the garments from the first maiden, their knives moving like streaks of silver fire, and thrust her naked toward the first horseman. He seized her by her dark braids and swung her across his saddle, clasping her slim, naked back to his leather-cuirassed chest. Simultaneously the ax-man struck in the head of the first cask and upended it above horse, rider, and maiden, drenching them all with gleaming oil. Then the rider twitched reins and dug in his spurs and set his mare galloping across the close-moored decks toward the flaming town. As the maiden became aware of the destination of the wild ride, she began to scream, and her screams rose higher and higher, accompanied by the rhythmic, growling shouts of the rider and the drumbeat of the mare's hoofs.

All these actions were repeated once, twice, thrice, quarce—the third horse slipped sideways in the oil, stumbled, recovered—so that the fifth rider was away before the first had reached his goal. The mares had been schooled from fillyhood to face and o'erlap walls of flame. The riders had drunk deep of the same mushroom wine as Edumir. The maidens had their screams.

One by one they were briefly silhouetted against the red gateway, then joined with it. Five times the flame of Sayend rose higher still, redly illuminating the small bay and the packed ship and the staring Mingol faces and glazed Mingol eyes, and Sayend expired in one unending scream and shout of agony.

When it was done, Edumir rose up tall in his fur robes and cried in trumpet voice, "East away now. Over ocean. To Rime Isle!"

Next day the Mouser and Fafhrd got their ships pumped out, warped to the docks assigned them, and work began on them early. Their men, refreshed by a long night's sleep ashore, set to work at repairs after a little initial grumbling, the Mouser's thieves under the direction of his chief lieutenant Pshawri and small Mingol crew. Presently there was the muffled thud of mallets driving in tow, and the stench of tar, as the loosened seams of *Flotsam* were caulked from within, while from the deck of *Sea Hawk* came the brighter music of hammers and saws, as Fafhrd's vikings mended upper works damaged by the icy projectiles of Khahkht's frost monstreme. Others reaved new rigging where needed and replaced frayed stays.

The traders' quarter, where they'd been berthed, duplicated in small the sailors' quarter of any Nehwon port, its three taverns, two brothels, several stores and shrines staffed and loosely administered by a small permanent population of ill-assorted foreigners, their unofficial mayor a close-mouthed, scarred captain named Bomar, from the Eight Cities, and their chief banker a dour black Keshite. It was borne in on Fafhrd and the Mouser that one of these fisherfolks' chief concerns, and that of the traders too, was to keep Rime Isle a valuable secret from the rest of Nehwon. Or else they had caught the habit of impassivity from their fisher-hosts, who tolerated, profited from them, and seldom omitted to enforce a bluff discipline. The foreign population had heard nothing of a Sea-Mingol eruption, either, or so they claimed.

The Rime Islanders seemed to live up to first impressions: a large-bodied, sober-clad, quiet, supremely practical and supremely confident people, without eccentricities or crochets or even superstitions, who drank little and lived by the rule of "Mind your own business." They played chess a good deal in their spare time and practiced with their quarterstaves, but otherwise they appeared to take little notice of each other and none at all of foreigners, though their eyes were not sleepy.

And today they had become even more inaccessible, ever since an early-sailing fishing boat had returned almost immediately to harbor with news that had sent the entire fleet of them hurrying out. And when the first of these came creaming back soon after noon with hold full of new-caught fish, swiftly salted them down (there was abundance of salt—the great eastern cliff, which no longer ran with hot volcanic waters), and put out to sea again, clapping on all sail, it became apparent that there must be a prodigious run of food fish just outside the harbor mouth—and the thrifty fishers determined to take full advantage of it. Even Groniger was seen to captain a boat out.

Individually busy with their supervisings and various errands (since only they could go outside the traders' quarter), the Mouser and Fafhrd met each other by a stretch of seawall north of the docks and paused to exchange news and catch a breather.

"I've found the Flame Den," the former said. "At least I think I have. It's an inner room in the Salt Herring tavern. The Ilthmart owner admitted he sometimes rents it out of a night—that is, if I interpreted his wink aright."

Fafhrd nodded and said, "I just now walked to the north edge of town and asked a grandad if he ever heard of the Hill of the Eight-Legged Horse. He gave a damned unpleasant sort of laugh and pointed across the moor. The air was very clear (you've noticed the volcano's ceased to smoke? I wonder that the Islers take so little note of it), and when I'd located the one heathered hill of many that was his finger's target (about a league northwest), I made out what looked like a gallows atop it."

The Mouser grunted feeling fully at that grim disclosure and rested his elbows on the seawall, surveying the ships left in the harbor, "foreigners" all. After a while he said softly, "There's all manner of slightly strange things here in Salthaven, I trow. Things slightly off-key. That Ool Plerns sailing-dory now—saw you ever one with so low a prow at Ool Plerns? Or a cap so oddly-visored as that of the sailor we saw come off the Gnampf Nor cutter? Or that silver coin with an owl on it Groniger gave me in change for my dubloon? It's as if Rime Isle were on the edge of other worlds with other ships and other men and other gods—a sort of rim. . . ."

Gazing out likewise, Fafhrd nodded slowly and started to speak when there came angry voices from the direction of the docks, followed by a full-throated bellow.

"That's Skullick, I'll be bound!" Fafhrd averred. "Got into what sort of idiot trouble, the gods know." And without further word he raced off.

"Likely just broken bounds and got a drubbing," the Mouser called out, trotting after. "Mikkidu got a touch of the quarterstaff this morn for trying to pick an Isler's pouch—and serve him right! I could not have whacked him more shrewdly myself."

That evening Fafhrd strode north from Salthaven toward Gallows Hill (it was an honester name), resolutely not looking back at the town. The sun, set in the far southwest a short while ago, gave a soft violet tone to the clear sky and the pale knee-high heather through which he trod and even to the black slopes of the volcano Darkfire where yesterday's lava had cooled. A chill breeze, barely perceptible, came from the glacier ahead. Nature was hushed. There was a feeling of immensity.

Gradually the cares of the day dropped away and his thoughts turned to the days of his youth, spent in similar clime—to Cold Corner with its tented slopes and great pines, its snow serpents and wolves, its witchwomen and ghosts. He remembered Nalgron his father and his mother Mor and even Mara, his first love. Nalgron had been an enemy of the gods, somewhat like these Rime Isle men (he was called the Legend Breaker) but more adventurous—he had been a great mountain climber, and in climbing one named White Fang had got his death. Fafhrd remembered an evening when his father had walked with him to the lip of Cold Canyon and named to him the stars as they winked on in a sky similarly violet.

A small sound close by, perhaps that of a lemming moving off through the heather, broke his reverie. He was already mounting the gentle slope of the hill he sought. After a moment he continued to the top, stepping softly and keeping his distance from the gibbet and the area that lay immediately beneath its beam. He had a feeling of something uncanny close at hand and he scanned around in the silence.

On the northern slope of the hill there was a thick grove of gorse more than man-high, or bower rather, since there was a narrow avenue leading in, a door of shadows. The feeling of an uncanny presence deepened and he mastered a shiver.

As his eyes came away from the gorse, he saw Afreyt standing just uphill and to one side of the grove and looking at him steadily without greeting. The darkening violet of the sky gave its tone to her blue garb. For some reason he did not call out to her and now she lifted her narrow hand crosswise to her lips, enjoining silence. Then she looked toward the grove.

Slowly emerging from the shadow door were three slender girls barely past childhood. They seemed to be leading and looking up at someone Fafhrd could not make out at first. He blinked twice, widening his eyes, and saw it was the figure of a tall, pale-bearded man wearing a wide-brimmed hat that shadowed his eyes, and either very old or else enfeebled by sickness, for he took halting steps and though his back was straight he rested his hands heavily on the shoulders of two of the girls.

And then Fafhrd felt an icy chill, for the suspicion came to him that this was Nalgron, whose ghost he had not seen since he had left Cold Corner. And either the figure's skin, beard and robe were alike strangely mottled, or else he was seeing the pale needle-clumps of the gorse through them.

But if it were a ghost, Nalgron's or another's, the girls showed no fear of it, rather a dutiful tenderness, and their shoulders bowed under its hands as they supported it along, as if its weight were real.

They slowly mounted the short distance to the hilltop, Afreyt silently following a few paces behind, until the figure stood directly beneath the end of the gallow's beam.

There the old man or ghost seemed to gain strength (and perhaps greater substantiality too) for he took his hands from the girls' shoulders and they retreated a little toward Afreyt, still looking up at him, and he lifted his face toward the sky, and Fafhrd saw that although he was a gaunt man at the end of middle age with strong and noble features not unlike Nalgron's, he had thinner lips, their ends downturning like a knowing schoolmaster's, and he wore a patch on his left eye.

He scanned around uncertainly, o'erpassing Fafhrd, who stood motionless and afraid, and then the old man turned north and lifted an arm in that direction and said in a hoarse voice that was like the soughing of the wind in thick branches, "The Widder-Mingol fleet comes on from the west. Two raiders harry ahead, make for Cold Harbor." Then he rapidly turned back his head through what seemed an impossibly great angle, as though his neck were broken yet somehow still serviceable, so that he looked straight at Fafhrd with his single eye, and said, "You must destroy them!"

Then he seemed to lose interest, and weakness seized him again, or perhaps a sort of sensuous languor after task completed, for he stepped a little more swiftly as he returned toward the bower, and when the girls came in around him, his resting hands seemed to fondle their young necks lasciviously as well as take support from their slim shoulders until the shadow door, darker now, swallowed them.

Fafhrd was so struck with this circumstance, despite his fear, that when Afreyt now came stepping toward him saying in a low but businesslike voice, "Didst mark that? Cold Harbor is Rime Isle's other town, but far smaller, easy prey for even a single Mingol ship that takes it by surprise. It's on the north coast, a day's journey away, ice-locked save for these summer months. You must——" his inter-rupting reply was "Think you the girls'll be safe with him?"

She broke off, then answered shortly, "As with any man. Or male ghost. Or god."

At that last word, Fafhrd looked at her sharply. She nodded and continued, "They'll feed him and give him drink and bed him down. Doubtless he'll play with their breasts a little and then sleep. He's an old god and far from home, I think, and wearies easily, which is perhaps a blessing. In any case, they serve Rime Isle too and must run risks."

Fafhrd considered that and then, clearing his throat, said, "Your pardon, Lady Afreyt, but your Rime Isle men, judging not only from Groniger but from others I've met, some of them councilmen, do not believe in any gods at all."

She frowned. "That's true enough. The old gods deserted Rime Isle long years ago and our folk have had to learn to fend for themselves in the cruel world—in this clime merciless. It's bred hard-headed-ness."

"Yet," Fafhrd said, recalling something, "My gray friend judged Rime Isle to be a sort of rim-spot, where one might meet all manner of strange ships and men and gods from very far places."

"That's true also," she said hurriedly. "And perhaps it's favored the same hard-headedness: how, where there are so many ghosts about, to take account only of what the hand can firmly grasp and can be weighed in scales. Money and fish. It's one way to go. But Cif and I have gone another—where phantoms throng, to learn to pick the use-ful and trustworthy ones from the flibbertigibbets and flimflammers —which is well for Rime Isle. For these two gods we've found——"

"*Two* gods?" Fafhrd questioned, raising his eyebrows. "Cif found one too? Or is another in the bower?"

"It's a long story," she said impatiently. "Much too long to tell now, when dire events press upon us thick and fast. We must be practical. Cold Harbor's in dismal peril and——"

"Again your pardon, Lady Afreyt," Fafhrd broke in, raising his voice a little. "But your mention of practicality reminds me of an-other matter upon which you and Cif appear to differ most sharply with your fellow councilmen. They know of no Mingol invasion, they say, and certainly nothing of you and Cif hiring us to help repel it—and you've asked us in your notes to keep that secret. Now, I've brought you the twelve berserkers you wanted——"

"I know, I know," she said sharply, "and I'm pleased. But you were paid for that—and shall get further pay in Rime Isle gold as services are rendered. As for the council, the wizardries of Khakkht have lulled their suspicions—I doubt not that today's fish-run is his work, tempting their cupidity."

"And my comrade and I have suffered from his wizardries too, I trow," Fafhrd said. "Nevertheless, you told us at the Silver Eel in Lankhmar that you spoke with the voice of Rime Isle, and now it appears that you speak only for Cif and yourself in a council of— what is it, twelve?"

"Did you expect your task to be all easy sailing?" she flared at him. "Art unacquainted with set-backs and adverse gales in quests. More-over, we *do* speak with the voice of Rime Isle, for Cif and I are the only councilpersons who have the old glory of Rime Isle at heart— and we are both full council members, I assure you, only-daughters inheriting house, farms and council membership from fathers after (in Cif's case) sons died. We played together as children in these hills, she and I, reviving Rim Isle's greatness in our games. Or sometimes we'd be pirate queens and rape the Isle. But chiefly we'd imagine ourselves seizing power in the council, forcibly putting down all the other members——"

"So much violence in little girls?" Fafhrd couldn't help putting in. "I think of little girls as gathering flowers and weaving garlands whilst fancying themselves little wives and mothers——"

"—and put them all to the sword and cut their wives' throats!" Afreyt finished. "Oh, we gathered flowers too, sometimes."

Fafhrd chuckled, then his voice grew grave. "And so you've inher-ited full council membership—Groniger always mentions you with respect, though I think he has suspicions of something between us— and now you've somehow discovered a stray old god or two whom you think you can trust not to betray you, or delude you with senile ravings, and he's told you of a great two-pronged Mingol invasion of Rime Isle preparatory to world conquest, and on the strength of that you went to Lankhmar and hired the Mouser and me to be your mercenary captains, using your own fortunes for the purpose, I fancy——"

"Cif is the council treasurer," she assured him with a meaningful crook of her lips. "She's very good at figures and accounts—as I am with the pen and words, the council's secretary."

"And yet you trust this god," Fafhrd pressed on, "this old god who loves gallows and seems to draw strength from them. Myself, I'm very suspicious of all old men and gods. In my experience they're full of lechery and avarice—and have a long lifetime's experience of evil to draw on in their twisty machinations."

"Agreed," Afreyt said. "But when all's said and done, a god's a god. Whatever nasty itches his old heart may have, whatever wicked thoughts of death and doom, he must first be true to his god's nature: which is, to hear what we say and hold us to it, to speak truth to man about what's going on in distant places, and to prophecy honestly— though he may try to trick us with words if we don't listen to him very carefully."

"That does agree with my experience of the breed," Fafhrd admitted. "Tell me, why is this called the Hill of the Eight-Legged Horse?"

Without a blink at the change of subject, Afreyt replied, "Because it takes four men to carry a coffin or the laid-out corpse of one who's been hanged—or died any other way. Four men—eight legs. You might have guessed."

"And what is this god's name?"

Afreyt said: "Odin."

Fafhrd had the strangest feeling at the gong-beat sound of that simple name—as if he were on the verge of recalling memories of another lifetime. Also, it had something of the tone of the gibberish spoken by Karl Treuherz, that strange otherworlder who had briefly come into the lives of Fafhrd and the Mouser astride the neck of a two-headed sea serpent whilst they were in the midst of their great adventure-war with the sapient rats of Lankhmar Below-Ground. Only a name—yet there was the feeling of walls between world disturbed.

At the same time he was looking into Afreyt's wide eyes and noting that the irises were violet, rather than blue as they had seemed in the yellow torchlight of the Eel—and then wondering how he could see any violet at all in anything when that tone had some time ago faded entirely from the sky, which was now full night except that the moon a day past full had just now lifted above the eastern highland.

From beyond Afreyt a light voice said tranquilly, attuned to the night, "The god sleeps."

One of the girls was standing before the mouth of the bower, a slim white shape in the moonlight, clad only in simple frock that was hardly more than a shift and left one shoulder bare. Fafhrd marvelled that she was not shivering in the chill night air. Her two companions were dimmer shapes behind her.

"Did he give any trouble, Mara?" Afreyt called. (Fafhrd felt a strange feeling at that name, too.)

"Nothing new," the girl responded.

Afreyt said, "Well, put on your boots and hooded cloak—May and Gale, you also—and follow me and the foreign gentleman, out of earshot, to Salthaven. You'll be able to visit the god at dawn, May, to bring him milk?"

"I will."

"Your children?" Fafhrd asked in a whisper.

Afreyt shook her head. "Cousins. Meanwhile," she said in a voice that was likewise low, but businesslike, "you and I will discuss your instant expedition with the berserks to Cold Harbor."

Fafhrd nodded, although his eyebrows rose a little. There was a fugitive movement in the air overhead and he found himself thinking of his and the Mouser's one-time loves, the invisible mountain-princesses Hirriwi and Keyaira, and of their night-riding brother, Prince Faroomfar.

The Gray Mouser saw his men fed and bedded down for the night in their dormitory ashore, not without some fatherly admonitions as to the desirability of prudent behavior in the home port of one's employers. He briefly discussed the morrow's work with Ourph and Pshawri. Then, with a final enigmatic scowl all around, he threw his cloak over his left shoulder, withdrew into the chilly evening, and strolled toward the Salt Herring.

Although he and Fafhrd had had a long refreshing sleep aboard the *Flotsam* (declining the shore quarters Groniger had offered them, though accepting for their men), it had been a long, exactingly busy, and so presumably tiring day—yet now, somewhat to his surprise, he felt new life stirring in him. But this new life invading him did not concern itself with his and Fafhrd's many current problems and sage plans for future contingencies, but rather with a sense of just how preposterous it was that for the past three moons he should have been solemnly playing at being a captain of men, fire-breathing disciplinarian, prodigious navigator, and the outlandishly heroic rest of it. He, a thief, captaining thieves, drilling them into sailorly and warlike skills that would be of no use to them whatever when they went back to their old professions—ridiculous! All because a small woman with golden glints in her dark hair and in her green eyes had set him an unheard-of task. Really, most droll.

Moonlight striking almost horizontally left the narrow street in shadow but revealed the cross-set beams above the Salt Herring's door. Where did they get so much wood in an island so far north? That question at least was answered for him when he pressed on inside. The tavern was built of the gray beams and planks of wrecked or dismantled ships—one wall still had a whaleback curve and he noted in another the borings and embedded shells of sea creatures.

A slow eyesweep around showed a half dozen oddly sorted mariners quietly drinking and two youngish Islers even more quietly playing chess with chunky stone pieces. He recalled having seen this morning with Groniger the one playing the black.

Without a word he marched toward the inner room, the low doorway to which was now half occupied by a brawny and warty old hag, sitting bowed over on a low stool, who looked the witch-mother of all unnatural giants and other monsters.

His Ilthmart host came up beside him, wiping his hands on the towel that was his apron and saying softly, "Flame Den's taken for tonight—a private party. You'd only be courting trouble with Mother Grum. What's your pleasure?"

The Mouser gave him a hard, silent look and marched on. Mother Grum glowered at him from under tangled brows. He glowered back. The Ilthmart shrugged.

Mother Grum moved back from her stool, bowing him into the inner room. He briefly turned his head, favoring the Ilthmart with a cold superior smile as he moved after her. One of the Islers, lifting a black rook to move it, swung his eyes sidewise to observe, though his head remained motionless and bent over the board as if in deepest thought.

The inner room had a small fire in it, at any rate, to provide movement to entertain the eye. The large hearth was in the center of the room, a stone slab set almost waist high. A great copper flue (the Mouser wondered what ship's bottom it had helped cover) came down to within a yard of it from out of the low ceiling, and into this flue the scant smoke twistingly flowed. Elsewhere in the room were a few small, scarred tables, chairs for them, and another doorway.

Sidewise together on the edge of the hearth sat two women who looked personable, but used by life. The Mouser had seen one of *them* earlier in the day (the late afternoon) and judged her a whore. Their somewhat provocative attire now, and the red stockings of one, were consonant with this theory.

The Mouser went to a table a quarter way around the fire from them, cast his cape over one chair and sat down in another, which commanded both doorways. He knit his fingers together and studied the flames impassively.

Mother Grum returned to her stool in the doorway, presenting her back to all three of them.

One of the two whorish-looking women stared into the fire and from time to time fed it with driftwood that sang and sometimes tinged the flames with green and blue and with thorny black twigs that spat and crackled and burned hot orange. The other wove cat's cradles between the spread fingers of her out-held hands on a long loop of black twine. Now and then the Mouser looked aside from the fire at her severe angular creations.

Neither of the women took notice of the Mouser, but after a while the one feeding the fire stood up, brought a wine jar and two small tankards to his table, poured into one, and stood regarding him.

He took up the tankard, tasted a small mouthful, swallowed it, set down the tankard, and nodded curtly without looking at her.

She went back to her former occupation. Thereafter the Mouser took an occasional swallow of wine while studying and listening to the flames. What with their combination of crackling and singing, they were really quite vocal in that rather small, silent room—resembling an eager, rapid, youthful voice, by turns merry and malicious. Sometimes the Mouser could have sworn he heard words and phrases.

While in the flames, continually renewed, he began to see faces, or rather one face which changed expression a good deal—a youthfully handsome face with very mobile lips, sometimes open and amiable, sometimes convulsed by hatreds and envies (the flames shone green a while), sometimes almost impossibly distorted, like a face seen through hot air above a very hot fire. Indeed once or twice he had the fancy that it was the face of an actual person sitting on the opposite side of the fire from him, sometimes half rising to regard him through the flames, sometimes crouching back. He was almost tempted to get up and walk around the fire to check on that, but not quite.

The strangest thing about the face was that it seemed familiar to the Mouser, though he could not place it. He gave up racking his brains over that and settled back, listening more closely to the flame-voice and trying to attune its fancied words to the movements of the flame-face's lip.

Mother Grum got up again and moved back, bowing. There entered without stooping a lady whose russet cloak was drawn across the lower half of her face, but the Mouser recognized the gold-shot green eyes and he stood up. Cif nodded to Mother Grum and the two harlots, walked to the Mouser's table, cast her cloak atop his, and sat down in the third chair. He poured for her, refilled his own tankard, and sat down also. They drank. She studied him for some time.

Then, "You've seen the face in the fire and heard its voice?" she asked.

His eyes widened and he nodded, watching her intently now.

"But have you guessed why it seems familiar?"

He shook his head rapidly, sitting forward, his expression a most curious and expectant frown.

"It resembles you," she said flatly.

His eyebrows went up and his jaw dropped, just a little. That was true! It did remind him of himself—only when he was younger, quite a bit younger. Or as he saw himself in mirror these days only when in a most self-infatuated and vain mood, so that he saw himself as unmarked by age.

"But do you know why?" she asked him, herself intent now.

He shook his head.

She relaxed. "Neither do I," she said. "I thought you might know. I marked it when I first saw you in the Eel, but as to why—it is a mystery within mysteries, beyond our present ken."

"I find Rime Isle a nest of mysteries," he said meaningfully, "not the least your disavowal of myself and Fafhrd."

She nodded, sat up straighter, and said, "So now I think it's high time I told you why Afreyt and I are so sure of a Mingol invasion of Rime Isle while the rest of the council disbelieves it altogether. Don't you?"

He nodded emphatically, smiling.

"Almost a year ago to the day," she said, "Afreyt and I were walking alone upon the moor north of town, as has been our habit since childhood. We were lamenting Rime Isle's lost glories and lost (or man-renounced) gods and wishing for their return, so that the Isle might have surer guidance and foreknowledge of perils. It was a day of changeable winds and weather, the end of spring, not quite yet summer, all the air alive, now bright, now gloomed-over, as clouds raced past the sun. We had just topped a gentle rise when we came upon the form of a youth sprawled on his back in the heather with eyes closed and head thrown back, looking as if he were dying or in the last stages of exhaustion—as though he had been cast ashore by the last great wave of some unimaginably great storm on high.

"He wore a simple tunic of homespun, very worn, and the plainest sandals, worn thin, with frayed thongs, and a very old belt dimly pricked out with monsters, yet from first sight I was almost certain that he was a god.

"I knew it in three ways. From his insubstantiality—though he was there to the touch, I could almost see the crushed heather through his pale flesh. From his supernal beauty—it was . . . the flame-face, though tranquil-featured, almost as if in death. And from the adoration I felt swelling in my heart.

"I also knew it from the way Afreyt acted, kneeling at once like myself beside him across from me—though there was something unnatural in her behavior, betokening an amazing development when we understood it aright, which we did not then. (More of that later.)

"You know how they say a god dies when his believers utterly fail him? Well, it was as if this one's last worshipper were dying in Nehwon. Or as if—this is closer to it—all his worshippers had died in his own proper world and he whirled out into the wild spaces between the worlds, to sink or swim, survive or perish according to the reception he got in whatever new world whereon chance cast him ashore. I think it's within the power of gods to travel between the worlds, don't you?—both involuntarily and also by their own design. And who knows what unpredictable tempests they might encounter in dark mid-journey?

"But I was not wasting time in speculations on that day of miracles a year ago. No, I was chafing his wrists and chest, pressing my warm cheek against his cold one, prising open his lips with my tongue (his jaw was slack) and with my open lips clamped upon his (and his nostrils clipped between my finger and thumb) sending my fresh, new-drawn breaths deep into his lungs, the meanwhile fervently praying to him in my mind, though I know they say the gods hear only our words, not thoughts. A stranger, happening upon us, might have judged us in the second or third act of lovemaking, I the more feverish seeking to rekindle his ardor.

"Meanwhile Afreyt (again here's that unnatural thing I mentioned) seemed to be as busy as I across from me—and yet somehow I was doing all the work. The explanation of that came somewhat later.

"My god showed signs of life. His eyelids quivered, I felt his chest stir, while his lips began to return my kisses.

"I uncapped my silver flask and dribbled brandy between his lips, alternating the drops with further kisses and words of comfort and endearment.

"At last he opened his eyes (brown shot with gold, like yours) and with my help raised up his head, meanwhile muttering words in a strange tongue. I answered in what languages I know, but he only frowned, shaking his head. That's how I knew he was not a Nehwon god—it's natural, don't you think, that a god, all-knowing in his own world, would be at a loss at first, plunged into another? He'd have to take it in.

"Finally he smiled and lifted his hand to my bosom, looking at me questioningly. I spoke my name. He nodded and shaped his lips, repeated it. Then he touched his own chest and spoke the name 'Loki.' "

At that word the Mouser knew feelings and thoughts similar to those of Fafhrd hearing "Odin"—of other lives and worlds, and of Karl Treuherz's tongue and his little Lankhmarese-German, German-Lankhmarese dictionary that he'd given Fafhrd. At the same moment, though for that moment only, he saw the fire-face so like his own in the flames, seeming to wink at him. He frowned wonderingly.

Cif continued, "Thereafter I fed him crumbs of meat from my scrip, which he accepted from my fingers, eating sparingly and sipping more brandy, the whiles I taught him words, pointing to this and that. That day Darkfire was smoking thick and showing flames, which interested him mightily when I named it. So I took flint and iron from my scrip and struck them together, naming 'fire.' He was delighted, seeming to gather strength from the sparks and smouldering straws and the very word. He'd stroke the little flames without seeming to take hurt. That frightened me.

"So passed the day—I utterly lost in him, unaware of all else, save what struck his fancy moment by moment. He was a wondrously apt scholar. I named objects both in our Rime tongue and Low Lankhmarese, thinking it'd be useful to him as he got his vision for lands beyond the Isle.

"Evening drew in. I helped the god to his feet. The wan light washing over him seemed to dissolve a little his pale flesh.

"I indicated Salthaven, that we should walk there. He assented eagerly (I think he was attracted by its evening smokes, being drawn to fire, his trumps) and we set out, he leaning on me lightly.

"And now the mystery of Afreyt was made clear. She would by no means go with us! And then I saw, though only very dimly, the figure *she* had been succoring, tending and teaching all day long, as I had Loki—the figure of a frail old man (god, rather), bearded and one-eyed, who'd been lying close alongside Loki at the first, and I empowered to see only the one and she the other!"

"A most marvelous circumstance indeed," the Mouser commented. "Perhaps like drew to like and so revealed itself. Say, did the other god by any chance resemble Fafhrd?—but for being one-eyed, of course."

She nodded eagerly. "An older Fafhrd, as 'twere his father. Afreyt marked it. Oh, you must know something of this mystery?"

The Mouser shook his head, "Just guessing," and asked, "What was *his* name—the older god's?"

(She told him.)

"Well, what happened next?"

"We parted company. I walked the god Loki to Salthaven, he leaning on my arm. He was still most delicate. It seems one worshipper is barely enough at best to keep a god alive and visible, no matter how active his mind—for by now he was pointing out things to me (and indicating actions and states) and naming them in Rimic, Low Lankhmarese—and High as well!—before I named them, sure indication of his god's intellect.

"At the same time he was, despite his weakness, beginning to give me indications of a growing interest in me (I mean, my person) and I was fast losing all doubts as to how I'd be expected to entertain him when I got him home. Now, I was very happy to have got, hopefully, a new god for Rime Isle. And I must needs adore him, if only to keep him alive. But as for making him free of my bed, I had a certain reluctance, no matter how ghostly-insubstantial his flesh turned out to be in closest contact (and if it stayed that way)!

"Oh, I suppose I'd have submitted if it had come to that; still, there's something about sleeping with a god—a great honor, to be sure, but (to name only one thing) one surely couldn't expect faithfulness (if one wanted that)—certainly not from the whimsical, merry and mischievous god this Loki was showing himself to be! Besides, I wanted to be able to weigh clearheadedly the predictions and warnings for Rime Isle I hoped to get from him—not with a mind dreamy with lovemaking and swayed by all the little fancies and fears that come with full infatuation.

"As things fell out, I never had to make the decision. Passing this tavern, he was attracted by a flickering red glow and slipped inside without attracting notice (he was still invisible to all but me). I followed (that got me a look or two, I being a respectable councilwoman) and pressed on after him as he followed the pulsing fire-glow into this inner room, where a great bawdy party was going on and the hearth was ablaze. Before my eyes he melted into the flames and joined with them!

"The revelers were somewhat taken aback by my intrusion, but after looking them over with a smile I merely turned and went out, waving my hand at them and saying, 'Enjoy!'—that was for Loki too. I'd guessed he'd got where he wanted to be."

And she waved now at the dancing flames, then turned back to the Mouser with a smile. He smiled back, shaking his head in wonder.

She continued, "So I went home, well content, but not before I'd reserved the Flame Den (as I then learned this place is called) for the following night.

"Next day I hired two harlots for the evening (so there'd be entertainment for Loki) and Mother Grum to be our doorman and ensure our privacy.

"That night went as I'd guessed it would. Loki had indeed taken up permanent residence in the fire here and after a while I was able to talk with him and get some answers to questions, though nothing of profit to Rime Isle as yet. I made arrangements with the Ilthmart for the Flame Den to be reserved one night each week, and like bargains with Hilsa and Rill to come on those nights and entertain the god and keep him happy. Hilsa, has the god been with you tonight?" she called to the woman feeding the fire, the one with red stockings.

"Twice," that one replied matter-of-factly in a husky voice. "Slipped from the fire invisibly and back again. He's content."

"Your pardon, Lady Cif," the Mouser interposed, "but how do these professional women find such close commerce with an invisible god to be? What's it like? I'm curious."

Cif looked toward them where they sat by the fire.

"Like having a mouse up your skirt," Hilsa replied with a short chuckle, swinging a red leg.

"Or a toad," her companion amended. "Although he dwells in the flames, his person is cold." Rill had laid aside her cat's cradle and joined her hands, fingers interweaving, to make shadow-faces on the wall, of prick-eared gigantic werewolves, great sea serpents, dragons, and long-nosed, long-chinned witches. "He likes these hobgoblins," she commented.

The Mouser nodded thoughtfully, watching them for a while, and then back to the fire.

Cif continued, "Soon the god, I could tell, was beginning to get the feel of Nehwon, fitting his mind to her, stretching it out to her farthest bounds, and his oracles became more to the point. Meantime Afreyt, with whom I conferred daily, was caring for old Odin out on the moor in much the same way (though using girls to comfort and appease him 'stead of full-grown women, he being an older god), eliciting prophecies of import.

"Loki it was who first warned us that the Mingols were on the move, mustering horse-ships against Rime Isle, mounting under Khahkht's urgings toward a grand climacteric of madness and rapine. Afreyt put independent question to Odin and he confirmed it—they were together in the tale at every point.

"When asked what we must do, they both advised—again independently—that we seek out two certain heroes in Lankhmar and have them bring their bands to the Isle's defence. They were most circumstantial, giving your names and haunts, saying you were their men, whether or not you knew it in this life, and they did not change their stories under repeated questioning. Tell me, Gray Mouser, have you not known the god Loki before? Speak true."

"Upon my word, I haven't, Lady Cif," he averred, "and am no more able than you to explain the mystery of our resemblance. Though there is a certain weird familiarity about the name, and Odin's too, as if I'd heard them in dreams or nightmares. But however I rack my brains, it comes no clearer."

"Well," she resumed after a pause, "the two gods kept up their urgings that we seek you out and so half a year ago Afreyt and I took ship for Lankhmar on Hlal—with what results you know."

"Tell me, Lady Cif," the Mouser interjected, rousing himself from his fire-peerings, "how did you and tall Afreyt get back to Rime Isle after Khahkht's wizardrous blizzard snatched you out of the Silver Eel?"

"It transpired as swiftly as our journey there was long," she said. "One moment we were in his cold clutch, battered and blinded by wind-driven ice, our ears assaulted by a booming laughter. The next we had been taken in charge by two feminine flying creatures who whirled us at dizzying speed through darkness to a warm cave where they left us breathless. They said they were a mountain king's two daughters."

"Hirriwi and Keyaira, I'll be bound!" the Mouser exclaimed. "They must be on our side."

"Who are those?" Cif inquired.

"Mountain princesses Fafhrd and I have known in our day. Invisibles like our revered fire-dweller here." He nodded toward the flames. "Their father rules in lofty Stardock."

"I've heard of that peak and dread Oomforafor, its king, whom some say is with his son Faroomfar an ally of Khahkht. Daughters against father and brother—that would be natural. Well, Afreyt and I after we'd recovered our breath made our way to the cavern's mouth —and found ourselves looking down on Rime Isle and Salthaven from a point midway up Darkfire. With some little difficulty we made our way home across rock and glacier."

"The volcano," the Mouser mused. "Again Loki's link with fire." His attention had been drawn back to the hypnotic flames.

Cif nodded. "Thereafter Loki and Odin kept us informed of the

Mingols' progress toward Rime Isle—and your own. Then four days ago Loki began a running account of your encounters with Khahkht's frost monstreme. He made it most vivid—sometimes you'd have sworn he was piloting one of the ships himself. I managed to reserve the Flame Den the succeeding nights (and have it now for the next three days and nights also), so we were able to follow the details of the long flight or long pursuit—which, truth to tell, became a bit monotonous."

"You should have been there," the Mouser murmured.

"Loki made me feel I was."

"Incidentally," the Mouser said casually, "I'd think you'd have rented the Flame Den every night once you'd got your god here."

"I'm not made of gold," she informed him without rancor. "Besides, Loki likes variety. The brawls that others hold here amuse him—were what attracted him in the first place. Furthermore, it would have made the council even more suspicious of my activities."

The Mouser nodded. "I thought I recognized a crony of Groniger's playing chess out there."

"Hush," she counseled him. "I must now consult the god." Her voice had grown a little singsong in the later stages of her narrative and it became more so as, without transition, she invoked, "And now, O Loki god, tell us about our enemies across the seas and in the realms of ice. Tell us of cruel, cold Khahkht, of Edumir of the Widdershin Mingols and Gonov of the Sunwise. Hilsa and Rill, sing with me to the god." And her voice became a somnolent two-toned, wordless chant in which the other women joined: Hilsa's husky voice, Rill's slightly shrill one, and a soft growling that after a bit the Mouser realized came from Mother Grum—all tuned to the fire and its flame-voice.

The Mouser lost himself in this strange medley of notes and all at once the crackling flame-voice, as if by some dream magic, became fully articulate, murmuring rapidly in Low Lankhmarese with occasional words slipped in that were as hauntingly strange as the god's own name:

"Storm clouds thicken round Rime Isle. Nature brews her blackest bile. Monsters quicken, nightmares foal, niss and nicor, drow and troll." (Those last four nouns were all strange ones to the Mouser, specially the bell-toll sound of "troll.") "Sound alarms and strike the drum—in three days the Mingols come, Sunwise Mingols from the east, horsehead ship and human beast. Trick them all most cunningly—lead them to the spinning sea, to down-swirling dizzy bowl. Trust the whirlpool, 'ware the troll! Mingols to their deaths must go, down to weedy hell below, never draw an easy breath, suffer an unending death, everlasting pain and strife, everlasting death in life. Mingol madness ever burn! Never peace again return!"

And the flame-voice broke off in a flurry of explosive crackles that shattered the dream-magic and brought the Mouser to his feet with a great start, his sleepy mood all gone. He stared at the fire, walked rapidly around it, peered at it closely from the other side, then swiftly scanned the entire room. Nothing! He glared at Hilsa and Rill. They eyed him blandly and said in unison, "The god has spoken," but the sense of a presence was gone from the fire and the room as well, leaving behind not even a black hole into which it might have retired —unless perchance (it occurred to the Mouser) it had retired into *him*, accounting for the feeling of restless energy and flaming thought which now possessed him, while the litany of Mingol doom kept repeating itself over and over in his memory. "Can such things be?" he asked himself and answered himself with an instant and resounding "Yes!"

He paced back to Cif, who had risen likewise. "We have three days," she said.

"So it appears," he said, then, "Know you aught of trolls? What are they?"

"I was about to ask you that," she replied. "The word's as strange to me as it appears to be to you."

"Whirlpools, then," he queried, his thoughts racing. "Any of them about the isle? Any sailors' tales——"

"Oh, yes—the Great Maelstrom off the isle's rock-fanged east coast with its treacherous swift currents and tricky tides, the Great Maelstrom from whence the island gets what wood it owns, after it's cast up on the Beach of Bleached Bones. It forms regularly each day. Our sailors know it well and avoid it like no other peril."

"Good! I must put to sea and seek it out and learn its every trick and how it comes and goes. I'll need a small sailing craft for that while *Flotsam'* s laid up for repairs—there's little time. Aye, and I'll need more money too—shore silver for my men."

"Wherefore to sea?" her breath catching, she asked. "Wherefore must you dash yourself at such a maw of danger?"—but in her widening eyes he thought he could see the dawning of the answer to that.

"Why, to put down your foes," he said ringingly. "Heard you not Loki's prophecy? We'll expedite it. We'll drown at least one branch of the Mingols e'er ever they set foot on Rimeland! And if, with Odin's aid, Fafhrd and Afreyt can scupper the Widder-Mingols half as handily, our task is done!"

The triumphant look flared up in her eyes to match that in his own.

The waning moon rode high in the southwest and the brightest stars still shone, but in the east the sky had begun to pale with the dawn, as Fafhrd led his twelve berserks north out of Salthaven. Each was warmly clad against the ice ahead and bore longbow, quiver, extra arrow-pack, belted ax, and bag of provender. Skor brought up the rear, keen to enforce Fafhrd's rule of utter silence while they traversed the town, so that this breach of port regulations might go unnoticed. And for a wonder they had not been challenged. Perhaps the Rimelanders slept extra sound because so many of them had been up to all hours salting down the monster fish-catch, the last boatloads of which had come in after nightfall.

With the berserks tripped along the girls May and Mara in their soft boots and hooded cloaks, the former with a jar of fresh-drawn milk for the god Odin, the latter to be the expedition's guide across central Rime Isle to Cold Harbor, at Afreyt's insistence—"for she was born on a Cold Harbor farm and knows the way—and can keep up with any man."

Fafhrd had nodded dubiously on hearing that. He had not liked accepting responsibility for a girl with his childhood sweetheart's name. Nor had he liked leaving the management of everything in Salthaven to the Mouser and the two women, now that there was so much to do, and besides all else the new task of investigating the Grand Maelstrom and spying out its ways, which would occupy the Mouser for a day at least, and which more befitted Fafhrd as the more experienced ship-conner. But the four of them had conferred together at midnight in *Flotsam*'s cabin behind shrouded portholes, pooling their knowledge and counsels and the two gods' prophecies, and it had been so decided.

The Mouser would take Ourph with him, for his ancient sea-wisdom, and Mikkidu, to discipline him, using a small fishing craft belonging to the women. Meanwhile, Pshawri would be left in sole charge of the repairs on *Flotsam* and *Sea Hawk* (subject to the advisements of the three remaining Mingols), trying to keep up the illusion that Fafhrd's berserks were still aboard the latter. Cif and Afreyt would take turns in standing by at the docks to head off inquiries by Groniger and deal with any other matters that might arise unexpectedly.

Well, it should work, Fafhrd told himself, the Rime Islers being such blunt, unsubtle types, hardy and simple. Certainly the Mouser had seemed confident enough—restless and driving, eyes flashing, humming a tune under his breath.

Onwinging dawn pinkened the low sky to the east as Fafhrd tramped ahead through the heather, lengthening his stride, an ear attuned to the low voices of the men behind and the lighter ones of the girls. A glance overshoulder told him they were keeping close order, with Mara and May immediately behind them.

As Gallows Hill showed up to the left, he heard the men mark it with grim exclamations. A couple spat to ward off ill omen.

"Bear the god my greeting, May," he heard Mara say.

"If he wakes enough to attend to aught but drink his milk and sleep again," May replied as she branched off from the expedition and headed for the hill with her jar through the dissipating shadows of night.

Some of the men exclaimed gloomily at that, too, and Skor called for silence.

Mara said softly to Fafhrd, "We bear left here a little, so as to miss Darkfire's icefall, which we skirt through the Isle's center until it joins the glacier of Mount Hellglow."

Fafhrd thought, what cheerful names they favor, and scanned ahead. Heather and gorse were becoming scantier and stretches of lichened, shaly rock beginning to show.

"What do they call this part of Rime Isle?" he asked her.

"The Deathlands," she answered.

More of the same, he thought. Well, at any rate the name fits the mad, death-bent Mingols and this gallows-favoring Odin god too.

The Mouser was tallest of the four short, wiry men waiting at the edge of the public dock. Pshawri close beside him looked resolute and attentive, though still somewhat pale. A neat bandage went across his forehead. Ourph and Mikkidu rather resembled two monkeys, the one wizened and wise, the other young and somewhat woebegone.

The salt cliff to the east barely hid the rising sun, which glittered along its crystalline summit and poured light on the farther half of the harbor and on the fishing fleet putting out to sea. The Mouser gazed speculatively after the small vessels—you'd have thought the Islanders would have been satisfied with yesterday's monster catch, but no, they seemed even more in a hurry today, as if they were fishing for all Nehwon or as if some impatient chant were beating in their heads, driving them on, such as was beating in the Mouser's now: *Mingols to their deaths must go, down to weedy hell below*— yes, to hell they must go indeed! and time was wasting and where was Cif?

That question was answered when a skiff came sculling quietly along very close to the dock, propelled by Mother Grum sitting in the stern and wagging a single oar from side to side like a fish's tail. When Cif stood up in the boat's midst her head was level with the dock. She caught hold of the hand the Mouser reached down and came up in two long steps.

"Few words," she said. "Mother Grum will scull you to *Sprite*," and she passed the Mouser a purse.

"Silver only," she said with a wrinkle of her nose as he made to glance into it.

He handed it to Pshawri. "Two pieces to each man at nightfall, If I'm not returned," he directed. "Keep them hard at work. 'Twere well *Flotsam* were seaworthy by noon tomorrow at latest. Go."

Pshawri saluted and made off.

The Mouser turned to the others. "Down into the skiff with you."

They obeyed, Ourph impassive-faced, Mikkidu with an apprehensive sidewise look at their grim boatwoman. Cif touched the Mouser's arm. He turned back.

She looked him evenly in the eye. "The Maelstrom is dangerous," she said. "Here's what perhaps can quell it, if it should trap you. If needs must, hurl it into the pool's exact midst. Guard it well and keep it secret."

Surprised at the weight of the small cubical object she pressed into his hand, he glanced down at it surreptitiously. "Gold?" he breathed, a little wonderingly. It was in the form of a skeleton cube, twelve short thick gold-gleaming edges conjoined squarely.

"Yes," she replied flatly. "Lives are more valuable."

"And there's some superstition——?"

"Yes," she cut him short.

He nodded, pouched it carefully, and without other word descended lightly into the skiff. Mother Grum worked her oar back and forth, sending them toward the one small fishing craft remaining in the harbor.

Cif watched after them as their skiff emerged into full sunlight. After a while she felt the same sunlight on her head and knew it was striking golden highlights from her dark hair. The Mouser never looked around. She did not really want him to. The skiff reached *Sprite* and the three men climbed nimbly aboard.

She could have sworn there'd been no one near, but next she heard the sound of a throat being cleared behind her. She waited a few moments, then turned around.

"Master Groniger," she greeted.

"Mistress Cif," he responded in equally mild tones. He did not look like a man who had been sneaking about.

"You send the strangers on a mission?" he remarked after a bit.

She shook her head slowly. "I rent them a ship, the lady Afreyt's and mine. Perhaps they go fishing." She shrugged. "Like any Isler, I turn a dollar when I can and fishing's not the only road to profit. Not captaining your craft today, master?"

He shook his head in turn. "A harbor chief first has the responsibilities of his office, mistress. The other stranger's not been seen yet today. Nor his men either. . . ."

"So?" she asked when he'd paused a while.

". . . though there's a great racket of work below deck in his sailing galley."

She nodded and turned to watch *Sprite* making for the harbor mouth under sail and the skiff sculling off with its lone shaggy-haired, squat figure.

"A meeting of the council has been called for tonight," Groniger said as if in afterthought. She nodded without turning around. He added in explanation, casually, "An audit has been asked for, Lady Treasurer, or all gold coin and Rimic treasures in your keeping—the golden arrow of truth, the gold circles of unity, the gold cube of square-dealing. . . ."

She nodded again, then lifted her hand to her mouth. He heard the sigh of a yawn. The sun was bright on her hair.

By midafternoon Fafhrd's band was high in the Deathlands, here a boulder-studded expanse of barren, dark rock between low glacial walls a bowshot off to the left, closer than that on the right—a sort of broad pass. The westering sun beat down hotly, but the breeze was chill. The blue sky seemed close.

First went the youngest of his berserks, unarmed, as point. (An unarmed man really scans for the foe and does not engage them.) Twoscore yards behind him went Mannimark as coverpoint and behind *him* the main party led by Fafhrd with Maria beside him, Skor still bringing up the rear.

A large white hare broke cover ahead and raced away past them the way they had come, taking fantastic bounds, seemingly terrified. Fafhrd waved in the men ahead and arranged two-thirds of his force in an ambush where the stony cover was good, putting Skor in charge of them with orders to hold that position and engage any enemy on sight with heavy arrow fire but on no account to charge. Then he rapidly led the rest by a circuitous and shielded route up onto the nearest glacier. Skullick, Mara, and three others were with them. Thus far the girl had lived up to Afreyt's claims for her, making no trouble.

As he cautiously led them out onto the ice, the silence of the heights was broken by the faint twang of bowstrings and by sharp cries from the direction of the ambush and ahead.

From his point of vantage Fafhrd could see his ambush and, almost a bowshot ahead of it in the pass, a party of some forty men, Mingols by their fur smocks and hats and curvy bows. The men of his ambush and some dozen of the Mingols were exchanging high-arching arrow fire. One of the Mingols was down and their leaders seemed in dispute. Faf quickly strung his bow, ordering the four men with him to do the same, and they sent off a volley of arrows from this flanking position. Another Mingol was hit—one of the disputants. A half dozen returned their fire, but Fafhrd's position had the advantage of height. The rest took cover. One danced up and down, as if in rage, but was dragged behind rocks by companions. After a bit the whole Mingol party, so far as Fafhrd could tell, began to move off the way they'd come, bearing their wounded with them.

"And now charge and destroy 'em?" Skullick ventured, grinning fiendishly. Mara looked eagerly.

"And show 'em we're but a dozen? I forgive you your youth," Fafhrd retorted, halting Skor's fire with a downward wave of his arm. "No, we'll escort 'em watchfully back to their ship, or Cold Harbor, or whatever. Best foe is one in flight," and he sent a runner to Skor to convey his plan, meanwhile thinking how the fur-clad Steppe-men seemed less furiously hell-bent on rapine than he'd anticipated. He must watch for Mingol ruses. He wondered what old god Odin (who'd said "destroy") would think of his decision. Perhaps Mara's eyes, fixed upon him with what looked very much like disappointment, provided an answer.

The Mouser sat on the decked prow of *Sprite*, his back to the mast, his feet resting on the root of the bowsprit, as they re-approached Rime Isle, running down on the island from the northeast. Some distance ahead should lie the spot where the maelstrom would form and now, with the tide ebbing, getting toward the time—if he'd calculated aright and could trust information got earlier from Cif and Ourph. Behind him in the stern the old Mingol managed tiller and triangular fore-and-aft mainsail handily while Mikkidu, closer, watched the single narrow jib.

The Mouser unstrapped the flap of the small deep pouch at his belt and gazed down at the compact, dully gold-gleaming "whirlpool-queller" (to give a name to the object Cif had given him) nested inside. Again it occurred to him how magnificently spendthrift (but also how bone-stupid) it was to make such a necessarily expendable object of gold. Well, you couldn't dictate prudence to superstition. . . . Or perhaps you could.

"Mikkidu!" he called sharply.

"Yes, sir?" came the answer—immediate, dutiful, and a shade apprehensive.

"You noted the long coil of thin line hanging inside the hatch? The sort of slender yet stout stuff you'd use to lower loot to an accomplice outside a high window or trust your own weight to in a pinch? The sort some stranglers use?"

"Yes, sir!"

"Good. Fetch it for me."

It proved to be as he'd described it and at least a hundred yards long, he judged. A sardonic smile quirked his lips as he knotted one end of it securely to the whirlpool-queller and the other end to a ring bolt in the deck, checked that the rest of the coil lay running free, and returned the queller to his pouch.

They'd been half a day sailing here. First a swift run to the east with wind abeam as soon as they'd got out of Salthaven harbor, leaving the Rimic fishing fleet very busy to the southwest, where the sea seemed to boil with fish, until they were well past the white salt headland. Then a long slow beat north into the wind, taking them gradually away from the Isle's dark craggy east coast, which, replacing the glittering salt, trended toward the west. Finally, now, a swift return, running before the wind, to that same coast where a shallow bay guarded by twin crags lured the unwary mariner. The sail sang and the small waves, advancing in ranked array, slapped the creaming prow. The sunlight was bright everywhere.

The Mouser stood up, closely scanning the sea immediately ahead for submerged rocks and signs of tides at work. The speed of *Sprite* seemed to increase beyond that given it by the wind, as though a current had gripped it. He noted an eddying ahead, sudden curves in the wave-topping lines of foam. Now was the time!—if time there was to be. He called to Ourph to be ready to go about.

Despite all these anticipations he was taken by surprise when (it seemed it must be) an unseen giant hand gripped *Sprite* from below, turned it instantly sideways and jerked it ahead in a curve, tilting it sharply inward. He saw Mikkidu standing in the air over the water a yard from the deck. As he involuntarily moved to join the dumbfounded thief, his left hand automatically seized the mast while his right, stretching out mightily, grabbed Mikkidu by the collar. The Mouser's muscles cracked but took the strain. He deposited Mikkidu on the deck, putting a foot on him to keep him there, then crouched into the wind that was rattling the sails, and managed to look around.

Where ranked waves had been moments before, *Sprite* at prodigious speed was circling a deepening saucer of spinning black water almost two hundred yards across. Dimly past the wildly flapping mainsail the Mouser glimpsed Ourph clinging with both hands to the tiller. Looking again at the whirlpool he saw that *Sprite* was appreciably closer to its deepening center, whence jagged rocks now protruded like a monster's blackened and broken fangs. Without pause he dug in his pouch for the queller and, trying to allow for wind and *Sprite*'s speed, he hurled it at the watery pit's center. For a space it seemed to hang glinting golden-yellow in the sunlight, then fell true.

This time it was as if a hundred giant invisible hands had smote the whirlpool flat. *Sprite* seemed to hit a wall. There was a sudden welter of cross-chopping waves that generated so much foam that it piled up on the deck and one would have sworn the water was filled with soap.

The Mouser reassured himself that Ourph and Mikkidu were there and in an upright position so that, given time, they might recover. Next he ascertained that the sky and sea appeared to be in their proper places. Then he checked on the tiller and sails. His eye falling away from the bedraggled jib lit on the ringbolt in the prow. He reeled in the line attached to it (not very hopefully—surely it would have snagged or snapped in the chaos they'd just endured) but for a wonder it came out with the queller still tightly knotted to the end of it, more golden-bright than ever from its tumbling it had got in the rocks. As he pouched it and laced tight the soggy flap, he felt remarkably self-satisfied.

By now waves and wind had resumed something like their normal flow and Ourph and Mikkidu were stirring. The Mouser set them back at their duties (refusing to discuss at all the whirlpool's appearance and vanishment) and he cockily had them sail *Sprite* close inshore, where he noted a beach of jagged rocks with considerable gray timber amongst them, bones of dead ships.

Time for the Rime-men to pick up another load, he thought breezily. Have to tell Groniger. Or perhaps best wait for the next wrecks— Mingol ones!—which should provide a prodigious harvest.

Smiling, the Mouser set course for Salthaven, an easy sail now with the favoring wind. Under his breath he hummed, "Mingols to their deaths must go, down to weedy hell below." Aye, and their ships to rock-fanged doom.

Somewhere between cloud layers north of Rime Isle there floated miraculously the sphere of black ice that was Khahkht's home and most-times prison. Snow falling steadily between the layers gave the black sphere a white cap. The falling snow also accumulated on and so whitely outlined the mighty wings, back, neck, and crest of the invisible being poised beside the sphere. This being must have been clutching the sphere in some fashion, for whenever it shook its head and shoulders to dislodge the snow, the sphere jogged in the thin air.

Three-quarters of the way down the sphere, a trapdoor had been flung open and from it Khahkht had thrust Its head, shoulders, and one arm, like a peculiarly nasty god looking sidewise down and out of the floor of heaven.

The two beings conversed together.

KHAHKHT: Fretful monster! Why do you trouble my celestial privacy, rapping on my sphere? Soon I'll be sorry that I gave you wings.

FAROOMFAR: I'd as soon shift back to a flying invisible ray-fish. It had advantages.

KHAHKHT: For two black dogs, I'd—!

FAROOMFAR: Contain your ugly self, granddad. I've good reason to knock you up. The Mingols seem to lessen in their frenzy. Gonov of the Sunwise descending on Rime Isle has ordered his ships double-reef for a mere gale. While the Widder-raiders coming down across the Isle have turned back from a force less than a third their size. Have your incantments weakened?

KHAHKHT: Content you. I have been seeking to assess the two new gods who aid Rime Isle: how powerful, whence they come, their final purpose, and whether they may be suborned. My tentative conclusion: They're a treacherous pair, none too strong—rogue gods from a minor universe. We'd best ignore 'em.

The snow had re-gathered on the flier, a fine dust of it revealing even somewhat of his thin, cruel, patrician features. He shook it off.

FAROOMFAR: So, what to do?

KHAHKHT: I'll refire the Mingols where (and if) they flinch back, never you fear. Do you, meanwhile, evade your wicked sisters if you're able and work what devilish mischief you can on Fafhrd (it's he that's cowed the Widder-raiders, right?) and his band. Aim at the girl. To work!

And he drew back into his black, snow-capped sphere and slammed the trapdoor, like a reverse jack-in-the-box. The falling snow was disturbed in a broad downward sweep as Faroomfar spread wings and began his descent from the heights.

Most commendably, Mother Grum was waiting in the skiff at the anchorage when Ourph and Mikkidu brought *Sprite* breezing in neatly to make fast to the buoy and furl sail under the Mouser's watchful, approving eye. He was still in a marvelously good mood of self-satisfaction and had even unbent to make a few benign remarks to Mikkidu (which puzzled the latter mightily) and discourse sagely by whimsical fits and starts with the wise, if somewhat taciturn, old Mingol.

Now sharing the skiff's mid thwart with Ourph, while Mikkidu huddled in the prow, the Mouser airily asked the hag as she sculled them in, "How went the day, Mother? Any word for me from your mistress?" When she answered him only with a grunt that might mean anything or nothing, he merely remarked with mild sententiousness, "Bless your loyal old bones," and let his attention wander idly about the harbor.

Night had fallen. The last of the fishing fleet had just come in, low in the water with another record-breaking catch. His attention fixed on the nearest pier, where a ship on the other side was unloading by torchlight and four Rime-men, going in single file, were bearing ashore what were undoubtedly the prizes of their monster (and monstrous) haul.

Yesterday the Rimelanders had impressed him as very solid and sober folk, but now more and more he was finding something oafish and loutish about them, especially these four as they went galumphing along, smirking and gaping and with eyes starting out of their heads beneath their considerable burdens.

First went a bent-over, bearded fellow, bearing upon his back by its finny tail a great silver tunny as long-bodied as he and even thicker.

Next a rangy chap carrying by neck and tail, wound round and over his shoulders, the largest eel the Mouser had ever seen. Its bearer gave the impression that he was wrestling with it as he hobbled—it writhed ponderously, still alive. *Lucky it's not twined about his neck,* the Mouser thought.

The man after the eel-carrier had, by a wicked handhook through its shell, a giant green crab on his back, its ten legs working persistently in the air, its great claws opening and closing. And it was hard to tell which of the two's eyes goggled out the farthest, the shellfish's or the man's.

Finally a fisherman bearing overshoulder by its bound-together tentacles an octopus still turning rainbow colors in its death-spasms, its great sunken eyes filming above its monstrous beak.

Monsters bearing monsters, the Mouser epitomized with a happy chuckle. *Lord, what grotesques we mortals be!*

And now the dock should be coming up. The Mouser turned round in his seat to look that way and saw . . . not Cif, he decided regretfully after a moment . . . but at any rate (and a little to his initial surprise) Hilsa and Rill at the dock's edge, the latter bearing a torch that flamed most merrily, both of them smiling warm welcomes and looking truly most brave in their fresh paint and whore's finery, Hilsa in her red stockings, Rill in a bright yellow pair, both in short gaudy smocks cut low at the neck. Really, they looked younger this way, or at least a little less shopworn, he thought as he leaped up and joined them on the dock. How nice of Loki to have sent his priestesses . . . well, not priestesses exactly, say temple maidens rather . . . no, not maidens exactly either, but professional ladies, nurses and playmates of the god . . . to welcome home the god's faithful servant.

But no sooner had he bowed to them in turn than they put aside their smiles and Hilsa said to him urgently in a low voice, "There's ill news, captain. Lady Cif's sent us to tell you that she and the Lady Afreyt have been impeached by the other council members. She's accused of using coined gold she had the keeping of and other Rimic treasures to fee you and the tall captain and your men. She expects you with your famed cleverness, she told me, to concoct some tale to counter all this."

The Mouser's smile hardly faltered. He was struck rather with how gayly Rill's torch flickered and flared as Hilsa's doleful words poured over him. When Rimic treasures were mentioned he touched his pouch where the queller reposed on its snipped-off length of cord. He had no doubt that it was one of them, yet somehow he was not troubled.

"Is that all?" he asked when Hilsa had done. "I thought at least you'd tell me the trolls had come, against whom the god has warned us. Lead on, my dears, to the council hall! Ourph and Mikkidu, attend us! Take courage, Mother Grum—" (he called down to the skiff) "—doubt not your mistress' safety."

And linking arms with Hilsa and Rill he set out briskly, telling himself that in reverses of fortune such as this, the all-important thing was to behave with vast self-confidence, flame like Rill's torch with it! That was the secret. What matter that he hadn't the faintest idea of what tale he would tell the council? Only maintain the appearance of self-confidence and at the moment when needed, inspiration would come!

What with the late arrival of the fishing fleet the narrow streets were quite crowded as they footed it along. Perhaps it was market night as well, and maybe the council meeting had something to do with it. At any rate there were a lot of "foreigners" out and Rime Islers too, and for a wonder the latter looked stranger and more drolly grotesque than the former. Here came trudging those four fishers again with their monstrous burdens! A fat boy gaped at them. The Mouser patted his head in passing. Oh, what a show was life!

Hilsa and Rill, infected by the Mouser's light-heartedness, put on their smiles again. He must be a grand sight, he thought, strolling along with two fine whores as if he owned the town.

The blue front of the council hall appeared, its door framed by some gone galleon's massive stern and flanked by two glum louts with quarterstaves. The Mouser felt Hilsa and Rill hesitate, but crying in a loud voice, "All honor to the council!" he swept them inside with him, Ourph and Mikkidu ducking in after.

The room inside was larger and somewhat more lofty than the one at the Salt Herring, but was gray-timbered like it, built of wrecks. And it had no fireplace, but was inadequately warmed by two smoking braziers and lit by torches that burned blue and sad (perhaps there were bronze nails in them), not merrily golden-yellow like Rill's. The main article of furniture was a long heavy table, at one end of which Cif and Afreyt sat, looking their haughtiest. Drawn away from them toward the other end were seated ten large sober Isle-men of middle years, Groniger in their midst, with such doleful, gloomily indignant, outraged looks on their faces that the Mouser burst out laughing. Other Islers crowded the walls, some women among them. All turned on the newcomers faces of mingled puzzlement and disapproval.

Groniger reared up and thundered at him, "You dare to laugh at the gathered authority of Rime Isle? You, who come bursting in accompanied by women of the streets and your own trespassing crewmen?"

The Mouser managed to control his laughter and listen with the most open, honest expression imaginable, injured innocence incarnate.

Groniger went on, shaking his finger at the other, "Well, there he stands, councilors, a chief receiver of the misappropriated gold, perchance even of the gold cube of honest dealing. The man who came to us out of the south with tales of magic storms and day turned night and vanished hostile vessels and a purported Mingol invasion—he who has, as you perceive, Mingols amongst his crew—the man who paid for his dockage in Rime Isle gold!"

Cif stood up at that, her eyes blazing, and said, "Let him speak, at least, and answer this outrageous charge, since you won't take my word."

A councilman rose beside Groniger. "Why should we listen to a stranger's lies?"

Groniger said, "I thank you, Dwone."

Afreyt got to her feet. "No, let him speak. Will you hear nothing but your own voices?"

Another councilman got up.

Groniger said, "Yes, Zwaakin?"

That one said, "No harm to hear what he has to say. He may convict himself out of his own mouth."

Cif glared at Zwaaken and said loudly, "Tell them, Mouser!"

At that moment the Mouser, glancing at Rill's torch (which seemed to wink at him) felt a godlike power invading and possessing him to the tips of his fingers and toes—nay, to the end of his every hair. Without warning—in fact, without knowing he was going to do it at all—he ran forward across the room and sprang atop the table where its sides were clear toward Cif's end.

He looked around compellingly at all (a sea of cold and hostile faces, mostly), gave them a searching stare, and then—well, as the godlike force possessed every part of him utterly, his mind was perforce driven completely out of himself, the scene swiftly darkened, he heard himself *beginning* to say something in a mighty voice, but then he (his mind) fell irretrievably into an inner darkness deeper and blacker than any sleep or swound.

Then (for the Mouser) no time at all passed . . . or an eternity.

His return to awareness (or rebirth, rather—it seemed that massive a transition) began with whirling yellow lights and grinning, open-mouthed, exalted faces mottling the inner darkness, and the sense of a great noise on the edge of the audible and of a resonant voice speaking words of power, and then without other warning the whole bright and deafening scene materialized with a rush and a roar and he was standing insolently tall on the massive council table with what felt like a wild (or even demented) smile on his lips, while his left fist rested jauntily on his hip and his right was whirling around his head the golden queller (or cube of square dealing, he reminded himself) on its cord. And all around him every last Rimelander—councilmen, guards, common fishers, women (and Cif, Afreyt, Rill, Hilsa, Mikkidu, needless to say)—was staring at him with rapturous adoration (as if he were a god or legendary hero at least) and standing on their feet (some jumping up and down) and cheering him to the echo! Fists pounded the table, quarterstaves thudded the stony floor resoundingly. While torchmen whirled their sad flambeaux until they flamed as yellow-bright as Rill's.

Now in the name of all the gods at once, the Mouser asked himself, continuing however to grin, *whatever* did I tell or promise them to put them all in such a state? In the fiend's name, *what?*

Groniger swiftly mounted the other end of the table, boosted by those beside him, waved for silence, and as soon as he'd got a little of that commodity assured the Mouser in a great feelingful voice, advancing to make himself heard, "We'll do it—oh, we'll do it! I myself will lead out the Rimic contingent, half our armed citizenry, across the Deathlands to Fafhrd's aid against the Widdershins, while Dwone and Zwaaken will man the armed fishing fleet with the other half and follow you in *Flotsam* against the Sunwise Mingols. Victory!"

And with that the hall resounded with cries of "Death to the Mingols!" "Victory!" and other cheers the Mouser couldn't quite make out. As the noise passed its peak, Groniger shouted, "Wine! Let's pledge our allegiance!" while Zwaaken cried to the Mouser, "Summon your crewmen to celebrate with us—they've the freedom of Rime Isle now and forever!" (Mikkidu was soon dispatched.)

The Mouser looked helplessly at Cif—though still maintaining his grin (by now he must look quite glassy-eyed, he thought)—but she only stretched her hand toward him, crying, flush-cheeked, "I'll sail with you!" while Afreyt beside her proclaimed, "I'll go ahead across the Deathlands to join Fafhrd, bringing god Odin with me!"

Groniger heard that and called to her, "I and my men will give you whatever help with that you need, honored council-lady," which told the Mouser that besides all else he'd got the atheistical fishermen believing in gods—Odin and Loki, at any rate. *What* had he told them?

He let Cif and Afreyt draw him down, but before he could begin to question them, Cif had thrown her arms around him, hugged him tight, and was kissing him full on the lips. This was wonderful, something he'd been dreaming of for three months and more (even though he'd pictured it happening in somewhat more private circumstances) and when she at last drew back, starry-eyed, it was another sort of question he was of a mind to ask her, but at that moment tall Afreyt grabbed him and soon was kissing him as soundly.

This was undeniably pleasant, but it took away from Cif's kiss, made it less personal, more a sign of congratulations and expression of overflowing enthusiasm than a mark of special affection. His Cif-dream faded down. And when Afreyt was done with him, he was at once surrounded by a press of well-wishers, some of whom wanted to embrace him also. From the corner of his eye he noted Hilsa and Rill bussing all and sundry—really, all these kisses had no meaning at all, including Cif's of course, he'd been a fool to think differently—and at one point he could have sworn he saw Groniger dancing a jig. Only old Ourph, for some reason, did not join in the merriment. Once he caught the old Mingol looking at him sadly.

And so the celebration began that lasted half the night and involved much drinking and eating and impromptu cheering and dancing and parading round and about and in and out. And the longer it went on, the more grotesque the cavorting and footstamping marches got, and all of it to the rhythm of the vindictive little rhyme that still went on resounding deep in the Mouser's mind, the tune to which everything was beginning to dance: "Storm clouds thicken round Rime Isle. Nature brews her blackest bile. Monsters quicken, nightmares foal, niss and nicor, drow and troll." Those lines in particular seemed to the Mouser to describe what was happening just now—a birth of monsters. (But where were the trolls?) And so on (the rhyme) until its doomful and monstrously compelling end: "Mingols to their deaths must go, down to weedy hell below, never draw an easy breath, suffer an unending death, everlasting pain and strife, everlasting death in life. Mingol madness ever burn! Never peace again return!"

And through it all the Mouser maintained his perhaps glassy-eyed smile and jaunty, insolent air of supreme self-confidence, he answered one repeated question with, "No, I'm no orator—never had any training—though I've always liked to talk," but inwardly he seethed with curiosity. As soon as he got a chance, he asked Cif, "Whatever did I say to bring them around, to change their minds so utterly?"

"Why, you should know," she told him.

"But tell me in your own words," he said.

She deliberated. "You appealed entirely to their feelings, to their emotions," she said at last, simply. "It was wonderful."

"Yes, but what exactly did I say? What were my words?"

"Oh, I can't tell you *that*," she protested. "It was so all of a piece that no one thing stood out—I've quite forgotten the details. Content you, it was perfect."

Later on he ventured to inquire of Groniger, "At what point did my arguments begin to persuade you?"

"How can you ask that?" the grizzled Rimelander rejoined, a frown of honest puzzlement furrowing his brow. "It was all so supremely logical, clearly and coldly reasoned. Like two and two makes four. How can one point to one part of arithmetic as being more compelling than another?"

"True, true," the Mouser echoed reluctantly, and ventured to add, "I suppose it was the same sort of rigorous logic that persuaded you to accept the gods Odin and Loki?"

"Precisely," Groniger confirmed.

The Mouser nodded, though he shrugged in spirit. Oh, he knew what had happened all right, he even checked it out a little later with Rill.

"Where did you light your torch?" he asked.

"At the god's fire, of course," she answered. "At the god's fire in the Flame Den." And then she kissed him. (She wasn't too bad at that either, even though there was nothing to the whole kissing business.)

Yes, he knew that the god Loki had come out of the flames and possessed him for a while (as Fafhrd had perhaps once been possessed by the god Issek back in Lankhmar) and spoken through his lips the sort of arguments that are so convincing when voiced by a god or delivered in time of war or comparable crisis—and so empty when proclaimed by a mere mortal on any ordinary occasion.

And really there was no time for speculation about the mystery of what he'd said, now that there was so much to be done, so many life-and-death decisions to be made, so many eventful trains of action to be guided to their conclusions—once these folk had got through celebrating and taken a little rest.

Still, it would be nice to know just a little of what he'd actually said, he thought wistfully. Some of it might even have been clever. Why in heaven's name, for instance, and to illustrate what, had he taken the queller out of his pouch and whirled it around his head?

He had to admit it was rather pleasant being possessed by a god (or would be if one could remember any of it) but it did leave one feeling empty, that is, except for the ever-present Mingols-to-their-deaths jingle—that he'd never get shut of, it seemed.

Next morning Fafhrd's band got their first sight of Cold Harbor, the sea, and the entire Mingol advance force all at once. The sun and west wind had dissipated the coastal fog and blew it from the glacier, on the edge of which they were now all making their way. It was a much smaller and vastly more primitive settlement than Salthaven. To the north rose the dark crater-summit of Mount Hellglow, so lofty and near that its eastern foothills still cast their shadows on the ice. A wisp of smoke rose from it, trailing off east. At the snowline a shadow on the dark rock seemed to mark the mouth of a cavern leading into the mountain's heart. Its lower slopes were thickly crusted with snow, leading back to the glacier which, narrow at this point, stretched ahead of them north to the glittering gray sea, surprisingly near. From the glacier's not-very-lofty foot, rolling grassy turf with occasional clumps of small northern cedars deformed by the wind stretched off to the southwest and its own now-distant snowy heights, wisps of white fog blowing eastways and vanishing across the rolling sunlit land between.

Glimpses of a few devastated and deserted hill farms late yesterday and early this morning, while they'd been trailing and chivvying the retreating Mingol marauders, had prepared them for what they saw now. Those farmhouses and byres had been of turf and sod solely, with grass and flowers growing on their narrow roofs, smokeholes instead of chimneys. Mara, dry-eyed, pointed out the one she'd dwelt in. Cold Harbor was simply a dozen such dwellings atop a rather steep hill or large mound backed against the glacier and turf-walled— a sort of retreat for the country-dwellers in times of peril. A short distance beyond it, a sandy beach fronted the harbor itself and on it three Mingol galleys had been drawn ashore, identified by the fantastic horse cages that were the above-deck portion of their prows.

Ranged round the mound of Cold Harbor at a fairly respectful distance were some fourscore Mingols, their leaders seemingly in conference with those of the twoscore who'd gone raiding ahead and but now returned. One of these latter was pointing back toward the Deathlands and then up at the glacier, as if describing the force that had pursued them. Beyond them the three Steppe stallions free from their cages were cropping turf. A peaceful scene, yet even as Fafhrd watched, keeping his band mostly hid (he hoped) by a fold in the ice (he did not trust too far Mingol aversion to ice) a spear came arching out of the tranquil-seeming mound and (it was a prodigious cast) struck down a Mingol. There were angry cries and a dozen Mingols returned arrow fire. Fafhrd judged that the besiegers, now reinforced, would surely try soon a determined assault. Without hesitation he gave orders.

"Skullick, here's action for you. Take your best bowman, oil, and a firepot. Race ahead for your life to where the glacier is nearest their beached ships and drop fire arrows in them, or attempt to. Run!

"Mara, follow them as far as the mound and when you see the ships smoke, but not before, run down and join your friends if the way is clear. Careful!—Afreyt will have my head if aught befalls you. Tell them the truth about our numbers. Tell them to hold out and to feint a sortie if they see good chance.

"Mannimark! Keep one man of your squad and maintain watch here. Warn us of Mingol advances.

"Skor and the rest, follow me. We'll descend in their rear and briefly counterfeit a pursuing army. Come!"

And he was off at a run with eight berserks lumbering after, arrow-quivers banging against their backs. He'd already picked the stand of stunted cedars from the cover of which he planned to make his demonstration. As he ran, he sought to run in his mind with Skullick and his mate, and with Mara, trying to make the timing right.

He arrived at the cedars and saw Mannimark signaling that the Mingol assault had begun. "Now howl like wolves," he told his hard-breathing men, "and really scream, each of you enough for two. Then we'll pour arrows toward 'em, longest range and fast as you can. Then, when I give command, back on the glacier again! as fast as we came down."

When all this was done (and without much marking of consequences—there was not time) and he had rejoined Mannimark, followed by his panting band, he saw with delight a thin column of black smoke ascending from the beached galley nearest the glaciers. Mingols began to run in that direction from the slopes of the beleaguered mound, abandoning their assault. Midway he saw the small figure of Mara running down the glacier to Cold Harbor, her red cloak standing out behind her. A woman with a spear had appeared on the earth wall nearest the child, waving her on encouragingly. Then of a sudden Mara appeared to take a fantastically long stride, part of her form was obscured, as if there were a blur in Fafhrd's vision there, and then she seemed to—no, did!—rise in the air, higher and higher, as though clutched by an invisible eagle, or other sightless predatory flier. He kept his eyes on the red cloak, which suddenly grew brighter as the invisible flyer mounted from shadow into sunlight with his captive. He heard a muttered exclamation of sympathy and wonder close beside him, spared a sidewise glance, and knew that Skor also had seen the prodigy.

"Keep her in sight, man," he breathed. "Don't lose the red cloak for one moment. Mark where she goes through the trackless air."

The gaze of the two men went upward, then west, then steadily east toward the dark mountain. From time to time Fafhrd looked down to assure himself that there were no untoward developments requiring his attention of the situations at the ships and at Cold Harbor. Each time he feared his eyes would never catch sight of the flying cloak again, but each time they did. Skor seemed to be following instructions faithfully. The red patch grew smaller, tinier. They almost lost it as it dipped into the shadow again. Finally Skor straightened up.

"Where did it go?" Fafhrd asked.

"To the mouth of the cave at the snowline," Skor replied. "The girl was drawn there through the air by what magic I know not. I lost it there."

Fafhrd nodded. "Magic of a most special sort," he said rapidly. "She was carried there, I must believe, by an invisible flier, ghoul-related, an old enemy of mine, Prince Faroomfar of lofty Stardock. Only I among us have the knowledge to deal with him."

He felt, in a way, that he was seeing Skor for the first time: a man an inch taller than himself and some five years younger, but with receding hairline and a rather scanty straggling russet beard. His nose had been broken at some time. He looked a thoughtful villain.

Fafhrd said, "In the Cold Waste near Illek-Ving I hired you. At No-Ombrulsk I named you my chief lieutenant and you swore with the rest to obey me for *Sea Hawk*'s voyage and return." He locked eyes with the man. "Now it comes to the test, for you must take command while I seek Mara. Continue to harry the Mingols but avoid a full engagement. Those of Cold Harbor are our friends, but do not join with them in their fort unless no other course is open. Remember we serve the lady Afreyt. Understood?"

Skor frowned, keeping his eyes locked with Fafhrd's, then nodded once.

"Good!" Fafhrd said, not sure at all that it was so, but knowing he was doing what he had to. The smoke from the burning ship was less —the Mingols seemed to have saved her. Skullick and his fellow came running back with their bows, grinning.

"Mannimark!" Fafhrd called. "Give me two torches. Skullick!—the tinder-pouch." He unbuckled the belt holding his longsword Gray-wand. He retained his ax.

"Men!" he addressed them. "I must be absent for a space. Command goes to Skor by this token." He buckled Graywand to that one's side. "Obey him faithfully. Keep yourselves whole. See that I'm given no cause to rebuke you when I return."

And without more ado he made off across the glacier toward Mount Hellglow.

The Mouser forced himself to rise soon as he woke and to take a cold bath before his single cup of hot gahveh (he was in that sort of mood). He set his entire crew to work, Mingols and thieves alike, completing *Flotsam*'s repairs, warning them that she must be ready to sail by the morrow's morn at least, in line with Loki god's promise: "In three days the Mingols come." He took considerable pleasure in noting that several of them seemed to be suffering from worse hangovers than his own. "Work them hard, Pshawri," he commanded. "No mercy to slug-a-beds and shirkers!"

By then it was time to join with Cif in seeing off Afreyt's and Groniger's overland expedition. He found the Rimelanders offensively bright-eyed, noisy, and energetic, and the way that Groniger bustled about, marshalling them, was a caution.

Cif and Afreyt were clear-eyed and smiling also in their brave russets and blues, but that was easier to take. He and Cif walked a ways with the overland marchers. He noted with some amusement and approval that Afreyt had four of Groniger's men carrying a curtained litter, though she did not occupy it as yet. So she was making the men pay for yesternight's false (or at least, tactless) accusations, and would cross the Deathlands in luxurious ease. That was more in his own style.

He was in an odd state of mind, almost feeling himself a spectator rather than a participant in great events. The incident of the stirring speech he had made last night (or rather the oration that the god Loki had delivered through his lips while he was blacked out) and didn't remember (and couldn't discover) a word of still rankled. He felt like the sort of unimportant servant, or errand boy, who's never allowed to know the contents of the sealed messages he's given to deliver.

In this role of observer and critic he was struck by how grotesque was the weaponry of the high-stepping and ebullient Rimelanders. There were the quarterstaves, of course, and heavy single-bladed spears, but also slim fishing spears and great pitchforks and wickedly hooked and notched pikes, and long flails with curious heavy swiples and swingles a-dangle from their ends. A couple even carried long narrow-bladed and sharp-looking spades. He remarked on it to Cif and she asked him how he armed his own thief-band. Afreyt had gone on a little ahead. They were nearing Gallows Hill.

"Why, with slings," he told Cif. "They're as good as bows and a lot less trouble to carry. Like this one," and he showed her the leather sling hanging from his belt. "See that old gibbet ahead? Now mark."

He selected a lead ball from his pouch, centered it in the strap and, sighting quickly but carefully, whirled it twice round his head and loosed. The *thunk* as it struck square on was unexpectedly loud and resounding. Some Rimelanders applauded.

Afreyt came hurrying back to tell him not to do that again—it might offend god Odin. Can't do anything right this morning, the Mouser told himself sourly.

But the incident had given him a thought. He said to Cif, "Say, maybe I was demonstrating the sling in my speech last night when I whirled the cube of square dealing around on its cord. Do you recall? Sometimes I get drunk on my own words and don't remember too well."

She shook her head. "Perhaps you were," she said. "Or perhaps you were dramatizing the Great Maelstrom which will swallow the Sun Mingols. Oh, that wondrous speech!"

Meanwhile they had come abreast of Gallows Hill and Afreyt had halted the march. He strolled over with Cif to find out why and for farewells—this was about as far as they'd planned to come.

To his surprise he discovered that Afreyt had set the two men with spades and several others to digging up the gallows, to uprooting it entire, and also had had its bearers set down the litter in front of the little grove of gorse on the north side of the hill, and part its curtains. While he watched puzzledly, he saw the girls May and Gale emerge from the grove, walking slowly and carefully and going through the motions of assisting someone—only there was no one there.

Except for the men trying to rock the gallows loose, everyone had grown quite silent, watchfully attentive.

In low undertones Cif told the Mouser the girls' names and what was going on.

"You mean to say that's Odin god they're helping and they're able to see him?" he whispered back. "I remember now, Afreyt said she was taking him along, but—Can *you* see him at all?"

"Not very distinctly in this sunlight," she admitted. "But I have done so, by twilight. Afreyt says Fafhrd saw Odin most clearly in the dusk, evening before last. It's given only to Afreyt and the girls to see him clearly."

The strange slow pantomime was soon concluded. Afreyt cut a few spiny branches of gorse and put them in the litter ("So he'll feel at home," Cif explained to the Mouser) and started to draw the curtains, but, "He wants *me* inside with him," Gale announced in her shrill childish voice. Afreyt nodded, the little girl climbed in with a shrug of resignation, the curtains were drawn at last, and the general hush broke.

Lord, what idiocy! the Mouser thought. We two-footed fantasies will believe anything. And yet it occurred to him uneasily that he was a fine one to talk, who'd heard a god speak out of a fire and had his own body usurped by one. Inconsiderate creatures, gods were.

With a rush and a shout the gallows came down and its base up out of the earth, spraying dirt around, and a half dozen stalwart Rimelanders lifted it onto their shoulders and prepared to carry it so, marching single file after the litter.

"Well, they *could* use it as a battering ram, I suppose," the Mouser muttered. Cif gave him a look.

Final farewells were said then and last messages for Fafhrd given and mutual assurances of courage until victory and death to the invader, and then the expedition went marching off in great swinging strides, rhythmically. The Mouser, standing with Cif as he watched them go toward the Deathlands, got the impression they were humming under their breaths, "Mingols to their deaths must go," and so on, and stepping to its tune. He wondered if he'd begun to say those verses aloud, so that they'd picked it up from him. He shook his head.

But then he and Cif turned back alone, and he saw it was a bright day, pleasantly cool, with the breeze ruffling the heather and wildflowers waving on their delicate stems, and his spirits began to rise. Cif wore her russets in the shape of a short gown, rather than her customary trousers, and her dark golden-glinting hair was loose, and her movements were unforced and impulsive. She still had reserve, but it was not that of a councilman, and the Mouser remembered how thrilling last night's kiss had been, before he'd decided it didn't mean anything. Two fat lemmings popped out just ahead of them and stood on their hind legs, inspecting them, before ducking behind a bush. In stopping so as not to overrun them, Cif stumbled and he caught her and after a moment drew her to him. She yielded for a moment before she drew away, smiling at him troubledly.

"Gray Mouser," she said softly, "I am attracted to you, but I have told you how you resemble the god Loki—and last night when you swayed the Isle with your great oratory that resemblance was even more marked. I have also told you of my reluctance to take the god home with me (making me hire Hilsa and Rill, two familiar devils, to take care of him). Now I find, doubtless because of the resemblance, a kindred hesitation with respect to you, so that perhaps it is best we remain captain and councilwoman until the defense of Rime Isle is accomplished and I can sort you out from the god."

The Mouser took a long breath and said slowly that he supposed that was best, thinking meanwhile that gods surely interfered with one's private life. He was mightily tempted to ask her whether she expected *him* to turn to Hilsa and Rill (devils or no) to be comforted, but doubted she would be inclined to allow him a god's liberties to that degree (granted he desired such), no matter how great the resemblance between them.

In this impasse, he was rather relieved to see beyond Cif's shoulder that which allowed him to say, "Speaking of she-demons, who are these that are coming from Salthaven?"

Cif turned at that, and there true enough were Rill and Hilsa hurrying toward them through the heather, with Mother Grum plodding along behind, dark figure to their colorful ones. And although it was bright day three hours and more, Rill carried a lit torch. It was hard to see the flame in the sunlight, but they could mark by the way its shimmer made the heather waver beyond. And as the two harlots drew closer, it was evident that their faces were brimming with excitement and a story to tell, which was poured forth on their arrival and on the Mouser asking drily: "Why are you trying to light up the day, Rill?"

"The god spoke to us but now, most clearly from the Flame Den fire," she began, "saying 'Darkfire, Darkfire, take me to Darkfire. Follow the flame—:'" Hilsa broke in, "'—go as it bends,' the god said cracklingly, 'turn as it wends, all in my name.'"

Rill took up again, "So I lit a fresh torch from the Flame Den blaze for him to travel in, and we carefully marked the flame and followed as it leaned, and it has led us to you!"

"And look," Hilsa broke in as Mother Grum came up, "now the flame would have us go to the mountain. It points toward her!" And she waved with her other hand north toward the icefall and the silent black scoriac peak beyond with its smoke-plume blowing west.

Cif and the Mouser dutifully looked at the torch's ghostly flame, narrowing their eyes. After a bit, "The flame *does* lean over," the Mouser said, "but I think that's just because it's burning unevenly. Something in the grain of the wood or its oils and resins——"

"No, indubitably it motions us toward Darkfire," Cif cried excitedly. "Lead on, Rill," and the women all turned sharply north, making for the glacier.

"But ladies, we have hardly time for a trip up-mountain," the Mouser called after protestingly, "what with preparations to be made for the Isle's defense and tomorrow's sailing against the Mingols."

"The god has commanded," Cif told him overshoulder. "He knows best."

Mother Grum said in her growly voice, "I doubt not he intends us to make a closer journey than mountaintop. Roundabout is nearer than straight, I ween."

And with that mystifying remark the women went on, and the Mouser shrugged and perforce followed after, thinking what fools these women were to be scurrying after a burning bush or branch as if it were the very god, even if the flame *did* bend most puzzlingly. (And he *had* heard fire speak, night before last.) Well, at any rate, he wasn't really needed for today's repairs on *Flotsam;* Pshawri could boss the crew as well as he, or at least well enough. Best keep an eye on Cif while this odd fit was on her and see she—or her three strangely sorted god-servants—came to no harm.

Such a sweet, strong, sensible, ravishing woman, Cif, when not godstruck. Lord, what troublesome, demanding and captious employers gods were, never a-quiet. (It was safe to think such thoughts, he told himself, gods couldn't read your thoughts—everyone had *that* privacy—though they could overhear your slightest word spoken in undertone—and doubtless make deductions from your starts and grimaces.)

Up from the depths of his skull came the wearisome compulsive chant, "Mingols to their deaths must go," and he was almost grateful to the malicious little jingle for occupying his mind troubled by the vagaries of gods and women.

The air grew chilly and soon they were at the icefall and in front of it a dead scrubby tree and a mounded upthrust of dark purplish rock, almost black, and in its midst a still blacker opening wide and tall as a door.

Cif said, "This was not here last year," and Mother Grum growled, "The glacier, receding, has uncovered it," and Rill cried, "The flame leans toward the cave!" and Cif said, "Go we down," and Hilsa quavered, "It's dark," and Mother Grum rumbled, "Have no fear. Dark is sometimes best light, and down best way go up."

The Mouser wasted no time on words, but broke three branches from the dead tree (Loki-torch might not last forever) and shouldering them, followed swiftly after the women into the rock.

Fafhrd doggedly climbed the last, seemingly endless slope of icy stone below Mount Hellglow's snowline. Orange light from the sun near setting beat on his back without warmth, and bathed the mountainside and the dark peak above with its wispy smoke blowing east. The rock was tough as diamond with frequent hand-holds—made for climbing—but he was weary and beginning to condemn himself for having abandoned his men in peril (it amounted to that) to come on a wild romantical goose-chase. Wind blew from the west, crosswise to his climb.

This was what came of taking a girl on a dangerous expedition and listening to women—or one woman, rather. Afreyt had been so sure of herself, so queenly-commanding—that he'd gone along with her against his better judgment. Why, he was chasing after Mara now mostly for fear of what Afreyt would think of him if aught befell the girl. Oh, he knew all right how he'd justified himself this morning in giving himself this job rather than sending a couple of his men. He'd jumped to the conclusion it was Prince Faroomfar had kidnapped Mara and he'd had the hope (in view of what Afreyt and Cif had told about being rescued from Khahkht's wizardry by flying mountain-princesses) that Princess Hirriwi, his beloved of one glorious night long gone, would come skimming along sightlessly on her invisible fish-of-air to offer him her aid against her hated brother.

That was another trouble with women, they were never there when you wanted or really needed them. They helped each other, all right, but they expected men to do all sorts of impossible feats of derring-do to prove themselves worthy of the great gift of their love (and what was that when you got down to it?—a fleeting clench-and-wriggle in the dark, illuminated only by the mute, incomprehensible perfection of a dainty breast, that left you bewildered and sad).

The way grew steeper, the light redder, and his muscles smarted. The way it was going, darkness would catch him on the rock-face, and then for two hours at least the mountain would hide the rising moon.

Was it solely on Afreyt's account that he was seeking Mara? Wasn't it also because she had the same name as his first young sweetheart whom he'd abandoned with his unborn child when he'd left Cold Corner as a youth to go off with yet another woman, whom he'd in turn abandoned—or led unwittingly to her death, really the same thing? Wasn't he seeking to appease that earlier Mara by rescuing this child one? That was yet another trouble with women, or at least the women you loved or had loved once—they kept on making you feel guilty, even beyond their deaths. Whether you loved them or not, you were invisibly chained to every woman who'd ever kindled you.

And was even *that* the deepest truth about himself going after the girl Mara?—he asked himself, forcing his analysis into the next devious cranny, even as he forced his numbing hands to seek out the next holds on the still steepening face in the dirty red light. Didn't he really quicken at thought of her, just as god Odin did in his senile lubricity? Wasn't he and no other chasing after Faroomfar because he thought of the prince as a lecherous rival for this delicate tidbit of girl flesh?

For that matter, wasn't it Afreyt's girlishness—her slenderness despite her height, her small and promising breasts, her tales of childhood make-believe maraudings with Cif, her violet-eyed romancing, her madcap bravado—that had attracted him even in far-off Lankhmar? That and her Rime Isle silver had chained him, and set him on the whole unsuitable course of becoming a responsible captain of men—he who had been all his days a lone wolf—with lone-leopard comrade Mouser. Now he'd reverted back to it, abandoning his men. (Gods grant Skor keep his head and that some at least of his disciplines and preachments of prudence had taken effect!) But oh, this lifelong servitude to girls—whimsical, innocent, calculating, icicle-eyed and hearted, fleeting, tripping little demons! White, slim-necked, sharp-toothed, restlessly bobbing weasels with the soulful eyes of lemurs!

His blindly reaching hand closed on emptiness and he realized that in his furious self-upbraiding he'd reached the apex of the slope without knowing it. With belated caution he lifted his head until his eyes looked just over the edge. The sun's last dark red beams showed him a shale-scattered ledge some ten feet wide and then the mountain going up again precipitous and snowless. Opposite him in that new face was a great recess or cavern-mouth as wide as the ledge and twice that height. It was very dark inside that great door but he could make out the bright red of Mara's cloak, its hood raised, and within the hood, shadowed by it, her small face, very pale-cheeked, very dark-eyed— really, a smudge in darkness—staring toward him.

He scrambled up, peering around suspiciously, then moved toward her, softly calling her name. She did not reply with word or sign though continuing to stare. There was a warm, faintly sulfurous breeze blowing out of the mountain and it ruffled her cloak. Fafhrd's steps quickened and with a swift-growing anticipation of unknown horror whirled the cloak aside to reveal a small grinning skull set atop a narrow-shouldered wooden cross about four feet high.

Fafhrd moved backwards to the ledge, breathing heavily. The sun had set and the gray sky seemed wider and more palely bright without its rays. The silence was deep. He looked along the ledge in both directions, fruitlessly. Then he stared into the cave again and his jaw tightened. He took flint and iron, opened the tinder-pouch, and kindled a torch. Then holding it high in his left hand and his unbelted ax gently a-swing in his right, he walked forward into the cave and toward the mountain's heart, past the eerie diminutive scarecrow, his foot avoiding its stripped-away red cloak, along the strangely smooth-walled passageway wide and tall enough for a giant, or a winged man.

The Mouser hardly knew how long he'd been closely following the four godstruck females through the strangely tunnel-like cave that was leading them deeper and deeper under the glacier toward the heart of the volcanic mountain Darkfire. Long enough, at any rate, for him to have split and slivered the larger ends of the three dead branches he was carrying, so they would kindle readily. And certainly long enough to become very weary of the Mingols death-chant, or Mingol jingle, that was now not only resounding in his mind but being spoken aloud by the four rapt women as if it were a marching, or rather scurrying song, just as Groniger's men had seemed to do. Of course in this case he didn't have to ask himself where they'd got it, for they'd all originally heard it with him night before last in the Flame Den, when Loki god had seemed to speak from the fire, but that didn't make it any easier to endure or one whit less boresome.

At first he'd tried to reason with Cif as she hurried along with the others like a mad maenad, arguing the unwisdom of venturing so recklessly into an uncharted cavern, but she'd only pointed at Rill's torch and said, "See how it strains ahead. The god commands us," and gone back to her chanting.

Well, there was no denying that the flame was bending forward most unnaturally when it should have been streaming back with their rapid advance—and also lasting longer than any torch should. So the Mouser had had to go back to memorizing as well as he could their route through the rock which, chill at first, as one would expect from the ice above, was now perceptibly warmer, while the heating air carried a faint brimstone stench.

But at all events, he told himself, he didn't have to *like* this sense of being the tool and sport of mysterious forces vastly more powerful than himself, forces that didn't even deign to tell him the words they spoke through him (that business of the speech he'd given but not heard one word of bothered him more and more). Above all he didn't have to celebrate this bondage to the inscrutable, as the women were doing, by mindlessly repeating words of death and doom.

Also he didn't like the feeling of being in bondage to women and absorbed more and more into their affairs, such as he'd felt ever since accepting Cif's commission three months ago in Lankhmar, and which had put him in bondage, in turn, to Pshawri and Mikkidu and all his men, and to his ambitions and self-esteem.

Above all, he didn't like being in bondage to the idea of himself being a monstrous clever fellow who could walk widdershins round all the gods and godlets, from whom everyone expected godlike performance. Why couldn't he admit to Cif at least that he'd not heard a word of his supposedly great speech? And if he could do that walk-widdershins bit, why didn't he?

The cavernous tunnel they'd been following so long debouched into what seemed a far vaster space steaming with vapors, and then they were suddenly brought up short against a great wall that seemed to extend indefinitely upward and to either side.

The women broke off their doom-song and Rill cried, "Whither now, Loki?" and Hilsa echoed her tremulously. Mother Grum rumbled, "Tell us, wall," and Cif intoned strongly, "Speak, O god."

And while the women were saying these things, the Mouser stole forward rapidly and laid his hand on the wall. It was so hot he almost snatched back his hand, but did not, and through his palm and outspread fingers he felt a steady strong pulsation, a rhythm in the rock, exactly as if it were itself sounding the women's song.

And then as if in answer to the women's entreaty, the Loki torch, which had burnt down to little more than a stub, flared up into a great seven-branched flame, almost intolerably bright—it was a wonder Rill could hold it—showing the frighteningly vast extent of the rock face. Even as it flared, the rock seemed to heave under the Mouser's hand monstrously with each pulsation of its song and the floor began to rock with it. Then the great rock face bulged, and the heat became monstrous too, and the brimstone stench intensified so that they were all set a-gagging and a-coughing even as their imaginations envisioned instant earthquake and cave-brimming floods of red-hot lava exploding from the mountain's heart.

It says much for the Mouser's prudence that in that short period of panic and terrified wonder it occurred to him to thrust one of his frayed branches into the blinding flame. And it was well he did so, for the great god-flame now died down as swiftly as it had flared up, leaving only the feeble illumination of the burning branch of ordinary dead wood afire in his hands. Rill dropped the dead stub of her burnt-out torch with a cry of pain, as if only now feeling how it had burned her, while Hilsa whimpered and all the women groped about dazedly.

And as if command had questionless passed to the Mouser with the torch, he now began to shepherd them back the way they had come, away from the strangling fumes, through the now-bewilderingly shadowy passageways that only he had conned and that still resounded with the dreadful rock music aping their own, a symphony of doom-song monstrously reverberated by solid stone—away toward the blessed outer light and air and sky, and fields and blessed sea.

Nor was that the full measure of the Mouser's far-sighted prudence (so far-sighted that he sometimes couldn't tell what was its aim), for in the moment of greatest panic, when the stub of Loki-torch had fallen from Rill's hand, he had thought to snatch it up from the rocky floor and thrust it, hardly more than a hot black cinder, deep into his pouch. It burnt his fingers a little, he discovered afterwards, but luckily it was not so hot that his pouch caught fire.

Afreyt sat on a lichened rock outside the litter on the broad summit-pass of the Deathlands (near where Fafhrd had first encountered the Mingols, though she didn't know that) with her gray cloak huddled about her, resting. Now and again a wind from the east, whose chilliness seemed that of the violet sky, ruffled the litter's closed curtains. Its bearers had joined the other men at one of the small fires to the fore and rear, built with carried wood to heat chowder during this evening pause in their march. The gallows had been set down by Afreyt's direction and its base and beam-end wedged in rock, so that it rested like a fallen-over "L," its angle lifting above the litter like a crooked roof, or like a rooftree with one kingpost.

There was still enough sunset light in the west for her to wonder if that was smoke she saw moving east above the narrow crater of Mount Hellglow, while in the cold east there was sufficient night for her to see, she was almost sure, a faint glow rising from that of Mount Darkfire. The eastwind blew again and she hunched her shoulders and drew the hood of her cloak more closely against her cheeks.

The curtains of the litter parted for a moment and May slipped out and came and stood in front of Afreyt.

"What's that you've got around your neck?" she asked the girl.

"It's a noose," the latter explained eagerly, but with a certain solemnity. "I braided it, Odin showed me how to make the knot. We're all going to belong to the Order of the Noose, which is something Odin and I invented this afternoon while Gale was taking a nap."

Afreyt hesitatingly reached her hand to the girl's slender throat and inspected the loop of heavy braid with uneasy fascination. There, surely enough, was the cruel hangman's knot drawn rather close, and tucked into it a nosegay of small mountain flowers, somewhat wilted, gathered this morning on the lower slopes.

"I made one for Gale," the girl said. "She didn't want to wear it at first because I'd helped invent it. She was jealous."

Afreyt shook her head reprovingly, though her mind wasn't on that.

"Here," May continued, lifting her hand which had been hanging close to her side under her cloak. "I've made one for you, a little bigger. See, it's got flowers too. Put back your hood. You wear it under your hair, of course."

For a long moment Afreyt looked into the girl's unblinking eyes. Then she drew back her hood, bent down her head, and helped lift her hair through. Using both hands, May drew the knot together at the base of Afreyt's throat. "There," she said, "that's the way you wear it, sung but not tight."

While this was happening, Groniger had come up, carrying three bowls and a small covered pail of chowder. When the nooses had been explained to him, "A capital conceit!" he said with a great grin, his eyebrows lifting. "That'll show the Mingols something, let them know what they're in for. It's a grand chant the Little Captain gave us, isn't it?"

Afreyt nodded, looking sideways a moment at Groniger. "Yes," she said, "his wonderful words."

Groniger glanced back at her in similar fashion. "Yes, his wonderful words."

May said, "I wish I'd heard him."

Groniger handed them the bowls and swiftly poured the thick, creamy soup.

May said, "I'll take Gale hers."

Groniger said gruffly to Afreyt, "Sup it while it's hot. Then get some rest. We go on at moonrise, agreed?" and when Afreyt nodded, strode off rather bumptiously, cheerily rumble-humming the chant to which they'd marched all day, the Mouser's—or Loki's, rather.

Afreyt narrowed her brows. Normally Groniger was such a sober man, dull-spirited she'd once thought, but now he was almost like a buffoon. Was "monstrously comical" too strong an expression? She shook her head slowly. All the Rime-men were getting like that, loutish and grotesque and somehow bigger. Perhaps it was her weariness made her see things askew and magnified, she told herself.

May came back and they got out their spoons and fell to. "Gale wanted to eat hers inside," the girl volunteered after a bit. "I think she and Odin are cooking up something." She shrugged and went back to her spooning. After another while: "I'm going to make nooses for Mara and Captain Fafhrd." Finally she scraped her bowl, set it aside, and said, "Cousin Afreyt, do you think Groniger's a troll?"

"What's that?" Afreyt asked.

"A word Odin uses. He says Groniger's a troll."

Gale came excitedly out of the litter with her empty bowl, but remembering to draw the curtains behind her.

"Odin and I have invented a marching song for us!" she announced, stacking her bowl in May's. "He says the other god's song is all right, but he should have one of his own. Listen, I'll chant it for you. It's shorter and faster than the other." She screwed up her face. "It's like a drum," she explained earnestly. Then, stamping with a foot: "March, march, over the Deathlands. Go, go, over the Doomlands. Doom!—kill the Mingols. Doom!—die the heroes. Doom! Doom! Glorious doom!" Her voice had grown quite loud by the time she was done.

"Glorious doom?" Afreyt repeated.

"Yes, Come on, May, chant it with me."

"I don't know that I want to."

"Oh, come on. I'm wearing your noose, aren't I? Odin says we should all chant it."

As the two girls repeated the chant in their shrill voices with mounting enthusiasm, Groniger and another Rime-man came up.

"That's good," he said, collecting the bowls. "Glorious doom is good."

"I like that one," the other man agreed. "Doom!—kill the Mingols!" he repeated appreciatively.

They went off chanting it in low voices.

The night darkened. The wind blew. The girls grew quiet.

May said, "It's cold. The god'll be getting chilly. Gale, we'd better go inside. Will you be all right, cousin Afreyt?"

"I'll be all right."

A while after the curtains closed behind them. May stuck her head out.

"The god invites you to come inside with us," she called to Afreyt.

Afreyt caught her breath. Then she said as evenly as she could, "Thank the god, but tell him I will remain here . . . on guard."

"Very well," May said and the curtains closed again.

Afreyt clenched her hands under her cloak. She hadn't admitted to anyone, even Cif, that for some time now, Odin had been fading. She could hardly see even a wispy outline any more. She could still hear his voice, but it had begun to grow faint, lost in wind-moaning. The god had been very real at first on that spring day when she and Cif had found him, and found that there were two gods. He'd seemed so near death then, and she'd labored so hard to save him. She'd been filled with such an adoration, as if he were some ancient hero-saint, or her own dear, dead father. And when he had caressed her fumblingly and muttered in disappointment (it sounded), "You're older than I thought," and drifted off to sleep, her adoration had been contaminated by horror and rejection. She'd got the idea of bringing the girls (Did that make her a monster? Well, perhaps) and after that she'd managed very well, keeping it all at a distance.

And then there'd been the excitement of the journey to Lankhmar and the perils of Khahkht's ice-magic and the Mingols and the renewed excitement of the arrival of the Mouser and Fafhrd and the realization that Fafhrd did indeed resemble a younger Odin—was *that* what had made god Odin fade and grow whisper-voiced? She didn't know, but she knew it helped make everything torturesome and confusing—and she couldn't have borne to enter the litter tonight. (Yes, she was a monster.)

She felt a sharp pain in her neck and realized that in her agitation she'd been tugging at the pendant end of the noose beneath her cloak. She loosened it and forced herself to sit quietly. It was full dark now. There *were* faint flames flickering from Darkfire and Hellglow too. She heard snatches of talk from the campfires and bits of the new chant and laughter as the story of that went round. It was very cold, but she did not move. The east grew silvery-pale, the milky effulgence domed up, and at last the white moon edged into view.

The camp stirred then and after a while the bearers came up and unwedged Odin's gallows and lifted it up and the litter too, and Afreyt arose, unkinking her stiff joints and stamping her numbed feet, and they all marched off west across the moon-silvered rock, shouldering their grotesque weapons and the two larger burdens. Some of them limped a bit (after all, they were sailors, their feet unused to marching) but they all went on briskly to the new Odin-chant, hunching their backs against the east wind, which now blew strong and steadily.

Fafhrd had just kindled his second torch from the ember-end of the first and his surroundings had grown warmer, when the lofty passageway he was following debouched into a cavern so vast that the light he bore seemed lost in it. The sound of the cast-away torch-stub hitting rock awakened distant faint echoes and he came to a stop, peering up and around. Then he began to see multitudinous points of light as stars, where flakes of mica in the fire-born stone reflected his torch, and in the middle distance an irregular pillar of mica-flecked rock and on its top a small pale bundle that drew his eye. Then from far above he heard the beat of great wings, a pause, then another beat —as though a great vulture were circling in the cavernous dark.

He called, "Mara!" toward the pillar and the echoes came back and amongst them, shrill and faint, his own name called and the echoes of that. Then he realized that the wing-beat had ceased and that one of the high mica-stars was getting rapidly brighter, as though it were swiftly traveling straight down toward him, and he heard a rush in the air as of a great hawk stooping.

He jerked his whole body aside from the bright sword darting at him and simultaneously struck with his ax just behind it. The torch was torn from his grasp, what seemed like a leather sail struck him to his knees, and then there was a great wing-beat, very close, and another, and then the shrill bellow of a man in agony that despite its extremity held a note of outrage.

As he scrambled to his feet, he saw his torch flaring wide on the rocky floor and transfixing it the bright sword that had struck it from his grasp. Wing-beat and bellowing were going off from him now. He set his boot on the torch handle, preparatory to withdrawing the sword from it, but as he went to take hold of the latter, his fingers encountered a scaly hand, slenderer than his own, gripping it tightly, and (his groping fingers ascertained) warmly wet at the wrist, where it had been chopped off. Both hand and blood alike were invisible, so that although his fingers touched and felt, his eyes saw only the sword's hilt, the silver cross-guard, the pear-shaped silver pommel, and the black leather grip wrapped with braided silver wire.

He heard his name spoken falteringly close behind him and turning saw Mara standing there in her white smock looking woebegone and confused, as if she'd just been lifted from the pillar's top and set down there. As he spoke her name in answer, a voice came out of the air beside Mara and a little above her, speaking in the chilling and confounding tones of a familiar and beloved voice turned hateful in nightmare.

The sightless mountain princess Hirriwi said, "Woe to you, barbarian, for having come north again without first paying your respects at Stardock. Woe to you for coming at another woman's call, although we favor her cause. Woe for deserting your men to chase this girl-chit,

whom we would have (and have) saved without you. Woe for med-
dling with demons and gods. And woe upon woe for lifting your
hand to maim a prince of Stardock, to whom we are joined, though he
is our dearest enemy, by bonds stronger than love and hate. A head
for a head and a hand for a hand, think on that. Quintuple woe!"

During this recital, Mara had moved to Fafhrd, where he knelt
upright, his face working as he stared at and hearkened to emptiness.
He had put his arm about her shoulders and together they stared at
the speaking gloom.

Hirriwi continued, her voice less ritually passionate, but every
whit as cold. "Keyaira heals and comforts our brother, and I go to
join them. At dawn we will return you, journeying upon our fish of
air, to your people, where you will know your weird. Until then, rest
in the warmth of Hellfire, which is not yet a danger to you."

With that she broke off and there was the sound of her going away.
The torch flickered low, almost consumed, and great weariness took
hold of Fafhrd and Mara and they lay down side by side and sleep
was drawn up over them from their toes to their eyes. Fafhrd, at last
thought, wondered why it should move him so strangely that Mara
clutched his left hand, bent up beside his shoulder, in both of hers.

Next day Salthaven was a-bustle so early and so wildly—so fantastically—with preparations for a great sailing that it was hard to tell
where the inspirations of nightmare and worry-dream ended and
those of (hopefully) wide-eyed day began. Even the "foreigners" were
infected, as if they too had been hearing the Mingols-to-their-deaths
chant in their dreams, so that the Mouser had been impelled against
his better judgment to man Fafhrd's *Sea Hawk* with the most eager of
them under Bomar their "mayor" and the Ilthmart tavern-owner. He
made Pshawri their captain with half the thieves to support his authority and two of the Mingols, Trenchi and Gavs, to help him con
the ship.

"Remember you are boss," he told Pshawri, "Make them like it or
lump it—and keep to windward of me."

Pshawri, his new-healed forehead wound still pink, nodded fiercely
and went up to take up his command. Above the salt cliff the eastern
sky was ominously red with sunrise, while glooms of night still
lingered in the west. The east wind blew strongly.

From *Flotsam*'s stern the Mouser surveyed the busy harbor and his
fleet of fishing boats turned warships. Truly, they were a weird sight,
their decks which had so recently been piled with fish now bristling
with pikes and various imromptu weapons such as he'd seen

Groniger's men shoulder yesterday. Some of them had lashed huge ceremonial spears (bronze-pointed timbers, really) to their bowsprits —for use as rams, he supposed, the Fates be kind to 'em! While others had bent on red and black sails, to indicate bloody and baleful intentions, he guessed—the soberest fisherman was a potential pirate, that was sure. Three were half wreathed in fishnets—protection against arrow fire? The two largest craft were commanded by Dwone and Zwaaken, his sub-admirals, if that could be credited. He shook his head.

If only he had time to get his thoughts straight! But ever since he'd awakened events (and his own unpredictable impulses) had been rushing, nay, stampeding him. Yesterday, he'd managed to lead Cif and the other three women safely out of the quaking and stinking cave-tunnels (he glanced toward Darkfire—it was still venting into the red sky a thick column of black smoke, which the east wind blew west) only to discover that they'd spent an unconscionable time underground and it was already evening. After seeing to Rill's hand, badly burned by the Loki-torch, they'd had to hurry back to Salthaven for conferences with all and sundry—hardly time to compare notes with Cif on the whole cavern experience. . . .

And now he had to break off to help Mikkidu instruct the six Rimeland replacements for the thieves they'd lost to *Sea Hawk*—how to man the sweeps and so forth.

And *that* was no sooner done (matter of a few low-voiced instructions to Mikkidu, chiefly) than here came Cif climbing aboard, followed by Rill, Hilsa, and Mother Grum—all of them save for the last in sailorly trousers and jackets with knives at their belts. Rill's right arm was in a sling.

"Here we are, yours to command, captain," Cif said brightly.

"Dear . . . councilwoman," the Mouser answered, his heart sinking, "*Flotsam* can't sail into possible battle with women aboard, especially—" He let a meaningful look serve for "—whores and witches."

"Then we'll man *Sprite* and follow you after," she told him, not at all downcast. "Or rather range ahead to be the first to sight the Sunwise Mingols—you know *Sprite*'s a fast sailer. Yes, perhaps that's best, a women's fighting-ship for soldieresses."

The Mouser submitted to the inevitable with what grace he could muster. Rill and Hilsa beamed. Cif touched his arm commiseratingly.

"I'm glad you agreed," she said. "I'd already loaned *Sprite* to three other women." But then her face grew serious as she lowered her voice to say, "There is a matter that troubles me you should know. We were going to bring god Loki aboard in a firepot, as yesterday he traveled in Rill's torch——"

"Can't have fire aboard a ship going into battle," the Mouser responded automatically. "Besides, look how Rill got burned."

"But this morning, for the first time in over a year, we found the fire in the Flame Den unaccountably gone out," Cif finished. "We shifted the ashes. There was not a spark."

"Well," said the Mouser thoughtfully, "perhaps yesterday at the great rock face after he flamed so high the god temporarily shifted his swelling to the mountain's fiery heart. See how she smokes!" And he pointed toward Darkfire, where the black column going off westward was thicker.

"Yes, but we don't have him at hand that way," Cif objected troubledly.

"Well, at any rate he's still on the island," the Mouser told her. "And in a sense, I'm sure, on *Flotsam* too," he added, remembering (it made his fire-stung fingers smart anew) the black torch-end he still had in his pouch. That was another thing, he told himself, that wanted thinking about. . . .

But just then Dwone came sailing close by to report the Rime fleet ready for action and hardly to be held back. The Mouser had perforce to get *Flotsam* underway, hoisting what sail she could carry for the beat against the wind, and setting his thieves and their green replacements to sweeping while Ourph beat time, so that she'd be able to keep ahead of the handier fishing craft.

There were cheers from the shore and the other ships and for a short while the Mouser was able to bask in self-satisfaction at *Flotsam* moving out so bravely at the head of the fleet, and his crew so well disciplined, and (he could see) Pshawri handling Sea Hawk nicely enough, and Cif standing beside him glowing-eyed—and himself a veritable admiral, no less, by Mog!

But then the thoughts which he hadn't had time to straighten all day began to cark him again. Above all else he realized that there was something altogether foolhardy, in fact utterly ridiculous, about them all setting sail so confidently with only one hairbrained plan of action, on nothing more than the crackling word of a fire, the whisper of burning twigs. Still he had a compelling feeling in his bones that they were doing the right thing and nothing could harm them, and he would peradventure find the Mingol fleet and that another wonderful inspiration would come to him at the last minute. . . .

At that moment his eye lit on Mikkidu sweeping with considerable style in the bowmost steerside position and he came to a decision.

"Ourph, take the tiller and take her out," he directed. "Call time to the sweeps.

"My dear, I must leave you for a brief space," he told Cif. Then taking the last Mingol with him, he went forward and said in a gruff voice to Mikkidu, "Come with me to my cabin. A conference. Gib will replace you here," and then hurried below with his now apprehensive-eyed lieutenant past the wondering glances of the women.

Facing Mikkidu across the table in the low-ceilinged cabin (*one good thing about having a short captain and still shorter crew, it occurred to him*) he eyed his subordinate mercilessly and said, "Lieutenant, I made a speech to the Rime Islers in their council hall night before last that had them cheering me at the end. You were there. *What did I say?*"

Mikkidu writhed. "Oh, captain," he protested, blushing, "how can you expect——"

"Now none of that stuff about it being so wonderful you can't remember—or other weaseling out," the Mouser cut him short. "Pretend the ship's in a tempest and her safety depends on you giving me a square answer. Gods, haven't I taught you yet that no man of mine ever got hurt from me by telling me the truth?"

Mikkidu digested that with a great gulp and then surrendered. "Oh captain," he said, "I did a terrible thing. That night when I was following you from the docks to the council hall and you were with the two ladies, I bought a drink from a street vendor and gulped it down while you weren't looking. It didn't taste strong at all, I swear it, but it must have had a tremendous delayed kick, for when you jumped on the table and started to talk, I blacked out—my word upon it! When I came to you were saying something about Groniger and Afreyt leading out half the Rimelanders to reinforce Captain Fafhrd and the rest of us sailing out to entice the Sun Mingols into a great whirlpool, and everybody was cheering like mad—and so of course I cheered too, just as if I'd heard everything that they had."

"You can swear to the truth of that?" the Mouser asked in a terrible voice.

Mikkidu nodded miserably.

The Mouser came swiftly around the table and embraced him and kissed him on his quivering cheek. "There's a good lieutenant," he said most warmly, clapping him on the back. "Now go, good Mikkidu, and invite the lady Cif attend me here. Then make yourself useful on deck in any way your shrewdness may suggest. Don't stand now in a daze. Get at it, man."

By the time Cif arrived (not long) he had decided on his approach to her.

"Dear Cif," he said without preamble, coming to her, "I have a confession to make to you," and then he told her quite humbly but clearly and succinctly the truth about his "wonderful words"—that he simply hadn't heard one of them. When he was done he added, "So you can see not even my vanity is involved—whatever it was, it was Loki's speech, not mine—so do you now tell me truth about it, sparing me nothing."

She looked at him with a wondering smile and said, "Well, I was puzzled as to what you could have said to Mikkidu to make him so head-in-the-clouds happy—and am not sure I understand that even now. But, yes, my experience was, I now confess, identical with his—and not even the taking of an unknown drink to excuse it. My mind went blank, time passed me by, and I heard not a word you said, except those last directions about Afreyt's expedition and the whirlpool. But everyone was cheering and so I pretended to have heard, not wanting to injure your feelings or feel myself a fool. Oh, I was a sheep! Once I was minded to confess my lapse to Afreyt, and now I wish I had, for she had a strange look on her then—But I didn't. You think, as I do now, that she also——?"

The Mouser nodded decisively. "I think that not one soul of them heard a word to remember of the main body of my—or, rather, Loki's talk, but later they all pretended to have done so, just like so many sheep indeed—and I the black goat leading them on. So only Loki knows what Loki said and we sail out upon an unknown course against the Mingols, taking all on trust."

"What to do now?" she asked wonderingly.

Looking into her eyes with a tentative smile and a slight shrug that was at once acquiescent and comical, he said, "Why, we go on, for it is your course and I am committed to it."

Flotsam gave a long lurch then, with a wave striking along her side, and it nudged Cif against him, and their arms went around each other, and their lips met thrillingly—but not for long, for he must hurry on deck, and she too, to discover (or rather confirm) what had befallen.

Flotsam progressed out of Salthaven harbor and the salt cliff's lee to the Outer Sea where the east wind smote them more urgently and the swells and the sunlight struck their canvas and deck. The Mouser took the tiller from sad-faced Ourph and that old one and Gib and Mikkidu set sail for the first eastward tack. And one by one *Sea Hawk* and the weirdly accoutered fishing boats repeated their maneuver, following *Flotsam* out.

That selfsame east wind which blew west across the southern half of Rime Isle, and against which *Flotsam* labored, farther out at sea was hurrying on the horse-ships of the Sunwise Mingols. The grim galleys, each with its bellying square sail, made a great drove of ships, and now and again a stallion screamed in its bow-cage as they plunged ahead through the waves, which cascaded spray through the black, crazily-angled bars. All eyes strained west-ahead, and it would have been hard to say which eyes glared the more madly, those of the fur-clad, grinningly white-toothed men, or those of long-faced, grimacingly white-toothed beasts.

On the poop of the flagship this frenzy looked in a more philosophical direction, where Gonov discoursed with his witch-doctor and attendant sages propounding such questions as, "Is it sufficient to burn a city to the ground, or must it also be trampled to rubble?" and contemplating such answers as, "Most meritorious is to pound it to sand, aye, to fine loam, without burning at all."

While the strong westwind that blew east across the northern half of the island (with a belt of squalls and fierce eddies between the two winds) was hurrying on from west across trackless ocean the like fleet of the Widdershins Mingols, where Edumir had proposed this query to his philosophers: "Is death by suicide in the first charge, hurling oneself upon the foeman's virgin spear, to be preferred to death by self-administered poison in the last charge?"

He hearkened to their closely-reasoned answers and to the counter-question: "Since death is so much to be desired, surpassing the delights of love and mushroom wine, how did our all-noble and revered ancestors ever survive to procreate us?" and at last observed, his white-rimmed eyes gazing east yearningly, "That is all theory. On Rime Isle we will once more put these recondite matters to the test of practice."

While high above all winds Khahkht in his icy sphere ceaselessly studied the map lining it, whereon he moved counters for ships and men, horses and women—aye, even gods—bending his bristly face close, so that no unlawful piece might escape his fierce scrutiny.

By early morning sunlight and against the nipping wind, Afreyt hurried on alone through heather dotted by stunted cedars past the last silent hill farm, with its sagging gray-green turf roofs, before Cold Harbor. She was footsore and weary (even Odin's noose around her neck seemed a heavy weight) for they'd marched all night with only two short rest-stops and midway they'd been buffeted by changing winds reaching tornadic strength as they'd passed through the transition belt between the southeastern, Salthaven half of Rime Isle, which the east wind presently ruled, and the northwestern, Cold Harbor half, where the equally strong west wind now held sway. Yet she forced herself to scan carefully ahead for friend or foe, for she had constituted herself vanguard for Groniger and his grotesquely burdened trampers. A while ago in the twilight before dawn she'd gone from litter-side up to the head of the column and pointed out to Groniger the need of having a guard ahead now that they were nearing their journey's end and should be wary of ambushes. He had seemed unconcerned and heedless, unable to grasp the danger, almost as if he (and all the other Rime men, for that matter) were intent only on marching on and on, glaze-eyed, growling Gale's doom-chant, like so many monstrous automatons, until they met the Mingols, or Fafhrd's force. Failing those, she believed, they would stride into the chilly western ocean with never a halt or waver, as did the lemming hordes in their climacteric. But neither had Groniger voiced any objection to her spying on ahead—nor even concern for her safety. Where *was* the man's one-time clear-headedness and prudence?

Afreyt was not unversed in island woodcraft and she now spotted Skor peering toward Cold Harbor from the grove of dwarf cedars whence Fafhrd had launched yestermorning's brief arrow-fusillade. She called Skor's name, and he whipped around nocking an arrow to his bow, then came up swiftly when he saw her familiar blues.

"Lady Afreyt, what do you here? You look weary," he greeted her succinctly. He looked weary himself and hollow-eyed, his cheeks and forehead smudged with soot above his straggly russet beard, perhaps against the glare of glacial ice.

She quickly told him about the Rimeland reinforcements approaching behind her.

His weariness seemed to lift from him as she spoke. "That's brave news," he said when she had done. "We joined our lines (I'm now making the rounds of them) with those of the Cold Harbor defenders before sunset yesterday and have the Mingol fore-raiders penned on the beach—and all by bluff! The mere sight of the forces you describe, strategically deployed, will cause 'em to take ship and sail away, I think—and we not lift a finger."

"Your pardon, lieutenant," she rejoined, her own weariness lifting at his optimism, "but I have heard you and your fellows named berserkers—and have always thought it was the way of such to charge the enemy at the first chance, charge wolf-howling and bounding, mother-naked?"

"To tell the truth, that was once my own understanding of it," he replied, thoughtfully rubbing his broken nose with the back of his hand, "but the captain's changed my mind for me. He's a great one for sleights and deceits, the captain is! Makes the foe imagine things, sets their own minds to work against 'em, never fights when there's an easier way—and some of his wisdom has rubbed off on us."

"Why are you wearing Fafhrd's sword?" she asked, seeing it suddenly.

"Oh, he went off yestermorning to Hellglow after the girl, leaving me in command, and he's not yet returned," Skor answered readily, though a crease of concern appeared between his brows, and he went on briefly to tell Afreyt about Mara's strange abduction.

"I wonder at him leaving you all so long to shift without him, merely for that," Afreyt commented, frowning.

"Truth to tell, I wondered at it myself, yestermorning," Skor admitted. "But as events came on us, I asked myself what the captain would do in each case, and did that, and it's worked out—so far." He hooked a middle-finger over a fore-one.

There came a faint tramping and the whispers of a hoarse chant and turning they saw the front of the Rime column coming downhill.

"Well, they look fearsome enough," Skor said, after a moment. "Strange, too," he added, as the litter and gallows hove into view. The girls in their red cloaks were walking beside the former.

"Yes, they are that," Afreyt said.

"How are they armed?" he asked her. "I mean, besides the pikes and spears and quarterstaves and such?"

She told him those were their only weapons, as far as she knew.

"They'd not stand up to Mingols, then, not if they had to cover any distance to attack," he judged. "Still, if we showed 'em under the right conditions, and put a few bowmen amongst 'em. . . ."

"The problem, I think, will be to keep them from charging," Afreyt told him. "Or, at any rate, to get them to stop marching."

"Oh, so it's that way," he said, raising an eyebrow.

"Cousin Afreyt! Cousin Afreyt!" May and Gale were crying shrilly while they waved at her. But then the girls were pointing overhead and calling, "Look! Look!" and next they were running downhill alongside the column, still waving and calling and pointing at the sky.

Afreyt and Skor looked up and saw, at least a hundred yards above them, the figures of a man and a small girl (Mara by her red cloak) stretched out flat on their faces and clinging to each other and to something invisible that was swiftly swooping toward Cold Harbor. They came around in a great curve, getting lower all the time, and headed straight for Skor and Afreyt. She saw it was Fafhrd and Mara, all right, and she realized that she and Cif must have looked just so when they were being rescued from Khahkht's blizzard by the invisible mountain princesses. She clutched Skor, saying rapidly and somewhat breathlessly, "They're all right. They're hanging onto a fish-of-the-air, which is like a thick flying carpet that's alive, but invisible. It's guided by an invisible woman."

"It would be," he retorted obscurely. Then they were buffeted by a great gust of air as Fafhrd and Mara sped past close overhead and still flat out—both of them grinning excitedly, Afreyt was able to note as she cringed down, at least Fafhrd's lips were drawn back from his teeth. They came to rest midway between her and Groniger at the head of the column, which had slowed to gawk, about a foot above the heather, which was pressed down in a large oval patch, as if Fafhrd and Mara were lying prone on an invisible mattress wide and thick enough for a king's bed.

Then the air travelers had scrambled to their feet and jumped down after an unsteady step or two. Skor and Afreyt were closing in on them from one side and May and Gale from the other, while the Rimelanders stared openmouthed. Mara was shrieking to the other girls, "I was abducted by a very nasty demon, but Fafhrd rescued me! He chopped off its hand!" And Fafhrd had thrown his arms around Afreyt (she realized she'd invited it) and he was saying, "Afreyt, thank Kos you're here. What's that you've got around your neck?" Next, without letting Afreyt go, to Skor, "How are the men? What's your position?" All the while the staring Rimelanders marched on slowly and almost painfully, like sleepers peering at another wonder out of a nightmare which has entrapped them.

And then all others grew suddenly silent and Fafhrd's arms dropped away from Afreyt as a voice that she had last heard in a cave on Darkfire called out like an articulate silver trumpet, "Farewell, girl. Farewell, barbarian. Next time, think of the courtesies due between orders and of your limitations. My debt's discharged, while yours has but begun."

And with that a wind blew out from where Fafhrd and Mara had landed (from *under* the invisible mattress, one must think), bending the heather and blowing the girls' red coats out straight from them (Afreyt felt it and got a whiff of animal stench neither fish nor fowl nor four-legger) and then it was as if something large and living were taking off into the air and swiftly away, while a silvery laughter receded.

Fafhrd threw up his hand in farewell, then brought it down in a sweeping gesture that seemed to mean, "Let's say goodbye to all that!" His expression, which had grown bleakly troubled during Hirriwi's speaking, became grimly determined as he saw the Rime column marching slowly into them. "Master Groniger!" he said sharply. "Captain Fafhrd?" that one replied thickly, as one half-rousing from a dream. "Halt your men!" Fafhrd commanded, and then turned to Skor, who made report, telling his leader in somewhat more detail matter told earlier to Afreyt, while the column slowly ground to a halt, piling up around Groniger in a disorderly array.

Meanwhile Afreyt had knelt beside Mara, assured herself that the girl wasn't outwardly injured, and was listening bemused as Mara proudly but deprecatingly told the other girls about her abduction and rescue. "He made a scarecrow out of my cloak and the skull of the last little girl he'd eaten alive, and he kept touching me, just like Odin does, but Fafhrd cut off his hand and Princess Hirriwi got my cloak back this morning. It was neat riding through the sky. I didn't get dizzy once."

Gale said, "Odin and I made up a marching song. It's about killing Mingols. Everyone's chanting it." May said, "I made nooses with flowers in them. They're a mark of honor from Odin. We're all wearing them. I made one for you and a big one for Fafhrd. Say, I've got to give Fafhrd his noose. It's time he was wearing it, with a big battle coming."

Fafhrd listened patiently, for he'd wanted to know what that ugly thing around Afreyt's neck was. But when Mara had asked him to bend down his head, and he looked up spying the curtained litter, and recognized the uprooted gallows beyond it, he felt a shivery revulsion and said angrily, "No, I won't wear it. I won't mount his eight-legged horse. Get those things off your necks, all of you!"

But then he saw the hurt, distrustful look in the girls' eyes as Mara protested, "But it's to make you strong in battle. It's an honor from Odin." And then the look of concern in Afreyt's eyes as she gestured toward the litter, its curtains fluttering in the wind (he sensed the grim holiness that seemed to emanate from it), and the look of expectation in the eyes of Groniger and the other Rimers, made him change his mind. He said, making his voice eager, "I'll tell you what I'll do, I'll wear it around my wrist, to strengthen it," and he thrust his left hand through the noose and after a moment May tightened it. "My left arm," he explained, lying somewhat, "has always been markedly weaker than my right in battle. This noose will help strengthen it. I'll take yours too," he said to Afreyt with a meaningful look.

She loosened it from around her neck with feelings of relief which partly changed to apprehension as she saw it tightened around Fafhrd's wrist beside the first noose.

"And yours, and yours, and yours," he said to the three girls. "That way I'll be wearing a noose for each of you. Come on, you wouldn't want my left arm weak in battle, would you?"

"There!" he said when it was done, gripping the five pendant cords in his left hand and whirling them. "We'll whip the Mingols off Rime Isle, we will!"

The girls, who had seemed a little unhappy about losing their nooses, laughed delighted, and the Rimers raised an unexpected cheer.

Then they marched on, Skor scouting ahead after remembering to give Fafhrd back his sword, and Fafhrd trying to put some order into the Rimers and keep them quiet—although the wind helpfully blew the drum-noise of their chant from the beach. The girls and Afreyt dropped back with the litter, though not as far as Fafhrd wished. The company picked up a couple of Fafhrd's men, who reported the Mingols massing on the beach around their ships. And then they mounted a slight rise where the lines extended south from the fortress-hump of Cold Harbor, Fafhrd and his men holding back the now overeager Rimers. A mounting cry of woe came from the beach beyond and they all beheld a wonderfully satisfying sight: the three Sea Mingol galleys launching into the wind, forward oars out and working frantically while small figures gave a last heave to the sterns and scrambled aboard.

Then came an arresting cry from Cold Harbor and they began to see out in the watery west a host of sails coming up over the horizon: the Widder-Mingol fleet. And with the sight of it they became aware also of a faint distant rumbling, as of the hoofbeat of innumerable war-horses charging across the steppes. But the Rimelanders recognized it as the voice of Hellfire, threatening eruption where it smoked blackly to the north. While to the south churned high-domed clouds, betokening a change of wind and weather.

The Gray Mouser fully realized that he was in one of the tightest spots he'd ever been in during the course of a danger-dappled career —with this difference, that this time the spot was shared by three hundred friendly folk (even dear, thinking of Cif beside him), along with any number of enemies (the Sun-Sea-Mingol fleet, that was, in close pursuit). He'd raised *them* (the Mingols) with the greatest of ease and was now luring them so successfully to their destruction that *Flotsam* was last, not first, of the Rime Island fleet, which was spread out disorderly before him, *Sea Hawk* nearest, and within arrow range of the pursuing Mingols, who came in endless foaming shrieking whinnying numbers, their galleys sailing faster with the wind than he. Moments ago one of the horse-ships had driven herself under with excess of sail, and foundered, and not a sister ship had paused to give her aid. Dead ahead some four leagues distant was the Rimic coast with the two crags and inviting bay (and blackly smoking Darkfire beyond) that marked the position of the Great Maelstrom. North, the clouds churned, promising change of weather. The problem, as always, was how to get the Mingols into the Maelstrom, while avoiding it himself (and his friends with him), but he had never *appreciated* the problem quite so well as now. The hoped-for solution was that the whirlpool would turn on just *after* the Rimers and *Sea Hawk* and he had sailed across it, and so catch at least the van of the close-crowding Mingol fleet. And the way they were all bunched now, that required perfect, indeed God-like timing, but he'd worked his hardest at it and after all the gods were supposed to be on his side, weren't they?—at least two of them.

The horse-galleys of the Mingols were so close that Mikkidu and his thieves had their slings ready, loaded with leaden ball, though under orders not to cast unless the Mingols started arrow fire. Across the waves a stallion screamed from its cage.

Thought of the Maelstrom made the Mouser look in his pouch for the golden queller. He found it, all right, but somehow the charred stub of the Loki-torch had got wedged inside it. It was really no more than a black cinder. No wonder Rill had burned herself so badly, he thought, glancing at her bandaged hand—when Cif had stayed on deck, the harlots, and Mother Grum, had insisted on the same privilege and it seemed to cheer the men.

The Mouser started to unwedge the black god-brand, but then the odd thought occurred to him that Loki, being a god (and in some sense this cinder was Loki), deserved a golden house, or carapace, so on a whim he wrapped the length of stout cord attached to it tightly round and round the weighty golden cube and knotted it, so that the two objects—queller and god-brand—were inextricably conjoined.

Cif nudged him. Her gold-flecked green eyes were dancing, as if to say, "Isn't this exciting!"

He nodded a somewhat temperate agreement. Oh, it was exciting, all right, but it was also damnably uncertain—everything had to work out just so—why, he could still only guess at the directions god Loki had given them in the speech he had forgotten and none else had heard. . . .

He looked around the deck, surveying faces. It was strange, but everyone's eyes seemed to flash with the same eager juvend excitement as was in Cif's . . . it was even in Gavs', Trenchi's, and Gib's (the Mingols) . . . even in Mother Grum's, bright as black beads. . . .

In all eyes, that is, except the wrinkle-netted ones of old Ourph helping Gavs with the tiller. They seemed to express a sad and patient resignation, as though contemplating tranquility from some distance a great and universal woe. On an impulse the Mouser took him from his task and drew him to the lee rail.

"Old man," he said, "you were at the council hall the night before last when I spoke to them all and they cheered me. I take it that, like the rest, you heard not one word of what I said, or at best only a few—the directives for Groniger's party and our sailing today?"

For the space of perhaps two breaths the old Mingol stared at him curiously, then he slowly shook his bald dome, saying, "No, captain, I heard every last word you spoke (my eyes begin to fail me a little, but my ears not) and they greatly saddened me (your words) for they expressed the same philosophy as seizes upon my steppe-folk at their climacterics (and often otherwhen), the malign philosophy that caused me to part company with them in early years and make my life among the heathen."

"What do you mean?" the Mouser demanded. "A favor—be brief as possible."

"Why, you spoke—most winningly indeed (even I was tempted)—of the glories of death and of what a grand thing it was to go down joyfully to destruction carrying your enemies with you (and as many as possible of your friends also), how this was the law of life and its crowning beauty and grandeur, its supreme satisfaction. And as you told them all that they soon must die and how, they all cheered you as heartily as would have my own Mingols in their climacteric and with the selfsame gleam in their eyes. I well know that gleam. And, as I say, it greatly saddened me (to find you so fervent a death-lover) but since you are my captain, I accepted it."

The Mouser turned his head and looked straight into the astonished eyes of Cif, who had followed close behind him and heard every word old Ourph had spoken, and looking into each other's eyes they saw the same identical understanding.

At that very instant the Mouser felt *Flotsam* beneath his feet slammed to a stop, spun sideways to her course, and sent off circling at prodigious speed just as had happened to *Sprite* day before yesterday, but with a greater force proportionate to her larger size. The heavens reeled, the sea went black. He and Cif were brought up against the taffrail along with a clutter of thieves, whores, witches (well, one witch), and Mingol sailors. He bid Cif cling to it for dearest life, then found his footing on the tilted deck, and raced past the rattling whipping mainsail (and past young Mikkidu embracing the mainmast with eyes tight shut in ultimate terror or perhaps in rapture) to where his own vision was unimpeded.

Flotsam, Sea Hawk, and the whole Rime fleet were circling at dizzying velocity more than halfway down the sides of a whirlpool at least two leagues wide, whose wide-spinning upper reaches held what looked like the entire Mingol fleet, the galleys near the edge tiny as toys against the churning sky, while at the maelstrom's still-distant center the fanged rocks protruding through the white welter there were like a field of death.

Next below *Flotsam* in the vast wheel of doom spun Dwone's fishing smack, so close he could see faces. The Rimers clutching their weird weapons and each other looked monstrously happy, like drunken and lopsided giants bound for a ball. Of course, he told himself, these were the monsters whose quickening Loki had envisioned, these were the trolls or whatever. And that reminded him of what, by Ourph's irrefutable testimony, Loki intended for them all and peradventure for Fafhrd and Afreyt also, and all the universe of seas and stars.

He snatched the golden queller from his pouch and seeing the black cinder at its heart thought, "Good!—rid of two evils at one stroke." Aye, but he must pitch it to the whirlpool's midst, and how to get it there, so far away? There was some simple solution, he was sure, it was on the tip of his unseen thoughts, but there were really so many distractions at the moment. . . .

Cif nudged him in the waist—one more distraction. As he might have expected, she had followed him close against his strictest bidding and now with a wicked grin was pointing at . . . . of course, his sling!

He centered the precious missile in the strap and motioning Cif to the mast to give him room, tried out his footing on the tilted deck, taking short dancing steps, and measuring out distance, speed, windage, and various imponderables with his eyes and brain. And as he did those things, whirling the queller-brand about his head, dancing out as it were the prelude to what must be his life's longest and supremest cast, there danced up from his mind's darkest deeps words that must have been brewing there for days, words that matched Loki's final four evil couplets in every particular, even the rhymes (almost), but that totally reversed their meaning. And as the words came bobbing to the surface of his awareness he spoke them out, softly he thought, though in a very clear voice—until he saw that Cif was listening to him with unmistakable delight at each turn of phrase, and Mikkidu had his shut eyes open and was hearing, and the monstrous Rimers on Dwone's smack had all their sobering faces turned his way. He somehow had the conviction that in the midst of that monstrous tumult of the elements his words were nevertheless being heard to the whirlpool's league-distant rim—aye, and beyond that, he knew not how far. And this is what he spoke: "Mingols to their deaths must go? Oh, not so, not so, not so! Mingols, draw an easy breath. Leave to wanton after death. Let there be an end to strife— even Mingols relish life. Mingol madness cease to burn. Gods to proper worlds return."

And with that he spun dancingly across the deck, as though he were hurling the discus, the queller-brand at the end of his sling a gold-glinting circlet above his head, and loosed. The queller-brand sped up gleaming toward the whirlpool's midst until it was too small for sight.

And then . . . the vasty whirlpool was struck flat. Black water foamed white. Sea and sky churned as one. And through that hell of the winds' howling and the waves' crash there came a rumbling earth-shaking thunder and the red flash of huge distant flames as Darkfire erupted, compounding pandemonium, adding the strokes of earth and fire to those of water and air, completing the uproar and riot of the four elements. All ships were chips in chaos, glimpsed dimly if at all, to which men clung like ants. Squalls blew from every compass-point, it seemed, warring together. Foam covered decks, mounded to mast tops.

But before that had transpired quite in *Flotsam's* case, the Mouser and some others to, gripping rail or mast, eyes stinging with salt sea, had seen, mounting for a few brief moments to the sky, from the whirlpool's very midst as it was smitten flat, what looked like the end of a black rainbow (or a skinny and curving black waterspout impossibly tall, some said afterwards) that left a hole behind it in the dark clouds, through which *something* maddening and powerful had vanished forever from their minds, their beings, and from all Nehwon.

And then the Mouser and his crew and the women with them were all fighting to save themselves and *Flotsam* in the midst of an ocean that was all cross chop and in the teeth of a gale that had reversed direction completely and now blew from the west, carrying the thick black smoke from Darkfire out toward them. Around them other ships fought the same fight in a great roiling confusion covering several square leagues that gradually sorted itself out. The Rime fishing boats and smacks (somewhat larger) with their handier rigs (and *Flotsam* and *Sea Hawk* too) were able to tack southwest against the wind and set slow courses for Salthaven. The Mingol galleys with their square sails could only run before it (the heavy seas preventing the use of oars) away from the sobering chaos of the dreadful isle whose black smoke pursued them and their dreary drenched stallions. Some of the horse-ships may have sunk, for *Flotsam* fished two Mingols out of the waves, but these were unclear as to whether they had been swept overboard or their ships lost, and far too miserable to seem like foes. Ourph, smiling serenely, later brought them hot chowder, while the west wind cleared the sky. (Regarding the winds, at the moment of decision the west wind had spilled south, blowing out all along the east coast of Rime Isle, and the east wind had spilled north, driving away from the whole west coast of the island, while the belt of storm between had rotated clockwise somewhat, causing wild, veering whirlwinds in the Deathlands.)

At the same instant as the Mouser slung the queller-brand, Fafhrd was standing on the seaward turf-wall of Cold Harbor, confronting the Widder-Mingol fleet as it neared the beach and brandishing his sword. This was no mere barbarian gesture of defiance, but part of a carefully thought-out demonstration done in the hope of awing the Sea-Mingols, even though Fafhrd admitted (to himself only) that the hope was a forlorn one. Earlier, when the three Mingol advance-raiders had departed the beach, they had made no move to join with or await their fleet, although they surely must have sighted its sails, but had instead rowed steadily away south as long as eye followed. This had made Fafhrd wonder whether they had not taken some fright on the isle which they had not wanted to face again, even with the backing of their main force. In this connection he had particularly remembered the cries of woe and dread that had come from the Mingols as Groniger's Rime Islers had topped the rise and hove into their view. Afreyt had confided to him how during the long march overland those same countrymen of hers had come to seem monstrous to her and somehow bigger, and he had had to admit that they made the same strange impression on him. And if they seemed bigger (and monstrous) to him and her, how much bigger might they not appear to Mingols?

And so they had taken thought together, Fafhrd and Afreyt, and had made suggestions and given commands (supplemented by bullyings and blandishments as needed) and as a result Groniger's reliefforce was posted at intervals of twenty paces in a long line that began far up on the glacier and continued along the ramparts of Cold Harbor and along the rise and stretched off for almost a league south of the settlement, each Isler brandishing his pike or other weapon. While betwixt and between them all along were stationed the defenders of Cold Harbor (their countrymen, though lacking their aura of monstrousness) and Fafhrd's berserks, to swell their sheer numbers and also to keep the Salthaven Islers at their posts, from which they still had a dreamy, automatonlike tendency to go marching off. Midmost on the broad ramparts of Cold Harbor, widely flanked by Groniger and another pike-waver, rested Odin's litter with the gallows propped over it as in the Deathlands, while around it were stationed Fafhrd, Afreyt, and the three girls, the last waving their red cloaks on long rakes like flags. (Anything for effect, Fafhrd had said, and the girls were eager to play their part in the demonstration.) Afreyt had a borrowed spear while Fafhrd alternately shook his sword and the cords of the five nooses drawn around his left hand—shook them at the massed Mingol ships nearing the harbor. Groniger and the other Islers were shouting Gale's (or Odin's) doom-chant: "Doom! Kill the Mingols! Doom! Die the heroes."

And then (just as, on the other side of Rime Isle, the Mouser hurled his queller-brand, as has been said) the whirlwinds betokening the reversal of gales moved across them northward, whipping the red flags, and the heavens were darkened and there came the thunder of Hellfire erupting in sympathy with Darkfire. The sea was troubled and soon pocked to the north by the ejecta of Hellglow, great rocks that fell into the waves like the shouted "Doom! Doom!" of the chant in a great cannonading. And the Widder-Mingol fleet was retreating out to sea under the urging of the wind that now blew off the shore—away, away from that dreadful burning coast that appeared to be guarded by a wall of giants taller than trees and by all the powers of the four elements. And Hellfire's smoke stretched out above them like a pall.

But before that had all transpired (in fact, at the same instant as, a hundred leagues east, a black rainbow or waterspout shot up to the sky from the whirlpool's center) Odin's litter began to rock and toss on the ramparts, and the heavy gallows to twitch and strain upward like a straw or like a compass needle responding to an unknown upward magnetism. Afreyt screamed as she saw Fafhrd's left hand turn black before her eyes. And Fafhrd bellowed with sudden agony as he felt the nooses May had braided (and decorated with flowers) tighten relentlessly about his wrist as so many steel wires, contracting deeper and deeper between arm bones and wrist bones, cutting skin and flesh, parting gristle and tendons and all tenderer stuff, while that hand was resistlessly dragged upward. And then the curtains of the litter all shot up vertically and the gallows stood up on its beam end and vibrated. Suddenly something black and gleaming shot up to the sky, holing the clouds, and Fafhrd's black severed hand and all the nooses went with it.

The the curtains fell back and the gallows crashed from the wall and Fafhrd stared stupidly at the blood pouring from the stump that ended his left arm. Mastering her horror, Afreyt clamped her fingers on the spouting arteries and bid May, who was nearest at hand, take knife and slash up the skirt of her white smock for bandages. The girl acted quickly, and with these folded in wads and also used as ties, Afreyt bound up Fafhrd's great wound in its own blood and staunched the flow of that while he watched blank-faced. When it was done, he muttered, " 'A head for a head and a hand for a hand,' she said," and Afreyt retorted sharply, "Better a hand than a head—or five."

In Its cramping sphere Khahkht of the Black Ice smote the sharply curving walls in Its fury and tried to scratch Rime Isle off the map. It ground together the pieces representing Fafhrd and the Mouser and the rest between Its opposed horny black palms and scrabbled frantically for the pieces standing for the two intrusive gods—but those two pieces were gone. While in far Stardock, maimed Prince Faroomfar slept more easily, knowing himself avenged.

A full two months after the events before-narrated, Afreyt had a modest fish-dinner in her low-eaved, violet-tinted house on the north edge of Salthaven, to which were invited Groniger, Skor, Pshawri, Rill, old Ourph, and of course Cif, the Gray Mouser, and Fafhrd—the largest number her table would accommodate without undue crowding. The occasion was the Mouser's sailing on the morrow in *Sea Hawk* with Skor, the Mingols, Mikkidu, and three others of his original crew on a trading venture to No-Ombrulsk with goods selected (purchased and otherwise accumulated) chiefly by Cif and himself. He and Fafhrd were sorely in need of money to pay for dockage on their vessels, crew-wages, and many other expenses, while the two ladies were no better off, owing yet-to-be-determined sums to the council—of which, however, they were still members, as yet. Fafhrd had to travel no distance at all to get to the feast, for he was guesting with Afreyt while he convalesced from his maiming—just as the Mouser was staying at Cif's place on no particular excuse at all. There had been raised eyebrows at these arrangements from the rather straight-laced Islers, which the four principals had handled by firmly overlooking them.

During the course of the dinner, which consisted of oyster chowder, salmon baked with Island leeks and herbs, corn cakes made of costly Lankhmar grain, and light wine of Ilthmar, conversation had ranged around the recent volcanic eruptions and attendant and merely coincidental events, and their consequences, particularly the general shortage of money. Salthaven had suffered some damage from the earthquake and more from the resultant fire. The council hall had survived but the Salt Herring tavern had been burned to the ground with its Flame Den. ("Loki was a conspicuously destructive god," the Mouser observed, "especially where his métier, fire, was involved." "It was an unsavory haunt," Groniger opined.) In Cold Harbor, three turf roofs had collapsed, unoccupied of course because everyone had been taking part in the defensive demonstration at the time. The Salthaven Islers had begun their homeward journey next day, the litter being used to carry Fafhrd. "So some mortal got some use of it besides the girls," Afreyt remarked. "It was a haunted-seeming conveyance," Fafhrd allowed, "but I was feverish."

But it was the short store of cash, and the contrivances adopted to increase that, which they chiefly talked about. Skor had found work for himself and the other berserks for a while helping the Islers harvest drift-timber from the Beach of Bleached Bones, but there had not been the anticipated glut of Mingol wrecks. Fafhrd talked of manning *Flotsam* with some of his men and bringing back from Ool Plerns a cargo of natural wood. ("When you're entirely recovered, yes," Afreyt said.) The Mouser's men had gone to work as fishermen bossed by Pshawri, and had been able to feed both crews and sometimes have a small surplus left to sell. Strangely, or perhaps not so, the monster catches made during the great run had all spoiled, despite their salting-down, and gone stinking bad, worse than dead jellyfish, and had had to be burned. (Cif said, "I told you Khahkht magicked that run— and so they were phantom fish in some sense, tainted by his touch, no matter how solid-seeming.") She and Afreyt had sold *Sprite* to Rill and Hilsa for a tidy sum; the two professionals' adventure on *Flotsam*, amazingly, had given them a taste for the sea-life and they were now making a living as fisherwomen, though not above turning a trick at their old trade in off hours. Hilsa was out night-fishing this very evening with Mother Grum. Even the foe had fallen on hard times. Two of the three fore-raiding Sea-Mingol galleys that had rowed off south had put into Salthaven three weeks later in great distress, having been battered about by storms and then becalmed, after having fled off ill-provisioned. The crew of one had been reduced to eating their sacred bow-stallion, while that of the other had so far lost their fanatic pride along with their madness that they had sold theirs to "Mayor" Bomar, who wanted to be the first Rime Isle man (or "foreigner") to own a horse, but succeeded only in breaking his neck on his first attempt to ride it. (Pshawri commented, "He was—*absit omen* —a somewhat overweening man. He tried to take away from me command of *Sea Hawk.*")

Groniger claimed that Rime Isle, meaning the council chiefly, was as badly off as anyone. The bluff harbor master, seemingly more hardheaded and skeptical than ever for his one experience of enchantment and the supernatural, made a point of taking a very hard line with Afreyt and Cif and a very dim view of the latter's irregular disbursements from the Rime treasury in the isle's defense. (Actually he was their best friend on the council, but he had his crustiness to maintain.) "And then there's the Gold Cube of Square Dealing," he reminded her accusingly, "gone forever!" She smiled. Afreyt served them hot gahveh, an innovation in Rimeland, for they'd decided to make an early evening of it what with tomorrow's sailing.

"I wouldn't be too sure of that," Skor said. "Working around the Beach of Bleached Bones you get the feeling that everything washes ashore there, eventually."

"Or we could dive for it," Pshawri proposed.

"What?—and get Loki-cinder back with it?" the Mouser asked, chuckling. He looked toward Groniger. "Then you'd still be a cloudy-headed god's-man, you old atheist!"

"That's as may be," the Isler retorted. "Afreyt said I was a troll-giant for a space, too. But here I am."

"I doubt you'd find it, dove you never so deep," Fafhrd averred softly, his gaze on the leather stall covering his still bandaged stump. "I think Loki-cinder vanished out of Nehwon-world entire, and many another curious thing with it—the queller (after it had done its work) that had become his home (Gods love gold) and Odin-ghost and some of his appurtenances."

Rill, beside him, touched the stall with her burnt hand which had been almost as long as his stump in healing. It had created a certain sympathy between them.

"You'll wear a hook on it?" she asked.

He nodded. "Or a socket for various tools, utensils, and instruments. There are possibilities."

Old Ourph said, sipping his steaming gahveh, "It was strange how closely the two gods were linked, so that when one departed, the other went."

"When Cif and I first found them, we thought they were one," Afreyt told him.

"We saved their lives," Cif asserted. "We were very good hosts, on the whole, to both of them." She caught Rill's eye, who smiled.

"When you save a suicide, you take upon yourself responsibilities," Afreyt said, her eyes drifting toward Fafhrd's stump. "If on his next attempt, he takes others with him, it's your doing."

"You're gloomy tonight, Lady Afreyt," the Mouser suggested, "and reason too curiously. When you set out in that mood there's no end to the places you can go, eh, Fafhrd? We set out to be captains, and seem in process of becoming merchants. What next? Bankers?—or pirates?"

"As much as you like of either," Cif told him meaningly, "as long as you remember the council holds Pshawri and your men here, hostage for you."

"As mine will be for you, when I seek that timber," Fafhrd said. "The pines at Ool Plerns are very green and tall."